Let The Rivers Clap Their Hands

Rube Wrightsman

Photos by Sandy Compton

An Author's Note

Many of the places, settings and establishments in this book are real, or were real in the time frame of the story. In some cases I used a touch of literary license, but tried to stay true to their essence. It is my hope that no one connected with these locations is upset or disrupted by their appearance. I used them in the story because I am quite fond of them and nothing fictional could compare.

The two disasters in the story actually happened on the dates and times they are depicted. In remembrance of the many victims I have attempted to describe the tragedies with as much historical accuracy as possible.

All of the characters, with the exception of John Wayne, The Fabulous Moolah, and Vardalia's mother, who is based on a real, and locally well-known Melungeon moonshine maker, are fictional.

Out of respect to the Apsaalooke, I gave all tribal characters on the Crow Reservation traditional Crow names. Many current tribal members have these same last names but in all cases, my characters have no association with any real people. If any person has the same name as someone in the book, it is by pure and unintended coincidence.

From the Book

There's somethin' in us, Deke, that makes us diff'ernt. We don't care about careers or retirement or goin' ta basketball games or none a' that kinda stuff. It's almost like we can't stand knowin' what we'll be doin' in a year, or a month, or even ta'morrow. Sometimes I think the only normal I'll ever have is the setting on my washin' machine an' that's only if I ever have a washin' machine."

Heading out of town Shelly noticed a large statue of a man on horseback. "What's that, Deke?" she said. "Let's go take a look at it." Shelly walked up to the statue, envious of the rider leaning forward in the saddle, hat brim bent back, spurring on his galloping steed. "It's a tribute to the Pony Express," she called to Deke, who had stayed in the truck. "It says here we been drivin' on the Pony Express Highway."

"I wonder why we ain't seen any of 'em yet," Deke said.

Take him over to the fire," Alvin Yellowtail said to Robert and Jeremy, and pointed to where the flames still burned by the dance circle. "And put more wood on it."

"Ohhhhhh nohhhhh!" Deke pleaded as they hauled him in tow across the camp. "Don' burn me at the stake… ohhhhh please, don' do that, I jest hate fire!"

"Maybe fire will help get some answers out of you," Robert Backbone told him.

Balanced and ready, Shelly didn't hold the knife in front of her like an amateur where it could be easily taken, but kept it protected along the back of her thigh, blade down, ready to slash or stab at whatever target presented itself.

"I'm tellin' ya… if ya git close I'm gonna kill ya," Shelly warned him.

Manufactured in the United States of America

ISBN: 978-1-886591-33-2
Library of Congress Control Number: 2024916039

For more information:

Rube Wrightsman
P.O. Box 476
Hot Springs, MT 59845
406-741-3430
sagehillrube@hotmail.com

BLUE CREEK PRESS

Heron, Montana
www.bluecreekpress.com

Acknowledgements

The most thanks go to my wife, Mary Ann, for her patience, kindness and wisdom. She encouraged me to keep writing and generously edited every chapter as it came off the printer. Then she read the whole thing again. Now, that's love.

It would be impossible to thank everyone who contributed to this book. I owe so much to those who read the monstrous first draft: Bill Martin of Troy and Pom and Kathi Collins, of Trego, Montana. Your positive comments were greatly appreciated. Very special thanks goes to Carol Peters of Spokane, who edited that first manuscript and set me straight on how much better the book could be. Thanks to Kandi Staley for the kind words and the fastest proof-read ever.

M'lin Kendrick of Hot Springs; your encouragement came when it counted most. Huge thanks to Sunday Dutro; your editing was much needed and well heeded. Cherry Lanigan, from Bingara, New South Wales Australia, did more to help than I can repay. My publisher, Sandy Compton, did a great job and tolerated my pickiness.

For the cover and frontispiece photos, Madeline Finley, a Shelly Stamper in her own right, played the part to perfection. Thanks. A heap of gratitude to Paul Overman for use of the car.

To Stewkey Hackett, I'm much obliged. Not only has he put up with me since college, but graciously drove me around Norwood and Cinncinati in what must have seemed a frivolous undertaking.

No acknowledgment would be complete without thanks to the two people who first encouraged me to write. Christa Powell showed me how magical the process of writing could be. And Ted Seaman, who late one night at a campfire, convinced me I should write a newspaper column, and then set me up with Ron and Susan Smith of The Valley Press in Plains, Montana, kicked the whole thing off.

Finally, though I met them well before I ever thought of being a writer, I owe a debt to a couple of my literary and real-life heroes, Ken Kesey and Ed Abbey. Both were considerate and kind to an enthralled fan and the time I spent with them is still vivid and cherished.

If there is magic on this planet,
it is contained in water.
Loren Eiseley

Chapter 1

Sunshine burst over the eastern hills up river, exploding against Shelly Stamper's eyelids as she lay sleeping on the damp stone. Irritated, she turned her face away from the harsh light and forced both eyes open, then sat up and lowered the hood of her sweatshirt. She reached into her knapsack, pulled out the gray ball cap that had *Mack Trucks* written on the front and tugged it on tightly. For a moment she stared at the water cascading over the ledge beside her, following the torrent downstream through the twisting canyon. Sucking in a breath of cold air, she stood up, stretched her long frame heavenward and grabbed for the sky with both hands. "Well, I'm here," she hollered over the roar of the water, "reckon I better git on with it." With one swift motion she picked up her knapsack, slung it over her shoulders and started tracking along the rocky ledge in long, purposeful strides toward the tree-covered slope that led to the highway.

Atop a grassy ridge surrounded by forested hills, the meager settlement of Peapatch looked out over the brier-choked valleys and gritty coal towns below. Its state was uncertain, because Peapatch Road wove around the Virginia-West Virginia state line like two mating vipers. Until 1939 Peapatch had a post office, but its loss never diminished Peapatchers' pride in their community. Perched well above the trash-cluttered hollers and mining towns, orderly Peapatch held to its lofty dignity. On evenings when the air grew heavy and the smoke from woodfires and coal plants advanced through the bottomlands like an army of dirty wraithes, the residents of Peapatch watched it roil below, enjoying starlight while those in the valleys around them hunkered in grimy vapor until morning, when the Devil released his grip on the countryside and gave it back to the coal companies.

As dependent on coal as everyone else, Peapatch clung to its sense of self-determination, though the town was in decline and everyone knew it. After the post office closed the only public structures were the small community center and the steepleless white church that just said 'Shiloh', its iron bell hung frugally from a pole in front. Unincorporated and without defined boundaries, Peapatch's population had always been indeterminate, but clearly it was diminishing, even while the coal towns thrived.

Many of the young people, including those who went to work in nearby mines, preferred the comparative social bustle of the valley. And though most of Peapatch's tight-knit core of mature citizens stayed put, they eventually became residents of the dark and quiet confines of the Shiloh churchyard. In either case, they were not being replaced. Uppity Virginia had never honored Peapatch on its roadmap but by 1960 it had disappeared from the West Virginia map as well.

On the west end of Peapatch, near the summit of the winding hill where Peapatch Road crossed Route 635 and climbed out of Wimmer Gap, the Stamper house sat. Two-storied, white and square, almost stately by local standards, the house lay south of the road by necessity, but north of the state line by intention, plumbed there by Shelly's grandfather, Lemuel Stamper. Though most of the Stampers' twenty acres lay in Virginia, they considered themselves West Virginians and Lem Stamper wanted to make sure that's where his offspring were born. This made the Stampers hillbillies instead of Southerners. Genetics and lifestyle would have made them hillbillies anyway, but Shelly was always grateful the designation was official.

Shelly's daddy, Cletus, started at the coal mine when he was seventeen but he didn't stay on the pick and shovel for long, because whenever a machine quit moving or began acting up, Clete could usually tinker it into running right again. One day the foreman walked up and took the pick right out of Clete's hand.

"Yor a maint'nence man, now," he said, handing Clete a leather tool belt. "Put this'n here belt on. It comes with more pay."

Tree-tall lanky, slightly buck-toothed and friendly going, Cletus Stamper was an easy man to like, and for Shelly, a man to love like no other she would ever meet. His mind functioned like his limbs, smooth and oiled, the iron strength only showing when it needed to. A man of patient understanding, Clete accepted God's will and trusted his days to unfold in the Lord's good time, believing that if he lived rightly, most of them would be to his favor.

Shelly's mama, Ethel, was solid as a feral razorback. Thickset and swarthy, her large head was framed by tight ringlets of black hair and held a pair of unsettling blue eyes set so deep under her dark brows that they shone like pale lights from a cave. A Kentuckian from Olive Hill, she'd done a stint of professional wrestling in the late 1940's and early 50's, her brush with fame being when she wrestled The Fabulous Moolah to a draw in the Mansfield, Ohio Armory. Clete was up from Peapatch, visiting his cousin Houstan, who lived in nearby Shelby, and they went to the match. Most of the crowd lined up to get Moolah's autograph but Clete stretched a long arm through the ropes and asked Ethel to sign his program. When she returned his smile he asked for her phone number and Ethel gave it to him.

Together, they raised seven kids. Shelly came first, in October of 1955, just nigh of Clete and Ethel's first anniversary. Ethel wanted to settle near her family in Kentucky but she was a practical woman. Wrestling never sported her much money and Clete had a good paying job and a large house. His mother had died ten years before and his father, Lemuel, battered from a life of mining, could no longer take care of the little farm on his own. Clete's only sibling, Vertnor, lived up in Gallipolis, Ohio, and the unspoken assumption was that the property would be Clete's when Lemuel passed.

Ethel's pop, Floyd Cooper, had died when Ethel was seventeen. Driving home one misty night with an open jug of stump liquor on the seat beside him, he goosed his V-8 Ford too enthusiastically on a curve and smacked into a maple tree as big around as an oil drum. His widow, Emma, called Grammy since her first grandchild, still got his railroad pension and kept the homestead on Tick Ridge in good order, but Ethel worried. Until 1967, the house had no indoor plumbing and was heated only by wood. Ethel had some consolation in that her two younger sisters still lived in Olive Hill and looked after their mother dotingly, sometimes living with her when they were between husbands.

Wanting her children to know easy rolling Kentucky, not just the harsh mining country of southern West Virginia, Ethel packed her growing family into the car at every chance and headed north to the gentle hills around Tick Ridge. She never much cared for the craggy ruggedness of McDowell County. The first time she saw the sharp clefts and deep, narrow ravines it looked to her like after God had created the mountains he turned his back and Satan went to work on them with an ax. Her only relief was that Lemuel Stamper had built their home on the top of a green ridge instead of in some dirty holler or trashy coal town with its close-packed houses and jacked-up derelict vehicles.

Ethel never said it to Cletus, but she was determined that not one of her children ever work a day in a coal mine or marry a man who did. She never could shake the feeling that coal people weren't just rugged, like their mountains, but that deep inside of them might be real savagery. She saw it in the way they took offense to the smallest slight, even if no insult was meant, or how they were ready to fight, even kill, over any affront to their pride. And talk about clannish. You had to be careful saying anything about a relative or friend of the person you were talking to. It was also considered bad manners, and often inviting trouble, to head up into a holler unless you already knew the locals and were on friendly terms.

Cletus, naturally, never saw coal people like this. "We got our customs, Ethel, like ever'body else. We might be a little more set on some of 'em. An' we got our pride. Ya cain't take that from the folks down here. Been times that was all we had left."

"Pride!" Ethel almost spat the word. "There's people down here who'd kill their neighbor over a wrong word or a jug a' likker. You know there is, Cletus."

Clete couldn't argue, he'd seen it happen. "Ah know yer right about some of it, Ethel, but you don't know what it was like in the mines back in daddy's day, 'fore the union come in, when miners were still paid in comp'ny store scrip. If'n them miners hadn'ta stood up to the coal companies – an' a lot a' times they got shot down fer it – we wouldn't have this house or the life we got."

Ethel and Cletus were both right, for nowhere in the United States did miners stand up to the coal companies or the owners put them down with the brutal violence that took place in southern West Virginia. The Matawan Massacre happened up in Mingo County along the Tug Fork, and the Battle of Blair Mountain, where miners took on the Baldwin-Felts Detective Agency, the Logan County Sheriff's Office, the West Virginia State Police and even the U.S. Army, was fought just two counties away. Well over a hundred people died and Clete's father, Lemuel, had been in the thick of it.

This was also feuding country. The Hatfield-McCoy fiasco, also fought along the Tug Fork, lasted nearly 30 years and took dozens of lives on both sides. Many living people still remembered it and Shelly grew up listening to their stories. Even in the 1950's, people spoke of the feud softly, never joked about it or said anything bad towards either side, as if a spark might still be smoldering, ready to flame at any excuse.

The folks around Peapatch, though, were a gentler lot than the ones 'down yonder', as they were usually referred to, and treated Ethel well. Not that she gave people much choice. Ethel's wrestling history was soon known, and her blunt manner and dark, boulder-like appearance dissuaded most of the local hellions from tangling with her. But more than that, she was Clete Stamper's wife and Lem Stamper's daughter-in-law and no two men were more respected in McDowell County. Lem liked Ethel the first time he met her and Ethel liked him too, but it was in Lemuel she first encountered that unyielding steely pride beneath the easy manner and polite words. Then she saw it in Cletus and vowed that it wouldn't get passed on to their children.

Shelly's birth cemented Ethel's place in the family. Lemuel lived long enough to get to know his first granddaughter and see Cletus Jr. born less than a year later. Ethel was expecting a third when Lem died in 1958 at the age of eighty, shortly after Shelly's third birthday. Throughout her life, Shelly carried only one memory of him: sitting on his knee Halloween night, dressed up like a little cowgirl and Lem bouncing her like she was on a horse just before he went upstairs to a sleep he never woke up from.

Shelly grew up exploring the lush, rugged countryside around the Stamper property. Usually alone, she ranged as far as Ethel would allow - or she could get away with - in a land and time where children were free to ramble terrain that included fast flowing creeks, cliffs, railroad tracks, climbable trees and poisonous snakes.

When Shelly wasn't roaming she was usually with her father. Like most Appalachian boys, Cletus loved cars and trucks. He tinkered with his own constantly and from a young age learned he could pick up extra cash by working on other peoples'. At times over a dozen vehicles sat on the Stamper property, awaiting repair. When the big dump truck arrived Ethel put her foot down.

"But Ethel," Clete protested, "Ah make toler'ble money doin' this."

"I don't care, I ain't livin' in no junkyard. You got two weeks to git 'em gone. If they ain't, I'll take the tractor and haul 'em off when you're at work."

The next evening after dinner, Clete pulled his '49 Dodge Power Wagon into his shop behind the house and blue arcs from his welder flashed in the windows until eleven that night. Three days later Clete drove the pickup out of the shop with a sturdy hoist jutting from its bed along with a large, weatherproof metal toolbox. From then on, Cletus became the local itinerant mechanic. Everbody was happy, especially Shelly, because now she got to go with her daddy when he went to 'do some fixin'.

Clete's true passion was diesel engines. Most coal trucks were company owned and maintained, but a few local boys ran their own dumps or logging rigs. Every owner did some repair, but when it came to a rebuild or overhaul, all of southern McDowell County knew that Clete Stamper was "the best they is."

Shelly also loved big trucks. By the age of five she'd learned how to help her daddy, bringing him tools then climbing up on the fender to watch him work. She even learned fractions, having to know the difference between an 11/16 and a 3/4-inch wrench. Sometimes she'd climb into the cab and take the massive steering wheel in her tiny hands, pretending she was hauling a load down the highway. But nothing excited Shelly more than when Clete would take the rig out for a drive to test his repairs. She'd let out a delighted scream as soon as the diesel coughed to life and the truck trembled with power. It was all Clete could do to make Shelly sit down as he wound the truck through the tight mountain curves, gearing up and down and working both shift levers at once.

The preferred truck in the mountains was the Mack B-61: ruggedly elegant with its rounded contours and heavy frame. "Ah like all trucks," Clete told Shelly as they rolled along, the rebuilt Thermodyne diesel purring like a 2,000 pound lion, "but these Macks are sum'thin else."

"Can I have one someday, Daddy, when I git older?" Shelly asked.

"Reckon ya kin, darlin'. If'n that's what ya really want."

"It's what I want."

Shortly before she turned six an event occurred that Shelly Stamper certainly did not want, even though she had heard rumors of its imminence for years. Despite having been thoroughly warned and preparations made for weeks in advance, when it descended upon her one sunny morning in early September, she was not ready for the unrelenting tedium of the whole business. Shelly went to War; more precisely, the elementary school in War, West Virginia. She had been to War many times before as it was the nearest town to Peapatch with a range of services, but Shelly had never previously been confined there; made a prisoner of War, restrained, told to "sit at your desk, young lady, stay quiet and study until the bell rings." Her teacher, Mrs. Weller, was a substantial woman who looked to Shelly to be of an age where she may have given Stonewall Jackson his first grammar lesson. In the ensuing struggle, Frieda Weller had an unfair advantage, for she had dealt with many Shelly Stampers over the years while Shelly had never crossed swords with any Mrs. Wellers.

Each morning, after they stopped to visit Cliff, Clete's good friend who owned a local gas station, Clete dropped Shelly off at school on his way to the Devil's Fork Mine outside of Warriormine. On Shelly's third day of school the principal phoned Ethel to ask why Shelly was absent. Ethel's shriek alerted him that Shelly's absence was unplanned and the War Police Department didn't find her until mid-afternoon, out of sight down the steep banks of the Dry Fork, playing happily in the water. After that, Clete had to walk Shelly into the school building each morning.

When Cletus and Ethel came to the first of what would be many, many school meetings with Mrs. Weller, she told them that Shelly was a quick, even an eager learner, especially with reading and numbers. Shelly's problems were that she wouldn't stay at her desk, didn't like to be told what to do and enjoyed fighting with other children.

"Ain't that normal?" Clete asked.

Both Ethel and Mrs. Weller assured him it wasn't.

Despite her scrapes Shelly managed good grades, though she sat in the corner nearly as often as she occupied her own desk. That was okay with Shelly, who reckoned that if you were stuck inside a school all day, one chair was as good as another.

Shelly's aptitude for learning was not accidental. She got more from her daddy than just a love of trucks, for Cletus Stamper was a rare sort of individual in southern West Virginia: a reader and a philosopher. He had a curiosity for all that nature encompassed and though a devout Christian, never became so enamored of the Bible or Pastor Scoggins' preaching that he discounted science. Clete was fascinated by the way the land, water, and air all worked together with the plants and animals to make an operational planet. Certainly he chalked it up to the hand of God, but he wanted to know how the whole shebang functioned and that wasn't what the Bible was meant to explain.

As much as Clete loved mountain air and the light that was the source of life, it was in the dank blackness of the mine that his passion soared, growing so strong in him that sometimes he had trouble concentrating on his work. He was awed and overwhelmed whenever he tried to conceive the extent of the ages the earth had spanned, and in the deep coal shafts all around him was the hard evidence. When underground, Clete became immersed in time. "Three hun'ernt million years ago," he told other miners, "was when this'n here coal started ta form. Jus' think about that, three hun'ernt million years. An' here we are, standin' right in the middle of what was growin' on earth back then."

He'd pick up a chunk of coal and squeeze it in his bare hand, feeling how it was different from other rock, and how this squeezing had turned trees and plants, and even some animals, he reckoned, into this black substance. Sometimes Cletus thought he could see what the earth was like when this coal was alive: hot and humid, the air dripping with swampy rankness: mosses, trees and ferns covering the boggy landscape. Clete also knew all about the arthropods and tetrapods from that time: dragonflies a yard wide, scorpions two feet long, and lizard-like amphibians up to thirty feet long. When Clete took Shelly to see *Journey to the Center of the Earth* on a Friday evening just before she started school, he was so entranced that he went back on Saturday and watched it again by himself.

What fascinated Cletus most was that coal still had life in it from three hundred million years ago and could put that life into motion again. It gave off light, kept people warm and turned the wheels that powered factories: "Hep'n people t'day," as he put it. Sometimes, when no one was around, he'd switch off his miner's lamp and let the darkness settle through him, feeling in this silent blackness how it was before Creation. Clete had no fear of the mines: their deadly gasses, fires and explosions, cave-ins and rock falls. Nor did he fear lightless eternity. Alone and quiet, hundreds of feet underground, rounded by a blackness so complete it clutched at a man's soul, it was just him and God, and coal was evidence that the Lord planned it out in the beginning. A line from one of Clete's favorite songs went: "Like a fiend with his dope and a drunkard his wine, a man will have lust for the lure of the mine," and Clete knew it was true.

To Ethel, not a damn thing was fascinating about coal or coal mines. Mining was a dirty, dangerous business that made men sick, crippled, hard-edged and too often dead and she was bent on getting Cletus working above ground. Clete couldn't smoke in the mine, so he chewed Union Workman tobacco when underground. The rest of the time he puffed Lucky Strikes.

Clete tried to hide it, but Ethel had seen the greasy brown blobs that he coughed up. "'Tween that coal dust you breathe all day an' them coffin nails you smoke, you ain't gonna be long fer this world," she groused. "These kids need a daddy growin' up, an' I wouldn't mind havin' ya around awhile longer."

"My dad did both all 'is life and lived ta be eighty," Clete told her, but he knew his lungs were getting worse. His doctor had warned him; "If you want to stay above ground, you've got to stop workin' underground. And if you don't give up those Luckies, you're not going to be lucky much longer."

Ethel's concerns went beyond Clete's lungs. Every year brought a stream of mining accidents and disasters to West Virginia. The worst had been 1925 when 686 miners died, but even in the 1950's and 60's miners died by the score every year. She waited for her chance, vowing that someday she'd get Cletus out of the mine.

But as 1962 approached, Ethel's most immediate problem was Shelly's behavior in school. She and Clete now had four kids and she was pregnant again. Ethel couldn't devote all of her time to one child and the staff at War Elementary School felt the same way. Clete still brought Shelly to school, but she rode the school bus home. By October she'd been banned from the bus for fighting and since Shelly couldn't be left unsupervised, she had to wait for an hour in the principal's office until Clete could pick her up from work. It was hell for Shelly, and whether she was six or later on when she was sixty, Shelly Stamper never suffered hell on anyone's account that she didn't create hell for them.

Clete had an idea. His good friend, Clifton Collins, owned a Mobilgas station one block from the school and Shelly could wait for him there. Cliff and Shelly were buddies and Shelly hopped with excitement when told. After school she went directly and without problems – for Ethel let her know she'd be back in the principal's office if there were any – to Cliff's where he presented her with a lollipop if she behaved. This wasn't an issue, because Cliff, though spare with his words and generous by nature, was tough as girder iron and took nonsense from no one. When he saw that Shelly knew tools and loved helping, he made her his official 'number one assistant'.

That solved one problem. Ethel addressed Shelly's other behaviors by telling her if she didn't have any trouble at school that week, she could go to the Saturday matinee, but she didn't always make it, for in a town named War, she was far from the only kid who liked to scrap.

"We cain't blame Shelly fer ev'ry fight she gits in," Cletus told Ethel, taking Shelly's side, as usual. "Other kids start 'em too, y'know. You wouldn't want yer daughter runnin' away, now would ya?"

"She could walk away," Ethel said.

"Jus' like you use ta do, Ethel?" Clete said, laughing.

But Shelly did regulate her pugnacity to where she didn't miss any movies she really wanted to see. From the previews she knew the upcoming shows and soon both the Stampers and the school staff considered bribing the local theater into showing a Roy Rogers film every week. Shelly liked Roy and Dale Evans, of course, but her real love was for Trigger and Dale's horse, Buttermilk, and soon a new problem arose.

"Whatcha gonna be when you grow up, Shelly?" Clete would ask her.

"I wanna be a cowboy."

"Ya can't be a cowboy," Ethel would remind her, "You're a girl."

"Then I wanna be a cow*girl*."

"Ah thought you wanted ta be a truck driver," Cletus would say.

"I can do both," Shelly insisted. "I wanna be a truck drivin' cowgirl. When do I git my horse?"

"It ain'ta gonna' happen," Ethel'd tell her. "We got too many kids to start in acquirin' horses."

Shelly begged for a horse, pleaded and whined: for her birthday, for Christmas, even Valentine's Day. "I'll pay fer it, Mama. I'll go ta work in the mine on weekends an' after school ta buy a horse."

That set Ethel's copper skin to blazing. "They don't let girls work in coal mines," she said. "An' if this world had any sense they wouldn't let boys or men work in 'em neither."

Half a mile east of the Stampers lived an older couple named Clemens who had a lazy brown quarter horse that served as a pasture ornament. They called him Tramp because he liked to escape from his rickety jackleg fence and wander the neighborhood. Whenever he got close to the Stampers, Shelly led him back home. Though discouraged by Ethel, Shelly, now ten, would go over to their place, take carrots or apples, and lean over the fence and pet him. But no matter how many times Shelly asked the Clemens, they would not let her ride Tramp.

"Quit askin' 'em," Ethel told her sternly.

"They're mean," Shelly said, and stomped her foot.

"They are not," Ethel said, " they're jest old an' set in their ways. They never had kids and don't want ta be worryin' about ya gittin hurt."

Then the story got around that the Clemens' were moving: selling out and going to Florida. Shelly worried horribly about what would become of Tramp. He wasn't a young horse or worth much and one day after school when Shelly was at Cliff's, she overheard somebody tell him, "Jack Clemens tol' me t'other day they still hain't found nobody ta take that horse a' their'n. They's prob'ly gonna hafta put 'im down."

Cliff came back into his garage and found Shelly bawling inconsolably. She also cried the entire way home with Clete. "We can't let 'em, Daddy," she wailed. "They can't shoot Tramp. It ain't fair. He ain't done nothin' ta deserve bein' shot. How can them old people be so mean?"

"It'll be okay, honey," Clete told her, "It'll be okay, Ah promise."

Shelly was still crying with her face buried in her hands when they pulled into the driveway. When she looked up, Tramp was standing in one of the fenced lots that made up part of the Stamper's twenty acres.

"Yer mama went an' got 'im today," Clete told her. "We talked about it las' night."

Tramp came with some old tack and a battered saddle that fit neither horse nor rider well, so Shelly often rode him bareback: 'Indian style' as they called it. Shelly knew nothing about riding except what she'd seen in the movies, so she fell off a lot at first, but always hopped right back on. Wiry and fearless, she was a natural and soon was riding Tramp across any terrain that wasn't fenced off. She also discovered that Tramp wasn't lazy at all, merely bored, and though seventeen years old, still had plenty of gumption when urged on. And Shelly urged him on plenty. She rode Tramp nearly every day after school and on weekends ranged as far as she could go.

Ethel imposed only three rules: that she not miss church or Sunday dinner and that she stay off the highway. "You can cross it, but there's too many hills an' curves fer you to be ridin' on it. Them trucks an' cars can't see ya."

With a horse of her own, Shelly was not as interested in watching movies on Saturday and Ethel feared losing that leverage. But after Ethel banned Shelly from riding Tramp for a week because she'd blackened the eye of a girl two years older than herself, Ethel knew she had found behavioral paydirt. Shelly would also do anything for a new piece of tack and over the next two years she acquired new bridles, bits and a lead rope, but she still had the same saddle, which was now dangerously decrepit.

Cletus had relatives scattered throughout the north, particularly Ohio, and he enjoyed visiting them. Though sober and industrious at home, Clete enjoyed a drink and cuttin' up now and again but didn't think it proper to do it locally, especially around Ethel or where Preacher Scoggins would catch wind of it. He often took Shelly, and later on, Clete Jr., along. Ethel knew what was going on, and though set against drinking, allowed Cletus to take the two older children "so long as you don't put them kids in no danger," which Cletus never did.

His most common destination was Gallipolis, Ohio, to visit his older brother. Vertnor was a happy sort who played fiddle and he would have other musicians over when Clete came. Clete couldn't play music but he sang a little and could dance an Appalchian flatfoot and do a hillbilly stomp like nobody's business. Shelly joined in and by the time she was eleven could match Clete step for step.

Shelly's favorite part of the drive up from Peapatch – and Junior's least enjoyable - was crossing the Silver Bridge over the Ohio River between Point Pleasant, West Virginia and Gallipolis. Fifteen hundred feet long, slim and graceful, the aged span was regularly given a thick coat of shiny aluminum paint that maintained, at least, its name. Arching high above the river like a tired old dragon trying to keep its belly out of the water, the structure was prone to an unsettling swaying motion and an occasional bout of the shakes, especially in a stiff wind, that earned it a local nick-name: the Monster of Beauty.

Adding to this, stop lights just before both the north and south ramps meant that traffic often backed-up on the narrow two-lane road-bed, where drivers and passengers got to fully experience the bridge's rhythm. Southern West Virginia had nothing like it and Shelly enjoyed soaring over the big river. To her it felt like the car was flying. She even loved being marooned by a red light, especially on the long center span between the two giant steel towers, where she could look far down and watch the boats and barges furrowing the chocolate water. Junior trembled like the bridge and felt like he was going to throw up.

"Quit bein' setch a baby," Shelly told him, but Clete tried to ease his fear.

"It's aw'right. This ol' bridge moves a little, but that's what it was built ta do. If it warn't safe they wouldn't let people cross it."

A year or so back, Shelly had spied a small tack shop just past the ramp where the bridge touched down on the Ohio side of the river. The next day Clete drove her there and she coaxed him into buying her a halter. After that the tack shop became a stop on every trip, though Clete made it clear that most of the time it was for looking only. This was okay with Shelly, because she was happy just to visit with the owner, Bev, an elderly, but knowledgable horsewoman who had actually known Roy Rogers.

"You really knew him?" Shelly asked, when she first found out. "He's mah fav'rit cowboy."

"I certainly did," Bev told her. "I used to let Lennie ride my horse when he worked in a shoe factory and lived with his folks on a houseboat in Portsmouth."

"Lennie?" Shelly asked.

"Sure," Bev said. "Leonard Slye. That's Roy's real name."

When Shelly and Clete got outside, Shelly said, "Daddy, I don't know as Roy Rogers is my fav'rit cowboy no more."

"How come?"

" 'Cause he's really Leonard Slye from Portsmouth."

Cletus knelt down and cupped his hands around Shelly's shoulders. "That should make you like him even more."

"It should?"

"Honey, anybody named Leonard Slye who works in a shoe factory and then becomes King of the Cowboys deserves a whole mountain of respect. It jus' shows you, darlin', that somebody who works at it kin be whatever he," and here Clete looked his daughter straight in the eye, "or *she*, wants ta be."

In early December Clete and Shelly stopped at the tack shop on a trip up to Vertnor's and Shelly was immediately drawn to a used saddle for sale on consignment. When she sat on it, Shelly could tell the saddle was built for a behind like hers and that it would fit Tramp. The price was $75 and Bev said, "That saddle's worth a lot more than that, but the owner needs Christmas money and wants a quick sale. It won't be here long."

Clete could see that Shelly dearly wanted the saddle but he had previously warned her, "We cain't be stoppin' by here ev'ry time we come up ta Gallipolis if yer gonna beg for sum'thin an' throw a fit over not gittin it."

When he told Ethel about the saddle they agreed to buy it for Shelly's Christmas present.

Shelly whooped with delight when they told her. "How soon kin we go back ta Gallipolis, Daddy? I'm 'fraid that saddle won't be there. You heard what Bev said about it goin' quick."

This was on Monday evening.

"The first day off Ah can git is Friday, honey," Cletus said, "but you oughta call an' find out if that saddle's still there 'fore we head up all that way."

On Tuesday Shelly called Bev. "Yeah, it's still here," Bev told her, "but some people are interested. A couple of folks are trying to get the money together and I told them it's strictly first come, first serve."

"We got the money, we jes can't git there before Friday. Can't ya hold it for me till then?

On the other end of the line, Bev was silent.

"It's my Christmas present," Shelly said. "Daddy's drivin' me up jes ta git it."

After another long pause, Bev said, "Alright, Shelly. I know how badly you want that saddle, and it fits you better than anybody else."

"Thank you, Bev, thank you," Shelly said. "You don't know how much that saddle means ta me."

"Oh, I think I do," Bev answered. "I was a girl with her first horse once too, you know." Then Bev said, "Listen, Shelly, I need to close right at five on Friday and I can't be open this Saturday because I have to go to a funeral."

"We'll be there, I promise," Shelly said. "Won't hell ...I mean heck, nor high water keep me from it."

Ethel arranged for Shelly and Junior to take that Friday off from school and Shelly was up before first light, getting everything ready so they could leave as soon as possible. She woke Junior up early too.

"It's still dark, Shelly. Let me sleep awhiles."

"Git up," Shelly told him, "an' git ready or I'll pour water on ya."

Downstairs, she pestered Clete till he finally said, "Dang, girl, at least let me finish breakfast 'fore we git on the road."

"I packed us a lunch," Shelly said, "So's we won't have ta stop nowhere."

"Now, honey, you know we gotta go ta Logan County first an' see yer cousin Wilbur. He owes me a little money an' I need ta git it while Wilbur still has it, cuz he don't have it long."

"I know Daddy, that's why we need ta be goin'."

"Settle down a mite, we got plenty a' time. It ain't all that far ta Wilbur's."

But to Shelly it seemed far. Even in those early hours, highways 80 and 52 were clogged with slow moving coal trucks. Throughout the raw, sunless morning they crawled north, and then, when they arrived at Wibur's ramshackle digs on Buffalo Creek Road near Saunders, he wasn't home.

"Hih' be back shortly," his heavily pregnant girlfriend, Shirl, said. "He just went ta check on sump'thin'."

An hour and a half went by and Shelly was going bonkers. "Let's go, Daddy, let's jes go. There ain't no tellin' when dumb old Wilbur'll be back."

"Hih' be here directly," Shirl told Shelly, "an' Wilbur ain't dumb."

"I've heard you tell 'im he was a hund'ert times," Shelly said.

Shirl thought a second. "Well, he ain't *old*." She turned to Clete. "He's got yor money with 'im an' he's fetchin' ya a present." She rubbed a palm over her bulging belly as she stirred a cast-iron pot on the woodstove. "Wilbur won't be late fer lunch, Ah'm cookin' 'im up some squirrel an' ramps. Y'all wanna stay?"

"Shor do," Cletus and Junior said at the same time Shelly said, "No!"

At ten till noon Wilbur's rusted-out Chevy pickup roared up to where the driveway ended fifty yards from the house. Clete and Shelly went out to meet him while Junior stayed inside and sampled the squirrel. Wilbur jumped out of the cab grinning. "Howdy, uncle Clete," he said, then put his hands under Shelly's armpits and lifted her high off the ground. "An' you too, cuzzin Shelly."

"Put me down," Shelly hollered, "we gotta git goin', we're late."

Junior walked up and Wilbur yelled, "Hey to ya, Junior," and lifted him over his head and spun him like a propeller.

"Still playin' banjo?" Junior called down to him.

"You betcha. Daddy'd tan me if I ever quit." Wilbur's 280 pounds shook as he laughed and set Junior back on the ground. "Sorry ta keep y'all waitin' so, but I had ta grab a coupla' things for ya ta take up ta pa's." Wilbur pulled a wad of small bills from his torn jeans. "Here's the money ya loaned me, Clete," he said, then reached through his open pickup window and handed Clete two one-quart mason jars full of clear liquid. "An' this here's some in'terst on the loan."

Shelly looked at Clete. "Now I know why we came ta Buffalo Holler."

They slowly wound north, through small towns that Cletus knew to be tax-enhancing speed traps. Traffic remained heavy and the curvy, hilly roads offered scant opportunity to pass. Shelly grew frantic and her mood as glum as the sun-deprived day. "We ain't gonna make it in time," she said, icily.

"We'll pick up some speed when we git on Route 35," Clete told her, but they didn't. It looked like all of southern Ohio was coming to Charleston for Christmas shopping and all of Charleston going to Ohio. Then they had to wait at two sections of road repair.

"I ain't gonna git that saddle," Shelly said to her dad. "An' it's all 'cause you wanted likker. Goin' ta Wilbur's was clear outa the way and you know it."

Clete did know it, and he had to admit, if only to himself, that going to Wilbur's had been a mistake. Normally they would have had plenty of time, but today it felt like some unseen force was working against them.

When Clete sighted the Ohio River valley at twenty minutes before five, he reckoned they'd make it. But Clete didn't figure on Point Pleasant having a rush hour, which on Friday afternoon pushing up against Christmas, it surely did. Then he remembered the stoplight right before the ramp onto the Silver Bridge. Oh, Lord, he said to himself, let us hit that light green.

Junior sat silent, squeezed in the middle of the front seat and queasy as usual about going over the bridge. Shelly looked anxiously out the side window, chewing on her lip and cracking her knuckles. The overcast day had deepened to a slate-gray gloom, not yet darkness, but one long, continuous shadow that cast its pall over the land. The first snow flurries blew in and a blast of wind gusted down the wide valley, rattling the stark trees along the near bank and making their black, leafless branches shudder in violent spasm.

As they worked their way up to the traffic signal ahead it went red. With a brittleness in her voice that Clete had never heard before, Shelly said, "If I don't git that saddle causa' you stoppin' for moonshine Daddy. . ."

Clete's heart went to his throat, but he cut her off. "Don't darlin', please don't. Ah'm tryin' mah best to git us there." When the light changed green and the line of traffic began moving Cliff said, "We're gonna make it, Shelly."

Shelly looked at her watch; they still had ten minutes.

But consistent with the hapless day, a couple of the coal-heaped semis ahead were slow in getting moving, and with three vehicles in front of them, the light went yellow. Two of the cars passed under it as Shelly yelled frantically, "Run it, Daddy, run it!"

Cletus stepped on the gas peddle, but the car in front of them stopped.

Shelly's front teeth bit into her lip and she couldn't hold back tears. In the colorless dusk, Shelly looked across the wide, murky river to Ohio where the tack shop sat, less than a mile away. But with cars and semis lined end-to-end on the bridge's roadbed and halted by the holiday traffic backed up on the far side, her saddle may as well have been in Siberia. Shelly didn't say anything but her face was as steely as the suspension bridge that towered in front of them. She glared at the structure malevolently, as if it was to blame for her not getting the saddle. Then Shelly wiped the tears off her cheeks and turned the stare on her father.

"Ah'm sorry, honey," Cletus said, "Ah'm real sorry," and was near to tears himself. Not knowing what else to say, Clete stared at the stoplight, trying to will it to turn green. From somewhere over near the Ohio side of the river he heard a strange *Ping!* like a shearing or breaking of metal. The light changed and the car in front of them drove onto the ramp but Clete, whose ears were attuned to un-natural sounds from years of working in the mine, just watched and listened to the massive iron creature before them.

"Go on, Daddy," Shelly yelled, "the light's green," but Clete kept his foot on the brake.

The sound came to them first: a grating, metallic creaking followed by a deep rumbling groan rising out of the earth. Their Pontiac trembled slightly, then shuddered with an unholy vibration. Junior started screaming as Shelly's eyes went white and wide as saucers.

The suspension bridge's far tower began tilting to the right; tilting, tilting, tilting, then went over, twisting the roadbed along the entire length of the span upside down, hurtling its load of cars and trucks into the dark river one hundred feet below where they struck the water with horrible thuds, each making its own explosion that shattered the river's smooth surface. The Silver Bridge then began a slow and terrible ballet of self-destruction as it collapsed, smashing into the river and sending up plume after giant plume of violent spray along the entire width of the Ohio. The crashing and rending of metal grew to a deafening roar, blasting through the thick air with a force that shook the Stamper's car.

Transfixed, they watched as the tower directly in front of them, pulled by the steel suspension bars still attached to the far tower, toppled into the river with a thunderous impact, casting a huge fountain of brown water high into the air. As a final act to the tragedy playing out before them, the truss span of the ramp leading to the doomed tower fell with a loud ripping and crunching of girders, first dropping, and then crushing the cars and trucks that had been sitting at the stop light in front of them.

Junior sat crying and shivering, trying to catch his breath and Clete leaned over and wrapped his arms around his son.

"Oh, Daddy, Daddy!" Shelly yelled.

Cletus remained silent. He didn't have words for something this terrible. When the awful grinding and mangling of steel subsided, Clete, Junior, and Shelly got out of the car to look, unbelieving, upon the wreckage before them. The scale of the disaster was gargantuan, otherworldly, frightening in its size. The Stamper's stood gaping, barely able to breathe, as the wind coming off the river, cold as the air from a tomb, whipped against their faces.

And then other, even more horrifying sounds, replaced the bridge's death roar. From the nearby ramp came the screams of those trapped in the tangled girders, and faint, yet clear, through the dense air they heard the helpless and terrified cries of those still alive in the deathly cold water of the Ohio River.

Shelly's saddle didn't seem important to her anymore. "Daddy," she said between sobs, "is God punishin' them people?"

Cletus held onto his silence for a moment. "No, honey, God's not punishin' them people. It's jus' their time ta go …an' not ours."

Chapter 2

Every year at Christmas Vertnor and his son Wilbur returned to the Stamper house for several days. Vertnor was fifteen years older than Cletus and looked nothing like him. Bandy-legged, barrel chested and balding, he had a set of buckteeth so gapped and protruding people said he could eat corn on the cob through a picket fence.

Despite a run of bad luck, Vertnor laughed easy and often. He married in 1942, shortly after joining the Army and from early 1943 on was in the middle of some of the toughest fighting in Africa and Europe. In January of 1945 the Sherman tank he commanded tangled with a German Panther and lost. Two crewmen died and Vertnor's right hand was mangled. He lost three-quarters of his pinky, one-half of his ring finger, and a fourth of his middle finger but he could still bow a fiddle and counted himself lucky. Whenever anyone from up north asked him what happened to his hand Vertnor would tell them, "Dontcha' know, that's how they teach us fractions in Wes' Virginia."

In early 1947 Vertnor's wife died three days after Wilbur was born. Vertnor and Clete's mother had died two years before, so Vertnor and baby Wilbur moved back into the family home in Peapatch where old Lemuel helped raise Wilbur. In 1953, the year before Cletus married Ethel, Vertnor took a welding job up in Gallipolis, partly because he knew a number of musicians there.

Foremost of these was a mandolin and guitar picking Black man named Benjamin Franklin Webber with whom Vertnor had played music before the war. Ben had been raised in western North Carolina and liked an emerging style of mountain music that would come to be known as bluegrass. Vertnor moved into a house three doors away from Ben and paid his wife to look after Wilbur while he was at work or away playing music. People who stopped by the Webber house at mealtime were often surprised to see a large, plump, alabaster boy sitting at the long table amidst seven skinny Black children as if a snow goose had deposited its egg, cuckoo style, in a raven's nest. None of Ben's children liked 'hillbilly music', so as soon as Wilbur was old enough to hold an instrument they thrust a banjo into his hands. Wilbur played in their band until he met Shirl Hatfield at age sixteen, quit school and went to live near her family in Logan County, a little northwest of Peapatch.

Shirl and Wilbur moved into a small cabin up Buffalo Holler where Wilbur soon hunkered down to a life of hunting, fishing and playing the banjo. From Shirl's relatives he learned the fine art of making moonshine (she was, after all, a Hatfield) and when absolutely necessary he drove a truck or operated heavy equipment.

Shelly loved her uncle Vertnor like all git out, but thought cousin Wilbur, eight years her senior, was an overly rambunctious, underly intelligent, boob. Her first vague memory of him was at grandpa Lem's funeral where Wilbur, then eleven, bawled so loud he nearly disrupted the service. Shelly also never understood why her father went to visit Wilbur so often, usually when Ethel took the kids to her mother's in Kentucky. "How come you go ta Wilbur's, Daddy, 'stead a' goin' ta Grammy's with us?"

"Cuz Ah like ta hunt an' fish with him and Shirl's family. They're a lot a' fun," Clete told her.

"Wilbur's dumb."

"Wilbur ain't nare as dumb as he acts," Clete said. "An' he has a tougher time than he lets on, never havin' had a mother. Losin' his gran'pa Lem was real hard on Wilbur too, cuz Lem hep'd raise 'im up."

"I wish you'd go ta Kentucky with us."

"Now honey, Ah spend lots a' time with you an' the family. Ah promised Vertnor I'd look in on Wilbur now an' agin. He needs it more'n ya know, Shelly."

———————————————

Despite the Silver Bridge disaster, the Stampers worked hard to make this Christmas a joyous one. Vertnor came on the 23rd and Wilbur and

Shirl arrived on the 24th. Ethel went to great lengths to get everyone into the Christmas spirit but beneath the gaiety she saw the sorrow in Junior, Shelly and Clete. Vertnor had also been affected, having crossed the bridge hundreds of times and knowing some of the people who were lost.

Shelly played along with her little siblings who still believed in Santa Claus, but she had to force her smiles and laughs.

"I know it's gotta be hard, seein' that happen in front a' ya like that," Ethel told her, "but our family was spared."

Shelly was old enough to understand what this Christmas must be like for the families of those people who were in the cars and trucks that had fallen from the bridge. "I know, Mama. I'm thankful."

On Christmas morning Shelly trooped down the maple staircase and saw a big lumpy present under the lower branches of the Christmas tree. She knew right away it was a saddle, but when she unwrapped it and saw that it was *the* saddle, her tears came. "How?" she said, looking up at Ethel and Cletus.

"Reckon you owe most a' the thanks to your uncle Vertnor," Clete said. "Ah ask'd 'im if he could pick it up that Monday mornin' an' meh'be come up with an excuse why he'd be a little late fer work."

After the hugs and thank yous Shelly asked, "Can I try it out? It ain't all that cold outside."

"Not till after Christmas dinner," Ethel told her. "If you take off on Tramp with that new saddle you might forget about comin' in ta eat."

Dinner started at one and Shelly hoped it would be over quickly, but unforeseen circumstances delayed her ride. On holidays the Shiloh Church members took turns inviting Reverend Scoggins, who was single, to their festivities. He had known Wilbur for many years and had met Shirl several times after they began living together, or as Preacher Scoggins preferred to call it, "fornicating without a license." So when Reverend Scoggins arrived for dinner and saw that Shirl was swollen like a late summer tick but still wore no wedding band, he asked her, as he forked his second piece of breast meat from the large oval turkey plate, "When is your child due?"

"Nare aroun' two weeks," Shirl replied, ladling cranberry sauce into the valley between her corn and butter beans.

"Are you working now?" the preacher asked Wilbur.

Wilbur, who was moving a scoop shovel full of mashed potatoes from the bowl onto his plate, was taken unawares. "Uh, ah … meh'be …"

Shirl had stretched both arms to the center of the table, and as she drew them back with a Parker House roll in each hand, answered for Wilbur. "The Pittston Coal Comp'ny's buildin' a big dam on the crick above us an' they offered Wilbur steady work runnin' dozer. He's gonna take the job, aincha Wilbur?"

Wilbur didn't answer. He was watching the big plate of turkey go around, hoping no one took the last drumstick before it got to him.

"Ain't that right, Wilbur?" Shirl said louder.

The turkey plate made it to Junior, who was seated beside Wilbur, and as Junior took the platter in both hands, Wilbur snatched the drumstick. "Tha's right, darlin'," Wilbur said, and smiled sweetly at his frowning cousin.

Shirl and Wilbur turned to their plates and began eating, hoping Reverend Scoggins would do the same, but he was on a mission.

"Have you chosen the child's name?" the preacher asked as he scooped out dressing from the bowl Ethel handed him.

"Notchet," Shirl answered, as she buttered a roll on both sides and stuffed it into her mouth.

"Cain't," Wilbur said, raising the drumstick to his face.

"How come?" Junior asked, his mind working on how to get the drumstick away from Wilbur before he bit into it.

" 'Cause'n we don't rightly know if it's gonna be a boy or a girl," Shirl told him as she closed her lips around a large spoonful of buttered corn and gravy. Frankly, she was getting tired of all this talk when there was eatin' to be done.

Preacher Scoggins swallowed some butter beans then looked up and said slowly, "I was referring to the baby's *last* name."

Wilbur's fork slipped and penetrated his carefully constructed mashed potato reservoir. Gravy cascaded through the broken dam, washing away his cranberry sauce and drowning low-lying kernels of corn. He quickly grabbed his knife, and using it like a miniature version of the D8 Cat he sometimes operated, tried to repair the leak. No one took outright offense, but the adults at the table knew that more had been breached than just Wilbur's mashed potatoes.

As usual, Wilbur struggled. He'd filled his impoundment pond to the brim and when he brought mashed potatoes from another part of the wall to repair the breach, it weakened that section so that more gravy poured out. Trying to stem the flood and answer the preacher's question at the same time had him befuddled.

Shirl, who would have preferred a dragline to a fork, had just scooped up a load of gravy covered mashed potatoes. She halted the fork in mid-air.

"Ah know yor a'wonderin' why we ain't married, Preacher. It's account a' he ain't ast me."

All eyes turned to Wilbur, who had given up on repairing his dam and was loading casualties onto his fork and rushing them to his belly. Flustered, he said the first thing that came into his mind, "Uh … I didn't know ya wanted me to."

Shirl was levering another mouthful into the air. "Well … Ah do," she said, without taking her eyes from her fork.

Wilbur knew that everyone in the room was watching him, waiting for an answer. "Wouldja pass me the mashed taters?" he asked Cletus and began building another resevoir. Finally he said, "Aw'right then, I reckon we could."

"Could what?" Shirl said, still not looking up.

"Git married," Wilbur answered.

"Air you askin' me?"

Heads swiveled from Wilbur to Shirl like a tennis match. Wilbur only hesitated briefly. "Reckon I am," he said.

Shirl put her fork down and looked at Wilbur. "Then you ask me proper."

Wilbur halted his dam construction. He looked into Shirl's green eyes and said so earnestly that everyone stopped eating. "Will ya marry me, Shirl?"

Shirl returned his tenderness and added a heap of her own. "Yes Ah will, Wilbur."

A respectful silence fell upon those gathered. As they were turning back to their plates, Reverend Scoggins held up a forkfull of stuffing and told them, "I can perform the ceremony right after dinner. All the legal documents are out in my car."

After everyone finished eating Ethel and the three girls began clearing away dishes. Normally, Shirl would have helped, but she announced, "Ah need ta git ready for my weddin'," and headed to the side bedroom she and Wilbur were staying in.

The menfolk moved furniture aside in the living room and set up chairs. Cletus placed a dozen Christmas candles around the room and told Reverend Scoggins, "Ah thought it'd make the ceremony look more solemn."

"If you want a Catholic wedding," the preacher said, only half joking, "I don't speak Latin."

Shirl walked into the room wearing lipstick, makeup and a bright green satin maternity dress that matched her eyes. She'd untied her ponytail and her light-red hair fell to her shoulders. She was a big woman, but not obese, and folks said she 'carried her weight well', for she was strong and active. Now she looked serene, the glow of her smile outdoing the Christmas tree. This was her moment and she intended to make the most of it. Everyone in the room told Shirl how beautiful she looked, and they meant it.

A few moments later Wilbur came down from the upstairs bathroom. Cletus had loaned him a tie, which didn't clash *too* badly with the flannel shirt he wore. He had slicked his black hair straight back and if the smile on his round face didn't quite equal Shirl's glow, everyone agreed that Wilbur, 'didn't look half bad for a Stamper'.

Wilbur gawked at his bride like he was seeing her for the first time. "Where'd ya git that dress, Shirl? It sure is purty. Near as purty as you."

"Ah got it in Welch the day the doctor tol' me Ah was pregnant. Been totin' it aroun' ever' since just in case you wanted ta git married."

"Wish I'd brung some better clothes," Wilbur said.

"You don't need no better clothes, ya look just fine ta me," Shirl said, and took Wilbur's hand in hers.

Preacher Scoggins deftly took over, directing everyone not in the wedding party to be seated. He herded Wilbur and Shirl to the forefront and opened his Bible. The ceremony was simple but tasteful, and though the preacher packaged the message in flowery words, his meaning was clear: You're married until you're dead.

When the reverend presented the newlyweds to the world as Mr. and Mrs. Wilbur Stamper, Shelly let out an audible sigh and was about to get up, but before she could escape, the preacher launched into a sermon. After he'd finished sermonizing, Ethel resumed control and announced pie and ice cream. Shelly gobbled hers and looked anxiously at her mother. "Can I go, now?" she asked.

"Yes, honey, now you kin go," Ethel told her.

Shelly flew up the stairs and in less than a minute bounded back down like a bolt of lightning. Clad in jeans, a heavy jacket and a cap, she scooped up her new saddle and was out the door.

"What was that streak?" Preacher Scoggins asked, as Shelly tore by.

"That was a Wes' Virginia road-runner," Vertnor said.

As soon as the sermon was over, Wilbur and Shirl headed for their bedroom. Preacher Scoggins watched aghast, thinking they were going to consumate their marriage right then, but shortly they emerged and Cletus and Vertnor ducked into the room.

Wilbur never came to holidays empty handed and this Christmas he'd brought two quarts of his best amber moonshine. One jar was hidden under a pillow in the spare bedroom he and Shirl were staying in. Another was squirreled away in the first floor bathroom. Ethel didn't raise a fuss so long as the booze stayed hidden and nobody got outright drunk. The drinkers tried to abide, but the Thanksgiving before last Ethel thought they were hitting the jar too hard and when Cletus went to the cupboard on the back porch where Wilbur had stashed the moonshine, it was gone.

"Let's have us a weddin' reception," Vertnor said. "Go gitch yor banjo, Wilbur."

"Hold on," Reverend Scoggins said.

"Cain't we play music on Christmas, Preacher?" Wilbur asked.

"Not till I get back."

The minister gathered up his wedding gear and hustled out to his car. Five minutes later he returned with a guitar case and unpacked a D-45 Martin.

"Lordy-be, that's a beauty," Vertnor said, and launched into "Shady Grove," on his fiddle.

Shelly rode out into the December afternoon, settling into the soft leather of her new saddle. As she walked Tramp past the house, multicolored lights from the Christmas tree in the window cast a splotch of color into the gunmetal day. From inside came music and the high-lonesome voice of her father, "I saw the li-i-ight, I saw the li-i-ight, " that became fainter and fainter until she could no longer hear it.

She and Tramp ambled west on Peapatch Road, down the twisting grade to where it crossed Highway 635 at Wimmer Gap. The intersection was in the middle of an S curve than made for a dangerous crossing. She halted at the pavement, looked both ways, then put her heels into Tramp's flanks and cantered across. Shelly continued west for half a mile on the narrow road that climbed away from the highway until she reached an abandoned logging trail that wound upward through thick forest to an open ridge. At the top of the ridge she pushed Tramp to a gallop then pulled up just short of a clump of trees on the far side.

Her view to the south was interrupted by a high ridgeline, but in the north, the hills of McDowell County rolled away before her. Though not yet four o'clock, the countryside was in shadow, the sunlight blocked by frothy layers of clouds. Some of the distant hollers were already purple and filling with wispy haze. Shelly sat for a moment, looking at her county, trying to get the horrible images of the Silver Bridge collapse out of her mind. Then she knew where she needed to go, and if she hurried, could get there and back before dark.

Less than two miles away was her special place. A small, un-named creek plunged down a narrow ravine of black stone and rushed through a level, open glade of grass that was surrounded by gnarled trees. The spot was accessible on horseback and Shelly had been there many times. She eased Tramp down the slope and into the forest.

By the time Shelly entered the glade the winter afternoon was slipping into dusk. Even in the daytime, when cascading yellow light filled the circle, this place gave her the spooks, and when she thought about coming here at night, her skin tingled. Shelly walked Tramp around the open circle, maybe eighty feet in diameter, and after twice jumping him over the little creek, dismounted. She let the horse stick his muzzle into the fast flowing water and drink, then led him over to the trees and tied the halter beneath Tramp's bridle to a small oak, leaving him enough rope to nibble at the wet grass.

Patches of snow dotted the ridge where Shelly had stopped earlier, but here the ground was bare. She walked to where the glade narrowed and butted up against the mountain. Through a deep cleft in the dark stone, the creek tumbled ledge over ledge from somewhere high above. Shelly scrambled up and over several small boulders until she was twenty feet into the slot but where she could still watch Tramp. Beside a head-high waterfall she sat down on a large rectangular black stone and then turned and looked up into the narrow fissure where the creek gushed from the mountain. The gloom was too deep for her to see to the top, but she knew the creek made a sharp right turn into a narrow cleft of jagged stone. Several times she had tried to climb there, seeking the origin of the rushing stream that danced its way down the rocks, but Shelly never could reach that spot where the creek bent back and out of sight. The ravine was too steep, the wet rock too slippery, and tantalizingly close to the top, where the water gushed into the light and took its first leap, a twelve-foot vertical slab of black granite guarded the crevice like a massive, immovable troll. Even when Shelly climbed the hills above the creek, she could not see down into where the stream began, as if its mother mountain wanted this child to remain a mystery.

Shelly closed her eyes and listened, letting her mind flow with the cascading water. After a few minutes, she opened her eyes and saw that the shadows in the glade had deepened and the ravine above her was shrouded in sable. It was time to go. She climbed out of the crevice and walked back into the tree-lined circle, now so cloaked in winter twilight it resembled a dim grotto. The surrounding oaks loomed menacingly, their crooked branches writhing in the breeze and Shelly imagined spirits lurking behind their dark trunks. A shiver darted up her spine and she hurried toward Tramp, but something made her stop and look at the little creek one more time.

Shelly stared into the swirling water, following it downstream with her eyes, thinking that where the little creek went was as mysterious as where it came from. At the point where the stream disappeared in a thick haze of forest she thought she saw a glimmer of colored light. The light quickly went out and a minute later appeared again before it vanished like a will-o'-the-wisp. Baffled by the enchanting glow Shelly started walking along the bank, pushing aside branches and weaving in and out of trees.

She followed the creek into the forest until she reached the spot where she'd seen it vanish. There, the water settled into a still pool before dropping over a natural barricade of stones and rushing on into the woods.

Through an opening in the trees a narrow shaft of light illuminated the pool and Shelly gazed at her reflexion in the flat water. Entranced, Shelly forgot where she was and when she glanced up, realized she was boxed in by a maze of gnarled, mishappen oaks and willows. The surrounding thicket was so dense with twisted branches Shelly felt like she had been led into a trap or stumbled onto an ogre's mountain fortress.

From downstream, a gust of wind whipped the still water into a series of ripples that broke her reflexion into a shimmering prism. When the pool settled, new images appeared and with sudden clarity Shelly saw where the little stream traveled: to places dark and unknown, light and airy, wild and civilized. She saw where the creek merged with the Tug Fork, then the Big Sandy, which flowed north to the Ohio, the river that had swallowed all those poor people. Further downstream this water became part of the great Mississippi, a river she had long dreamt of seeing. On it flowed, no longer a tiny creek in the mountains, until it reached the ocean, becoming part of the vast, wide world, for that was the creek's destiny. Shelly saw her own reflexion again and knew that her destiny was the same as the creek's, to leave these mountains and become part of the wider world. She'd seen her future and her body tingled with energy.

Shelly followed the creek back to the glade, got on Tramp and turned him toward the forest, trusting his eyes to guide her in the dusk. She climbed slowly out of the vale, trying to dodge the brush and briars that were nearly indistinguishable from patches of shadow. Often she had to back Tramp out of thick tangles and by the time she reached the path that led to the highway stars sprinkled the black sky. Shelly stopped her horse and looked up, trying to recognize the constellations her father had taught her. She saw the Big Dipper and enough of the Little Dipper to locate the North Star, but didn't see her two favorites; the tight little cluster of the Pleiades or the great square of Pegasus, the winged horse. She turned Tramp toward the east and home.

––––––––––––––––––––

Before she even got to the driveway, Shelly heard music blaring from the lighted house, louder, but not as pure as when she rode out. The playing continued as she unsaddled Tramp and rubbed him down. On her way to the house, Shelly went into the pen where Clete kept his two hounds, Homer and Jethro. They bounded over, eager for a warm hand on their flanks in the cool night, and Shelly knelt down and petted them. She opened the back door and walked through the kitchen, stopping beneath the arched doorway that led into the living room. The revelers were heartily swatting out the "Mule Skinner Blues." Reverend Scoggins was gone: out the door, Shelly guessed, as soon as he realized they were drinking. Wilbur and Vertnor were whipping the song along with some quick licks and Cletus was carrying the lyrics and trying to dance, but was having trouble staying on his feet. Shirl, who only knew half the words, and whose singing Vertnor once compared to "a hound dog with his balls caught in a steel trap," made up for her vocal deficiencies with volume.

Cletus looked over at Shelly when the song ended. "C'mon in 'n join us, honey," he said.

Shelly looked at the group but remained silent, hesitant about crossing the living room to the staircase.

"Hey, cuzzin, how 'uz yor horsey ride?" Wilbur hollered as he reached down and opened his banjo case. He lifted out a jar, had a swig and handed it to Shirl, who did likewise then passed the moonshine to Clete and Vertnor.

They ain't even hidin' their likker now, Shelly thought. An' they got it close to 'em so's Mama can't take it away.

She headed into the living room, wanting to get up the stairs, and when she passed by her father, he reached out for her. "Hey, honey, why'ncha stay 'n sing wi' us awhile. Meh'be we cou' dance us a flatfoot ta'gether."

Shelly sidestepped away from Clete and when he tried to take a step toward her he let go of the hutch he was clinging to and nearly fell down. His face was flushed, his red eyes sad and bleary with drink. "Come o'r here'n gi' me a hug, Shelly," he said.

"I'm tired, Daddy, I'm goin' up ta my room," Shelly told him and bounded up the stairs.

———————————

Shelly opened the door to her bedroom and was surprised to see the rest of the family: Ethel, Junior, Sarah, Mack, and Sadie, sitting clumped together on her bed. The three younger kids had their backs against the wall and were wrapped in blankets while Junior, clad in blue pajamas, sat cross-legged in the middle of Shelly's feather mattress. Each pair of hands, except for Ethel's, which held a book, cradled a mug of steaming hot chocolate.

Ethel had her back propped against the tall maple headboard. The attached reading lamp cast a narrow, soft-yellow beam onto the book she was reading aloud from while two candles from the earlier wedding sat on Shelly's dresser and bed table, bouncing shadows off the darkened walls. Ethel stopped reading when Shelly entered and waited until she had taken off her coat, hat and boots and settled onto the bed, snug among her siblings and wrapped in a quilt, the chill from her night ride still in her bones.

When Ethel saw that Shelly was shivering, she took a nearly full mug from the nightstand and passed it to Shelly. "I can't, Mama, that's your's," Shelly said, but Ethel put the warm cup against Shelly's chest and held it there until Shelly took it from her hands. "Thanks, Mama."

"I hoped you'd git back in time ta join us," Ethel said, and Shelly understood why her mother had gathered the children in her room.

Ethel started reading again from one of Shelly's favorite books, *The Wind in the Willows*. Her strong voice was soothing and her soft, northern Kentucky accent strangely fit the story set in the English countryside. In the flickering candlelight, the broad, dark form of Ethel herself was cut straight from a fairytale. She had read this Yuletide chapter aloud to Shelly and Junior once before, but the younger children were hearing it for the first time. Shelly was glad to find that she had come in near the beginning of the story, just when, as Mole and Rat were trudging through the winter night, in dire want of dinner and warm rest, Mole's nose caught the tingling, electric summons of his former, and much loved, abandoned home.

A raucous clamor, led by Shirl's baying, rose from the floor below, but Ethel seemed to not hear it. Using only her will, she turned her children's attention away from the din and drew them into the magical world of two gentle and sentient animals seeking shelter and food, and upon finding those comforts, heartily sharing their good fortune with a troop of caroling field mice.

But it was good to think he had this to come back to, this place which was all his own, these things which were so glad to see him again and could always be counted upon for the same simple welcome.

Ethel closed the book and Mack asked her, "What's that chapter called agin, Mama?"

"'Dulce Domum'," Ethel said.

"What's 'at mean?" Sarah asked.

"It means 'sweetly at home'," Ethel replied, "just like we are, right now."

Later, after Ethel had tucked Junior and Mack into their room and Sarah and Sadie into theirs, she came to Shelly.

"Mama, how come yor lettin' 'em do that downstairs?" Shelly asked her.

" 'Cause I didn't want a big fight in front a' y'all on Christmas," Ethel said.

"I don't think I can sleep with all that racket goin' on."

"Don't you worry none about that, Shelly," Ethel said, as she bent and blew out a candle. "That crew downstairs is about ta be done for the night an' they won't ever be doin' it in this house again. Not if they want us livin' here."

That last sentence frightened Shelly, as she had never considered her mother and father seperating for any reason. She listened as Ethel's solid footsteps descended the stairs. Above the maelstrom of music and singing Shelly heard shouting. The music stopped and Shelly heard more shouting and then arguing and yelling. Within a few minutes silence rose from the ground floor, filling Shelly's room just as the noise had.

Shelly pulled the covers tighter around her. She was back at the dark glade, hemmed round by spectral oaks and gazing into the little creek that ran unfathomably into the future. But now Ratty and Mole were there as well, gaily scampering about the twilit grove, laughing as they danced around Tramp's hooves, while Tramp bent down his long neck and twisted his great head to watch, amused at their antics.

The weird feeling that had been growing in Shelly since the collapse of the Silver Bridge was stronger than ever and she felt that tonight, this Christmas, was the last night of her old life and when she awoke in the morning, all would be different. For Shelly now knew, that like Mole, she would someday forsake this narrow home for the stage of the wider world, and while she may at times be able to look back and view her old self and her old life, there would always be a gauzy layer of mist that prevented her from ever truly returning. Yet just before sleep took her into the new world of morning, Shelly's final thought was of how, even as bedlam prevailed below, her mother had preserved Christmas for her children.

Chapter 3

Nineteen-sixty-eight was as turbulent for Shelly Stamper as it was for the rest of the country. Back before Christmas, Ethel'd had 'the talk' with her, explaining what would soon be happening in her body and how boys fit into the scheme. Shelly was already feeling the changes take place and sometimes her insides hurt, but in late February she started experiencing pain far beyond what Ethel had described. In March Ethel took her to a doctor in Welch who casually told Shelly this was common for girls beginning their periods and would soon pass, but it didn't.

Since she'd gotten Tramp, Shelly's school behavior had improved but when she was hurting she got into trouble and fights. When the pain was so intense she couldn't go to school, Shelly prowled the house like a wounded panther, looking for trouble with anyone who crossed her path. Ethel was as frustrated as Shelly and did everything she could to help her daughter, but she was also adamant. "I know ya hurt, honey, an' we'll do ever'thing we can ta help, but ya can't take it out on other people."

The new year, however, gave Cletus and Ethel more to worry about than just their oldest daughter. As the Stamper family sat together in their living room and watched, the news became more gruesome every month. In late January the Viet Cong and North Vietnamese Army launched the Tet Offensive. Three servicemen from McDowell County had already been killed in Vietnam and in February another one died. In April, Martin Luther King Jr. was assassinated and riots, some deadly, broke out in over one hundred cities and towns. Ethel was particularly upset by King's death. Clete and Ethel both supported the civil rights movement and the Stamper children had been raised to understand that all people are equal and should be treated so. Shelly had heard her mother get into terrible arguments with people who were prejudiced.

In May, another serviceman from the town of War was killed in action. Each evening the news carried stories of protests and riots on the streets or in the universities. Just after school let out for the summer, Bobby Kennedy was shot. Ethel took that hard too. She had hoped he'd become president, as she figured he'd stop the war. Shelly also liked him, but part of that was because she thought he was cute.

Everyone was relieved when the school year ended. Shelly was able to ride Tramp or hike whenever her insides weren't hurting too badly. She had outgrown Roy Rogers and Dale Evans and now imagined she was an Indian. One day as Ethel was hanging laundry, Shelly, wearing warpaint and a feather, dashed up on Tramp like a Commanche and grabbed two fresh towels off the clothesline.

"What're you doin', young lady?" Ethel yelled.

"This is a raid," Shelly hollered.

"Not with my clean linens, it ain't," Ethel said.

"What would I want with takin' dirty ones?"

"You'd best not be stealin' any of 'em," Ethel told her.

"When your're an Indian it ain't stealin'," Shelly said, "it's raidin'."

"Whatever ya call it, you bring them towels back here right now."

Shelly threw a leg over Tramp's neck and lit easily on the ground. When she brought the towels over Ethel said to her, "How come your're an Indian now? Ain't you a little old ta be play-actin'?"

"It jes suits me, I reckon," Shelly said and shrugged her shoulders.

Ethel hung the towels up then looked closely at her daughter. "You been spendin' too much time in the sun," she said. "Your face an' arms are burnt."

"No they ain't," Shelly said, lifting up her shirt to show Ethel that she was the same color all over. "My skin's jes gittin' darker, kinda like your's. I figger'd it was part a' growin' up." Then Shelly laughed. "Maybe I really am part Indian."

Ethel didn't laugh. She put her thick hands under Shelly's armpits and lifted her off the ground until their faces were level. Nose to nose, she stared deeply into Shelly's eyes, like she was trying to read her spirit. Hypnotized by her mother's gaze, Shelly felt helpless. Finally Ethel put her down. "You go on an' play," she said.

Ethel never said another word about the incident and Shelly didn't ask, but she never forgot the intensity in her mother's eyes that day and years would pass before she understood the reason. This wasn't the first time Shelly'd witnessed her mother's odd behavior. She and Junior had talked about Ethel's sudden mood changes and times when Ethel would go off alone and sit silently for hours. Shelly asked Clete about it.

"Don't guess Ah understand some things about Ethel much better'n anybody else," he answered. "But Ah saw it in 'er right away."

"Didja ever ask mama about it or wonder what's goin' on?"

"Oh, Ah've wonder'd plenty," Clete told Shelly, "but Ah've never ask'd. If Ethel wanted ta tell me, she would. All Ah know is she's diff'ernt. The rest a' her fam'ly ain't like her at all. Ah do believe that's part a' what drew me to 'er, though."

Once in a while Cletus could still talk Shelly into going with him when he worked on a truck engine. "C'mon an go with me ta'day," he'd say, "and give 'at ol' horse a' yours a rest. Ah'm fixin' ta rebuild a Mack engine an' could use some hep."

That usually worked, for as much as she loved to ride, Shelly still liked trucks. With their heads bent over a diesel, Shelly and Clete could talk like they always had. Shelly loved telling her father about special places in the mountains she had found, and was usually surprised to find that Clete already knew them.

"Ah'd guess mah daddy and his daddy, an' likely mah mom an' her mom went ta them places, too, Shelly. That's what kids've always done 'roun here, explore these mountains."

Clete and Shelly also talked about what they saw on the news.

"Things are changin' purty fast out in the world. We ain't seein' 'em too much in McDowell County, leastways not yet, but they'll be comin' here too."

"I know, Daddy."

"Does it worry ya, Shelly?"

"A little."

"Ah know these are rough times ta grow up in, but that ain't noth-in' new, honey. Ah had mah own troubles an' your momma had hers, but things worked out for us. Mah folks an' gran'folks had it real hard up in these hills, but somehow daddy still built a nice house an' raised a lovin' family." Clete concentrated on torquing several bolts. "Bad things come ta ever'body once in a while, 'at's jus' how life is."

"You mean like all them people on the Silver Bridge?"

"Sometimes, Shelly, there ain't no accountin' fer what happens, but ya gotta remember that ever' one a' them people did a lot a' good things before that day, an' the good they did is more important than the day they died."

"Some people do bad things, Daddy. We see it all the time on the news."

Clete tightened two more bolts. "Well, that's what news people do, honey. They make money by showin' bad things."

"But all that bad stuff really happens, don't it?"

"It does, Shelly. This world's never been an easy place ta live in. What matters is how you live in it an' that you per'tect them close to ya."

"How do ya do that?" Shelly asked.

"Ya make a place that's safe."

"Like our house?"

"Ah reckon," Clete said, picking up a pair of pliers. "But there's more to it'n that. It's a way a' thinkin', Shelly. Ya make a space aroun' ya that's safe fer them people an' things ya care about, like kinfolk an' good frien's. But it kin even be yer dogs … or yer horse. An' ya don't let nothin' bad happen inside this space."

"But sometimes things happen ya can't stop, Daddy, like that bridge fallin'."

"Well, that's kinda what Ah'm talkin' about, but it's a hard thing ta explain." Clete laid the pliers on the Mack's fender. "When Ah heard that strange noise on the other side a' the bridge it was like Ah knew sum'thin was wrong so Ah didn't go on it. Ah almost did … an' jus' thinkin' about that bothers me more'n you'll ever know … but Ah didn't."

"So you knew the bridge was gonna fall?" Shelly asked.

"Oh, no … nothin' like that." Clete said. "Ah jus' knew after hearin' that noise that goin' onta the bridge might be puttin' you an' Junior in danger."

"But how'd ya know?"

"That's the tricky part, Shelly, ya have ta work at it. First, ya git it inta yer mind that yer gonna per'tect the things ya love, then ya don't ever let that outa yer mind, not even fer one second. After a while that way a' thinkin' becomes natural to ya, like breathin'.'"

"Does that way a' thinkin' have a name?" Shelly asked.

"Not that Ah ever heard of. But it's a funny thing, Ah kin tell right away when somebody else has it."

"Like who?"

"Cliff at the gas station has it," Cletus said. "Him an' his family are part a' my per'tected space an' we're part a' his. That's why Ah always felt good about leavin' you with 'im."

"That way a' thinkin' sounds like a good thing, Daddy," Shelly said, smiling. "Maybe I could learn how ta do it."

Clete smiled back at his daughter. "Meh'be ya could, Shelly, but there's a lot more to this than jus' thinkin' about it."

"Like what?"

"Well ... if you think sum'thin bad is about ta happen ta somebody that you swore you'd per'tect, then you gotta step up an' stop it ... right away."

Shelly nodded. "I think I understan' that, Daddy."

Clete locked his eyes into Shelly's. "What Ah'm sayin' to ya, honey, is that once you've made up yer mind about this, then ya have ta stand by it ... an' ya cain't never back away. An' if'n the time comes, then you might have ta die ... or meh'be even kill somebody."

Shelly looked into her father's eyes and nodded again. "I understand, Daddy."

––––––––––––––

One subject Cletus and Shelly did not discuss were her ongoing 'girl troubles', but Shelly's agony bothered Clete almost as much as it did Shelly. "Cain't we do more ta hep her?" Clete asked Ethel one night after he'd watched Shelly fight back tears all afternoon. "Ah'm worried, Ethel. Ah don't think 'at doctor up in Welch knows what he's a'talkin' about."

"He don't," Ethel said. "I'm worried too. There's somethin' not right inside her. Shelly ain't makin' this up, she's as tough a' girl as I ever was. Look at how she comes home with black eyes an' busted lips from fightin' an' don't say a word about it. Or falls off that dang horse and gits right back on, rubbin' her bruised-up shoulder or backside an' laughin' the whole time."

"What're we gonna do?"

"Take her to a better doctor," Ethel answered. "I been askin' around an' heard a' one down in Bluefield." Then she added, almost as an aside, "I pro'bly oughta' see one myself."

"You okay, Ethel?"

"Never better. It's just that I'm pregnant agin."

In early August Ethel took Shelly to Bluefield. She made the appointment for 8:30 in the morning and Shelly was still half asleep when Ethel pulled her out of bed at five and they hit the road before seven. Ethel had arranged for a neighbor to come over and mind the kids and also fix dinner, as she didn't expect to be home in time.

"How come yer gonna be gone so long?" Cletus asked Ethel. "It ain't but an hour an' a half ta Bluefield."

"It's 'spose ta be a nice day," Ethel told him. "I thought me an' Shelly might do a bit a' gaddin' around after her exam. That'd give us a chance ta talk."

'Gaddin' around', was not something Ethel did, but Clete agreed that it was a good idea.

The examination was long and thorough but when Doctor Rosbery was finished he gave Shelly and Ethel news they didn't want to hear. "From your description of the symptoms and the physical examination I believe you have endometriosis. It's rare in girls your age, but not unheard of."

"What's the cure?" Shelly asked.

"We can try to manage the pain, but there is no absolute cure. Even the diagnosis is not exact."

"Will it get better or worse as she gets older?" Ethel asked him.

"There's no way of knowing."

"What do ya know?" Ethel said, frustrated.

"I know that no other doctor can likely tell you any more than I can," Doctor Rosebery replied. "But I can tell you this; endomitriosis gets worse more often than it gets better … if that's what Shelly has."

"Then what do I do?" Shelly asked.

"The options are neither good nor assured to work. Some women have found that getting pregnant relieves the symptoms."

"Gittin' pregnant is not an option," Ethel told him.

"Surgery to remove the reproductive organs often helps, but it's not a guaranteed cure."

"I know your're 'spose ta be a good doctor," Ethel said, "but you ain't doin' us much good."

"I wish I could do more," Doctor Rosebery said, "but here's what I want you to do." He handed Ethel two small sheets of paper. "Here's a prescription for pain medication that works for some of my patients. And here is the phone number for a woman gynecologist up in Charleston. She's very busy so you won't get in to see her right away, but I suggest you take Shelly for a second opinion. Endometriosis is a difficult diagnosis in a girl Shelly's age."

Shelly and Ethel left the clinic a few minutes after ten and got back in the Pontiac. In spite of the sunny morning, both felt downcast over the examination and did little talking until Ethel continued southeast on Highway 19 instead of turning north toward Peapatch.

"Where we goin', Mama?" Shelly asked. "You missed the road."

"We're in no hurry ta git back," Ethel said. "I reckoned you an' I could ramble around some, seein's it's such a nice day."

"Okay, Mama," Shelly agreed. "Any place special?"

"Not really, honey. This area's real pretty down here an' you an' I ain't been out ta'gether for a while."

Shelly worked up a smile but she was puzzled, driving about aimlessly was not her mama's way at all. But as Ethel had hoped, she and Shelly talked, and Ethel tried to ease her daughter's concern about what the doctor had told them. "Ever'thing'll be alright, darlin'. Me an' your daddy'll do whatever we need to ta help ya."

An hour later, when Ethel stopped to look at a road map for the third time, Shelly knew her mother was heading for some unstated destination. "Where we goin', Mama? I know you got some place in mind."

"I just don't want ta git us lost," Ethel said.

It was well past noon when they slipped into Tennessee and Shelly's stomach was rumbling. "I'm hungry Mama, when we gonna have lunch?"

"There's a town up here a ways," Ethel said. "They'll have a café."

Ethel turned onto a road that roughly paralleled the Clinch River until they came to Sneedville. She pulled into the first gas station they saw and Ethel told the attendant, a scarecrow looking teenager with an acne splotched face, to "fill er up." Ethel and Shelly got out to stretch and Ethel noticed that the first thing the kid did was check out their rear license plate. He cranked the pump back to zero, inserted the nozzle into the Pontiac, and then leaned back against the pump and began gnawing a half eaten Snickers bar he'd pulled from his oil-stained shirt.

"Nice day we're havin'," Ethel said to him.

He looked absently at Ethel, peeled the candy wrapper down and sank his front teeth, rat-like, into the chocolate.

Ethel walked up close to the kid. "How 'bout you check our oil and wash the windshield since we're gittin gas here."

The kid stuffed the Snickers in his pocket and went and lifted the Pontiac's hood. Ethel followed and watched as he checked the dipstick. After wiping the windshield he went back to the pump and ran it up to an even seven dollars, then just stood and looked at Ethel.

"I'll pay inside," she said.

Shelly leaned against the car and watched her mother pull money out of her purse and hand it to an older man she guessed was the owner. She couldn't hear what Ethel said but it looked like she asked the man a question and he raised his arm and pointed down the road. Then Ethel asked him another question and the man turned his back and walked away without answering. When Ethel got back in the car Shelly could see she was agitated, but all Ethel said was, "He said there's a good place ta eat down the road."

The man lied. As Shelly and Ethel were leaving the café Shelly said, " I feel kinda sick, Mama."

"Whyn't you lay your head over an' try ta sleep some," Ethel told her. "You had ta git up awful early and what you went through in Bluefield was mighty tiring."

"That stuff they called lunch didn't help none," Shelly said. She put her head against the side window and tried to sleep but Ethel made two more stops in Sneedville and Shelly opened her eyes to watch. Ethel was asking people questions, but both times she was either ignored or rebuffed. Finally Ethel got back into the car and drove to the Hancock County Courthouse.

"I might be in there fer a while," Ethel said. "You git some sleep, honey."

Half an hour later Ethel got back into the Pontiac. "What's goin' on, Mama?" Shelly asked. "What are you lookin' for?"

Ethel took a couple of breaths. "A place I heard about a long time ago."

"What kinda place?"

"A school, Shelly, that's all I know about it."

"Why we goin' there?"

Again, Ethel deliberated. "I've just always wanted ta see it, that's all."

For the first time, Shelly suspected her mother wasn't telling her the truth.

Ethel pulled away from the courthouse and turned off the main drag onto Route 63 heading north. After a series of climbing curves and switchbacks, the highway leveled and a few miles later Ethel turned east onto a narrow gravel road. The road ran through a fertile valley between two ridges and she continued on until they came to a small cluster of buildings. Ethel pulled into a gravel driveway as Shelly curiously looked around. One white building had a bell tower and arched windows and was obviously a church. On each side of it sat a small house. A larger stucture, set back from the others, was three stories high and filled with windows. Several adults were walking around the grounds or doing maintenance work, but as it was summer break no children were in sight.

"Can I go with ya, Mama?" Shelly asked when Ethel opened the car door.

"You don't feel good, honey. I think it best you wait here in the car an' rest."

"Do I have to?"

Ethel eyes were gentle, but her voice was firm. "Yeah, Shelly, ya do."

Shelly watched Ethel approach a tall, dignified looking man who was carrying a cardboard box full of books. By his dress and manner, Shelly guessed that he was a minister, or perhaps a teacher. Then a young, thin woman came out of the school carrying a mop and a bucket and walked by the Pontiac. She looked at Shelly and smiled, but didn't say anything. Shelly had never seen anyone who looked like the woman. Her skin was deep chestnut brown, similar to a medium-dark Negro, but her strong, unique features were like a White person's and her eyes were deep-set, with the same steel-gray irises as Shelly's. Fascinated, Shelly watched the woman until she disappeared into the church.

The man with the books and Ethel went into the school together and Ethel didn't come out for almost forty-five minutes. When she got back into the car Ethel didn't say anything, just stared silently over the steering wheel at the school.

"You alright, Mama?" Shelly asked her, but Ethel didn't answer.

After a while Ethel started the car, turned around in the driveway and drove back the way they came. She remained quiet all the way through Sneedville and Shelly let her be, content to watch the scenery. When they got to the intersection at Kyles Ford, Shelly turned away from the side window. "Mama?"

Ethel looked over at her. "I'm sorry for not bein' more talkative. Are you feelin' any better?"

"Yeah, Mama. I think that rest helped."

"Thanks for waitin' in the car," Ethel said, and put her hand on Shelly's arm. "You been real good today through all a' this, and I 'preciate it, honey."

"Okay, Mama, but I don't understand it."

Ethel's face had a distant look, but she focused a smile on her daughter. "I'm not sure I do either," she said.

The pills that Doctor Rosebery prescribed gave Shelly some relief but only for a while. Ethel made an appointment with the gynecologist in Charleston but the soonest Shelly could get in was in late December. For a short time, however, both Shelly and the country enjoyed a respite from a season of torments. Then in late August, about the same time as Shelly's medication stopped working, the nation was shattered by the Democratic Convention in Chicago. The nightly televised images of rioting, teargas and beatings were not what the Stampers, nor most Americans, had come to expect as part of the electoral process.

Cletus and Ethel barely understood what hippies were; now they were confounded by Yippies, as members of the radical and disruptive

Youth International Party were known. When the Yippies ran a hog they named Pigasus for president, demanding that he receive the same media coverage and recognition from the Democratic Party as its other candidates, Ethel and Cletus feared the country was going crazy.

But the country's trauma soon seemed trivial and far away to the Stampers in that summer of 1968 compared to when, right after the Democratic Convention had wrapped up and school was about to begin, Shelly lost Tramp under circumstances so terrible and tragic that they were never spoken of in her presence again.

Chapter 4

With Tramp gone, her insides hurting and fearing she may need surgery, Shelly started the eighth grade at the most despondent time of her life. A month later she turned thirteen and soon took on the habits of a mountain teenager. She became surly, her language grew coarse, and she started smoking cigarettes. Many of her class-mates were older than Shelly because they had flunked and shortly after turning thirteen Shelly began running with one of them. She had known Tommy Kegley since she was in second grade, but as Shelly progressed through the grades and Tommy didn't, their socializing be-came more frequent.

Greasy-haired, tough talking and proud-strutting Tommy Kegley, at five foot seven and 135 pounds, had been the toughest and most feared kid in the War Elementary School, mostly because he was the oldest. His fame reached its peak in the sixth grade when he was six-teen and got into a fistfight with the principal over a parking issue.

"You can't park your car here, Tommy," Mr. Wilkins told him. "The grade school parking lot is for teachers and staff, not students."

Tommy scowled. "Ah been at this school longer'n anybody but you an' two teachers," he told the principal. "That oughta' count for sump'thin."

"And Bill, the custodian," Mr. Wilkins reminded him, smiling.

"Ah'm parkin' here anyway," Tommy said. "Whether you lak it or not."

"I'll have it towed, Tommy, and it'll cost ya' twenty bucks to get it back." Mr. Wilkins chuckled. "And your old heap isn't worth more than two or three tows."

The principal could have insulted Tommy's parentage, his intelligence, or his legitimate claim to either with impunity, but Tommy wouldn't take anybody ridiculing his 1954 Ford coupe. He wound up and planted his fist square on the old man's chin. Tommy's aim had been unerring, but his judgement was far from the mark, because the former WVU Mountaineer defensive tackle received Tommy's punch with barely a blink, then knocked Tommy through his open door and into the next office, where he bounced against the wall and sank down on his backside, unconscious. The school secretary looked over at him, let out a chortle, and resumed typing. Far from destroying Tommy's reputation, the incident enhanced it and no grudge was held on either side. Like gentlemen duelists, both parties had taken a fair shot, although Tommy let it be known that when he grew a little more, he was "gonna come back an' knock Wilkins on 'is ass."

When Shelly transferred to Big Creek Junior High School in seventh grade Tommy was in the eighth and they became friends. The next year Tommy was still in the eighth grade and they were now classmates. On the surface, Shelly and Tommy Kegley appeared to be opposites, but both were going through hard times, and shared misery can be its own attraction. Tommy was allowed to park in the junior high lot, as by eighth grade half the students were old enough to drive. Shelly had outgrown being driven to school by her father and when she was thrown off the school bus for fighting, Tommy offered to pick her up in the morning and drive her home each day. Ethel didn't like the situation one bit.

Two weeks later Tommy asked Shelly to go to a Saturday matinee. Afterwards they drove around in his car until ten that night when he had to take Shelly home because he was nearly out of gas. They went out again the next weekend and Tommy asked Shelly if she'd sit close to him when they were in his car. His reputation was suffering from being seen with a girl who was snuggling against the passenger door instead of him. Shelly understood, and now it looked to everyone, including Clete and Ethel, like she and Tommy were going steady.

"We ain't goin' steady," Shelly insisted, when Ethel confronted her. "We jes run aroun' together. What's wrong with that?"

"He's nineteen an' you're thirteen!" Ethel yelled.

"But we're in the same grade," Shelly answered, all innocence.

"That just means he's dumb. You an' him got nothin' in common."

"Tommy ain't dumb," Shelly protested. "He jes don't like school."

"He's a troublemaker," Ethel said.

"So am I," Shelly answered, smiling. "That's what we got in common."

Two days later Ethel ran into Tommy at the grocery store when he was buying cigarettes. "I 'preciate you givin' Shelly a ride back an' forth ta school," she told him.

"It's mah pleasure," Tommy replied politely.

Ethel backed Tommy into a corner between the produce and frozen foods and put her face an inch from his. "The way old Wilkins flattened your ass won't be nothin' compared ta what I'll do to ya if anything happens to my little girl."

Shelly, however, was no longer little. In the sixth grade she commenced a growing spurt and was now taller than Tommy, who had not grown a lick since his fight with the principal. Her bones also thickened, and though still gangly, she was sinewy as dock rope. Shelly had always loved physical exertion and despite her rebellious attitude, never balked at doing hard chores, delighting in the strength her growing body was generating. About this time, Shelly also acquired her distinctive walk. No one ever accurately described or labeled her gait but the mechanics were certainly not feminine, suggesting more of an animalistic rhythm and power somewhere between a jungle cat and a Komodo dragon.

Other changes were taking place in Shelly, also. Her hair, always blonde, began turning light brown and her olive skin took on a bronze hue that set off her flat-gray eyes. This gave Shelly a formidible, exotic look that made her appear older than her years, a useful trait when hanging around Tommy Kegley's crowd.

All of Tommy's friends were older than Shelly and most had quit or been booted from school. They were wild and tough, and despite her tender age, Shelly was expected to keep up.

"I sure hate ta see Shelly runnin' with that bad crowd," Ethel told Cletus.

"The mothers of all them other kids are sayin' that too, Ethel," Cletus said, "only they're a' blamin' Shelly fer bein' part a' the bad crowd their kid is runnin' with."

Most of the time Shelly was still polite to Clete and Ethel and played with her younger siblings like the big sister she had always been. But as soon as she climbed into Tommy's car, Shelly turned surly and feral. She came home late, smelling of cigarette smoke and booze, often with her clothes torn and her face bruised and bloody.

Besides Shelly, Ethel also had to contend with Junior's emerging adolescence. He took up smoking in the fifth grade and sometimes smelled of alcohol when he came home. Ethel was galled to no end, but knew she was fighting a culture that hadn't appreciably changed since Daniel Boone came over the Cumberland Gap. Whenever she confronted Shelly the result was the same. "Your're a'headed for trouble, young lady, an' one a' these days you'll find more'n your're lookin' for."

"How d'ya know how much I'm lookin' for, Mama?"

"You're gittin' a smart mouth on ya, too."

"I ain't doin' nothin' you didn't do."

"I wadn't drinkin' an' runnin' around with wild grown-ups when I was thirteen, like you are," Ethel said, her voice rising.

"I know ya weren't, Mama. You waited till you was seventeen, then run off with a carny-man an' did it."

Ethel's concern for Shelly's involvement with Tommy Kegley and the crowd he ran with was well deserved. Tommy still lived with his parents, who were both abusive drunks, and even in his childhood, never provided him with more than life's bare necessities. His primary income came from doing odd jobs, but Tommy also had a reputation as a thief, though not a malicious one. None of his friends had finished high school and most were destined for an early death, prison, or at best a life of impoverished misery.

Tommy's own rowdiness was often limited by his lack of money. Knowing that Shelly was painstakingly honest, he was careful not to steal anything in her presence or talk about his thievery, for the truth was, he had completely fallen for this girl who never failed to back him up and was acquiring a hefty reputation of her own. Tommy was, however, confused by how much romantic interest Shelly had in him. They smooched and groped, but Shelly always drew a line, and Tommy never knew from night to night where the line would be drawn.

With her own pregnancy, Ethel had less time to focus on her two older children and then, on November 20, the Consol No. 9 coal mine near Farmington, West Virginia blew up, killing 78 men. For Ethel, it was the last straw. Clete's coughing was getting worse and his nightly hack-fests worried the entire family.

"Ain't a thing wrong with me," Clete told them. "Ev'ry year Ah go for my physical an' the doc says Ah'm jus' fine."

Ethel knew better; Clete wasn't fine at all. Maybe the doctor hadn't yet diagnosed him with anything specific, but it was coming. She went to Clete's foreman and friend, Henry Bearden, on the sly. "Henry, we got ta git Clete workin' in fresh air. He's coughin' somethin' awful an' I don't think he's gonna make it much longer underground."

"Ah know it, Ethel," Henry agreed. "Ah've seen his breathin' gittin' worse with ev'ry yare. Ah'll see what I can arrange, but Clete won't wanna do it."

"This ain't about what Cletus wants," Ethel said, "it about what he needs."

The next morning Henry went into the company office and that afternoon he rode the mantrip back to where Clete was repairing a gathering arm loader.

"Ah got some good news for ya," Henry said with a big smile.

"What might that be?" Cletus asked, looking up from his work.

"You'll be workin' up top from now on."

"Ah'm happy raht here, Henry."

Henry and Clete looked at each other in the light of their head-lamps until Henry said, "Thar ain't really no choice to it, Clete." He pointed to the roof of the tunnel, "Them fellers up in that office yonder said they need ya on top a'working on diesels."

Cletus was silent for a moment. "Ah know what's goin' on, Henry, an' Ah don't lak it … but Ah 'preciate it." Henry nodded his head and Cletus asked, "Do ya s'pose, Henry, when we ain't too busy, meh'be Ah could come down here fer a little while an' work on sum'thin back in one of these tunnels when there ain't nobody else aroun'?"

"Yeah, Clete, Ah reckon ya could. Thar's likely some piece a' junk down here nobody else could fix up as well as you."

"An' Ethel don't have ta know a thing about it," Clete added.

"B'lieve me," Henry said, "she won't."

The Stampers, along with much of the country, plunged into December looking forward to Christmas and New Years, but also wanting 1968 to be over with. Shelly was especially anxious about her upcoming doctor's appointment.

The day after Christmas break began the seven Stampers, with Ethel bulging with number eight, wedged themselves into the Pontiac and headed north to Charleston. They stayed that night with Clete's aunt Viv, his mother's baby sister, filling up all the beds and couches. The next morning Ethel drove Shelly into the center of the city to see the specialist.

Dr. Rita Marlowe, M.D., GYN., Ph.D., was tall and gaunt with the figure of a plank, but her self-assurance and caring showed with her first words. "Please, come in and sit down. If I appear blunt it is only because I have other patients scheduled and I do not like to keep people waiting. I will give you the best medical treatment I am able to and I care about you as a patient and as a person."

Shelly and Ethel liked her immediately, yet when all was done, Doctor Marlowe had little more to offer than Doctor Rosebery in Bluefield. "I concur with Doctor Rosebery that you have endometriosis, Shelly," she said. "I can give you a different kind of pain medication. It works for some people and not for others."

"Am I gonna need an operation?" Shelly asked.

"Possibly," Doctor Marlowe said. "If you were over forty and had a family, I would recommend surgery immediately. But you're one of the youngest patients with this I've seen and I cannot in good conscience do that. Sometimes, endometriosis does improve, or at least the symptoms lesson. I believe that someday you will want a hysterectomy, but I advise waiting. I know the pain is difficult to bear, Shelly, but I don't believe you want to forsake the chance of having children if you don't have to."

Shelly nodded her head in agreement. "I can live with it a while longer."

From Charleston the Stampers swung over to Olive Hill to have an early Christmas celebration at Grammy's house with Ethel's kin. They returned home a few days before Christmas and Ethel called all parties to let them know that drinking would not be tolerated this year, but their presence was expected. Vertnor, Wilbur and Shirl arrived together on the 23rd. Shirl climbed out of the back seat, all smiles and bounce, with baby Earlene plugged into a nipple. She looked at Ethel's bulging abdomen and said, "Looks like it's yor turn this year."

If anyone thought that Ethel harbored ill feelings from last year, Ethel soon put those thoughts to rest. On the day Vertnor arrived, she phoned Reverend Scoggins and invited him to dinner that evening, promising there'd be no liquor and asking him to bring his guitar. After the meal Ethel drew everyone into the living room where the big spruce tree blazed with colored lights and tinsel. Wilbur, Vertnor and the Reverend unpacked their instruments and the entire family sang or hummed along. Clete and Shelly danced until the walls shook and the other kids joined in. For once, Ethel let the children stay up as long as they wanted and when they drifted off to sleep, she carried them to their beds.

On Christmas Eve, further enchantment arrived from beyond the world, gifted by three silver suited Magi. Instead of a radiant star in the east, astronauts Frank Borman, James Lovell, and William Anders sought the Moon and then circled it ten times round. On the ninth, they took turns reading from the Book of Genesis.

Like most of America, the Stampers, joined this year by Tommy Kegley, followed their journey on live television, the first humans in history to leave the bounds of earth. When mission commander Frank Borman finished with, "And from the crew of Apollo 8, we close with good night, good luck, a Merry Christmas, and God bless all of you, all of you on the good earth," he was not signing off to the troubled and turbulent year of 1968, but offering a message of hope for the coming year and all the years ahead.

As the encapsulated crew turned toward home, a quarter million miles away, in the Stamper house as well as many others around the world, to the usual Christmas prayers of thanks was added another: "Please, God, bring them home safe."

And He did.

Chapter 5

Nineteen-sixty-nine began quietly for both the country and the Stamper family. When Richard Nixon was sworn in, Clete, who had voted for him, said, "Ah don't know 'zactly how he's gonna handle Vietnam, but he was Ike's vice-president, so at least ya know he's honest."

"Whoever's president, I just want 'em to get us outa this war," Ethel said. She had voted for Hubert Humphey,

Junior, who was too young to vote, said, "I was hopin' George Wallace would win. He'd a'ended this war by bombin' that North Vietnam ta smithereens."

In March, Charles, called Charlie from his second day, was born just as a sumptuous spring was coming into the mountains. Shelly still did her chores, but now that Junior and Sarah were old enough to help out, spent more time with Tommy Kegley. Tommy had gone to the Stampers for both Christmas Eve and Christmas Day, but Shelly's invitation had more to do with Tommy's toxic home situation than with their relationship. Tommy left his usual brash swagger on the doorstep and was invariably polite, humbled by the Stamper's graciousness. Shelly noticed with amusement, however, that he always sat as far away from Ethel as he could.

In truth, Ethel felt sorry for Tommy and except for the time at the grocery store, was polite to him. She didn't like her daughter being with him, but Shelly's grades stayed up, she still read at bedtime, worked around the house and sometimes went on long walks into the mountains. Ethel knew she'd never change Tommy but despite being occupied with a newborn, schemed to limit Shelly's involvement with him. She knew better than to clamp down too much or she might lose Shelly for good. Ethel had seen it happen many times and her own history of running off from home was evidence enough. But if Ethel feared Shelly and Tommy might run away together, her worries were for nothing. Though Tommy would have done anything Shelly agreed to, she had no such intentions and before summer was over, Ethel's concerns were moot.

———————————

One sweltering afternoon in late May, the junior high principal, backed up by the superintendant, pulled Tommy into his office. "Tommy," the principal began, "you had all F's this year. We can't pass you on to the ninth grade."

"Yor a liar," he told the principal. "Ah had a D in phys-ed. 'At oughta be enough right there ta git me passed."

"This is your second time in the eighth grade, Tommy," the superintendant said.

"Ah know that. Ah kin count. Ah ain't stupid."

The superintendant cleared his throat. "We know you're not stupid, Tommy," he said, almost kindly. "But you're twenty years old now … and with grades like this, you'll never get out of the eighth grade. Your teachers said you never did one lick of work all year."

"What about mah seen'yority?"

"Uh … school isn't like a union job," the principal said.

"It oughta be," Tommy told him, "'At'd only be fair."

Harsh sunlight blazed through the office window, baking everyone in the cramped room.

"What we're trying to tell you, Tommy," the principal said, wiping sweat from his face, "is that you're never going to get into high school."

"Then gimme my diploma an' we'll call 'er good," Tommy said. "Otherwise Ah'll show up agin next year."

Both men looked quizzically at the boy – or man - in front of them. The white shirts beaneath their sports coats were soaked with perspiration.

"Jus' 'fore she died," Tommy said, "my granny made me promise Ah'd git my diploma from school, an Ah aim ta do it."

That morning Tommy had slicked down his thick black hair with a handful of stale lard from the frying pan on the stove. In the stifling heat, the rancid mixture had liquefied and several viscuous, off-white flows, enhanced with flecks of skillet grit, oozed from Tommy's hairline. The substance moved slowly at first, then gained momentum as it ran down Tommy's face. At first fascinated, then repulsed, the principal and the superintendant watched the flow progress but when the vile substance sent forth a great stench, the men quickly took a step backwards. The principal and superintendant looked at each other and their thoughts silently colluded.

"We can do this for you," the superintendant said, stifling a gag. "We'll give you a certificate that says you went through the eighth grade."

Tommy curled his lip as his mind worked the deal over. A droplet of the gruesome pomade fell from Tommy's chin and plopped on the principal's desk.

"It'll look just like a diploma," the principal said quickly. "We'll even put it in one of those blue and yellow folders, just like a diploma."

"In fact, it will be a diploma … almost," the superintendant added.

Tommy thought on the offer. Another drop fell. Finally Tommy nodded his head in assent. "Good e'nuff," he said.

After that, whenever Tommy applied for a job and the application asked for his education level, Tommy always filled in the blank truthfully: 14 years.

———————————

With the prospect of Vietnam hovering over the young males, the summer of 1969 was a binge of wild hellraising. McDowell County had already lost seven men and though few boys feared going, they wanted to have fun before they left.

Parties, often at the end of abandoned logging roads, went on every night and usually developed along the same lines. Drinking beer and smoking marijuana progressed to hard liquor and other drugs which led to screwing, fights, or car races.

Since school let out, Shelly was seldom home and Clete and Ethel knew there was no controlling her. Plenty of girls Shelly's age had already quit school to shack up with their older boyfriends and though

Clete and Ethel were fairly sure Shelly wouldn't do that she made it plain she'd come and go as she pleased. Ethel worried that Shelly would get pregnant but when she broached the subject, Shelly stopped her with a laugh. "Ya don't need to worry about that, Mama. Me an' Tommy ain't doin' it."

But if Shelly and Tommy weren't doing *it*, they were doing everything else. Tommy was old enough to legally buy beer, but seldom had money, so he preferred to swipe his old man's or his mother's. He also knew enough local moonshiners to acquire some of their product by helping them run it off or doing odd jobs. Tommy's big dream was to be a moonshine runner like Robert Mitchum's character, Luke Doolin, in his favorite movie, *Thunder Road*. More than anything else, Tommy loved driving fast, and even when he wasn't racing, drove like he was being chased by the law.

His 1954 Ford coupe was old and battered but Tommy was mechanic enough to get as much out of the L-Head V-8 as it could give. He'd removed the muffler and exhaust and traded some work for a used set of chrome Lake Pipes, and though far from the fastest car around, Tommy's gutsy driving skill earned him and the car a local reputation.

In southern West Virginia, car wrecks killed even more young people than the war, as alcohol and drug fueled drivers roared from party to party or raced each other over treacherous mountain roads. This worried Ethel even more than the thought of Shelly becoming pregnant, as her father had died while driving drunk, and if she'd known what Shelly did two days after summer vacation began, she would've had a fit.

Sidled up to Tommy in the front seat, Shelly wriggled her body against his and asked, "Tommy, will ya teach me ta drive? I wanna learn from a pro."

"It'd be mah pleasure," Tommy said, and by early July he had enough confidence in Shelly's driving that he let her use his car to go up against another girl in a drag race. Shelly lost, but a week later she beat a twenty-year old woman who was driving her own Chevy and the week after that, won a three car road race against two other girls, racing from Cucumber to Squire down Route 16 at three in the morning.

Shelly was hooked; only the thrill she got from fighting compared, and she got plenty of that, too.

With this older crowd the fights were more serious. Though small, Tommy was a good fighter and taught Shelly a lot of moves and tricks, but he warned her, "Look out, them other girls know 'em too."

Most of the fights were with people from other towns, especially Welch or Bluefield. Even at thirteen, Shelly was taller than most of the other girls, but they were usually heavier and much older. Even so, Shelly more than held her own. Once in a while she'd even fight a boy if he'd done or said something crude to her. Some fights were squared-off matches, even pre-arranged challenges, but many were impromptu brawls and in these, Tommy Kegley taught Shelly a lesson that she never forgot; once you know a fight is coming, don't hold back. Hit your opponent first and keep attacking until your adversary is beat. It was something Shelly saw again and again: that the one who strikes first usually wins.

As the crazy summer of 1969 wore on, Tommy Kegley's lack of funds became more of a problem. His sporadic odd jobs barely made him enough for gas, but now, tradition and pride obliged Tommy to spend money on his girlfriend. Adding to his woes, Tommy could no longer steal because of Shelly's honest company. Officially he still lived with his parents, though in warm weather Tommy sometimes slept in the back seat of his car rather than be drug into their drunken fights. He ate only what he could forage as his mother had not provided him with a meal since he was weaned.

Shelly also had no income except for the few dollars Clete slipped her when Ethel wasn't looking. If Tommy hadn't worked that week, their dates were meager fare. Sometimes, for lack of gas, they could only drive a few miles and park at some overlook nestled in the woods, share a beer or two Tommy'd swiped from home, talk and make out.

Now that Tommy had officially "gradge-iated," as he called it, he was eligible for full-time work. He was not without practical skills, and his swaggering attitude aside, most local people liked him. Several of them offered Tommy employment.

"How come you don't take one a' them jobs?" Shelly asked. "You're outa school now."

" 'Cause Ah kin do better'n that," Tommy said. "They ain't offerin' to pay me what Ah'm worth."

But as July collided into August, Tommy's gas gauge and wallet rested on empty so often that Shelly began curtailing their outings. One Friday afternoon Tommy phoned Shelly to tell her he was broke and his gas tank was so low he couldn't get to her house. "Meh'be we both could jus' hitchhike inta War an' hang out."

"Maybe you could jes git a job," Shelly told him. "Call me when ya got money to take me out."

Tommy walked out, got into his Ford, and drove to the highway from his parent's house in Coon Branch Holler, climbed the grade then shut off the engine and freewheeled the long descent into War. As his coupe silently coasted under the Mobilgas sign and came to a stop beside the regular pump at Cliff's filling station, Cliff came out and stared at the face looking up at him. "If'n yor fixin' ta ask me for some free gas ya ain't a'gittin' any."

With his arm resting confidently on the door, Tommy looked up at Cliff through the open window of his Ford and took a Raleigh he'd swiped off his mother's bedstand out of his shirt pocket. He tapped the end of the cigarette on his steering wheel before he stuck it in his mouth and puffed it to life with the glowing end of the dashboard lighter. Skewing his head toward Cliff, Tommy glanced up at him with one eye. "Ah didn't come to ask ya for free gas. Ah come to ask ya for that job ya offered me las' month."

"I thought you was too good fer it," Cliff said.

"Ah ain't too good for it," Tommy said, "but Ah'm good e'nuff."

Cliff and Tommy had a long history. As a kid, Tommy did chores for Cliff for pop and candy. When Tommy was eleven, Cliff caught him stealing two GooGoo Clusters. He whaled Tommy's bottom and told him he couldn't come into the station for a month. Emmit Kegley, Tommy's dad, rampaged into Cliff's and kicked the office door open. "Nobody whups my kid's ass but me!" he yelled at Cliff, who was bent over a motor.

Cliff looked up casually from the engine of the Buick he was working on. "Wal' that ain't true, Emmett, 'cause Ah jus' did it. An' if'n you broke my door, Kegley, Ah'll whup yor ass too."

Before he was married, Clifton Collins was the terror of every road-house within drinking range of War. Not much larger than average, Cliff looked like he'd been forged from iron and was widely known as 'nobody to mess with'. But Emmett Kegley was a fool, and a drunken one at that. No stranger to brawls himself, he was no taller than Tommy, but was stout as an oak whiskey barrel.

The two men glared at each other. "Ain't nobody talks ta me like that," Emmett growled and picked up a foot and half long ratchet. "Ah'm gonna part yor hair, grease monkey."

Cliff let Emmett come on, and when he was four feet away, threw a can of solvent in his face, stepped in and landed a walnut-hard fist to Emmett's jaw. Emmett knew it was coming and swung the ratchet at the same time, the handle glancing off Cliff's shoulder. Emmett staggered from Cliff's punch but kept his feet. He brought the wrench back for another blow but Cliff moved in close and jack-hammered his elbow into Emmett's round, hairless skull, then brought a knee up, with all his weight behind it, into Emmett's lower abdomen. Emmett dropped the ratchet and fell to his knees. Cliff drew his fist back to give Emmett another good one but Emmett covered his face with both hands and rasped out, "Don't hit me no more!"

Winded and in agony, Emmett grabbed at the fender of the Buick to keep from falling onto his face. "If'n you'd treat yor boy better and give him somethin' once'd in a while, he wouldn't have ta steal," Cliff told him.

Between gulps of air Emmett managed to gasp, "What I do with mah family is mah own goddam business ...an' you stay outa it."

"An' you stay out a' my fillin' station."

Later, Cliff heard that Emmett took the beating he got out on Tommy, who was so busted up he couldn't go to school for three days. Cliff vowed that if he ever got the chance to kill Emmett Kegley, he wouldn't pass it up.

When Tommy got older he started fighting back against Emmett so fiercely that Emmett quit beating on him. Tommy's mother, Effie, never needed any help against Emmett because she started half the fights herself, and what she lacked in bulk she made up for by her expert use of household weaponry.

Tommy worked at the station until closing time that Friday and Cliff advanced him a tank of gas and ten dollars. He drove straight to Shelly's with the news of his job and they headed off into the crimson sky of a West Virginia sunset. As they sped along the winding highway toward Welch with all four windows down, Tommy tore open a fresh pack of Winstons and handed two of them to Shelly. She lit them with the dashboard lighter and passed one to Tommy. Each took a long drag then tipped back their beer bottles.

From the open window, Shelly watched the tree-covered hills roll by, tinged mauve and purple in shadow. The forest ran unbroken from the ridgetops down to the edge of the asphalt. Several times they crossed railroad tracks that jumped suddenly out of the trees. None of them had crossing lights, but Tommy never slowed or even looked when he shot across. More than once when riding with Tommy, Shelly had seen trains approaching but he was unconcerned when she mentioned it. "If ya go over the tracks fast e'nuff, trains can't gitch ya," he told her, laughing.

By the time they pulled into the Welch A&W drive-in for dinner, stars were spackling the sky. They polished off the rest of the six-pack that Tommy had bought in War then drove to a roadside store where Tommy bought a half-case of Falstaff, Shelly's favorite beer. While cruising around Welch, they fell in with some locals. Tommy was in such a good mood that he got into a fight with one of them, a high school football player, and though the boy was much bigger, Tommy fought so ferociously that they finally called it a draw.

The next day Shelly told her family about Tommy getting a job at Cliff's.

" 'bout time," Ethel said.

As soon as Clete was alone with Shelly, he pulled his wallet out and handed her a five-dollar bill. "You an' Tommy have a good time tonight," he said.

And they did. They headed south to Bluefield where Tommy and Shelly both raced with the local hot-rodders and Shelly beat up a 16 year old girl who had called her a "dumb-ass Peapatch bean-pole," getting no worse for herself than a fat lip. By Sunday afternoon, when

Tommy came by to pick up Shelly, they were both broke and Tommy's gas tank was so low they couldn't go more than a few miles away.

"Gotta save some ta git back'n forth ta work," he told Shelly.

They drove to one of their favorite spots, a ledge that overlooked a gorge where a railroad trestle jutted between sharp, black shale cliffs that harbored a bustling creek. Tommy got out of the car and opened the trunk then came back and stuck his head into the open window.

"Lookee what Ah got," he said, holding up a six-pack of Budweiser bottles.

"Where'd ya git those?" Shelly asked.

"Took 'em outa one a' them Bluefielder's back seats las' night whilst they was all watchin' you fight that gal."

"Ya should'na done that, Tommy."

Tommy smiled and winked. "Ya wanna git in the back seat?"

Shelly thought on it. "Let's jes talk for a spell."

Tommy got back into the car, slid under the steering wheel and scootched tight against Shelly. He put the top of a Budweiser on the lip of the open ashtray and brought his palm smartly down against it. The cap dropped onto the floor and he handed the bottle to Shelly and opened a beer for himself.

"Beer always tastes good," he said, "but stolen beer tastes better."

"Ya shouldn't steal, Tommy, not even from Bluefielders," Shelly told him, then put the bottle to her lips and tipped it back.

Tommy swilled half his Bud, set it on the floorboard and took Shelly in his arms. After their first long French kiss Shelly saw that the front of Tommy's pants were bulging out and when his hands slid under her shirt it looked like he was trying to smuggle a summer sausage into a movie theater. Tommy worked at massaging Shelly's little boobs like he thought handling them might make them grow. Still locked in kiss, he reached his right hand down and undid the snap on Shelly's jeans. Shelly lay back on the seat as Tommy slid his fingers under her cotton panties and began a gentle, but dedicated manipulation. Soon Shelly was wriggling and moaning and Tommy started dry humping her. Just before the point where Shelly knew she would not be able to stop, when pleasure overrode all sense, Shelly disengaged from Tommy's mouth, shouted, *"Nuff!"* and sat up. Still panting, she zipped up her jeans and smoothed out her clothes.

Tommy was sucking in fast, desperate breaths. "Ah gotta take a walk," he said, reaching for the door handle. He hurried toward the woods and disappeared behind a thick maple. Shelly tried not to envision what was happening on the other side of the tree. A few minutes later, Tommy returned, still breathing hard. He got in the car, grabbed his Budweiser and drained it in one swallow.

"Tommy," Shelly said, by way of sympathy, "I ain't goin' all the way. I'm only thirteen."

"How soon ya gonna be fourteen?" he asked.

Shelly didn't answer and after a short silence Tommy held up his empty bottle. "Ya want another beer?" he asked.

"Notch'et. I still got half a' this one left."

Tommy returned with two more beers anyway. He popped the cap off one, took a swig, then leaned his head against the back of the seat and stared at the furry dice hanging from his mirror.

"You excited 'bout your new job?" Shelly said, trying to get Tommy's mind off sex.

"Not really. It's a job, but it ain't what Ah wanna do."

"What do ya wanta do?" Shelly asked.

"Don't know ... but it'd have ta be sump'thin exciting."

"You're old enough ta be drafted an' sent ta Viet Nam," Shelly said. "That'd be exciting ... if ya didn't git killed."

"Ah ain't scared a' bein' drafted," Tommy said. "Ah might even like it. The Army can't treat me no worse'n my ol' man has."

From deep in the woods came the long, heavy blast of an air horn, followed by two shorter toots. Tommy and Shelly knew what was coming but they still looked down into the gorge to watch. Sunlight glazed the surrounding hills but the canyon was deep enough in shadow for them to see a wave of yellow light sweeping along the trackside forest. From a narrow cleft in the trees came a glaring, cyclopean headlight that grew bigger and bigger, swaying easily as the train rumbled closer. The horn sounded again, and when the train rounded a curve just before the trestle, the engines appeared in silouette: the graceful and rounded contours of a Norfolk & Western EMD F-7 diesel backed by two cab-less B units and another, rearward facing A unit, dragging a loaded string of coal cars that stretched away into the dark trees.

"Don't see many a' them ol' covered wagon lookin' diesels no more," Tommy said.

"I wish I was on it," Shelly told him, and took a drink from her beer. "Sittin' on top a' that front coal car an' lettin' the wind blow over me as it gits dark and the stars come out."

"Goin' where?" Tommy asked.

"Anywhere I never been," Shelly answered. "Out west, maybe. Some wild place on the prairie or in the mountains that ain't too settled yet."

"Would ya gitcha' another horse?" Tommy said, then regretted his words as Shelly's breath caught in her lungs.

"Ah'm sorry, Shelly," he said. "Ah wasn't thinkin'."

"It's okay, Tommy. I know ya didn't mean nothin by it." Shelly turned to watch the coal cars go by and when the caboose passed a man standing on the back platform waved to them and Shelly and Tommy waved back.

On Monday morning Tommy again coasted his Ford down the grade into War but a block from Cliff's station he started his engine so Cliff wouldn't know he was nearly out of fuel. When Cliff advanced Tommy the gas and ten dollars on Friday he told him, "Don't ast me fer more. You git paid next Friday after work. 'Sides learnin' to work here at the station, you need ta learn r'sponsibility."

Despite grousing to Shelly about the job, Tommy loved working at the gas station. He understood cars but also had an eagerness to please the customers. Whenever a car or pickup rolled up to the gas pumps, Tommy ran outside to be of service. "Fill 'er up? Check 'at ol'? Looks lak 'at left rear might need some air."

On Tuesday, as Cliff was sharing the lunch his wife had brought him with Tommy, he said, "Them tires on yor coupe are about shot. Ah gotta set a' good used ones in the back that Ah'll give ya if'n yor still workin' here on Friday."

That Thursday afternoon, Cliff got backed-up by two cars that needed immediate repair. "Ah have ta take my wife an' boy up ta Welch tonight fer his gran'ma's birthday party," he told Tommy, "an' Ah need to git these cars done an' outa here. If'n you wanna stay late an' help, Ah'll give ya time an' a half."

Tommy stayed until they were done. "We'll put them tires on yor car tomorrow," Cliff said, as he hurried out the door.

Tommy drove up the grade north of War then turned onto the dirt track known as Coon Branch Holler to his parent's tarpaper covered house, knowing he barely had enough gas to get into work on Friday. When Tommy saw that neither of his parents were home, he dug through the filth-encrusted cubboards, found some breadcrusts and made himself two Jiff and jelly sandwiches. As he was heading to his room, his old man's pickup clattered up in front and his parents climbed out, both clutching a bottle of beer.

"Hold up, boy," Emmett said, as he came through the door.

"Ah was jus' goin' to my room," Tommy told him.

"We got some things to say to ya first," Tommy's mother said.

Effie, as scrawny as Emmett was round, popped into the doorway and stood beside her husband. She gripped her beer bottle in one hand and a cigarette in the other, taking turns sucking on them.

"You git paid tomorra," Emmett said, "if that sum'bitch yer workin' for don't cheat ya out of it."

"Cliff won't cheat me," Tommy said.

"You don't say his name in this house. It's bad 'nuff yer workin' there, but if you need ta call 'im sump'thin, then call 'im what he is: a sum'bitch. An' you kin tell 'im Ah said that."

"Tell 'im yor'self," Tommy answered.

"Here's what Ah'll tell you," Emmett said. "Long as yer stayin' here you need to start payin' fer yer keep."

"Ah intended to help out," Tommy said.

"Not jest fer what yer usin' now, but fer all we done give ya in the past."

"That won't come ta much," Tommy said.

Emmett's eyes narrowed. "Don't chew git smart-ass with me."

Effie lifted her empty beer bottle and pointed it at Tommy. "Half," she said. "We figger half a' what that s.o.b. is payin' ya oughta be 'bout right." She went to step out of the doorway but had to grab the frame to keep from falling. "An' we want it tomorrow night 'fore you go anywheres."

Tommy looked at his parents. "Is that all?"

"No," Emmett said. "Tell 'im about yer brother, Effie."

"Yeah, Ah forgot," Tommy's mother said. "Hop called here yesterday. He wants ta talk to ya right away. Said it's important an' you need ta call him back." Effie tossed her empty bottle on the floor where it skittered away to join a pile of others. "If yor fixin' to call from here it's long distance, so you'll hafta pay fer the call when ya git yor money tomorrow."

Tommy took his sandwiches into the living room, sat down on the couch in the one spot the springs weren't poking through then picked up the phone and dialed his uncle. Even though Hop could be gruff, Tommy liked his uncle and wished he'd been born into Hop's family instead of his own. He'd been on partial disability since World War II and his wounds kept him from doing steady work, but not coon hunting or running his part-time business: Hop's Tire & Bible, which he operated out of a small corrugated steel building outside of Dwarf, Kentucky, near Hazard. Hop also distilled some of the finest moonshine in eastern Kentucky, but unlike his sister Effie, seldom touched alcohol, save to sample his own product for quality. Having found God as a wounded and pinned down Marine on the beach in Tarawa, Hop also did a little preaching when the Spirit moved him or if requested to sermonize where financial remuneration was offered.

Until 1959 Hop drove his own liquor into Tennessee and North Carolina, when he got tagged and spent two years in federal prison. A few years later he resurrected the still the revenuers never found and started running off special batches for a few trusted and high paying customers. His son Melvin, five years Tommy's senior, now did the transporting.

Tommy admired and envied his older cousin and listened reverently to Melvin's stories of hauling moonshine, most of them greatly exagerated because since his incarceration, Hopwood Branstool had become a very careful man. Whenever Tommy pleaded with Hop to let him make a run, Hop would tell him, "Hit ain't that I don't trust ya, Tommy, hit's that I don't need ya. We only run-off aroun' a dozen batches a yare, an' Melvin hauls 'em in." So when his uncle Hop answered the phone with his customary, "Yeah, whatchoo want?" Tommy was holding his breath in anticipation.

"It's me uncle Hop, Tommy."

"What took yeh so long teh call?"

"Ma jus' tol' me two minutes ago."

"At's 'bout raht fer her. You still in'trested in doin' a little work fer me?"

"You mean runnin …"

"Shutchure mouth. We're on the phone here, people might be listenin'." Hop was even more abrupt than usual. "Mah shit-fer-brains son Melvin totaled his car the night 'fore last an' broke his leg. He cain't drive."

Tommy's heart pounded with excitement and blood raced to his head.

"Ah took some special *honey*, if yeh git mah drift, from my hives the other day," Hop said, "fer this big singin' star, 'cause he's havin' a giant ol' party fer this gol' record he got and wants a batch a' mah *honey* fer the celebration. Ah'll pay yeh two hunderd dollars teh take it inta Nashville."

"Ah sure kin help ya out, uncle Hop," Tommy said, thrilled darn near breathless, "Ah gotta work tomorrow, but Ah kin be at your place on Saturday."

"No good," Hop said. "His party starts tomorra an' is gonna last all weekend. Ah promised him mah stuff would be in Nashville by tomorra mornin'. If you cain't do it, Ah'll drive it in mah'self but Ah shor'ly don't want to."

"Ah think Ah kin git off work ta do it," Tommy said.

"Hain't no thinkin' to it," Hop said, his voice rising. "Hit's yes or no raht now. This ol' boy pays top dollar for mah product, an' Ah mean *top* dollar, but it has got teh be thar when he says. He don't tolerate no fuckin' aroun'."

Tommy had never heard his Christian uncle use that word before and he knew Hop was serious. His brain was racing in a furious effort to make the right decision. Besides the chance to be a moonshine runner, two hundred dollars was over two week's wages. With a grubstake like that he could get his own place and then maybe Shelly would … .

"Ah'll do it, uncle Hop," Tommy said.

"If you hain't here bah two a.m., Ah'm takin' this *honey* in mah'self, an' don'choo ever ast me agin."

"Ah'll be there," Tommy said, but Hop had already hung up.

As soon as he put the phone down, Tommy realized the job wasn't as simple as he had imagined only a minute before. He had no gas. He had no money. His tires were bald. He would have to get off work and talk Cliff out of some gas. Tommy cleared the lump from his throat before calling Cliff's home number but the phone rang and rang and rang ... until Tommy remembered that Cliff was going to Welch and wouldn't be back until late. He gnawed at the crusty sandwiches as he thought the matter over, then picked up the phone again and dialed. Junior Stamper answered.

"Hey, Junior, this is Tommy. Is yor big sister home?"

"Unforch'nately," Junior said, as Shelly elbowed him aside and took the receiver.

"Shelly," Tommy said, before she'd even said hello, "Ah need ta go ta my uncle Hop's in Kentucky right away. Ah'll be back by tomorrow night with enough money so's we kin have us a weekend like all git out."

"Why ya goin' tonight? What about work tomorrow?" Shelly asked.

"Ah can't say on the phone, Shelly. It's kinda like an emergency."

Tommy had told Shelly about his uncle Hop. "You be careful, Tommy," she said.

"Ah will," Tommy said, then added, "Ah love you, Shelly."

After a pause Shelly said, "I think a lot a' you too, Tommy."

That wasn't the answer Tommy wanted, but he'd take it. "When Ah git back Ah'll have me some real money ... an' maybe we kin git married."

Shelly breathed a couple of times before she answered. "You be careful, Tommy. You jes be real careful."

Tommy laid the receiver in its cradle and walked warily back into the kitchen. His parents were arguing out on the porch as Tommy quietly opened the fridge door, took two beers from the fresh case his old man had just put there, stuffed them down his pants and walked out to his car.

"Where you goin'?" his dad said.

"Out."

"What'd Hop want?" Effie asked.

"Jus' ta talk to his favorite nephew," Tommy said as he got in his Ford.

"Bullshit!" Emmett hollered.

"That's what we did, aw'right" Tommy answered as he started the engine.

The gas gauge had been on empty for two days and Tommy kept his fingers crossed as he drove to the highway and ascended the grade above War. At the summit the motor sputtered and then quit. Tommy eased the shifter into neutral and coasted down the hill and through town until he came to Cliff's station. The Ford stopped twenty feet from the regular pump and Tommy got out and pushed it the rest of the way.

He walked around to the back door, picked up a rock and broke out a pane, then reached in, unlocked the door and went inside. In Cliff's office, Tommy switched on the gas pumps, unlocked the front door and went back outside. As he stood filling his tank, the soft light of gray evening was settling over the town as cars cruised past the station. Most everybody in War already knew that Tommy worked for Cliff and likely wouldn't question his presence there after closing time, and Tommy had a ready answer if they did. Several folks waved as they drove by and Tommy smiled and waved back, but nobody stopped. Still, he felt mighty bad, and a little scared, at what he was about to do.

After checking his car's oil, Tommy went back into the garage area and dug behind a stack of old tires where he knew Cliff hid forty dollars in small bills and coins for making change each day. He stared somewhat longingly at the four tires Cliff was going to give him, wishing he had time to put them on right then. Returning to the front office area, Tommy pulled a dozen Cokes from the cold water of the pop machine and put them into a cloth poke he took from under the counter. He found a second bag and filled it with GooGoo Clusters and Moon Pies, then walked over to the cigarette case and added a carton of Winstons. Satisfied he had what he needed for the run, Tommy picked up the clipboard Cliff used for scheduling, pulled a fresh sheet of paper from the bottom and placed it on top. With the stubby lead of a chewed pencil he wrote:

CLIFF I hop whut Im doing is alrite. I hav a famly emurgincy in kentuky. I neded gas and munny to git ther and bak. I wil work xtra hard nextd week and pay yu for wat I tok. Sory abote the bak dor windo I will fiks it. Tommy

After turning off the pumps Tommy relocked both the front and back doors. Two passers by waved to him as he walked around to the front of the station and he returned their greeting. Tommy looked solemnly at his black Ford coupe. He dug in his back pocket for his hanky and wiped a smudge of oil off the driver's side Lake Pipe then got in. Before starting the engine, Tommy opened the carton of Winstons, took out a pack and carefully tore off the top corner. He tapped the pack on his steering wheel until a lone cigarette popped out then pulled it from the pack with his mouth and lit it with the dashboard lighter. Tommy rolled the rest of the pack up in the sleeve of his white t-shirt, glanced into his rearview mirror and stroked a hand over his slick, black hair.

He leaned down for one of his old man's beers from the passenger side floorboard and knocked the cap off on the edge of the ashtray. After taking a long pull from the bottle, Tommy turned the ignition key, then cocked his head and listened in satisfaction to the steady, reassuring rumble of the old, but well-tuned mill under the hood. He spun the car around and tooled down the main drag of War, arm slung out the window and smiling, blowing cigarette smoke into the passing air of a summer evening. Tommy climbed the grade he had descended only a few moments before, his hood pointing straight into a notch between the mountains where the low sun ignited the sky, feeling that now, right now, was the beginning of what was going to be a big change in his life.

Chapter 6

Tommy kept to the main roads but not the speed limit as his black coupe raced over the asphalt between War and Dwarf, Kentucky. It was a little after 1 a.m. when Tommy passed the old steel building with the sign out front for Hop's Tire & Bible and turned onto the dirt lane 100 feet further down the road. Ten feet from the highway Tommy's headlights illuminated the first sign in Hop's long driveway: *NO TRESPASSING! DONT COME HERE UNLESS YOURE ASKED.* Thirty yards further, the second sign was more welcoming: *THE BRANSTOOL FAMILY – Hopwood & Marie, Melvin, Hazel, Sally & JESUS.*

Brush and willow swatted the sides of Tommy's car as he barreled along the narrow lane and when he roared up and skidded to a stop in front of Hop's house his arrival was announced by a comet tail of dust and the barks and bays of a dozen hounds. Hop was waiting outside in bib overalls and the dust enveloped him in a cloud of grit that glimmered in the porchlight. He glowered at Tommy through the open window of his coupe. "Listen, *dumbass,* you mighta drove lak Satan's sister a'gittin here, but when you git *them* in yor car," Hop pointed to a stack of cardboard boxes, "you drive the speed limit an' not a mile more the whole way inta Nashville. Yeh got that?"

"Yes, uncle Hop," Tommy said obediently, and reached for the ignition key.

"Don't shut 'er off yet," Hop said. "We hain't loadin' yeh up till Ah check out a few thangs. Is yor driver's license in order?"

Tommy nodded.

"Lemme see," Hop said. He took Tommy's license and examined it in the headlights. Then he walked around the Ford to see that all the lights were working and had Tommy test the blinkers and brake lights. Hop looked at the tires and shook his head. "Them tar'rs hain't worth a good-damn. Ah've seen rubbers with more tread on 'em 'an that."

"They'll make it ta Nashville, uncle Hop," Tommy said.

"They better."

To fit all twenty-five cases of Mason jars into the trunk, Tommy and Hop removed everything else, including the spare tire, and put it in the Ford's back seat. After they'd carefully packed in the last carton, Hop stepped back and whistled low at the way the car's backend drooped. "Ah don't lak it," he said. "'At's a dead give-away. Melvin's got stouter springs an' heavy duty shocks on his car, but the ass-end on this thang sags as much as mah wife's."

"How much is in there?" Tommy asked.

"Three hun'dert quarts," Hop replied. " 'At's nare six hun'dert pounds."

Now Tommy let out a low whistle.

"You hain't gonna outrun much with that in the back," Hop said, "so don't gitch yor'self in a position whar' yeh even need teh try." Then, as if he was reading Tommy's mind, he added, "This hain't *Thunder Road*."

After Tommy got in and started the engine, Hop said to him, "Pull over yonder to the tank an' Ah'll top yeh off so's yeh don't have teh stop fer gas. Wouldn't be nothin' open now, anyhow." After he filled the tank Hop asked, "You got gas money fer the trip back?"

"Yessir," Tommy said.

Hop handed Tommy a piece of paper with the address to a Piggly-Wiggly store on the north side of Nashville. "The man yor a'meetin' will be drivin' a blue '68 Eldorado. He knows what yor drivin' an' he'll meetcha in the parkin' lot an' lead yeh to a safe spot he knows whar' you kin transfer the product inta his car."

"Oh boy," Tommy said, "Ah can't wait ta meet this famous singin' star. Who is it?"

Hop shook his head slowly back and forth a few times and looked away at the horizon of hills barely visible against the scattered stars. "Ah know mah sister hain't very smart," he said, "an' Ah wouldn't own a pig as dumb an' dirty as that drunken som'bitch she married, but Ah'd always kinda hoped his short little dick hadn't filtered out what few brain cells thar was in his jizzim when he made you."

Tommy just looked at his uncle.

"What Ah'm sayin', boy, is don't be so stupid. You hain't gonna meet that singin' star or ever know who he is, cause Ah hain't a'tellin' yeh. Them kind a' people lak teh give out illegal likker so's ev'body'll think thar outlaws, but they let lesser folks take the real chances fer 'em."

"Oh," Tommy said quietly. Then he added, "Don'choo worry uncle Hop. Ah'll do this right an' Ah'll bring back ever' penny a' the money they give me."

Hop looked off into the dark hills again, pinched one nostril and blew the other into the dirt. He turned back and said to Tommy, a little softer now, "Tommy, they don't pay you. They pay me. But you deliver that product on time an' git back here in one piece and Ah'll pay yeh what Ah said." Then he put his thick hand on Tommy's shoulder. "You obey all the laws an' be careful."

"Ah will. Ah promise, Hop."

Hop's hand tightened until Tommy winced in pain. "You may be kin," Hop said, "but if'n anythang goes wrong, nobody better find out whar this hootch come from."

Hop released his grip and Tommy swallowed hard. "Ah wouldn't say nothin', uncle Hop," he said.

Tommy depressed the clutch and eased the shifter into first gear. "Oh, hell," Hop said to him, "Ah almost fer'got. If thangs turn bad, you might be a'needin' this."

Hop dipped into the front of his bibs and pulled out a black object that Tommy thought – and hoped – was a pistol, but when he reached for it through the open window, his uncle handed him a Bible.

While loading the trunk, Hop had given Tommy specific instructions as to his route of travel: "Stay in Kentucky long as yeh kin. The cops roun' here are easier goin' than 'em Tennessee boys. An' if'n you do git stopped, say 'yessir' an' 'no sir' an' do what they tell yeh to."

Tommy drove west through the quiet night, seeing little traffic. In many places trees came abreast of the road and his greatest concern was slamming into a deer or some other critter big enough to cause serious damage. A few miles past London he nailed a possum and fifty miles later swerved to miss a cat, but otherwise, his run was uneventful. The towns he passed through were boarded up for the night and the only police car he saw was parked beside the pumps of a closed filling station, the cop's head tilted back, dozing peaceably.

Still, Tommy was excited to be hauling moonshine out of the Kentucky hills, just like Luke Doolin in *Thunder Road*. He didn't have any gimmicks on his car, like in the movie: a bumper that detached when the revenuers locked onto it, or a knob on the dash that released a stream of oil to wreck who's chasing you, but after he'd made a few runs maybe he'd put those on. But tooling through the night with a trunk full of white lightning, window down and the air blowing back against his face, making good money for the first time in his life, Tommy felt every bit like the savvy-cool character Robert Mitchum played so well. Now he could treat Shelly to all the things she deserved and when he got back, he'd ask her to marry him.

The night wore on and the air cooled but Tommy still drove with the front windows down. To stay alert he sucked on Coke's, munched his candy bars and lit one cigarette after another. By 3 a.m. the air blowing through his car had chilled to the point that Tommy pulled over and put his leather jacket on. The few stars that salted the sky above his uncle Hop's place had disappeared and an hour and a half later, just before he rounded Glasgow and turned south toward Tennessee, a light drizzle spattered on his windshield and moistened the black highway ahead of him.

Twenty-five miles before the Tennessee line, Tommy pulled into a gravel turnout at the top of a hill to empty his bladder. Droplets of cold rain fell onto his greased hair and ran down the back of his neck. Looking east, he saw the first hint of the coming day on the low edge of the horizon and when a pair of headlights coming from the south rounded a curve in the highway up ahead, Tommy was taken by surprise.

Caught in the middle of his act, Tommy stopped the flow, gave two quick shakes, a tuck and a zip, and was scooting around the front of his Ford when the car passed and his headlights illuminated the Kentucky State Police emblem on the door. He jumped in his coupe, threw it into gear and was not even back on the highway when he saw the cop's brakelights in his rearview mirror and watched him perform a neatly executed bootleg one-eighty in the middle of the road. Before Tommy was up to running speed the trooper's headlights were locked on his tail. For three miles Tommy ran steady at just below the speed limit, keeping his fingers crossed that if he didn't break any laws the cop behind him would back off, but then red flashes from the police car's rooftop rotator started bouncing off his rearview mirror.

Tommy pondered his options. Being pulled over in an old car like his with West Virginia plates and a sagging rear-end driving through Kentucky in the middle of the night, by a curious cop who's got nothing else to do would surely be trouble. The feeling rose in his gut that he would not be let off with a lecture for peeing beside the road. With Tennessee not far away, Tommy decided to keep driving at the speed limit and hope the Kentucky patrolman would have to give it up when they got to the state line. For another two miles it looked good, but on the next straightaway the cop gunned his engine and started around. Tommy guessed the trooper would try to cut him off, so he tromped the pedal. Just as the nose of the patrol car passed his back tire, Tommy swerved in front of the officer, forcing him to lock up his brakes to avoid a collision. Now the cop was mad.

So began a sinuous tango as the two cars weaved from lane to lane, the trooper trying to pass and Tommy blocking him at each attempt. Tommy had his V-8 mill wound tight but his loaded down '54 Ford was no match for a state police car. He figured his only chance would be to outdrive or outsmart the cop on his tail. At this time of night, Tommy guessed there wouldn't be any more cops between him and Tennessee and for a while his own driving skill and the wet, curvy road kept the state patrolman at bay. But the cop knew every inch of that highway and when the road straightened out the trooper knew he had a long straightaway ahead of him with no oncoming traffic and he made his move.

He flipped on his siren to give Tommy a jolt and swung out into the left lane to pass. Tommy veered over to block but the trooper braked, cut right, and then stomped his accelerator. Before Tommy could react, the cop was right beside him. Instead of passing, however, the angry patrolman, whose window was also down, looked over and jabbed the air with his index finger, motioning for Tommy to pull over. Tommy looked at the trooper who'd just outfoxed him and watched him for a second. His Ford was running at full-bore but Tommy knew the cop still had plenty of spare horsepower under his hood, and if he got out in front, would block him from getting to the state line.

Tommy knew exactly what to do. Just like in *Thunder Road*, Tommy took the lit cigarette from his mouth and flicked it directly at the cop's face. But unlike in the movie, where Luke Doolin's cigarette hit his pursuer on the cheek and caused him to crash, Tommy's cigarette hit the airstream between the two cars and disappeared. Damn!

The cop laughed, goosed the gas pedal and started to pull ahead of Tommy's coupe. But he didn't reckon with something that every cop should know: that those who run from the law have more to lose than the cops chasing them have to gain and will go to desperate lengths to escape.

Though it pained him to do it, Tommy was left with only one option and he took it without hesitation. Before the trooper got clear of him, Tommy slammed his right front fender into the patrol car's rear door panel and then dodged left to avoid the trooper's hood as it swung in front of him. The move took the cop by surprise, knocking his rear end into the loose gravel at the side of the road. Fighting against disaster, the trooper managed to keep out of the ditch but he couldn't overcome momentum and his car spun round like a dervish, making two complete circles on the wet pavement. Working the gas, brakes, and steering wheel with concerted precision, the patrolman not only stayed on the road, but as his car was completing its final revolution, he tromped the gas and cranked the wheel so that the patrol car emerged from the whoop-de-do with its tires smoking rubber and once again heading south.

In the mirror, Tommy watched the patrolman's maneuvers with a sort of awe and as the cop's headlights and red flashing rotator closed the distance between them, Tommy took a swig from the Coke bottle between his knees and lit another cigarette. The cop came up on him so fast that Tommy thought the trooper was going to ram him, but he fastened himself a carlength behind and stayed put. Tommy was pretty sure the cop wouldn't make any more attempts to pass him for a while but he had no doubt that the chase had now taken on a seriousness, maybe even a deadliness, that it had not had before.

For the next few miles the Kentucky patrolman hugged Tommy's rear end like a stout lady's girdle. Seeing no sense in blowing up his engine, Tommy eased up and ran at a steady 85, but still pushed his old coupe hard on the curves, hoping the cop would make a mistake. The closer they got to Tennessee the more the rain picked up, and though hard drops spackled against his cheek, Tommy kept his side window down, not wanting to dim his senses or be robbed of the reality of what was taking place on this lonesome black highway. The sounds of the chase ran through him like a country song; the siren, the hard running engines, the squeal of tires on the curves and the slap, slap, slap of his windshield wipers playing in time with the patrol car's blinking top light. Being chased by the law with a trunk full of moonshine was every bit like he had imagined and Tommy felt like he was in his own movie, watching himself perform.

When he passed the 'Welcome to Tennessee' sign, Tommy's face lit into a smile, but the grin disappeared when he saw that the Kentucky trooper stayed with him. The patrolman still made no attempt to pass and even backed off several car lengths. A little past Westmoreland Tommy found out why.

Coming onto a straight patch of highway after rounding a blind corner, Tommy was confronted by a Tennessee Highway Patrol car sitting sideways in the road with its flashers on. A Mountie hatted trooper stood behind it holding a shotgun. Tommy cranked his steering wheel and swerved hard left, putting his two driver's side tires in the dirt and clipping the front bumper of the state patrol car, shearing it off. The jolt caused Tommy's coupe to do a hopping little minuet as he fought to get back on the pavement and then Tommy heard the blast from the twelve-gauge as buckshot blew out his back window. Bits of shattered glass hit the back of his head and neck and ricocheted off the windshield.

The Ford had just regained its footing on the roadway when Tommy saw too late that the Tennessee cop had chosen his spot well, for he had parked just before a left-hand ninety-degree turn. Tommy hit the curve on the inside lane doing 75. His bald tires skated on the wet asphalt and he slid sideways across the road and into the gravel. Fortunately for Tommy, the gravel slowed his car some before its back end hit a tree that demolished the right rear fender and popped the trunk open. Tommy jerked the steering wheel to get back on the pavement, but he overcorrected and the Ford lurched onto its side, then over on its top, and slid ninety feet down the slick highway to the sound of grinding metal and crunching glass to where it finally came to rest upside down in the middle of the road, leaving a trail of mangled cardboard, shattered Mason jars, and the sweet, sinful smell of mountain moonshine in its wake.

A moment later a cut and bruised, but otherwise uninjured Tommy Kegley crawled from the scrunched passenger window of his overturned car. Haloed by the white glare from a police car's spotlight, he looked up into two of the biggest gun barrels and maddest faces he'd ever seen. With a cigarette still in his mouth, Tommy grinned. "Ah give y'all a mighty good run there fer awhile," he said, just before the wooden stock of a shotgun whacked him upside the head.

"That's for my bumper," the Tennessee cop said.

The Kentucky trooper looked at his Tennessee counterpart and told him, "Looks like this feller hit his noggin' purty hard in the wreck."

Just before consciousness deserted him it went through Tommy's mind that even Robert Mitchum couldn't a' done it better.

Chapter 7

Most mornings when Cletus passed through War on his way to work at Warriormine, he stopped to have a cup of coffee with Cliff. The filling station was always open by seven and Cliff made coffee for the gaggle of early-risers who liked to stop and ratchet-jaw. On this Friday, Clete was earlier than usual and Cliff was still alone, silently working his own jaw. He showed Cletus Tommy's note, but didn't say anything.

"What all'd 'e take?" Clete asked.

"A tankfull a' gas, Ah reckon," Cliff said. "My change makin' money, some Cokes, a few candy bars, and a carton a' cigarettes. And he broke some glass in the back door gittin' in."

Cletus finally said what he knew Cliff was thinking. "Ah wonder if Shelly know's anythin' about this?" He walked over to the counter, picked up Cliff's phone and dialed. When Ethel answered he told her he wanted to talk to Shelly.

"She's still sleepin'," Ethel said.

"Gitter up," Clete said, and told Ethel what had happened at Cliff's.

"You bet I will," Ethel answered.

The way Ethel pulled her out of bed Shelly knew there was trouble.

"When's the las' time you saw Tommy or talked with 'im?" Clete asked.

"He phoned me last night, aroun' nine," Shelly anwered. "Why?"

"What'd you two talk about?"

Shelly hesitated and Clete said, "You don't need ta think it over. You jus' need ta tell me the truth."

Shelly didn't want to lie, but she didn't want to give Tommy up either. "Tommy said he had an emergency in Kentucky an' had ta leave right away but that he'd be back late today."

"Is that all?" Clete said.

"Yeah," Shelly answered, though that really wasn't true. "What's wrong, Daddy?" Shelly asked, playing the 'daddy' card.

"He broke inta Cliff's station an' stole money an' some other stuff."

"He didn't say nothin' about that. He knows I wouldn't put up with it."

Clete softened. "Ah know ya wouldn't, honey." He hung up the phone and looked at Cliff. "You gonna call the cops?"

"Naw, Ah don't 'spose. Ah owe Tommy 'bout as much fer the work he done as what he took. From his note it sounds like he's comin' back. Ah'll deal with 'im then."

Throughout the morning a relentless stream of curious locals flowed through Cliff's station.

"Aintch ya mad about it?" most of them asked.

"Whada' you think?" Cliff answered.

"Whatcha fixin' ta do to 'im if 'e comes back?"

"Don' know. Guess Ah'll hafta wait an' see why 'e did it."

"You gonna beat Tommy's ass like ya did 'is ol man's?"

"Only if 'e asks fer it."

"Didja lose a lotta money, Cliff?"

"Not as much as Ah'm losin' by not gittin any work done answerin' all these questions."

A few minutes after he came on duty at 9 o'clock, Bud Click, the War police chief, heard about the burglary and stopped by.

"Don't bother makin' a report, Bud," Cliff told him, standing under a Chevy lifted high on the rack "Ah ain't pressin' charges. Ah'm too busy."

At 3 p.m. the chief returned and walked into the garage area while Cliff was stretched underneath a pickup. Cliff saw the bottom half of his uniform trousers. "Yeah, Bud?" he said.

"You wanta hear the story?" Bud asked.

Cliff slid his trolley out from under the vehicle, got up and wiped his hands on a shop rag. "Shor. Ya want a pop an' some tater chips?"

"Shor," the chief answered.

They went out into the office area and Cliff pulled a bottle of Nehi Cream Soda from the cooler and handed to the chief then pulled out a big bag of chips from under the counter and held it out. Bud reached deep into the bag and his long, bony hand came out like a clamshell bucket full of potato chips.

"I got a call from the Tennessee Highway Patrol," he told Cliff. "They're holdin' Tommy in Nashville. He won't say nothin' ta nobody, but from his license they saw that he's from here."

"What they got 'im on?" Cliff asked.

"He's in a heap a' trouble. Kentucky's chargin' Tommy for peein' on a public roadway, eludin' the law, damagin' state property, an' assault. He rammed a state police car an' tried ta run it off the road." Bud stuck some chips in his mouth and crunched them. "Tennessee's nailed 'im on destruction of state property. Guess he smacked a Tennessee patrol car while runnin' a road block." Bud swallowed the chips then took a drink of cream soda.

"Whew," Cliff let out a low whistle. "That ain't good."

"They didn't think so, either," Bud said. "The trooper shot out Tommy's back winda'. Then Tommy hit a tree and rolled his car over an' totaled it."

Cliff took a swig from his Royal Crown Cola. "Is Tommy okay?"

"A might scraped up an' contused," the chief said. "Accordin' ta them, he sustained a head injury that left him unconscious for awhile, but he's okay now."

"How come Tommy done all this?" Cliff asked.

"The federal charges against him per'ty much answer that question," Bud said. "They're stickin' him for transportin' moonshine."

"Well, that explains his family emergency," Cliff said.

On his way home from work Cletus stopped by Cliff's station and got the low-down. When he told Shelly, she said, "I'm goin' for a walk up in the woods."

"Ah wantcha home by suppertime," Clete told her. "You don't need ta go worryin' your mama an' me." Then he said, "Ah'm sorry about Tommy, honey."

Four weeks passed and no more was heard from or about Tommy Kegley. August edged into September and the first Wednesday after school began, Shelly was changing out of her school clothes when the phone rang. Ethel answered and called Shelly down from her room. Looking rankled, Ethel handed the phone to Shelly. "It's Tommy. He called collect."

"Thanks for takin' the call, Mama." Shelly said as she put the receiver to her ear. "Tommy, you alright?"

"Hi, Shelly," Tommy said. "You alone?"

"I can be." Shelly picked up the phone and stretched the cord into the next room. Ethel frowned but didn't follow.

"Where are ya?" Shelly asked.

"Nashville."

"You still in jail?"

"Naw. They wouldn't let me call ya from jail cause you ain't kin."

"Well, where ya callin' from then?"

"Ah'm callin' from a phone booth in the Nashville recruiter's office."

"Whatcha doin' there?"

"Waitin' for a bus ta take me ta Parris Island," Tommy answered.

"Wow!" Shelly said. "We talked about goin' ta France someday."

"This ain't that one. This un's a base for the United States Marines."

"You in the Marines?"

"Yep," Tommy said proudly.

"What about all your trouble?"

"That's what landed me in the Marines. After they all saw Ah warn't gonna tell 'em nothin' about the moonshine, they started deal makin'. All the lawyers from both sides, an' even the ol' judge 'imself, sampled Uncle Hop's juice; Ah recken jus' to make shor it could be used as evidence. An' when they tasted it ever'body concluded Ah was only haulin' the stuff."

"How'd they figger?" Shelly asked.

"Well," Tommy said, and chuckled, "they all said Ah was too dumb ta make booze that good. Anyway, the judge's nephew is a Marine recruiter so they all agreed if Ah'd sign up they'd de-fer my charges." Tommy laughed again. "An' Ah heard they divvied up the evidence, leastwise, all that warn't broke."

"Didja call your uncle yet?" Shelly asked.

"No," Tommy answered, more serious now. "Ah'm gonna write 'im a letter from boot camp. Ah reckon he can't come git aholt a' me there."

"You think he'd do somethin' bad to ya if he could? From what you told me about 'im, I wouldn't want your uncle mad at me," Shelly said.

"Ah don't know, Shelly. What happened really warn't all my fault … an' Ah didn't tell nobody where the moonshine come from." Tommy paused. "And uncle Hop was in the Marines too. That might settle him a little, 'specially if Ah come back a war hero."

"Listen, Tommy, don't you do nothin' stupid if ya git sent to Viet Nam. Keep your head down an' don't take no more chances than ya got to."

"Ah'll be alright," Tommy said. "In a way, Ah'm kinda lookin' for'ard to it. But what Ah really wanta talk about is you an' me after Ah git out. Ah signed up for three years, will ya wait for me?"

"Three years is a long time, Tommy."

"Ah know. But you'll be sixteen by then an' we kin git married an' nobody say a thing against it."

For a moment Shelly didn't say anything. "Tell ya what, Tommy," she finally said; "I promise that for the next three years I won't marry nobody."

"Good e'nuff'," Tommy agreed.

———————

Shelly received several short, barely legible letters from Tommy during his basic training and always answered them. The last one she got was when he finished his advanced infantry course and stated he'd be shipping out for Viet Nam soon. Then Shelly heard from him no more, though as Clete told her, if anything bad happened to him over there, word would certainly come back.

Now a high school freshman, Shelly hung out with her own classmates and settled down some. She went on dates but never had a steady boyfriend, and though her classmates drank, partied and raised some hell, their doings were tame compared to Tommy's crowd. Once again she hiked in the hills or went with Cletus on repair jobs and even resumed attending church.

Except for a few after school and weekend fights, Shelly's freshman year passed without serious trouble. In April of 1970, Ethel gave birth to her seventh and last child, Rose, and after a wet May, the Stamper household was looking forward to a quiet and pleasant summer. Summer vacation had barely started, however, when Shelly's 'girl problems' became worse than ever. Ethel made an appointment for her in August.

Clete's coughing had also intensified and Ethel set him up to see a lung specialist in Charleston the same day Shelly was to see Dr. Marlowe. "Ain't no need fer all that fuss, Ah feel fine," Clete protested, but Ethel told him, "Shut up, you're goin'. The only good thing about workin' in a mine is ya got medical in-shorance."

Junior, Sarah, and Mack stayed with Cliff and his wife for a few days while the rest of the clan went to Charleston. After two days of tests the doctor told Clete, "You've got emphysema. It's not terminal – yet, but if you don't give up smoking, it will be."

Shelly's news wasn't much better. "We are nearly out of options," Doctor Marlowe explained to her and Ethel. "I can increase your pain medication but you will probably suffer some side effects like irritability and drowsiness. If your symptoms don't improve the only course of action is surgery."

"And then she wouldn't ever be able ta have kids," Ethel said, a statement more than a question.

"That is correct," Doctor Marlowe said. "This is something you need to consider. I cannot – and will not – make that decision for you."

As Shelly was buttoning up her clothes to leave, Rita Marlowe stuck her long nose close to Shelly's blouse. "You didn't tell me you were a smoker."

"She's never told me, neither," Ethel said, "but I know about it."

"You need to stop," the doctor told her.

"What's that got ta do with my other problems?" Shelly said.

"We're trying to help you in any way we can, Shelly," Dr. Marlowe said gently. "Quitting smoking won't make your pain go away, but it might reduce it. Wouldn't that be nice?"

After returning from Charleston, Ethel constantly got on Clete, Junior, and Shelly about their smoking.

"Lee' me alone," Junior said. "Ah ain't sick, they are."

"You will be if ya keep it up," Ethel told him.

Junior and Shelly were never allowed to smoke around Ethel, and now Clete began going outside to get away from her harranging. One September evening after dinner as the setting sun was flaring with a final burst of color, Shelly returned from a short hike and saw Clete in the kennel with his two hounds, sucking on a cigarette and coughing between each puff. Shelly opened the gate and went inside. "How come you git ta smoke around here an' me an' Junior can't?" she said.

"Cuz Ah'm the boss," Clete told her.

"We all know better'n that," Shelly said. "Maybe I oughta take this up with the real boss."

Clete squatted down on his haunches and hawked out a string of roupy coughs as he petted the dogs. "Y'all best not do that," he said. "She's makin' it mighty tough on me as it is."

"That's cause Mama knows it's killin' ya."

"An' she's worried it'll kill you someday, too," Clete said. He tried, unsuccessfully, to stifle the raspy hacks that came up from his lungs. "An' it hurts me sum'thin awful ta think a' you coughin' like this."

"But it's killin' you *now*," Shelly said, staring at the ground. She raised her head and Clete saw that his daughter was crying. "We don't wanta lose you, Daddy," Shelly said. "I'd give anything if you'd quit smokin'."

"Well, Ah'd give anythang if *you'd* quit smokin'," Clete shot back.

Shelly stopped crying. "Really?"

As soon as she said it, Cletus knew he'd been had. Shelly didn't need to say the words, but she did anyway. "I'll quit smokin' if you do."

"That ain't fair," Cletus said. "Ah been smokin' a long time. It's way harder fer me ta stop."

"I don't care," Shelly said. "You said you'd do anything if I'd quit."

Clete quit playing with the dogs and stood up. He squinted into the western sky's blazing display of violet and gold. "When?"

"Right now," Shelly said without hesitation.

"*Now?*" Clete asked, caught offguard.

"You're the one who always told me, 'Once ya make up your mind ta do somethin', ya need ta do it right away or ya might not do it a'tall'," Shelly said

Cletus looked at his daughter, who seemed to have grown out of childhood right before his eyes. He gave two sharp coughs, took a long draw on his Lucky Strike then ground it into the soil with the toe of his work shoe. "Aw'right," he said, "Let's do it."

"We need ta take some kinda oath," Shelly told him. "So it's official."

Clete chuckled. "Yeah, Ah reckon that would hep us keep to it."

"How 'bout we swear on a Bible, Daddy. We can go down to the church an' do it."

Cletus sucked in his breath and for once didn't cough it out. The Bible was sacred to both of them. "Okay," he finally said.

So father and daughter walked to the Shiloh Church that was always unlocked. They went up to the pulpit where the preacher's own Bible lay open and Shelly put her hand upon it and Cletus covered her hand with his. Both swore in the presence of God to never smoke another cigarette so long as they lived and then went to the wastebasket where Clete tossed the remainder of his Luckies into it. Shelly pulled out the Winston's hidden in her sock and tossed them in as well.

In the soft gloaming of mountain twilight they strolled home and if the evening breeze that wafted over them now smelled sweeter, it wasn't only because the air was no longer tainted with Clete's cigarette smoke. A joy hung round them that they had done this together, a feat neither could have accomplished alone. Like the child that part of her still was, Shelly took hold of her father's hand. They came into the house like that and when Shelly kissed Clete on the cheek and said, "I'm goin' up to my room an' read fer awhile, Daddy," Ethel knew something important had taken place.

Cletus told her the story and Ethel said, "Shelly's been fixin' to quit fer a couple a' weeks now."

"You mean she planned …?" Clete said, as his mind worked out the details of what had just taken place.

"Yep," Ethel answered. "Likely clear down to the tears an' the Bible."

Quitting was hard on Cletus, but he didn't complain. When he was having a rough time, he'd go out to the kennel with his two coon dogs, but if he complained to them, they kept it to themselves. One time Ethel came outside to fetch the laundry off the line and saw Clete shaking and sweating. "I know this is hard fer ya," she said, "but me an' the kids do appreciate it. And maybe you'll git ta see your gran'kids, now."

Clete looked at her and nodded.

After a couple of months Clete adjusted to life without cigarettes but Shelly's endometriosis continued to worsen and neither giving up smoking nor increased medication alleviated the pain. As her sophomore year progressed, sometimes her insides hurt so badly that she couldn't go to school. Ethel made another appointment for Shelly over Christmas vacation, but Dr. Marlowe had nothing left to offer. Shelly was now missing so much school that her grades fell. Her social life disappeared and on the days she felt better, just wanted to go up in the hills and be alone.

One Saturday in April, when sunshine filled the air and the rest of the Stamper family played and laughed in the yard, Shelly lay in bed, hurting so terribly she was crying. Throughout the day her family came to see her, offering sympathy and treats, but Shelly chased them away. "Lee' me alone. I jes wanna die in peace."

Shelly expressed that thought so often that Ethel feared she might mean it. Shortly before suppertime, Ethel went to Shelly's room and refused to leave. "We've *got* to do som'thin, honey," Ethel said. "I'm worried about what this is doin' to ya ...an' I'm afraid a' what you might do to yor'self."

"I know, Mama," Shelly said, "but it hurts so bad I can't stand it no more."

Ethel sat down on the bed and took her daughter's hand. They sat quietly for a while as Shelly cried lightly. "I want that operation, Mama," she said.

In early June Shelly had a hysterectomy. She healed quickly and by July was back cavorting with friends and scrambling around the mountains. In the middle of August she helped her father rebuild a diesel engine.

"Lessee," Cletus said, as they were leaning over the motor, "yer 'bout old enough ta git a driver's license."

"I'd like ta do that," Shelly said.

"Well then, Ah need to be a'teachin' ya how ta drive."

"I already know how ta drive, Daddy. Tommy taught me."

"An' look where his drivin' got him. Ah need ta teach you how ta drive in a way that won't gitcha throw'd in jail."

"Could ya teach me ta drive one a' these?" Shelly asked, slapping the Mack's solid fender with her hand, not really expecting her father to say Yes.

"Tell ya what, you learn on a little rig first, like my Powerwagon, then when ya git yer license, I'll teach ya ta drive a big one."

Shelly ran her eyes down the length of the tandem axel B-61. "You really mean it?" she said.

"Shor, why not? Folks expect me ta try these rigs out after Ah rebuild 'em. They wouldn't care if'n you drive a little, long as Ah'm with ya."

Throughout that summer and on into autumn and winter, seldom a week passed that Cletus and Shelly didn't go out driving. Once in a while Junior went along and Clete let him have a turn at the wheel. Sometimes they took the family car, now a Ford station wagon, but more often drove Clete's old 4x4 Dodge Powerwagon. Shelly wanted to learn how to use the boom that Clete had built in the bed so they'd hoist the station wagon and tow it around.

Clete taught Shelly how to change tires, tune-up the engine, change the oil and spark plugs, adjust the valves and timing and how to make emergency repairs. Besides the twisting highways around Peapatch, they drove the treacherous dirt roads back in the mountains. Sometimes they'd have to chain up all four tires to make it back to asphalt and returned home covered in mud, but laughing.

After Shelly turned sixteen in October she began pestering Clete to take her driver's test. The license bureau in Welch was only open on weekdays so Shelly would need to miss school and Clete a day of work. Coal production had picked up that autumn and Clete was working ten-hour weekdays and Saturdays.

"Ah can't git a day off right now, honey," Clete told her, "an' the boss says the mandatory overtime'll prob'ly keep on till after the first a' the year."

Shelly looked at her father, clearly unhappy.

"Ethel could take ya," Clete offered.

Shelly pouted. "I want you ta take me."

"Ah wanna take ya, too," Clete said, "but sometimes we don't git ever'thang we want."

Shelly opened her mouth to say something, but Clete went into a long coughing fit and she stayed silent.

Just as Clete's boss had said, the overtime continued through December. The only Saturday Cletus got off was Christmas. When Vertnor, Wilbur and Shirl arrived the day before, Shirl was pregnant. "Looks like it's your turn agin," Ethel said.

———————————

Shelly jumped into 1972 eager for her driver's license but Clete's overtime continued through January. "You said after the first a' the year, you'd git some time off," Shelly told him indignantly.

"We're still mighty busy," Clete said, "but Ah'll try." Two days later he came home from the mine and announced, "Well, Ah finally got a day off."

"When?" Shelly said, ecstatic with joy.

"Tuesday, February 29th. Ah told 'em since it was an extra day a' the year they could afford letting me have it off," Clete said, laughing.

Shelly arranged to miss school that day and for the next two Sundays she and Clete went driving so she could practice for her test. On Sunday, February 20th, the sun rose resplendent and by late morning had warmed the hills and valleys with a golden glow that plainly said spring is coming. When Cletus and Shelly took to the roads after church and Sunday dinner, they were able, for the first time since autumn, to roll the windows down and drive with their arms resting on the door panels.

"What kinda drivin' should we do today, Daddy?" Shelly asked, smiling. "I could use some work on my parallel parkin'."

"Yer plenty good enough," Clete said. "Let's find us a nice highway an' enjoy the afternoon. It's too nice a' day ta stay in one place."

Shelly and Clete turned south onto Highway 16, passed lazily through Cucumber, Newhall and Squire, crossed the Virginia border into Bishop and meandered their way west. They stopped twice for pop and once for ice cream as the afternoon wore on. The lustrous sun of morning faded only slightly when a line of wispy, willow thin clouds edged in front of it. All along their route, people were outside, on porches or in their yards, smiling and waving to anyone who passed. Near Castlewood they pulled off at a farmhouse that was having a yard sale and Cletus bought Shelly a gray baseball cap with a bulldog and *Mack Trucks* written on the front.

"Here's the hat," Clete told her, "you'll have ta git the truck yer'self."

North of Dante, Clete and Shelly joked at the way the sun balanced on the tip of a distant peak, like it might tumble off if the wind blew too hard.

"Reckon we oughta start headin' fer home," Clete said. "Ethel won't want us late fer supper. Take a right when ya get ta 83 up here."

Traffic was considerably heavier on that road but after Grundy it thinned out again. Cletus and Shelly had chattered away all day, but now they drove through the tree-shadowed hills in a comfortable silence. Clete rolled the side window up halfway and leaned his head against it. He couldn't take his eyes off his daughter as she muscled the Powerwagon through the curves and grades, clutching and working the four-speed shifter.

"What?" Shelly said.

"Ah'm jus' watchin' ya drive," he said, "at how good ya are an' how much ya like doin' it."

Sunlight blazing through a gap in the hills reflected off Shelly's light brown hair that spilled from her new hat and cascaded between her shoulder blades. As she cranked the steering wheel, the muscles beneath her bronze skin rippled in her forearms and triceps. Clete watched his daughter's face as it alternated in light and shadow with each turn of the highway. Maturity had not only made her body bigger, but had firmed her jawline and chin, making them square and solid. He reflected how Shelly had gotten her mother's dark skin, but not her black hair or striking, deep-set blue eyes. From him came her light brown hair but who she got her gray eyes from was a mystery. Clete reckoned that many a man would be smitten by those eyes, but few would ever tell her she was beautiful.

"Yer a'gittin big," Cletus said, when he saw that Shelly was uneasy at his staring. "Yer taller'n most boys."

"Not as tall as you, Daddy."

"Ah hope ya never are. Six-five wouldn't look good on a girl." Then Clete nodded towards her upper torso. "An' judgin' by yer arm muscles an' them wide shoulders, yer likely tougher'n a lotta boys too."

"You an' Mama both got muscles an' wide shoulders," Shelly told him.

Cletus laughed, and then coughed a couple of times. "Ah'm jus' happy you didn't get my buckteeth," he said, grinning a mouthful of them at Shelly. "Or worse yet, my brother's."

"Junior shor did," Shelly said and grinned back at Clete. Then she stopped smiling. "I ain't very girly am I, Daddy?"

"You'll be plenty girly when ya need ta be," Clete said, and then wondered if Shelly might take that wrong.

"I don't even walk like a girl. People say I walk like a big lizard."

"You don' walk like no lizard," Clete said, "but you do walk with *purpose*. A lot a' people don't know where they're a'goin' most a' the time, but you always know where yer goin' ...an' why."

"It don't always feel like that ta me," Shelly said.

"Well, it looks that way ta other people, an' that counts fer a lot."

"Sometimes," Shelly said, "sometimes ... I think that when I grow up, like git outa school an' all, men ain't gonna like me."

"Boys like you jus' fine, Shelly," Cletus said, surprised to hear his daughter talk like this. "You git calls an' go on dates."

"Not with any a' the guys I really want to."

"Do ya hint that you'd like 'em ta call ya?"

"I try," Shelly said, "but I don't git much chance, cause they're always hangin' around the girls who really *are* good lookin'."

"Shelly, yer a fine lookin' girl. Why would ya even think ya weren't?"

"You jes think I'm good lookin' cause yor my daddy," Shelly said, and sank her front teeth into her bottom lip.

"That ain't the reason a'tall," Cletus told her, but secretly he wondered if Shelly had read his mind a few minutes earlier.

"It ain't jes that," Shelly said, her lip quivering. "Ev'rybody at school knows I can't have babies."

Clete was searching for an answer when Shelly pulled into a gravel turnout, put the shifter into neutral, then laid her head on the steering wheel and began sobbing. Clete sat silent, not sure how to respond.

He'd certainly seen his daughter cry before, but not like this, coming out of nowhere. He scooched over on the seat beside her and wrapped both of his lanky arms around her shoulders. "Ah know it's hard on ya, Shelly," he said, "but at least you don't have 'at horrible pain no more."

"It jes hurts in a diff'ernt way now," Shelly said between sobs. "Knowin' I won't have kids an' that decent men won't ever wanta marry me cause I can't give 'em a family." Shelly's body shook and she looked up from the wheel into her father's eyes. "An' you can't tell me it ain't true."

Cletus knew it was true, especially in mountain culture, and it wouldn't do for him to lie. Shelly put her head back down on the steering wheel and continued to cry. Clete tightened his arms around his daughter and squeezed her shoulders. "Yer right, honey, Ah cain't lie to ya 'bout that," he said, "but Ah kin tell ya some thangs that are true."

Clete eased Shelly off the steering wheel and looked into her eyes.

"It's true that you are good lookin', in yer own way … an' nobody else's. There are decent men who will love ya an' wanta marry ya. Ah know you don't b'lieve it now, honey, but someday you'll see Ah'm right."

Shelly looked at him, trying to stifle her crying.

"An' here' sum'thin else that's true. Yer strong an' tough an' stubbern as hell. You *will* make yer way in this world," Cletus laughed a little, "cuz you won't tolerate nobody standin' in yer way."

Shelly sniffed a couple of times and attempted a small smile.

"Ah think it's also true," Clete said, "that it won't be the same way other girls make their way in the world … cuz you don't want it ta be."

Shelly pulled a red handerchief from the back pocket of her jeans.

"An' one more thang that's true," Clete said, as Shelly dabbed the tears off her face. "Yer a'hurtin' over this now an' that's understandable, but when you think on it, an' it may take ya awhile's, meh'be even a few years, but when ya do, Ah think it's true you won't ever wanta be any'thang but what you are … Shelly Stamper."

Shelly nodded a couple of times but didn't say anything. She blew her nose on the handkerchief and stuffed it back into her pocket, then put the stiff-framed old Powerwagon into gear and eased onto the highway. By the time they crossed the line back into West Virginia and

the sun had dipped behind the western hills for the day, she and Clete
were talking and laughing like nothing had happened. But of course,
it had, although it wasn't until years later that Shelly fully understood
how important that day, and that conversation with her father had
been, and wished with all of her heart that she could tell him so.

Chapter 8

That next week Shelly bounded around the house like a big jack-rabbit, excited to be getting her driver's license the Tuesday after. Cletus was back to working forty hours a week at the mine and Shelly told him, "Since you ain't workin' this weekend, we kin go drivin' *both* Saturday an' Sunday. I wanta work on my parkin'. They make ya do that ta pass the test."

"We'll, see," Clete said, "but yer parkin' is jus' fine, quit worryin'."

"I still wanta practice, Daddy, jes ta be sure."

When the phone rang at a quarter to ten on Thursday night, after the young kids were in bed, Shelly eyed it with suspicion. Ethel answered and then handed it to Cletus. "It's your brother," she said.

Clete was on the line for twenty minutes, listening and saying things like,"It's 'at bad, huh?" and "Yeah, well Ah reckon Ah could if'n you think it'd hep 'im."

"What's Vertnor want ya to do?" Ethel asked, when Cletus hung up.

"Go over ta Wilbur an' Shirl's this weekend."

"Daddy!" Shelly said, "You promised we'd go drivin'."

"Ah didn't promise nothin'. Ah said we'd see."

Shelly's pout was on. "I'm 'fraid I ain't gonna git my license now."

"Ah'll be back Sunday evenin' an' we'll git yer license on Tuesday jus' like we planned," Clete said. "An' you won't have a lick a' trouble … less'n you've make up yer mind to."

"Why's Vertnor want ya ta go?" Ethel asked.

"Coupla reasons," Cletus said. "Wilbur ain't workin' much late-ly an' he's drinkin' hard. Vertnor thinks he might even be a'smokin' some a' that whacky-weed, an' that stuff'll either kill ya or make ya crazy. With Shirl's baby due in a few weeks, Vertnor wants me ta git 'im straightened out."

"How come *you* got ta go?" Shelly asked. "Why don't Vertnor go?"

"Vertnor was fixin' ta go, but he come down with the flu," Clete said. "'Sides not feelin' good, he don' wanna give the flu ta them, 'specially little Earlene. Saturday's her fourth birthday an' they're havin' a party that afternoon. Since Vertnor cain't be there he figger'd it'd be nice if Ah was."

"*Earlene,*" Shelly said and sneered. "Nobody other'n Wilbur'd name a girl Earlene."

"Wilbur named 'er after Earl Scruggs," Clete said, "his favorite banjo player."

"Least he didn't name 'er Scrugglene," Shelly said. "Wilbur's dumb e'nuff ta do that. I still don't see why you hafta go."

"Cuz Wilbur needs hep an' he's kinfolk too. Vertnor said meh'be me an' Wilbur could go fishin' an' Ah could talk with Wilbur an' git 'im walkin' right again. Vertnor tol' me that Wilbur listens ta other folks better'n he does his own daddy." Clete looked at Shelly. "Kinda' like some a' mah own kids."

Shelly glared at Clete until he told her, "If'n that lip a yer's drops any more it's gonna drag on the floor."

"I don't see why it's your job ta go over an' pull Wilbur's fat head outa his fat ass," Shelly yelled and stomped her foot down.

Ethel put her finger an inch from Shelly's nose. "You don't talk like that in this house! Gitch yor'self upstairs an' ta bed. Your part in this conversation is over."

Shelly glowered at her mother but didn't move.

Ethel met Shelly's challenging glare with her own unflinching eyes. "Now!" she shouted, "or you'll be goin' ta bed with a sore bottom. You ain't too old ta have it an' I ain't too old ta give it to ya."

Just as Ethel was about to take hold of her, Shelly turned and ran up the stairs. Ethel walked over to the big window in the living room and pointed outside. "You really wanta' go fishin', Cletus? It's rainin hard an' it's 'spose ta keep rainin' all weekend."

"Fish bite in the rain," Clete said. "They don't mind gittin wet."

The next morning Shelly came down to breakfast late and her words to Ethel were clipped and surly. Cletus had already left for work and as Shelly got up from the table to get her coat, she glanced out the kitchen window into the rainy morning and saw that her father's pickup was still in the driveway. "How come the Powerwagon's still here?" she said to nobody in particular.

"Cause Daddy drove the station wagon t'day," Junior said. "He's leavin' fer Wilbur's straight from work. When he called this smornin' ta let 'em know he was comin', Shirl said if he was gonna be there fer dinner, she'd cook up a coupla possums Wilbur shot las' night. We all said bye to him 'fore he left." Junior licked his lips. "Ummm, possum; shor wish Ah was goin' with 'im."

Shelly put on her jacket and looked at her brother. "You are sech a hillbilly."

Shelly didn't come home after school, but around 5:30 she called Ethel. "I won't be home for dinner. I'm goin' out with some friends."

Ethel didn't like it, but all she said was, "Be careful, honey."

That night Shelly was anything but careful. By nine o'clock she was drunk and even her friends were wary of her edgy anger. A little after midnight she insulted a heavy-set girl from Coalwood who was known for her strength. The girl splatted a fist against Shelly's cheek, knocking her down with a punch that should have taken the fight out of a lumberjack, but Shelly climbed to her feet, bellowing with wild rage and worked the girl over so badly that several boys finally jumped in and pulled her off.

A little past 3:00 a.m. Shelly's friends dropped her off where Peapatch Road intersected the highway and though a steady drizzle poured from the starless sky, Shelly insisted on walking the rest of the way home. To keep the hat Clete bought her from becoming drenched, Shelly tucked it inside her jacket, letting the water run down her face. By the time the dark outline of the Stamper home appeared, she was soaked.

The frigid water and raw air helped sober her up. The entire side of her face was throbbing and Shelly put a hand to her cheek and felt the swelling. The girl's a loudmouth, Shelly thought, and a bully who picks on smaller girls. But Shelly knew she'd started this fight and felt a pang of guilt. She'd been in a bad mood all day, still mad from last night, she reckoned, and just wanted to fight.

Shelly turned into the Stamper driveway and walked over to Clete's pickup. The Powerwagon sat soaked and dripping in the night, like an old horse unable to find shelter. As the rain pattered off its metal skin, Shelly felt sorry for the wet pickup and wished she'd gotten up that morning to see her daddy off.

The dreams began early the next morning: strange, spectral visions that woke Shelly up. She looked at her alarm clock then rolled over and covered her face with a blanket. Usually the sounds of raucuous little kids made sleeping in late on Saturday mornings difficult, but on this morning the house was quiet. Every time Shelly tried to go back to sleep she heard the phone ring downstairs.

A few minutes before ten, Shelly gave it up and climbed out of the sack. She pulled on some old jeans and a shirt then went into the upstairs bathroom and after using the can, wet a washcloth and looked in the mirror. The entire left side of her face ached from the bulging purple lump that flowered on her cheek and she knew Ethel would glower and the kids tease her and ask about the fight. She washed her face in cold water and walked slowly down the long staircase that entered into the living room, surprised that none of her little brothers and sisters were watching cartoons. Rain still spackled against the roof and windows so she knew they weren't outside. As Shelly stepped from the last stair the phone rang and Ethel rushed passed her to answer it. She glanced at Shelly but didn't say anything.

Shelly walked into the kitchen and saw her siblings arranged around the big wooden table, all silent. Breakfast was long over and Shelly wondered at the reason. When they looked up she expected the usual comments about her battle bruise, but no one said a thing, or acted like they even noticed. Everyone's eyes followed Shelly as she walked to the stove, poured a cup of coffee and gingerly took a sip. She turned around to face the assembled group. "What?" she said, a little grumpily.

"The dam broke," Mack said.

"Huh?" Shelly asked.

"That gret big coal slag dam 'bove Wilbur an' Shirl's bursted," Sarah said.

Shelly realized that some of her siblings were quietly crying. "When?" she asked.

"Sometime this mornin'," Junior said. His eyes were also wet. "Meh'be aroun' eight or so."

"Is Daddy an' Wilbur an' them all okay?" Shelly asked.

"We ain't heard from nobody yet," Mack said as he sniffed and wiped the tears off his face with the back of his hand.

The punch she'd been hit with the night before was nothing compared to the blow that slammed into Shelly's gut. Ethel came back into the kitchen and Sarah asked in a quavering voice, "Was that Daddy?" but Ethel's silence and the look on her face told everyone that it wasn't.

"We got a call from uncle Vertnor jus' 'fore nine," Junior told Shelly. "Folks from near Wilbur's called 'im an' said Saunders got wiped out right away and the flood's still goin', takin' out all a' them little towns down from it."

Shelly knew that Wilbur and Shirl's place was only a little ways downstream from Saunders, and bordered Buffalo Creek.

"Reckon word got aroun', cuz the phone's been ringin' ever' since," Junior said, "mostly with people wond'rin about Wilbur an' Daddy."

The phone rang and Ethel closed her eyes, as in prayer, then hurried into the living room to pick it up. Everyone around the table went silent, hoping this was the call they'd been praying for, the call from Cletus, their indestructible Daddy, calling to say that, yes, it was bad, it was real bad, but that he and Wilbur and Shirl and little Earlene were all safe and he'd be home tomorrow.

A few minutes later, Ethel walked back into the kitchen, her face strained, and told everyone, "That was Henry Bearden, your Daddy's foreman. He jest heard."

Nine year-old Sadie began openly crying. "Ah'm worried about ar' Daddy bein' drown'd in that big flood," she said between sobs.

Beside her, eleven year-old Mack put his arms around his little sister. "You don' have ta worry about Daddy gittin drown'd," he told her through his own tears. "He's tall 'nuff ta keep his head above all that water."

Shelly ran from the room. Ethel went upstairs and found her under her blankets, sobbing. "I never said goodbye," Shelly said, choking. "Daddy thinks I'm mad at 'im."

"He don't think any such thing," Ethel said, and laid her hand on Shelly's shoulder. "Now you come on back down. Your place is with the rest a' the family. Your brothers an' sisters need you with 'em just as much as they need me. I'd like ta hide my head under the covers too, but I can't an' neither can you."

Shelly sat up and she and Ethel hugged. Her mother's body was trembling and Shelly knew she was crying too; the first time Shelly'd ever seen it.

What scared Shelly most was that she had seen the dam. It was monstrous big and ugly. It wasn't at all like a real dam, just a humongus heap of coal slag hundreds of feet wide and thick and high, dumped between two ridges to impound polluted wastewater. Wilbur took her and Clete and Junior up to see the dam after it was built. He'd taken a job on the dam running a bulldozer and was actually proud of the black, hideous thing. "Look at the size a' it," Wilbur bragged. "That dam ain't a' goin' nowhar'."

Ethel and Shelly came back into the kitchen and Shelly sat down. She couldn't stop looking at the empty chair at the head of the table where her father always sat.

"I'll make ya som'thin ta eat," Ethel said.

"Thanks anyway, Mama, but I ain't hungry."

The phone rang again and Ethel rushed to get it while the others breathed silent prayers for the umpteenth time that morning. Ethel talked into the phone for some minutes and everyone knew it wasn't good news or their mother would have shared it with them immediately.

"That was Vertnor," Ethel said when she returned to the kitchen. "He still don't feel good cause a' the flu, but his friend Ben, who helped raise Wilbur, is gonna drive him down ta Logan County an' see what they can find out." Ethel poured a cup of coffee and sat down in her usual spot opposite Clete's chair. "Vertnor says he'll call soon as he can ta let us know what's goin' on."

––––––––––––––––––

As word spread that Cletus had gone to Buffalo Creek, the Stamper phone rang throughout that dreadful afternoon. Just before 2:00 Pastor Scoggins arrived and stayed for two hours. At around 4:30 the rain stopped and Shelly said, "Mama, kin I go out fer a short walk? I won't be gone long, I promise."

Junior joined her and as they were returning they passed the Shiloh Church. "Let's go in," Shelly said.

They went up to the pulpit and placed their palms on the open Bible. "This is the Bible Daddy an' I swore on that we'd quit smokin'," Shelly said.

After saying a prayer, they walked out of the church and stood for a moment, looking up at the gray sky that loomed over the distant hills. Not a single ray penetrated the swollen, bruised clouds that roiled from one horizon to the other. When they returned home Shelly and Junior recognized a neighbor's car parked in the driveway. Bill and Maude Hutchins, who lived at the far end of Peapatch, were in the kitchen and had brought a huge platter of fried chicken. More friends and neighbors, also bearing food, came by as day turned to evening. Ethel expressed her gratitude and tried to sound hopeful. "We ain't gonna hafta cook till July," she told them.

Cliff from the service station stopped by and when he saw that all Ethel had was the old pickup, he drove back into town and returned with his wife driving their second car, a big, nice-running Lincoln, and left it for Ethel to use.

At 6:40, Vertnor called. "It's awful," he said, his voice trembling. "As bad as eny'thing Ah saw in the war. Thar's a lot of folks, over a hun'ert, they know of's been killed, an' a whole lot more still missin'."

Ethel listened quietly as Shelly sat beside her on the couch. "Any news of ..." she tried to ask, but she couldn't finish the sentence.

"Nobody's hear'd a thing about Clete or Wilbur an' Shirl ... or mah little gran'daughter," Vertnor said, knowing what Ethel was trying to ask. He had to stop and compose himself. "The police an' fire an' them won't let eny'body git too close, so me an' Ben's jus' bin watchin' from the hillsides an' goin' ta all the shelters they got set up, askin' ever'body we kin." Vertnor paused.

"We took this hill road ... whar's we could see down inta the flood," Vertnor said, trying to form words. "Pert' near the whole town a' Saunders is gone ... washed away." He hesitated, the words sticking in his throat. "An' where Wilbur and Shirl's place was … thar ain't nothin' … jus' mud an' slag …nothin' left a'tall."

Vertnor broke down and began weeping.

Ethel let him cry for a few minutes and then asked, "Is there anything we can do, Vertnor, anything at all ta help?"

The voice on the other end was silent for a moment.

"Ah cain't think of a thing," Vertnor said, when he was finally able to answer, " 'cept ta pray."

Friends came by until about 8:30 and Pastor Scoggins stopped again and stayed until 9:00, but when he departed and the family was alone, a pall of sorrow settled over the Stamper home. As Ethel, Shelly, and Junior were helping the younger kids into bed, it started raining again, reminding everyone of the cause of this calamity. The little ones were tucked in with prayers and promises, but after only a few minutes Ethel couldn't stand hearing them crying in their beds. Shelly refused to go to her bedroom, insisting on sleeping on a couch in the living room where she could listen for the phone, so Ethel let Sarah sleep near her on the other couch. She put Mack into bed with Junior and gathered up Rose, as well as Charley and Sadie into the big bed with her, for what everyone knew was going to be a very long night.

Chapter 9

The Stamper's phone started ringing shortly after eight the next morning, but the calls were from friends and distant relatives offering hope and prayers and wondering if any more news had come. Some in the family talked of going to church, but when the time for the service came, no one wanted to leave the house. Pastor Scoggins stopped by when church was over but didn't stay long. He said he'd be by later, and if they wanted, conduct a Sunday service at the house. A few minutes after he left, Vertnor called, but he hadn't learned anything new.

Towards noon, people began coming by with food and Ethel laid out the table and encouraged everyone, visitors and family, to have a Sunday dinner together. At 3:00 o'clock Reverend Scoggins arrived, carrying his Bible, and Ethel told him, "Yes, the family would like him to do a prayer service." The other visitors left to give the Stamper family privacy, and a few minutes after four, shortly after the last prayer, the phone rang. It was Vertnor.

He wasn't crying, but his hesitation and trembling voice told Ethel that he was shaken to the core. Ethel could also hear other voices in the background.

"Ah'm at the school here in Logan," Vertnor said. "They got 'em a place set up fer people ta stay who lost their houses."

"Ya heard anything, Vertnor?" Ethel asked.

"Yeah," Vertnor said. "Wilbur an' Shirl an' Earlene are here too."

Shelly came into the living room and sat beside her mother on the couch.

"Are they alright?" Ethel asked, biting her lip at not hearing Clete's name.

"Ah reckon," Vertnor said. "They're wet an' cold but other'n that okay. They got stranded on a hillside all night. One a' them big Army trucks hauled 'em out this mornin' an' Ben an' I found 'em here a little while ago."

Ethel forced herself to ask: "Any news about Cletus?" The silence on the other end of the phone seemed eternal. "Vertnor?" Ethel finally asked again.

Vertnor took a deep breath. "Ah better let Wilbur tell ya, Ethel."

In the background Ethel heard Wilbur's quaking voice. "Ah cain't Pa. Ah don't think Ah kin do it."

"You need to, son. You was thar an' saw it. Ethel needs ta hear about it straight from you so she knows what happened."

Ethel held the receiver out from her ear a couple of inches so Shelly, who was sitting up against her, could hear.

"Here's Wilbur," Vertnor said, as if he were introducing him.

"Pa?" Ethel and Shelly heard Wilbur say.

"Wilbur?" Ethel said, and when she got no response said, "Wilbur, I know it's hard, with what y'all been through, but ya gotta tell us what happened."

In the kitchen, Cletus Junior got up from his chair to come into the living room and Ethel yelled, "Junior, you stay there." She called to Preacher Scoggins, who was also in the kitchen, "Reverend, would you keep ever'body out there. I'll be in directly an' tell y'all what's goin' on."

"Ethel … " Wilbur finally said.

"Yeah, Wilbur?"

"Ethel … Ah'm sorry …" Wilbur blubbered, choking on each word. "Ah'm so sorry … Ah cain't … hardly talk."

After several seconds of silence Ethel heard Vertnor say, "Go ahead, son."

"Please, Wilbur," Ethel told him in a steady voice, "you need ta tell me what happened. We hafta know."

The sober tone of Ethel's voice steadied Wilbur some. He took several deep breaths, and though crying, was able to talk.

"It come so quick," he said, "the water … "

Wilbur stopped again, sobbing.

"Ya need ta tell 'er, son," Vertnor said.

"Aw'right, Pa, Ah'll try," Wilbur said and took a couple more breaths. "Me an' uncle Clete was jus' fixin' ta head out fishin' ... when we heard a horn honkin' at the end a' the driveway. We went down ta see what it was an' thar was this pickup fulla people from Saunders yellin' and screamin', 'The dam broke! The dam broke!'

Ah didn't b'lieve 'em," Wilbur said, crying again. "Ah didn't think nothin' could break thet big dam .... But Clete said, 'we got ta git Shirl an' Earlene' and he started runnin' back to the house. When we got thar he started yellin' at Shirl ... an' me too ... 'Git to the car, raht now,' he kep' sayin', 'Raht now!' We'd all be dead if it wern't fer him doin' that."

Wilbur paused and Ethel could hear him crying.

"Shirl tried ta go back to the bedroom an' git her old fam'ly albums, but Clete wouldn't ler 'er. He grabbed up Earlene an' stuck 'er in Shirl's arms. 'Thar ain't time ta grab nothin',' he told 'er. 'Git to the car, now'."

Wilbur broke down again.

"But we didn't make it," he sobbed. "Halfways thar the water come. It rose so fast we couldn't git ta the car ... an' the car pro'bly wouldna' got us out by then anyways. Clete holler'd at us ta make fer the hill, cause it was closer'n the car, but that water was a'risin so fast ... an' with all the trash n' stuff slammin' us, it was hard jus' ta walk through it." Wilbur stopped, remembering the scene, and choked again.

Ethel looked at Shelly, who was catatonic with shock, as if she already knew what Wilbur was going to tell them.

"Ah made it up first ... " Wilbur said, strugging to talk, "an' turned ta hep Shirl git up the slope, but she's so big with bein' pregnant, an' all, she was havin' a real hard time. She was holdin' Earlene in one arm an' Ah had 'er bah the other one tryin' ta pull er' up 'at hill, but most a' her was still down in the water. Uncle Clete was b'side 'er, hep'in ta git 'er up that steep bank ... but the water was gittin deeper all the time."

Once more Wilbur stopped to compose himself.

"We near had it," he said. "We *almost* made it. Oh, God. Shirl's feet slipped in all that mud an' water an' Earlene come raht outa' her arm. Mah little girl jus' floated off in all that water and stuff. Lord, Ah couldn't stop it! Ah give Shirl's arm a gret big yank an' pulled 'er up then started runnin' after Earlene ... but she was too far out in the water fer me ta grab 'er ... an' Ah cain't swim."

Now the story spilled out of Wilbur, rapid and breathless.

"Uncle Clete was halfways up the bank bah then an' coulda' made it ... *he coulda' made it* ... but he jumped in the water an' startin' swimmin' after Earlene. Ah run along the bank best Ah could, keepin' up ... an' saw Clete grab holt a' Earlene. Thar was more an' more w-water comin' all the t-time," Wilbur said, trembling so hard he was stuttering. "An' we went awhiles till he got c-close to the bank whar Ah was ... an' he jus' give Earlene a toss ... Ah reckon with all the strength 'e had left ... an' Ah caught her."

Wilbur stopped, out of breath, and began crying hard.

"Wilbur?" Ethel said.

"Oh Lord ... oh God, Ethel ... A whole bunch a' stuff in the water come by raht then an' took 'im. It jus' swep' uncle Clete away."

Giant sobs heaved up from Wilbur's lungs as Ethel sat silent. Shelly turned away from the phone and stuck her face deep into the soft back of the couch to keep from screaming.

As Ethel was about to say his name again, Wilbur said, "Ah run along the bank, a'holdin' on ta Earlene an' tryin' to find Clete."

Wilbur's voice rose to a high pitch. "Ohhh ... that water jus' kep' gittin higher an' higher an' thar was houses, whole houses floatin' by ... with people ... p-people Ah knew ... a'lookin' out the winda's an' yellin' fer help. Later Ah seen them houses all smashed up aginst that big bridge down yonder from us ... an' Ah heard that all them people died."

He stopped, out of breath, and for a minute only Wilbur's sobs came over the phone. After a while he said, still crying, "But Ah never saw uncle Clete no more after he tossed Earlene to me. Ah'm sorry, Ethel .... Ah'm so sorry ... "

Wilbur began bawling so hard he could no longer talk and out in the kitchen, the rest of the family knew. The Stamper children began crying as Reverend Scoggins went from one to the other, trying to comfort them and fighting hard not to break down himself.

Wilbur's voice rose to a wail, loud enough that it carried into the kitchen. "Uncle Clete saved mah baby ... he saved mah baby," Wilbur cried, over and over. "Uncle Clete saved mah baby."

Chapter 10

Clete's battered body was found on Tuesday, the day he and Shelly were supposed to drive to Welch to get Shelly's driver's license. Ben and Vertnor had stayed on to help take care of Wilbur and Shirl and Ben identified Cletus so that Vertnor wouldn't have to see his brother so mangled.

Besides many of Shirl and Wilbur's friends, Shirl lost several kinfolk; the Hatfields were hit hard by the disaster. Where her and Wilbur's house had been, nothing remained but brown mud and coal slag. The Stamper's station wagon was located, barely identifiable, over two miles from where it had been carried away by the surging water.

On Saturday, Clete's funeral took place at the Shiloh Church, which could not accomodate all the mourners. Experienced as he was at eulogizing close friends, Reverend Scoggins cried nearly as much as everyone else. After Cletus was lowered into the hillside plot beside his mother and father, a number of the family's inner circle gathered at the Stamper house for dinner.

Ethel's sisters, Nellie and Gladys, and nine of their twelve children had driven down from Olive Hill in two cars the night before with Ethel's mother. Grammy got a bed but the others sprawled on couches and blankets scattered throughout the home. After the funeral Ethel coaxed them to come back to the house and eat but they had a long drive ahead and wanted to get home.

Wilbur, Shirl and Earlene, as well as Vertnor and Ben had been staying at the Stamper house since Wednesday, when Clete's body was brought to the funeral home in War. Ben, especially, had been a blessing, helping with the funeral arrangements and doing whatever work needed done around the house, sharing his good nature and kindness with a family so much in need of both.

At the dinner Vertnor said to Ethel, "Ah guess we'd all best be gittin' on home tomorra'. They'll be a'wantin' me an' Ben back ta work on Monday."

"Thanks fer stayin'," Ethel told Vertnor and said to Ben, "I don't know how ta thank you fer all ya done. You missed a week a' work an' ya got a big family ta feed an' take care of."

Ben stopped eating and wiped his mouth with a cloth napkin. "Ethel, I've always thought of this family like my own."

Ethel turned to Wilbur and Shirl. "You an' Earlene can stay here long as ya like. If ya want to, you can make this your home. We'll make room."

Shelly winced at sharing the house with Wilbur and Shirl and breathed a quiet sigh when Vertnor spoke up. "Thas' mighty generous of ya ta offer, Ethel," he said, "but we already made plans fer 'em ta move in with me at Gallipolis. Ah got room an' Ah'm pretty shor we kin find Wilbur a job thar."

Whatever had been thought of as normal at the Stamper home was now gone, but on Monday Ethel made the kids return to school, though none of them wanted to go. "We need ta git on with life," she told them, "an' the sooner we start, the better."

That evening, after everyone else was in bed, Shelly asked her, "How we gonna git by, Mama?"

Ethel was honest with her. "We're alright fer a little while. We got some money saved up and Clete had insurance through the union, but since he didn't die on the job, it ain't a lot. We'll hafta tighten our belts and sell some things."

"What about the coal comp'ny that built the dam?" Shelly asked. "Won't they hafta pay for all them people they killed and the houses they destroyed?"

Ethel was quiet for a moment, letting her rage settle before she spoke. "I already saw it on the news. Pittston is callin' this 'an act of God'. They're sayin' all that rain put more water in the resevoir than it could hold. The Governor an' state legislature's goin' along with 'em on it."

For the first time in her life, Shelly felt like getting a gun and shooting people.

———————————

Springtime came into the mountains with a whoosh of sunshine and dazzling promise, like Mother Nature were apologizing for the dreadful weather and tragedy she had flung at them in February. The deciduous trees roared with newfound color and even the evergreens jumped to life more vigorously than usual. Throughout the wildlands of southern West Virginia ferns and flowers, bushes, brambles, and mosses that had kept quiet all winter and then gobbled dirt and rain until the equinox, now decided, as though word had come to them through the underground, to burst forth in a mighty vernal explosion. One morning the people of McDowell County rose and looked out of their bedroom windows to a world of black and white and after breakfast stepped out of their kitchen doors into Oz.

On a fine and sunny afternoon in late March, Shelly came home from school and found that Clete's Powerwagon was gone from the driveway. Though she had not driven it since the week before Clete died, Shelly hoped it would become hers. "Where's the pickup?" she asked, when she came into the kitchen, where Ethel was baking rolls for dinner.

Ethel turned toward Shelly with flour-covered hands. "I traded it ta Cliff fer the Lincoln he loaned us."

A spasm of anger shot through Shelly. "How couldja, Mama?"

"I had to, Shelly. We need us a car that we can fit ever'body into. That Lincoln is worth three times what that ol' pickup was. It was a mighty nice thing fer Cliff ta do."

"I wanted ta take my driver's test in that truck."

"Cliff'll loan ya the truck fer that," Ethel said.

"I don't wanta license no more!" Shelly yelled and ran out the door.

———————————

In early April, Henry Bearden dropped by to bring Ethel some things from Clete's locker at work. When Ethel invited him to stay for dinner he accepted. A few days later Ethel ran into Henry at the grocery store in War and mentioned how a recent windstorm had loosened some of the shingles on their roof. Henry said he'd be more than happy to stop by on Saturday and nail them back on. When he arrived to do the repair work, he not only brought his tools, but a large ham and a gallon of ice cream as well. He stayed for supper that evening also, the ice cream setting him in good favor with the Stamper kids – except Shelly, who remained silent throughout the meal and left the table as soon as Ethel would allow it. When Henry accepted Ethel's offer to join them in church the next day, Shelly sat as far away from him as possible.

From there on Henry Bearden became a regular visitor to the Stamper home. He never arrived without food or some other needed item and on Saturdays worked with Junior and Mack around the house. On Sundays, after noontime dinner, Ethel and Henry went off together in Henry's car, leaving Junior, who was now fifteen, to mind the other children for a few hours. Shelly usually attended church, even if she'd been out late the night before and Ethel was insistent she be at Sunday dinner, but other than that, Shelly spent very little time at home on the weekends. Her dislike of Henry, or at least his keeping company with Ethel, was openly apparent.

"What's wrong with Henry?" Junior asked Shelly one day. "You never talk to 'im."

"Can't you see what's goin' on?" Shelly shot back.

"Ah see it well as you," Junior said, "but that ain't no reason fer you ta be so snotty to 'im. He's good ta ev'rybody."

"For now," Shelly said, and walked away.

After Clete's funeral, Shelly's absences from school increased. Sometimes she skipped to go tramping in the mountains, but even in the midst of a gorgeous spring, she found no relief from her sorrow. More often, Shelly blew school to drink and party. Once again she started running with the older crowd she had known through Tommy Kegley. Along with the fights and drugs, they spent a lot of time in bars, their favorite being a rowdy, brawling roadhouse down by Cucumber called Rattler's Den. With her height, tawny skin, and confident, surly demeanor, sixteen-year-old Shelly was never questioned about her age.

As spring drew on and Ethel and Henry Bearden openly courted, Shelly's behavior at school deteriorated. She missed more days than she attended and when at school, refused to do any work, disrupted class, and fought constantly. Near the end of April the principal called Ethel and told her that Shelly was failing every subject and about to be suspended.

Ethel met with the principal and school counselor and they suggested Shelly get professional help. Ethel agreed, but when the idea was proposed to Shelly she hackled up in defiance. "I won't go," she yelled. "You'll hafta tie me to the chair, cause I'll run out." To show she meant it, Shelly got up and ran out of the room.

Later, Ethel tried to talk to her. "Shelly, ya only got a few weeks a' school left. At least do enough ta pass. Next year you'll be a senior and 'fore ya know it you'll be graduated." Shelly didn't sass back, but her behavior didn't change.

Ethel felt frustrated and helpless, but she had six other kids to fret over and they were also having trouble since Clete's death. Adding to her problems, the savings were almost gone. Henry Bearden, as well as friends and neighbors, tried to help out, but Ethel was part of a proud culture that disdained charity. With Charlie and Rose not yet of school age, Ethel couldn't go to work. She briefly considered moving back to her mother's in Olive Hill, but that would gain her nothing. At least in Peapatch they had a large house that was paid for.

Despite her attitude, Shelly did odd jobs and contributed money for household expenses, for she still cared about her brothers and sisters. Some of the neighbors also began hiring Junior, and even Mack to work for them. Sarah was now old enough to babysit, but the money they made was not nearly enough for what the family needed.

Henry Bearden was a widower who'd lost his wife to breast cancer fifteen years earlier. They never had children and though he was shy around kids, he enjoyed their lively presence. A fairly small, compact man, Henry had somewhat of a strut to his manner, and though he generally spoke only when he needed to, he measured his words and meant them. Four years older than Clete, Henry had been made foreman shortly after Cletus started at the Devil's Fork Mine and Clete was glad for Henry's promotion, knowing he was a fair man who cared about the other miners. They'd become good friends over the years and Henry had visited the Stamper home many times, where he was always a welcome guest.

Clete's death hit Henry mighty hard and he wracked his brain on how he might help the Stamper family. As a single man with a good job and no desires for pretense or material wealth beyond his needs, Henry lacked not for money, but he well knew the accepted limits of offering help. After Ethel had asked him to dinner twice and then to join the family at church, Henry saw the path before him and stepped to it with his characteristic determination.

On the first Sunday in May, Henry joined the Stampers at church but bid them goodbye at the end of the service and was not present for the noon dinner.

"Where's Henry?" Sadie asked, after they were all seated at the table.

"I asked him not ta come today," Ethel said. "There's som'thin we need ta talk about as a family."

Everyone continued eating, but they remained silent, knowning their mother was about to tell them something important. Ethel put her fork down and laid her thick, brown hands on the table. "Las' Sunday," she began, "after dinner when me an' Henry was out drivin', he asked me ta marry 'im."

Everyone stopped eating and looked at their mother. The blood rose in Shelly's face and she was about to say, I hope ya said no, when Ethel said, "I told 'im I would."

"When?" Junior asked quietly.

"Next Sunday," Ethel answered. "Here at the church. I already talked to Reverend Scoggins. It'll be a small ceremony; just the family and a few friends."

Everyone was silent, trying to digest what this would mean to the Stamper household, until Shelly spoke up. "You shoulda' ask'd us first."

Ethel peered into Shelly's eyes for a few seconds then looked at each of her children in turn. "I thought about it," she said, but offered no more.

The Stamper kids remained quiet, dazed at Ethel's sudden announcement. Only Shelly's feelings could be read by the flush of anger on her face.

"Henry's a good man," Ethel told her children. "Y'all have known him a long time. He was your daddy's friend as well as his boss, an' they always got along fine."

"Ain't this kinda soon?" Junior asked.

Ethel had never been good at deception, not with others and even less with herself. "We've got to live, Junior," she said. "I'm grateful for you kids helpin' out the way ya do, but it ain't enough ta git us by on."

"Are we broke, Mama?" Sarah asked.

"Not yet, honey," Ethel told her, "but we ain't all that far from it."

Ethel looked around the table at her children again. "I swore I'd never marry another coal man ... but Henry's a foreman an' ain't down in the mine all the time. He makes good money as a foreman, too."

"Are you marryin' Henry fer 'is money?" Mack asked.

Ethel didn't answer right off, searching for the proper words. "If Henry wasn't a good man," she said, "no amount a' money could make me marry 'im. But he *is* a good man."

"As good as Daddy?" Sadie asked.

"Ain't no man as good as Daddy," Mack said, turning to his sister.

Shelly was trembling, but stayed silent.

"Henry's a generous man," Ethel continued. "He tol' me about the money he's got saved. He tol' me we could use his savings for any a' you kids who wanta go to college." Ethel looked at Shelly, "After ya graduate high school."

Ethel watched each of her children, trying to gauge their feelings. When no one spoke up she said, "If anybody's got questions, now's the time ta ask."

"Will we hafta call 'im 'Daddy'? Sarah asked.

"He wants to be called Henry," Ethel answered.

"Will he be 'lowed ta spank us?" Sadie wanted to know.

"Henry said he don't wanta do that," Ethel told the kids, "lessen there ain't no other way." She watched the relief in the faces around her. "But," she went on, "if you do som'thin' really bad an' I ain't here ... Henry's gonna have to punish ya. Otherwise some a' ya won't behave." The relief in one or two faces disappeared.

"But," Ethel said, very serious now, "you got my word, I won't ever let 'im be mean or do nothin' to ya that's wrong."

Shelly's eyes went wide and her fists tightened.

"I know Henry ain't your Daddy ... and he never will be," Ethel continued, "but I want each one a' you kids to promise me you'll treat him nice." The kids just stared until Ethel said, "Right now."

Beginning with Junior, each of the Stamper children, except for Rose, who was too young, and Shelly, who was too stubborn, said, "I will, Mama."

Ethel and Shelly glared at each other, but neither wavered. The other kids were now staring at Shelly, also.

"You got to promise, Shelly," Sarah said," we all did."

Shelly swallowed hard and lowered her eyes. "I will too, Mama," she said, then got up and ran out the back door.

She went into the pen with Homer and Jethro, Clete's hounds, and sat down in the dirt between them. Tears ran down her face as she hugged and petted the dogs, who looked almost as forlorn as she did. After a while she stood up and walked down the road to Wimmer Gap, crossed the highway and disappeared into the forest on the other side. She got back to the house shortly before suppertime and when she came in the back door, Henry was in the kitchen, helping Ethel prepare the meal. Her brothers and sisters were talking and laughing with him as if nothing had changed.

"Supper's almost ready, ya better git washed up," Ethel said to her.

Shelly looked at Ethel, then at Henry, and back to Ethel again. "Alright, Mama," she said.

Throughout the next week Henry came to supper every evening and each time moved more of his belongings into the house. He had arranged to rent out his own home and so brought no furniture except for a large tilt-back chair. On Saturday he made two trips, taking Junior with him to help, and after the second run was unloaded he said, "Well, Ah think that's about got 'er."

The wedding was scheduled for eleven on Sunday morning, an hour after the regular service. Vertnor and Ben, along with Wilbur and Shirl, and Ethel's family, all phoned and said that they wouldn't be able to attend, but gave their blessings to the matrimony, understanding Ethel's need to look after her children. Cliff was there with his wife and boy, along with half a dozen Peapatch neighbors and two men who worked at the mine and were friends of both Clete and Henry. All were invited to dinner afterwards, but declined.

Halfway through the meal, Sarah asked her mother, "Are we still Stampers or are we Beardens now?"

Shelly bristled.

"You all are still Stampers," Ethel said, "but my name is legally Bearden."

Henry felt obliged to say something. "Ah know this is tough on you kids, losin' yor daddy like ya did, then havin' me movin' in so soon. Ah cain't replace Cletus, an' Ah won't try. Ah've always liked ev'ry one a' ya, an' Ah'll learn ta love ya." Sadie and Mack smiled at Henry and encouraged, he went on. "An' Ah'll be good as kin be ta your mother, and treat each a' you the best Ah know how. Ya got mah promise on it."

The other kids nodded their assent, but Shelly knew he was lying. It ain't gonna be like that after a while, she thought. That night she didn't sleep a lick, her mind wild with thoughts of what was going on in Ethel and *her Daddy's* bedroom. She considered sneaking down stairs and listening at their door, and then pounding on it and telling them to stop.

The next morning Shelly caught the school bus along with her brothers and sisters. Her attendance had become so sporadic that friends would no longer stop by to pick her up. But when the bus arrived at school, Shelly took off in the other direction. She'd done this before, but on this Monday, Junior and Sarah saw a change in their sister; she just didn't care any more.

"Come on back ta school, Shelly," Sarah pleaded.

"Nope," Shelly said.

"Where ya goin?" Junior called after her.

"Won't know till I git there," Shelly hollered back, "an I might not even know then."

"You ain't gonna pass if ya keep missin' school like this," Ethel told Shelly when she walked in the back door a few minutes before suppertime.

"Don'tchoo tell me what ta do," Shelly said. "You didn't graduate so you got nothin' ta say about it."

All through supper Shelly stayed silent, glaring at Henry sitting in Clete's chair. Whenever one of the other kids spoke to him or smiled at something he said Shelly fixed them with the evil eye. After dinner Shelly joined her sisters in doing the cleanup, but remained sullen.

"What's wrong, Shelly?" Sadie asked.

"What ain't wrong?" Shelly shot back.

When the dishes were finished, Shelly bounded the stairs three at a time to her room. Ethel followed and for twenty minutes the Stamper house vibrated with their yelling. Ethel descended the staircase shaking with anger and saw that her two youngest were crying.

"Ah'm sorry fer bringin' this on," Henry said.

Ethel sat down on the couch, hugging Charlie in one arm and Rose in the other. "You didn't bring it on. It'd a'happened whether you were here or not."

"What're we gonna do?" Henry asked.

"I don't know, Henry. I love Shelly, but we can't have her rippin' up the family like this."

Shelly went to school on Tuesday but never spoke a word all day. That evening at supper she demanded to eat up in her room but Ethel told her, "You'll eat at the table with the rest a' the family or not at all."

"I'll take the 'not at all'," Shelly said and jogged up the stairs. After dinner several of Shelly's siblings sneaked food to her and, to Ethel's great irritation, joined Shelly in her room, listening to music and dancing.

On Wednesday Shelly skipped school and didn't come home until supper was over. She wordlessly went up to her room and began playing records on her stereo. Within a few minutes Sarah, Mack, and Sadie joined her. Ethel could hear them laughing and guessed that Shelly was trying to turn them against Henry.

Shelly went to school on Thursday but her sulkiness continued. By lunchtime her classmates had had enough and a few of the boys began discussing what it would take to get Shelly to talk.

"Bet if'n somebody grabbed 'er tit she'd say som'thin'," one of the boys said, with a laugh.

"Reckon so," they agreed, "but who's gonna do it?"

None of them, that was for sure, but then their eyes fell upon Jem Hardin, a gangly and unkempt special-ed student. After some eager encouragement by his peers and the offer of a communally collected five dollars and eighty-two cents, Jem was good for a go. When Shelly got up from where she was sitting alone and returned her lunch tray, Jem met her head on as she was making for the exit to cut class for the rest of the day.

"Hi, Shelly," Jem said, then grabbed Shelly's left breast and twisted it like a doorknob.

Shelly's right fist came up so fast that some students claimed they never witnessed the punch, only a screaming Jem writing on the cafeteria floor, two of his rotten front teeth sheared off and Shelly walking away, her knuckles dripping blood onto the tiles.

For the rest of the day Shelly disappeared but she hitchhiked home in a downpour and straggled into the kitchen a little after nine, looking like she'd fallen into the ocean, a handkerchief wrapped around her swollen right hand.

"The school called," Ethel told her. "They said we might hafta pay for that boy's teeth you knocked out ta'day."

"Did they tell ya why I done it?"

"They did," Ethel said, "an' I told the principal they could git the money from them boys that put 'im up to it. That five-dollars an' some they give 'im ta grab you ain't gonna cover fixin' his teeth."

When Shelly heard that she felt bad about hitting Jem and wished she'd knocked them other kids's teeth out instead.

"The principal said you're suspended for the rest a' the year," Ethel told her. "He want us ta come in an' meet with 'im tomorrow."

"I ain't goin'," Shelly said and headed up to her room.

On Friday morning, while Shelly was still in bed, Ethel took Charlie and Rose and drove the Lincoln into War to meet with the school principal and the guidance counselor. When she got back home Shelly was gone. Shelly didn't come home until Sunday evening when she sauntered through the kitchen door in the middle of supper, ragged looking and drunk. She made a point of smiling and saying hello to everyone but Henry and Ethel then made straight for her bedroom. After the meal was over Mack, Sadie, Sarah and Junior joined her and they played records and danced with the door closed.

Ethel rapped on Shelly's door. "Can I come in?" she asked.

"Sootch your'self," Shelly called to her over Ferlin Husky's singing.

Ethel didn't really want to talk to Shelly in the company of her brothers and sisters, but hoped there wouldn't be a fight if they were present. "Can I turn the music down?"

"If ya got to," Shelly said.

"I went to the school today," Ethel began, squeezing herself onto the bed between Mack and Sadie. "They tol' me you're gonna hafta go ta summer school an'make up what ya flunked if ya wanta be a senior next year."

"Hell's bells," Shelly said, laughing, "I ain't hardly been goin' now, why would I go in the summer?"

Part of Ethel wanted to reach over and backhand Shelly and the other part wanted to put her arms around her daughter and hold her. "How can you just throw away eleven years a' schoolin', baby?" Ethel said softly, and before Shelly could answer added, "an' don't tell me that I did it. You ain't me an' never did a thing in your life b'cause I did it."

"You're right, I ain't you," Shelly said, her voice rising with anger, "an' I'll do what the hell I want whether you like it or not."

Ethel held up her hand. "Please, Shelly,' she said quietly, "I didn't come in here ta fight with ya … an' it hurts your brothers an' sisters real bad when we yell at each other."

Shelly's jaw was about to open but nine-year old Sadie reached over and took her hand. "Don't cuss like that an' holler at Mama, Shelly," Sadie told her.

"It ain't right fer you ta be mean to our mom" Mack said. "We ain't allowed to an' you shouldn't neither."

Shelly took a couple of breaths. "Okay, Mama," she said, "we won't fight over it … but I still ain't goin' ta summer school."

"You gonna go back next yare in the 'leventh grade agin?" Junior asked.

"Nope, I won't do that," Shelly said.

"Then watcha gonna do?" he persisted.

"I don't rightly know. Maybe git a job." Shelly turned to Ethel. "I'll leave if ya want me to. I can be packed by morning."

A chorus of pleas rose from the kids, begging Shelly to stay. Finally, Ethel said, "I don't want ya ta leave. Let's just see how things work out for a while."

To make sure everyone knew she was still Ethel, she looked at Shelly and said, "You made a promise that you'd be nice ta Henry, an' I *will* hold ya to that."

"I ain't said a bad word to 'im yet," Shelly said.

Ethel got up and left the room, closing the door behind her. "An' I won't say a bad word to 'im ... or any other word, neither," Shelly told her siblings.

Little changed. The memory of Clete still permeated the Stamper home and Ethel often came into a room to find one of her children crying. But for the most part, the kids tried to get on with life and none of them held it against Henry Bearden for marrying their mother; except Shelly. Watching Henry go into the master bedroom every night, knowing he was lying on the same feather mattress that Cletus had slept on with Ethel and doing the same things to her, never set right with Shelly. She rejoined the family at meals, but couldn't stand to look at Henry sitting in Clete's chair at the head of the table, like he was now the boss.

Only Shelly understood, or thought she understood, what Ethel meant when she had told her children, "I won't ever let 'im do nothin' to ya that's wrong," and it made Shelly suspicious, as if Ethel knew something about Henry she wasn't telling the rest of them. Shelly kept a wary eye on Henry until she got to thinking he was keeping too much of an eye on her. She also felt like warning Sarah and Sadie, and for all she knew, maybe even Junior and Mack, about what Henry might try.

Shelly kept her promise to Ethel and didn't fight with Henry or even sass him, but she also kept her promise to herself and ignored him. It rankled Ethel to no end and though she didn't say anything, the tension between her and Shelly was unrelenting.

With the end of the school year, the Stamper children were emancipated for the summer but they were also expected to do chores around the house and property. Like Cletus, Henry enjoyed fixing things up and farming on the side and Ethel put it in plain words that the older kids would do their part.

When Shelly was home, she only helped with the chores she felt like doing and refused to work with Henry. Most days and nearly every night, she was off boozing and carousing. Often she came home drunk and sometimes she didn't show up for two or three days at a time. Then she spent most of the time up in her bedroom, usually joined by her sisters and brothers.

Halfway into June, Ethel announced that they were going to Olive Hill for a week. Henry had vacation coming and she wanted her family to meet him.

Shelly said flat out, "I ain't goin'."

"Don'tcha wanta see Grammy and yor aunts an' cousins?" Junior asked.

"Nope," Shelly answered. "I got better things ta do."

Apparently so, for when the family returned, the inside of the Stamper house was trashed. Cigarette butts (and roaches) littered the home. Crushed cans and broken bottles of beer and whiskey were strewn throughout. A number of items were missing and some of the furniture was overturned or damaged. Every bed had been slept in. Not surprisingly, Shelly was gone. Two days later, after dinner was over, she walked through the back door and into the empty kitchen, sat down at the table and waited for the storm.

Junior entered first. "How could ya, Shelly?" he said. "You gotcha any idea how much that hurt Mama? What it did ta us all, even the little ones?"

Before she could answer, Mack and Sarah, and then Ethel came into the kitchen. Nobody sat down and Shelly could feel their eyes boring into her. Ethel was shaking and her dark face had turned a deep maroon with restrained anger.

Shelly forced herself to meet their eyes. "I'm sorry," she said. "I'm real sorry. It wasn't 'spose ta git like it did. Somehow ev'rything got outa hand an' I couldn't stop it. But I'm sorry."

"That's cuz you was drunk an' crazy as ever'body else," Sarah said.

"Prob'ly drunker an' crazier," Junior added.

Shelly's siblings were madder at her than they'd ever been, but they feared what would happen when Ethel started in.

Shelly looked up at her. "You can do whatever ya want to me, Mama," she said. "If ya need to beat me, go ahead, I won't fight back.

You can beat me as much as ya want." Then she looked at Junior, Mack and Sarah. "An' you all can beat on me too, cause I deserve it."

The second hand on the wall clock ticked away as the two women stared at each other. Finally, Shelly said, "Go ahead, Mama, do whatcha got to. I don't care no more."

Out in the living room Sadie got up from the couch and started to come into the kitchen but Henry scooped her up. "Y'all come back in here an' hang out with me an' we'll watch the TV t'gether," Henry told her.

Shelly lowered her head and said, to all of them now, "There ain't nothin' here for me no more, not in this county, anyways. Maybe not in the whole world."

"*We're* here for ya, Shelly," Junior said. "We're mad at ya, real mad, but we're still here for ya."

"Thanks, Junior, but I need ta leave." Shelly looked at her mother. "Ta'morrow."

When Sarah and Mack realized they were about to lose their big sister, perhaps for good, they had to fight back tears.

"Shelly," Mack said, "we kin help ya, you don't have ta leave."

"No," Shelly answered him, "Junior's right. What I done was real bad an' hurt ev'rybody. I'm 'fraid that if I stay I'll jes keep doin' things that hurt y'all."

Ethel, who had calmed down, now spoke. "Mack is right, too, Shelly," she said. "We can git ya some help."

"No, Mama," Shelly said to her, "I need ta leave ...'fore we stop lovin' each other."

––––––––––

Now that she'd made her decision Shelly slept soundly, but Ethel got little rest that night. Shelly set her alarm for 4:30 a.m. and was dressed and downstairs by five, planning to slip away before the others were up to avoid the tearful goodbyes. But as she tiptoed into the dark kitchen heading for the back door, she saw the blocky form of her mother drinking coffee at the table

"You ain't leavin' without breakfast," Ethel said.

"I wanta go 'fore the others are up," Shelly told her.

"You will," Ethel assured her. "I got ever'thing already cooked and warmin' in the oven."

Over eggs, mush, and bacon, the two women talked easily.

"Any idea where you're goin'?" Ethel asked.

"Nope."

"If ya git up north, you can always stop at Grammy's or Vertnor's."

Shelly nodded that she understood but said, "Ain't plannin' to."

"Anything I can do ta talk you out a' this, honey?"

"Nope."

"I'll give ya a ride inta War. Be easier for ya ta hitchhike from there."

"No thanks, Mama. I gotta start from here. It's jes somethin' I need ta do."

Shelly finished off her breakfast, got up and took her plate to the sink and rinsed it off. "Guess I better be goin, Mama," she said, putting on her jacket and the hat that Clete had bought her. Shelly hoisted her knapsack onto her back and went to pick up her suitcase.

Ethel opened the fridge and got out a paper bag that held two sandwiches. She stuck them into the top of Shelly's knapsack then reached into her apron pocket and pulled out five twenty-dollar bills. "This'll git ya started, at least," she said, holding them out to Shelly.

Shelly shook her head in refusal. "I can't take that, Mama," she said. "It wouldn't be right. I oughta be givin' you money for what I done to the house."

"You got ya any money at all?" Ethel asked.

"A little," Shelly answered. "But don't worry, Mama, I'll be okay, I'm tough, jes like you."

The two women hugged so long that both had trouble letting go. The full impact that she might never see her daughter again fell hard on Ethel, especially after losing Cletus. She briefly considered physically trying to stop Shelly from going out the door, but knew there'd be a fight as wild as the one she'd had with The Fabuous Moolah the night she met Clete.

———————

First light was hazing the eastern ridges as Shelly walked down Peapatch Road toward Wimmer Gap. When she arrived at the highway, Shelly paused only briefly before deciding she'd point her thumb north. She had the urge to go into War and have a last cup of coffee with Cliff at the station, but could only imagine his reaction to her leaving home.

No cars or trucks came by as the sun slowly pushed the darkness away. After twenty minutes enough light had come into the sky that Shelly saw she was standing at the exact spot where Tramp had so horribly thrashed and died nearly four years ago, and where his dark blood had stained the asphalt until the spring rains finally washed it away. A sob rose up from her gut and just as Shelly was about to burst into tears, a set of headlights swung around the corner, and when they swept over the tall girl standing on the roadside gravel, the brakelights came on and the car stopped to pick her up.

Chapter 11

Choking back emotion, Shelly grabbed her suitcase and jogged to the car. She got into the front seat and the driver, a middle-aged man in a shabby suit, said, "Hi, little lady," and stuck out his hand for Shelly to shake. "My name is Sylvester, but my friends call me Sylie."

I'll bet you are, Shelly thought, but she shook the man's hand and knew right away that she needed a ready story for why she was hitch-hiking. Being a sixteen year old with no destination was a sure recipe for trouble.

"My name is Juniper, but my friends call me Junie," Shelly said. "I jes turned twenty-one las' week and I'm headin' up ta Columbus, Ohio, ta take a job at my uncle's bank."

Sylvester said he was a traveling salesman and kept up a steady banter. Shelly felt like asking him if the stories and jokes about his pro-fession were true but she didn't have to, because Sylvester launched into a series of his amorous escapades. At the town of Gilbert, Shelly insisted on getting out, as Sylie was becoming creepy. Daylight had overtaken the sky when Shelly set her suitcase down on the berm of Highway 52, the two-lane road that she and her father had traveled so many times. She wasn't sorry when the young woman who picked her up said, "I'm getting off Route 52 up here and going to Pike County Kentucky."

"Me too," Shelly said.

All that morning Shelly hitched short rides through eastern Ken-tucky, avoiding interstates where she'd have trouble with the cops. She explored the small towns she got dropped off in. Some were attractive and friendly, but none appealed to her and besides, she was still too close to home. At noon she sat down on a patch of grass and reached into her pack for the sandwiches Ethel had made. Her hand bumped against her framed, autographed photo of Ferlin Husky, then felt something else. Ethel had secretly stuck Clete's Bible into her knapsack and Shelly thumbed through the pages as she ate.

As she was swallowing the last bite, a beatup Chevy hardtop with two teenage boys in the front stopped. "Need a rahd?" the passenger yelled.

"Okay," Shelly said, getting up. When the passenger got out, indicating for her to get in the middle, Shelly shook her head. "Thanks for the offer," she told him, "but I'll ride shotgun or not at all."

"Ah think she knows ya, Berl," the boy said to the driver, then laughed. "Wahl, Ah ain't ridin' queer, so Ah'll jus' hop in the back."

Shelly got into the front seat and turned sideways, leaning her back against the door so she could watch both boys, but within a few miles she had relaxed. Berl and Mort were a pair of backwoods jokers and soon Shelly's nostrils filled with the acrid smell of cheap weed. Mort passed her a joint, and after taking a long toke, Shelly told them the truth of her circumstance and the boys were awed at her audacity.

"You gotcha some *balls*," Mort said, as he put flame to a second reefer.

Berl looked Shelly up and down then turned to Mort in the back. "I don' think so, Mort. You know even less about women than I thought ya did."

All three erupted into stoned laughter that continued till the boys let Shelly off in Carlisle where they were going to help Berl's mom paint her house. "Don't fall off no ladders," Shelly called as they drove off.

Shelly then made her first miscalculation. A very old farm couple gave her a ride and Shelly closed her eyes in the back seat. Still stoned, Shelly fell asleep and didn't notice when they turned onto a gravel road that ran to their ancient farmstead. Only when they turned into their driveway, seemingly oblivious to Shelly's presence, did she wake up and realize her mistake.

"Can ya let me out?" Shelly said, sitting up with start.

"Oh ... okay," the old man said, and braked to a stop.

Shelly had no idea how far they'd driven on the gravel road, but she started walking in the direction they'd come, hoping a ride would come along. The mid-afternoon sun blazed down and after a few miles Shelly was thirsty and sweating. She took off her *Mack Trucks* hat and tucked it into her knapsack to keep perspiration from staining the liner then wiped her forehead with her handkerchief. Several miles later she came to a brook that scuttled through a culvert beneath the road. She walked down to the bank and swallowed half a dozen handfuls of water and then dipped her head into the creek. Shelly took off her shoes and socks, lay back on the thick grass and let her feet dangle in the cool water, pondering her new life as a hobo. After a spell she sat up, slurped more water, and started walking again.

Finally she reached a paved county road and a middle-aged woman picked her up. The woman was a high-school teacher and overly curious about Shelly's age and reason for hitchhiking, but took her into a small town named Oddville. Another series of short hops got Shelly onto U.S. Highway 27, a busier road than she wanted, but the sun was heading toward the horizon in the west and Shelly was having thoughts about her destination.

The next car that stopped, occupied by two large and boisterous Black women, took Shelly across the Ohio River and into the middle of Cincinnati, a city she'd never seen before. Shelly had been on the road for over fourteen hours. She was tired and hungry and knew her hitchhiking was done for the day.

Wandering aimlessly as evening settled in, Shelly drifted into Norwood, a separate incorporated city surrounded by Cincinnati. As she stood on the sidewalk wondering where to spend the night, a large, well-built man who looked in his early twenties, came up and said with a self-assured smile, "You look lost."

"I been loster," Shelly told him.

"Whatcha doin' in Norwood," the man asked, nodding toward the knapsack and suitcase at Shelly's feet.

"I ain't decided yet if I'm doin' anything in Norwood," Shelly said.

"Whatcher name an' where ya from?"

Shelly hesitated, but saw no reason to lie. "Shelly Stamper from Wes' Virginia."

"Ah'm Jim Stidhams from Kentucky," the man said, "but Ah been in Norwood three years now."

"That's why your accent sounds like Mama's," Shelly told him. "She's from Olive Hill."

"Why, hell, Ah'm from Morehead, jus' down the road from Olive Hill," Jim said, his smile lighting up. "What was yor mama's last name?"

"Cooper," Shelly answered, without thinking. "My grandma's name is Emma. I got a couple a' aunts there too, Nellie and Gladys."

A look of happy recognition spread over Jim Stidhams' face. "I think Ah met 'em, leastwise yer grandma. Where's she live in Olive Hill?"

"Jes outside a' town, up on Tick Ridge."

"Why, shor," Jim said, "Ah know who they are. The Coopers are real well liked aroun' Carter County."

"That'd be them," Shelly said, and Jim offered to buy her a drink.

A few minutes later he reeled Shelly into a dive called Hillbilly Heaven. Central to the establishment was a raised stage where a scantily clad young lady with acne and a pinched smile contorted herself to country music. The joint was packed and only two stools were open at the bar. A lean, scraggly-bearded man with long stringy hair falling out of his dirty white cowboy hat sat between the two empty seats. Jim Stidhams went up to him. "Move over, Dickhead," he said.

The man took his eyes off the dancer, sat his can of Strohs down and looked at Jim defiantly. His started to say something but Jim put his caloused hand on the man's shoulder and squeezed. "Me an' this lady are gonna set down here … ta'gether."

"Oh, sure man, sure," the man said and quickly slid a stool over.

Jim motioned for Shelly to sit on the stool furthest away from the man, and then sat down, bumping longhair with his elbow. "Whatcha want?" he asked Shelly.

Shelly looked at Jim then turned and said straight on to the barmaid, "Gimme a George Dickel on the rocks."

The woman brought it without questioning her age. Shelly sipped her sour mash and let Jim yabber in her ear while she watched the sequine-bikinied dancer.

Jim was used to women listening when he talked and he found Shelly's distraction with the dancer irritating.

To get her attention he said, "Jeet yet?"

"Huh?"

"Jeet yet?" Jim said again.

"Nope."

"Want sumpthin'?"

"Sure. Two cheeseburgers and fries … an' another Dickel."

"You got 'er," Jim said and motioned to the barmaid.

Shelly looked closely at her companion. He was at least her height, around six-one or six-two, with a strapping body. His thick black hair, heavily greased and combed straight back, reminded her of the fifth-wheel on a semi tractor, but Shelly had to admit; Jim Stidhams was not a bad looking fella, not bad looking at all.

When the food came, Shelly gobbled one burger and then the other, but she couldn't take her eyes off the dancer. After the girl's set ended and she stepped off the stage Shelly got up and asked her how much she made each night, including tips. Shelly's eyes went wide when the girl told her.

"Why, hey," Shelly said, "I can dance good as you. Who owns this joint?"

The girl pointed to a bald, rotund character stuffed into a Nauga-hyde recliner near the stage. "Bussy does."

Shelly walked over to him and when he looked up, said, "Mr. Bussy, I dance better'n that girl that was up there a minute ago. Can I have a job?"

Bussy stared at Shelly with his white, bulging eyes for a minute, then lowered his gaze to her feet. Slowly he levered his round head back up, checking every inch of this long girl in the tight jeans. "You ken start tomorra night et eight," Bussy said, when his eyes finally got back to Shelly's, although he had made his decision by the time they'd reached her belt buckle.

Shelly celebrated her new job and new life by getting drunk and then going home with Jim Stidhams and losing her virginity. The next night she pulled on a borrowed sequined bikini and danced for the drunken and highly appreciative crowd, many of whom would've been even more excited if they'd known she was only sixteen. She spent that night with Jim, too, and the next. When Jim asked Shelly if she wanted to move in with him, she agreed. Shelly wanted a man in her life and two and a half weeks later, when Jim asked her another question, Shelly considered his proposal only briefly before she answered, "Okay, I reckon we could."

The next Sunday Jim drove Shelly to a Quonset hut with a sign above the door that read *The True Savior Gospel Church* where his uncle Clyde preached. After the sermon and collection Shelly became Mrs. James Stidhams. When the ceremony was over Reverend Clyde asked Shelly to tell the congregation what she was most grateful for. "I'm grateful yor leavin' all them snakes in their cages till after me and Jim are gone," she told him.

Shelly certainly never planned to be dancing nearly naked in front of boozy strangers, but she was a natural. In Hillbilly Heaven pleasing the crowd was more important than dancing ability and Bussy, the owner, saw right away that this tall girl from the hills had *presence*, which is what *attitude* tries, but always fails, to achieve. Shelly instinctively knew how to use her sinuous body to maximum effect. Once in a while, if the music was right, she'd do a hillbilly stomp or a flatfoot and have half the crowd on their feet trying to follow along. Unlike most of the other dancers who took stage names, Shelly reckoned her own name was just fine, so she stuck with it. But the name she did have trouble calling herself was Shelly Stidhams.

Jim Stidhams made his living as a scrapper. Scrappers locate and then obtain metal and resell it to scrap yards, 'obtaining' being the key to their success. A scrapper might buy the metal or get it for nothing by saying, "I'll haul that junk off for you." If no one's around or the ownership in doubt, a scrapper might just haul the stuff off, the concept of theft not entering his mind. A true master like Jim Stidhams might even get the owner to pay him for carting it away as trash.

Scrapping was a chancy profession, but scrappers enjoyed their bit of glamour. They were the professional gamblers of the hillbilly world; freewheeling, high-rolling Mavericks for a few nights then cadging draft beers until their next score. The scrapper life fit Jim Stidhams well because he did what he liked, kept his own hours and answered to no one, including his new bride.

Two weeks into the marriage, Shelly came home from Hillbilly Heaven when her set ended at 2 a.m. and Jim was gone. Sometime after noon he drifted through the door, bleary-eyed and wrung out. Shelly demanded to know where he'd been.

"None a' yer goddam business," Jim told her as he got a Blatz from the fridge, plopped down on the couch and turned on the TV.

A week later Shelly asked Jim if she could borrow his pickup to go to the store.

"Thought you didn't have a license," he said.

"I don't," Shelly answered, "but we need groceries."

"I'll take ya to the store when *Bonanza's* over."

"If you'd let me use your truck ta git my license," Shelly said, "ya wouldn't have ta be bothered."

Jim looked up from the TV. "You go no reason ta be drivin'," he said, then drained off his Blatz and tossed the empty into a corner. "Cause there's nowhere you need ta be goin' without *me*."

So it began. When Jim made a bundle on scrap, he would be gone for two or three days. At first Shelly thought he might just be out on a binge with the boys, but then word of his dalliances began drifting back to her. When Jim was home they fought.

"I'm gittin' sick an' tired a' all this arguin'," Shelly told him, "but I won't stand for you screwin' other women."

Nothing changed and Shelly finally accepted that Jim was a hopeless cause so she ignored him the way she'd ignored Henry Bearden, turned away from him in bed and began saving her money. That's when the real trouble started.

Jim had the attitude of, hey, babe, we're married, we share our money, but the only money that ever got shared was Shelly's. She paid the rent, water, electric and bought all the food. Jim told her, "I'll ketch ya next time I sell a load a' scrap," but he never did; his scrap money was gone after each spree.

He took to helping himself to Shelly's purse when she wasn't looking, so she opened a bank account in her maiden name and stopped keeping cash at home. That made him near berserk and their arguments got worse, to the point that he began physically threatening her. "Don'tcha ever do it," Shelly warned him. "I'm tellin' ya, Jim, I won't take it, not even once."

Only four months after Reverend Clyde had told them, in a solemn ceremony witnessed by thirty-seven parishioners, six rattlesnakes and two water moccasins, "What God has joined together let no man rend asunder till death do you part," Jim and Shelly's union was sundered, not by death nor by man, but by women. Shelly guessed close to a dozen of them.

On the sly, Shelly rented an apartment, and one morning Jim came home from a three-day romp to an empty trailer. Shelly did him the courtesy of leaving a note, weighted down with her pawnshop wedding band: *Don't say you weren't told!*

In Jim Stidhams' world, women didn't walk out on their husbands, especially if their husband was Jim Stidhams. He knew Shelly was dancing that night and showed up at the bar full of rage and whiskey. Storming to the foot of the stage, he loosed a wild barrage of threats and insults at Shelly as she danced. When the song was over Shelly hopped down from the stage and called to Dixie behind the bar, "Can ya shut off the music for a minute? Me and Jim got ta settle somethin'."

What followed forever stamped Shelly into the lore of Norwood's hillbilly bars, the story still making the rounds long after she was gone, with Jim grown to the size of Paul Bunyon and Shelly Queen of the Amazons. Crazy dangerous as Jim was, Shelly stepped up to him. "You need ta leave," she said. "We'll talk about this when I ain't workin'."

"We'll talk about it NOW!" Jim roared into Shelly's face. "No wife a' mine walks out on me! You walk yer ass back ta that trailer right now and you don't leave it till Ah say so."

Hillbilly Heaven got quieter than anyone could remember.

"You don't tell me what ta do," Shelly said, surprising everyone with her calmness. "I walk where I want when I want. I shoulda' walked out on you the first night ya didn't come home. An' from now on when you can't find no tramp ta go fuck, you can go fuck your'self."

Normally that would have gotten a good laugh from the crowd but Jim backhanded Shelly hard across the face, the viciousness of the blow more horrific because the girl facing him looked so vulnerable in her near nakedness.

"Gal, don't you ev-" Jim bellowed, but that was as far as he got.

When Shelly uncorked her best left hook she didn't give it any more thought than a rattlesnake gives to striking somebody who's stepped on its tail. The smart, bright crack of Shelly's knuckles to Jim's jawbone was heard throughout the hushed tavern. As usual, Jim's jaw was open, and shattered nicely.

Jim went down on his backside in the middle of the floor, stupefied, holding his cheek with both hands. "Yuh … b … b … broke … m … muh … jaw."

Rubbing her smarting fist, Shelly said, "Well a' course I did, dumbass. Didja think I was jes gonna let ya hit me?"

The crowd now felt free to laugh and they did for the rest of the night.

"You can start the music up again," Shelly hollered over to Dixie then got back on the stage and began dancing.

As Jim painfully climbed to his feet, Dixie walked around the bar and pointed to the door. "We don't allow no men to hit women in here," she told him. "You gitcher ass out, Stidhams, an' stay out."

If Shelly could've raked in as much in tips every night as she did that night she would have been a rich woman. Now with employment, her own place to live and Jim Stidhams out of her life, Shelly could have soared. Instead, she dove.

Chapter 12

Shelly never could explain why her life took the turn it did after she left Jim Stidhams. Whatever she expected from marriage certainly hadn't happened with Jim and she didn't expect marrying another man would make it happen either, whatever *it* was. Still grieving for Cletus, and without friends or family near, she was more alone than she'd ever been. Leaving Norwood, at least for the present, was not an option. Shelly knew she'd been lucky to land a well-paying job and if she struck out on the road again, would likely become a penniless derelict instead of a self-supporting one. But other than saving money for a car, she had no plans for the future, or for that matter, wasn't sure if she even had a future.

If she had to take a nosedive, though, Shelly picked a good town to do it in. Norwood, Ohio was hopping in the early 1970's. The General Motors assembly plant was running at full bore and half of Norwood was from Appalachia. There was money and good times to be had. Shelly got in on some of the former and way too much of the latter. She had always liked being around men, but now developed an unhealthy craving for their company. No doubt, losing her father had a lot to do with it, but even as a kid, she spent most of her time with boys, playing sports at recess and later on, drinking and raising hell. What Shelly liked to do best with other girls was fight them.

After Shelly broke the sex barrier her first night in Norwood, the love making between her and Jim gushed forth like a geyser, but once she realized that love was absent and Jim Stidhams was just screwing her, the passion was gone. Even after Shelly found out Jim was cheating and stopped having sex with him, she was never lured into infidelity as long as she and Jim were living together as man and wife. Once their separation became official, which it did with Shelly's left hook, the opening that Jim had made in Shelly's wall of virtue widened into a massive and unguarded breach. Drunk and drugged, Shelly might as well have shouted from the stage each night, as if she were King Henry, "Once more unto the breach, dear friends!"

Suckered by any man who showed her attention and treated her decently, Shelly could be sacked as easily as a quarterback whose offensive line had walked off the field. Men trod on each other's toes to buy Shelly liquor and she took nearly every drink offered. Through Tommy Kegley's crowd, Shelly had been introduced to drugs, but with the exception of marijuana, avoided most substances.

The men she met now loaded her up on cocaine, LSD, mushrooms, and pills. Drugs weren't just for hippies anymore and young hillbillies were no longer satisfied by 'white lightnin' or even weed. Rowdy and lewd by her second set, come closing time, Shelly was usually too grogged to walk back to her upstairs apartment on Ivanhoe Avenue. Not that it mattered, because men lined up like taxis at an airport to drive her home.

Shelly slept with men because that's what they wanted and she liked their attention, but sex had no real meaning to her. Many men pestered her to be their steady girlfriend and some even proposed marriage. They bought her drugs, booze, food, clothes and much else and Shelly let them, but she rejected all suiters. While still with Jim, Shelly had turned seventeen and though legally too young to drink, or even work in a bar, had long since stopped thinking of herself as a "girl". By Christmas time she had been apart from Jim for five weeks and was well into her self-destructive life style. Despite her reckless ways, though, Shelly Stamper maintained two good habits: she never missed work and she saved her money.

Christmas of 1972 fell on a Monday and though Hillbilly Heaven was closed on that day, the party on Christmas Eve was a doozy. Shelly wasn't dancing that night, as Sunday and Monday were her days off, but she came to the party. It was Shelly's first Christmas away from home and she went out of control early, getting so screwed up on liquor and drugs that some of the customers were worried about her.

Early on Christmas morning Shelly awoke hungover to the call of her bladder and was pleased to find she was in her own bed and not that of a stranger. Though still too dark to see the form clearly, Shelly knew that a man lay asleep beside her but she had no idea who he was. Whatever had taken place the night before was lost to memory.

When she returned to her bedroom, Shelly crawled back into bed and lay awake, thinking of past Christmas's. Only a year ago she had hopped from bed and scrambled downstairs to open presents with her family, never imagining that two months later, her father would be dead.

As she lay remembering, the first shards of gray light inched around her thick curtains and Shelly saw that not one man, but two, lay naked and askew among the tangled covers. One of them, a pudgy, unkempt fellow, stirred and turned his head toward Shelly.

Smiling, he said to her as a Christmas greeting, "God-damn, man, that shor wuz a fine Shelly sam'wich we had las' night."

Shelly exploded. Swearing, screaming, and flailing her fists, she drove the men from her bed and her apartment with barely a chance to grab their clothes. After she'd slammed the door behind them, Shelly covered her own naked body with a dingy robe then went to the fridge, grabbed a Falstaff longneck and started drinking.

In the six months since she'd left, Shelly had only called home three times: the day after she got to Norwood and found work (in a restaurant, she'd said), when she and Jim were married, and at Thanksgiving, when she told her mother she'd left Jim. Shelly knew she should call home since it was Christmas, Ethel and the others would be expecting her to, but she couldn't force herself to walk to the phone booth, and by noon she was too drunk anyway.

As the bleak Ohio winter wore on into a spring that eventually became a blistering summer, Shelly continued, month after month, charging full-tilt into a storm of drugs, sex, alcohol and craziness. Her face took on a different look, no longer just strong and solid, but now hard and worn: seventeen going on thirty. No place she ordered a drink ever thought of asking her for an ID, and nobody, including Shelly, could remember the last night she had been straight or slept alone.

One mid-August Friday evening, when neither the swirling overhead fans nor the open door facing out onto Montgomery Road could remove the humid swelter from Hillbilly Heaven, Bussy motioned Shelly over to his recliner before she started her shift. "Get y'self a chair, Shelly," he said, "there's some things I got to be sayin' to yeh."

Shelly had worked for Bussy for over a year now and she couldn't claim to know this unusual man much better than that first night when she'd asked him for a job. Their conservations were usually pertinent to the business at hand, but when they drifted into the personal, Shelly was always surprised that Bussy knew a great deal more about her than she had ever told him. Of Bussy, Shelly knew little, except that he was from Kentucky, had minimal education, and that his last name was Fellows, for the man seldom spoke of himself and kept a firm wall between his business and personal life.

Shelly grabbed a chair from a nearby table and set it close to Bussy's big Naugahyde tilt-back so she could hear him over the music, then waited for him to speak.

"I'm gittin' to be worry'n about yeh, Shelly," Bussy said. "You're hittin' it hard ev'y night and yeh can't keep on doin' this way."

"I know it, Bussy," Shelly said, lowering her eyes. "Are ya gonna fire me?"

Bussy put his stubby index finger under Shelly's chin, lifting it gently so her eyes met his. "Shelly, ain't no girl in all a' Norwood what could bring in half the business you do, but I'd fire yeh in a minute if'n it'd stop yeh from ruin'n y'self. Without no job you'd end up dead in some gutter, which I'm feared might happen anyway."

Shelly nodded, knowing Bussy was right.

Bussy remained quiet for a moment, letting what he had said sink in. "I'm a'guessin' your friends' been tellin' yeh this, too," Bussy said, "an' yeh oughta be listen'n to 'em."

"Ain't nobody been tellin' me nothin'," Shelly said. "I don't have any friends."

It was true. Since Shelly's split with Jim Stidhams and subsequent deterioration, she had simply been the wildest character in a realm full of other wild characters. Few thought of her behavior – or their own

– as self-destructive. Far from trying to slow her down, the male clientele of Hillbilly Heaven spurred Shelly on with booze and drugs. To most of the women, Shelly was nothing more than a crazed and feared rival and the sooner she got worn out and ugly – or died – the better.

Bussy continued holding Shelly's chin up, forcing her to look into his bulbous eyes. After a moment he removed his hand and pointed to a wrung out floozy trying to maintain her equilibrium on a nearby barstool. "Jerri use't to dance here," he said.

Shelly knew Jerri, at least a little bit, as Jerri never missed a day at Hillbilly Heaven, but Shelly's attempts at conversation with her had never gone far. If Jerri's pickled brain was capable of anything other than drunken mumbles, Shelly was not aware of it.

"Like me, she gots the sugar," Bussy said, and when Shelly gave him a puzzled look, he clarified. "Diabetes, thet's why I dasn't drink. But havin' sugar don't slow Jerri down none."

Shelly turned and looked at Jerri, who swayed in rhythm to some melody playing in her brain only, a rum and coke in one hand and a trembling cigarette in the other. Beside her, some paunchy gomer was buying drinks as fast as Jerri could suck them down. Shelly couldn't imagine anyone watching, let alone paying, to see this scrawny old wraith wiggle around in a bikini.

"How long ago'd she dance here?" Shelly asked, and scrunched up her face.

"'Bout ten ye'ers ago," Bussy said. "She ain't all thet much over thirty."

Shelly thought she saw amoebic movement in Bussy's opaque eyeballs as he fondly remembered: "Jerri use't to be real per'ty."

Bussy put his finger under Shelly's chin again. "Stay doin' like y'are too long," he said, "an' after awhiles it comes to be the only thing yeh know … and yeh never get away fum it."

"I guess I know that, Bussy, but I jes keep doin' it anyway an' I don't even rightly know why." Shelly felt embarrassed, having Bussy lecture her. She averted her eyes. "I wanna stop, but it seems like I don't know how, or what I'd do then."

"Yeh don't have to quit dancin' to quit killin' y'self," Bussy said. "We got dancers what hardly drink … an' don't do drugs."

Shelly took a long time to answer. "Maybe … if I made you a promise not ta git so … " Shelly wanted to say 'fucked up,' but instead said, "wild ev'ry night … maybe that would help me straighten out."

"Shelly," Bussy said, "It ain't me you gots to promise, it's y'self … 'cause it's your mind what needs made up to do it." Then he added, "And made up to do it now."

Shelly smiled. "I remember Daddy used ta say, 'when ya make up your mind ta do somethin', you got ta start doin' it right away, otherwise ya might not do it a'tall'."

Bussy didn't answer and Shelly wondered if he had heard her. Finally he said, "I know 'bout your daddy an' how he died savin' thet little girl."

Shelly looked at Bussy, amazed that he knew this. Then Bussy said, "An' if he was he'er now, he'd give his life to save his own little girl."

That got Shelly's attention. It was though a wind from Peapatch had blown straight into her soul, bringing all the memories and love from that place with it. Along with much else, Shelly couldn't remember the last time she'd cried, but now the tears came and she let them. When Shelly was able to catch her breath, she said to Bussy, to herself, and to her Daddy … "I promise."

She stood up and started to walk away then stopped and turned around. Shelly went back to Bussy's chair and planted a big kiss and two teardrops on the top of his hairless round head. "Thank you, Bussy," she said.

That night Shelly only had three drinks and refused all drugs. When patrons asked her if she was okay, she answered, "I'm okay'er than I been in a long time."

At two, when her last set was over, Shelly went into the back room and put street clothes on. Half a dozen men were waiting when she came out but Shelly made it plain to them she was walking home alone and anyone who followed would end up horizontal, but not in the way he was hoping for.

The late night air had lost its humid stuffiness, and as Shelly walked west on Montgomery Avenue her mind cleared. For the first time in a long while, she began to think about the rest of her life. Twice, cars pulled over to the curb and men asked Shelly if she needed a ride. "Ah don't need nothin'," she told them.

Fifteen minutes after she left the bar, Shelly turned onto the quiet and leafy sidestreet that led to her apartment on Ivanhoe Avenue. As she climbed the dark staircase to her second story flat, sober and alone, a feeling of serenity enveloped her. She stopped and listened, listened to nothing, and the sound of it was beautiful. Her own breathing filled the confined space around her and Shelly sucked in the darkness, not the darkness of despair that she had been living with, but a darkness in which anything was possible and each person made his or her own light. It was the same feeling that Cletus had known at the bottom of a mineshaft and Shelly knew that she was strong again.

———————————

The next morning Shelly climbed out of bed, confident and fresh with hope. She decided to go car hunting.

After getting dressed, she chomped a bowl of cornflakes and hit the street. Having no transportation, Shelly had to limit her search to the three car lots near her apartment. By one o'clock she was tired of walking in the heat and fed up with salesmen trying to sell her junk. Disgusted, she decided to call it quits for the day and have a burger. Hillbilly Heaven was only a few blocks down the street and she'd barely sat down at the bar when a man two stools away looked over and said, "Hiya, Shelly."

She turned to see a grinning face framed by a scraggly beard and long, stringy hair that fell from beneath a dirty white cowboy hat. The man's right hand curled around a can of Strohs beer and his left hand held a cigarette. Like half the men in the bar, he carried his cigarettes rolled up in the sleeve of his tattered tee shirt but the big belt buckle with the embossed image of John Wayne and the scuffed cowboy boots clicked in Shelly's memory. She recalled seeing the man around, but couldn't for the life of her remember his name. Shelly was pretty sure she'd never slept with him.

"Hi," she said back to the man, and then turned away, hoping to get the bartender's attention to order a burger and a Coke.

"Whatchya' up to today?" the man asked her.

What Shelly was not up to was having a conversation, especially with this dude, but neither did she want to be rude to someone who was only trying – so far, at least – to make friendly small talk. After all, that's what a good part of her tips depended on.

"Lookin' for a car," she answered.

"Havin' any luck?" he persisted.

Shelly knew she was now in a conversation whether she wanted to be or not. "I've been ta three lots and they all try ta sell me the ones they wanta git ridda. The other lots are too far for me ta walk to."

"I love ta look at cars," the man told her, "an' I know a lot about 'em, too. B'sides drivin' truck fer a livin' I race modified stock cars. Tell ya what, I ain't doin' nothin' this afternoon, I can drive ya around ta some other car lots."

As the man talked, Shelly began remembering him. He was the one Jim Stidhams had made move over the first night she was in Norwood. Several times he had spoken to her and tipped her when she was dancing. She also recalled hearing from somebody that he'd lived with a short, plump woman named Debbie but that they'd broken up. Still, the man's name was lost to her.

Shelly thought over his offer. She did want to look at more cars but the afternoon was getting hot and she had no desire to hike for miles on roasting pavement. The man smiling at her looked harmless enough and even if he did make an attempt at a hustle, Shelly knew she'd have no trouble brushing him off. "Okay," she told him, "but I wanta git a burger first. I'll buy you one too since you're drivin' me."

After they'd finished their burgers the man led Shelly outside to a souped-up 1966 Pontiac GTO fitted with an air scoop and racing slicks. Red and yellow flames streamed along the blue sides and boldly emblazoned above the flames was the car's nom de guerre, *el Diablo de acero.*

"Whadaya think a' my goat?" the man said as he opened the door for Shelly.

"Your what?" Shelly asked.

"My goat, my GTO?"

"It's cool," Shelly answered. "I've always wonder'd, what does GTO stand for?"

The man's face went panicky as he struggled for an answer. "Uh, Going To Ohio."

After Shelly got in the man asked her, "What kinda car ya lookin' for, anyway?

"Somethin' nice," Shelly said. "Maybe a little sporty but reliable."

"I know jest the place. There's a big car dealer about four miles from here that's got a bunch uv'em." The driver punched the accelerator, and constantly revved the high-out 400-inch engine under the hood as he weaved through traffic. As they pulled into the car lot he turned to Shelly. "Now listen, I done this sorta' thing a whole lot and I know how ta handle these salesmen-types, so you jest go along with whatever I say, okay?"

Before they'd even shut their car doors, a crewcut salesman wearing a bowtie appeared from nowhere. Dapper and smiling, he started his spiel while still on approach.

"Hello and good afternoon," he said. "My name is Harvey Baldridge, but you can call me Harv. Who do I have the pleasure of helping to find the right car today?"

Shelly's escort stepped up to meet him. "This is Shelly, she dances at Hillbilly Heaven and I'm Deke, Deke McConahay. I drive race cars."

Harvey's face did the impossible as his grin widened another two inches. He grabbed Deke's hand. "I think I may have heard of you on the racing circuit, Mr. McConahay," he said. "You're not the one they call Daredevil Deke, are you?"

Deke's face erupted into a grin nearly as wide as Harvey's. "Uh, could be. Yessir, that could be me, alright."

Now the man's name came back to Shelly. She remembered his former girlfriend, Debbie, introducing him and she also recalled other customers mentioning his name, but he wasn't called Daredevil Deke, he was called Dickhead Deke. Shelly also wasn't happy that he had introduced her as a bar dancer. She wasn't ashamed of her job, but didn't see what that had to do with buying a car.

Still pumping Deke's hand the salesman nodded to Shelly. "Ma'am," he said, and then turned back to Deke. "Well I certainly am proud to meet you, Daredevil Deke, and if you don't mind me saying so, you are with a mighty fine lady today. But then, you race car drivers always do get the best lookers."

Deke went all grinny at the compliment and Harvey looked at Shelly, expecting her to do the same, but she just glared at him, thinking, *this fella actually could polish a turd an' then talk ya into buyin' it.*

Harvey cut loose of Deke's hand. "So, what are you nice folks looking for today?"

"Well, Harv," Deke said, "Shelly here is my fee-an-cee, and I said I'd buy 'er a car for our weddin'. I was hopin' you'd cut us a deal an' all, seein' it's a weddin' present."

Shelly turned and looked at Deke, weighing whether to laugh at his ridiculous attempt at deception or just slap the shit out of him right now and get it over with.

"Deke," the salesman said, "being you're a race car driver, I know better than to try to put anything over on you, and as it's a wedding present for this beautiful young dancer here, I'll make you a special deal; my own wedding present to the two of you." He shook Deke's hand again. "Follow me," he said.

When Harvey turned away Deke gave Shelly a big, knowing wink and a thumbs up. Shelly followed behind, thinking, Deke, he's playin' you like a pi-ana.

Deke and Harvey became so engrossed talking cars and deals that twenty minutes passed before they noticed Shelly wasn't with them anymore. They found her in another part of the lot, sitting in a green 1965 Mustang GT. She looked up at Harvey and said, "I kinda like this one."

"She's a sweet little pony car," Harvey told her. "And you'll like this," he said to Deke as he walked around to the front and opened the hood, "a 289 V8."

Deke looked at the clean engine. "Shitfire," he said, "that's nice."

"Can I drive it?" Shelly asked.

"Why certainly," Harvey told her. "I'll go get the keys and be right back. Just as a matter of policy, you understand, I'll need to see your driver's license."

"I don't have one yet," Shelly said. "But I drive real good; my daddy taught me."

"Oh, I am so sorry, Shelly," Harvey told her, disappointment in his voice. "But it's our policy as well as the law. I'd lose my job if I let you drive one of our vehicles."

"Well, I can drive it," Deke said, "and Shelly could see how it runs. I even got my chauffeur's license cuz I'm a professional truck driver … on weekdays when I ain't drivin' race cars."

When Harvey came back with the keys, Deke slid behind the steering wheel and Shelly walked around to the passenger side. Harvey opened the door and as Shelly went to climb in Harvey bent the bucket seat forward for her to get into the back. "There you go, little lady," Harvey said to her, though Shelly was a solid five inches taller than him.

Only one day before, Shelly might have knee'd the little bastard in the groin and told him, You git your saggy ass in the back seat, I'm the one buyin' this car, but in her new-found ways Shelly was trying to be 'lady-like' and already it was pissing her off. She folded herself into the tiny back seat, her chin resting on her knees.

Deke twisted the key, listened to the engine's steady pulse for a few seconds, eased the floor-shifter into low and rumbled the Mustang toward the car lot's exit. Glancing right and left, he saw that cars were coming from both directions and punched the pedal to the floor. The two rear Goodyear's squealed their displeasure at leaving forty feet of hide on the pavement as Deke spun a left turn into the far lane, throwing Harvey and Shelly sideways.

"JESUS CHRIST!" Harvey screamed, as Deke shifted into second, hitting sixty as he buzzed by a 35 mph speed limit sign. "WHAT THE HELL ARE YOU DOIN'! THIS AIN'T THE RACE TRACK. SLOW DOWN!"

"Jest makin' sure it'll burn rubber," Deke said.

"Well, it will," Harvey told him. Composing himself, he said, "Sorry about yelling like that. It's just that I'm not used to riding with a race car driver like yourself, Deke. I trust your driving skill, but we have to obey the law or I'll get in trouble."

"Oh sure, sure, I understand, Harv. I kinda fergot myself there an' thought I was back on the track."

Shelly had a lot of questions she wanted to ask Harvey about the car, but the men in front jabbered nonstop, ignoring her when she tried to speak. Twenty minutes later when they pulled back into the car lot, Shelly'd had a bellyfull.

Deke was giddy with the Mustang. "Oh, she's sweet, Shelly, she's real sweet. Let's buy 'er. You'll give us a good price on it, won'tcha Harv?"

"So low it will probably get me in trouble with my boss. But for a lovely couple like yourselves, about to be married, I'll take that chance."

"Ya hear that, Shelly. C'mon, let's buy this baby right now."

Shelly looked at Deke and Harv. "I ain't buyin' nothin' today," she said. "Let me outa this sardine can."

So you drive a truck?" Shelly said on the way back to the bar. "What kind?"

"I drive a dump truck right now," Deke answered, "but I can drive anything. Drivin's what I do best." He shot a sly grin at Shelly. "Well, *almost* what I do best."

Shelly ignored the inference. "I always wanted to learn how ta drive a truck," she said. "Daddy used ta work on trucks an' take me drivin' with 'im. He was gonna teach me ta drive the big ones but then ... " Shelly turned to look out the GTO's side window.

As Deke slowed down for a red light he said, "I could teach ya ta drive mine."

"You own it yor'self?" Shelly asked.

"Sure do. All paid for and ever'thing."

As Deke edged the Pontiac over to the curb and shut off the engine, Shelly asked, "What about me not havin' a driver's license?"

"I'll help ya git that too," Deke said, smiling.

When Deke and Shelly walked into Hillbilly Heaven a thick-set swarthy man with massive hands and forearms who was shooting pool in the back looked at Deke, laid his cue on the table, and strode determinedly toward him.

Deke's eyes went wide. "Shelly," he said hastily, "I got some personal business ta discuss with this guy. Can ya excuse me?" and he rushed to head him off.

Shelly overheard Deke say to him, "Over here, man, over here. Can we talk over here?" as he scurried to a far corner where no one could hear them.

"Where you been with my car, McConahay?" the man said in a Mexican accent. "When I said you could test drive *el Diablo de acero* I meant for ten minutes, not the whole fucking afternoon. You're going to buy it now, *si?*"

"Sure Doguillo, sure. I wanna buy it," Deke told him. "It's jest gonna take me a few days ta git the money together. Don't s'pose I could drive it till then, could I?"

Doguillos's huge head swelled with the molten blood of rage. "You ... " he pointed at Deke with his thick index finger, "*cabron* ... you told me yesterday you had the money. For no other reason would I let an *estupido* like you dirty the seat of *el Diablo de acero* with his *lanudo culo*."

Clenching his heavy brown hands, Doguillo battled the urge to wrap them around Deke's throat and squeeze until Deke turned the color of a pickled beet.

"I jest wanted ta make sure my girlfriend over there," Deke said, nodding in Shelly's direction, "liked the car before I bought it."

"Hah! Shelly, *your* girlfriend?" Doguillo said, and let out a harsh laugh. "Your *polla* is the only one here that Shelly has never seen. Give me my keys and go away. If I wasn't on probation, McConahay, I'd stuff your face in the toilet where your *cabeza de mierda* belongs."

Doguillo went back to shooting pool as Deke joined Shelly, who was drinking a Coke at the bar. He sat down and ordered a double Jack Daniels and a can of Strohs.

"What was goin' on back there, Deke? Doguillo looked like he was about ta jack your jaw."

"Doguillo can jack my rabbit," Deke said, puffing up like a blowfish. "An' if he bothers me agin I'll fix his wagon but good."

Shelly was about to say, If Doguillo hears you say that he'll knock ya into next week, but instead said, "Deke, did ya really mean it about teachin' me how ta drive your dump truck?"

"Sure did," Deke answered. "If I say somethin', I mean it."

"When can I start?" Shelly asked.

"Uh, well … " Deke said, looking puzzled, "I reckon we'd have ta figger out a time ta do it."

My dancin' hours are from eight till two at night with Sundays an' Mondays off. I don't need all that much sleep an' I can take a nap before comin' in ta work. I could go with ya ev'ry day."

"Yeah … well … I guess maybe ya could," Deke said.

"Great," Shelly told him. "You can pick me up at my place Monday mornin'. I live at 222 Ivanhoe, apartment C."

"Uh … okay …I guess."

"I really appreciate this, Deke," Shelly said as she slurped the remains of her Coke. "I better be gittin on home, I gotta work tonight. See ya Monday."

"Uh …yeah," Deke said. "Reckon so."

Shelly got up and walked out the door and into the bright sunshine that engulfed Montgomery Road. As she passed the GTO parked at the curb, she was surprised Deke hadn't offered her a ride home.

Chapter 13

At 8:23 a.m. on Monday, a yellow tandem axel dump truck rumbled up outside of Shelly's apartment building.

"Wow," Shelly said, admiring the truck as she hoisted herself into the cab, "it's a Brockway. One a' the mines near us ran Brockways. They're tough rigs."

"I see ya already know somethin' about trucks," Deke said.

"Oh yeah, I like trucks. How come your truck says Norwood Sand and Gravel on the side? I thought you owned it."

"Oh, I do, Shelly. I lease it out to 'em an' they want their name on it."

Deke steered with his left hand, which also held a cigarette, and with his right hand, manipulated the shifter. Between shifts, he reached into a greasy paper bag and lifted out fingers full of a crumbly pink mixture that he stuffed into his mouth.

"Whatcha eatin'?" Shelly asked.

"Baloney an' crackers," Deke answered, chewing. "I eat breakfast in the truck so's I don't have ta git up so early."

Still with a mouthful, Deke told Shelly that the first run of the morning was spreading gravel on a private driveway about six miles away.

"Ya ever drove a heavy truck before?" he asked.

"Nope," Shelly answered.

"These big rigs are way harder ta drive than cars an' pickups, an' ever' trucker has his own style," Deke said as he deftly maneuvered the loaded rig through heavy morning traffic, adding a good many flourishes for Shelly's benefit.

"Couldja explain to me what your doin'?"

"Sure. I'll teach ya the shiftin' first," Deke said and pointed to the shift lever. "This here tranny's called a crashbox 'cause it ain't synchronized. Ya gotta have the speed an' rpm's jest right then git the gears matched up."

"Do ya double-clutch?"

"Ya can," Deke said, "but after awhiles ya jest float the gears without usin' the clutch."

"Sounds hard," Shelly said. "Reckon Ah oughta learn ta double clutch first. How do ya do that?"

"Well, ya clutch once ta take it outa gear and once ta put 'er back in. But ya can't push down much or you'll put the clutch brake on. Ya only do that when yer startin' out from a stop."

"Is it the same for downshifting?"

"Ya work the clutch the same," Deke said. "But when ya shift up ya let off on the gas and when ya downshift ya give 'er some juice then kinda tickle it into gear."

Shelly watched for several blocks. "How many gears are there?"

"This here's an Eaton 13 speed. It's got a three-position splitter with low, direct and overdrive. It ain't a real common gearbox, but I kinda like it."

"Is that why ya have it on your truck?"

"On my truck?"

"You said the truck was yours."

"Oh, yeah. Sure, I had it installed special."

"Do ya use all the gears?" Shelly asked.

"Depends on where yer drivin' an' how much of a load ya got on."

Shelly watched closely as Deke explained the gears and by the time they reached the driveway where they were to spread the gravel she understood the gear pattern. Deke slowly backed up the dump truck and stopped a few feet from the garage door. "The driveway looks close to a hunderd feet long so I reckon three inches deep should be about right," he said.

"Did you do the math for that in your head?" Shelly asked.

"Naw," Deke said, "I ain't too good at math but when ya do this fer a spell ya know how far a load'll spread. Ya gotta git the tailgate set right, your dump bed tilted jest so, an' your speed matched up. It takes a real expert ta do it."

He got out and set the tailgate spreader chains to open only a few inches then climbed back into the driver's seat and engaged the PTO. The Cummins diesel reverberated throughout the cab as Deke depressed the accelerator and put the truck into gear then moved the hoist control lever to raise the bed. He eased the clutch out and as the Brockway slowly moved forward he reached out the open window, pulled on a rope and tripped the tailgate latch. Watching the spread in his side mirror, Deke carefully raised the dump bed as he drove. When the truck reached the end of the driveway there was a perfect trail of level crushed white stone in its wake. The result was beautiful and Shelly told him so.

Deke smiled and tipped his dirty straw cowboy hat. "Thank ya, ma'am."

On the way back to the gravel pit Shelly noticed that Deke was acting fidgety. "What's the matter?" she asked.

"Well, uh, Shelly, ya see, even though I own the truck an' all, the company's got rules I have ta follow and one of 'em is I can't haul no passengers."

"Jeeze, Deke, why didn't ya say so ta begin with. I don't wantcha ta lose your contract."

"It's no big deal out here on the road, but inside their yard I don't think they'd like it. Could I jest drop ya off close by then pick ya up after I git loaded?"

"You sure it's okay Deke? I wouldn't feel right if ya got in trouble."

"Naw, there won't be no trouble, an' if there is, they'll git over it."

Deke dropped Shelly off at a small store two blocks from the Norwood Sand and Gravel Company pit. She bought a can of Coke then waited on the sidewalk, debating whether or not she should keep riding with him. Several other yellow Norwood Sand and Gravel trucks passed and after twenty minutes another came down the road and she saw Deke behind the steering wheel, his index finger up his nose, digging away. Deke dislodged his finger, downshifted and pulled to a stop beside Shelly.

Before she could say anything, Deke flashed a huge grin and hollered over the idling diesel, "Good news, Shelly. We're blue-topping fer a big pavin' job about twenty-five miles from here. It'll be easier ta teach ya how ta drive an ya won't have ta wait here so much."

"You sure it's okay, Deke?"

"It's okay, other driver's take their girls along on these long hauls. Hop in, I'm backin' up traffic sittin' here."

Shelly got into the cab and as soon as they were moving Deke looked over and winked. "Sometimes," he said, "drivers tell stories about what happens when their girlfriends are ridin' with 'em."

Her qualms returned and Shelly was about to tell Deke to pull over and let her out, when he said, "You can drive on the way back. It's easier with an empty truck."

Shelly looked out over the hood to the Brockway emblem: a Huskie dog pulling in trace, as Deke worked the gears and splitter, revving the Cummins diesel to a steady purr. She had to drive this truck, at least once.

At the highway job the road foreman gave Deke instructions on where and how thick to spread the gravel and after Deke dumped the load he drove a mile from the job site and pulled into a turnout. He put the truck into neutral and pulled out the yellow parking brake button to a whoosh of air. "The traffic ain't too heavy out here," he said to Shelly, "but when we git back inta the city, I better drive till you get the hang of it."

They traded seats and Shelly's entire perspective changed. Watching someone else drive was one thing, but sitting behind the big steering wheel and driving tons of moving steel through traffic, with so many other things to do at once, was as intimidating as it was exhilarating. Shelly looked down at the road. "Boy, ya sure set up high in this thing," she said, nervously.

"Yeah," Deke said, "these 359 Brockways have real tall cabs." He puffed on his Camel and watched Shelly as she went over driving the truck in her mind. "You'll be alright. Jest do it like I showed ya an' watch the traffic."

"Okay," Shelly said and reached for the shift lever. Then she remembered Deke picking his nose, but not even snot on the gearshift could stifle Shelly's thrill of finally getting to do what she'd longed for since childhood.

"Push that yella' button in ta take the air brake off," Deke said, pointing. "Check the air pressure gauge, then push the clutch the whole way down an' put 'er inta second. I usually start in third when I'm empty, but if ya start out in a lower gear it won't be as likely ta stall."

Shelly followed Deke's instructions but the grinding that followed made Deke chuckle. "Ya have ta get a feel fer where the gears are," he said. "Let up on the clutch a mite an' try it."

The shift lever went in and Shelly eased the dump truck onto the highway.

"Now go ta third," Deke said.

Concentrating on double clutching, Shelly grabbed the shifter and aimed for third gear but the gearshift failed to go in and rattled in her hand.

"Yer rpm's are too high," Deke told her. "Watch the tach and let 'em drop to around 1200."

Shelly let up on the accelerator then looked to make sure the truck wasn't drifting across the centerline. When she glanced down at the tachometer, the rpm's had dropped to 900.

"Give 'er a little more gas," Deke said, "but let off jest before ya shift."

As Shelly was about to clutch, a horn honked behind her. She was doing 14 mph in a 55 zone. Watching the tailgating car in the side mirror while trying to steer, Shelly depressed the clutch and tried once more to get the Brockway into third. Her rpm's had dropped again and Shelly coasted along in neutral, losing speed. She revved the accelerator and pushed harder on the shifter, trying to jam it into gear.

"Don't try ta force it," Deke said. "That's the biggest mistake sodbusters make. You lost yer road speed now so yer gonna have ta stop and put 'er back inta second."

Four cars were now backed up behind her and honking. "Where'd this traffic come from all uvva sudden?" Shelly said.

"Screw 'em, they'll git over it," Deke said, as he leaned out the side window and flipped his cigarette butt, and then his middle finger at the drivers.

Shelly pulled over to the side of the road and the cars behind shot around. She got the Brockway rolling in second again and Deke said, "Shift now." Shelly clutched into neutral and Deke leaned over, put his hand on top of hers, said, "Clutch" and then guided her smoothly into third gear. He did the same for fourth and fifth.

They drove along in fifth and Deke directed Shelly to pull over at each turnout so she could practice going through the gears. Shelly bit her lip in concentration and though she didn't say so, was giddy with excitement. After eight or nine times of working the Brockway up through fifth, she was catching the gears regularly. "Okay," Deke said, "I think yer ready ta try the splitter. Pull over an' I'll explain it."

Shelly guided the truck into the next turnout.

"The splitter ain't that hard ta use," Deke told her. "Ya got five speeds in low range, four in direct, an' four in overdrive; that's why it's a thirteen speed. The splitter only talks to the tranny in neutral. Like when yer goin' from fifth ta sixth, ya move the splitter from low ta direct then put yer shifter back inta what was second gear an' that makes it sixth."

"Do ya switch your splitter before ya take it outa fifth or after?" Shelly asked.

"It works either way. It won't kick in while yer still in fifth, ya gotta go ta neutral ta make the splitter work, but ya can't wait till yer in sixth or you'll still be in second."

"I thought you said this wasn't hard."

"It ain't," Deke said. "After ya take the shifter outa fifth an' put it in neutral, jest move that black button one position over. Then work yer clutch again and go back inta second gear an' you'll be in sixth. Work yer way up through the gears an' that'll take ya ta ninth in direct. Then do the same thing with the splitter in overdrive. If ya get inta trouble, move the splitter back ta low and go inta fifth. That's the sweet gear, the one ya go into if yer havin' a problem."

Shelly struggled using the splitter but finally made her way up to eleventh gear and 40 mph. She was wary of going any faster and whenever she met oncoming traffic, especially large trucks, drifted to the right.

"Don't git over so far," Deke warned. "If you put the front wheel off the road it'll pull us inta the ditch."

Despite her nervousness, driving the Brockway was as exciting as Shelly imagined it would be. As they approached Cincinnati the traffic grew heavier.

"Ya better let me take 'er from here," Deke said. "They're gonna be a'wondrin' back at the yard what happened to me."

"You won't git in no trouble, will ya, Deke?"

"Naw, I'll make up somethin' if they ask."

Shelly got out of the cab and they changed seats. Deke lit up a cigarette and as he was working the gears up to speed asked, "Well, whadaya think of it?"

A gigantic smile covered Shelly's face. "This is what I wanta do."

Deke dropped Shelly off, went and got another load of gravel and after they'd dumped it, let Shelly drive again until they neared the city.

"Hey, Shelly," he said, without taking the cigarette from his mouth, "how about us havin' dinner t'gether after work?"

Shelly thought the question over. "Tell ya what, Deke, I'm real grateful for this. Ev'ry day we're drivin', I'll buy us lunch, an' after we're done, I'll treat ya ta supper."

That was the answer Deke wanted, but not exactly in the way he wanted it.

"Speakin' a' which," Shelly said, "where ya wanta go for lunch?"

"White Castle. There's one up here on Montgomery."

Shelly didn't like White Castle's little square hamburgers, but she agreed to his request. After lunch Deke dropped Shelly off again and picked her up fifteen minutes later. "We're only gonna git two loads in the morning and two after lunch," he said. "You won't have all that much waitin' time as long as we're on this blue-toppin' job."

Coming back from the last load of the day, Shelly was driving well enough that Deke let her go part way into Cincinnati. After they'd exchanged seat positions Shelly asked, "Where ya wanta eat supper?"

"White Castle."

"Ya ever eat anywhere else?"

"Not really."

"I can't eat there twice ev'ry day, Deke," Shelly said. "There's other places."

 "I don't wanna eat in no other places," Deke said.

"Why not?"

"They might not be any good."

"But ya might like 'em better," Shelly said.

"An' I might not," Deke argued.

Shelly gave in and as she and Deke were having dinner at White Castle she asked him, "When d'ya think I'll be ready ta drive the truck loaded?"

"Real soon. Yer pickin' this up fast."

"You gonna let me spread the gravel too?"

"Sure. That's part a' learnin' ta drive a dump truck, ain't it?"

"Won't them fellas on the job site think it's strange seein' me do that?"

"Maybe," Deke said, "but they'll git over it."

By Wednesday Shelly was driving so well that as they were having lunch at White Castle, Deke said, "I think yer ready ta drive with a load a' gravel on."

After Deke got loaded he drove until they were out of town then let Shelly take over. "Wow," she said, after stalling the truck twice, "it's a lot diff'ernt."

A mile before the construction job Deke took the wheel, but at the site he had Shelly get out and he showed her how to set the spreader chains on the tailgate. The road foreman came over and Deke said to him, "I'm breakin' in a new driver. The gover'ment made us hire a woman." Even Shelly had to laugh at that.

On Friday morning Deke let Shelly spread a load of gravel and the result was less than perfect. When the foreman and the state highway inspector gave them dirty looks Deke hollered out the window, "Regulations. The gover'ment says we gotta have 'er."

The state inspector, an unpleasant squinty-eyed fellow with a head so pointed that his hard hat sat six inches above his eyebrows, yelled back, "She better learn to do it right pretty damn quick."

With each load, Shelly got better and what Deke told the foreman soon got around. Most construction workers already knew that companies with federal contracts were being pressured to hire women and minorities. The other Norwood Sand and Gravel drivers knew Deke was lying but they understood his motives and stayed quiet.

By Monday afternoon the foreman quit frowning at Shelly's spreads and the state inspector's nasty look settled into his usual scowl. Barely a week after she'd started, Shelly was driving all day except for going into the company yard. Deke still coached her on the finer points but she was learning fast.

"Shitfire, Shelly, yer gittin' real good at this," he told her, flipping the stub of his Camel out the window, "fer a girl." Shelly shot him a look and he hastily added, "who ain't even got 'er license yet."

On Thursday morning Shelly came out of her apartment wearing the gray *Mack Trucks* hat that Clete had bought her. Deke got down from the cab so Shelly could drive and watched silently as she approached.

"Mornin', Deke," she said. Deke stood mute, as if struck dumb, then finally muttered, "Hi, Shelly."

Shelly walked around Deke and reached for the grab bar to pull herself up into the truck. "I like that hat, Shelly," Deke said. "It looks good on ya. It matches yer eyes."

"It's kinda special. I didn't wanta wear it till I could handle the truck all by myself."

Instead of going to the passenger side as he usually did, Deke stood and watched Shelly climb into the cab. After she'd closed the door, Shelly looked down at Deke, who was still staring up at her. "You comin' along ta'day, Deke?"

Deke stood as if he hadn't heard. "You comin'?" Shelly said again.

"Uh, yeah ...yeah," Deke said. He trotted around to the passenger door, climbed in the cab and stared at Shelly with a slack-mouth gaze.

There must have been magic in that hat, for when Shelly grasped the steering wheel and put the truck in gear, all nervousness and doubt about her ability or right to be driving the big dump truck disappeared. She chugged the Brockway through heavy morning traffic like she'd been doing the job forever. After she'd spread the day's first load of gravel the road foreman gave her a slight smile and for once, the state inpector did not glower. In fact, the only person who did not notice how well Shelly was driving was the one sitting beside her. He stared at Shelly with the same gape-jawed gawk that he'd been wearing all morning.

When Shelly emerged from her apartment building that morning wearing the *Mack* hat, Deke had not just been dumbstruck at the change in her, he'd been double plus dumbstruck. As she walked towards him, every movement in her limber, purposeful stride bespoke of her eagerness to climb into the truck and get at it. And when a waft of morning breeze lifted and rippled the long hair that flowed from beneath the enchanted ballcap and Shelly gave a little shake of her strong-featured face to clear the hair away from her eyes, then said, in her melodius, husky voice, "Mornin', Deke," his switch was tripped.

Somehow, Deke got words to come out of his mouth as he turned to watch Shelly pull herself up into the cab. He had seen this same girl dancing near naked over a hundred times, and he had lusted, oh yes, Deke had lusted. Yet on this morning, it was if he were seeing the *real* Shelly Stamper for the first time, and he fell like a tub of bricks for what he saw.

As Shelly climbed into the truck, Deke ogled her every movement and noted each feature. Her sinewy, tawny arms and the ripple of muscle beneath the cotton fabric that covered her sleek form. The way her wide shoulders tapered to a slender waist. How her faded jeans rode up between the rounded firm cheeks of her magnificent butt, then molded around her strong thighs. Deke nearly groaned aloud. And there he had stood, smitten, transfixed, sucked down the rabbit hole, until Shelly called to him from the cab and asked if he were coming along.

Coming back from the road job, Shelly glided the dump truck along confidently as Deke continued staring at her. As they entered the city she asked, "You okay, Deke? You been actin' a little strange ta'day."

Deke took a few seconds to answer. "Uh, yeah …yeah, Shelly, I'm jest fine."

As Shelly went to downshift for a stoplight, Deke reached over and put his hand on top of hers. "Let me help ya with them gears, Shelly."

Shelly shook his hand away. "I'm fine, Deke. This ain't my first day."

Embarrassed, Deke stayed quiet until they got to the store where Shelly waited. When Shelly pulled over Deke said to her, "Uh, I reckon it'd be okay if you went inta the company yard with me."

"I don't think that's a good idea, Deke."

"They'll git over it," he said absently.

"Nope," Shelly said, as she opened the door. "I ain't sure what's goin' on with you, but I ain't doin' it."

The morning's second load was a repeat of the first, but when they went to White Castle for lunch, Deke insisted on buying.

"Well, ya kin if ya want," Shelly said, "but our deal was I'd buy lunch an' supper."

"No, let me buy," Deke insisted. "I can do it, I got money. I got lotsa money."

All that afternoon Deke got as close to Shelly as he could and sought any excuse to touch her. As they were returning from the day's last spread, Shelly was fed up, and when Deke said, "I'll buy ya dinner at White Castle t'night," Shelly told him, "I ain't goin' ta White Castle, I'm eatin' at the Quatman Café. You can go wherever ya want."

"Oh, I'll go ta the Quatman," Deke said. "I been wantin' ta try it."

As they entered the restaurant, Deke told Shelly, "This joint's purty fancy," then rushed to pull out a chair for her. To Shelly's horror he tried to play footsie under the table and his fawning manner and idiotic attempts at cultured small talk had her near crazy. By the time Shelly paid the bill, over Deke's repeated insistence to let him buy, she was thoroughly fed up and creeped out.

"Let me drive ya home," Deke said as they were leaving.

"You know I always walk home after supper, Deke, it ain't that far."

"Then let me walk ya home, jest ta be sure yer safe."

"Ain't no need for that … an' you know it."

"Oh, I don't mind," Deke insisted, as he hurried ahead to hold the door open. "I don't mind a'tall, Shelly. I can walk ya home, I got time."

"Urrrrrr …" Shelly growled, her patience gone. "I'm walkin' home alone. See ya ta'morrow."

But Shelly was wrong. Two hours later, when she walked from the dressing room onto the stage, Deke McConahay was sitting at the nearest table. "Hi, Shelly," he called, a can of Stroh's in one hand, a cigarette in the other and two empty shot glasses in front of him. Deke stayed until closing time, cheering Shelly as she danced and pestering her during breaks. When her last set ended, Deke tried, without success, to drive her home.

Friday was a repeat of Thursday. Shelly came close to telling Deke to stop acting like an idiot or she was done, but held off because she loved driving the Brockway. On Saturday Shelly reckoned she'd get a reprieve, but late that morning she heard a rapping on her door. Just as she was about to open it, Deke's voice came from the other side.

"Shelly, you home?"

Her first instinct was to call back, No, I'm not here right now, but instead she tiptoed back into the bedroom and stayed silent until the pounding stopped. That night at work, a drunken, leering Deke pestered her until closing time.

Sunday was the only day that Shelly neither danced nor hauled gravel and she was looking forward to the day off, but now she had to avoid Deke. The day was sunny but not overly hot and Shelly walked around Norwood and into Cincinnati, browsing and going into whatever shops were open. She returned to her apartment in early evening and decided to call home on her newly installed telephone. For over an hour she talked with her family, telling them about driving the dump truck. Everyone asked her the same question: "When we gonna see ya agin', Shelly?"

"Soon," Shelly promised, "Soon."

Shelly was about to hop in the shower when there came a loud and persistent knocking at her door. She remained quiet and then heard Deke's voice, desperate and drunk; "Shelly, Shelly, I wanna see ya."

After several more knocks the knob turned as Deke tried to enter, but Shelly was keeping her door locked all the time now. Ta'morrow, she said to herself, ta'morrow ... I'm takin' care a' this.

When the yellow Brockway lurched to a stop in front of Shelly's apartment on Monday morning, it was a haggard and hungover Deke McConahay who crawled from the cab. He managed a feeble, "Hi, Shelly," but after getting into the passenger seat, fell into a deep slumber. He didn't even have his greasy bag of baloney and crackers and despite the morning chill, Deke's B.O. was so bad that Shelly drove with the window down. After spreading the first load, Shelly pulled up to the store where she got out and shook Deke awake. "You need to go git more gravel," she told him.

"Uhhhhhh," Deke groaned, and when Shelly climbed out of the truck, Deke clumsily crawled over the dump levers and shifter into the driver's seat.

"Are you okay ta drive?" she called up to him.

"I made it here, didn't I?" Deke said as he revved the diesel and drove off.

Shelly thought about just walking away but she wanted to give Deke a chance to straighten out, or at least explain to him why she was finished. When Deke returned, Shelly was waiting for him with a cup of coffee and a look that meant business.

"Thanks, Shelly," Deke said, as he climbed down from the cab and took the coffee. But as soon as they were in the truck, Deke looked over and asked, "Since you ain't dancin' t'night, how about we git together after work?"

"Listen, Deke," Shelly said, "I don't know what's goin' on with you these last few days, but it's gotta stop."

"Whadaya mean, Shelly?"

"You know what I mean. You keep sayin' an doin' stupid things an' starin' at me like I got three eyes or somethin'."

"You got beautiful eyes, Shelly," Deke said.

"That's what I mean, right there." Shelly geared down for a red light and when she came to a stop said, "What's got inta you, anyways Deke?"

They looked at each other across the width of the cab. "Don't ya know, Shelly?"

"Yeah, I reckon I do," Shelly said, as the light turned green and she rumbled through the intersection. "But it still has ta stop. You can't be starin' at me all the time or botherin' me at work or comin' by my place on weekends."

"How'd ya know I was at your place? Nobody ever answered the door."

" 'Cause other people told me you was there," Shelly lied.

Deke remained quiet. At the next red light Shelly said, "I'm tellin' ya, Deke, if you don't stop all this bullshit right now, I ain't comin' with ya no more."

Deke sat stonefaced for the rest of the day, even through lunch and dinner. On Tuesday, Deke returned Shelly's morning greeting, but remained sullen and untalkative. He spoke a few words on Wednesday, but most of the time sat in the cab with his arms folded, looking out the window with a hurt look on his face. When Deke returned from getting gravel after lunch, Shelly thought she smelled alcohol on his breath and when she got into the truck for the final afternoon haul there was no question of it. By the second morning run on Thursday, Deke smelled of booze and coming back from the first spread after lunch he lifted up his pantleg and pulled a pint of Jack Daniels from his cowboy boot.

"Deke, whatcha doin'?" Shelly asked him as he took a jolt from the bottle. "You can't be drinkin' on the job."

"Why?" he said. "I ain't drivin', you are."

"You gotta drive back an' get gravel an' somebody might smell it on ya."

"Fuck 'em, they'll git over it."

"They can take your contract away, Deke."

"They kin jack my rabbit."

As they were coming back from spreading the last load of the day, Shelly pulled over at the corner of Ivanhoe Avenue and said, "Deke, I ain't eatin' out ta'night. I jes wanta go home an' rest up before I go inta work."

Deke frowned and Shelly thought he was about to cry, but he quietly clambered over the controls and got into the driver's seat. Shelly watched him drive away, her mind made up that tomorrow would be her last day.

On Friday morning, Shelly was waiting at the curb when Deke arrived, stinking and hungover. Except for when he had to go into the yard and get gravel, Deke slept the morning away, his filthy cowboy hat tipped over his eyes and his pointed boots resting on the dash. His long hair was dirty and tangled and he had on the same unwashed clothes he'd been wearing for two weeks. Just before lunch, Deke took a full pint of Jack Daniels from his boot, cracked the seal and took a swig.

"Ya can't be doin' that, Deke," Shelly said to him.

"It's my truck, I'll do what I want."

Shelly had decided not to tell Deke she was through until the final run, as she wanted to enjoy her last day of driving as much as possible. They had lunch at White Castle and after he picked up a load of gravel, Deke drank steadily as Shelly drove to the job site. On their way back into town Deke pulled a reefer from his shirt pocket and lit it up. He passed the joint over to Shelly but she shook her head no.

As Deke drove off to get more gravel, Shelly wondered why nobody at the pit ever noticed his condition. The truth was simple. Deke never had to get out of the truck or interact with anyone at Norwood Sand and Gravel. He drove up to the gravel pile and his uncle, who ran the loader, (and who had gotten Deke his job) dumped three buckets of gravel into the bed of the truck and Deke drove away.

After Shelly got back into the truck and Deke had crawled to the passenger side, he immediately lit another fat doobie and took a pull from what little remained of the pint. Shelly figured it was time to give him the news. As they reached the edge of the city, she told him, "Deke, I think I've learned as much about drivin' a dump truck as I can. This'll be the last day I go with ya."

Swaying in his seat, Deke drunkenly glared at Shelly.

"But I'm grateful to ya for lettin' me do this," she said, "an' for what ya taught me. I mean that, Deke; thanks."

Deke's eye's flashed anger. "You don' know shit about drivin' truck," he said, holding his joint in one hand and waving the nearly empty pint at Shelly with the other. "I know fif'y times more'n I taught ya."

"I know enough for now," Shelly answered. "I need ta git my driver's license, then maybe I can work at learnin' more."

"How come you won' be my girlfrien'," Deke said, "even af'er all I done fer ya?"

His tone was belligerent and his mouth had curled into a mean sneer.

"What ya mean is, 'Why won't I let ya screw me?'" Shelly responded, matching Deke's tone.

"Well, you let ever' other man in Norwood screw ya, even when they ain' done nothin' for ya like I done." Deke looked at Shelly and his eyes moistened. "What's so wrong with me?"

In spite of her rising anger, Shelly understood Deke's pain and answered kindly. "Deke, there's nothin' wrong with you. Before Bussy had that talk with me, I'd a' gone home with you jes as soon as them other men, sooner'n some, but you was with Debbie then. By the time we met I'd changed my ways."

Deke looked at her, almost pleading. "Well how come ya hadda change yer ways jest after the man before me 'stead of jest before the man after me?"

Shelly had to work that out.

"Them things Bussy said really hit me hard, Deke. I knew I had to change an' the only way ta do it was right then. If I'd a' put it off, even for one night, I'd a' jes kept on the way I was. You understand that, don'tcha, Deke? It ain't nothin' against you. I like ya Deke, I really do, but I ain't ready to be nobody's girlfriend right now."

Deke heard Shelly's words but it didn't matter. All the hurt, all the longing, and all the rejection that he'd ever known welled up inside of him. "Tha' migh' be so," he choked out. "Maybe it ain' yer fault an' the time jest wadn't right, but shitfire an' dammit all ta hell anyways, how come when I wan' sum'thin, when I really, really wan' sum'thin, I never kin git it?"

A mighty sob escaped from Deke's constricted throat and great big tears rolled down his grimy cheeks. Shelly reached over from the shifter and put her hand on Deke's arm. "You will, Deke, someday ya will git the thing ya really want, I jes know ya will."

"Fuck som'day," Deke snarled. "How come nothin' good's ever come ta me so far? An' now yer leavin'." Deke swilled the last of the Jack Daniels and tossed the empty bottle out the window. He wiped the tears from his face. "I wan' mah truck back," he slobbered. "Righ' now. I wan' it back."

"Huh?" Shelly said in amazement. "You can't drive. Yor drunk ... and stoned."

"I don' care," Deke shouted. "It's mah truck an' I'm drivin' it. You stop righ' now or I'm takin' the wheel from ya! We'll fight fer it righ' here in the cab."

That didn't leave Shelly much choice, so she pulled over and let Deke drive. She thought about hitchhiking home but it was a long way and she still hoped she might talk some sense into Deke. But as Shelly feared he would do, Deke told her, "Now I'm gonna' show yew how ta drive truck."

Missing and grinding gears, double clutching, triple clutching, quardruple clutching, Deke revved the loaded Brockway to its limit: 25 tons of mass, momentum, and potential mayhem blustering down the highway. Shelly hung on and prayed he'd keep the monster out of everyone else's way.

Deke high-balled the truck to the construction site and charged onto the unfinished roadbed in a cloud of dust, then got out and stumbled to the back of the bed. Instead of latching the tailgate chains to the spread position, in his drunkenness Deke unhooked them so the tailgate would swing open all the way. He climbed into the cab, missing the door handle twice, then tipped his greasy cowboy hat back and smirked at Shelly. Deke punched the clutch to the floor, jammed the gear lever and splitter into direct reverse and staring straight ahead, tromped the accelerator. The Brockway let out a lion's roar and trundled backwards, gathering force.

"Where ya goin'?" Shelly yelled to Deke.

"Ta dump the fuckin' gravel, whadaya think?" Deke yelled back.

Shelly glanced into her side mirror and saw a blue and white State Department of Highways pickup truck sitting directly in their path.

"DEKE! DON'T HIT THE ..." she screamed as the loaded gravel truck broadsided the pickup, but the jolt and crunch of metal drowned out her words. The collision slowed, but did not halt the renegade dump truck's regress. Deke pushed the pickup sideways for 30 feet before he braked the Brockway to a stop. In her mirror Shelly saw that the passenger side of the state pickup was as demolished as if a locomotive had punched it.

Deke engaged the PTO, jerked the dump lever and as the bed tilted he reached out and yanked the rope to the tailgate latch. The Brockway unencumbered itself of 28,000 pounds of crushed and sorted gravel onto the highway department pickup, covering the entire cab and most of the bed.

Construction stopped as the workers watched this spectacle play out. Seventy yards away the pointy-headed State Department of Highways inspector ran towards the dump truck, maniacally screaming and waving his arms.

"I think that fella there wants ta talk to ya, Deke. He looks real mad," Shelly said.

Deke looked at the inspector, puffing and bellowing as he ran at them. "He'll git over it."

Mashing the clutch to the floor, Deke rummaged for a forward gear and disengaged from the pickup, dragging its passenger-side door, which had somehow become attached to the back of the dump truck, in the dust behind him. The demented state highway inspector planted himself directly in the path of the Brockway to halt it, hopping up and down, yelling every profanity he knew and flailing his arms, looking for all the world like he was doing jumping jacks for exercise, his hard-hat bouncing up and down on the apex of his head.

Deke never veered, but kept the truck headed straight at the crazed man, pedal to the floor. "DEKE! DON'T HIT HIM!" Shelly screamed, and was about to wrench the steering wheel to the right when the inspector dove for the dirt, leaving his hardhat and one final blast of blasphemy hanging in the air. Shelly looked in the mirror and saw him in the midst of the trailing dust cloud, up and running after the dump truck, shaking his fist and still screaming. When the door from his destroyed pickup shook loose from the back of the Brockway, he tripped over it and tumbled face first in the dirt again.

Pumping the clutch like he was keeping time to a fiddle tune, Deke ran the length of the construction project, grinding away on the crashbox in search of higher gears and leaving a rooster tail of dust in his wake. By the time he bounced the empty truck over the hump that led back onto the asphalt he was running in overdrive. Satisfied that the job had been done right, Deke smirked to himself and reached a finger up to push his cowboy hat higher on his brow. He turned and looked at Shelly through eyes gone glassy and wild. "Now that's how ya fuckin' drive a dump truck," he said.

The entire way back Shelly stared at the windshield and uttered only six words: "Drop me off at my place." Occasionally she glanced into her side mirror, expecting to see a police car's flashing lights behind them, but never did. When they got to Shelly's, she opened the cab door and looked over at Deke.

"Deke," she said to him.

"Yeah, Shelly?" he said, with a plaintive, almost pleading look.

Shelly smiled sweetly at him as she climbed from the cab. "You can let the dump bed down anytime now."

Chapter 14

That night at work, Shelly knew something had changed and she knew it on the first song. Most nights she bounded onto the stage like a panther, eager and ready to dance, but even though Hillbilly Heaven was packed and the crowd was revved, her own enthusiasm was gone from her like yesterday's oatmeal. All night Shelly danced like her mind was somewhere else. Her only enjoyable moment came when she punched out a drunk who'd put his hand down the back of her bikini.

On Saturday she sat around her apartment all day, not feeling like doing anything. She wasn't looking forward to work that night, but after having a shower, she grabbed the bag with her dancing gear and trooped down to Hillbilly Heaven for dinner and maybe find out if anyone had heard about Deke's stunt the day before.

The place wasn't crowded yet and Shelly took a seat at the bar. She'd just ordered catfish and fries when Debbie, Deke's ex, came up and sat beside her.

"Ya seen Deke since he clobbered that state pickup?" Debbie asked.

"I guess the word is out then?" Shelly said.

"Out!" Debbie roared with laughter. "All a' Norwood is talkin' about how Deke shit an' fell back in it, an' sayin' you were with him when he done it."

"Reckon so," Shelly said, seeing no use in denying what everybody already knew.

"How come you were ridin' with Dickhead?" Debbie asked.

"He was teachin' me to drive the truck," Shelly answered. "How come you were livin' with Dickhead?"

" 'Cause I didn't know Deke was like a baby robin, all mouth an' fulla shit. He even told me he was a race car driver an' I fell for it."

"Was he?" Shelly asked.

"Hell no! Like an id-jit, my brother, who's about as dumb as Deke, let him drive his modified stock car in a race one night. Turns out Dickhead had never drove one before. He got sideways in the first turn, wrecked my brother's car and took out four more drivers. They chased him right off the track and woulda killed him if they coulda caught him. That's when I threw his sorry, lyin' ass out."

Shelly seldom felt the need to explain herself, but she said to Debbie, "I mighta learned how to drive a truck from Deke, but he ain't my boyfriend an' never will be."

"Well, at least you got sense enough for that," Debbie said, and got up.

Shelly's dinner came but she didn't get much peace eating it. Everyone who walked by had a comment or wanted to chat about Deke's fiasco. "Any idea where he got off to?" people asked. "Ain't nobody's seen him since it happened."

Just as Shelly stuffed the last French fry into her mouth and was reaching for the dregs of her Coke, Bussy came out of his little room and locked eyes with her. He drumbled over and said, "Can I talk to yeh back in meh office, Shelly?"

"Shor," Shelly answered and got up and followed him.

Bussy planted himself in the chair behind his desk and looked up at Shelly. "I hear'd fum the po-leece, Shelly, about what happened. They come by today, lookin' for Deke … an' you too."

"How come they're lookin' for me? I wasn't drivin'."

"You're a witness an' they's gonna' want ya to testify."

"I won't," Shelly said.

"They done some checkin', Shelly. People's seen you drivin' thet truck an' yeh don't have a license." Bussy watched her with his bug eyes for a minute before he spoke again. "They also said they's per'ty sure you're under eighteen an' wondered why yeh been workin' in he'er all this time. They said they's gonna' call down to Wes' Virginia on Monday an' find out your birthday, and if you warn't eighteen they was comin' back an' there'd be trouble over it. Are yeh eighteen, Shelly?"

"No, but I will be in a coupla weeks."

"I'm feared thet ain't good enough," Bussy said. "Even after you're turned eighteen I dasn't have yeh dancin' no more. Them cops'll bother me caus' yeh danced in he'er when you was under age. I can't chance losin' meh license."

"I'm real sorry, Bussy. I sure hope ya don't git in no trouble over it."

"Oh, it'll be aw'right," Bussy said after a long pause, "long as they don't see yeh in he'er no more. I might have to grease some wheels for awhile." Bussy paused again. "Leeg'ly, you ain't spose to even be in a bar drinkin' soda pop til you're eighteen. An' yeh gots to be twenty-one to drink whiskey … which you been doin'."

They looked at each other in silence until Shelly said, "I been thinkin' about gittin' away an' maybe doin' somethin' else, Bussy."

"Thet'd be a good thing for yeh, Shelly, 'specially with this mess you're in. I know you was jest with Deke to learn how to drive thet truck, but I known him for awhile, an' things never go right with thet boy."

Shelly smiled. "Well, I shor know that now, Bussy," she said, "but what's done is done and I'm done with Deke. The only thing he'll ever see a' me again is my foot kickin' 'im in the ass."

Bussy chuckled then opened a desk drawer and pulled out an envelope. "If things was normal, Shelly, I'd give yeh thirty days a' notice, but since I dasn't do thet I paid yeh an extra month."

"You don't need ta do that," Shelly said. "I got money in the bank."

Bussy held the envelope out and said, "You brung in so much business I wouldn't feel right cuttin' yeh loose an' not givin' yeh sum'thin."

Shelly took the envelope and thanked him then stood up to leave.

"We're all gonna miss yeh 'round he'er, Shelly," Bussy said. "An' I'm gonna' miss yeh, too."

Shelly stepped around the desk and gave Bussy a hug, her chin resting on the top of his bald head. "I'm gonna miss this place an' you too, Bussy," she said, and ran out the door.

Chapter 15

Sunday morning blossomed bright, the warm autumn air beckoning, but Shelly Stamper didn't answer its call. She stayed in bed with the curtains closed until noon. After leaving Hillbilly Heaven the night before, she'd gone to another bar down the street until closing time then bought a six-pack of Falstaff and went home, where she watched old black and white tear-jerkers until four-thirty in the morning.

Shelly crawled from bed, tugged on some rumpled clothes, had a bowl of cornflakes and took to the streets, walking aimless in the early afternoon sunshine. She missed her family and longed for the country, where she could clambor through forests and go barefoot in creeks, but feared if she went back home, she might never leave. The only thing Shelly knew for certain was that she was not going back to dancing in bars.

Her walk took her past the corner store where she had waited while Deke got more gravel. She went in and bought a can of Coke, and as she stood outside sipping on it, couldn't help wondering what had happened to Deke. Certainly, she didn't miss him, but she did miss driving the big Brockway. Shelly knew the chance of becoming a truck driver anytime soon was not good. Most companies didn't hire drivers unless they were at least twenty-one and had certified training or experience. The other hard fact was that many employers wouldn't hire women truck drivers.

In the September twilight Shelly walked back to her apartment. Restless, she turned the TV on and off half a dozen times then began straightening up her bedroom. Buried in her sock drawer she found

Clete's Bible that Ethel had stuffed into her knapsack. Despite her unsaintly lifestyle, Shelly had never stopped believing in God, though the only time she'd been to church since leaving home was when she and Jim were married. She picked up the Bible and thought about her sins. Even back in Peapatch, she was no Apostle, but in Norwood she'd sinned more than a horde of heathens and she wondered if God was punishing her.

Shelly went to the kitchen, made a ham sandwich and came back into her living room. Flipping on a light, she sat down on the couch and thumbed through her father's Bible as she ate, hoping to find a passage of Holy Scripture that would give her guidance. Darkness settled over Norwood and the night air crept into her apartment, squeezing out what little heat remained from the day. She got up and closed the windows then went back to the couch and continued searching the Good Book.

Nine o'clock edged into ten but no Biblical word spoke to Shelly's needs. Neither Moses nor David offered useful counsel. Even Solomon was silent. Shelly jumped to the New Testament. Surely Jesus'll have something to say, she thought, he's full of advice.

But He didn't. Frustrated, Shelly said, "Well, maybe I ain't doin' this right. Maybe I oughta have more faith in the Lord and let Him show me the passage that'll guide me."

She closed her eyes, opened the Bible to a random page, circled her finger in the air and plopped it down. Shelly opened her eyes and read: *Let the rivers clap their hands. Let the mountains sing together for joy.* "Well, that don't help much," she muttered, then read it again. "Maybe there's some kinda meaning to it I don't understand."

"Lord," Shelly said, raising her voice to make sure God heard, "it's Sunday night an' I'm holdin' the Bible in my hands an' askin' for help. I hate ta bother You on Your day a' rest, 'specially since it's gittin' late, but I'm in a real pickle, God. I don't know what ta do or where ta go."

Shelly put the Bible down, placed her palms together and looked at the ceiling.

"Thank you God that I'm still alive and healthy after all the bad things I done … an' I'm sorry for most of 'em. You had ta be lookin' out for me or I wouldn't be here no more … an' I'm grateful."

Shelly waited for her words to reach Heaven.

"I really don't like askin' favors as I've always believed people should do for themselves, but all I want is a chance, God, some way ta git outa this tangle I'm in now. I don't expect too much, the way I been carryin' on an' all. I know You work in mysterious ways an' I might not even know it if You send me a sign, but I want one anyway, jes one thing that'll give me a shot at a better life. Amen."

Shelly reached over, flipped the lamp off and reclined her head against the back of the couch, letting the darkness settle around her. She listened to her heartbeat and thought about her blood: Stamper blood, her daddy's blood and her mama's blood coursing through her body, giving her strength. This blood ain't gonna quit flowin' through me for a long time, she thought, and till it does I ain't gonna' quit neither.

The throb of Shelly's heartbeat increased until it became a loud pounding. Alarmed, she sat upright, and realized someone was beating on her door.

"This is jes what I don't need right now," she said as she turned the light back on and got up. She undid the bolt and opened the door to gaze upon a ghastly spectre, hideous and haggard, its eyes wide with terror, standing in her doorway.

"DEKE! What are you doin' here?" Shelly shouted, more startled than angry

"Ya gotta let me come in, Shelly," Deke pleaded, trembling. "They're after me."

"Who?" Shelly asked, blocking the doorway with her body.

"Ever'body," Deke said, his eyes darting nervously down both sides of the hallway. His left cheek twitched and drool ran from the side of his mouth.

"Please, Shelly," he whined, "I need ta use yer phone."

"What for?"

"To call my brother so's he kin help me out."

Shelly looked at Deke and her lip curled in revulsion.

"Ohhhh ... please Shelly, I'm des'sprit. Yer the only person I can trust. All I wanna do is make a phone call."

"Okay," Shelly said, "you can use the phone, but then ya gotta leave."

Deke scurried in then quickly grabbed the door and closed it behind him.

"What happened after ya dropped me off Friday?" Shelly asked, her curiosity now tweaked.

"Oh, Shelly," Deke moaned, "somebody out at the road job musta phoned the company about what I done, cuz when I pulled in ta the gravel pit, a whole buncha bosses come runnin' outa the office yellin' and screamin' at me somethin' awful. I was so scared I jest jumped outa the truck and started runnin'. I ran ta my pickup an' took off fast as I could."

"Did ya stop the dump truck 'fore ya jumped out, Deke?" Shelly asked

"Uh … no I didn't, Shelly. I was too scared. The truck kept goin' till it run inta the company office building."

"Oh Lord, Deke. It wasn't really your truck, either, was it? It was theirs. You jes made that up about havin' a contract an' all."

Deke looked down, ashamed to meet Shelly's eyes. "Yeah, it was their truck."

"Ya gotta quit lyin' like that, Deke. It don't work out. Never."

"I know it, Shelly, an' I'm sorry. I hope it didn't bring no trouble ta you."

"I lost my job over it."

"How come?" Deke asked, "You didn't do nothin' wrong."

"The cops come by Hillbilly Heaven lookin' for you an' told Bussy I was too young ta be workin' there."

"Oh Shelly, I'm real sorry," Deke said. "Whadaya gonna do now?"

"I don't rightly know, Deke. I'm feelin' perty lost right now, too. In fact, I was waitin' on a sign from God when you knocked on the door."

"I didn't mean ta inta'rupt you an' God, Shelly, but I'm des'sprit. Worse'n I ever been before."

"Do you even remember what ya did at the job site, Deke?" Shelly asked.

"Well, I sorta recall backin' into somethin', but it didn't seem like any big deal, so I jest dumped the load a' gravel and drove off, like I always do."

"Ya backed into a pickup truck, Deke"

"I know it now," Deke said. "My uncle Charlie, the loader operator, came by my place Friday night and tol' me it belonged to the state guy who was the inspection supervisor fer the whole job. Charlie said I completely de-molished the pickup when I hit it, then dumped my load a' gravel on it ta boot. I guess the construction guys thought it was real funny cuz the inspector's a big prick."

"Oh Lord, Deke," Shelly said again.

"Charlie said when I ran from the truck it kinda destroyed a lotta offices when it hit 'em an' totaled the dump truck too. He tol' me I needed ta clear out fast cuz the company called the cops an' even the county persecutor and is gonna' have me arrested and persecuted on felony destruction a' property or somethin' like that. Charlie said they smelled marijuana smoke in the cab and thought I mighta been drinkin' too, but they ain't got no witnesses fer that. Do they, Shelly?"

"Nah, you know I wouldn't say nothin' to 'em, Deke."

"Charlie said they was gonna put me in prison if they found me, so I quick like threw my guns and some other stuff in a duffel bag an' left. I hid my truck down by the rail yard and been sleepin' in it the las' two nights."

"What about your GTO?" Shelly asked.

"GTO?"

"The one you drove me to the car lot in," Shelly reminded him.

'Oh, yeah, that GTO. I sold it, Shelly. Made real good money on 'er too."

Shelly glared at Deke. "You never owned that GTO, did ya?"

"I almost did, Shelly. I was hopin' ta buy it."

"That don't count. It wasn't yours and you should'na told me it was. It's that kinda lyin' that got ya inta this mess."

"It wadn't lyin' that got me in this fix, Shelly, it was my feelin's fer you. I let ya drive the dump truck so I could be near ya... an' then I went real crazy over ya."

"Don'tcha start acusin' me now, Deke. You offered to teach me ta drive a dump truck before I ever asked ya."

"I ain't blamin' you, Shelly, not one bit. It's my fault, one-hunderd percent." Deke's eyes softened. "I love ya, Shelly, an' I can't help it."

"I'm sorry, too, Deke. I didn't want that ta happen."

"I know ya didn't, but shitfire, I'm scared what they're gonna do ta me. I didn't mean ta wreck that feller's pickup, even if he is a prick. An' I sure didn't mean to destroy the company offices or their truck. They never treated me bad. I feel sick ever' time I think about it."

Shelly thought about the majestic yellow Brockway, now wrecked, and felt a little sick herself.

"Now I feel even worse cuz you lost yer job over what I done," Deke said.

Shelly looked at the pathetic figure who stood before her. "Whatcha gonna do now, Deke?" she said.

"That's what I come by for Shelly. I need ta use yer phone ta call my brother."

"Ain't it kinda late? It's after ten-thirty."

"Nah, he lives in Montana. It's two hours earlier out there."

"You never told me ya got a brother in Montana?"

"Yeah," Deke said, "he's six years older'n me an' we ain't much alike. He's a Christian with a wife an' kids an' owns his own loggin' truck, a real nice Peterbilt."

"What's his name?" Shelly asked.

"Zeke. He's helped me out a few times before when I was in trouble but I sure hate askin' 'im again. I don't know what else ta do. Bein' sent off ta prison ain't somethin' I could handle."

Shelly agreed with that.

Deke went on. "A coupla months ago, when I told Zeke I was drivin' dump truck and doin' real good at it – which I was then – he said if I ever wanted to come ta Montana he could likely git me on drivin' a log truck. He'd teach me first in his rig. Zeke said they're always lookin' for log truck drivers out there in Montana cuz it's a hard job up in them mountains."

Shelly and Deke stood looking at each other and after a minute Shelly said, "Shor, Deke, you can use the phone ta call your brother. Reckon I owe ya that much anyways for teachin' me ta drive that dump truck."

"Thanks, Shelly. You might be savin' my life lettin' me do this."

Shelly picked up her phone and handed it to Deke. "You can take it inta the other room if ya want," she told him. "The cord's long enough."

Deke took the phone and headed for the bedroom.

"Uh … Deke, would it be too much ta ask a little favor of ya?"

"Why no, Shelly, not a'tall. I'd do anything fer you."

"Well," Shelly said, hesitating, "maybe I shouldn't ask it."

"Tell me what it is," Deke said. "It'd make me feel good ta help you out."

"I hate ta mention it, Deke, but do ya 'spose you could ask Zeke if there'd be any way I could git a job in Montana drivin' a log truck; or any kind a' truck for that matter. You know, like if I ever decided ta go out there someday."

"Why sure, Shelly. I'll ask muh brother about it."

Deke sat down on Shelly's bed and dialed his brother's number. When Zeke answered, Deke tried to make pleasant small talk, but his brother sensed the despair in his voice. "You can stop the chatter, Deke. Whadja do now and whadda ya want?'

"Zeke," Deke said, at the point of tears, "I hate askin' fer favors, I jest hate it, you know that, but …"

"How come you keep doin' it then?" Zeke cut in.

"I don't have no choice, Zeke. I had a' accident with the dump truck on Friday."

Zeke breathed in. "Ah jeeze, Deke."

Deke paused to steady his voice. "An' then, a little while later, I had another one … an' I think it mighta been worse'n the first one."

"Did ya hurt or kill anybody, Deke?"

"Naw, I didn't do nothin' that bad, Zeke, but some stuff got wrecked."

"Like what?"

Deke hesitated. "A state highway pickup, the dump truck I was drivin' an' the company's office building."

Deke heard a long, labored sigh on the other end of the line.

"Were ya drunk, Deke, or usin' any drugs when ya did all this?"

"Not much, Zeke, really, not much a'tall. An' I don't think they got any proof even if I was … which I wasn't … too much."

"Deke, I can't keep haulin' you outa things like this. You're twenty-four years old now. You gotta start takin' responsibility."

"I know, Zeke, I know it," Deke said, sobbing, "an' I'm ready ta do that, I really am. But I can't do it here. They called the law, Zeke, an' they wanna throw me in prison for this stuff I accidentally wrecked. They even got the county persecutor after me."

"So what is it you're askin' me to do for ya, Deke?"

"I wanna come out ta Montana, Zeke. You told me I could. You asked me ta do it lots a' times. Said you'd teach me ta drive log truck and help me git a job doin' that. You also said that if I was around you, maybe I wouldn't screw up so much. That's all I want, Zeke, is ta do what you been askin' me to."

The phone was quiet on the Montana end.

"You still there, Zeke?"

"I'm still here, Deke. I'm thinkin' it over." After a few seconds Zeke said, "You still shackin' up with that woman ... what's her name, Debbie?"

"Oh no, Zeke, not a'tall," Deke answered hastily. "I come ta realize we was livin' in sin jest like you said, so I left. I'm all by m'self now, Zeke."

Zeke was in a quandary. He had made that offer to Deke, more than once, and he meant it, but now Deke was on the run from the law.

"Ya promised me, Zeke. You said, 'come out here an' learn ta drive a log truck.'" Deke broke down completely. "Yer the only chance I got left, Zeke," he blubbered into the mouthpiece.

Zeke knew the risks of having Deke in Montana and letting him drive his truck, but he was a Christian man and Deke was his brother. "Okay," he finally said. "You can come out, but there's gonna be some rules. And if you break 'em, even a little, Deke, it's done. You're on your own. Got it?"

"I understand, Zeke, I understand."

"You can stay with me till ya get enough money for your own place, but you can't be drinkin' or using drugs. You need to stop lyin' and you hafta go to church with us."

"I kin do all that, Zeke. All a' that an' more. I wanna do them things. That's the kinda life I really want, Zeke. Jest like you got."

"This is the last time, Deke."

"I know it, Zeke, and I'm thankful to ya, to you an' the Lord, for givin' me one more chance."

Zeke didn't say anything and after a few seconds, Deke said, "Uh, there's one more thing, Zeke, and I hate ta ask it, I really do, but I might need a little money ta git there. I ain't got but three dollars. I never got my paycheck yet for them las' two weeks I worked an' I likely owe the company more for the pickup an' the dump truck an' the office that got wrecked than I got comin' on my check."

"You do that math all by yourself, did ya Deke?"

"Listen Zeke, I don't need much. Jest enough for gas an' ta pick up some baloney an' crackers for the way out."

"You realize, don't ya Deke, that I'm tryin' to support a family and pay off my logging truck?"

"I know that, Zeke, an that's why I'm sorry for askin."

"Don't ya have anything you could sell or pawn?"

"Jest my guns. I got eight guns, but I can't sell them, I like 'em too much."

"Yeah, Deke, you can sell them. And if ya wanta come to Montana you will sell them. Take them to the pawnshop tomorrow. That'll give ya enough money to get here and then some. You need to take responsibility for what ya done … and I need ta go ta bed now on account a' I gotta be up at four-thirty. If you decide to sell your guns and come out here, I'll do just what I said. Good bye, Deke."

The phone went dead. Deke had stopped crying by the time he came out of the bedroom but his eyes were wet and red. He leaned against the doorway, exhausted.

"Well?" Shelly asked.

"Zeke says I can come out. He'll teach me ta drive his log truck an' fix me up with a job."

"I'm glad for ya, Deke" Shelly said, but her voice was flat.

"I guess so," Deke answered, "but he wouldn't send me no money fer the trip so the only way I can get there is ta sell my guns … an' I really don't wanna do that." Deke sniffed and drew his arm across his nose. "I know you got a bank account, Shelly," he said. "I don't s'pose you could stand me some cash to git ta Montana?"

A low growl rose from Shelly. "Uuurrr …how dare you!" Deke took a step back as Shelly wagged her finger at him. "How fucking dare you!"

"I'm sorry I asked, Shelly. I didn't mean to make ya mad."

"How can you be so selfish? You destroyed thousands an' thousands a' dollars worth a' other people's property," Shelly raged, "an' if they catch ya yor lookin' at prison. Here's your brother offerin' you a way out, riskin' himself an' his truck to help ya an' all you kin think about is havin' to sell your guns. Don't you ever think a' nobody but yor'self?"

Deke started crying and backpedaled around the room with Shelly in close pursuit.

"Quit bawlin' like a damn baby. You can sell a few ol' guns an' run away from all the trouble you caused. You git ta go out west an' drive a log truck. I never did one thing wrong, but what'll I be doing while yor truck drivin' in Montana? Huh? I got no job, no car an' no place to go. I oughta be the one cryin', Deke McConahay, not you!"

Shelly stopped to catch her breath.

"You'll be eighteen soon," Deke said. "You can get a job dancin' at some other bar then. With the body you got, any place'd hire ya."

"I ain't goin' back into some dirty dive ev'ry night," Shelly shouted with renewed fury, "wigglin' around near naked in fronta a bunch a' drunk men, all of 'em thinkin' about dickin' me. Damn you anyway, Deke McConahay," Shelly screamed, "you got nothin' to cry about, so shut the fuck up!"

Deke stopped crying ... and Shelly started. Spreading his long arms, Deke moved towards Shelly to embrace her but she backed away and raised her fists.

"Don'tchoo dare putch your hands on me!"

Deke stopped in his tracks. "Yer right, Shelly. I know yer right. I'll sell my guns t'morrow an' go ta Montana an' make somethin' outa myself. Maybe someday I'll git my own log truck, or a whole fleet a' log trucks, an' you'll think better a' me and come out ta Montana. I could teach ya ta drive my log truck. You might even git yer own truck someday too."

Shelly quit crying and looked at Deke like she was trying to remember something.

Deke continued. "Zeke's told me how purty it is where he lives. There's great big mountains with snow on 'em, an' wild rivers an' waterfalls. He says it's still kinda like the Old West an' you can do about anything ya want out there if ya work hard at it."

Now Shelly remembered what she had been trying to think of.

"Deke," she said, wiping her eyes, "did ya ask your brother if he thought I could git a job drivin' truck too, you know, like if I ever went out there sometime?"

Deke's eyes went wide with the remembrance that he forgot.

"Oh yeah, Shelly, I asked 'im. Zeke told me there's all kinds a' truck drivin' jobs in Montana. He said that with the experience you got from me teachin' ya, you could likely git a job out there real easy. Zeke said he'd even help ya out learnin' ta drive his log truck an' findin' a job if ya ever come out someday."

"Really? Zeke would teach me ta drive his log truck an' help me find a job?"

"Uh … yeah … I reckon so … " Deke said, feeling like he'd had this conversation with Shelly before.

Shelly stared at Deke. His brother's description of Montana had put visions into her mind: a vast land of rivers, mountains, wild beauty and opportunity, still open and free, where a person with grit could become whatever he or she chose. Montana. Shelly even liked the sound of it, the way the word rolled on her tongue. The idea welled up in her as big as the state itself and the words slipped out before Shelly even knew she'd said them. "I wanta go to Montana with ya."

Deke gaped at Shelly in disbelief. Such was his discombobulation over her request that Deke's mind traveled to a seldom visited part of his brain, the tiny spot where reason and sense resided. For a moment he remained quiet, engaged in thought, and for once, the thoughts that Deke's mind begat were not intercepted and altered by his pecker. "Shelly, I'd love ta take ya," he said. "I'd just love to … but I can't."

Shelly couldn't believe her ears. "Why? I got money for my share a' the trip."

"It ain't that, Shelly. An' sayin' this might be the hardest thing I ever done in my life, even harder'n sellin' my guns t'morrow, but I gotta be honest with ya."

Deke removed his dirty white cowboy hat and ran his fingers through his long, greasy hair, as if he were about to do some – as Davy Crockett called it – speechifyin'.

"Shelly, I'd give anything, anything a'tall to have you go with me out ta Montana, but I can't do it. It'd be too hard on me with you sittin' beside me the whole time an' us bein' t'gether at night but you not bein' my girlfriend or nothin'. I'd be miser'ble every single minute. Kinda like how you said you'd be if ya had to go back ta dancin'."

Deke shuffled back and forth on his feet, curling up the sides of his cowboy hat, like he was wringing his words from it.

"That's what drove me crazy, Shelly … drove me ta drinkin' an' tokin' up on the job, bein' so close to ya like that, but not bein' able ta do nothin' about it. I never done that kinda stuff before when I was workin'.

"I know you think all I want is ta screw ya but it ain't so. My feelin's fer you are real. I wanna hold ya an' tell ya how much I love ya … an' do stuff t'gether … all a' them things that boyfriends an' girlfriends do. If I can't be yer boyfriend then I need ta not be near ya a'tall or I'll jest go back ta bein' all messed up. I promised my brother I wouldn't do that no more an' I gotta keep my word. I'm sorry, Shelly."

Shelly looked at Deke like she had just watched an orangutan recite The Gettysburg Address. This was the first time he'd been completely honest with her and Shelly looked past the bedraggled stray in her living room and saw the human being that stood before her. Deke was not inherently revolting or ugly, and if he trimmed his hair and beard, showered and put on some nice clothes, he wouldn't be a bad looking man. Not up there with Ferlin Husky, but tolerable. Deke's eyes had moistened and Shelly saw, or thought she saw, kindness and caring in them. Maybe, with some prodding, Deke could be straightened out.

"Is that the only reason ya won't take me, Deke?" she asked.

Before he answered, Deke thought of how he'd made everything up about Zeke teaching Shelly to drive and finding her a job. He also knew that if he arrived at his Baptist brother's house with Shelly in tow, Zeke would give him the boot.

"Yeah, Shelly, I swear it is," he lied.

"Okay, Deke. If I can go ta Montana with ya I'll be your girlfriend."

Deke's head almost exploded. His jaw fell and his brain whirled round like someone had dropped it into a blender. He nearly twisted his cowboy hat in half.

"Do ya really mean it, Shelly?"

"I mean it … Deke," Shelly said slowly, wondering what had gotten into her.

Deke put his crinkled hat back on and covered the two steps between them in a flash. He threw his arms around Shelly and hugged her close to him, feeling, finally, her warm female body pressed against his. Shelly didn't resist or back up, but she kept her arms at her sides.

"Ohhhhh" Deke moaned, then excitedly said, "I'll change my ways, Shelly. I'll change the way I am. I'll change what I am. If ya want, I'll even change who I am. An' I'll be real good to ya, I promise, Shelly. I'll do whatever ya want, I swear."

Deke's world had again aligned to its normal order: the little head did the thinking for the big head, and once Shelly saw it, she knew she was holding a straight flush to Deke's pair of threes.

"That's right, Deke," she told him, "ya will. Leastwise if you want me ta stay bein' your girlfriend, ya will."

"Uh, Shelly," Deke said into her ear, "do ya s'pose we could start bein' boyfriend and girlfriend right now?"

"No!" Shelly said, extricating herself from Deke's grasp. "We don't start bein' boyfriend an' girlfriend till after we leave for Montana." Shelly took a step away from Deke. "You gotta prove ta me that ya really meant all them things you was sayin'. And there's conditions too, Deke."

Deke was mighty let down, especially as part of him had already come up. But after holding Shelly against him Deke was willing to go along with anything. "What kinda conditions?" he asked.

"Firstly," Shelly said with authority, "you need ta change your ways about lyin'. That GTO wasn't yours an' neither was the Brockway. You weren't no race car driver, neither. You only drove one once and ya wrecked it."

"Ya got my word as a gentleman," Deke told her, solemnly raising his right hand, "and a scholarman too. From this day on ever'thing I say'll be the gospel truth, and I'll swear to it on a Bible."

Shelly looked over at Clete's Bible, still lying on the table from where she had been reading it earlier. She picked the Good Book up and thrust it toward Deke. "Okay," she said, "swear to it."

As Shelly held it, Deke placed his palm on the Bible and said, "I swear on this Bible that I won't lie no more."

Deke went to remove his hand but Shelly put her hand over his and held it fast.

"You also gotta swear that ya won't fool around with other women while I'm your girlfriend, an' that ya won't git all messed up on liquor an' drugs like ya do."

"Would that mean I can't take a drink or smoke a little weed now an' again?"

"That ain't what I'm sayin', Deke. I mean you can't git all screwed up on it so's you don't know what yor doin', like what happened on Friday."

"Okay," Deke said, drawing a long breath. "I swear not ta screw no women ... this don't include you does it, Shelly?"

Shelly was beginning to wonder if she was doing the right thing making Deke swear on the Bible. "No, Deke, just other women," she said.

Deke began once more. "I swear not ta screw no other women but Shelly, leastwise as long as she keeps lettin' me screw her ... "

"Deke!"

Deke gulped, wanting to get this over with. "An' I promise not ta get all fucked up on booze an' dope no more. But I might still have me a little bit now an' then."

"Deke," Shelly said, "yor talkin' ta God – with your hand on the Bible, my daddy's Bible. Swearin' on the Bible don't mean usin' swear words."

"Oh, sorry about that," Deke said and continued. "Lord, fer'give me them bad words. I meant what I said but not the words I said it in."

Shelly put the Bible back on the table and Deke said to her, "We done with all the conditions now?"

"No," Shelly said, not particularly happy at how the Bible swearing had gone. "I got two, no, three more."

"Three more? That's a whole bunch, Shelly."

"They won't be that hard ta do," Shelly said, as Deke began to frown. "First."

"This one ain't the first," Deke interrupted, "it's the fourth."

"Alright then, fourth. We both pay our own way on the trip. We split ev'rything down the middle."

"I wanna do that too," Deke said.

"Fifth," Shelly said. "I want ya ta take me back ta Peapatch for a few days so I can see my family."

"We'll do it. I understand ya wantin' that, Shelly."

"And last," Shelly said. "I wanta take our time gittin' ta Montana. I ain't hardly been nowhere in this country and I don't wanta jes blow through it on the interstate. We gotta drive on back roads so we can meet people. We can even stop at some friendly bars if you don't git drunk or stupid. I wanta stay in little towns too, not in cities, an' eat at real rest'ernts run by real people, not them phoney ones like McDonalds. An' I wanta stay in nice, clean motels."

Thinking about that last request made Deke want to hit the road right then. "Why sure, Shelly, all that sounds real good ta me. That's how I like ta travel, too," Deke said, as if he had actually done it. "We'll take as long as ya want goin' ta Montana."

"An' when we git in the West," Shelly continued, "the real West, I wanta meet some cowboys an' Indians and maybe even ride a horse. I wanta have fun on this trip."

"Oh, that'd be great, Shelly, that'd be real great," Deke agreed, grinning. "You got me all fired up about this trip, now. I've always wanted ta go out west an' fight outlaws an' In'juns an' cross deserts and mountain passes in snowstorms. It'll be real excitin' Shelly, jest like we're pioneers."

Shelly tilted her head back and laughed. "Deke, that sounds plenty exciting, but I don't think none a' that's gonna happen. You been watchin' too many westerns. This ain't 1873, it's 1973, an' that kinda stuff quit happenin' a hund'ert years ago."

"I reckon," Deke said, "but, shitfire, yer right about me lovin' westerns. They always been my favorite movies, 'specially the ones with John Wayne. That's why I got him on my belt buckle."

Shelly was in a good mood now, too. "Oh, I 'spose we'll have us a few adventures, Deke. I hope so, too."

"I want some real adventures, Shelly," Deke said. "I hope we git ourselves in some real tough fixes where a man has ta prove up. Since yer my girlfriend now ... or about ta be ... you need to know what kind a' man I am when the chips are down, an' that I can take care a' myself , an' you too, if need be."

Shelly almost laughed until she saw how serious Deke was. "This trip is gonna be somethin', Deke, I jes know it," she said, smiling.

Then she remembered something and stopped smiling. "There's one last thing, Deke, an' I'm dead cold serious about it."

"You jest said that other'n was the last," Deke said.

"Well, it wasn't," Shelly told him. "No dope on the trip, an' I mean it. I ain't endin' up in no dirt-floor calaboose two thousand miles away."

"Okay," Deke said. "I ain't got none anyway. I smoked it all up when I was hidin' out in my pickup."

"All right, then," Shelly said, "we got us a deal."

"Deal," Deke said, and moved in to give Shelly a kiss, but Shelly quickly stuck out her hand and said, "Shake on it."

After they'd shaken hands Deke said, "Shelly, you ain't said nothin' about it, but I got no place ta go t'night. Can I stay here?"

"Reckon so, Deke. If the law's really after ya, we better git goin' ta'morrow. You can sleep on the couch."

Deke looked glum but didn't say anything.

"Listen, Deke," Shelly said, "you gotta understand that this all come about real sudden. It'll take me a while ta git used to it, but once were travelin' to Montana we'll sleep together. I won't keep puttin' ya off … an' that's a promise."

"I understand, Shelly," Deke said, even though he didn't.

"Do ya need to git some stuff outa your truck tonight?"

"I do," Deke answered, "an' I don't wanna leave my truck parked out on the street. If the cops see it, they'll know I'm here."

"I think yor worryin' way too much about the cops, Deke, but if it'll make ya sleep easier, there's an old garage behind the building here that nobody uses."

Shelly and Deke went downstairs to where his pickup sat curbside. Deke opened the door of a 1962 Ford half-ton that had seen better days – probably by 1963. Motley and brindled with rust, the poor beast rested wearily on its worn shocks and sported dents like spots on a leopard.

"I hope you won the demolition derby it was in," Shelly said.

"This ol' pickup might look a little rough, Shelly, but she'll make it ta Montana. Leastwise, I'm purty sure she will," Deke replied.

Deke got in and cranked the engine. The starter made a loud grinding sound before it finally took hold. They drove around back to the alley and Shelly had Deke pull into a doorless garage. Deke climbed into the cluttered back of his pickup and unlocked the hasp on a large, sturdy wooden bin that was bolted to the front of the bed. He reached in and handed a heavy duffel bag down to Shelly.

When they got back to the apartment, Shelly pointed him to a door. "There's the bathroom if ya wanta clean up."

"Okay," Deke said, and stood looking at her.

"Deke," Shelly said, "I don't want ya to take this wrong, but since we're gonna be together I need ta tell ya somethin'. Yor not a bad lookin' man, but if ya trimmed your hair and beard some, took a shower an' put on some clean clothes, you'd look a whole lot better. It'd make our relationship a lot more enjoyable ... when it happens."

Deke didn't say anything and Shelly couldn't tell if he was hurt, mad, or just didn't know what to say. Finally she said, "Tell ya what, Deke, you give me your dirty clothes an' I'll wash 'em up in the laundry down the hall whiles you take a shower." She grabbed the spread from the couch and handed it to Deke. "You can wear this till your clothes are dry."

Deke hesitated. "Okay, Shelly," he said and went into the bathroom. Two minutes later he opened the door a crack and tossed out his clothes. An hour and a half later, Deke stood before Shelly, scrubbed down and in clean duds, and if not quite a new man, he was at least better than the old one.

Shelly smiled approvingly. "Deke, I think we're off to a good start." She drew in close to give him a kiss and grimaced. "Didja brush your teeth when you were in there?"

"Uh, I don't have a ... what I mean is, I fergot ta grab my toothbrush when I left in a hurry." Sensing that he wouldn't get the kiss, Deke said, "Maybe I could borrow yers."

Not ready for that close of a relationship - now or ever - Shelly said, "Hang on a second, I got a spare one you can have," and went into her bedroom.

"Here ya go," she said, handing Deke the toothbrush. "There's toothpaste on the counter ... an' mouthwash too."

Deke came out of the bathroom smiling, hoping for the kiss, but Shelly said, "We better git some sleep, there's a whole lot we gotta do ta'morrow." She made up the couch for Deke to sleep on and turned to go into her bedroom. "See ya in the morning, Deke."

"Do ya reckon I could kiss ya goodnight, Shelly?"

Shelly looked at Deke, suddenly aware that soon they'd be doing a whole lot more than just kissing. "I 'spose ya kin," she said and walked over to him.

Deke put his arms around Shelly and pressed his lips to hers. Shelly cradled Deke's head in her hands and returned his kiss, not as passionately as Deke had hoped for, and his probing tongue failed to penetrate her sealed lips, but it was a start.

Shelly disengaged from the kiss, went into her bedroom and closed the door. She knew she needed to sleep, but lay in the dark, listening to the night sounds of Norwood outside her window. This past weekend had been a blurred and swirling dream.

Don't that jes beat all, she thought, ta'morrow I'm off to start a new life in Montana.

Chapter 16

Monday, September 17, 1973

Shelly popped awake at 6:30, got dressed and woke up Deke on the couch. He'd slept with his clothes on, ready to bolt if the cops showed up and told Shelly, "I'm purty much ready ta go. Whyn't you get yer stuff ready and I'll cook breakfast."

Deke searched the fridge and cupboards and half an hour later presented Shelly with a plate of ham, fried eggs, waffles, and toast. It was good and Shelly was impressed. "Deke, you can cook," she said. "I thought you ate baloney and crackers ev'ry morning."

"That's only when I'm workin'," Deke said. "After Zeke left for the Army I had ta help raise my little sister an' I cooked breakfast for 'er ever' day."

Shelly sat down at the table and ate with Deke and then began sorting and packing as he cleaned up and washed the dishes. By 7:45 Shelly was making good progress.

"I'm gonna call home ta let 'em know we're comin'," she told Deke.

"Ain't it kinda early?"

"Nah, it's Monday morning. Everbody'll be up gittin ready for school."

Shelly took the phone into her room and closed the door. She wasn't sure what Ethel would say, or if she'd even be welcome when Ethel found out she was bringing a man along. Half an hour later Shelly came out and told Deke, "They're expectin' us for dinner. Mama says she'll hold it till we git there if it ain't too late."

Shelly's household items were limited and by a quarter past nine she had her possessions sorted into three piles. "This goes ta Montana," she told Deke, pointing at her loaded knapsack and suitcase. Indicating the second heap, she said, "All this is junk an' we can put it in the trash bin by the alley. I can give the rest a' this stuff to Mrs. Wallace down the hall. She ain't got much an' there's things here she could use."

Shelly turned toward her door and Deke headed for the bathroom. "Gotta take a leak," he announced, "my eyeballs are floatin'."

"Deke, you don't hafta inform me about what yor gonna do in the ..."

Shelly's words and Deke's trip to the toilet were interrupted by pounding on the apartment door.

"It's the cops," Deke whispered. "Don't let 'em in."

"It ain't the cops, Deke. What would they be doin' here at this time a' the mornin'?"

Deke only heard the first four words because he shot into the bedroom and skittered under the bed. Shelly was laughing at Deke when she opened the door but her laugh died when two badges were thrust in her face. Behind them were two plain clothesmen ... very plain clothesmen.

"I'm Sergeant Long, from the Norwood Police Department" the short one said. "Are you Shelly Stamper?"

Shelly touched the top of her head. "The whole way up ta here."

"And I'm officer Sweet" said the tall one, who's facial expression suggested he was anything but. "Why were you laughing?"

" 'Cause I knew it'd be the cops," Shelly answered, then forced another laugh when she told them, "An' I know why yor here."

Long said "Good" at the same time Sweet said, "You do?"

Shelly answered Sweet. "Course I do. It's about that drunk I punched at Hillbilly Heaven Friday night fer goosin' me. Look, fellas, I didn't mean to hit 'im so hard, but I ain't lettin' nobody stick his finger up my butt."

Long and Sweet stared silently at Shelly, either at a loss for words or else perversely picturing the scene. Shelly stretched out her long arms, indicating they should put the cuffs on her wrists. "But I'm guilty of it," she said. "Take me ta jail."

"Uh, that's not why we're here ma'am," Sweet said, sounding confused.

Long covered for him. "We're looking for Deke McConahay."

"You an' half a' Norwood," Shelly said, and laughed again. "I heard about what he done on Friday."

"You can cut the crap right now," Sergeant Long said. "We know you were with him and we have evidence that drugs and alcohol were involved."

"I ain't sayin' if I was or if I wasn't," Shelly said, "but it don't matter, 'cause I didn't do none of it anyhow."

"There are witnesses who saw you driving that dump truck over the course of several weeks before the incident occurred," Sweet said. "We checked and you don't have a driver's license."

"Yeah, well, ya never caught me at it if I did," Shelly said, her humor gone. "If yor gonna arrest me then do it right now and git it over with."

"We didn't come here for you, Shelly," Long said, easing off. "We came on the possibility McConahay might have run here to hide or maybe you know where he is."

"He didn't an' I don't," Shelly said with what she hoped was finality.

Under the bed, Deke heard every word and breathed a quiet sigh that Shelly didn't give him away, but he desperately had to pee.

"Harboring a fugitive is a felony," Long said. "Don't get yourself in trouble over a worthless piece of dirt like McConahay."

Deke stiffened.

"Listen, I'll give it to ya straight," Shelly said, trying to sound the way she'd heard people talk to cops in the movies. "This is the last place that lyin', deceitful, skunk Deke McConahay would come."

Deke grimmaced.

"After what he done, an' gittin my good name involved in it – even though I might not a' been there – he knows that whatever the law's gonna do to 'im I'll do way worse if I git to 'im first."

"We believe you, ma'am," Sergeant Long said, smiling.

"But just to make sure he didn't slip in when you weren't home, we'd like to check your apartment," Sweet said, trying, but failing miserably to live up to his name.

Curled up and cramped, Deke was terrified that they were going to search the apartment and nearly as afraid that he would wet himself. He gritted his teeth and clamped his knees together.

"Ya got a search warrant?" Shelly said, moving to block their entry.

"No," Long answered, "but if McConahay isn't here, what are you worried about? If we don't find him here then you're in the clear and we can look somewhere else."

"You won't find 'im here, I am in the clear, and you kin look somewheres else," Shelly said. "I got girly stuff in here that I don't want y'all pawin' through. I'm a modest woman. Either git a search warrant or go away. I got things ta do."

Both cops knew that Shelly was a bar dancer and they looked at her with disgust.

"All right, Shelly," Sergeant Long said, "Here's a card with my phone number on it. If you see Deke McConahay call me."

Shelly ignored the card. "I don't need your card. If I see Deke McConahay I won't be callin' you, you'll be callin' the coroner."

The two men looked at the tall, rawboned woman plugging the doorway, then looked at each other, thinking, Hmmm, maybe this girl would kill McConahay … and that would be okay too.

Both cops put an index finger to their foreheads, nodded to Shelly in unison, said "Good day, ma'am," then turned and walked down the hall.

Deke struggled from beneath the bed and ran into the bathroom. He came out trembling. "Shitfire, that was close. If I hadn't a' crawled under the bed, they'd a' got me. How soon can we git goin'?"

"Well, les' see; I need ta give this stuff ta Mrs. Wallace and carry this other pile downstairs to the trash. Reckon I oughta tell the landlady I'm leavin' an' clean the place up some." Shelly paused, thinking. "I'll need ta go to the bank an' cash the check Bussy give me and take out some money for the trip."

"That's a lot ta do," Deke said, frowning.

He frowned even more when Shelly said, 'An' we gotta stop at the pawn shop so's you can sell your guns."

"I jest wanna git outa Norwood," Deke said nervously. "Clean out of Ohio, really. Once'd I'm in another state I'll be a whole lot safer."

Shelly opened the door and peeked out cautiously. "I'm gonna take these things to Mrs. Wallace," she told Deke. "Keep the door locked." After she returned, Shelly looked at the junk pile. "I better carry this stuff down by myself so nobody sees ya."

Shelly made two trips. When she finished Deke was in obvious distress.

"I'm scared shitless them cops are gonna come back, Shelly. Can we hurry up an' git outa here." ·

"Alright," Shelly said. "Reckon we don't have time ta clean this place up proper. I'll let the landlady know I'm leavin' an' she can keep some a' the deposit."

Shelly returned from the landlady's and gave one final look around her apartment. She opened the door to her refrigerator and hiding behind the mustard was a lone can of Falstaff beer. While stuffing it into her knapsack she noticed a picture that had fallen face down on the counter. "Oh Lordy," she said, "I almost forgot this," and walked over and snatched the photograph.

"What is it?" Deke asked.

"It's my autographed picture a' Ferlin Husky that he signed for me at the state fair," Shelly said, looking at the photo. "I can't b'lieve I almost walked off without it." She opened her suitcase and carefully tucked the picture away. "Well, I guess that's it, Deke, we can leave now."

Shelly grabbed her knapsack and suitcase and Deke picked up his duffel bag. As soon as Shelly opened the door, Deke pushed past her and ran down the hall and the stairway. When Shelly got to the truck, Deke was waiting, looking scared and breathing hard. He dug under the seat and pulled out a ratty, oil-stained sweatshirt and put it on, cinching the hood tight around his face. In the glovebox he found a pair of mirrored sunglasses with a cracked lense.

"Is all that git-up necessary, Deke?" Shelly said, laughing. "You look like you escaped from the nut house."

Without a word, Deke got behind the steering wheel, depressed the clutch and twisted the key. Nothing. "Ohhhh ..." Deke moaned. "Please ... please start."

Shelly's heart missed a beat but she steadied herself. "Think Deke, think. What could it be? A dead battery?"

"Likely not, Shelly," Deke said, tears of frustration pooling in his eyes. "I jest bought one from a guy at work an' he tol' me it was good."

"Let's look under the hood."

Deke hoisted the bonnet. Both battery cables were disconnected.

"Oh yeah," Deke said, "I fergot. I took 'em off last night when I came back down so's nobody could steal it. Purty smart, huh?"

Shelly shook her head. "Brilliant Deke, jes brilliant."

They got in the cab and Deke turned the key. For thirty seconds the starter coughed and spit. "Don't worry," Deke said, "it purt' near always starts."

Finally the engine came to life.

"I thought we might hafta do CPR on this thing," Shelly said.

Deke backed the Ford out of the garage and into the alley, pulled onto the street and gave it gas. "I'm headin' straight fer the Ohio River bridge, the sooner we git across'd it the better."

"Ain't you forgettin' somethin', Deke?"

"What?"

"I gotta go to the bank first an' you need ta sell your guns."

Deke flinched.

"My bank's only down the street a ways," Shelly said, "an' I'll only be in there a minute or two." She looked at Deke. "But in that outfit you better wait in the truck or they'll think yor there to rob it."

After the bank, Deke drove to a pawnshop he knew about in Finney-town, nervously checking his rear-view mirror every two seconds. After he parked on a sidestreet Shelly said to him, "You ain't wearin' that git-up inside, are ya?"

"You bet. They might rec'nize me an' call the cops."

"You ain't John Dillinger, Deke," Shelly said. "I ain't seen your picture up in no post offices."

"How d'ya know? You been in any post offices since I became an outlaw?"

"Deke, you gotta git rid a' that goofy outfit or they will call the cops. You look like a fifteen year old boy buyin' his first pack a' rubbers."

"Alright, I'll take my sweatshirt off," Deke said, "but I'm keepin' the glasses." He looked in the mirror. "They look good on me."

He got the duffel bag that contained his guns — two pistols, four rifles, and two shotguns — out of the wooden trunk in the bed and lugged it into the shop. Twenty minutes later he returned carrying a much lighter duffel bag. "I couldn't sell my Winchester .30-30," he told Shelly. "It's a pre '64 model that my daddy give me on my twelfth birthday, jest b'fore him an' mom died in a car wreck. An' they weren't gonna give me hardly nothin' for my double-barrel 10 gauge 'cause they said it's got old style Damascus barrels, so I kept it too. I kinda wanted ta keep it anyway 'cause it belonged ta my great-grandpappy an' he kilt a Jenkins with it.

"What's a Jenkins?" Shelly asked. "I don't believe I've ever seen one."

"Jenkins was a family us McConahays were feudin' with a long time ago. An' we still don't like each other much. Anyways, I got $820. Now I jest wanna git the hell out of Ohio."

This time the Ford fired right up, as if it also wanted to get the hell out of Ohio. Deke sweated his way through Cincinnati with Shelly constantly reminding him to keep to the speed limit. When the massive, century old stone towers of the Roebling Bridge peaked into view over the rooftops, Deke's relief was palpable. He smiled at Shelly and said, "It looks like we made -

"DEEEEEKE!!!"

Deke looked at Shelly in alarm.

"DEEEEEKE!" she screamed again. "PULL OVER!"

"What's wrong?" Deke asked.

"You got ta pull over right now, Deke," Shelly cried. "I jes remembered, I ain't Shelly Stamper."

"Sure ya are. Who else would ya be?" Deke asked as he pulled to the curb.

"I'm Shelly Stidhams. Me an' Jim are still married. I got ta git divorced before I can start a new life in Montana."

"Can't ya divorce Jim in Montana after we git there?" Deke said.

"Nope. I need ta start my new life bein' who I really am."

Deke put the shifter in neutral and turned to Shelly. "I'm a wanted man, Shelly. We're only two blocks from Kentucky an' freedom. You can't do this ta me."

"Nope," Shelly said again, crossing her arms and jutting her chin out. "I come ta Ohio as Shelly Stamper an' I'm leavin' Ohio as Shelly Stamper."

Deke looked at the bridge up ahead and tried not to cry.

Shelly said nothing, her will set in concrete.

"Where'd ya git married at?" Deke asked.

Shelly thought for a minute. "I think it was called the The True Savior Gospel Church. Jim's uncle Clyde married us."

Deke, who had been through one or two of these rituals himself, asked, "Did ya git a marriage license or fill out any papers an' file 'em with the state recorder?"

"Nope. We just got up in front a' the preacher an' said our vows."

"Then ya ain't legally married," Deke said.

"Sure I'm legally married, we did it in a church an' all."

"Shelly, you ain't *legally* married unless ya get a marriage license and file it with the state. Did them cops ask fer Shelly Stidhams or Shelly Stamper?"

"Shelly Stamper."

"Well, see," Deke said, "yer not really married 'cause nobody legal even knows about your weddin'."

"God knows, an' He's legal," Shelly said. "Like I told ya, we done it in a church."

"Alright," Deke said, "tell ya what. We'll go find the preacher that married ya an' you can tell him – and God – yer gittin' divorced. How about that?"

"I don't think the preacher'd go fer that, Deke. When he married us, he said it was till death do us part."

"Well, how about this then? We go back ta that church right now an' you put your right hand on the church and swear your divorce on it, jest like I did with the Bible last night."

Shelly thought it over. "Yeah, I could do that."

Turning away from Kentucky nearly tore Deke's heart out, but back they went into Norwood, driving in circles as Shelly tried to remember where the church was located. "I know it was near some old railroad tracks," she said, as Deke muttered to himself.

"If we can git close to it, maybe we'll see the steeple," Deke said.

"Oh, it ain't got no steeple, Deke, it's jes this half-round metal thing."

Deke's face lit up. "Why, shitfire, I got mar … uh … I know right where it is."

Deke hid his pickup behind the empty church and they walked around to the front. The door was locked but the front window was propped open and covered only by a screen. As reverently as she knew how, Shelly placed her right palm on the front of the church and shouted into the open window.

"God, I'm here ta divorce Jim Stidhams. I wanta be Shelly Stamper again. Preacher Clyde said our marriage was 'sposed to be forever but Jim kept goin' out and screwin' other women and not comin' home. I won't put up with that, God, an' I know You wouldn't either. I promise, God, me and Jim will be divorced till death do us part and I'll be more careful next time. I was only sixteen when I married Jim Stidhams and it was wrong. I'm seventeen now and know better. So now I swear and declare on Your church, God, that me and Jim Stidhams is *officially* divorced in Your eyes. Amen."

Deke added his "Amen."

They got back into the pickup. The battery cranked at the starter and Deke sweated in apprehension until the engine fired up. As they drove through Cincinnati for the second time Deke was beside himself with fear. His knees were shaking and his head swiveled round looking for cops. Shelly was now almost as nervous. When they again caught sight of the Roebling Bridge towers Deke exhaled in relief and then checked the rearview mirror and saw a police car following them.

"Shitfire! It's the cops," Deke said, and his entire body began trembling.

Shelly looked in the side mirror and forced down her own rising panic. "Jes be calm, Deke, an' drive normal," she said. Then Shelly remembered who she was talking to. "No Deke, don't drive normal the way you normally drive normal, drive normal the way normal people drive normal."

Deke's stomach balled into a knot. Neither he nor Shelly could take their eyes from the mirror. Six blocks to the bridge, five, then four: "I think we might make it," Deke said shakily.

Shelly gave him a weak thumb's up. "There's the ramp," she said when they were two blocks from the bridge. "Them cops'll have ta turn aroun' 'cause they can't go inta Kentucky."

The scream of a siren shattered the air behind them and Deke and Shelly's heads nearly hit the roof. Red flashing lights reflected against the pickup's windshield.

"I think I'm gonna shit muh pants," Deke said.

"Don't do that, Deke. That won't help nothin'."

"Ohhhhhhhh," Deke wailed as tears ran down his cheeks. "I'm too scare't ta stop. We gotta make a run fer Kentucky."

"Don't do nothin' stupid, Deke," Shelly pleaded. "You promised me ya wouldn't."

Just as Deke started to tromp the accelerator two cars went by in the opposite lane of traffic and the police car whipped a u-turn and sped off. Shelly twisted around and watched the cruiser disappear, siren singing and top lights winking goodbye to them. "Them cops weren't after us a'tall, Deke. They had somewhere's else ta go and was waitin' ta turn around."

Deke wanted to pull over and calm down but they were already headed up the bridge ramp. With hands trembling and bowels pleading, Deke somehow kept himself together. When they reached the center of the bridge Shelly began laughing. They floated over the broad, brown Ohio River more on a cloud than a bridge and by the time they were descending the far side, Deke had calmed down and was smiling. As they sailed passed the 'Welcome to Kentucky' sign, he and Shelly let out whoops of joy.

"We made it, Deke," Shelly exclaimed. "I almost wanta shout and sing."

"Me too, Shelly," Deke said, as some of his old cockiness returned. He yelled "Yehaw! We're goin' ta Montana!" and started singing to the tune of "The Old Chisholm Trail":

"Well I went downstairs, ta get a glass a' cider

There sat a cockroach jackin' off a spider

Gonna tie my pecker to my leg, to my leg, gonna tie my pecker to my leg."

Shelly turned toward Deke with a *look* – which he mis-interpreted as wanting him to continue.

"Got my eyes on the road and my foot on the gas

A hand fulla pussy and a fist fulla ass

Gonna tie my pecker to my leg, to my leg, gonna tie my pecker to my leg."

Shelly gave Deke another *look* but this time she added, "Alright, Deke, you don't hafta sing no more. I git the idea."

Deke quit singing. "We gotta stop soon," he said, "I really need ta blow a load."

"I got an idea," Shelly said, "besides you not singin' no more. It's a little before noon, let's stop an' have lunch."

Colonel Sanders had obligingly placed a chicken stand only a few miles ahead. Deke whipped the Ford in close to the front entrance and raced for the bathroom.

Shelly went in and ordered a bucket of chicken, along with mashed potatoes and gravy and coleslaw and by the time Deke came out of the bathroom the meal was ready. Shelly wanted to ask Deke if he'd washed his hands, but she didn't, and tried not to think about it. Instead, she said, "This one's on me, Deke. Whadaya want ta drink?"

"I'll have me a big RC Cola."

They went back to Deke's pickup, glad to once again be in Appalachia. Shelly dipped into the bucket and pulled out a drumstick. Deke snaked a hand towards her and giggled. "Mind if I grab a breast?"

"The last guy who did lost his teeth," Shelly said, as she pulled one out of the bucket and thrust it into Deke's reaching fingers.

Deke gnawed on the chicken until he'd reduced it to a greasy carcass and went to throw it out of the truck's open window.

"Don't do that!" Shelly yelled at him. "That's litterin'. Ain't you got no manners a'tall, Deke?"

Deke held up the remains as if inspecting them. "Reckon I do," he said and dropped the bones on the floor at Shelly's feet.

Shelly shook her chicken leg at him. "Sometimes, Deke, I jes don't get you. You act like an animal."

"Chistamighty, woman, but yer hard ta please," Deke said, wiping his hands on his jeans.

Shelly'd heard men say 'woman' like that before. She didn't like it, but she also didn't feel like having a big fight. "Let's jes git goin'," she said. "I got family waitin'."

"Sounds good ta me," Deke agreed, and turned the key.

AAARRRRRUH-RUH-RUH-RUH-AAARRRRRUH-RUH-RUH-RUH-AAARRRRUH-RUH-RUH-RUH

Now that the Ford had gotten the hell out of Ohio it was content to stay right where it was.

AAARRRRRUH-RUH-RUH-RUH-AAARRRRRUH-RUH-RUH-RUH-AAARRRRUH-RUH-RUH-RUH

"Don't worry," Deke said, "the battery's strong."

AAARRRRRUH-RUH-RUH-RUH – AAARRRRRUH-RUH-RUH-RUH-AAARRRRRUH-RUH-RUH-RUH –

Deke held off for a minute to let the pickup catch its breath. "She'll turn over. She always does."

He twisted the key and coaxed the Ford's engine one more time.

AAARRRRRUH-RUH-RUH-Ruh – Ruh...ruh ....ruh ... ...ruh ...

The truck was quiet for a second, then went ...ruhruhruh ...in a quick shudder that was its death rattle.

Shelly poleaxed Deke with her eyes. "How come ev'rything you do, Deke, ev'ry damn thing, turns out like this?"

Glaring at Shelly, Deke unrolled the pack of Camels from his t-shirt sleeve and lit one, then got out and lifted the hood of his truck.

"Lookin' at the motor ain't gonna do no good, Deke, the battery's dead," Shelly called from the open window as a newer model Chevy pickup pulled in beside them. She glanced over and saw a good-looking young man behind the wheel, who turned her way and smiled. Before he could turn the truck off, Shelly jumped out. "Howdy," she said to him, grinning. "My brother's truck won't start. Couldja jump us?"

Deke heard what she said and his face tightened.

"Sure," the man in the Chevy said, "I'd be happy to."

He maneuvered his pickup closer to Deke's heap then got out and opened his hood. "My name's Bobby Lee," the man said to Shelly as he was hooking up his jumper cables. "I own a custom auto shop in Cincinnati. What's your name?"

"Shelly," she answered. "I been livin' in Norwood."

"Why, heck," Bobby said, "that makes us neighbors." He reached into his shirt pocket. "Here's a business card for my shop," he said, and handed it to Shelly. "When you get back to Norwood, give me a call. Maybe we could got out to dinner."

"I'd be my pleasure ta do that, Bobby Lee," Shelly said with a big smile.

Deke stood scowling and silent, his idle hands stuffed in his front pockets. When the cables were in place he got into his truck and turned the key. The Ford took up its mantra: AAARRRRRUH-RUH-RUH-RUH-AAARRRRRUHRUH-RUH-RUH-AAARRRRUH-AAAAAAARRRRRRRRUH

Bobby Lee looked into the passenger window, grinned at Deke and said, "If you'd get a Chevy this wouldn't happen. Course then I wouldn't a' met your cute sister."

Deke just glared at him and kept cranking the ignition.

Eventually the old Ford started and as Bobby Lee unhooked the cables, Shelly gave him a kiss on the cheek and said, "Thanks, Bobby Lee."

As they exited the parking lot, Shelly asked, "How's the gas?"

Frowning, Deke didn't answer, but after a while he glanced at the gauge. "We're gonna need some purty soon."

"Let's fill 'er up at the next station," Shelly said. "Reckon we can't shut the motor off, though, till we git ta Peapatch."

They ate the rest of their lunch as they drove. When Deke pulled into a gas station twenty minutes later, Shelly packed the trash into the empty chicken tub and tossed it into a garbage can. "See, Deke," she said, "this ain't so hard."

Deke looked at her but didn't say anything.

They drove along Route 8, paralleling the Ohio River and twice Shelly pestered Deke to keep to the speed limit. The first colors of autumn tinged the trees around them and Shelly stuck her head out the side window, taking in the scent of Kentucky as the wind blew through her hair. Scattered fields and tobacco barns popped through openings in the dense foliage. In some spots the trees came right up to the edge of the road and leaned over it, trying to touch their leafy kin on the other side of the highway.

Just before Maysville Shelly directed Deke to cut over a winding ridge on road 576 where they dropped onto Highway 9. When it turned south at Vanceburg and entered Carter County, Shelly thought about going to see her grandmother in Olive Hill, only a few miles away, but knew that would make them late for the dinner Ethel was preparing. South of Ashland, Deke and Shelly crossed the Big Sandy and entered West Virginia, following the river along the Kentucky border on Route 52.

Deke had remained sullen and pouting since lunch but Shelly didn't mind, preferring the mountain scenery to Deke's chatter. As they drove along she thought of what a difference even a small river could make. The Kentucky side of the Big Sandy was covered with huge, stinking oil refineries, but even when they petered out, the difference in the two states was striking. Kentucky remained rolling and gentle, but in West Virginia ridges too steep and rocky for farming stetched to the East as far as she could see. Coal plants rose along the riverbank, heaped trucks came at them steadily in the oncoming lane and a double set of railroad tracks for coal trains ran between the highway and the river.

More than just the landscape had changed. Most of the northern Kentucky farms were ordered and neat, but with each mile they drove into West Virginia more litter covered the roadsides. Derelict vehicles, often sitting on cement blocks, cluttered yards and driveways in front of rundown houses or house trailers. Dirt tracks led into the trees and ended abruptly at heaps of rubbish. Still, Shelly felt like she was coming home.

They rolled south through dinky communities with strange names like Crum and Steptown, and into Mingo County. After Kermit came its unlikely suburb, East Kermit, where they stopped at a filling station with an attached convenience store. While Deke filled up the gas tank, Shelly went into the store to get some snacks. When they got back into the truck she handed Deke a paper bag filled with baloney and crackers.

"Here, Deke, I got ya somethin'."

Deke looked into the sack and said, "Did ya git any beer? I sure would like some."

Shelly's face hardened. "Deke, you can't show up at Mama's drunk. Last night you made me some promises about straightin' up an' I need ta know right now if ya really meant 'em."

They stared at each other but Deke remained silent. Shelly could tell he was still mad about the incident with Bobby Lee at Kentucky Fried Chicken but she didn't give an inch.

"Alright, then," she said, opening her door, "I'll git my stuff outa the back an' hitch-hike the rest a' the way home."

Deke backpeddled in full retreat. "Oh, I didn't mean drinkin' the beer right now, Shelly. I meant fer later, like maybe takin' some to yer kinfolk outa politeness."

"Mama don't allow alcohol in our house," Shelly said.

"Oh, sure, Shelly, sure, I understand."

"Come on, cheer up, Deke. You don't need beer to make ya happy, we got an adventure ahead of us."

"Reckon yer right," Deke said, a slight grin coming back to his face. "There's jest a whole lot a' stress in me right now, an' I might need a little help stayin' on the tracks."

Now Shelly smiled. "Guess I can do that for ya." Then she said, "There's somethin' else we need ta talk about 'fore we get ta Peapatch. Mama ain't happy with you an' me bein' ta'gether like we are. It's nothin' against you personal, Deke, but Mama says we gotta stay in diff'ernt rooms an' act appropriate when we're there."

"What's that mean, 'act appropriate'?" Deke asked.

"You know, like we can't be kissin' or huggin' or touchin' each other. An' you got ta watch your language, too … 'specially around the kids."

Deke's lower lip jutted out. "Shitfire, Shelly, I'm startin' ta wonder if you an' me are ever gonna be boyfriend an' girlfriend."

"It'll happen when we git on the road ta Montana, Deke. You didn't expect you was gonna diddle me in Mama's house with my little brothers an' sisters right there an' all, didja?"

"No, I reckon not," Deke said as a horn blared, reminding him that he was blocking a gas pump.

Further down the highway Shelly directed Deke through Williamson and just beyond town told him to turn right onto Route 49. "We'll go down through Matewan an' back inta Kentucky and then Virginia an' catch highway 83."

"Is that way faster?" Deke asked.

"I don't know, but it sure is pert'ier. We'd best not waste any time, though, if we wanta make Peapatch by supper."

As Deke was making the turn onto Route 49 he said, "I can step on 'er if ya want an' we'll make us some real good time."

"Don'tchoo even think of it," Shelly fired back, "or I'll be outa this truck an' walkin. Route 49 ain't nothin' ta mess with, 'specially when ya never drove it before."

"You sure are stubborn about gittin' yer way," Deke said, but he was smiling.

"That's 'cause my way's the right way," Shelly said, smiling back, "instead a' your way, the wild, dumb-ass hillbilly way that always gets ya inta trouble."

Deke turned to Shelly, serious now. "I never liked bein' called a hillbilly, even by my own kind."

"I always been proud a' bein' a hillbilly," Shelly told him, "but I guess that comes from my daddy. He called us 'mountain folk' sometimes but said that was just a fancy name for a hillbilly. When I hear somebody say that word, or call me that, I guess it's how they say it that matters. Some people say it funny, some people say it proud, and some people say it mean. If they say it mean ta me, or belittlin', I git mean right back with 'em, but I reckon the word itself don't bother me none."

"I guess," Deke said, but he sounded unconvinced.

Shelly laughed again. "I know yor from Tennessee, but I never heard ya say exactly where."

"A place called Kingston Springs, near Nashville."

"You still got kin there?"

"Jest my sister who lives in Nashville. My folks died in a car wreck when we were young. Us kids was raised by our aunt and uncle, but we don't see 'em no more."

"Oh, that's right, " Shelly said. "I remember now how ya told me you learned to cook by helpin' ta raise your sister."

"She's six years younger'n me," Deke said, "an' had a hard time, even harder'n me, when our folks was killed. She was only six."

Deke took a couple of breaths. "I reckon it was good of 'em ta take us in like they done, but we didn't like the way our aunt an' uncle raised us. They was real strict, religious strict. Zeke tried ta stay at home after he got outa high school, workin' at a local job an' all, but after a year or so he couldn't take no more an' joined the Army. I sure wanted ta leave too, but I knew what it'd do ta my little sister, so I stayed there an' finished my schoolin', even though I wadn't much good at it."

"Ya ever see your sister?"

"Not too much. I think it's been two years now, but we still git on real good. Jest after I finished up with school, my aunt sent 'er down to the store ta fetch some bread an' milk. These bikers from Nashville were stopped there fer gas. My sister got ta talkin' to 'em and one of the bikers asked 'er if she wanted ta come along with 'em. Don't reckon he knew, or even cared, that she was only fourteen. She got on his Harley an' rode off with 'im; left the bread an' milk sittin' right there on the counter."

"Didn't your aunt an' uncle call the police?" Shelly asked.

"Naw, I don't reckon they cared one way or t'other. They was more in'trested in gittin' the bread an' milk back. She called up Zeke, who was in Montana by then, and told 'im she was stayin' in Nashville an' not goin' back home. Soon's he called an' tol' me about it I took off too."

"Is she still with the bikers?"

"Yeah. Zeke talked to 'er not long ago; they still keep in touch. Zeke's never been too happy about it though, 'cause they're a real tough bunch."

"Ya wanta go see her 'fore we head to Montana?"

"Naw, I wouldn't know how ta find 'er anyways. She's moved since I seen 'er last. I can phone 'er when we get to Zeke's."

Deke soon found out that Shelly was right about Route 49. Tortuous and narrow, it climbed from the valley hugging the side of a sheer ridge, and though the view below was stunning, Deke had little time to look. In some places the hillside had sloughed off, taking part of the road with it, and Deke had to swerve around the gaps that fell steeply away for several hundred feet. Where the road dipped into hollers, battered single-wide trailers and small, tarpaper covered houses edged right up to the roadway, having nowhere else to go. When they got to Matewan Shelly said, "A whole lot a' bad stuff happened here with the miners and the coal companies. A bunch a' people got killed an' my gran'daddy was in the middle of it."

Shelly was going to tell Deke the story of the "Matewan Massacre" but he didn't look interested so she let it go. "Didja ever here about the Hatfield-McCoy feud?" she asked a couple of miles later.

"Yeah."

"That happened right around here, too," Shelly said, but Deke gave no sign of interest in hearing about that either.

They continued on through Thacker and Edgarton. At Freeburn they crossed back into Kentucky, headed south on Route 194, and a few miles past Stopover, entered Virginia. "Jes think, Deke," Shelly said, "we been in four states so far ta'day."

Deke thought on that before he answered. "Other'n Tennessee, these are the only four states I ever been in."

Shelly grinned at him. "Well, perty soon you'll be in a whole lot more."

The narrow road continued twisting through the hills and several times Shelly gave Deke directions at intersections with no markings.

"A fella could git his ass lost around these parts," Deke ventured.

"A lot have," Shelly said, "but after Hurley we"ll hit 83 an' that's a better road."

And it was – but they didn't stay on it for long. When a small sign for Route 639 appeared on the right, Shelly told Deke to turn, and once again they climbed a steep track barely one lane wide that ventured into a maze of precipitous hills. 639 had more curlicues than a bag of pretzels and while Deke worked hard at the steering wheel, brakes, clutch, and gearshift, Shelly quietly gazed out the window. No matter how many times she traveled this road, she never grew tired of how it spiraled up through the magnificent stretch of forest. On this autumn afternoon each tree flaunted its beauty and every opening in the canopy provided a view over the flaming landscape below.

By the time they reached the top of the ridge the sun had dropped enough that the distant hills had turned to a gray-dappled purple and coming down the eastern slope they often drove in shade. A few scattered houses appeared beside the road and cows grazed on open splotches of grass. Every few miles, the markers of some small cemetery sprouted on a hilltop like white mushrooms.

When 639 became Route 616, otherwise known as Peapatch Road, Shelly tightened and sat up straight. She stared out the side window and thought about how much she had changed since she'd left Peapatch and silently wondered if her family had also changed. In her few phone calls home, she had not been honest about dancing in a bar and had told her family that Hillbilly Heaven was a restaurant. More than once she'd run into men from McDowell County and without doubt some of them went back home and talked about Shelly's true occupation and what she did after closing time. Her other concern was what

her family would think about her coming back home with Deke McConahay. If Deke pulled one of his calamitous boners she'd never be able
to show her face in southern West Virginia again.

The sky was now a dull, gunmetal gray and after a few more miles
Shelly said, "Be careful here, Deke, there's a stop sign an' a dangerous
crossing jes up ahead."

"Where are we?" he asked.

"Close ta home. This road goes ta Peapatch, right past our house."

Deke slowed and they dropped down a slope to an intersection
where the roads angled out every which-a-way. "This is Wimmer
Gap," Shelly said and pointed across the highway to a narrow road
that wound up through the trees. "Yonder is Peapatch."

After they'd climbed out of the gap and topped the ridge, Deke
asked, "Where's the town?"

"Yor a'lookin' at it," Shelly said, laughing.

Lights from scattered houses shone here and there, but even in the
pale gloaming, Deke could see how Peapatch hovered on the ridgetop
and fell away so steeply on the Virginia side that a wrong step might
send a careless wayfarer tumbling halfway to Georgia. When they
parked in front of the Stamper home, it was both larger and nicer than
Deke had expected. "This is a fine-lookin place," he said.

"We ain't all peckerwoods like folks up north think we are," Shelly
said.

Warm yellow light beamed from the windows and no sooner had
Deke cut the engine than the porch light came on, casting a welcoming
beacon across the yard and driveway. The back door opened and Ethel
walked out. "Come on in, supper's all ready," she called.

Shelly was barely out of the truck when she was mobbed by her six
younger siblings. Cletus Jr. was now an inch taller than Shelly and he
threw his lanky arms around her. "Hi Shelly," he said. "Ah'm seventeen
now, same age as you – fer a month, anyways."

Rose was barely two when Shelly left. Now she was three and a half
and a running, jabbering wonder. She hugged Shelly's knees. "Sheh-
wee, Sheh-wee," she said, until Shelly bent down and scooped her up.

Shelly couldn't stop her tears. She looked at the chattering kids
and thought of baby birds in a nest, heads tipped up with their mouths

open and wished she could hug them all at the same time. Shelly wiped her eyes and glanced at Deke standing off to the side, looking uncomfortable. "I want ya all ta meet my friend, Deke," she said.

Deke was disappointed Shelly had said 'friend' instead of 'boyfriend' but he smiled at everybody and said, "Hi."

Twelve-year-old Mack didn't let big sister off that easy. "Is Deke yor boyfrien'?"

Shelly deflected him. "What d'you know about things like that, Mack? You already got yor'self a girlfriend?"

"No Ah don't," he shot back, "an' Ah never will."

"Ah got a boyfriend," Sadie shouted over the ruckus. "His name's Jimmy an' he's two years older'n me."

"You keepin' comp'ny with an' older man, are ya?" Shelly said, laughing.

"It's okay, Shelly," Sadie told her, "cuz we're in the same grade, jis like you an' Tommy were."

"Ev'rybody quiet for a minute," Shelly said, "whiles I introduce ya. Deke, this is Clete Jr, an' here's Sarah, she's fourteen. This one's Sadie, eleven, an' the mouthy one is Mack. What are ya now, Mack, nine?"

"No," he protested, "Ah'm twelve, nare' on thirteen an' you know it, too."

"This here's Charlie, who's four." Shelly stopped speaking as Charlie walked solemnly over to Deke and shook his hand. "Hey, Deke," he said.

"An' the one I'm holdin' here is Rose. She's three." Rose bashfully turned her head away and hid her face in Shelly's shoulder.

Ethel had remained near the back door and Henry was now standing beside her. Shelly put Rose down and walked over to them, but when Deke didn't follow, she walked back and led him by the arm, the kids trailing in a herd. Shelly and Ethel embraced for a long time then Shelly introduced her to Deke. Deke stuck out his hand to shake but Ethel threw her meaty arms around him and hugged until Deke thought his ribs were about to crack. Ethel looked into Deke's desperate eyes. "Good ta meet ya," she said without smiling.

Just as Deke was about to cry out, Shelly noticed his distress. "I shoulda warned ya, Deke," Shelly said with a giggle, "Mama's trademark wrasslin' move was the bearhug."

Ethel let go and Deke sucked in air to catch his breath. Shelly turned him to face Henry Bearden, who stuck out a firm hand and said pleasantly, but with authority, "Welcome to our home, Deke."

Everyone went into the warm kitchen where supper baked in the oven and simmered on the stove. While the other kids gathered around Shelly, Junior went up to Deke and said to him, "When Shelly called home a few weeks ago she said you was teachin' her ta drive a dump truck. That's mighty good a' you, Deke. Shelly's always lak'd doin' that kinda stuff."

"Uh, yeah," Deke said, wondering how much Shelly's family knew. "That's how Shelly an' I got ta know each other."

"You still drivin'?"

"Naw, I quit so's I could go ta Montana an' drive a loggin' truck."

"Wow," Clete Jr said. "Is Shelly gonna do that too?"

"That's what she wants ta do," Deke said.

Ethel and Sarah placed the hot food on the big kitchen table. Henry said grace and Ethel added thanks about her family being together again. She tried to maintain order, but the kids were too excited over Shelly's homecoming to stay quiet. They wanted to know all about Shelly's life 'in the big city' and about Deke. Shelly deferred questions about her job in the 'nightclub', as she now called her workplace, while Deke, knowing he couldn't lie in front of Shelly and that the truth would not do at all, muttered along as best he could.

After dinner Deke and Junior sat out on the front porch smoking cigarettes and a short while later, Henry joined them and lit his pipe. Ethel didn't approve, but she knew men would be men, and the best she could do was to make them go outside. Junior wanted to know all about Deke's adventures and with Shelly now inside, Deke regaled him with stories of trucking, race car driving and bar fights. Henry mostly stayed silent, except for shooting Deke an occasional question that left him stumbling for an answer.

Inside, Shelly laughed and tussled with her brothers and sisters while catching up on local news with Ethel, who asked nothing about her life in Norwood. Rumors had floated back to her from Ohio, but people who knew the truth never dared tell Ethel the stories they'd heard, but Ethel could guess.

At 9:30 Ethel said, "You kids got school tomorrow and I already let ya stay up a half hour later'n usual. Now git yor'selves ta bed. Sarah, you help Rose and Charlie."

"Where am I sleepin', Mama?" Shelly asked.

"When Junior turned sixteen we gave him your old room so's he could have one to himself," Ethel told her. "There's a featherbed on the floor for you in Sarah and Sadie's room. We fixed a place for Deke in the parlor so's he won't be bothered if he wants ta sleep in."

Shelly got snuggled into the old featherbed mattress, the same one her grandparents had slept on, but Sarah and Sadie chattered away at her in the dark.

"Listen," Shelly finally told them, "you two june-bugs hafta get up and go ta school ta'morrow and I need some sleep. When you get home from school we can talk all ya want. Goodnight."

Chapter 17

Tuesday, September 18

Shelly dressed quietly in the dark before her sisters were up and went down the maple staircase into the kitchen where Ethel was beginning her morning routine. Ethel poured her a cup of coffee and Shelly walked over to the fridge, topped the coffee off with milk and said, "What can I do ta help?"

"Set yor'self down," Ethel told her. "You're a guest."

Ethel said it to make Shelly feel welcome, but to Shelly it was a reminder that this was no longer her home.

"I can't jes sit an' do nothin'," Shelly said, and started helping Ethel fix breakfast.

Several minutes later Henry walked in and Ethel set his breakfast in front of him.

"Mornin', Shelly," he said. "Did ya have a good sleep?"

"I did," Shelly answered.

Ethel set a plate of eggs and a bowl of oatmeal on the table and pointed for Shelly to sit down. "You better eat now 'fore the kids come pourin' in."

Shelly sat down two chairs away from Henry. Shelly and Ethel talked and Ethel and Henry talked, but Shelly never said a word to Henry. When he'd finished eating, Henry got up, took his dishes to the sink and lifted his jacket off the peg by the back door. "It's time ta be a'scootin'. Ah don't want mah crew gittin thar' ahead a' me," he said, then walked over to Ethel and they kissed.

"You didn't do that with Daddy," Shelly said when the door closed behind Henry.

"I know I didn't," Ethel said, "an' I'm sorry for it ev'ry day. Henry might be a foreman but he still goes down in the mine. I don't want a phone call some day an' then feel bad 'cause I never said goodbye to 'im."

As soon as the words were out, Ethel knew she shouldn't have said them. Shelly's face reddened but before Ethel could apologize, Sarah and Sadie bounded down the stairs and into the kitchen.

"Mornin', Shelly," they both shouted as they ran over and hugged her.

Ethel put their breakfasts in front of them and said to Shelly, "Honey, would you run upstairs an' drag those two boys outa bed."

Shelly hustled up the stairs and pounded on the door of her old bedroom, which was now Junior's. "Ah'm up," he answered sleepily.

Knowing he'd still be asleep, Shelly didn't bother knocking on Mack's door. She entered his room silently and pounced on the form under the covers. "Wake up, Mack!" Shelly yelled. "There's a tornado comin' an it's right outside the house!"

Startled, and now wide-awake, Mack tried to sit up, but Shelly kept him pinned beneath the blankets. "Hurry, hurry up!" Shelly kept hollering, not letting him out from under the covers. "It's a tornado!"

Mack struggled like a trapped wildcat, yelling, "Leh' me up, Shelly, leh' me up!" until Shelly began laughing so hard she rolled off the bed.

"That wuz mean," Mack said after he'd sat up, but he was smiling.

"C'mon, kid," Shelly said, getting up from the floor, "you gotta get ready for school. I know how much ya love it."

"Shit on school. Ah don't love it, Ah hate it."

"Where'd you learn that bad word?" Shelly said.

"From you, 'fore ya left home. An' a whole lot worse ones 'an that. You wanna hear 'em."

"Nope," Shelly answered, "don't need to. I already know 'em."

Shelly sat on the bed as Mack dressed. "Turn yor back," he said, "Ah need ta put on clean underwear."

"You kin turn aroun' now," Mack said as he was pulling on his jeans. He looked at his sister. "Ah miss ya, Shelly. Almost as bad as Ah miss Daddy."

Shelly got up and hugged her brother. "I miss you too, Mack. I miss all a' you so much that sometimes I can't hardly stand it."

Mack's hug was nearly as crushing as his mother's. Of all the Stamper children, he most resembled Ethel, with dark skin, curly black hair and striking blue eyes. In the time Shelly had been gone he had grown thickset and powerful.

"How come ya don't stay aroun' here then?" Mack said. "You don't need ta go allaway out ta Montana, 'specially with that Deke guy."

"Yeah, I do, Mack. I don't know how to explain it to ya, 'cause I can't explain it to myself, but I know I need ta go."

Shelly waited while Mack went into the bathroom and then they went downstairs.

Ethel stuck breakfast in front of Mack. "If you don't hurry you'll miss the bus," she told him, "an' then you know what's gonna happen."

"Ah know. Ah'll hafta go fetch a switch fer you ta wale me with," Mack said. He tried to sound unconcerned, but he began gobbling his breakfast.

Soon, the kitchen became a flurry of activity as the four school kids grabbed coats, lunches and homework and trooped out the back door, Junior pushing Mack ahead of him. From the back yard came the baying of a hound.

Shelly's ears perked up. "I only hear one dog."

"Honey," Ethel said, "Homer died. There wasn't nothin' really wrong with 'im. I reckon he just died of sadness from missin' Clete."

Shelly bit her lip. "How's Jethro?"

"He's sad, too. You oughta go out an' cheer 'im up."

"I will, Mama," Shelly said, staring into her coffee.

Ethel sat down at the table with her coffee cup. "Darlin', you told us ya married a man named Jim right after you got to Ohio. Are ya still married?"

"No, Mama. I divorced Jim."

"Officially divorced him?"

"As officially as I married 'im."

Ethel raised her eyebrows and then sat her coffee down and went upstairs to get Rose and Charlie. Deke came into the kitchen at twenty past eight as Ethel was making breakfast for them. "I see most of the house ain't up yet," he said.

Before Ethel could answer, Shelly said, "The rest are gone off ta work or school"

"Take a seat," Ethel told him. "I'll make ya breakfast soon as I finish with the young'uns here."

"What all we fixin' ta do today?" Deke asked Shelly.

"That," Shelly told him.

"What?" Deke asked, perplexed.

"What you jes said, fixin'. After we git showered an' cleaned up we'll take your truck down ta Cliff's garage an have him go over it and fix whatever needs fixin'."

"I can fix it m'self, Shelly. I'm a good mechanic."

"How long you had this truck, Deke?"

"Six years."

"Then how come ya ain't already done it?"

Deke looked down, swirling his coffee.

"And when it gits back from Cliff's we're gonna clean out the cab. I ain't ridin' ta Montana in no pigsty."

As Ethel sat Deke's breakfast in front of him, Shelly asked, "Mama, can you go ta town with me an' Deke an' drive us back after we leave his truck at Cliff's?"

"Sure, honey, I got a few things ta do there anyway."

"I'm gonna go upstairs an' take a shower," Shelly told Deke. "You can take one in the bathroom down here. There's clean towels in the cabinet."

After her shower, Shelly came back downstairs and Deke was sitting in Henry's lounger with his feet kicked up, reading one of Mack's comic books. "Didja git showered?" she asked.

"Naw, I'll do it when we get back," he answered, not glancing up.

Ethel came into the room with Rose and Charlie in tow. "Y'all ready ta go?"

"Reckon so," Shelly answered, but the look on her face told Ethel she wasn't happy about something.

Shelly and Deke climbed into his pickup and Deke turned the key. The starter growled for half a minute before the engine finally turned over as Ethel sat in the Lincoln, shaking her head. They followed her into War and when Deke pulled into Cliff's station, Shelly jumped out and gave Cliff a hug. Deke walked up and Shelly turned loose of Cliff. "This is Deke," she said.

Cliff met Deke's eyes, but didn't smile. "Deke," he said, and nodded, but didn't offer to shake hands.

"We're goin' ta Montana in this truck," Shelly said, "an' it needs ta make it the whole way. I don't wanta hafta finish the trip in a Conestoga."

Cliff looked over at the truck. "Ah do mechanic'n, not miracle workin'."

Deke started to say something, but Shelly shook her head 'No' at him. He stared at the ground, pushing dirt around with the toe of his boot.

"We're gonna walk around town some, Cliff," Shelly said. "Maybe when we git back you can tell us what all needs done ta that critter ta keep it alive."

"Ah'll do it," Cliff said and turned to Deke. "Leave the key in it."

Late morning sunshine traded off with shade and a mild, pleasant breeze blew through town as Shelly and Deke strolled along War's main drag. Shelly noticed several stores that had been open when she left were now closed and boarded up. As they walked along, Shelly either said "Hello" or stopped to chat with nearly everyone they passed. When they came to the War Room Café, Shelly said, "Let's go in an' git a cup a' coffee."

"I already had two at yer place," Deke answered.

"Me too," Shelly told him. "I jes wanta see people. I didn't think I'd ever miss this town, but now that I don't live here, I kinda do."

The joint was bustling with the late breakfast crowd sipping coffee and chatting. Most of the customers looked up and called friendly greetings to Shelly as she and Deke settled onto two stools at one of the horseshoe shaped counters. A short, compact woman came over with a wet cloth in her hand and said, "Let me clean y'all off."

"I'm okay, Opal, but Deke here could use a scrubbin'," Shelly told her.

Opal laughed as she wiped off the counter then returned with the two cups of coffee Shelly had ordered. "Is this the feller yer goin' ta Montana with?"

"That's what people around town been tellin' me," Shelly said.

"Som'body tol't me yor a'goin' out there ta be a lumberjack, or sump'in lak 'at," a man across from Shelly said as he dipped a wad of tobacco into his cheek.

"Somethin' like that, Rollie," Shelly answered.

"I hear't they still got wild Injuns thar," the man beside Rollie said.

"I hope so, Del, 'cause I wanta meet some."

"Yeah, well you best be a'cuttin' off 'at long hair a' yor'n, Shelly, 'cause it might be real temptin' to 'em."

A chortle went around and when it had subsided, Shelly said to the crowd in general, "This is Deke."

Most folks nodded and one or two said, "Deke."

A stocky man wearing a UMW Union cap sitting beside Deke stubbed out his Pall Mall in the ashtray then turned to Deke. "What's yor stake in this?"

Shelly knew the man – everybody called him by his last name, Millar. He and Clete had worked at the same mine but Shelly heard he'd retired.

Deke just sat looking at the man, dumbfounded by his directness.

"Huh?" Millar said to him, "Whutchoo got in this?"

Everyone near Deke turned to look, waiting for him to answer.

"Uh … I got a brother in Montana," Deke finally said.

"So, I might have a brother in Tim-buck-too," Millar said, "but that don' mean I'm a'takin' Shelly thar."

"Tell Millar what your brother said he was gonna do," Shelly said.

"Oh …right," Deke said. "He's gonna teach us ta drive his log truck an' help us find jobs."

A number of heads nodded in acceptance, but Millar bent forward on his stool and looked past Deke to Shelly. "You talked to this brother a' his, didja?"

Now Shelly felt uncomfortable. "Nope," she answered, trying to sound confident, "but I heard Deke make the call to 'im."

Deke squirmed on his seat, wondering how much of his conversation with Zeke Shelly had heard.

"Uh-huh," Millar said, and resumed downing his cornbread and butter beans.

"We better git goin', Deke," Shelly said, looking at her Timex.

"I didn't much like that place," Deke said when they were outside.

"Aw, those folks are fine, they jes care about what happens to me."

"I care about ya too, Shelly."

"I know ya do, Deke," Shelly said, as she looked up and down Main Street. "Let's cross to the other side. It's sunnier over there."

They hadn't gone twenty paces when Shelly stopped in her tracks. A man with a unique swagger was walking toward them. "As I live an' breathe," Shelly yelled and took off running. The man looked up and grinned at her, but never changed his stride.

Short and wiry, with a black crewcut, the man wore nice clothes, but there was something in his manner that Deke disliked. When he and Shelly locked in a vibrant embrace and kissed each other long and hard, *maybe even French kissed!* Deke hated him immediately. They finally broke off and Shelly turned to Deke. "This is Tommy," she said, beaming at the man.

"Howdy," Tommy said, sticking out his hand.

Deke took Tommy's hand and was surprised at the little man's strength.

"This is my friend, Deke," Shelly said, and once again, Deke caught Shelly's absence of the word 'boy' in front of 'friend'.

"Hi, Tommy," Deke forced himself to say.

"Tommy got in trouble runnin' moonshine so he joined the Marines an' went off ta Vietnam," Shelly told Deke.

Now Deke really hated him.

"How long you been out?" Shelly asked Tommy.

"Ah ain't out. Ah re-upped fer another stint an' Ah'm home on leave."

"Somebody told me you got shot up some," Shelly said.

"They tol' ya right. One a' them little som'bitches popped me in the shoulder. It still troubles me some." Tommy rubbed his shoulder and stretched his left arm out a time or two. "But I nailed him good, an' a few a' his buddies too. They give me a Purple Heart an' a Silver Star an' tol' me Ah was a damn good Marine and hoped Ah'd stay in the Corps." Tommy smiled at Shelly and then at Deke. "An' so Ah done it."

"I'm glad ya come out alive," Shelly said and threw her arms around him again. "I was worried about ya after you wrecked your car runnin' from the law an' they shot at ya an' all."

"I done that a time or two," Deke said, but nobody looked at him.

Shelly loosed Tommy from her embrace but kept a hand on his shoulder. "I'm goin' ta Montana."

"So Ah heard."

"So ev'rybody's heard," Shelly said, a little irritated. "I don't know how word got around so fast."

"Me an' Shelly's goin' out there t'gether," Deke said. "My brother's gonna. . ."

"The three years I promised ta wait are up, Tommy," Shelly said, as she looked into his eyes.

Deke's jaw tightened.

"Ah know," Tommy said and laughed. "It don't matter none. Ah'm engaged now."

"I figgered a handsome Marine like you'd be hooked up," Shelly said and winked at him.

Deke turned and walked over to an empty store and gazed in the window.

"Met a girl in the Air Force last year," Tommy said. "We're stationed apart an' don't see each other real often, but when we do we make up fer it."

"You stayin' at your folks' place while yor here?" Shelly asked.

"Yeah, but it's jest Ma's place now. My ol' man got killed 'bout a year ago. He was out huntin' an' some other hunter mistook him for a deer, or more likely a pig, but nobody ever found out who done it."

"I'm sorry," Shelly told him.

"Hell, Ah ain't. Best thing that ever happened. Ma quit drinkin' an' joined the Baptist Church. She's even workin' for 'em, takin' care a' the church an' cleanin' it up."

"Your ma, cleanin' up the church?"

"Ah know, ain't that a kick. She even keeps the house cleaned up now and the church give her some better furniture."

Shelly had to know. "Didja ever call your uncle Hop?"

"Took me till Ah got them medals ta git up the nerve," Tommy answered. "He was still mad as hell but tol' me that since Ah done good in the Marines an' didn't give 'im up, he wouldn't shoot me, anyways."

Tommy and Shelly both laughed.

"Ah gotta git on down ta Cliff's," Tommy said. "I'm havin' lunch with 'im."

"Reckon you an' Cliff settled accounts, then?"

"When Ah come back for mah ol' man's funeral last year – which Ah only done cuz mah sergeant made me – Ah went ta see Cliff. Ah 'pologized an' tried ta pay 'im for all a' what Ah took an' the broken winda', but he wouldn't take a penny. Then Cliff said a real strange thing ta me. He said Ah didn't owe 'im one cent for what happened at the station, but I owed 'im for sumpthin' else, but he wouldn't tell me what it was, an' said he never would."

Shelly and Deke continued their walk around War and an hour later ran into Ethel and the kids. They all piled into the Lincoln and drove back to Cliff's. Charlie and Rose jumped out of the back seat and ran up to Cliff, yelling their greetings. He bent down and picked one up in each arm.

"What's the verdict?" Shelly asked, looking toward the Ford.

"I don't reckon it'll need much done to it," Deke cut in.

Cliff walked over to the truck still carrying Rose and Charlie. "Yor gonna want new tar'rs. These are almost bald and as far as yor goin' it'd be a lot safer."

"We sure do, Cliff," Shelly said, as Deke was shaking his head 'No'.

Cliff nodded toward the engine under the raised hood. "The mill is fair, but it needs a complete tune up, plus a new starter, hoses, belts, air, oil an' fuel filters, plugs, points, an oil change an' a lube job. The u-joint is bad an' both the fuel pump an' water pump oughta be replaced. Ah'd put in a new battery, too, this one's about shot."

"That much, huh?" Shelly asked, and Cliff nodded.

"It shouldn't need alla' that, it's been runnin' fine fer me," Deke said. "An' I know it don't need no battery, I jest bought a used one. I think you might be tryin' ta run up the bill on us."

Shelly and Ethel glared at Deke; ashamed they were with him.

"That truck does need it," Cliff said. His voice was even but his eyes hard and dangerous. "An' if'n you want, Ah'll show ya ev'rything that's wrong with it. For Shelly's sake Ah wish it didn't need all that work, but this'n here truck ain't been taken care of or had much maint'nance done to it."

Deke puffed out his chest. "I take *good* care a' this truck an' work on it all the time," he said loudly, rising up on his toes.

For a few seconds Cliff watched Deke's posturing. He placed the two children back on the ground. "Maint'nance *talk* don't do much for a truck," he said.

Deke glowered at Cliff and clenched his fists, shifting his weight back and forth on his feet. Just as he was about to say something that would've gotten him hurt, Shelly stepped in front of him. "We got ta git on home an' start dinner. When can we pick up the truck, Cliff?"

Cliff never took his eyes off Deke. "Lessee," he told Shelly, "this is Tuesday. I'll have 'er done by Thursday; Friday at the far end."

"Alright, and thanks, Cliff. See ya then." Shelly turned to leave but Deke stood fuming, trying to look menacing.

"Hang on a second," Cliff said.

He ducked into the garage and came out with several lollipops in his hand. He passed one to Charlie and one to Rose. "Thank you, Cliff," they said and smiled.

He reached out his hand toward Deke. "Here, I got one fer you too."

Deke's face turned bright red. Ethel grabbed him by his shirt collar and pulled him to the car. "You better not say nothin' bad in front a' these little kids."

For the rest of the afternoon Deke sulked while Shelly and Ethel laughed and chatted, fixed supper and ignored him. Deke tried to play with Rose and Charlie but they didn't want anything to do with him, either. Finally Shelly said, "Why don't you take Jethro for a walk, Deke. He needs the exercise."

In the forlorn hound Deke found a companion. As they walked along Peapatch Road and onto the side lanes that dipped into the valleys, Deke lamented to Jethro all the slights and wrongs that had been done to him throughout his life. The dog patiently listened and then bayed out his own sorrows. When they returned to the house, both felt better and supper was on the table.

Earlier, when Henry and the school kids had arrived home, Ethel took Henry aside and told him how Deke had insulted Cliff. Henry's normally placid face tightened. "Ah'm not havin' that Ethel. Cliff's our frien' an' he's been good ta us an' the kids."

"I know," Ethel said. "I don't like it any either but it's only for a few days. Shelly's mighty ticked-off too, but her heart's set on goin' ta Montana."

Henry ignored Deke at supper and afterwards, when Deke and Junior went out on the porch to smoke, Henry didn't join them. Through the porch screen, he could hear Deke's bragging and when Henry couldn't stand it any longer he turned the radio on loud enough to drown him out.

Chapter 18

The next morning Deke stayed in bed again until Henry and the school kids were gone. By the time he dragged into the kitchen, breakfast was over and Ethel and Shelly were on to other chores. "There's coffee in the pot an' you can fix yor'self whatever ya want," Ethel told him over the noise of the vacuum cleaner.

"Got any baloney an' crackers?" Deke asked.

"We got Saltines," Ethel answered, barely looking at him, "but no baloney."

Deke grabbed a cup of coffee and made a peanut butter and jelly sandwich then stepped outside where Shelly was chopping firewood.

"What're we doin' today?" he asked.

Steadying a chunk of wood on the block, Shelly said, "Well ... we could go for a hike up in the mountains."

"I don't really like hikin' all that much," Deke told her, "an' me an' high places don't git along."

"Okay. We could go call on some a' my old friends."

Deke wondered how many of her old friends were old boyfriends. "Naw, I don't reckon I'd care for that."

"Well, whata' you wanta do?" Shelly asked him.

"It's yer homeplace," Deke said. "I'll do whatever ya want to."

Shelly straightened up and glared at Deke, who wisely stayed quiet. "Go ask Mama if there's some work you can do aroun' here," she said and went back to chopping.

A few minutes later Shelly looked out by the roadside. Deke was down on his hands and knees in the ditch, pulling weeds as Ethel stood over him, pointing to other places around the homestead that needed weeding.

After an hour of chopping Shelly was warmed up for some real exertion. She walked over to Deke. "Ah'm gonna hike to the top a' yonder mountain," she told him, pointing at a peak several miles away. "You wanta come along?"

He frowned and shook his head 'no.'

Shelly went into the house and came out a few minutes later wearing a knapsack, a canteen and a large sheath knife at her belt. As she strode by Deke, she tossed him a pair of leather gloves. "Here, ya better wear these," she said, "or you'll git blisters," and took off down Peapatch Road at a jog.

Three hours later she stood on the peak known as Johnson's Knob, surveying Appalachia. To the northwest a ridge dropped sharply into the glade that was her special place. The day was still young enough that she could reach it and be home by supper.

As Shelly edged down the holler that led to the glade her mind must have been elsewhere, for when she stepped out of the brushy forest into the open, sunlit circle, she was taken by surprise. She blinked several times then walked to where the brook flowed away into the dense woods. The summer had been dry and the stream was shrunken and languid, barely a foot wide. She pushed her way downstream through the close-packed trees and tangled undergrowth. The magical pool was now a brown morass of thick mud.

Turning around, she hiked back upsteam to the steep chasm where the stream tumbled from the mountain. A thin veil of water dropped sullenly onto the rocks, barely making a sound.

Shelly climbed to her seat on the square, black stone and dipped her hand into the feeble current, then swung round and looked up into the narrow cleft to the top of the gorge. The creek was so low that she might be able to climb the dry rock and see where the water emerged from the mountain, or at least get to the huge granite slab that guarded the portal and peek beyond it. As much as she had always longed to look upon that secret fissure, she now had no desire to see it in this depleted condition.

Edging her way down the chasm and into the open, Shelly stood in the center of the sun-parched circle, so harshly different than when she'd ridden here that Christmas day in the haunted twilight. The tree where Tramp had stood, happily munching on the damp grass, was now uprooted and lying on the ground, the grass around it brown and dry. Shelly knew it was time to leave. She took one last look before plunging into the gnarled trees that ringed the glade and made her way toward home.

As Shelly approached the house, Deke was sitting by the road, smoking a cigarette and picking his nose. He was wearing some of Clete's old work clothes, now sweat-stained and spattered with white paint. "Whatcha been up to?" Shelly called to him.

"Just finished paintin' the fu …the toolshed," he answered wearily.

Shelly sat down beside him. "We'll do somethin' fun ta'morrow, I promise."

Deke pinched out a small smile. They sat quietly for a spell, Shelly pensive and Deke too exhausted for conversation. When the kids saw that Shelly was back they rushed outside and jumped on her, wrasslin' beside the road until Henry drove up. "Reckon we better go inside an' git washed up for supper," Shelly said.

Half an hour later, as Ethel and the two older girls were putting supper on the table, Junior still wasn't home. "He comes in later ever' day," Ethel told Shelly when his battered Chevy pulled up outside. Ethel gave Junior the cold-eye as he strolled through the back door, but all she said was, "Git washed up, it's suppertime."

Junior walked past her without replying, but he grinned at Shelly. When he returned from the bathroom and sat down, Henry said grace and people began passing around bowls and platters of food. "Ah got mah driver's license right after you left," Junior told Shelly as he handed her the bowl of string beans. "Ah 'spose you got yor commercial license, seein's you was drivin' a dump truck."

"I'm waitin' ta get my driver's license in Montana," Shelly said.

Ethel sat the platter of fried potatoes down hard and stared at Deke. "You let my daughter drive a dump truck without her even havin' a driver's license?"

Deke stopped gnawing his pork chop and looked desperately at Shelly.

"It ain't his fault, Mama," Shelly said. "I asked 'im to teach me."

"He's older an' should know better," Ethel said, still glaring at Deke.

"Daddy was way older'n Deke, an' he let me drive all the time," Shelly answered.

"I see you ain't lost that smart mouth on ya," Ethel said, then lowered her head and began eating.

As supper was ending, Deke turned to Shelly. "You wanna go out after dinner with me an' walk the dog?"

"I already walked plenty ta'day, Deke. I'm gonna help Mama clean up the kitchen. Maybe Junior'll go with ya."

Junior nodded that he'd go.

Shelly did her best to lighten Ethel's mood as they cleaned up after dinner and when they were alone, Shelly told her, "Mama, I don't mean to make ya mad or hurt your feelins' any."

Ethel wiped her wet hands on a dishtowel and tossed it onto the counter. "I know ya don't Shelly, but I ain't gonna lie to ya; I ain't one bit happy about this situation with you an' … " Ethel paused, not wanting to say Deke's name.

Shelly walked over and put her arms around Ethel's thick shoulders. "I don't know as I am either, Mama," she said, "but I gotta see it through."

Before she went to sleep that night, Shelly resolved to be nicer to Deke, so when he trailed into the kitchen at 8:30 the next morning she cooked him a breakfast of cornmeal mush with maple syrup and fried ham. As she sat the plate in front of him the phone rang in the living room and Shelly hurried to answer it.

"That was Cliff," Shelly told Deke when she came back into the kitchen. "He said your truck won't be ready till ta'morrow afternoon. Some other things come up that he had ta work on first."

Deke scrunched up his face. "I was hopin' ta git my truck back so's we could do somethin' today."

"We can," Shelly answered, smiling. "Cliff said he'll loan me Daddy's old Powerwagon. I could show ya some a' my fav'rit spots an' maybe even stop at a couple a' places for a quick beer."

Deke's face lit up. "I'd like that."

Shelly heard footsteps and turned to see Ethel, Rose, and Charlie coming down the stairs, dressed for town. "Can I catch a ride with ya inta Cliff's?" she called to Ethel.

"Hurry up," Ethel called back, "we're leavin' right now."

"Can I come along?" Deke said, as Ethel made for the back door without acknowledging him.

Ethel turned to say something but Shelly interceded. "You stay here an' finish your breakfast, Deke, then take Jethro for a walk."

An hour later, as Shelly was pulling the grade where Peapatch Road left Route 635, she saw a tall, longhaired man wearing a cowboy hat with a dog on a leash up ahead. Shelly stopped beside them and called out the open window, "Hey, good-lookin', ya wanta ride?"

Deke looked at her and grinned then Shelly said to the dog, "That feller who's walkin' ya can come along too."

Deke looked puzzled. "Oh … I get it now," he said.

Shelly laughed. "Both a' you good-lookin' boys can git in."

After they arrived at the house Deke put Jethro into his pen then came back to admire the '49 Dodge pickup. "That's a beaut. I like that towin' hoist in the bed."

"Daddy built that," Shelly said. "I was mad at Mama when she traded this truck ta Cliff, but he's been good to it an' uses it for his business."

"I can tell it's in real good shape," Deke admitted.

"You all ready ta go?" Shelly asked.

"Sure am."

"Hang on a second, I wanna git somethin'," Shelly said. She shot into the house and came back out wearing her *Mack Trucks* ballcap. "The last time I drove this truck was when Daddy bought me this hat, a week 'fore he died," she told Deke. "That's why it's so special to me."

Deke stared at Shelly bug-eyed but didn't move.

"You ain't gonna start that crap up again, are ya, Deke?" Shelly said.

"I can't help it, Shelly, that hat does somethin' to ya when ya put it on."

"Seems more like it does somethin' ta you when I put it on," Shelly said. "Now git in the truck an' stop actin' goofy."

Deke climbed in the truck, but Shelly could see that he tried to cop a look whenever he thought she wasn't watching. At Wimmer Gap, Shelly hesitated, pondering which direction to go. Finally Deke asked, "Which way we goin'?"

Shelly pursed her lips. "Let's go up ta Greenbrier country. I ain't been there for a long time."

She turned north toward Bradshaw, aiming to cut over to Yukon and up to Welch. "There really ain't no fast way ta get to the Greenbrier from here," she told Deke. "All these roads in southern Wes' Virginia jes twist aroun' in ev'ry which direction."

"Uh, Shelly, when you s'pose we could stop an' git us a beer?" Deke said as they were coming into Welch.

"It ain't even eleven o'clock yet," Shelly said, sorry she'd mentioned beer earlier.

"I didn't mean right now," Deke said quickly, "maybe later on."

From Welch, they wound a circuitous path north into Wyoming County and east through the Irish sounding burgs of Tralee and Killarney. Shelly cranked the big steering wheel, constantly shifting gears and enjoying every second of driving Clete's old Dodge. As they passed through Odd, Shelly said, "We likely coulda taken a faster way, but I ain't been up in these parts for a spell and wanted to see 'em again."

At one o'clock Deke and Shelly crossed the bridge over the New River near Hinton. "Down yonder's the New River Gorge," Shelly said, pointing north. "People say it's a real wild stretch a' water."

"I sure wouldn't like that," Deke told her. "I can't swim all that well."

"I'd like ta see the gorge," Shelly said. "an' I'm a good swimmer, but after watchin' the Silver Bridge fall in, rivers seem ta put some kinda spell on me. But I do love 'em."

"You actually saw the Silver Bridge fall in the river?" Deke asked. "I remember hearin' about that."

"We was next in line ta go over it," Shelly said, and as they drove around Hinton looking for a lunch spot, she told Deke the story. Deke listened, but Shelly could tell that he was also watching for a place with a beer sign in the window. When they saw one, Deke pointed. "Let's stop here," he said, "it looks like they got good food."

Before he even looked at the menu Deke ordered a Strohs. "Never hear'd of it," the waitress told him.

"How about Budweiser?" Deke asked. When the woman nodded Deke told her, "Bring me two."

The waitress looked at Shelly. "Two cheeseburgers, fries, and a Coke," she said and then asked Deke, "You gittin' anything ta eat?"

"Uh ... sure," he said, "same as you ... but not the Coke."

Halfway through his second burger Deke ordered another Bud and would have ordered a fourth had Shelly not hustled him out of the joint. "Deke, I know you been wantin' some beer, but this trip ain't gonna be a drunk run."

Back on the highway, Shelly said, "This road follows the Greenbrier River over ta Ronceverte but a most a' the time you can't see the river." Deke was quiet but Shelly kept up a line of chatter. "They say the Greenbrier's the longest river in the East that ain't been dammed up in some way."

"You ever been on it?" Deke asked.

"Nope," Shelly said. "Daddy an' I used to come here an' fish it sometimes, but always from the bank." She looked through a patch of rustling cottonwoods to a stretch of shining, swift flowing water coursing under steep banks and then turned her attention back to the highway and chuckled.

"What?" Deke asked her.

"Oh, I was jes thinkin' 'bout somethin' kinda funny."

"Well, you gonna tell me?"

"Alright," Shelly said. "Tommy Kegley told me when he was fourteen – he was still in the third or fourth grade then – him an' some other kid were hitch-hikin' through here an' saw a boat sittin' on the bank."

Deke didn't want to hear any stories about Tommy Kegley, but since he'd asked, he was stuck listening.

"They decided ta steal it an' as they was floatin' away from the bank the guy it belonged to ran up hollerin' at 'em. He couldn't catch 'em 'cause they was too far out in the water but he kept runnin' along an' yellin' ta beat the band. Tommy an' this other kid jes laughed an' gave the guy the finger an' the las' thing they heard 'im yell was 'It ain't the boat I'm worried about'."

"That ain't so funny," Deke said.

"I ain't done with the story," Shelly told him. "There was even a cooler full a' beer in the boat an' Tommy and this kid was havin' a merry ol' time fer a coupla miles jes driftin' along an' drinkin' beer. Then they saw this big rock wall comin' up and heard a bunch a' rapids.

"Turns out, Tommy said, they'd come to a place called Bacon Falls. The boat starts goin' ev'ry which a way, a bouncin' up an' down and fillin' full a' water. Perty soon it takes a dive an' sticks b'tween two big rocks, straight up an' down an' jes stays there. They git throwed in the river an' barely make it ta shore. They was wet an' cold an' didn't know where they were. It took 'em all night ta make it to a road an' they thought for sure they was gonna freeze ta death."

Shelly laughed, but Deke said, "I still don't think it's that funny."

"Maybe ya had ta hear Tommy tell it."

"I don't wanna hear Tommy tell it," Deke said.

"Ya didn't hear Tommy tell it, ya heard me tell it."

"An' I didn't think it was funny."

"Urrrrrr," Shelly growled. She remained silent until they neared Talcott. "You ever hear that song 'bout John Henry, the steel drivin' man?"

"Sure," Deke answered.

"Well, it happened right here," Shelly said as she made a turn off the highway and drove alongside a double set of railroad tracks.

"What happened here?" Deke asked.

"John Henry's race with the steam drill."

Deke looked at Shelly uncomprehending.

"That's what the song's about," she said.

"Oh."

Shelly stopped the pickup near a pair of newer, mile long railroad tunnels and a smaller, much older one no longer in use. She pointed to a weathered plaque commemorating John Henry's feat. "Here's where it happened Deke, where John Henry beat the steam drill in a race an' then died, right in that old tunnel."

Deke looked at the tunnel, then at Shelly, as if he still didn't understand. "You mean he raced the drill to the other end a' the tunnel, runnin' 'long side of it?"

"No, Deke! He raced it drillin' holes in the side a' the rock ta put in dynamite."

"Why'd he do that?"

"I don't know why he did it, Deke. He jes did it. An' he beat the steam drill too, then he laid down his hammer an' he died."

"Well that sounds like a purty stupid thing ta do," Deke said, laughing. "I think this story's way funnier'n 'at other one you told."

"Urrrrrrrr."

They'd barely got back on the highway when Deke said, "That beer's got to me. I need ta pee."

Shelly turned onto a dirt track that led into the forest. As with so many places in Appalachia this one ended in a pile of rubbish and discarded furniture. "I jes don't understand why people do this," Shelly said.

"Do what?"

"Make messes like this in the woods."

Deke shrugged.

"Don't it bother you, Deke, seein' this?"

"Not really. There's plenty more woods."

Deke got out and took care of business and when he returned he said casually to Shelly, "This is kind of a purty spot."

"No it ain't, it's fulla trash."

"Well I mean, other'n that … an' there ain't nobody around," he said slyly, and winked. "That truck seat's big enough fer us ta do it on."

Shelly glared at him.

"Well, you said we'd start bein' boyfriend an' girlfriend once we got on the road," Deke said, almost pleading, "an we been on the road all day now."

"First of all," Shelly said, "that seat ain't big e'nuff for two midgets ta do *it* on. An' second of all, which is gonna be *last* of all, I said we'd start bein' boyfriend an' girlfriend after we got on the road ta Montana, which we ain't. To be exact, right now we're headin' *away* from Montana."

Shelly got back into the Powerwagon and slammed the door to let Deke know the matter was ended. Deke stood silent beside the open passenger door as Shelly revved the motor. When Deke didn't take the hint she said to him, "You goin' with me or you stayin' here with this rubbish pile you seem ta be so fond of?"

Deke climbed into the pickup but sulked until they got to Ronceverte. They pulled into a park where the Greenbrier River flowed fast and clear beneath tall, leafy maple trees, and then got out and walked over to the river. Shelly took off her shoes and socks, sat down on the bank and let her feet dangle in the cool water. She leaned back, stretched out her long torso and turned her face into the afternoon sunshine. "I could learn ta love this river," she said, "'specially since it ain't all damned up."

"This all we gonna do today?" Deke asked. When Shelly didn't answer, Deke nudged her with his elbow and said it again, louder.

"Oh, sorry," Shelly said. "Sometimes when I get around rivers, they jes kinda carry me away. What was it you said?"

"I said, 'is this all we gonna do today?'"

"What else you wanta do?"

"I thought we was gonna stop at some places."

"You mean for beer?"

"Well, you said we would," Deke reminded her.

"Alright, Deke. I know a tavern down by Cucumber I think you'd like."

Shelly put on her shoes and socks and they got into the pickup. She turned onto Route 219 and stayed on it the whole way to Peterstown. Taking U.S. 460 they crossed Bluestone Lake and re-entered McDowell County a pinch after four o'clock. When they pulled into the nearly full parking lot of a flat-roofed, squalid establishment called Rattler's Den Shelly told Deke, "We can't spend a lot a' time here, 'cause we need to git back for supper."

As soon as Shelly shut off the engine they heard yelling. Half a dozen cars away, a stringy-haired blond woman and a stocky man in bib-overalls were hollering at another man who stood with his head bent over his bloodied white t-shirt. The bleeding man looked up and said something to the woman and the other man hit him hard in the face. He bounced against the side of a car and went down and out of sight as the woman unleashed a torrent of angry swearing at him.

"This place can git a little rough sometimes," Shelly said.

"Don't worry, I can take care a' myself," Deke said, "an' you too, if need be. I been in plenty a' these kind a' joints." He lit a cigarette and rolled his t-shirt sleeves up over his shoulders, exposing his bare arms.

Shelly opened the tavern door and they stepped into a shadowy cavern of darkened forms and faces. Everyone in the bar turned to look at them and several hands went up to wave at Shelly. Though her eyes were not yet adjusted enough to identify their faces, Shelly waved back.

The joint was shabby to an extreme. Holes, likely from fists, punctured the walls at regular intervals. Peeling paper and loose wires dangled from the unpainted ceiling. No two tables or chairs were alike and at least two of the chairs lay tipped over on the floor, which was cluttered and filthy. Bottles, cans and glasses, many of them turned over and leaking, covered every table, whether anyone was sitting there or not. Dingy and derelict as the place was, the patrons looked even worse.

Only one bartender served the crowd, a middle-aged balding man wearing a short white towel tucked into the front of his pants, apron-like, to denote his rank. Alcoholic skinny, with one missing incisor, Oney Mills poured drinks and handed out beer in the same dark gray work clothes he'd worn at the mine before it caught fire and closed. Early on in the bar business he'd decided that cleanup and maintenance offered no chance of profit, and as he was disinclined toward those tasks anyway, Oney limited his labors to the dispensation of alcohol.

He kept an open bottle of Miller beside the cash register behind the bar, and every time Oney rang up a sale he took a swig. On this day, the register was banging like a trolley bell and Oney was tuned up and smiling.

"Hey, High-pockets," he called out to Shelly before she and Deke were halfway to the bar. "How you bin, sweet-thang? We all miss ya."

"Been good, Oney, I been real good," Shelly said as they shook hands and Oney set an open bottle of Falstaff in front of her.

"Ya know I keep this stuff around jus' fer you, Shelly," Oney said. "Nobody else drinks this shit."

"This is Deke," Shelly told Oney, and as Deke stuck out his hand to shake, Oney asked him, "What kin I git for ya?"

"Got any Strohs?" Deke asked.

"Even I don' carry that crap," Oney said and laughed. "You look more lak' a Bud man ta me, anyways", he said, and without asking, pulled a bottle of Budweiser from the cooler and set it in front of Deke. Shelly paid Oney for the beers and he punched the register, took a pull from his Miller and hustled off to refill the drinks of three women who were yelling for service.

Deke and Shelly turned around to check out the crowd. After a couple of minutes Shelly said, "I'm gonna walk aroun' an' say 'hi' to folks. Ya wanta come with me?"

"Naw, I'll stay here," Deke answered.

Deke leaned his back against the bar and watched Shelly move among the patrons, talking, laughing and even tussling in raucus horseplay. With some discomfort, he saw that he was the only man in the bar with long hair. Several men made eye contact and stared at him until Deke averted his eyes. He tipped his cowboy hat up, Paul Newman style, and stuffed his NASCAR t-shirt into the front of his jeans so everybody could see his John Wayne belt buckle and know what manner of man they were dealing with.

One guy in particular, a rough-hewn, craggy-faced character wearing a grimy MOPAR ballcap, kept staring at Deke. Grease stains covered his clothes and his face was blackened with coal dust from where he'd just come from the mine. The man was drinking cans of Pabst and had about ten empties in front of him at a crowded, noisy table. Like Deke, the sleeves of his t-shirt were rolled up to his shoulders, but unlike Deke, this ol' boy had shoulders three ax handles wide and arms like suspension bridge cables. Deke tried to look everywhere except in his direction, but the man continued glaring at him.

Finally Deke turned around and faced the back bar. He ordered a second beer and tried to make talk with Oney, but Oney was too busy to keep up a conversation. Deke shot a quick look over his shoulder and saw that the man was not only still looking at him, but now he was standing up. He reared back and let out a roar that sounded like Godzilla trying to do the rebel yell. "He'er's mah hat," he hollered, tossing his cap onto the floor in front of him, "Eny som'bitch in this bar got the balls ta step on it?"

When nobody answered, he looked straight at Deke. "How 'bout yew at the bar," he shouted, "the girl in the white cowboy hat?"

Deke quickly turned around and faced the back bar again.

"'At's raht, asshole, yew better turn around. Meh'be Ah'll jus' come up there an' step on yor hat … while yor head's still in it."

Deke squeezed his head down between his shoulder blades, turtle-like, and his sphincter puckered up till it hurt. From somewhere in the crowd came a woman's voice: "I don't need balls ta step on your hat, Luther, I jes don't wanta get my boot dirty."

"Who said that?" Luther yelled, turning to look in the direction of the voice.

"Who the hell you think said it, you big, retarded hillbilly?"

Luther scowled, then smiled. "Is that yew, Shelly?" he said.

"At your service," Shelly said, stepping away from the group of people she'd been talking with.

"Why hell," Luther said, "git on over he'er an' Ah'll buy ya a beer."

Deke relaxed and let out a quiet sigh until Luther added, "Soon's Ah stomp this faggot's ass at the bar. Ya wanna help? Ah think thar's a'nuff fer both of us if'n Ah don't take too much out of 'im."

"Can't do it, Luther," Shelly said. "That fa … uh, I mean that guy at the bar's with me."

"Is he, if it is a *he*, yor boyfrien'?"

Deke, who had ventured to turn around, waited for Shelly's answer.

"It don't matter," Shelly said. "He come in here with me."

"Why, shit," Luther said. "Reckon Ah'll jus' whup 'im on mah own then."

"Can't do it, Luther," Shelly told him again. "Like I said, we come in here ta'gether. You'll hafta git through me first."

"Ah don' wanna beat yew up, Shelly, jus' him."

"I don't want ya to beat me up, neither, Luther, but yor gonna have ta fight me ta git to him."

"Damn!" Luther said. "Thangs shor do git comp-ul-cated 'round here enymore."

Rattler's Den went quiet as the drinkers watched and listened.

"Oney, bring me two cans a' Blue Ribbon," Shelly called toward the bar.

Oney hurried over and handed them to Shelly and she passed him two one-dollar bills. "Keep the change," she said to the smiling barman.

Shelly walked up to Luther and stuck one can of Pabst in each of his massive hands. "Here's a better use for your fists than usin' 'em to hurt somebody you don't even know," Shelly said and gave him a peck on the cheek.

"C'mon, Deke," she hollered, "we need to git on home for supper."

After they were in the truck and had driven a few miles Deke said, "Thanks for doin' that back there, Shelly."

"That's okay, Deke. I drug ya in there, reckon it was the least I could do."

"Yeah, I'm sure glad I didn't have ta hurt that fella, spesh'ly since he was a friend a' yers," Deke said.

Shelly looked at Deke to see if he was serious. Deke was leaning back in the seat with one boot resting on the dashboard, his hat tipped high on his forehead. He was looking at his bare left arm, watching his biceps flex as he squeezed his fist.

Chapter 19

After lunch at the War Room Café on Friday, Ethel pulled the Lincoln into Cliff's station followed by Shelly in the Powerwagon. Deke's pickup was parked under the Mobilgas sign, ready to go. Ethel opened the back door and Charlie and Rose piled out. "Kin we have a lollipop, Cliff?" they hollered.

"Now see what ya got started," Ethel said as Cliff handed one to each of them. "You kids go lick them suckers in the car," she told them. "We got things ta talk about."

Cliff walked to the Ford and started it up then opened the hood to show them the work he'd done.

"It sounds good, Cliff," Shelly said as they listened to the engine.

Back in the station Cliff handed Shelly the bill. "If'n it was anybody but you this bill woulda been twice'd that. Ah give ya the parts at cost an' didn't charge ya fer all a' mah time."

"You didn't need ta do that, Cliff," Shelly said, "I got money in the bank."

"That's awright, you may need that money out th'air in Montana. Jus' don't spend it on the guy that's takin' ya." Cliff turned to Ethel. "How come yor a'lettin' this girl go all the way out th'air with that … well, Ah'm a Christian man, so Ah better not say it."

"I can't stop her, Cliff, anymore than I coulda stopped her from takin' off before. Shelly might only be seventeen but look at 'er – she's tall as a tree. Least this time she ain't hitch-hikin' and she knows where she's goin' and what she wants ta do when she gits there."

"She mighta grow'd tall as a tree," Cliff said, "but that don't mean she's grow'd deep as a tree." He looked at Shelly. "Ah've had fellas come in here an' tell me stories about you up in Norwood. It ain't no secret what you was doin'. Meh'be goin' ta Montana's a good thing for ya, but Ah don't like who yor a'goin' with. You got family and friends here, Shelly, an' ya oughta think about stayin' around, least fer a while."

Ethel flinched when Cliff mentioned Shelly's doings up in Ohio, but didn't say anything.

"I know yor worried an' mean well, but I can't stay," Shelly said. "I still think about Daddy too much when I'm aroun' here. It's like I keep expectin' ta see 'im in those places we used ta go. I also don't wanta end up as some man's 'woman', without ever havin' a life a' my own."

"I was your daddy's woman," Ethel said, "and we had us a fine life."

"Don't tell me that, Mama. You married Daddy when you was twenty-four, seven years older'n me. An' 'fore that you was a wrassler and traveled all over and did more'n some people do their whole lives. I want that same thing."

"See what I told ya," Ethel said, looking at Cliff.

"I know headin' off with Deke ta Montana don't look good, but I need ta at least try ta make my'self inta what I wanta be. An' if I fail, then I'll try somethin' else.

"We jest worry about you bein' with Deke, honey," Ethel said. "He ain't a good man fer you."

"Ah never thought Ah'd be a'sayin' this to a seventeen year old girl," Cliff said, "but Ah think you'd do better goin' ta Montana on yor own than goin' as Deke's woman – which is what people will think when you two show up t'gether."

"I ain't Deke's woman, Cliff, and I never will be. I jes need a way to get ta Montana an' I don't have a car or a driver's license."

"Ah'll fix ya up with a good car, or a pickup if ya want, an' take ya ta git yor license. Then you won't need that guy," Cliff said.

"Deke's jest usin' you, honey," Ethel added.

Shelly looked down at the scuffed linoleum floor. "No he ain't, Mama, I'm usin' him an' I ain't proud of it. It was me who asked Deke if I could go with 'im ta Montana. I even wonder if what I'm doin' is fair ta Deke. He ain't always like what you saw the other day. Sometimes he's real nice and does things right."

"It ain't those times your mama and me are frettin' about, Shelly," Cliff said. "It's those other times that are gonna git Deke, and maybe you, inta trouble." Cliff paused, looked at Ethel then back to Shelly. "Folks tell me a lotta things, Shelly. I hear'd about what happened up in Ohio with Deke an' why he had ta leave."

Ethel nodded her head, indicating Cliff had told her about the fiasco.

"That ain't the kinda' thing you need ta be mixed up in," Cliff said. "It could folla' you the whole way ta Montana."

Shelly took a breath, trying to figure out how to explain why she *had* to go, and go now. "There's more to it than Deke jes drivin' me ta Montana. His brother Zeke owns a log truck an' he's gonna teach Deke an' me how ta drive it an' help us git jobs. Deke said so right after he talked to 'im. Zeke knows a whole lot a' people there an' he's real well thought of. If I ain't with Deke, none a' that'll happen."

Shelly looked at Cliff and then at her mother, trying to make them understand. "It's what I wanta do. Here's my chance ta do it an' I need ta grab that chance while it's there. I ain't 'fraid a' what'll happen if I do this, I'm 'fraid a' what might happen if I don't. I *will* survive – both Montana and Deke McConahay."

The debate was over. Cliff even smiled a little when he said, "Well, yor Clete's girl aw'right, stubb'ern to the bone."

Shelly wrote out a check for the repair bill and handed it to Cliff. He took it and said, "You know that if ya ever need enything, we're here."

"That's right, honey," Ethel said, and turned to leave.

"Hold up a minute," Cliff said. "Ah got one more thing ta say ta Shelly."

"Yeah, Cliff."

"Ah know what yor sayin' about still missin' yor daddy so bad. Ethel an' me had ta go through that too, ya know. Ya never git somebody like Clete outa yor heart, an' ya don't want to, but you gotta keep from havin' it on yor mind all the time."

"Cliff's right," Ethel said. "You need ta close that circle 'fore ya leave."

"Mama, I need ta close a lot a circles."

"Honey, whyn't you go up to the churchyard an' have yor'self a nice long talk with Cletus. Tell 'im all about what yor doin' and how ya feel. I've done it – more'n once – an' it helps a lot."

"That'd be a good idea, Shelly," Cliff said.

"Okay, I will," Shelly said. She and Cliff hugged and said goodbye and as Shelly headed to Deke's pickup she told Ethel, "When ya git home, Mama, tell Deke not ta worry about his truck an' that I'll be along in a little while."

––––––––––––––––––

Earlier that morning, Deke sauntered from his makeshift bedroom in the parlor at a quarter till nine and found a note on the kitchen counter.

Deke –
We all went into War to do some shopping and get your truck this afternoon. Make whatever you want for breakfast and lunch. Mama says there's still weeds to pull along the driveway.
Shelly

Deke was irked at not getting to pick up his own truck and make sure that the work had been done right, but he helped himself to the coffee pot and had a bowl of Cap'n Crunch. He went into the living room, turned on the TV, planted his butt in Henry's recliner and watched cartoons all morning. Around noon he made a peanut butter and jelly sandwich for lunch then read Mack's old comic books for almost two hours. A little before two he took Jethro for a walk, but when he returned, Ethel and the kids had arrived home and Ethel immediately set him to pulling weeds.

When Deke heard the sound of his F-150 coming down Peapatch Road he stood up to greet Shelly as she pulled into the driveway. "Where ya been? Yer mom got home a long time ago," he said through the truck's open window.

Shelly's eyes were red, like she'd been crying. "You alright?" Deke asked.

"I'm fine, Deke. I jes had ta go do somethin'."

"Oh," Deke said, reckoning that was all the answer he was going to get. He ran his eyes along the length of his pickup. "Can I drive it, Shelly? I wanna see how she runs."

"Shor," Shelly said, scooting over to the passenger side, "but we can't go far, it's close ta suppertime."

"It drives good," Deke said, before they even got to the highway. After turning onto Route 635 he wound out the engine. "Wow." After a couple of miles he turned to Shelly. "How much was the bill?"

"With the new tires it was $620, Deke."

Deke's eyes narrowed and he frowned.

"Listen, Deke," Shelly said gently, "nearly all that was fer parts, new tires an' a battery. Cliff didn't charge us hardly nothin' for his labor. Even after payin' your half, you'll still have plenty a' money left to git ta Montana."

"When we leavin', anyway?" Deke said. "I'm real anxious to git on the road ta Montana so's we can start bein' boyfriend an' girlfriend."

"In a coupla days, Deke. I wanta go ta church an' have Sunday dinner with my family 'fore we go."

That night a number of friends and neighbors stopped by the Stamper house to see Shelly before she left for Montana. Deke was clearly uncomfortable and stayed on the front porch, smoking cigarettes. After the visitors had left and the smaller kids put to bed, Ethel and Shelly were alone in the kitchen. "I ain't tryin' ta hurry ya," Ethel said, "but y'all got any idea when yor fixin' ta leave?"

"I'd like ta be on the road by Sunday or Monday."

"Yor stickin' around for church an' Sunday dinner, I hope."

"I was plannin' to, Mama."

"Shelly," Ethel said, "there's som'thin I been puttin' off tellin' ya 'cause it ain't good news. You need to go up ta Olive Hill an' see Grammy."

"I was thinkin' 'bout doin' that."

"She had a stroke," Ethel said, and Shelly drew in her breath. "It wadn't a real bad one, but she don't git around like before."

"How come ya didn't tell me sooner, Mama?"

"It only happened three weeks ago an' since I knew you was comin' home I figgered it'd be best ta tell ya in person."

Shelly bit down on her lower lip.

"The bad part," Ethel continued, "is that her doctor said she might have more strokes an' they could be worse'n this one."

"Okay, Mama, I'll go see 'er. Me an' Deke can leave here right after Sunday dinner an' be in Olive Hill by suppertime."

"I'll call up there tomorrow an' let 'em know yor comin'," Ethel said.

———————————

On Saturday morning Shelly took Deke outside and they cleaned out and washed the interior of his truck but he refused to part with most of the junk in the bed. That afternoon, Ethel and Henry drove up to Welch to visit Henry's mother, who was in a nursing home. Shortly after they left, Shelly told Deke, "Would you mind takin' Jethro for a walk? I wanta talk ta my brothers an' sisters about some family things."

Shelly made popcorn and gathered everybody around the kitchen table. They told stories and laughed until Shelly brought the conversation around to what she really wanted to talk about. "How y'all doin' with Henry?" she asked.

Eleven-year-old Sadie spoke up first. "We all still miss Daddy somethin' awful, Shelly," she said, "but Henry's nice to us."

"Does Henry ever spank ya?"

Everybody shook his or her heads 'no' except for Mack.

"He spanked me once'd when Mama was gone," Mack said, "but he don't spank near as hard as Mama does."

"What'd ya do ta get spanked?" Shelly asked.

"Ah broke yonder picture winda," Mack said, pointing towards the living room, "kickin' mah football in the house."

Shelly had trouble not laughing. "I'd a' spanked ya too."

"We all wanted ta wale on 'im," Junior said. "It happened the day after Christmas an' it was cold in here. He's jus' lucky Henry got to 'im first."

Sarah, just turned fourteen, understood why Shelly was asking about Henry. "We're all more afraid a' Mama than we are a' Henry," she said. "Even Junior. Las' June he got too sassy with 'er and she wrassled him down and stuck his head in the pig's waterin' trough, right in front a' all of us."

Clete Jr's face went red as everybody giggled. When he recovered his composure he said in a serious voice, "Ah know why yor askin' us all this, Shelly. You need ta understan', us Stampers don't jus' look out for ar'selves, we look out for each other, too. We're all branched from the same tree you are, big sister."

Shelly took Junior's hand in hers, surprised that he was already getting callouses. "I jes needed to know ev'rything was okay before I left."

After supper, as Deke and Junior sat on the front porch smoking, Shelly went looking for Henry. She found him out back looking up at the waxing moon that was hovering over the hills, smoking his pipe and petting Jethro. He turned when he heard footsteps. "Shelly," he said in greeting.

They stood silently for a moment, watching the moon slice through a pod of drifting clouds. "Ah never git tired of lookin' at the moon," Henry said. "Whatever troubles Ah might be havin', it settles me some."

"Henry," Shelly said, "I got somethin' to tell ya 'fore we leave."

Henry turned away from the sky and looked at Shelly.

"I'm sorry, Henry."

"For what, Shelly? Ah don't recall as you've done any wrong ta me."

"Maybe not now, Henry, but back before I left, I didn't treat ya very nice. Reckon I jes missed Daddy a whole lot."

Henry put his hand on the shoulder of the girl who stood almost a head taller than him. "Don't you worry one bit about it. Ah understan' how tough that was an' Ah don't have any bad feelin's over it. Ah lost my dad when Ah was even younger'n you. An' now my mom is in that place up in Welch an' she's doin' poorly. Life kin be awful rough at times, Shelly."

Shelly couldn't help herself. She threw her arms around Henry and said, "Thanks for taking care a' my family, Henry."

At 8:30 on Sunday morning, Shelly went into the parlor to wake Deke up and found him lying under the sheets reading one of Mack's comic books. "Is this what you been doin' ev'ry morning instead a' gittin' up?" Shelly asked.

"Uh ... jest fer a little bit."

"Well, c'mon, we're fixin' ta leave for church in fifteen minutes."

"You go on without me," Deke said, barely glancing up. "I don't need ta go. B'sides, I ain't had breakfast, yet."

"You need church more'n any man I know, an' we're havin' a big brunch right afterwards, so git up." Then Shelly asked, "You got any decent clothes for church?"

"Uh …not really. Other'n my guns an' huntin' gear, an' my flannel shirt an' jacket, I only grabbed a few things when I took off."

"You mean …" Shelly said slowly, "that you don't have any clothes other than what you been wearin'? Not even extra socks or underwear?"

"Uhhh …. no."

Shelly closed her eyes and took a deep breath. "Alright, then. Git dressed. We'll buy ya some new things next week after we're on the road."

Deke crawled out from under the sheets, embarrassed for Shelly to see him in his droopy white skivvies. After he dressed, Deke headed for the bathroom and was again embarrassed when he came out and found the entire Stamper family standing outside the door, waiting for him so they could leave.

As they nearly always did in good weather, the Stampers walked to the Shiloh Church, less than half a mile away. Reverend Scoggins was waiting at the open door, greeting parishioners as they arrived. He had been on vacation this past week, hiking in the Smoky Mountains, and so had not yet met Deke. Clearly happy to see Shelly again, the preacher gave her a long hug, and when Shelly introduced him to Deke, he vigorously shook Deke's hand and said, "I hear you and Shelly are going to Montana together."

"Uh … yeah … I guess so," Deke muttered.

Ethel stepped up to the minister. " We're havin' a meal right after the service today," she said, "so Shelly and Deke can git on the road. Would you care ta join us?"

"Why thank you, Ethel," he replied. "I'd be delighted to."

Twenty minutes after the Stampers returned from church, Reverend Scoggins pulled into their driveway in his black Buick. He spent a few moments in the kitchen chatting with Ethel, Shelly, Sarah, and Sadie, who were preparing the food, then went into the living room and made the rounds. Deke, who was not comfortable with any of the Stamper clan except Junior, was sitting by himself near a corner. After briefly talking with everyone else in the room, the preacher grabbed an empty straightback chair and placed it directly in front of Deke. "It's good finally getting to meet you, Deke," he began, thrusting his hand out for Deke to shake. "Especially after everything Ethel's told me about you."

Deke took the reverend's hand and gulped. After ten minutes of one-sided interrogation, Deke could think of nothing but escape. When Junior walked into the living room after changing out from his church clothes, Deke saw his chance. "Hey, Junior, ya wanna go out on the porch an' have a smoke?"

"Aw'raht," Junior said, and reached for the crumpled pack of Old Gold's in his shirt pocket.

Deke got up to walk around the minister, but he rose as well. "If you don't object," he said, "I'll join y'all on the porch. It's a nice morning and I could use a little air."

"Uh, yeah … sure," Deke mumbled as the three of them went out the front door.

In the kitchen, Shelly caught the preacher's move and nudged Ethel. They snickered at Deke's distress until they both remembered how Reverend Scoggins had married off Wilbur and Shirl right after Christmas dinner.

"We're about done here, Mama," Shelly said to Ethel. "You mind if I go out on the porch an' join that crew? I'm 'fraid if Preacher Scoggins gits Deke too confused, he might start tellin' the truth."

When everyone was seated at the table, the preacher kept to pleasant small talk and wished Shelly well on her adventure, never once breeching the subject of matrimony. Even the short time he'd spent with Deke had convinced him that Shelly was better off risking eternal damnation than becoming Mrs. McConahay.

After brunch, Reverend Scoggins bid farewell to Shelly and departed. Though she had little packing to do, the closer Shelly got to finishing, the more her siblings pestered her, not wanting to let Shelly out of their sight. When she was done packing, Shelly knew she needed to do one more thing and she needed to do it alone. "Mama, can you find somethin' for the kids ta do for a whiles," Shelly whispered to Ethel, "I wanna go out back 'fore we leave."

Though Shelly hadn't been there since that awful day in 1968, Ethel sensed immediately where she was going. "Ev'rybody go wash your hands," she called out, "an' we'll have some ice cream."

While the kids raced each other to the bathroom, Shelly slipped quietly out the back door. As she walked past the kennel Jethro came over and looked up at her with his sad eyes. "I'll be back in a minute an' pet ya, Jethro," Shelly told him and continued on to a small, dilapidated wooden shed.

She unhooked the rusty hasp and forced the sagging door open with her shoulder. The inside of the shed was dim in shadow, but enough light came through the open door and broken window for Shelly to make out every detail of the interior. Two bridles, a halter and a lead rope hung from pegs on the wall, and a saddle, once her special Christmas gift, rested on the rounded side of a raised and blanketed oil drum. The things on the wall weren't in bad shape, but vermin had gnawed the saddle until it was ruined. Shelly ran her palm over the chewed, dried-up leather and inhaled several slow breaths. She stepped over to the tack hanging along the wall and ran the leather lines and lead rope through her fingers. "Goodbye," she whispered and walked out the door, closing it behind her.

Shelly spent a good ten minutes with Jethro, talking to him, petting him and rubbing his round belly when he rolled over. When she came into the kitchen Ethel was putting the ice cream away. "Ya want some?" Ethel said.

"No thanks," Shelly answered, and then asked, "Mama, can you do me a favor?"

Ethel looked at Shelly and waited.

"Would you get rid a' that stuff a' mine out in the shed? Give away what ya can an' throw away the rest."

"Sure, honey," Ethel answered.

Shelly walked into the living room where everyone was finishing up their ice cream. "You 'bout ready ta go?" she said to Deke, who was licking his bowl clean.

Deke lowered the bowl enough to see over it. "In a minute," he said.

Followed by her family, Shelly carried her pack and suitcase out to Deke's truck. Deke grabbed the duffel bag with his guns in it from the parlor and tagged along behind. He climbed into the pickup bed and as he was stowing their belongings in the big wooden trunk, said to Shelly, "I'm rearin' ta git on with it," more enthusiastically than Ethel cared to hear.

Shelly hugged Henry and Ethel and just like when she had arrived her siblings formed a ring around her, hugging her and all talking at the same time. "Call us as soon's ya git there. When ya comin' back, Shelly? Are we ever gonna see ya a'gin?"

"Lordy," Shelly said, while passing out hugs, kisses, and head rubs, "I ain't goin' ta Jupiter, jes Montana. It ain't all that far away."

"Las' time ya left, ya only went ta Uh-hi-uh," Mack said, "an' ya never come back ta see us once'd ... an hardly called."

Shelly looked at her brother and saw herself; he didn't pull his punches. "I know I didn't, Mack, an' I'm sorry for it. I'll do better this time," Shelly told him, but they both knew it probably wouldn't happen.

Chapter 20

Shelly leaned out the open window, waving goodbye until the Stamper house disappeared from her view. As they pulled onto the highway at Wimmer Gap, Deke asked, "How long we stayin' at yer Grammy's?"

Shelly turned and noticed that the tip of Deke's nose was brown. "Whatcha got on your nose?" she asked.

Deke rubbed his index finger across his nose and then licked it. "Chocolate ice cream," he said, and smiled.

Shelly grimaced. "What if it a' been somethin' else an' you licked it?"

"Then I guess I'd a' found out it was somethin' else."

They drove a few more miles before Shelly said, "Well, you gonna wipe it off or leave it there till we git ta Montana?"

Deke pulled out his old snot rag, rubbed it across his nose two or three times and stuck it back in his pocket. "There, ya happy now?"

Shelly wasn't happy. She wasn't happy to be leaving her family and she wasn't happy that her grandmother'd had a stroke. "I'm only plannin' ta spend the night in Olive Hill," she said, answering Deke's original question. "We'll head for Montana bright an' early ta'morrow."

All afternoon Deke and Shelly drove with both windows down, letting the early autumn wind blow over them. Traffic was light and other than one stop for fuel, pop, and a restroom, they drove straight through. At a few minutes past four they crossed the bridge in Olive Hill and began climbing the winding road along Tick Ridge. After several miles, Shelly directed Deke to turn in at a driveway where three women were sitting in lawn chairs in front of weathered clapboard farmhouse. Two of the women got up and walked over to greet them, but the third, wrapped in a quilt, remained seated.

"Hi, Aunt Gladys. Hi, Aunt Nellie," Shelly called as she jumped from the truck and ran to greet them.

They were still embracing when Deke walked up, and after introducing him to her aunts, Shelly went over to the seated woman. "Grammy," she said, bending over to hug her grandmother, "how are ya doin'?"

"I bin better, but I'm gittin' by," the old woman said and smiled. "It's sa' good ta see ya agin', Shelly. I'm grateful ya stopped by b'fore headin' out west."

The two aunts walked over, trailing Deke in their wake, and Shelly asked them, "Where's all my cousins?"

"Gaddin' about somewhere's," Nellie answered.

"How many y'all got now?" Shelly wanted to know.

Her two aunts looked at each other and for a second Shelly thought they were going to start counting on their fingers. "Fourteen," Nellie answered, "twixt us."

Gladys elbowed her sister. "That av'erges out ta two per husband."

"It would if'n they were all from husbands," Nellie said, giggling.

Shelly led Deke over to the blanketed woman. "Deke, this is my grandmother, Emma, but we call her Grammy."

The old woman stuck out a boney hand for Deke to shake as Shelly went to the porch and got two more chairs. Grammy's stroke hadn't affected her mind or speech and for the next hour the five of them drank iced tea, joked, and shared stories. Neither of Shelly's aunts was overly religious and besides having multiple husbands, both had done their share of shacking up and wild living so they didn't judge Deke or Shelly for heading west together.

Deke soon relaxed and after the pent up week he'd endured in Peapatch, was eager to let his tongue run loose over some free-range embellishment. The aunts laughed easy and often and soon Deke was shoveling the bullshit. Shelly knew that whenever Deke took shovel in hand, he would sooner or later dig himself into a hole. Several times she tried to get the conversation onto firmer ground, but Deke had an audience. From telling about his brother in Montana, Deke moved on to his own truck-driving experience, boasting about how he'd taught Shelly to drive a dump truck.

Nellie leaned over and patted her niece on the knee. "I reckon Shelly gets that love a' trucks from her daddy."

Either Shelly had not sufficiently explained to Deke that these were her mother's relatives, that is, Coopers, not Stampers, or else Deke had forgotten, for he replied, "Yeah, I'm sorry I never got ta meet yer brother. Shelly's told me how nice 'e was."

"Brother?" Gladys and Nellie both said. "We don't have a brother." Laughing, they turned to Grammy. "Is there sump'thin you never told us, Mom?"

Shelly stepped in to rescue Deke. "Gladys an' Nellie are Mama's sisters, Deke, not Daddy's."

As usual, Deke chose to keep digging his hole rather than grab onto the proffered rope. Looking from Nellie to Gladys, Deke said, "You are?"

The two sisters' stoney expressions should have stopped Deke right there, but never a man to waste the opportunity to turn a simple mistake into a fiasco, Deke said, "You two don't look nothin' like Ethel." And when their angry looks still didn't register with him, Deke turned and said to their mother. "Grammy don't either."

In his blundering way, Deke had broached the only topic that could (and did) piss off Shelly's two fun-loving and easygoing aunts. Nellie and Gladys clammed up like their mouths were full of glue.

The matter had long been a sore spot in the Cooper family but Deke's confusion was understandable. In contrast to thickset Ethel's swarthy skin and black, curly hair, both aunts and Grammy were thin and light complected. Gladys especially, with her pale skin and wispy, straight flaxen hair, was almost wraith-like. Even Shelly had wondered at the striking difference, and though she'd never met grandpa Floyd, pictures of him depicted a slim, well-built man with fair hair and medium complexion.

"Oh ..." Deke finally mumbled. "I jest thought that ... uh ... well, you know ... "

Both aunts stood up from their chairs. "Y'all kin stay here an' talk," Nellie said, "'bout whatever ya want to. We're goin' inside an' fix supper."

Half an hour later Gladys leaned out the front door and announced the meal was ready. Shelly got up and walked to Grammy's chair to help her get up, but the old woman shook her head. "I kin walk on mah own," she announced. "It jes takes me a little longer ta git whar' I'm a'goin'."

At the dinner table, Deke tried to join in the conversation, but both aunts pointedly ignored him. When supper was over, Nellie, Gladys, and Shelly rose from the table and began cleaning up.

"Is there somethin' I can do ta help?" Deke asked.

"No," both aunts answered at once.

"Ya got a dog I can walk?" Deke said, hoping to get away for a spell.

"Where's Snowball?" Shelly asked Grammy.

"Lordy-bee, Shelly, Snowball died two and a half years ago," Grammy said. "You ain't been here in that long."

"I'm sorry, Grammy."

"It's okay, she was a good dog," Grammy said, "but she got old, like me."

"No, I meant I'm sorry about not comin' ta see ya in all that time."

"That's awright too, Shelly. I know how it is with young folks. They git to a sar'tin age and don't like hangin' aroun' with old people. I weren't no diff'ernt. The important thing is ya come ta see me now."

Shelly walked over from the sink and hugged her grandmother. "I wouldn't a' took off without comin' ta say goodbye, Grammy."

With no dog to walk, Deke planned his own exit. "I'm goin' out to the truck an' git our things," he said to Shelly, standing up. "I'll be back in a while."

Grammy pushed herself up from the table and began putting the dishes away that her daughters had washed and dried but Shelly could see that she was unsteady on her feet and in some pain.

"We kin do this for ya, Mom," Nellie told her, but Grammy didn't stop.

"I ain't helpless yet," she said.

Deke stayed outside, puttering around his truck until Nellie and Gladys were gone. After they'd left, he came in, carrying his duffel bag and Shelly's suitcase.

"You two kin sleep upstairs," Grammy said after Deke plopped the luggage down on the kitchen floor. "I moved inta the parlor down here after my stroke 'cause it's hard for me ta climb stairs."

When Deke saw that Grammy was putting him and Shelly together, a big grin spread over his face. "You bet," he said, as he grabbed the bags and quickly headed toward the stairway that led off the hall.

Shelly listened as Deke bounded the first few stairs. "Deke!" she called after him. "You can have the bedroom on the right. Put my suitcase in the one on the left."

The footsteps on the stairway stopped and for thirty seconds Shelly heard nothing. Then slowly, one heavy footfall at a time, they continued up to the landing.

When Deke returned from upstairs, Shelly and her grandmother had moved to the living room and Grammy was telling Shelly stories about her great-grandparents and other relatives that Shelly'd never heard before. "I reckon you need ta hear some a' this, Shelly, 'cause we might not see each other agin'."

"Don't say things like that, Grammy," Shelly told her, almost choking up. "You got a long time ta live an' I'll come back an' visit."

"You say that 'cause yor young an' kin still pretend," Grammy said, "but I'm old an' know better." She took Shelly's hand and smiled. "But none a' that matters. Yor here now an' we got this time t'gether."

Shelly managed a smile and she and Grammy talked for a while longer until Grammy said, "I know it ain't but eight-thirty, but I'm gonna go git ready for bed. I'm a whole lot more comf'terble layin' down anymore than sittin' up."

"Do ya need help with anything, Grammy?"

"Naw, I git on fine, but after I'm settled in bed, I want ya ta come in an' sit for awhiles. We got us more talkin' ta do. Deke kin watch television out here."

Grammy raised herself from the couch and hobbled into the kitchen. After a few moments she went into the bathroom and then the parlor. Shelly got up and turned on the old black and white TV, switching between the three channels until Deke settled on *Kung Fu*. Just as Caine was beating up seven racist cowboys Grammy called, "I'm ready for ya ta come in now, Shelly."

Shelly walked into the converted parlor where she and her siblings had spent many nights sleeping on blankets spread out on the floor. Now an iron-framed bedstead with Grammy's feather mattress, a nightstand, a dresser and a well-padded armchair filled the small room. Grammy pointed to a cup on the nearby nightstand. "I always have a cup a' 'sang 'fore I go ta sleep. It takes the rough edges off the day. I made one for you too."

Shelly picked up the cup of ginseng tea, took a sip and sat down in the chair beside the bed where her grandmother lay under a worn and faded quilt.

"I always wanted you ta have this quilt, someday," Grammy said. "My mama made it for me when I was only five or six so it must be close ta seventy years old."

"It's real perty," Shelly told her.

"It use't ta be," Emma said, knowing Shelly was merely being polite. "But it's all wrung out now 'cause years ago we washed ev'rything with lye soap."

"I'd still be proud ta have it ... someday."

"I'll tell Nellie an' Gladys ta save it for ya," Grammy said, "but don't count too many chickens on 'em ta do that."

Shelly laughed at her grandmother's expression, wondering if she was making a joke or had confused the old saying. They could hear the TV out in the living room and Grammy nodded toward the door. "You ain't gonna up an' marry that boy, are ya Shelly? When yor mama call't, she told me a few things about 'im."

"Nope, Grammy. I wouldn't marry Deke in a million years. Not even if somebody was holdin' a gun on me ta do it."

"Now thar'd be a switch, wouldn't it? The groom's daddy holdin' a shotgun on the bride," Grammy said and cackled over the thought of it.

Shelly laughed along with her grandmother and when they'd settled down Grammy said, "Aw, I don't think Deke's a bad sort, Shelly, he jes ain't for you. I ain't know'd 'im 'cept for today, but it seems like the good Lord, for whatever reason, put his head on a little crooked."

Shelly laughed again. "Grammy," she said, more serious now, "I'm sorry for those things Deke said ta'day."

"Ya never need ta apologize for somebody else's words, Shelly. 'Sides, Deke shor ain't the first one ta wonder why yor mother looks so diff'ernt'n the rest of us. Even when people warn't sayin' it d'rectly, we knew they was sayin' it behin't our backs."

Grammy took a sip of her ginseng tea. "After Nellie an' Gladys was born'd it got even worse, 'cause they was so light skinned an' fair-haired. Ethel got teased all the time by other kids, and even pestered on it from some a' the grown-ups 'roun here."

"I never knew that," Shelly said.

"Naw, Ethel wouldn't say nothin' now. She's real good at keepin' past things in the past. But it bothered her a lot when she was young. I think that's what made 'er so tough. If'n any kid teased her about bein' dark or called her a name, they was in a fight."

"I don't know if it's my place ta ask, Grammy, but you got any idea why Mama's so dark when the rest a' your family is light complected."

"If it ain't your place," Grammy said with a smile, "I don't know whose it would be." She reached across the bed and grabbed a second pillow. "Help me sit up here, will ya, so's I kin look at ya better." After she got settled, Emma looked deep into Shelly's gray eyes. "You must a' wondered about it before now, Shelly," she said, "'specially after ya grow'd up some?"

"Maybe I did a little," Shelly admitted, "an' about my own dark skin too. I jes reckoned there was some dark complected people on your side a the family."

"There ain't," Grammy said.

"Or maybe Floyd's family."

"His neither."

"Grammy, you didn't?" Shelly said, chuckling.

"Yor right," Grammy said, "I didn't ... Floyd did. That's what I call't ya in here ta tell ya about."

"Are you tellin' me, Grammy, that yor not really my ..."

"That's what I'm sayin', Shelly."

"Or that yor not Mama's real ... "

"Thet's right, I'm not."

Speechless, Shelly took a deep breath as the full impact of her grandmother's announcement hit her. Finally she said, "Does Mama know?"

"She does."

"Who else knows?"

"Purty much jes me an' Ethel, an' now you, Shelly."

"Do aunt Nellie and aunt Gladys know?"

"Lordy-bee," Grammy said, and laughed. "They'd be the last ones I'd tell. If'n they knew, the whole county'd know, an' Ethel'd never speak ta me agin."

"What about Mama's mother?" Shelly asked.

Grammy took another sip of her tea. "Nobody rightly knows what become of 'er. Leastwise none a' us do. Floyd weren't even sure of 'er last name."

Shelly stopped and let this information sink in. Then she remembered what started this conversation. "Was Mama's mother a Negro?"

"Partly. An' Indian too, with some other things throw'd in, maybe some kinda Turk or Portch-a-ghee. Nobody rightly knows for shor 'bout those folks Ethel come from. From what I'm told, they don't even know themselves." Emma sat her teacup down on the nightstand. "But Ethel's mama was nare dark as a Negro."

"You met 'er?" Shelly asked, surprised.

"Once'd ... the night she brought your mother."

This was all too much for Shelly. She exhaled then fell back into the cushioned chair. "So that means I'm part Negro?"

"Likely so."

"An' Indian too."

Grammy nodded.

"But how come ... how come you raised Mama, and not her real mother?"

"It's quite a story, but since I tol't ya this much, I reckon you wanta hear it all."

"Yeah, Grammy, I wanta know it," Shelly said.

"When me an' Floyd got married in 1926, he was a brakeman on the railroad, so's I got used to 'im bein' gone a lot. We lived up here then, 'cause both our families were Carter County people an' we liked bein' close to 'em, but a coupla years later, the railroad wanted Floyd to transfer down ta Tennessee an' learn ta be an engineer. It was more money for 'im, an' in them days you didn't refuse the railroad, so we moved to a place called New Tazewell. Floyd was gone even more then, 'cause he ran freight trains up through the Cumberland Gap and down through Knoxville as far as Chattanooga."

Grammy picked up a small white lace handerchief from her bed-stand and wiped her lips with it. "I always knew Floyd had a taste for likker, 'specially the home-made kind. Thar weren't no shortage a' moonshine 'roun east Tennessee, 'cause after the depression hit in 1929 a lot a' folks started in ta makin' it for extra money. But this one woman, 'bout twenty miles from our place in the hills above Sneed-ville, up on this spot they called 'The Ridge', was real well known for makin' the best stuff aroun'. There was so many stories about this woman even I'd heard of 'er. She was gret big an' fat, people said, but strong as a plough horse. Ev'rybody knew she made moonshine, and once'd in a while the law'd come and take whatever she had and bust up 'er still if'n they could find it, but they never arrested 'er, 'cause she was too big ta fit through the jail door."

Laughing, Grammy wiped her mouth again with the handerchief. "That's what people said, anyways, though I don't know as I b'lieve it all."

"It's quite a story," Shelly admitted.

"What I didn't know till later, was that Floyd was scuttlin' over there ta buy that big woman's likker an' stayin' 'roun for a coupla' days ta git drunk, then tellin' me he was on a train run. An' what I *really* didn't know was that big ol' woman had a young daughter that Floyd took up cavortin' with. Well, one night in the autumn a' 1930, aroun' nine-thirty at night, there come a'knockin' on the door of our house in New Tazewell. Floyd was away on a *real* train run, so's when I went to the door and saw this big, real strong lookin' dark woman standin' there, I was a might uneasy.

'Whata you want?' I said to her, not too polite."

'Ta give ya this,' she tol't me right back, not real friendly, either. 'It belongs ta Floyd'.

"She reached out an' handed me this bundle wrapped in a blanket, an' without even lookin' I reached out an' took it.

'What is it?' I said to 'er.

'It's Floyd's daughter,' she said. 'Mama died, so I needed ta git married. My husband says he ain't a'raisin some other man's baby, 'specially an outsider's.'

"When I first opened the door to 'er, I thought she was a Negro, but as my eyes adjusted to the light, I could see she weren't. She was sturdy and square built, likely still in 'er late teens. Her skin was dark but her lips and nose an' such, was like White people's, and eyes as blue as any I ever seen."

"Like Mama's," Shelly said, and Grammy nodded.

"I said to 'er, 'How come you know she's Floyd's?' and that girl laughed, but not happy-like, an' said, 'cause till I got married, he was the only man I was ever with.'

'Does he know about her?' I said.

'He knows,' she tol't me. Then she handed me this poke an' said, 'here's her clothes an' things.'

"She turned ta walk away an' I said, 'Does she have a name?'

"She barely turned her head aroun'. 'She does, but I ain't tellin' ya,' she said. 'You name 'er what ya want, she's yours now.'

"Aw, I had quite a time, figgerin' out what ta tell people about this baby jes showin' up at my house, when they know'd I weren't pregnant. It might not a' bin so bad if that woman was White, but in them days neither Negroes nor your mama's people could go ta reg'lar schools or git any kind a' decent work. It was lucky that Ethel weren't as dark as her mother, so's I made up a story that your mama was my sister's baby. I tol't folks my sister was dirt poor with no job an' the father'd run off so I said I'd raise the little girl. I don't know if'n ev'erbody b'lieved it, but leastwise one a' the neighbor women help'd me out since I didn't know much about raisin' a baby."

"What'd ya tell your own family?" Shelly asked.

"I wrote letters ta me an' Floyd's relatives up here an' made it sound like I hadn't tol't 'em 'cause I wanted the baby ta be a s'prise. Well, since I hadn't seen any of 'em for over a year, that weren't too bad, but some of 'em was put out 'cause I'd sprung the news on 'em like that.

"After a few years though, I found we was in a fix, 'cause when Ethel got ta be four or five she started gittin' darker an' I could tell some people was curious about what sort a' man my made-up sister had coupled with. I was sorely 'fraid that when it come time to put 'er in school they might make me try ta prove she was all White, an I couldn't do that. I tell ya, Shelly, once'd ya start inta lyin' 'bout sump'thin it jes gits harder'n harder ta keep that lie goin'. But I didn't have no choice if I wanted Ethel ta have a decent life, an' I don't regret doin' it one bit.

"So I started pesterin' Floyd ta git transferred back up here ta Kentucky. Luck'ly he had more seniority by then an' after six months or so, his transfer come through. People here might wonder about her bein' so dark, but it ain't unheard of for light skinned couples ta have a dark baby now an' then, so's we got by okay."

"What happened when grandpa Floyd got home and you was here with the baby?" Shelly asked.

"Aw, now that was a fine ta' do," Grammy said, and laughed out loud. "But I shor weren't laughin' about it then." She reached for her teacup and drained off what was left. "I wish I had some more 'sang tea."

"You want me ta make ya some, Grammy?"

"Naw, it's gittin' late. You jes stay here an' let me finish the story," Grammy said and set her cup back down.

"Soon's Floyd come in the door the next afternoon he heard the baby cryin', an' at first I thought he was gonna turn aroun' an' walk right back out. 'You git in here,' I yelled at 'im. 'Some big colored girl brought you a present las' night.'

Well, Floyd come in the room on tiptoes. He'd never seen the baby, he jes knew he'd got the girl pregnant, an' then she wouldn't see 'im no more. Floyd's first words were, 'Ya keepin' it?'

'Yeah, I'm keepin' the baby,' I tol't 'im. 'The only question is am I keepin' you.'

"See, I'd bin a'wantin' a baby. With Floyd bein' gone so much I was lonely an' I never did like socializin' with them Tennessee women all that much. We jes couldn't seem ta have one though, but it weren't for lack a' tryin'."

Grammy stopped her story and winked at Shelly.

"Aw, I chewed Floyd ta pernition an' back. He drug out the Bible an' swore on it he'd never done anythin' like this b'fore an' never would agin'. An' I couldn't jes up an' leave or even throw 'im out. This was 1930 an' there weren't no jobs for men, let alone women. I couldn't take some baby what weren't even mine back ta my fam'ly an' expect 'em ta take us in an' help raise 'er up. An' then the truth might come out that this little girl's mama weren't White, an' that wouldn't do, even in Kentucky."

Shelly reached across the bed and took Grammy's hand and held it.

"An' I didn't really wanta leave Floyd. We got on ta'gether an' he treated me good. Aw, he'd git drunk sometimes an' once'd in a while come home that way an' it bothered me, but he weren't mean or nothin'. He'd jes crawl inta bed an' sleep it off an' he never missed work over it."

Grammy looked at Shelly and shrugged her shoulders. "So I forgave 'im and we named the baby Ethel after my great-grandmother and got on with raisin 'er."

The old woman dipped her head, like the story was over, but Shelly's curiosity was aroused. "Grammy, did ya ever find out anything 'bout that girl who brought Mama?"

Grammy raised her head up. "Aw, I found out some things. A' course, I made Floyd tell me the whole story. He'd been goin' up ta that gret big woman's cabin to buy likker for some time an' she always had three or four a' her kids around ta help her, but never any menfolk. She weren't shy about tellin' Floyd she'd bin married a few times but said her last husband had died a few years b'fore. One a' the kids help'n out was the girl who brought the baby. Floyd said her first name was Vardalia but he never knew 'er las' name 'cause them kids had diff'ernt fathers, but it was likely Mullins, Collins, or Goins, 'cause near ev'rybody roun' there had one a' them names.

"After Floyd bought likker a few times him an' Vardalia got on talkin' terms. If her mama weren't feelin' well an' didn't want anybody up ta her cabin the girl'd bring the likker ta Floyd at this little settlement down in the valley that some church had set up for these people. Floyd said they had a school an' a church along the road down there."

Shelly stiffened at the memory of the strange trip she'd taken with Ethel the day she'd had her examination in Bluefield.

"Well, Vardalia an' Floyd got ta bein' more an' more friendly an' purty soon Floyd started bringin' 'er presents an' things. She'd never had no man do that for 'er 'cause most a' her people were so poor."

"You said this girl was in 'er teens, Grammy," Shelly said. "Floyd woulda been a lot older'n her."

"Floyd was a little over thirty an' a good lookin' man, Shelly. An' you know how some girls git all flattered by an' older man payin' attention to 'em."

Shelly nodded to that.

"I think Floyd got ta buyin' Vardalia nicer an' nicer things, stuff she'd never be able ta git otherwise. Accordin' ta Floyd, Vardalia's people was treated jes like colored's an' weren't allowed in the better stores. Purty soon, more was happenin' twixt Floyd an' Vardalia than jes buyin' moonshine an' talkin'. Floyd said he never planned on doin' what he did, but he got drunk an' it jes happened. That might a' bin so the first time, but it kept happenin' on a reg'lar basis afterwards. When this'd bin goin' on awhile's Vardalia told Floyd she was pregnant with his baby an' her mama was mad about it. He couldn't come aroun' no more an' she was done sellin' 'im likker."

Grammy shook her head. "I think Floyd was more trouble'd 'bout not bein' able ta buy that big woman's moonshine than he was about what he'd done to 'er daughter."

"Grammy," Shelly said, "you keep sayin' 'Vardalia's people' an' 'them people', but you ain't said what people yor talkin' about."

"Why landsakes," Grammy said, "I guess I didn't."

Shelly passed her teacup to her grandmother. "Here Grammy, you finish this, I don't need it."

Grammy took the cup in her palms and carefully sipped from it. "I don't know a whole lot about 'em, Shelly," she said. "Most a' it comes from what Floyd tol't me or what I could pick up from people in New Tazewell. Ya had ta watch out even askin' questions 'bout them people, like there was sump'thin wrong with even wantin' ta know. And a' course, with a dark baby that ev'rybody in New Tazewell knew weren't mine, I had ta be ext'er careful.

"Floyd said they was called Melungeons. He was a curious man and he'd ask'd Vardalia an' her mother how they'd come about an' why they looked like they did, but Floyd said they didn't know a whole lot 'bout themselves. They didn't even know what the word Melungeon right'ly meant or where it'd come from but they didn't much call themselves that 'cause other people used it as an insult. Vardalia tol't Floyd they couldn't vote or go ta White schools an' till them church people come in an' built that little settlement, most Melungeons never got any schoolin'. They kept ta themselves an' only married in their own group."

"Is it still like that?" Shelly asked.

"I think it's changed a lot, Shelly, but I don't know. I ain't bin down in that area for close ta forty years an' got no desire to go back."

Grammy raised her hand and lifted an index finger. "Floyd was real shor about one thing, though. He said we couldn't ever let anybody know Ethel's mother was a Melungeon or it'd go real bad for her an' meh'be us too. That's why I wanted ta git back up here where most people'd never even heard that word."

"I still don't understand what Melungeons are, Grammy," Shelly said.

"You an' ev'rybody else," Grammy told her, and laughed. "What they are an' where they come from seems ta be quite a mystery. They gotta be part Negro 'cause their skin is dark and Floyd said they tell 'bout mixin' with Indians. Other'n that nobody knows, but 'cause they got White features an' some of 'em have blue eyes, there's some purty crazy stories. Floyd said he worked with one fella on the railroad who actually thought they come from outer space."

"How old was Mama when you told her that her mother was a Melungeon?" Shelly asked.

"Oh Lordy, Shelly, we never tol't her. Me an' Floyd didn't want Ethel know'n anything about her not bein' my real child."

"How'd she find out?"

"Well now, I reckon that's the last part a' the story," Grammy said. "The night Ethel got dropped off here, when I unwrapped her blanket, there was a letter for Floyd underneath it. I ain't gonna lie an' say I didn't read it 'fore Floyd got home, 'cause I did. I reckon Vardalia musta' bin goin' ta that church school, 'cause she knew how ta write."

"What'd it say, Grammy?"

"Aw, Vardalia went on for quite a spell, really. 'Bout how she'd cared for Floyd an' thought he cared for her an' how mad she was at 'im. She reckon'd he'd jes bought her all them things so's he could have his way with 'er. She never mention'd the baby's name, but she shor 'nuff went on 'bout how she loved 'er an' was sad ta give 'er up and hoped Floyd an' me would raise her right. She signed 'er name 'Vardalia' but never wrote no las' name after it.

"When I give that letter ta Floyd I figger'd he'd read it an' throw it away, like he shoulda, but Floyd tucked that letter up somewheres an' forgot about it. After he hit that tree an' died we was goin' through his things an' Ethel found it an' read it. I was in the other room an' heard her cryin' then I heard her yellin' at me. It's jes a good thing her sisters weren't home at the time."

"Didja tell Mama the whole story then, Grammy?"

"I didn't have much choice at that point."

"How'd she take it?" Shelly asked.

"How you reckon she'd take it? Findin' out after seventeen years that I weren't her real mother an' that Floyd, who she loved like you did Cletus, did that to a teenage girl. An' this comin' right after he died from bein' drunk. I hugged Ethel an' tol't her how much I loved 'er an' she settled down some 'fore Nellie an' Gladys got back home, but she made me promise I'd never say a word about this ta them or anybody else. Like I said, Ethel always had trouble bein' teased 'bout her dark skin an' you know how tetchy teen-age girls kin be. Well, what with Floyd's dyin' an' then learnin' all this, your mama was knocked for a loop. Even as a young'n Ethel was tough minded an' good at not lettin' things git the best of 'er, but she never was the same after that. She'd always talked about bein' a nurse or a teacher an' she got good grades, but after that day, none a' that mattered to 'er anymore. She quit studyin' an' then took ta missin' school."

"Jes like I did after Daddy died," Shelly said.

"Ethel tol't me 'bout that, an' it bother'd us ta see it happenin' in you."

Grammy yawned but went on with her story. "One week this two-bit carnival come ta Olive Hill with all sorts a' peculyar things in it, like freaks an' chicken head eaters. They had 'em a coupla shaky old carnival rides for kids but they also had women an' midget wrasslers. After them women wrassled with each other they offered ta take on any a' the local girls an' Ethel entered. She didn't know any fancy moves, but Ethel was strong as a bear and knew how ta fight an' them other women wrasslers couldn't do a thing with 'er. Well, that slick feller who run the show started inta flatterin' your mama and tellin' her all sorts a' crazy things 'bout how he could turn her inta' a famous wrassler an' there'd be lots a' money in it for 'er. Jes like you, Shelly, your mama like'd ta fight. I think it released some a' the hurt inside her, an' she fell for that dandy's line. Sakes, but it broke all our hearts when that show pulled up stakes an' left town an' Ethel with it. An' her only havin' three months a' school left ta graduate."

"So Mama ran away ta join the circus," Shelly said.

"This weren't no circus, Shelly. It was lower'n any circus I ever seen."

"I know yor tellin' me this, Grammy, 'cause I kinda did the same thing."

"Yor right, Shelly, I am, but there's a lesson in this. Your mama's life came out jes fine even though she did sump'thin crazy an' your's kin too. It's what you do from now on that counts, not what ya did in the past."

"You think Mama believes that 'bout me?" Shelly asked.

"I think so, but she still worries over ya, 'cause that's what mamas do."

Grammy brought her hand up to her mouth and covered a yawn.

"After travelin' with this show for a coupla years, Ethel finally figgered out that huckster wern't gonna turn her inta nothin' but pregnant, but by then she'd learn't how ta wrassle from them other women. In them days after the war there was a lot a' wrasslin' goin' on an' it weren't hard for Ethel ta hook up with a real outfit an' git on the circuit. There really weren't much money in it till television come in later on, an' jes about the time Ethel was startin' ta git a name for herself, she met Cletus an' quit."

"Mama never told us kids much about her time in wrasslin'," Shelly said.

"That's 'cause Ethel was livin' on the wild side a' life, but I ain't gonna say too much about that," Grammy said, wiping her chin.

"Did you see Mama much in them days?" Shelly asked.

"A fair amount. Whenever Ethel was wrasslin' close by or had a few days off she'd drop in an' see us. Jes like with you, her sisters look'd up to 'er an' made a fuss whenever she got home. Sometimes she'd show up with a man, but a diff'ernt one each time. When she brought Cletus here I tol't her, 'Ethel, if you don't marry this one, it'll be the dumbest thing you never did.'

"Ethel said, 'He's already proposed. I jes thought I'd drag 'im by an' see what you thought of 'im.'

"I'll tell ya one thing, Shelly, me an' Ethel never fought. She was tough with other folks but always nice ta me. Even when she found out

I weren't her real mother, it didn't change a thing with us. An' she was good with Nellie an' Gladys, too."

"Ain't you breakin' your promise ta Mama by tellin' me all this, Grammy?" Shelly asked.

"I guess I am, Shelly, but we might not see one another agin'. I know you don't wanta hear this, but I ain't got all that long ta live. At least one person in this family b'side's your mama needs ta know this story, 'cause meh'be someday it should be passed on. I'm purty shor Ethel's never gonna talk about it, an' down the line, some a' her kids or gran'kids might think it's important."

"I already think it's important, Grammy," Shelly said.

"I reckon'd ya might, Shelly, an' it likely explains a few things that you'd seen or heard but didn't understand."

"Yeah, Grammy, it does. One time when I was twelve Mama drove me down ta this place in Tennessee for some reason she'd never tell me about."

Shelly told her grandmother the story of how Ethel had driven around Sneedville asking questions and afterwards taken her to this cluster of buildings with a school and a church up in the hills north of there. When Shelly described the dark-skinned, unusual looking woman with steel-gray eyes Grammy said, "I reckon that woman woulda been a Melungeon. An' I'd guess Ethel was lookin' for 'er mother, or leastwise information 'bout 'er."

"I don't think Mama found out anything," Shelly said. "We come straight home an' Mama was real quiet for most a' the way."

Grammy was yawning again, but Shelly still had one more question. "Do you an' Mama ever talk about this?"

"Never. After Ethel left home she wouldn't say another word about it. Over the years, if we was alone, I'd try ta bring it up, 'cause I figger'd she might do jes what you tol't me about, but each time Ethel'd clam right up. I do think, though, if Ethel'd found Vardalia, she'd a' tol't me, so I always figgered she didn't. An' I always reckon'd Vardalia don't wanta be found, knowin' it'd cause nothin' but trouble for her. She mighta even a' tol't people 'round there not ta say anything 'bout where she is."

Grammy paused, thinking back. "But when Ethel read that letter she knew Vardalia loved her an' didn't wanta give 'er up, and I think that in the years since, she's learn't ta love Vardalia an' it pains her ta know she'll never git ta meet 'er."

Shelly was still holding onto her grandmother's hand and she squeezed it gently as Grammy sighed and her eyelids closed. The old woman shook her head and blinked her eyes back open and Shelly leaned over and kissed her on the cheek. "Thanks for tellin' me all this, Grammy," Shelly said. "I don't think a' you no diff'ernt, it jes feels like I gained an extra gran'ma ta'night."

Grammy managed a tired smile. "I knew you'd be okay with knowin' this Shelly, an' could be trusted."

"I won't say nothin'," Shelly promised, "leastwise not till a long time has passed an', like you, I know it's the right thing ta do."

Shelly got up from her chair and walked to the doorway as Grammy lowered herself under the quilt. Just before Shelly switched off the light she told her grandmother, "But now I'm like Mama ... I wanta meet Vardalia."

Deke was tilted over on the couch, snoring with the television still going. Shelly sat down in an ancient rocker across from him and rested her head against the back. Her grandmother's story filled her mind, yet a feeling of serenity spread over her like a warm quilt. If she was part Melungeon, that meant she was part Negro ... and Indian too, which explained her dark skin. Far from being troubled, Shelly felt excited by the idea, like she was now exotic, and she wanted to tell people, but knew, of course, she couldn't.

But more than anything else, Shelly wanted to go out and get into Deke's truck and drive back to Peapatch. She imagined running into the house and waking Ethel up and hugging her, telling her mother how she knew the whole story and having a long talk with her. Then at daybreak the two of them would drive back to that little cluster of white buildings north of Sneedville, just like they'd done when Shelly was a child, but this time they wouldn't stop asking around or quit looking until they'd found Vardalia, and the three of them would hug and talk and laugh and tell stories about their lives until the sun peeped over the hills the next morning.

Chapter 21

Monday, September 24, 1973

Shelly trooped down the narrow stairway, turned the corner into the hall and was surprised to see Grammy and Deke already in the kitchen, chatting away as Deke cooked breakfast. She sat down at the table facing her grandmother. "Do you still cook for yourself, Grammy?"

"'Course I do," Grammy said, "but when Deke offered, I weren't gonna say no."

Deke sat plates of eggs, bacon and fried potatoes on the table and took a chair near Grammy. They laughed and talked throughout the meal, but Shelly couldn't shake the troubling notion that this might be the last meal she'd ever have with her grandmother. She knew that Grammy believed they'd never see each other again and Grammy had an uncanny knack of being right about such things.

After breakfast, Deke did the dishes while Shelly went back upstairs and finished getting ready. She picked up her suitcase to carry it downstairs then opened it and took out her *Mack Trucks* ballcap. When she walked into the kitchen Deke gawked at her with unsatiated lust, but Grammy saw right away how important the hat was to her. Shelly read her grandmother's questioning look. "Daddy bought me this hat the las' time we went out drivin' ta'gether. It's special to me."

"That's 'cause it makes you look an' feel like the woman yor gonna become," Grammy said. "An' I reckon Cletus knew that when 'e got it for ya."

Tears welled up in Shelly's eyes. "Deke," she said, handing him her suitcase, "could you take this out to the truck?"

Dense as Deke could be, he understood that Shelly wanted to say goodbye to her grandmother alone. "Bye, Grammy," he said as he took Shelly's suitcase and picked up his duffel bag.

"You git on over here an' give me a big hug," Grammy said with a smile. Deke sat the luggage down and Grammy stretched out her thin arms and gave him a long, heartfelt embrace and said, "Take care a' yor'self, honey."

A few minutes later Shelly walked out of the house wiping her eyes. The Ford's hood was up and Deke was checking the oil. "Is ev'rythin' packed an' ready ta go?" Shelly asked, and when Deke nodded that it was, she said, "Alright then, let's hit it."

They followed Tick Ridge Road west in the cool morning sunshine until it rejoined the highway. In Morehead Deke pulled into a Texaco station to fill up the tank and Shelly went inside and bought an atlas. After Deke had cleaned the windshield they drove two blocks to a grocery store where Shelly bought apples and bananas and Deke bought a carton of Camels and enough baloney and crackers to last a week.

"How come yor gittin' so much?" Shelly asked. "They got baloney an' crackers out west."

"I ain't takin' no chances," Deke informed her, lighting up a cigarette.

Back on the road, Shelly studied her new atlas. The layout of the highways was drawing them toward Lexington but Shelly didn't want to get tied up in a city. "When we git to Mount Sterling," she told Deke, "let's take Highway 460 and go ta Frankfort, I never been there."

Deke was jubilant at being on the road to Montana at last. He and Shelly were now officially boyfriend and girlfriend. Barely able to contain his excitement, he turned to Shelly with a big grin and a mouthful of baloney and crackers. "Sounds good ta me, little darlin'."

Half an hour later they were driving through Paris, Kentucky and Shelly said a little wistfully, "I wonder if I'll ever git to the real one."

"The real what?" Deke asked.

"Paris."

"You mean the one in France?"

"Yeah, Deke. That's kinda the one I had in mind."

"How come ya wanta go there?"

"Jes ta see it," Shelly answered. "Who wouldn't?"

"I don't partic'arly want to," Deke said.

"Wouldn't ya like ta see the Eiffel Tower an' the Louvre, or the Left Bank?"

"What's the Loov?" Deke asked. "An' why would anybody go all the way ta France ta see some bank, jest 'cause it's on the left?"

"The Louvre is a big, famous art museum," Shelly said, "an' the Left Bank is where artists an' poets hang out."

"Sounds ta me like they'd both be fulla French queers ... an' they're the worst kind," Deke said, flipping his lit cigarette stub out the window.

Deke's comment about queers irritated Shelly and she said, a bit harshly, "Don't put your butt out the window. You got an ashtray right here."

Deke began giggling. "Ya wanna see me really put my butt out the winda'? We did it all the time in Tennessee. We called it moonin'. If you wanna drive, I'll do it right now an' show ya."

"No, Deke, I don't wanta see it. In fact, I don't even wanta think about it."

"Well, since I'm drivin', Shelly, you could stick yer butt out the winda'. I bet a lot of people'd like ta see that. I know I sure would."

"Stop it! Sometimes, Deke, I swear, you sound like yor ten years old."

From the grin on Deke's face, Shelly had the uncomfortable feeling that he was picturing her bare rear end hanging out the side window.

"Ya ever been here before?" she said, trying to change the subject, as they drove into Frankfort.

"No," Deke answered, still smiling.

"Let's drive around an' look at it. It's the capitol of Kentucky, ya know."

"I didn't know that," Deke said. "I'm from Tennessee an' we got a diff'runt capitol there."

"Yeah, Deke, I reckon ya would."

Twenty minutes later they left Frankfort on Highway 60, intentionally avoiding Interstate 64 to the south. A little after noon they hit the outskirts of Louisville and were funneled onto I-64 anyway. Climbing the ramp leading across the Ohio River, this time with no police siren wailing behind them, Deke and Shelly laughed at the memory. Deke threw back his head and began singing:

"Oh the last time I seen 'er, an' I ain't seen 'er since
She was takin' on a bull through a barb wire fence
Gonna tie my pecker to my leg, to my leg, gonna tie my pecker ..."

"Deke, I don't want ta hear that stupid song no more," Shelly said, cutting him off.

"Guess I was jest happy ta be crossin' the Ohio River again." Shelly leaned back and put her feet on the dash. She *was* excited to be crossing the Ohio River, this time heading west, off to start a new life.

Coming down the ramp into Indiana Deke turned to Shelly. "I ain't never been west a' Kentucky before."

"Me neither," Shelly admitted, then asked, "You still worried about the law comin' after ya, Deke?"

The question caught Deke unawares. "I don't know. Guess I hadn't thought on it much ... till now."

Sorry she'd brought it up, Shelly said, "I don't reckon they'd come over state lines ta gitch ya, Deke. All ya did was have an accident ... or two."

"I s'pose yer right," Deke said, but he looked concerned.

They drove in silence through the built up area west of the river until Shelly said, "Let's git off this damn four-lane an' find us a real road." She looked at her atlas. "Route 150 looks perty good, Deke, take the next exit to the right."

Just off the interstate they saw a McDonald's.

"I'm hungry," Deke said. "Let's stop."

"You been eatin' crackers an' baloney all mornin'. How can you be hungry?"

"They don't count. I jes eat that ta keep myself goin'," Deke explained, then asked, "Ain't you hungry yet?"

"I guess so," Shelly said as Deke wheeled into the parking lot.

As he was finishing his second Happy Meal Deke said, "I'm gittin' tired from all this drivin'. Maybe we oughta git us a motel an' stop fer the day."

Shelly took a sip of Coke. "You can't be serious. It ain't but a quarter past one."

"Well, you said ya didn't wanna be in any hurry to git ta Montana an' this is kind of a nice spot." Deke waved his arm at the urban sprawl outside their table window. "There's a clean lookin' Motel 6 over yonder and with the McDonald's here we don't have ta worry about findin' a place fer supper an' breakfast."

"Nice? There's a noisy interstate pert' near right over our heads an' we're surrounded by trashy food joints an' gas stations." Shelly slurped the last of her Coke and stood up. "Let's go. I'm already tired a' cities."

Deke pouted as he followed Shelly out to the pickup. She hopped onto the back bumper and climbed into the bed. "Can ya hand me the key to the trunk?"

"Whadaya need?" Deke asked, as he reached his keys up to her.

"I'm puttin' my hat away."

"Uh … I was kinda hopin' you'd keep on wearin' that hat, Shelly," Deke said. "Even after we was at the motel t'night."

Shelly slammed the trunk lid shut and glared at Deke. "I ain't a'wearin' the hat Daddy bought me jes so's you can git turned on by it."

"Oh no, Shelly, I didn't mean that. I jest don't want ya ta catch cold or nothin'."

As they drove, Deke's eyes were fixed on Shelly more than they were the road. She tried to ignore his leers and watch the scenery, but the level redundancy of Indiana was far from enchanting. Glaciers had ground away whatever fetching geological features may have once been there and the small vales, drumlins and hillocks they'd left behind were puny compensation for their scourings. The farms and small patches of forest were charming, but in every direction the land had been tamed and made subservient: fenced and plowed into mediocrity.

They cruised through towns with Civil War sounding names like Fredericksburg and Chambersburg and Shelly wondered if the people were as orderly as the neatly constructed homes they'd built. She spoke to Deke only when his comments demanded an answer, keeping her face turned toward the side window to avoid his stares. As they came into the small burg of Prospect, Shelly swiveled around so she could see both sides of the street. At the intersection a sign pointed south to French Lick. Nodding toward the sign, Deke winked at her and said, "A French lick sounds kinda fun, maybe we oughta go there." Shelly turned away and resumed staring out the side window.

Past Vincennes they entered Illinois. Route 150 now became Route 50 but the scenery didn't change. With small towns every few miles and their well-enforced 25 mph speed limits, Deke and Shelly's progress was slow, and by the time they passed through Flora, twilight was beginning to infringe upon their day. Shelly looked at her watch. "It's after five, Deke," she said. "I 'spose we oughta stop at the next town and have supper then start lookin' for a place ta stay."

Deke, who had grown quiet over Shelly's prolonged silence, now brightened. "Oh that sounds good ta me, Shelly. That sounds *real* good."

Shelly managed to squeeze out a smile but she couldn't shake the unsavory feeling that Deke had been thinking of little else besides screwing her since they'd left Olive Hill that morning. Technically, this was not true, as Deke had thought of little else but screwing her since they'd met that early afternoon in mid-August when he'd driven her around to look at cars.

But Shelly could not remain dour for long, for as they wested into the beginnings of a sunset, the sky now began to do what the land had not: become magnificently beautiful. Contours of pink and mauve interspersed with the blue firmanent and the growing pods of clouds that had been trailing them all afternoon now came to the forefront. The scattered formations gathered themselves into a great cloud city of altocumulus castellatus, layered and turreted, mighty and pure, and began pushing the lowering sun out of the sky. As the sun dropped, it beamed yellow rays into the silken mass of onrushing clouds, dramatically filling their gray billows with golden striations that turned the distant horizon into a Kingdom of Glory. Salvation was down the road, and though Deke and Shelly likely had differing views of what constituted Heaven at that moment, it appeared to be just ahead and waiting.

They reached the eastern edge of Salem at 6:00 o'clock where blue neon script and a downward pointing arrow let them know that Doris's Oasis Cafe was open. The place was packed and the only available table had not yet been cleared. A waitress in a white uniform and a name tag that read 'Sue' hustled by and said, "I'll be right with ya."

She returned with two plastic glasses of ice water, a large tub and a wash towel. Smiling and chatting, she sat the water on the table and gathered up the dirty dishes. Deke and Shelly had already pulled menus from the rack against the wall and when Sue told them, "I'll take your order now," they rattled off their choices.

Twenty minutes later Shelly levered a fork into her gravy covered chicken-fried steak and mashed potatoes. "Now ain't this better'n McDonald's or White Castle?"

Deke shrugged. "It's purty good, I reckon."

They exited Doris's to a shadowy parking lot that was half empty. Salem's streetlights were now on and tossed a brittle yellow glow against the leafy billows of the oaks and maples that lined the highway. Deke drove slower than Shelly had ever seen him, cranking his head from side to side, looking for a motel. When they reached the downtown area, several stores were still open, but they saw no place offering accommodation. After leaving the business district Deke looked panicky, as it was now nearly seven o'clock. "Maybe we oughta try some a' these side streets," he ventured.

"I got a better idea," Shelly answered, when they passed a man walking an Irish setter. "Let's stop and ask this feller."

Deke halted the Ford when they were alongside the man and Shelly rolled her window down. "Howdy," she called. "Ya got any motels in this town?"

"Just one," he said, pointing in the direction they were heading. "It's a mile or three that way, on the edge of town."

"I sure hope they got a room left," Deke said, pulling back onto the road.

"It'll be fine, Deke," Shelly assured him.

As the streetlights and houses petered out, Deke began to fidget. "I think that guy with the dog was joshin' us, Shelly, there ain't no motel here."

Two miles later Shelly was starting to wonder also, but then they topped a rise in the highway and saw the outline of a long, low building up ahead. Deke and Shelly were almost to the entrance before they saw the small neon sign letting them know that they had arrived at the Mount Sinai Motel. Only after Deke whipped into the empty parking lot and came to a stop in front of the office did he and Shelly take note of the cardboard 'vacancy' sign in the window. Deke looked at the sign, saw that the office was open and turned to Shelly with a fawning smile. "Ummmmmmmmm."

Unsure how to respond to Deke's unctuous sigh, Shelly said, "Well, I reckon we're here," and opened the truck door far enough for the dome light to come on but didn't get out. She looked down at the atlas that lay open on her lap. "I sorta hoped we'd git across the Mississippi River ta'day," she said.

"Yeah, that woulda been nice, Shelly," Deke agreeably replied.

"If we keep goin', Deke, we could make it by early morning … an' I wouldn't mind drivin' if yor tired."

"NO! I didn't mean it like that," Deke exclaimed. "I like it right here."

Deke fixed Shelly with an oily smile and after a short, uncomfortable silence, Shelly pushed the truck door open. "If you wanta grab our bags," she said, "I'll go in an' see what kinda rooms they got."

"Oh sure," Deke said, his face erupting into a huge grin. "I need ta make the truck safe for the night, too."

Deke jumped out of the cab and Shelly heard him whistling away in the bed of the pickup as she opened the office door. The middle-aged woman who guarded the front desk was short and plump, yet formidable with her brown hair pulled back and wound into a severe bun. A large silver crucifix lay on her substantial bosom, so that Jesus reclined on his cross rather than hung from it, and with his arms stretched wide and feet crossed, looked downright relaxed as he gazed at the water marks on the ceiling. On the wall beside Shelly, Jesus also watched over the motel's transactions from a large, garish painting set into a heavy, gilded frame.

"Hello, ma'am," Shelly said politely and smiled.

"Good evening," the woman replied. "I'm Maud. What's your name, child?"

Shelly bristled but didn't say anything. She had hoped to complete the arrangements without Deke's assistance, but before she even got started he breezed through the door, duffel bag in one hand and Shelly's suitcase in the other.

"And what is your name, sir?" Maud asked, halting his momemtum.

Deke sat his load down and pulled up beside Shelly at the counter. Revving into manly action, he took charge of negotiations.

"My name is Deke, Deke McConahay," he began, bouncy and quick, like a 2-cycle engine powering a bullshit generator, "and this is Shelly. We're newlyweds on our way to Montana ta stay with my brother who's a minister out there."

Shelly guessed that Deke had noticed the Christian regalia, but was brainless as an empty coffee pot in sizing up the woman standing before him.

"We're a little short on money," he prattled on, ignorant that Maud's eyes were checking their hands for wedding rings, "an' I was wonderin' if maybe you could cut a deal fer me and my ..." Deke looked at Shelly and saw how red her face had gone, "blushin' bride."

Shelly was not blushing but was crimson with fury at Deke telling Maud they were newlyweds. Oblivious, he continued. "This is our first day on the road, ya see, an' we got us a long ways ta go an' all, an' I thought you might find yer way ta ... "

Maud held up her hand and stopped Deke in mid-sentence. "We do give special rates, Mr. McConahay, to our guests newly entered into *holy* matrimony. I will, of course, need to see a copy of your marriage license."

Deke cranked his throttle up a notch. "Oh, well, ya see now, we had ta leave it back at the courthouse in Wes' Virginia so's they could record it an' all an' the judge an' them said they'd send it out to us soon as they ... "

Maud cut Deke off again. "This is a Christian establishment and we hold to Christian values." She looked directly at Shelly: "and *morals*. I cannot let you have a room unless you have matrimonial proof."

"Ya gotta let us stay," Deke begged. "It's late an' we're tired an' we ain't seen a motel fer a hunderd miles an' might not see another'n."

Maud remained resolutely silent to Deke's pleading. In desperation, he put his hands together in supplication. "Please, lady, we come all this way an' need a place ta stay. We're jest like Joseph an' Mary."

Shelly turned to Deke. "No we're not. I ain't pregnant."

Deke's unfortunate comparison of himself and Shelly to the Savior's mother and father (or perhaps step-father) caused a dreadful transformation in Maude. Florid-faced and grim, she placed an open hand in front of Deke's nose. "No! No! No!" she said, "You are *not* like Joseph and Mary! You are sinners." At each 'No!' Maud jabbed her chubby palm closer to Deke's face, while her other hand clutched at the crucifix, her thick fingers constricting Jesus like an anaconda.

Only a moment before, Shelly was ready to brain Deke, but now she had half a mind to yank the picture of Jesus off of the wall and frame Maud's head with it. "Let's git outa here, Deke. We didn't wanta stay in this crummy rathole, anyway."

Shelly turned to go, but Deke didn't move. "What's the matter with you?" she hollered, but Deke's eyes remained fixed on Maud's hand, only inches from his nose.

Shelly picked up their luggage and bumped the door open with her butt. "C'mon, Deke," she yelled, but he didn't respond.

Maud tapped Deke on the forehead with her outstretched palm. "Begone with you!" she said, and without taking his eyes from her hand, Deke backpeddled through the open door.

"What's wrong with you anyways?" Shelly said, when they were outside.

Deke blinked a couple of times. "I dono," he mumbled. "Somethin' come over me ...like I was in a trance or somethin'."

As Deke's senses returned, he realized he'd been deprived of bedding Shelly. "You fat ol' hog," he screamed at Maud, who was still standing behind the desk, pointing her open palm at him. "You kin jack my rabbit."

Shelly tossed their bags into the truck bed and climbed into the cab where a trembling Deke fumbled for his keys. "Calm down," she told him, but Deke couldn't stop shivering.

"I can't. That ol' bitch put the hoo-doo on me. I wanna git outa here."

Deke depressed the clutch and turned the key. Nothing. He turned to Shelly in desperation. "She put the hex on my truck, too! Look at 'er. She's still got that hand a' hers facin' right at me an' givin' me the evil-eye."

Maud had moved to the front window where she stood behind the glass, arm extended.

"Let's git out an' see what the problem is with the truck," Shelly said.

"Not me," Deke said. "I ain't gittin' out with her standin' there castin' some spell on me."

"Oh, for the love a'. . ." Shelly muttered. "Deke, this ain't three hund'ert years ago and Maud ain't no witch that can turn us inta toads."

That jogged a memory from Deke's school days. "Shelly, ain't this the town, Salem, where they had so many witches they had ta start burnin' 'em?"

Shelly opened the truck door. "This ain't the same Salem, Deke, but maybe they oughta start." She walked to the front of the pickup and hoisted the Ford's hood. Even in the deep twilight the problem was obvious.

"Damn you, Deke," Shelly yelled. "You disconnected the battery again."

"I didn't want nobody ta steal the truck," Deke hollered back. "Reckon with that witch puttin' her curse on me I forgot."

"She ain't the curse," Shelly said, as she reconnected the cables. "You are."

They left the parking lot slinging gravel onto the office window as Maud stood behind it, following their exit with her open hand. Deke and Shelly gave Maud their hands in return, but showing only one finger.

Chapter 22

Deke and Shelly drove west in silence as the fullness of night overtook them. Only a few faint ochre shards remained of the gorgeous sunset they had witnessed earlier and by the time they'd reached Carlyle, twenty miles down the road, even those had slipped over the horizon. At Carlyle, and Sandoval before that, they had looked for motels, but neither town had one and no one knew of any further on. Deke became more morose with each failure.

"We'll find us a place, Deke," Shelly assured him as she flipped on the dome light and spread the atlas across her knees. "St. Louis and the Mississippi River ain't as far as I thought. Only about eighty miles from here."

"Ain't there nothin' b'fore that?"

Shelly looked at her map again. "Well, East St. Louis is only sixty miles away."

"I wanna stop at the first place we see an' I don't care where it's at," Deke said.

Shelly switched off the dome and leaned her head against the side window. Yard and barn lamps lit the passing farmsteads and their windows exuded warm, inviting light. The small towns they drove through felt cozy and secure, the sidewalks edged with friendly trees and a welcoming front porch on every home. The mid-west countryside, so boring in daylight, now felt serene and comforting, abiding within itself.

She turned away from the window. "Ya know, Deke, sometimes I think it'd be nice ta be normal."

"We're normal," he answered flatly.

"Compared to who, the Munsters?"

"No, Shelly, we're *normal*. We ain't nothin' like them kids in that special class they had at school."

"What I mean, Deke, is sometimes I wish I lived like regular people do."

"Well, I don't know, Shelly, I always thought a' us as re'glar people."

"That's 'cause the people we hang out with are as far away from normal as we are, Deke. Some of 'em even farther." Shelly pointed out the side window. "Do ya see these farms we been drivin' by and the houses in the little towns? That's how normal people live. They don't lie about bein' newlyweds an' git throwed outa motels. They don't smash inta the supervisor's pickup or destroy the comp'ny office and have the law after 'em. They don't dance near naked in front a' other people for a livin'."

"That's 'cause they got reg'lar jobs an' make more money'n we do."

"It ain't that, Deke. When you had that dump truck job, you made enough money ta live like these people. I bet there were guys workin' with ya who did."

"Yeah, my uncle Charlie has a wife an' kids an' his own house."

"See what I mean, Deke. Even though my dancin' job wasn't normal, I coulda lived decent if I'd a' wanted to. Nancy danced at Hillbilly Heaven an' she was married an' settled with three kids. But I never even thought a' havin' a life like that."

"You never thought a' havin' kids, Shelly?" Deke asked.

Shelly went quiet and closed her eyes. "I can't have kids, Deke. Things didn't go right for me so when I was fifteen I had an operation."

"I'm real sorry, Shelly, I didn't know."

"Well, it ain't somethin' I wear a sign around my neck advertisin'. But even if I could have kids, I don't think it'd change me, any more'n makin' decent money changed me ... or you."

Shelly looked out the window again. "Deke, they could give us one a' them nice houses, or even a farm, an' it wouldn't matter, 'cause after awhile we'd go back ta bein' what we are. We'd lose it or sell it or run away from it, or somethin', I don't know what, but we wouldn't live like them people do for long.

"An' it ain't 'cause we're young, or poor, or from the hills or any a' that. There's somethin' in us, Deke, that makes us diff'ernt. We don't care about careers or retirement or goin' ta basketball games or none a' that kinda stuff. It's almost like we can't stand knowin' what we'll be doin' in a year, or a month, or even ta'morrow. Sometimes I think the only normal I'll ever have is the setting on my washin' machine an' that's only if I ever have a washin' machine."

"Are you sayin' them people, the ones you call normal, are better'n us?"

"I don't think that, a'tall, Deke, but sometimes it does seem like we're livin' beneath 'em somehow. We might not look up ta them, but they shor look down on us. We're like them carp and catfish that swim aroun' on the floor a' lakes an' rivers, their heads goin' back an' forth like their always lookin' for somethin', but never findin' it."

"You mean bottom feeders?" Deke asked.

"Yeah, bottom feeders," Shelly said, her eyes lighting up. "That's us, Deke, we're bottom feeders. An' it ain't money or the houses we live in, it's *how* we live an' the way we think an' how we never feel settled. It's what we are an' we can't change ourselves any more'n a carp could."

"I ain't so sure about that, Shelly. I'm goin' ta Montana ta change."

"I think we're goin' west, Deke, 'cause we're the kind a' people who's always gone west. We need ta see what's there for us."

"Well, maybe."

"An' somethin' else, Deke, us bottom feeders know each other when we meet."

"We do?"

"Shor, Deke. There was this guy who run an old timey clothing store in Cincinnati that I used ta go to sometimes. He had real good taste in clothes, even women's clothes, so I asked 'im about it one time. He laughed an' said, 'Oh, don't you know I'm gay. Most people can tell.' I didn't know what that meant back then, so he told me, 'Gay means queer, but most of us like that word better.' Sometimes when I went in there an' he wasn't busy I'd talk to 'im, 'cause he was real int'resting."

Deke made a wry face. "Uhhrr, you talked to a queer?"

"Yeah, Deke, I talked to a queer. I didn't figure it was contagious."

"I don't know, Shelly, I heard that people who hang around queers too much can git that way themselves."

"If I caught anything from 'im, Deke, I hope you don't catch it from me."

"They ain't no goddam way," Deke said.

"Anyways," Shelly said, "this gay feller told me how people say that one queer can spot another one, even if they ain't actin' queer."

"Yeah, I heard 'at before," Deke said.

"He told me that a lot a' times it's true. That somehow they jes know."

"So what's that got ta' do with us?" Deke said. "All this talk about queers is makin' me sick ta my stomach."

"Well, that's what I was sayin' about bottom feeders, Deke, we jes sorta know each other."

"Long as that's the only way we're like queers," Deke said and lit a cigarette from the dash lighter.

Shelly went back to gazing out the side window and by 9:00 o'clock clusters of ranch-style and split-level homes had replaced the farms along the highway. A little further on the first darkened businesses appeared.

"Look's like we're gittin' close ta somethin'," Deke said. "We oughta be seein' a motel purty soon."

"Deke," Shelly said in a serious voice, "when we git to the next one, could we at least try ta act like normal people, even though I just got done tellin' ya how we're not?"

"I'm not sure I know what ya mean, Shelly."

"For a start, Deke, we don't need to try ta git 'em down on the price by lyin'. Not only didja promise me ya wouldn't do that no more, but it's embarrassin'."

"You lie too sometimes, Shelly," Deke said. "You tol' that guy back in Kentucky that we was brother an' sister. That's a lie."

"That was diff'ernt, Deke, we needed a jumpstart."

"He'd a' give us a jump anyway. You said that cuz ya wanted ta flirt with 'im."

Shelly winced at the memory. "Yor right, Deke, I shouldn't a' done that."

Deke was quiet for a moment. "Shelly, when ya said that, it was like you was ashamed he might think I was yer boyfriend."

"I didn't mean it ta sound like that, Deke," Shelly said, "an I'm sorry about it. Maybe we both could do a little better."

"That sounds real good ta me, Shelly," Deke said, and his face brightened, "cuz in a little while I really will be yer boyfriend. An' it's a good thing, too."

"Why is that, Deke?"

"Well, when we was drivin' inta that last place, I got real excited. An' when that witch woman turned us away we didn't git ta do nothin', an' now with us close to a motel agin, it's startin' ta build up in me, an', well, I might be gittin DSB, Shelly."

"What's that? I never heard of it."

"Dangerous Sperm Buildup," Deke said. "You girls don't have ta worry about it none, but it gits real bad in men sometimes. If it gits too bad, like it is in me right now, things git terrible sore an' ya turn blue."

Shelly flipped on the dome light and looked closely at Deke's face. "You don't look blue ta me a'tall, Deke."

"Oh, not all a' me. Jest them parts that're swelled near ta overflowin'."

"I don't know as I want any a' that dangerous sperm in me, Deke."

"It ain't dangerous ta you, Shelly. It's only dangerous ta me if I don't get rid of it," Deke said. "And soon."

"Deke, I know yor excited an' all, but this conversation ain't doin' much ta put me in the mood."

Deke eyes grew wide with terror. "Shelly, you wouldn't … "

"Relax, Deke. We're spendin' the night ta'gether, an' everythin' that goes with it. I'm jes sayin' maybe we could talk about somethin' a little more romantic as we're leadin' up to it. Us ladies do like romantic talk, ya know, an' this sure ain't it."

"It's jest that I been waitin' fer so long, Shelly."

"I know ya have, Deke. But sometimes you act so desperate."

"I ain't des'prit," Deke countered.

"Well, what would ya call it then?"

"I'd call it my love … and my desire fer you, Shelly. Don't you have some desire fer me too?"

Shelly thought about her promise not to lie. "'Course I do, Deke," she said after a few seconds, "otherwise I wouldn't be goin' to Montana with ya."

The answer was longer in coming than Deke would have liked, but he accepted it. "I'm glad ta hear that, Shelly, cuz we're gonna have us a real good time t'night."

As more industrial and commercial buildings appeared along their route, Deke slowed down and craned his neck in both directions. The first motel they saw was dark and had a CLOSED FOR THE SEASON sign out front. The next one was grandly lit but below its neon sign was a smaller one announcing NO VACANCY. The third motel they passed looked like it was constructed from old railroad boxcars, but not as roomy or clean. Deke wanted to stop anyway but Shelly told him she'd sleep in the truck before she'd stay there. They were close to the center of East St. Louis and Deke's anxiety level was in the red zone, so when they came to The Golden Jubilee Motor Hotel and the VACANCY sign was on, Shelly didn't quibble. She'd had a long day and was tired.

As Deke squeezed between two cars in the nearly full lot, he told Shelly, "I sure hope the people here in East St. Louis ain't a bunch a high-falutin' religious snoots like they was back yonder."

"Me too," Shelly said, "but jes in case, would ya mind lettin' me take care a' gittin' the room? We can't afford ta be turned down this late at night."

"Alright, Shelly," Deke agreed. "I'll git our bags and lock up the truck."

As they were getting out, Deke looked across the street to a brightly lit store with a yellow neon sign above the entrance that read: Moses John's Liquor Store. "Listen, Shelly, while yer dickerin' fer the room, I'll run over there an' git us some beer. Shitfire, I ain't had hardly any since we left Norwood and I'm almost as des'prit fer a beer as I am fer … well, you know."

"I thought you said ya weren't desperate."

"Oh, I didn't mean it like that, Shelly, I jest meant that I wanted a beer."

"When it comes ta romance, Deke, yor a reg'lar Cary Grant, ya know that?"

"Why, thankya'," Deke said smiling, and set off across the road at a trot.

"Git me some Falstaff if they got it," Shelly yelled and headed for the motel office.

Shelly's breath caught in her throat when she saw the big picture of Jesus on the wall, but shortly, a large, balding Black man with thick gray eyebrows came out from a back room. "You look tired, ma'am," he said and smiled, "can we get you a room for the night?"

As Shelly was about to answer, a skinny Black woman hurried through the front door and went behind the counter.

"Heavens, but we're busy tonight, Jordan," she said to the man.

"I hope ya still got a room left," Shelly said.

"Only two," the man answered, glancing down at the register.

"I'd like ta have one of 'em, if I could," Shelly told him.

"That's what we're here for," the woman said to Shelly, and then she stuck out her hand. "I'm Shelly and this is my husband, Jordan."

Shelly laughed as she shook her hand and then Jordan's. "My name's Shelly, too."

"Put her in number 12, Jordan," the woman said. "That's the nicer room."

Jordan reached under the desk, got out a form and began filling it out. "Is it only for the one night, Shelly, and is it just you?"

"It's jes for tonight," Shelly said, "but there'll be two of us in the room. Me an' … "

The office door flew open and a frantic looking Deke McConahay rushed in.

"Didja git the beer, Deke?" Shelly asked.

"I didn't git it," Deke puffed, out of breath. "That store's clear fulla nig … "

Then Deke saw Jordan and Shelly behind the counter and his mouth clamped shut with an instant case of lockjaw.

Shelly glowered at him. "This is Jordan and Shelly," she said, throwing each word at Deke like it was an ice pick. "An' they're lettin' us have the best room they got left."

She turned to Jordan and Shelly. "This is Deke McConahay, an' he's … he's … well, I don't know what he is."

Jordan and his wife looked at Deke but said nothing as Deke gulped and stared at the floor.

"Well," Shelly said to him, "you jes gonna stand there, Deke, or you got somethin' else stupid ta say?"

"I'll go git our stuff," Deke spluttered and ran out the door.

Shelly turned back to Jordan and Shelly, not knowing what to say. Jordan finished filling out the registration form as his wife pivoted on her heel and went into the room behind the office. "I'll just put that there are two people in the room," Jordan said, all trace of friendliness gone from his voice.

Shelly paid Jordan and he handed her the key. "You'll want to take everything valuable out of your truck tonight," he told her. "With that liquor store across the street we sometimes get the wrong kind of people around here."

"Thanks for lettin' me know, Jordan," Shelly said, taking the key. She wanted to say more, *needed* to say more, but feared any attempt to undo Deke's words would come out sounding ridiculous. Her eyes went to the halo'd portrait of Jesus on the wall and she nodded towards it. "I went ta church with my family in Wes' Virginia yesterday for the first time in a long while an' it felt good."

"My wife and I try to live like we think He'd want us to," Jordan replied.

"Listen, Jordan, I ain't like Deke a'tall. I'm jes ridin' with 'im out ta Montana so's I can git a job, an' I'm sorry for what he said … "

Jordan held up his hand to stop her. "I've heard it before."

———————————

Shelly walked out to the parking lot, where Deke was bent over his truck unhooking the battery cables. She considered slamming the hood down on his head, grabbing her things and taking off, but she was too tired. "I hope yor happy, sayin' what you did in there," she said.

"Well, I didn't see 'em when I come in and didn't know that they was … "

"What they are is good people and that's all that matters."

"No, what I mean is, I didn't know they was … "

"Oh, jes be quiet, Deke. I got half a mind ta take the other room ta'night an' then start hitchhikin' in the morning."

A look of alarm came over Deke's face. "You can't jest take off, Shelly. It ain't safe around here!"

Deke was on the verge of panic, but when Shelly grabbed her suit-case and pack and started toward the motel Deke saw she wasn't leav-ing and shut up.

"Jordan said we shouldn't leave nothin' valuable in the truck to-night," Shelly said over her shoulder.

"I already knew that," Deke answered.

Shelly opened the door to the room, set her bags down and went back to the pickup. Deke was in the bed, poking through the clutter.

"Whatcha doin'?" Shelly asked.

"Lookin' fer some rope so's I can tie down my spare tar'r."

"Oh, for the love a ... Deke, nobody's gonna take that old tire, there ain't enough tread on it ta bother with."

"I don't care," Deke said, "I'd feel better if it was roped down."

"Deke, if anybody really wanted it, which nobody would, they'd just cut the rope an' take it anyway." Shelly grabbed the toolbox from the bed. "Let's jes git in the room, Deke. All a' your bullshit is startin' ta wear me out."

Deke looked at Shelly. "Alright," he said, hopping down from the pickup bed, "I'll let 'er go fer t'night, but that tar'r better be here in the mornin'."

"If it ain't, I'll buy ya a new one," Shelly said, and headed to their room.

Other guests were in the parking lot, all of them Black. A young couple walked by, looked at Deke and Shelly curiously, but offered smiles and said hello. After they passed, Deke said, "Shelly, I don't think it's safe ta stay here."

"Shush yor'self, Deke," she snapped. "It's as safe as any other place an' I don't wanta hear about it no more."

Shelly flipped on the light to the room. It was small, but clean and well arranged. As she watched from the open doorway, Deke sat down on the bed and hurriedly took both guns from his duffel bag. He pulled out a box of ammunition and loaded the .30-30, then dug some more and found a small poke of 10 gauge shells. A heavy-set, well-dressed older Black man walked by the open door. "Evenin', miss," he said to Shelly and glanced into the room to speak to Deke, who was stuffing two shells into the chambers of the huge shotgun. "Oh, Lord," he said, and hurried past the doorway.

"Yor scarin' people, Deke," Shelly said.

"Me? Shitfire, I'm the one that oughta be scared. You need ta git inside an' lock that door."

Deke got up, pulled the door shut, locked and dead-bolted it. He walked to the window, flipped back the heavy drape and looked out into the parking lot. "I don't like stayin' here one bit," he said.

"Stop it, Deke. You embarrassed me ta no end with them nice people in the office an' I don't wanta hear no more a' your ig'nernt prejudice." She glared at Deke. "An' I want a beer."

"I ain't leavin' this room tonight fer nothin'," Deke said.

"You don't have ta go nowheres, Deke, I'll go git the beer."

"Oh no ya don't, Shelly," Deke said, and plastered himself against the door, arms spread wide. "You ain't goin' out there. There's no tellin' what might happen to ya. You could be killed … or worse yet, raped."

Shelly stood up. "Alright, then," she said, "I'll go take a shower."

She walked into the bathroom, closed the door behind her, stepped onto the commode, opened the window and climbed out.

Deke lit up a cigarette, took off his boots, and turned on the television. The 'Monday Night Movie' was *Zulu*. As Deke watched, several English officers in red uniforms anxiously discussed their hopeless and surrounded situation. The next scene jumped to British soldiers being skewered by howling, spear thrusting African tribesmen – thousands of them – who were not only killing the British, but also having a jolly time doing it. Deke stared open-mouthed at the carnage. He lunged for the off button on the television just as someone began pounding on the motel room door. Deke grabbed his Winchester off the bed and yelled, his voice high and nervous, "Who is it?"

A woman's voice answered. "It's the head a' the NAACP and I'm here to give ya a medal for all the work ya done helpin' us with civil rights."

Deke hesitated a moment. "Is that you, Shelly?"

"Yeah Deke, it's me. Open the door."

"I thought you was in the bathroom."

"Well, what you think an' what you know are diff'ernt things. Now let me in."

"Are ya by yer'self, Shelly?"

"No, Deke. I got four great big Black men with me that I met at the liquor store. I figgered we'd all party ta'gether tonight." When she didn't get a response, Shelly added, "I hope ya don't mind."

Silence.

"Open the door! It's gittin cold out here."

"Shelly, yer jest kiddin' about them … other people bein' with ya? Right?"

"YES! Now open the door!" Shelly roared and gave it a kick.

Still holding his rifle, Deke unlocked the door and cracked it open a few inches. Shelly pushed her way in, carrying a six-pack in each hand. "Would ya put that stupid gun down b'fore ya shoot somebody," she said.

Deke propped the .30-30 in a corner and resecured the door. "Shitfire, Shelly, I didn't know you was gone. Did anything bad happen to ya?"

"Not really, Deke, I only got raped twice. Heck, I was hopin' for at least three or four times."

"Don't say that, not even jokin', 'cause it ain't funny. It coulda happened to ya."

"An' if you'd a' gone for the beer, Deke, it could a' happened ta you. Now that would a' been funny."

"Stop it, Shelly. Quit makin' fun a' me."

"I can't help it, Deke. You get yor'self so riled up over nothin'."

"Well maybe I can't help it, neither. I never been in a place like this."

"Alright, Deke," Shelly said. "How about we jes have us a beer an' relax." She handed Deke a beer. "Here, I got ya some Strohs."

Deke opened his beer and sat down on the bed. "That's a good idea, Shelly. I got so wound up my DSB even went away." His eyes traveled down the length of Shelly's body. "But it's comin' back, real fast."

"I can't tell ya how glad I am yor sharin' that information with me, Deke," Shelly said, and popped the ring on her beer. She moved toward the television. "Maybe we could watch TV. There might be a good movie on."

"NO!" Deke shouted. "Let's jest talk fer a while. You know, like boyfriends and girlfriends are s'pose to."

"Okay, let's talk." Shelly sat down in the straight back chair beside the television and held up her beer. "Look, Deke, they even had Falstaff over there."

"How come you drink that stuff, anyway?" Deke asked. "Yer the only one I know who likes it."

"I'm hopin' it'll make me smarter," Shelly said. "I read somewhere's – or maybe heard – that Shakespeare drank Falstaff beer, an' he was perty smart."

"You really b'lieve drinkin' beer can make ya smarter?"

"Aw, I reckon not, Deke; if it could, you'd be Einstein. But I do think it's kinda cool drinkin' the same beer that Shakespeare used ta drink. Didja ever read any of 'is plays?"

"We were s'pose ta read *Romeo and Juliet* in high school but I jest kinda skipped through it. I sorta know what it's about, though."

"We read it in ninth grade," Shelly said. "Then our class put on a play about it."

"I bet you was Juliet," Deke said, "cuz you'd a' been the purtiest girl in class."

"Nope. They made me be this ol' nurse. I had ta wear all these funny lookin' clothes, an' even some kinda hood around my head like a nun."

Shelly paused, then chuckled. "All the boys hated it 'cause they had ta wear their long underwear bottoms. An' the ones that got killed in sword fights had ta lay there on the stage while people made speeches over 'em. Us girls laughed at that."

"All I know about it," Deke said, " is that a boy an' a girl fall in love and the grownups don't much like it. That's how I felt at yer family's place."

"*Romeo and Juliet* is more like if you'd a' fallen' for a girl from that family yours had been feudin' with. What's their name?"

"Jenkins," Deke said. "An' I really did that."

"You did?"

"I sure did. When I was sixteen I had a crush on Raylene Jenkins. I'd buy 'er pop an' candy jest so I could talk to 'er. I even asked 'er fer a date."

"So what happened?"

"Her older brother tol' me he was gonna' beat me up real bad if I didn't stay away from 'er."

"Jes 'cause you were a McConahay?"

"Coulda been," Deke said. "But he said Raylene was jest twelve an' I oughta be sparkin' girls my own age."

Shelly cringed. "Yeah, that could a' had somethin' ta do with it, Deke."

"Ya know, Shelly, I don't like hippies all that much, but I do agree with 'em on what they call free love. If two people care about each other, no matter who they are, why shouldn't they be allowed ta git together? Other folks shouldn't be a' judgin' 'em fer what they do."

"Jeepers, Deke, I never heard ya talk like this. Maybe yor more open minded than I thought."

"I try ta be, Shelly. I think of all men as my brothers."

"Even men who are gay?" Shelly asked.

"No way. I hate queers," Deke answered. "But other'n them I love ever'body."

"I thought ya jes said ya didn't like hippies."

"Naw, I don't care fer them too much, either, but I like ever'body else."

"I'm mighty glad ta hear that, Deke, 'cause you had me worried there for a while. It shor seemed like you was havin' trouble bein' aroun' Black people."

Deke didn't say anything.

"Well," Shelly said, "do ya think a' Black people as your brothers an' sisters?"

"That's diff'runt."

"How's it diff'ernt? They're jes people, same as us."

"No they ain't, Shelly, they're a whole lot diff'runt n' we are," Deke said, getting up to get another beer.

"Where'd you learn them ig'nernt ideas anyway? Ain't you ever known any Negroes?"

"Reckon not too much," Deke answered. "I seen some before, but never knew any. Guess most a' what I know comes from what my aunt an' uncle taught us. They tol' us some real scary stories about what coloreds do ta White folks ... or would do if they got the chance. They said ta stay away from 'em, that Black and White people weren't s'pose ta mix, an' that it said so right in the Bible."

"Deke, I bet the couple who run this motel, Shelly an' Jordan, know the Bible as well as your aunt an' uncle do, an' they don't believe that way."

Deke frowned.

"An' my family was all raised on the Bible, too, and we weren't taught nothin' like that." Shelly gathered her thoughts. "Deke, I know you had a hard time, losin' your parents an' all, an' your aunt an' uncle bein' real strict with ya. An' I understand you ain't been around dark skinned people, but you gotta git over this thing about 'em. Jes a minute ago you was sayin' that all men are brothers an' shouldn't be judgin' each other, an' that's a good way ta think."

Deke downed his Strohs and reached for another one. "How come you know so much about coons anyways? You weren't raised around 'em anymore'n I was."

Shelly's nostrils flared. "Deke, don'tchoo say that aroun' me no more, or even when yor not around me. That's a horrible thing ta call Black people. You might a' been taught that way when you was young, Deke, but yor a grown man now – or should be – an' there ain't no excuse fer you ta still be talkin', or even thinkin' like that."

Deke started to say something, but Shelly headed him off.

"To answer your question, my parents weren't as ... well, they weren't like your aunt an' uncle, even though we went ta church an' read the Bible too. My daddy's brother, Vertner, who lives up in Ohio, has a real good Black friend named Ben, an' we'd git ta'gether with 'im whenever we'd go up there."

Shelly took a swig off her beer. "Him an' my uncle played music ta'gether an' they was real good. Ben was always nice ta me, laughin' an' jokin' about how tall I was. Ben an' his wife also helped raise my cousin, Wilbur, an' anybody who can put up with Wilbur is better than a saint."

"Guess I never know'd anybody like that," Deke said.

"It's too bad ya didn't, 'cause maybe you'd think diff'ernt." Shelly looked at Deke, her eyes serious. "But if you keep thinkin' like ya do an' bein' afraid a' Black people, then you won't *ever* know anybody like that."

"I ain't scared a' ... Negroes," Deke said.

"Then how come you loaded your guns an' wouldn't go buy beer?"

" 'Cause there's so many of 'em. Don't it bother you bein' surrounded by all these ... coloreds?"

"I notice it, if that's what ya mean, but why would it bother me? I ain't had no more trouble with dark people than I've had with light people."

"You only knowed that one, Shelly, an' he was a friend a' yer uncle's. A lot a' the others ain't like that."

"I've known more colored people than jes Ben," Shelly said. "There were some Black guys that used ta come inta Hillbilly Heaven. Some even brought their girlfriends. You must a' seen 'em in there."

"Yeah, I seen em' in there, but I didn't talk to 'em."

"Well, ya should have, they were nice people. Most of the ones I met worked at GM. They were polite and tipped me real well. Their girlfriends were always polite ta me too. I never had a one of 'em git outa hand with me like some of my own people from the hills did when I was dancin'."

"You mean you let 'em watch ya dance?" Deke asked.

"What was I supposed to do, make 'em put a hood over their heads when they come in?" Shelly said. "I'm startin' ta think maybe yor the one that oughta have a hood over his head – a white one, and a sheet to go with it."

Shelly drained her Falstaff and flipped the empty can into the trash basket. "Deke, don't you realize yor lookin' at these people 'cause they got dark skin the same way some people look at us 'cause we're hillbillies."

"It ain't the same."

"Why?"

" 'Cause with us it ain't justa'fide."

"That's the dumbest thing I ever heard, Deke." Shelly got up and pulled another Falstaff from the pack.

"I don't b'lieve in slav'ry or nothin'," Deke said, "I jest don't think we oughta be mixin' t'gether all that much. Hand me another beer, wouldja."

Shelly reached a beer out to Deke. "Are you tryin' ta tell me," she said, a sharp edge to her voice, "that I shouldn't be friends with Black people?"

"I guess bein' friendly's okay, so long as ya don't git too close with 'em."

"Well, I have been close with Black people," Shelly said.

"Like who?"

"D'you remember that real tall guy named Marvin who used ta come inta Hillbilly Heaven sometimes?" Shelly said. "He wore this hat he called a porkpie."

"I r'member seein' 'im," Deke said.

"Well, me an' Marvin were friends. He was real nice."

Deke made a wry face. "How close a' friends?"

"It ain't really none a' your business how close a' friends we were, Deke."

"Didja ever screw 'im?"

Deke tossed the question out almost as a joke, for he knew that Shelly never would have done anything that bad, but when the question hung in mid air, defying gravity and several other laws of Deke's universe, his smirk turned to a look of worried concern.

"Yes, I did," Shelly finally said, "and not jes once either, but whenever he asked me to. Sometimes I even asked him."

At first Deke didn't say anything, but then he let out a long groan. "Ohhhhhhhhhh, Shelly, you didn't?"

"I shor did," Shelly said. "An' he was a good lover, too." She smiled at the memory. "A *real* good lover."

A shudder ripped through Deke. Tremors shot through his body until his toes were twitching. Slumping on the bed, Deke cradled his head in his hands, trying to stem the images racing through his mind. He knew who Marvin was: tall, well dressed, limber and smooth. Marvin had even said "hello" to him once. One time Deke overheard one of his hillbilly friends point at Marvin and say, "He shor is a cocksure son-of-a-bitch, ain't he?"

Cocksure! Deke didn't even want to think about what that meant. In fact, Deke didn't want to think about anything right now, he just wanted this whole conversation not to have happened at all. Deke's strangled words came out somewhere between a moan and a plea. "Ohhhhh, Shelly, how could ya do somethin' like that? Jest thinkin' about it makes me sick."

"Then don't think about it," Shelly said to him.

"I can't stop thinkin' about it," Deke said, close to tears. "I don't know if I can do it with ya now."

"Then don't. We can have us one a' them plutonic relationships. I don't mind one bit."

Deke fell back on the bed, wailing.

Shelly wondered what Deke would say if he knew she had found out the day before that she was part Negro. "Deke," she said, "I jes don't understand you. When you asked me ta be your girlfriend you knew that since I came ta Norwood more men went down on me than on the *Titanic*, an' that don't bother ya one bit. But now yor actin' nuts jes 'cause some of 'em were a diff'ernt color than you."

Deke sat up straight. "There was more'n one?"

"I ain't sayin' ... 'cause it don't matter."

"Ohhhhhhhhhhhh!" Deke fell back on the bed again.

Shelly got up from the chair. "I'm gonna really go take a shower now," she said, "an' then I'm gittin inta bed. If you still wanta do somethin' I reckon I will, jes 'cause I promised I would."

She took a bag from her suitcase and walked into the bathroom, closing the door behind her. Deke's eyes followed her every move. Twenty minutes later, Shelly came out wearing only panties and a bra, pulled back the covers and climbed into bed. "Are you gonna git cleaned up an' come ta bed or jes sit on top a' the spread all night?" she asked Deke.

Deke sniffed a couple of times and wiped his red eyes. "I sure wish I didn't know what I didn't know an hour ago," he said.

"Then ya shouldn't a' asked," Shelly told him.

"But I had ta know."

"Now ya know."

"But I wanted ta know that ya didn't. Couldn't you a' fibbed?"

"No, Deke. Like I told ya, I ain't gonna lie no more."

They stared at each other until Shelly said, "So right now, Deke, why don'tcha change the way ya feel about Black people. The problem would be solved, you'd be a better man for doin' it, an' you'd have my everlastin' respect."

"Don't ya respect me now?"

Shelly had no wish to dropkick the already suffering Deke, but neither was she going to lie. "Let's jes say that I don't respect some a' your ideas. No matter what we were taught growin' up, we all got ta learn new things."

Shelly waited for Deke's response, but when none came, she said, "Deke, this conversation ain't goin' nowhere an' I'm tired as all git out. Either you go clean up some an' we git it on, or I'm turnin' the lights out an' goin' ta sleep."

Deke didn't move and after a few seconds Shelly shook her head in disgust and reached for the light switch.

"Wait!" Deke yelped, and scurried into the bathroom. Two minutes later the toilet flushed and Deke walked out wearing only a droopy pair of once-white skivvies. He turned out the lights, peeled off his underwear and climbed under the covers beside Shelly. Determined to obliterate the images that throttled his brain, Deke took half a dozen breaths and reached over to touch the girl he had fantasized about since he had first seen her dance at Hillbilly Heaven. To his immense delight, Shelly had taken off her bra and underwear while he was in the bathroom and was naked beside him.

Deke let his hand glide cautiously down Shelly's sinuous body, fearing some misstep might disrupt the proceedings. He ran his palm back up Shelly's length, along her thigh and over her flat stomach. Still in disbelief that this was finally happening, Deke wanted to tell Shelly how much he loved her, flatter her, sweet-talk her, but was afraid he would sound foolish and break the spell. He reached out and cupped Shelly's shoulder and rolled her over on her side to face him. She did not resist. Then he enfolded Shelly in his arms and just held her tightly and quietly against him.

As Deke fought to repress the images of Shelly and Marvin, Shelly also tried to forget about Deke's McConahay's many inglorious shortcomings. His caresses were tender and Shelly knew that Deke truly cared for her. She let the present moment just happen and returned Deke's embrace.

They kissed, long, long and deep. This moment was all that Deke McConahay had imagined it would be ... and more. It was to be his night, after all.

To her amazement, Shelly discovered that she actually enjoyed making love with Deke. Not only was he well formed of frame and limb, but equally surprising to her, nothing in Deke's manner was clumsy or awkward. Shelly's body responded with a tingling desire that drove away her weariness.

Emboldened now, Deke's hands went wandering, exploring the heretofore unknown regions of Shelly's spectacular body that they had sought for so long. He felt the tension of youthful muscle beneath her skin, the upright righteousness of her breasts, the solid determination of her butt.

Shelly ran her hands over Deke as well, starting at his shoulders then dug her fingers into his back, massaging the muscles, moving down his torso to his hips. They lingered there for a moment then passed on to his thighs. Shelly was surprised at the firmness of Deke's body, for she had never thought of him as a muscular man. She put her right hand between Deke's legs and wrapped around him. Shelly thought Deke might need a little help keeping his compass needle pointing north, but found to her delight that he needed no assistance at all.

Deke shuddered with pleasure and fought off the urge to have his finale right then. Reluctantly, his hands left Shelly's buttocks and sought her most intimate part. Deke's fondling and digital insertion made Shelly giddy with passion and she rolled onto her back and arched her spine, pushing her pelvis against Deke's hand, wanting more.

As Deke continued thrusting with his finger, she became even more aroused. Her breaths came in quick, sharp gasps and moans eased out from between her lips, low at first, then louder as her ecstasy reached a crescendo. There were no thoughts at all now in Shelly's brain, only the immeasurable pleasure of what was happening in her own body. Shelly began quivering from head to toe, and just as she was about to orgasm, Deke removed his finger, wanting to share that sensation with her, their bodies pressed together.

Tossing off the restraining covers, Deke gazed at Shelly's nude form, shimmering and succulent in the shadows of the dimly lit room. He carefully eased himself on top of her, the aura of disbelief still clinging to him. This was the moment Deke had yearned and pined for and he was more ecstatic than he had ever been in his life. There was no sense of conquest or triumph over Shelly, only the richness of fulfillment. As Deke began penetration, the images of everything that had led up to this sweet instant flashed through his brain and a glowing warmth of self-satisfaction pulsed through him. All that he had endured to finally be with Shelly, truly *be* with her, had been more than worth his effort and hardships: all the torturous weeks of unfulfilled longing, the disaster with the dump truck and losing his job, being hunted by the police, his humiliation by Cliff at the garage and his rejection by Shelly's family.

All of this pain, Deke gladly would have borne again to be rewarded with this rapturous moment. Even the terrible agony he'd suffered only a short while ago when he found out that where he was sticking his whang, some big, black, cocksure son of a bitch had stuck his big, black cock … *an' it was pro'bly longer an' bigger an' harder'n mine and he went on screwin' her fer'ever an' ever and she screamed an' begged fer more an' he gave it to her all night long agin' an' agin' an' the black on his dick likely rubbed off on her an' some a' his stuff might still be in there …*

"OOHHHHHHHHHH!" Deke McConahay wailed, "I can't do it," and collapsed in a flaccid, sobbing heap on top of Shelly.

Chapter 23

Tuesday, September 25

Deke stayed in bed, motionless as a corpse, the covers pulled tight over his head, as Shelly got dressed and ready. When she came out of the bathroom, Shelly shook the form under the sheets. "I'm goin' over to the motel office," she said. "I saw a sign las' night that said they got a free continental breakfast, whatever that is. Ya wanta go?"

The head moved from side to side, indicating, "No!"

Ten minutes later Shelly was back, carrying two Styrofoam cups of coffee and a small paper bag. "You need ta git outa bed so's we can get goin'," she said. "I know ya feel bad about las' night but ta'day's a new day an' ya gotta face it. Here, I brought ya coffee and some things from that continental breakfast."

Deke slipped his head out from under the covers and sat up. He took the coffee, but eyed the paper bag with suspicion. "What's a continental breakfast?"

"I don't know for shor," Shelly answered. "Maybe it's what our continental soldiers ate during the Revolutionary War. Whatever it is, it ain't much. It's a wonder they whipped the redcoats on jes coffee an' donuts."

Deke shook his head. "I ain't hungry." He leaned against the headboard and sipped the coffee but showed no sign of stirring.

"It's after eight, Deke, we need ta git movin'," Shelly told him.

"Could ya hand me my underwear layin' there on the floor?"

Shelly eyed the dirty skivvies, remembering that they were Deke's only pair. "I'll let you git 'em," she said. "I need to go inta the bathroom and finish gittin' ready."

When Shelly came out, Deke was dressed and was putting his guns back in his duffel bag. He went into the bathroom, pee'd and flushed the toilet. "I'm ready," he said.

Shelly started to say something, then picked up her suitcase and pack. "Alright then, let's go."

They walked out of their room into a sunny and promising morning. The highway and nearby shops were already bustling. Just like the night before, Deke and Shelly were the only Caucasions in sight. Shelly pointed to the spare tire in the bed. "See Deke, I told ya nobody'd steal it."

As they were loading their gear into the wooden trunk, Deke glanced around nervously. "Maybe I oughta keep one a' my guns in the cab with us."

"Oh no you won't," Shelly told him. "If we git stopped by the law they'll haul us both off ta jail if they find a loaded gun in the truck."

Deke got into the driver's seat and pumped the gas a couple of times. "I can't wait ta get outa this place," he said. He depressed the clutch and turned the key. Nothing.

"Ya might wanta reconnect the battery," Shelly said with a grin.

Sulking, Deke got out and raised the hood. Before it was halfway open Shelly heard a loud scream and thinking Deke was hurt, jumped from the cab to see what was wrong. Deke had stopped screaming but his mouth remained open and Shelly followed his gaze to where both cables dangled in empty space; the new battery they'd bought from Cliff was gone. Deke's face purpled with rage and he began swearing violently. He pounded the fender, kicked the bumper, stomped the asphalt. Shelly was mad too, but didn't see any profit in throwing a fit. "You wait here, Deke, I'll take care of it," she said and walked to the motel office.

"Let me guess," Jordan said when Shelly walked in, "your battery's gone."

"How'd ya know?" Shelly asked.

"Fifth one this morning," Jordan said. "We try … we really try to do right by our customers, but that damn …" he caught himself, "that liquor store across the road attracts some desperate people. My wife and I feel terrible about it."

"I don't blame you folks one bit," Shelly told him. "This same thing happens in Wes' Virginia, too. How do I git another battery?"

"There's a NAPA store three blocks away," Jordan told her and sighed in exasperation. "I can drive you there."

As Shelly and Jordan left the parking lot in Jordan's car, Deke, still in the throes of his tantrum, saw them and stopped ranting. His eyes followed them with a steady, malevolent glare. Shelly felt like rolling down the window and yelling out, That's right, Deke, Jordan an' I are runnin' off together.

As they returned from the NAPA store Jordan told Shelly, "I'd better carry that battery over to the truck for you."

"I appreciate the offer, Jordan, but Deke's in a real bad mood over this."

"It's heavy," he cautioned.

"I'm one a' them big, strong hillbilly girls you mighta heard about," Shelly told him as she hefted the battery out of his car.

Jordan laughed.

"Thanks a lot," Shelly said to him. "If I'm ever through these parts agin' I'll stay at your motel, or leastwise stop in an' say 'hi' … I mean, if that's okay."

"Shelly, it'd be our pleasure."

Deke watched in dour silence as Shelly lugged the battery to his pickup, lifted it into the engine compartment and attached the cables.

"Reckon we can go now," Shelly said and smiled.

"Whadda you so goddam happy about?" Deke said.

" 'Cause we're on our way ta Montana," Shelly answered. "Let's git on with it."

To cross the Mississippi River they had to get on an interstate, but their late start spared them the morning rush hour. Gliding over the vast expanse of water helped lighten Deke's sour mood, but not enough for him to start singing, for which Shelly was grateful. When they reached the other side, Shelly turned to him with a grin. "We're officially pioneers now, Deke."

"Yeah, I reckon," he answered.

"Soon as we see a decent rest'ernt, I wanta stop," Shelly said. "That revolutionary breakfast didn't do much for me."

Deke nodded, but drove on in silence. At the next interchange a giant Howard Johnson's sign poked into the stratosphere.

"Let's stop there, Deke," Shelly said, pointing.

"I don't know, Shelly. I always heard that's a purty high class joint."

"Whatcha sayin', Deke, that we ain't good e'nuff ta go in there?"

"Oh no, nothin' like that. It jest might be a little spendy."

"Deke, I never been in a Howard Johnson's an' I've always wanted to. Ev'ry once in a while we at least oughta *try* ta stop actin' like bottomfeeders."

As they drove toward the restaurant Deke motioned down the road. "Hey, there's a MacDonalds right over yonder," he said.

"You can go there if ya want, but drop me off at the Howard Johnson's."

Deke pouted, but he pulled in and parked.

The place was packed. A party of four waited ahead of them and within five minutes half a dozen people stood in line behind them. Shelly gawked at the potted plants and listened to the soft, non-descript music while Deke fidgeted. He unrolled the pack of smokes from his t-shirt sleeve and lit one up. The hostess came and took the foursome ahead of them to a table, and now that they were in full view of the seated patrons, Shelly noticed that a number of them were staring at Deke. With his scraggly beard, long stringy hair, tattered jeans and t-shirt, he could easily be taken for a bum who had wondered in off the street. Deke sucked on his cigarette and looked around the room. "This waitin' in line's making me nervous."

"We'll be fine, Deke," Shelly told him. "They'll seat us in a minute."

"Maybe I oughta put my shirt tail in," Deke said and unsnapped his jeans. With a Camel dangling from his mouth, head down and skivvies showing, Deke didn't see the waitress come up. Shelly stood in mute embarrassment as the woman fought to control her facial muscles. When all was tucked, Deke looked up, took the cigarette from his lips and said, "There, that's way better."

The waitress put on the smile she had been saving for the rainy day that had clearly arrived. "We have a table for two ready," she said. Deke and Shelly followed her to a table that was already prepped with water, silverware and menus. "Coffee?" the waitress asked and both Shelly and Deke nodded yes.

Shelly flipped the pages of her glossy, photo-covered menu. "I must be hungry," she said, "ev'rything looks good."

As Deke scanned his menu, he said without looking up, "I never been in a place this fancy b'fore. It kinda makes me feel like a hick. An' las' night was the first time I ever stayed in a motel. Reckon that really does make me a hick."

Shelly laughed.

"How come yer laughin' at me? I can't help it we never went anywheres."

"I ain't laughin' at you, Deke," Shelly said. "I'm laughin' 'cause last night was the first time I ever stayed in a motel too." She picked up her water glass and held it out to Deke. "Let's have us a toast. Here's ta two hicks that finally made it across the Mississippi River." Deke picked up his water glass and clanked it against hers.

When their order came, Deke picked through his plate, eyeing each morsel before he put it in his mouth. "What's the matter, Deke, don'tcha like it?" Shelly asked.

"I ain't all that hungry," Deke said and looked up. "Shelly, are we really boyfriend and girlfriend? I know we're s'pose'd ta be, but it don't feel like it."

Shelly swallowed. "I said I'd be your girlfrend if ya took me ta Montana. I ain't gonna go back on my word, so I reckon we perty much are."

"It's that 'purty much' that's got me worried, Shelly. I mean, we didn't exactly coperlate our relationship las' night."

"We come close," Shelly said, trying to sound positive.

Deke picked up a forkful of hashbrowns, looked at it, and set it back on his plate. "What I mean is, Shelly, we don't act like boyfriend an' girlfriend. We don't kiss or touch, or put our arms around each other. You don't sit close ta me in the truck when we're drivin'."

"Deke, I ain't gonna ride ta Montana in the middle a' the front seat with the gear shift in my crotch. We ain't high-school kids."

"Yer only seventeen," Deke said.

"Not for long."

When Deke didn't respond, Shelly said, "Look, Deke, I don't mind if you touch or kiss me a little, long as it's done in a carin' way an' not a feelin' me up way. What I keep tryin' ta tell ya is that it'd be nice if you said or did romantic things more often. Boyfriends an' girlfriends do that for each other."

"Does that mean you'd say nice things ta me, too?" Deke asked.

"Yeah, I guess that means I'd say nice things ta you, too."

Deke smiled slightly. "I understand what yer sayin', Shelly, an' I'll try ta be more romantic." The expression on Deke's face changed. "Uh … I gotta go use the bathroom," he said. "Would ya wait for me?"

"I won't go ta Montana without ya, Deke, you got the keys to the truck."

"It's jest that I might be in there fer awhile," Deke said, getting up.

"That's good ta know, Deke. I'm always so glad when you share that information with me."

Twenty minutes later, as they walked to the pickup, Deke put his arm around Shelly's waist and leaned in to kiss her. Shelly didn't resist but turned her head so that the kiss caught her on the cheek instead of the mouth. She waited for Deke to open the passenger door for her, but he went to the driver's side, leaving her standing. "You shor know how ta romance a girl," she told him.

"Thank ya, Shelly," he answered politely.

Deke started up the Ford and Shelly draped the atlas across her knees. "Don't git back on the interstate," she said. "Let's take Highway 61. It looks interesting an' we need ta be further north anyway." A short while later they came to the town of Troy. "How 'bout that, Deke," Shelly said, "we're in Troy already. Let's drive around."

Deke drove down several side streets of the quiet, conventionally styled town. On Main Street they saw a sign for Wood's Fort Park and near it, a very old log cabin. "Let's git out an' go look at it," Shelly said.

While reading the historical marker by the cabin, Deke said, "It says this is Lincoln County. Zeke told me that Troy, Montana is in Lincoln County too."

They drove on to Bowling Green. On the main drag two black horsedrawn buggies rolled slowly toward them. The drivers had broad-brimmed straw hats, suspenders and beards while the women beside them wore full dresses and white prayer caps.

Deke braked the pick-up to a halt and stared. "What are those?"

"I think they're Amish people," Shelly said.

"I never seen nothin' like 'em," Deke told her.

"I never seen any either, but I've heard about 'em. There's a lot in Pennsylvania an' some in Ohio," Shelly said. "I don't know much about 'em except they're real religious an' hold ta old timey ways."

Deke continued gaping as the buggies approached. "How come them women are wearin' coffee filters on their heads?"

"I don't think those are really coffee filters," Shelly told him. "An' I also don't think it's polite ta stop in the middle of the street an' stare at 'em." The driver behind them agreed and loudly honked his horn.

When they came to the intersection of Route 54, Shelly looked down at her map. "I wanta drive along the Mississippi River," she said. "That river deserves more respect than jes crossin' over it. Let's go east ta Highway 79."

At the town of Louisiana they saw the Mississippi again, but then Route 79 took a turn west and left the river. In recompense, the highway twisted up into some beautifully forested hills, and twice Shelly had Deke stop so they could look out over the vast plain of the Mississippi. When they reached Hannibal, Shelly's desire to get close to the big river was fulfilled. As they entered the town, she told Deke, "I recall hearin' somethin' about Hannibal bein' famous but I don't remember for what."

"I've heard 'at name before," Deke said.

"Yor pro'bly thinkin' of the guy, Hannibal," Shelly said. "He was a general way back when and put some butt-whippin' on the Romans. This town Hannibal is famous for somethin' else."

Deke cruised slowly into Hannibal's business district and at Shelly's direction took a side street that pointed towards the river. At the base of a hill two bronzed boys carrying sticks strolled jauntily side-by-side.

"Now I remember!" Shelly yelled. "Stop the truck, Deke."

Before the wheels quit turning Shelly was out of the truck and scrambling up to the boys, but they responded neither in voice nor gesture, for they were, literally, bronze.

"It's Tom Sawyer an' Huckleberry Finn," she called to Deke. "This is the town where Mark Twain grew up."

Blank-faced and puffing on a Camel, Deke just looked up at the statue.

"Don't that mean nothin' to ya, Deke?"

"Well, I heard of 'im, but no, it don't really mean nothin' to me."

Likely in violation of some rule or city ordinance, Shelly pulled herself up onto Tom and Huck's pedestal and stood beside them.

"I wish we had us a camera, Deke," Shelly called down at him. "My brother Mack loves Huckleberry Finn. I'd love to send 'im a picture a' me standin' b'side him an' Tom." Shelly smiled. "Well, at least I can tell Mack how I met 'em." She patted both boys on the top of their heads and jumped down.

After they got back on Main Street they saw Mark Twain's boyhood home, along with other period structures and a museum, set back off the main drag along a street of brick. "Oh look!" Shelly said, pointing. When she realized Deke was going to drive right on by, she punched him in the arm. "You pull over right now. I wanta look at this."

"OW!" Deke said, rubbing his arm. "Ya didn't have ta hit me."

"I'll hit ya again if ya don't stop," Shelly told him. "I didn't come all this way ta drive past the house that Mark Twain grew up in."

"Alright, alright, I'll pull over."

Shelly dragged Deke from building to building, reading aloud each sign in front of them. When they came to a white fence Shelly pointed at it. "Look Deke, it's the fence that Tom Sawyer talked 'em boys inta paintin' for 'im."

Deke looked at the fence. "Well," he said, "they done a good job, it's still real white." He glanced at Shelly's watch. "The day's gittin on, Shelly, an' we ain't hardly gone anywhere."

"This is somewhere," Shelly said. "Don't ya wanta go inta the museum?"

"No," Deke told her. "They likely want a heap a' money jest ta see a bunch a' old stuff that most people woulda throwed away by now."

Deke's lack of enthusiam was contagious. Shelly exhaled a long breath. "Okay," she said, "I reckon we don't have to if yor that dead set against it, but there is one thing I'm gonna do 'fore we leave here."

"What's that?"

"Go down to the Mississippi River."

They got back into the truck and drove down Main until they saw a street where they could access the river. Deke parked again and he and Shelly got out and walked until they stood on the bank, looking across the expanse of water.

"Ain't it somethin'?" Shelly said. "I wish I could go ta all the places this water does."

Even Deke was awed. "Shitfire, it sure is big."

"It's gits a lot bigger," Shelly said. "The Missouri River an' the Ohio ain't even come into it yet."

Where the water lapped at the grass, Shelly knelt down and cupped her hands in the river. She splashed the water over her face and felt it come alive, like tiny rivulets of energy running down her skin. She splashed on more water, then looked out over the Mississippi, so immense it seemed a lake, and in an instant understood the pull and enchantment of the great river and was caught in its spell. Like Tom and Huck, Shelly wanted to cast herself adrift upon the current to see where the river took her. She dipped again and smoothed the water through her long hair, then stood up.

"How come ya done that?" Deke asked. "Yer face didn't look dirty."

"It wasn't," Shelly said. "I've jes always wanted ta wash my face in the Mississippi River. It feels good, ya oughta try it."

"No way," Deke said. "That river don't look all that clean ta me."

On their way back to the truck, Shelly went into a gift shop and bought a postcard of Tom and Huck's statue while Deke waited on the sidewalk.

"Can we go now?" he said when she came out.

Still dripping, Shelly took hold of the door handle. "Let's point this buggy west."

Shelly navigated them onto Highway 36 and after a few miles Deke asked, "How come you know about things like that feller Hannibal and Mark Twain, an' what rivers go inta the Mississippi? You quit school an' I done graduated … even though it took me till I was twenty."

"Them kinda things always int'rested me," Shelly said. "I didn't quit school 'cause I didn't like learnin', I left 'cause a' all the other stuff that was goin' on in my life. Both Daddy an' Mama liked ta read and I got that from them."

"We never had nothin' like that growin' up."

"It ain't too late for you ta start, Deke."

"I reckon," Deke said, and reached into his bag of baloney and crackers.

They drove steadily, stopping only for lunch and gas in Macon, but the frequent towns hindered them from making any real mileage. Deke chafed at the pace but Shelly was content, twisting her head to check out each little burg they drove through. They reached Cameron and the interchange to I-35 at 5:00 pm.

"Ya wanta go ta Kansas City?" Shelly asked, looking at her atlas.

"Is it like St. Louis?"

"Pro'bly."

"Then no, I don't wanna go there," Deke said.

From Cameron to St. Joseph, Highway 36 undulated like a roller coaster. Coming into St. Joseph they saw an A&W drive-in and Deke said, "I'm hungry."

"Me too," Shelly concurred, so they swung in.

Shelly thought Deke was eyeing the teenage carhops way too much, but when the food came it was good. As Deke finished off his third mug of frosted rootbeer, he said, "It's startin' ta git late. We need ta find us a motel soon."

As they drove through St. Joseph Shelly said, "Let's git away from the city ta'night, Deke, I think you'd be more comf'terble stayin' in a small town."

They crossed the Missouri River into Kansas where the landscape opened into farms and fields. When they didn't see any towns or motels Deke began to fret, but fifteen minutes later they entered Troy, their second one of the day. Though not large, it sported a decent looking motel. After checking in, Deke and Shelly drove to a nearby convienence store and bought snacks and two six packs of Grain Belt beer, which they'd never heard of before.

Though not as homey as the Golden Jubilee Motor Hotel, the room was pleasant and Shelly opened the windows and let the night breeze come in. They munched Oreos and chips and drank their Grain Belt, Shelly going one for one with Deke while they laughed and traded stories of growing up in the hills.

If Deke still harbored trepidations of Shelly's sexual history, he didn't let them show, and when darkness flowed into the room like a soft mist they left the lights off. A little past 10:00 o'clock the night air went from cool to chilly and Shelly closed the windows. She and Deke drained off the last of the beer and without further ado, fanfare, or drama, 'coperlated' their relationship; several times.

Chapter 24

Wednesday: September 26

The Grain Belt overtook Deke shortly after dawn. He went to the bathroom and got back into bed, where he lay awake, savoring the night before. As he listened to Shelly's steady breathing, Deke imagined what would happen when she awoke. Perhaps she'd reach out, take him in her arms and they'd make love until checkout time. Or maybe Shelly would open her eyes and wink at him, then, unable to contain her lust, throw the covers back and bend her lovely mouth over him and give him a morning jump-start.

"Mornin', Deke," Shelly said a few minutes later.

"Mornin', Shelly," Deke replied sweetly and smiled.

Shelly pulled the covers back and sat up, and just as Deke thought she was going to bend down and go to work on him, she got to her feet and went into the bathroom so fast that Deke didn't even get a good look at her bare butt.

Deke heard the toilet flush and he waited for Shelly to come out and get back into bed with him but then he heard the shower running. Thirty minutes later Shelly came out fully dressed in the clean clothes she'd laid out in the bathroom the night before. She walked over to Deke, leaned over and kissed him on the forehead, then put a bar of motel soap in his hand. "Your turn," she told him.

"My turn fer what?"

"Ta take a shower."

Deke wasn't happy, but he took the soap and went into the bath-room. When he came out, Shelly said, " Deke, do you ever brush your teeth?"

"Not too much."

"How come?"

"I don't wanna destroy the protective layer a' plaque."

Shelly didn't know whether to laugh or gag. "Listen, Deke, that ain't too good fer your teeth. Maybe we oughta stop an' get ya some toiletries."

"What's brushin' my teeth got ta do with the toilet?" Deke asked.

Shelly looked at Deke and saw that he was serious. "Let's jes hit the road."

Now that Deke was 'officially' Shelly's boyfriend, he took for grant-ed that certain privileges came with that title. As he followed Shelly to the truck, he said, "Yer lookin' good today, baby," and grabbed a handful of ass.

Shelly spun around and knocked his arm away. "You don't grab me like that!"

At the diner down the road, Shelly said, "It's your turn ta buy, Deke. I bought breakfast yesterday and ya still owe me for half the battery an' the motel in East St. Louis." Grumbling, Deke got out his wallet, paid for breakfast, and counted out the money he owed Shelly. They strolled outside into the sunshine and as Shelly was stretching her limbs before getting into the truck, she said, "When we git to a bigger town, Deke, I wanta stop at a department store."

"What for."

"Ta buy some clothes."

"Can I help pick 'em out?" Deke asked.

"Shor, Deke, that'd be great."

Highway 36 out of Troy was more undulating asphalt and vast farms like they'd seen the day before. Past Fairview, the road ran straight for such an unbroken stretch that when they reached Seneca they drove around town just to wake up and were pleasantly awed by its wide brick streets and historic buildings. Back on the highway, the road con-tinued its unbending path but Deke soon found a way to alleviate the boredom. Steering with his left hand, Deke smiled at Shelly and put his right hand on her knee. Shelly didn't say anything but when Deke's hand crept up her thigh, heading for territory that was not part of her leg, Shelly pried it off as if it were an alien creature.

"What's wrong?" Deke said. "There ain't nobody watchin'."

"You need ta be steerin' with both hands."

"Why? The road's straight."

"Well, ya never know. There might be a curve up here somewhere's."

"I can see fer over a mile."

"I don't care. Ya still need ta be safe."

"Ya know," Deke said slyly, "there's things girls can do ta boys while they're a'drivin'. An' on a straight road like this one, it wouldn't be dangerous."

"You might as well quitchor dreamin' 'bout that," Shelly told him, "'cause it ain't gonna happen."

Deke pouted as Route 36 continued straight all the way to Marysville. Heading out of town Shelly noticed a large statue of a man on horseback. "What's that, Deke?" she said, "Let's go take a look at it." Shelly walked up to the statue, envious of the rider leaning forward in the saddle, hat brim bent back, spurring on his galloping steed. "It's a tribute to the pony express," she called to Deke, who had stayed in the truck. "It says here we been drivin' on the Pony Express Highway."

"I wonder why we ain't seen any of 'em yet," Deke said.

Shelly got back in the pickup, opened the map and saw that, except for one jog, Route 36 remained arrow straight. "Deke, I can't take no more a' this boring road. Unless there's somethin' yor desperate ta see in Kansas, we oughta take 77 up here an' go north inta Nebraska."

"Dodge City's in Kansas, ain't it?" Deke said. "I wouldn't mind goin' there."

"What for? It's clean on the other side a' the state an' way to the south."

"Well, you know," Deke said, "Marshall Matt Dillon an' Miss Kitty an' all that."

"That was a TV show. I don't think they even filmed *Gunsmoke* in Dodge City."

"I don't know, Shelly, it looked purty real ta me. The Long Branch Saloon might still be there."

"Yor thinkin' of how Dodge City was a hund'ert years ago, Deke. I bet now it don't look no diff'ernt than any a' these towns we been goin' through."

"Yer likely right," Deke admitted, then stubbed his cigarette out in the ashtray.

"What'sa matter, Deke, yor lookin' a little glum?" Shelly asked him.

Deke was glum. Neither his 'official' girlfriend nor the state of Kansas was living up to his expectations. "Shitfire, Shelly, I jest kinda hoped things would be more like, well, you know, the West. I figger'd by now we'd be seein' ranches an' cowboys an' Injuns an' stuff like that. So far there ain't been nothin' but cornfields. This here statue's the only thing we've seen that even looks like the West."

"Maybe we ain't really in the West yet, Deke."

"I don't know. I've seen lotsa westerns that took place in Kansas." Deke lit a cigarette from the dashboard lighter. "You don't s'pose it's all gone, do ya?"

"I don't think any such thing, Deke," Shelly said. "It'll start lookin' more like the West on up here a ways."

Shelly was trying to cheer Deke up, but his words had put some doubt in her. At the edge of Marysville Deke and Shelly turned north onto Highway 77, but southeastern Nebraska was just like Kansas, except there were more small towns to pass through. They had lunch at a local café in Beatrice and after getting back on the highway Shelly said, "This road goes to Lincoln. I don't really wanta go inta a city, do you, Deke?"

"Not if we can help it," Deke replied.

At the intersection of Route 33 Shelly had Deke take a left towards Crete, but before they got there, she directed him back north on 103. Both roads were so straight and nondescript that when they bumped into I-80, even Shelly was ready to get Nebraska over with. Like the other roads, I-80 ran straight as a laser beam. Deke was content, rolling along at 80 plus, but after half an hour Shelly said, "Deke, I'm already fed up with this interstate. Git off up here at Route 81 an' we'll go north some more."

Highway 81 also ran linear until a few miles past Stromsburg, where a series of turns and more interesting scenery led into Columbus, but then it straightened out again all the way to Norfolk. At the first K-Mart, Shelly said, "Pull in, Deke, an' we'll shop for some clothes."

After a day of tedious driving, even the prospect of a K-Mart felt exciting, especially to Deke, who was picturing what under-apparel he would like to see on Shelly. But when she grabbed a cart and led him to the menswear section, Deke realized she had meant buying clothes for *him*.

Shelly halted Deke in mid-aisle and looked him up and down. "Let's start by gittin' ya a new shirt," she said.

"I like this shirt I got on."

"You wait here," Shelly told him. She returned carrying a red and yellow long sleeve, pearly snap-button shirt. "Lookee, Deke, here's a cowboy shirt. It's even got front pockets for ya ta put your cigarettes in."

"I don't like it," Deke said.

Shelly pointed to the dressing room. "Go try it on."

Frowning, Deke took the shirt. When he came out of the changing room, Shelly said, "Deke, you still got your old shirt on under it. Go back in there an' take it off." She walked over and grabbed a white t-shirt from a rack and handed it to Deke. "Here, put this on under your new shirt."

Five minutes later Deke stood motionless in front of Shelly as she straightened the collar and fiddled with the sleeves on his shirt. "It looks good on ya, Deke," she said.

"I don't like it," he said.

"Let's see if we can find ya some pants now."

"What's wrong with the ones I'm wearin'?"

Shelly jiggled Deke's pants at the waistline. "Looks like you take about a thirty-two," she said. "I'll be right back."

Shelly came back holding a pair of jeans in each hand. "Try these on."

"I don't wear Wranglers, I wear Levis," Deke told her.

"Yor in the West now, or close to it, an' out here men wear Wranglers."

"These are too stiff," Deke said, holding up the pants.

"How d'ya know till ya try 'em on?" Shelly said and pointed to the dressing room.

When Deke came out he didn't get three steps until Shelly called to him. "You need ta put your shirttail in."

Deke stopped and started to unsnap his jeans.

"Not out here," Shelly hollered.

Deke scowled and went back in to the changing room. A minute later he opened the door and walked over to Shelly like he was wearing two stovepipes. "I don't like 'em," he said. "They don't bend right an' they look funny on me."

"Didja try the other pair on?" Shelly asked him as she tugged and pulled at the shiny new britches.

"They're even worse'n these."

"They go perty good with that shirt."

Deke looked himself over. "I don't like either one of 'em."

"They don't go with that belt buckle at all," Shelly said, and put her index finger right on John Wayne's nose. "An' the leather's all frayed, too. Let's gitcha a new belt."

"Ain't no way!" Deke said, clutching the Duke with his right hand. "My brother Zeke give me this belt when he went off to the Army."

"I shor wouldn't trust that ratty ol' thing," Shelly said, "but I reckon you got your mind made up on it."

"We done yet?" Deke asked.

"No. We need ta get some hankies for when ya have ta blow your nose."

"I don't need ta blow my nose," Deke said.

"Well, there's times, Deke, when ya *should* blow your nose, instead a' pickin' it."

Shelly walked two aisles over and brought back three handkerchiefs. She looked at Deke and pursed her lips, calculating how many days it'd take them to get to Troy. "Don't go nowhere," she said. Five minutes later Shelly returned with two three-packs of boxer shorts and six pairs of socks.

"I don't wear that kind a' underwear," Deke said. "B'sides, 'at's more socks an' underwear than I ever owned in my life. I don't need that many."

"It's a clean pair for ev'ry day we're trav'lin," Shelly said, as she tossed them into the shopping cart. "How 'bout a new hat?"

"No!" Deke yelled, and grabbed his hat with both hands. "The one thing ya don't mess with is a man's hat. An' I'm keepin' my boots, too. Shitfire, they're jest gittin' broke in."

Shelly sighed. "Alright," she said. "I think that's about got it. Let's go find ya some toiletries an' git outa here."

"Don't you need anything?" Deke asked her. "Like maybe some red bikini panties or somethin'?"

Shelly glared at Deke. "I'm fine in that department, but thanks fer askin'."

She started pushing the cart down the aisle but when Deke didn't follow, she called, "C'mon, Deke."

"I need ta take these duds off," he said.

"Leave 'em on. Jes keep the price tags on so's they can check ya out."

After tossing some toiletry articles for Deke into the cart, Shelly headed towards checkout. As they waited in line, Shelly saw a trash can. She wadded Deke's old clothes into a ball and said, "I'll go throw these away since you won't be needin' 'em anymore."

"Oh no you don't!" Deke said, and reached out and grabbed the bundle away from Shelly. "I might jest want these again sometime. I'm keepin' 'em."

When Shelly told the gum-popping cashier that Deke was wearing the clothes he was buying, she rolled her eyes. "You gotta be shittin' me," she said, and made Deke come around by the register so she could check the tags.

As Deke clutched his old clothes to keep them away from Shelly, the checkout lady turned him around a couple of times and then made him bend down so she could see the label on his t-shirt. Two pimply teenage boys standing in line behind them watched and snickered the whole time.

"You're not wearin' new underwear, too, are you?" the checkout woman said. "If you are, you'll have ta drop those Wranglers so I can see the price tag."

The two boys waiting in line laughed and when Deke scowled at them, one gave him the finger.

"No, we got his underwear an' socks right here," Shelly told the woman, holding the packages up for her to see.

After she'd rung up the total, the cashier stood looking back and forth from Deke to Shelly. "Well?" she finally said.

"Pay the woman," Shelly told Deke.

"Me? You're the one who picked all these things out."

"Yor the one wearin' 'em. Pay the woman."

Deke mumbled something unintelligible as he took his old wallet from his back pocket and grudgingly lifted a fifty dollar bill from it's frayed innards.

"We shoulda got ya a new billfold too," Shelly said.

On the way to the truck, Shelly said, "Hold up, Deke, I wanta pull them price tags off so ya don't look like Minnie Pearl." When she'd finished, Shelly stepped back and looked him over. "Ya know, Deke, you don't look half bad."

"What about the other half?" Deke said, not one ounce of humor in his voice.

Shelly looked at her watch. "It's gittin' on suppertime. Let's go find someplace ta eat. I'll even buy'," she said, trying to cheer Deke up.

"Can we go to a drive-through? I don't want nobody ta see me."

They drove around until Deke spotted a Kentucky Fried Chicken with a take-out window. After ordering, they sat in the parking lot and ate in the truck. "This kinda reminds me a' that day we left Norwood an' ate at a KFC," Shelly said as she finished off a drumstick. "That was a perty wild day, huh, Deke?"

"That was the day you told that guy I was yer brother."

Shelly stopped eating. "I wouldn't do that again, Deke. I'd tell 'im that you were my boyfriend."

It was the first time Deke had heard Shelly say that, and goofy new clothes or not, he felt better and smiled.

After they'd finished, Shelly took the trash to a can and when she got back in the truck said, "This day's about done. I don't think there's much in the way a' towns west of here for a while. We oughta grab us a motel."

Since they were on one of Norfolk's main highways, there were a number to choose from. They settled on a Motel 6 and after checking in and unloading their luggage, Shelly said, "It ain't that late, let's go see a movie."

Deke didn't say anything.

"That's what boyfriends an' girlfriends do," Shelly told him. "Movie theaters are dark, nobody'll notice your new clothes."

At the front desk they got directions to the local theaters and after some discussion decided on *Deliverance*. Deke bounced his toes to the banjo music but Shelly could sense his rage and discomfort during the sodomy scene. "I liked that movie," Shelly said when they came out, "but it shor didn't make us hillbillies look too good."

"I'm glad those two guys got killed fer doin' what they did," Deke said. "They could shoot arrows through ever' queer in the world fer all I care."

Shelly thought of her gentle, intelligent gay friend who owned the old time clothing store in Cincinnati, but she didn't say anything.

On the way back they stopped and got a six-pack of Coors, which neither of them had ever tried, and as they were pulling into the motel parking lot Shelly said, "Deke, I know you don't like them clothes we bought ta'day, but they look good on ya."

Deke still looked doubtful.

"You ain't a bad lookin' man," Shelly told him, "an' puttin' on new clothes makes ya look all that much better." Shelly wanted to add; and if you'd brush your teeth, cut your hair an' trim your beard you'd look a whole lot better'n ya do now, but figured she'd save that for another day.

They got out of the pickup and Deke walked back to the bed and dug out a piece of thick rope.

"Are you plannin' to tie the spare tire down with that?" Shelly asked.

"After what happened the other night, you bet," Deke answered.

"Deke, there ain't nobody in the whole world who'd steal that old worthless tire. Let's jes go inside an' have a beer."

"Alright, I won't then," Deke said, "but I'm gonna diconnect the battery."

Shelly shook her head as Deke raised the hood and undid the cables. "There, that's the best I can do," Deke said, letting the hood drop. "I jest hope no jungle bunny steals it t'night."

Shelly cringed and thought; changin' the way Deke looks is gonna be easy compared to changin' the way Deke thinks.

Chapter 25

Thursday: September 27

First light had barely crept into the room when Shelly popped awake and headed to the bathroom. She came out, all showered and dressed, but Deke was still asleep. Shelly looked at his dirty skivvies and filthy socks on the floor then took a broom from the closet. She used a tissue to pick up Deke's socks, then skewered his underwear on the broom handle and carried them outside to a dumpster. Next, she laid out Deke's new clothes on a stand in the bathroom and set a razor, toothbrush, toothpaste, and trimming scissors on the sink counter. She woke Deke up by placing a kiss on his forehead.

After some cajoling, Deke took a shower and put on his new clothes, but didn't touch the toiletry articles. Shelly started to comment, but instead told him, "There's a Denny's over yonder, let go have breakfast."

"Sounds good ta me," Deke said.

During the night the weather had turned and Deke and Shelly opened the door to a cold, blustery wind coming at them from the west. Shelly squinted into the lashing gale as they walked to the restaurant. "I hope we start seein' some ranches an' cowboys ta'day."

"Me too," Deke said. "I'd like ta meet some cowboys. I think they'd take ta me real quick."

As they entered the restaurant, Deke lit a cigarette in his cupped hands and tipped his cowboy hat back. Glaring around the room through squinted eyes he told Shelly, "Nobody better say nothin' about these clothes or call me a dude or a pilgrim."

Ain't nobody gonna make fun a' ya, Deke," Shelly assured him.

After breakfast they went back to the motel room and Shelly started packing. Deke looked at the clock on the nightstand. "It ain't all that late, Shelly," he said. "We got over two hours till checkout time. I feel like climbin' back inta bed fer a while."

"That bed does look invitin', Deke," Shelly said, as Deke's face brightened. She looked at her watch. "It ain't all that early, either. By the time you finish brushin' your teeth, shavin', and trimmin' up your hair an' beard, it'll be time ta go. Too bad ya didn't do all that earlier."

Deke slunk into the bathroom. "Git them hairs growin' outa your ears and nose too," Shelly hollered through the closed door, but when Deke came out he didn't look one bit different.

Deke reconnected the battery and let the truck warm up while he and Shelly stowed their luggage in the wooden trunk and locked it. They drove through downtown Norfolk, which was about as exciting as dry cornflakes, then Shelly got out her map and directed Deke to Route 275. Traffic was light, but the highway and scenery were similar to those of the day before. Ahead of them a sky of plump gray pillows stretched to the horizon and the wind blew without mercy. They crossed the Elkhorn River just past Oakdale and the road became curvy. At Neligh, Shelly saw a sign for the Neligh Mill State Historical Site. "Let's go look at it," she said.

Shelly wanted to go through the mill but Deke was cold and bored. They walked around enough to stretch their legs and headed west again.

After Clearwater the asphalt ran straight and flat. The Elkhorn River paralleled their route, but Deke and Shelly only caught glimpses of its cottonwood-lined banks. Fields stretched from horizon to horizon and gravel roads ran endlessly linear from each side of the highway. They drove past small patches of wetlands and creeks but their slack water was muddy brown and brush-filled. Yet they struck Shelly as the only remaining natural features in a land that only a few generations ago had been wild.

A few miles past Ewing U.S. 20 merged with 275. The monotonous character of the road did not change, but the amount of traffic did. Before interstates, U.S. 20 had been one of the great east-west highways, traversing the country from Boston to Newport, Oregon. Officially the longest road in the United States at 3365 miles, at one time it was a major transportation artery and still smelled like diesel smoke. The trucks coming towards Deke and Shelly were long haul over-the-roaders: sleek Peterbilts, powerful Kenworths, and massive cabover White Freightliners. Deke and Shelly looked at each one, wishing they were wheeling it down the highway.

Tired of traveling in a straight line, Shelly directed Deke to drive around O'Neill but they found nothing interesting to stop for. West of town the highway started curving but the landscape didn't change. Shelly wanted prairie, sagebrush and open range but all they saw were cornfields, hay, and pasture. Where she'd hoped the sky would be broken by buttes and mesas, there were silos and grain elevators. Instead of wild, hellbent cowtowns with rowdy saloons and gambling halls were only farming hamlets with church steeples and water towers watching over the flat fields like bigheaded sentinels. As in Indiana and Illinois this land had been tamed and subdued, every last acre of it. At the edge of each town was a farm equipment dealer. Shelly had never paid much attention before, but now she saw them as arms dealers in the war against nature.

The only untamed element was the sky and even it was endlessly uniform. All morning, the rumpled cloud layer remained unbroken, an upside down ocean that stretched to a meeting point with the horizon and when you got there, started all over again. Beneath that sky, the wind came hard out of the west. It gave the day a heavy, leaden feeling that sucked away one's energy. When the road ran unbending after Stuart, Deke opened his mouth in a wide yawn and shook his head to get the blood moving.

"You doin' alright?" Shelly asked him.

"I'm gittin' bored. This country ain't much ta look at."

Shelly glanced over at the speedometer. "We're lucky, Deke, we git ta go through here at over 80 miles an hour. Jes think how it'd be travelin' like the pioneers did in an ox drawn covered wagon."

"Shitfire," Deke said, "that woulda been too slow fer me."

"I've read that there's places where you can still see the ruts their wheels made," Shelly said. "I can picture 'em, jes crawlin' along, slow, but determined, out ta make new lives for themselves, jes like you an' me."

"Reckon this place woulda been way diff'runt back then," Deke said.

"I wish I could a' seen it like the pioneers did, or better yet, the Indians," Shelly said, looking out the side window. "All wild prairie as far as you could see an' giant herds a' buffalo wanderin' through it."

"I woulda' liked ta live back then," Deke said, "in the Wild West."

"Me too, in a way," Shelly said, "but most women in the old West didn't have much in the way a' choices. If ya weren't married you were either a school marm or a whore. None a' that sounds too good ta me. I might a' been like Calamity Jane, wild an' free, jes goin' from place ta place an' bein' part of it."

"I'd a' been a gunslingin' outlaw or an In'jun fighter," Deke said, "like Jesse James or Wild Bill Hickock."

"How come ya want ta fight Indians, Deke? They ain't done nothin' bad ta you that I know of."

"That's jest what cowboys did back then."

"I thought cowboys herded cows, " Shelly said. "An' ain't you on the outs with the law enough already?"

Now a thousand miles and several states away, Deke felt safe enough to boast. "I don't mind bein' a wanted man. The law don't scare me one bit."

Shelly felt like reminding Deke of how he had almost soiled his pants when the police car was behind them in Cincinnati, something she was pretty sure neither Jesse James nor Wild Bill Hickock would've done.

At Bassett, where Route 183 intersected from the south, they stopped at an ancient gas station with a rundown convenience store.

"Reckon we could use some gas," Deke said, "an' I wouldn't mind grabbin' some baloney an' crackers if they got any."

"What about all those you bought in Kentucky?" Shelly asked.

"I finished them off yesterday."

A tall, lanky man wearing a weathered Stetson appeared at the driver's side window. "Fill 'er up?"

"With reg'lar," Deke told him, and when the guy asked, "Want me ta check the oil?" Deke said, "Sure."

As Shelly headed for the ladies room the man lifted the Ford's hood and hollered back to Deke, "Needs a quart."

"Okay," Deke told him.

"Better take an extra quart with ya. There aren't any gas stations for awhile."

"Alright," Deke said. "Ya got any baloney an' crackers inside?"

"The best in a hundred miles."

The attendant chatted up Deke like they were old buddies and when Shelly got back Deke said, "I'm goin' inside an' git some things. Morgan here's got somethin' he wants ta show me."

Shelly stood beside the truck, her jacket collar turned up against the blistering wind. Through the building's grimy windows she watched Deke and the attendant passing an object back and forth. Deke finally came out, dropped a quart of oil into the bed, and got into the cab holding a paper bag in one hand and a red calico bundle in the other. He sat the bundle on the seat then pulled a slice of baloney and three crackers from the bag and stuffed them into his mouth.

"Whatcha got there?" Shelly asked, nodding toward the red calico.

"Somethin' for Montana," Deke said smiling, and unrolled the bundle. He held up a cowboy style pistol in a holster and gunbelt. "When Morgan found out we were goin' ta Montana he told me this'd be jest the ticket fer a guy like me. Morgan said he could tell right away that I was somebody who could handle himself in a fix, an' that things could git purty rough out here sometimes."

"Is it loaded?" Shelly asked.

"Don't reckon so or Morgan woulda told me," Deke said, twirling the gun on his index finger.

"It looks kinda beat up, Deke. How much didja give for it?" Shelly asked.

"One-twenty-five."

"Whew. That sounds mighty steep."

"Well, it ain't. Morgan was askin' one-fifty, but when he saw my John Wayne belt buckle he dropped 'er ta one an' a quarter. 'From one cowboy to another', he said. Now that's my kind a' people. He even threw in a box of fifty shells fer practice, but I don't need any practice."

"It ain't very big," Shelly said, and Deke frowned as if Shelly was talking about his pecker.

"It's a Ruger Bearcat," Deke explained. "It's only a .22, but in the hands a' somebody who knows how ta use it – like me – it'll git the job done." Deke stuck the revolver into the front of his pants, then drew and cocked it as fast as he could.

"An' jes what job are you fixin' ta do with it, Deke?"

Deke stopped practicing his fast draw and tipped his hat brim up with the gun barrel. "Whatever job needs doin', little lady."

"The job that needs doin' right now is for you ta put that gun away and start drivin', 'cause yor makin' me nervous playin' with it like that. Anyway, how come yor buyin' more guns? Your money for this trip came from sellin' guns."

"My money's my own," Deke said testily. "And when we git ta Troy and I start drivin' log truck, I'll be pullin' down plenty." He cocked the pistol and pointed it out the window. "An' quit bein' so nervous. I been around guns all my life – an' anyway, it ain't loaded, see."

Deke flipped the side gate open and turned the revolver around for Shelly to look at. When her eyes went wide and her mouth fell open, Deke spun the revolver around and saw the glint of cartridges in the cylinder. The barrel now pointed directly at Shelly's face. "Damn you, Deke McConahay!" she screamed and ducked away. "You been playin' with a loaded gun all this time and pointed it right at my face."

Deke quickly put the gun back in the holster as Shelly berated him. "You are such an id'jit sometimes! You coulda shot me jes now or shot yor'self in the privates with your stupid fast draw. Maybe that woulda been a good lesson to ya."

"I'm sorry Shelly. I didn't know it was loaded."

"Well, ya coulda looked," Shelly told him. "You unload it right now."

"No way. An unloaded gun's about as good as a rubber with a hole in it."

"What's got a hole in it is your head, Deke. An' ya 'bout put one in mine. I'm tellin' ya, if you don't unload that gun, I'll toss it out the winda the first chance I git."

"Alright then, if it makes ya feel better," Deke finally said, as he took the gun from the holster and dropped the shells out of the cylinder. "But we're in wild country now and we'd be a lot safer if this gun was loaded."

"Wild? There ain't nothin' aroun' here but a bunch a' farmers."

"Well, sometimes these sodbusters git purty riled up. Didn't ya ever see *Shane*?"

"Oh, for the love a' … Let's jes git outa here, Deke."

Deke stayed quiet for the next few miles, dipping his hand in the paper bag beside him and shoving the contents into his mouth. As they approached the town of Ainsworth Shelly asked, "How can you eat so much a' that stuff?"

"Guess I jest like baloney an' crackers. But this here ain't all that good."

Shelly peered into the bag then pulled out a slice of baloney. "This baloney's green an' got slime all over it, Deke," she said, wrinkling up her nose.

"Reckon I shouldn't eat too much more of it, then," Deke said.

"Ya shouldn't be eatin' any of it."

Coming out of Ainsworth Deke went to reach into the paper bag again, but Shelly pulled it away from him. "Deke, that baloney's gonna make ya sick."

"I don't care. I'm hungry."

Shelly pulled some stale crackers out of the bag and handed them to Deke. "Here, eat these," she said and shoved the bag of baloney under the seat.

As Deke munched the outdated saltines, Shelly studied her atlas to see what was up ahead. What the map did not show was that they were edging up on a historical, almost fabled, dividing line, a demarcation between the humid continental part of the United States and the semi-arid side, a division that was not only climatic, but cultural as well. They were entering the rain shadow of the Rocky Mountains, where the Great Plains began; where the land was harsh and dry, life hard and uncertain, and where often in the past, neither loans nor insurance could be obtained by those living beyond this point. No guidepost or marker informed Deke or Shelly that they had crossed the boundary, but a few miles past Ainsworth they slipped over the 100th meridian. The next town down the road let them know that they were now officially in the West.

"Didja see that, Deke?" Shelly said, as they blew by a cluster of buildings set back off the highway.

"What?"

"That little town we jes went by. It looked like somethin' right outa the old West. I wanta go back an' take a look at it."

"Alright," Deke said and did a U-turn. "Maybe we can get somethin' ta eat there."

They turned onto the unpaved Main Street, which, except for several rutted tracks that ended in clumps of brush, interspersed with derelict vehicles and rundown houses, was the town's only street. Wooden boardwalks marched in front of a half score of square-fronted businesses, or former businesses, for the difference was not easy to tell. Prominent among the buildings was the large brick general store, which dominated the west side of the street. High over the entrance, faded black letters painted onto the brick stated, 'JOHNSTOWN MERCANTILE'.

"This must be Johnstown," Deke said.

"I won't argue," Shelly told him.

Deke parked across the street from the general store, in front of a row of small establishments, each one fronted by a hitching rail. He and Shelly got out and walked to the middle of the dirt street, sizing up the town. An unceasing wind whistled around the old buildings and blew through the tall weeds at their edges. From out of nowhere a dust devil sprang up, danced and whirled in the middle of Main Street and then skipped out of town as quickly and mysteriously as it had appeared. Deke and Shelly could barely believe what they were seeing: an 1880's ghost town, except that some of the ghosts might still be alive.

"We're either finally in the West, Deke, or the *Twilight Zone*," Shelly said.

North of the general store was a small post office and beside it a barbershop, which was only open two days a week. Twenty paces away an antique store languished and past that several other weathered structures sat in various states of disrepair. On the side of the street that Deke's pickup faced, a small, but sturdy looking bank, built of brick, anchored the south end. Attached to its flank was the Ace in the Hole Saloon and snug against it sat the Wild Rose Café. A little further on a neat and freshly painted building displayed a sign that said, 'Veterinary Clinic'. Beyond this were two more ramshackle constructions with their windows boarded over and at the edge of town a repair shop of some sort nestled amongst several acres of scrap equipment and machinery. The street then narrowed into a gravel track that continued north and endless into the distant prairie, possibly to the far side of the galaxy. The only solid evidence that humans inhabited the town were the four vehicles parked on the street: two beater pickups, a 1950's Desoto, and a John Deere 5020 tractor.

"Jumpin' Jesus," Shelly said, "this town looks like the real thing, not some fakey tourist trap."

"I wonder where the marshall's office is," Deke said.

"I don't think they got one, Deke."

"That bank looks like it'd be purty easy ta rob," Deke speculated.

"Are you outa your mind?"

"Oh, I ain't gonna do it, Shelly, I jest meant if some outlaw come through here an' wanted to."

They heard a door open and turned to look. A portly older man, wearing a high-brimmed Stetson and cowboy boots, sauntered across the boardwalk from the café and into the Ace in the Hole. Other than his boots clanking on the wooden planks, he made no sound nor turned his head to acknowledge them. Shelly watched the saloon door close behind him and wondered if he was real, or some sort of animated decoy that made periodic trips between the café and the bar to lure unwary travelers inside where they would never be heard from again.

Deke had no such reservations. "Let's eat," he said, nodding toward the Wild Rose Café. Shelly agreed and took a couple of steps toward the café, but Deke went over to his pickup, pulled off his jacket and tossed it inside, then started to open the hood.

"You ain't gonna disconnect the battery are ya?" Shelly said. "We can see the truck from inside."

"Jest figger'd I oughta secure it," Deke answered.

"We're out west now," Shelly said, as she walked to the truck bed and dug out a length of heavy rope. She eased Deke aside and closed the hood, looped the rope around the front bumper a couple of times, tied if off and did the same at the thick hitching post. "There, Old Paint is secured."

Thirty-five minutes later Deke and Shelly stepped out of the Wild Rose and onto the creaking boardwalk, full of the Daily Special: beans, bacon, and cornbread. Two saddled horses stood tied to the hitching post in front of the Ace in the Hole Saloon.

"Look at that," Deke said, but Shelly was already walking toward them.

She ducked under the rail and stood between the brown quarter-horse mare and the paint gelding, rubbing their muzzles, scratching them behind the ears, and talking to them like old friends. "I miss ridin'," she said to nobody in particular.

"Let's go in an' have us a drink," Deke said. "I bet there's a coupla cowboys inside."

"Or cowgirls," Shelly answered. "Alright, Deke, I reckon we could have us jes one ta celebrate bein' in the West."

"Lemme grab my jacket outa the truck," Deke said, "this wind's got me feelin' chilled."

Deke hopped down from the boardwalk and opened the driver's door as Shelly continued stroking and talking to the horses. She couldn't see what Deke was doing as the mare was standing between her and the pickup, but he was sure taking his sweet time just to put a coat on. Finally she heard the truck door slam and Deke climbed onto the wooden sidewalk and headed for the saloon door, his straw cowboy hat tipped back on his head and more strut than usual in his gait.

"I'm ready ta have a drink in a *real* cowboy saloon," he said.

Shelly gave both horses a pat, then jumped onto the boardwalk and followed Deke into the Ace in the Hole, unaware that he had taken the Ruger .22 from its holster, reloaded it and tucked it into the leather belt under his jacket.

Chapter 26

Everyone in the bar stopped talking and turned to look at Deke and Shelly, who stood gawking in the doorway. Dust covered horse tack, rusty tools, guns, mounted animal heads, and a barrage of knick-knacks clung to the walls and each item had a price tag. Half a dozen battered tables with ancient wooden chairs sat scattered throughout the small saloon. A massive wood stove commanded one side of the room. The grime covered front windows and 40-watt bulb above the back bar provided only enough light to let the bartender tell whiskey from gin and a fin from a sawbuck. Most of the customers had been looking at each other for so long they didn't need more wattage to tell who was who, and if anybody complained, Hazel, the proprietor, told them, "You shit-kickers don't spend enough money in here for me to buy more lights."

At one end of the bar sat a small, dark woman who looked like she hadn't moved from her stool in thirty years. She tugged hard at a menthol cigarette and had the rest of the pack lying beside her gin and tonic. The heavy-set cowboy who'd walk out of the café had placed himself beside her. Two stools away from them stood the two riders, leaning easy against the bar and watching Deke and Shelly with be-mused smiles.

Lean but sturdy, both men looked to be cowboys but they were as different as salsa and apple pie. The short one, barely out of his teens, wore a brown Stetson, a button down shirt, expensive cowboy boots with spurs, and snug, custom made trousers and had the tension of a coiled spring. His companion, older and more relaxed, was outfitted in Car-rhartt brown and a baseball cap, but his look and manner said, 'cowboy'.

"Well, have a seat," the bartender said. "It's not like there's standing room only in here." Deke started for the far end of the bar but she brought him up short. "C'mon down here and sit. I'm not walking halfway to Wyoming just ta sell two drinks. Nobody down here's gonna bite ya, and if they do," she poked her finger at the fellow wearing the Carrhartts, "Clem's the vet and he'll sew ya up."

"I do it sometimes," Clem said, "but I charge more for people than cattle and horses. They scream louder."

Shelly walked over to the empty stools and Deke followed. To his consternation, Shelly sat down beside the young cowboy and Deke squeezed in between her and the old fat man. When they were situated the vet leaned in front of his young partner and stuck out a hand to Shelly. "Guess you already know that I'm Clem," he said.

"I'm Shelly," she said, and Clem reached out his hand to Deke.

"I'm Deke, Deke McConahay," Deke told him, and quickly added, just so both cowboys knew, "an' Shelly's my girlfriend."

As Deke and Clem were shaking hands the other cowboy said, "If you knew where that hand had just been you might not be so eager to shake it."

Clem gave his companion a sideways look. "I was wearin' my long plastic glove and washed up afterwards."

As the young cowboy showed no inclination to introduce himself Clem did it for him. "This is Billy," he said, "but unless you're lookin' for trouble, don't call him 'the kid'. His family owns that big ranch just east of here. I just finished playin' 'bull' and Billy suggested we ride in for a drink. He's tryin' to sell me that dun mare out there and thinks if he gets me liquored up I'll pay the ridiculous price he's askin'."

Shelly extended her hand to Billy, who held it longer than Deke thought proper.

"I just wanted Clem to see what a good riding horse she is," Billy said, "and that even a piss-poor rider like him can handle her." Billy let go of Shelly's hand, but didn't extend it to Deke.

"Some of us don't get as much riding time in as others, we have to work for a living," Clem said.

"Well if ranchin's so easy, how come you gave it up to become a vet?"

"Because I felt guilty about takin' all that money for doing so little," Clem said.

"There's more bullshit in here than in our feedlot," Billy said, and everybody in the bar laughed.

It was just everyday rancher talk, but it sounded like the West and rang sweet in Shelly's ears. The bartender, however, heard it everyday. She pointed to the woman and the man sitting beside Deke. "Haddie here is my sister and this is Ralph. I'm Hazel, the owner, the bartender, and the law. Now that we got that out of the way, what can I get for you ladies?"

Deke blanched, wondering if that was just a western expression or if Hazel was making fun of his long hair. He ordered a Bud, then remembered he was in the West and changed it to a Coors. Shelly asked for a Falstaff.

"He don't come in here," Hazel said.

Down the bar Clem piped up. "He wouldn't. He died in *Henry V*."

Hazel looked at him. "It's too early for you to start spoutin' that Shakespeare shit, Clem." She turned back to Shelly. "Honey, all I have is plain beer and booze. If you want wine there's half a bottle of Boone's Farm somewhere in the cooler."

Shelly settled on a Coors.

"How come it's so dark in here?" Deke asked Hazel.

"So I can get the drop on anybody who comes through the door."

Deke laughed. "That's a good one," he said.

"You think she's shittin' you, don't ya?" Billy said, irritated at Deke's laughter. "This bar's been here since 1882 and there's been more than one shooting in here."

"This used to be a famous — and notorious — bar," Clem said, and pointed to an autographed picture of Buffalo Bill on the wall. "William F. Cody himself stopped by for a drink in 1894."

"That's right," Hazel said, "and now I maintain order." She reached under the bar and hauled out a .45 caliber Colt Peacemaker. Her small hand held the big pistol with an authority that left no doubt she'd put many rounds through the barrel. Deke's eyes got white and round and his laugh died in his throat. The regulars paid little attention, they'd seen Hazel jerk that gun out before under less friendly circumstances.

"So what do you two Ohio sodbusters think of the West so far?" Billy asked after Hazel put the hogleg back under the bar.

"How'd ya know we was from Ohio?" Deke said.

"Could be from the way you dress," Billy said, rudely looking Deke up and down. "Or … it could be from the way you walk, kinda light on your heels."

"Or," Clem said, "it could be from the license plates on your truck."

"Oh, sure," Deke said, fidgeting with his beer.

From the other side of Deke, Ralph asked, "Where are you two headed?"

"Montana," Shelly answered.

"I'm goin' there ta drive a loggin' truck," Deke said, making sure everyone in the bar heard him.

Irked that Deke hadn't mentioned her, Shelly said, "I'm gonna be drivin' a log truck, too,"

"A flatlander like you better be careful on those Montana mountain roads," Billy told Deke.

"I mighta been livin' in Ohio fer a spell," Deke said, looking past Shelly to Billy, "but I'm from Tennessee, an' we got mountains there too."

Billy sipped at his whiskey. "What you had in Tennessee was hills. What they've got in Montana is mountains. Big difference, bucko."

Deke's face went red and he sucked in his breath.

Shelly jumped into the fray. "Speakin' a' bein' flatlanders, I don't see no Alps aroun' here."

"We used to have mountains," Clem said. "Some pretty big ones."

"Really. What happened to 'em?" Deke asked.

"Back when I was a kid," Clem said, "Billy woulda been too young, but I'm sure Hazel, Ralph, and Haddie remember it, a big east wind come along in March and blew 'em all over into Wyoming."

"Oh yeah, I remember it," Haddie said, finishing off her drink and lighting up another smoke.

"None of us knew there was so much sky till that happened," Ralph said.

Deke and Shelly both laughed and as Deke was tipping his beer back, a sign above the bar caught his eye: JOIN OUR PISTOL CLUB.

"How do ya join the pistol club?" Deke asked Hazel, but Billy answered for her. "You drink till twelve, then piss till two," he said to Deke, then sniggered.

"I can't believe you fell for that one," Ralph told Deke, laughing. "It's older than this bar."

Deke flushed, then turned crimson when Billy asked Shelly, "Do you ride?"

"I can ride," Shelly said. "I used ta have my own horse."

"You want to take a turn on the mare?" Billy asked.

Deke cut in. "We gotta be goin', Shelly. The day's gittin on."

"No it ain't, Deke. It's not even two o'clock an' we ain't in no hurry a'tall. Remember how I said I wanted to have fun on the way ta Montana? Well, this is what I was talkin' about."

Taking that as a 'yes', Billy said to Clem, "You okay hanging out here until we get back?"

"I've got plenty to do at my office," Clem said. "You can come and get me when you're done and we'll ride back to your ranch."

Billy looked at Shelly and nodded towards the door. Shelly got up but Billy beat her there. "After you, Shelly," he said smoothly, holding the door open for her.

Hearing Billy say Shelly's name made Deke wince and he emptied his beer and followed them out with Clem behind him. After untying both horses Billy put his hands on Shelly's waist to help her into the saddle but Shelly said, "I can get on by myself."

When she was mounted Billy went to adjust her stirrups and took ahold of Shelly's calf. "Me an' Clem are about the same height," she told Billy, rising in the saddle, "they're okay."

"All right then," Billy said, "let's ride."

He walked around to the paint, put both hands on the saddle horn, and in one graceful leap, rolled into the saddle without first putting a foot into the stirrup. Billy looked down at Deke, who stood fuming with his hands in his pockets. "See ya later, *dude*," he said.

Billy reined the gelding around, walked him about ten steps and spurred him to a trot. Shelly did the same on the dun, posting a few steps behind Billy, amazed at the mare's smooth gait. They rode north up Main Street and by time they'd reached the scrap piles of the repair shop they were moving at a lope. Just before they turned onto a trail and disappeared from sight, a gust of wind blew in, carrying Shelly's happy laugh back with it. Deke stood watching, redfaced and silent, his insides broiling.

"Don't worry," Clem said, "your girlfriend just wanted to ride a horse again."

Deke turned and looked at him but didn't say anything.

"It'll be alright," Clem added, and stuck out his hand. "Nice to meet you, Deke. I'm going to walk up here to my office and catch up on a little business before they get back. Good luck to you and Shelly in Montana."

Deke shook Clem's hand but his mood was as low and dark as the sky above the Mercantile across the street. He went back into the bar and clanked his empty bottle down. "Gimme another one," he said and when Hazel sat the Coors in front of him, Deke looked at it for a second. "And a shot a' whiskey, too." Hazel lifted the bar whiskey from the well and started to take a shot glass off the shelf. "Make it a double," Deke said, and took a twenty from his wallet and laid it on the bar.

Everyone remained quiet, watching Deke as he lit up a Camel and sullenly drank his whiskey. After a spell Ralph said to Haddie, "What're you doing later?"

Hazel raised her eyebrows.

"What have you got in mind?" Haddie asked.

"Thought maybe you'd like to come down to my place for dinner?"

Hazel gave Ralph the old stink-eye, but kept quiet.

"Just picked up some prime Angus," Ralph said with a wink. "Nothing but the best for a lady like yourself."

Hazel stopped glowering at Ralph and turned to her sister. "Have you heard from your boy lately?"

Now it was Ralph's turn to give Hazel the evil eye.

"He called about a month ago," Haddie said, and exhaled an enormous blue cloud.

"Where is Johnny now?" Ralph asked.

"What d'you care, anyway?" Hazel answered for her sister.

"Well, I do," Ralph said indignantly.

"Like hell," Hazel told him.

"He's in California, Ralph," Haddie answered. "I've got his address if you want to write him."

"I don't know what I'd write to him about," Ralph said.

Hazel sneered at Ralph. "You could tell him you're happy he's outa jail."

"Well, I'm glad to hear it," Ralph said. "Does Billy know?"

"He knows," Haddie said. "Billy told me he wrote Johnny a letter telling him to come back; said they'd put him to work on the ranch."

From the other side of Ralph came a surely mumble. "Goddam Billy."

Everyone turned to look at Deke. He edged his empty whiskey glass toward Hazel and jabbed at it with his index finger, indicating she should fill it up again. Hazel reached for the whiskey bottle and poured another double, taking the money from Deke's change on the bar. Deke pulled the glass toward him and picked it up. "Goddam Billy," he said again. "They oughta be back by now."

"It's only been a few minutes," Haddie said. "Quit worryin'."

Deke lifted his glass, as if making a toast. "Billy can jack my rabbit," he said, and drank the double whiskey in one swig.

"Huh?" Haddie said and Hazel said, "What?"

"That was most of the problem right there," Ralph said.

"It was?" Haddie asked, thinking Ralph was referring to Billy jacking Deke's rabbit.

"It sure was," Ralph answered her.

Haddie and Hazel looked at each other, wondering if something was going on that they didn't know about, which was unlikely in Johnstown.

"Johnny palling around with Billy," Ralph continued, "and getting into trouble with him. And Johnny not having a rich pappy to jump him out of it like Billy does."

"That was *most* of the problem right there," Hazel said, looking straight at Ralph. "Johnny didn't have any pappy, leastwise one that would claim him – or help him out with *anything*."

Ralph stood up from the bar, his hand shaking under Hazel's glare. "I gotta take a whiz," he said.

After Ralph had walked away, Hazel whispered to her sister, "Don't you let that man talk you into goin' home with him. He's never done right by you … or Johnny."

"I'm not *going home* with him. He just asked me to dinner, that's all."

"It doesn't matter what a man asks you for at first," Hazel said, "once he's got you alone he'll be askin' for something else."

"What'd you say Billy's gonna be askin' Shelly for?" Deke asked Hazel.

"We weren't talkin' about Billy," Hazel said, irritated.

"Who *were* you talkin' about?" Ralph said, coming back to the bar and taking his stool.

"They was talkin' about Billy," Deke told him, "an' what that sum'bitch is gonna' ast' Shelly ta do once he's got 'er out there alone."

"No we weren't," Haddie said, exhaling another cloud.

Deke drained his bottle of Coors then motioned for another beer and a whiskey. Hazel was setting the Coors down when Deke got up, walked over to the big bell hanging above the bar and gave the rope a tug. "What's this for?" he said, as the clanging echoed throughout the bar.

"It means you're buying a round for the house," Hazel said as she poured Deke another double then set Ralph and Haddie up and helped herself to Deke's diminishing pile of money. Ralph and Haddie tipped their fresh drinks in thanks to Deke.

"Let me tell you about Billy," Ralph said to Deke, after he had taken a sip from his whiskey ditch.

"What about that worthless, goddam asshole Billy?" Deke asked.

"Billy's a kid," Haddie said, sticking up for her son's friend. "He's not really bad."

"That's jest what I thought!" Deke said, tossing off his double and bringing his fist down hard on the bar. "He thinks he's Billy the Kid an' that he's really bad."

"That's not what I said," Haddie tried to explain.

"You're right," Ralph said.

"'Course I am," Deke told him.

"No, I meant Haddie," Ralph said.

"How kin Haddie be Billy the Kid? It's 'at goddam Billy who thinks he's Billy the Kid." Deke pointed at Haddie. "She jest said so."

"I think you're confused," Hazel said to Deke.

"I ain't confused 'bout one thing," Deke told her. "That sum'bitch who calls hi'self Billy the Kid's been out 'ere with mah girlfrien' fer over an hour now." He pointed to his empty glass. "Gimme another."

"It hasn't been near that long," Hazel said, as she poured the whiskey. "They'll be back soon."

Picking up his shot glass Deke said, "An' when they git back, that goddam Billy the Kid's gonna fine' out he ain't t'only man in 'is bar wann'ed by the law."

Everybody looked at Deke and Ralph said, "Huh?"

"Thas' right," Deke said. "Thas' the real reason me'n Shelly ha' ta leave Ohio. Goddam law's af'er me. They done chased us through six states s'far an' ain't caugh' me yet. Ain' goin' to, neither."

Deke poured the whiskey down in one gulp and took a slug of beer. "Seh' me up agin', barkeep," he said. "Seh' us *all* up agin'. When Deke McConahay drinks, ever'body drinks." Deke took another twenty from his wallet then walked over to the bell and swatted it with his hand.

Hazel looked at Deke's money, shrugged, and did her duty.

"What are you wanted for?" Haddie asked.

"Cuz I'm a' outlaw." Deke said, "an a fas' draw expert wih' a gun."

Hazel put Deke's change on the bar and was about to ask him what he had done to become an outlaw, when the sound of galloping hooves interrupted the conversation. As the riders tied up the horses, their laughter could be heard inside the bar. The door swung open as Billy held it for Shelly, placing his hand on her back as she came through. "Me an' the mare almost beat you on that last run, Billy," Shelly said.

"Aw, I was being polite and takin' it easy, Shelly," he said, "but you're a good rider. C'mon, I'll buy you a drink."

Billy and Shelly were halfway to the bar before they noticed Deke. At the sound of the door opening, he dramatically tossed down his whiskey, loudly smacked the glass against the bar, then turned around to face them. He stood spread-legged, arms down by his sides, gunfighter style, swaying slightly, but poised and ready. Shelly and Billy stopped and looked at him. "Hi, Deke," Shelly said, "What's goin' on?"

Deke looked at her and then turned his scowl on Billy. "D'ya know who he is?"

"Yeah, Deke, he's Billy Stanton," Shelly said.

"No 'e ain'. He's Billy the Kid."

Billy turned rose red, every muscle coiling tight.

"He is not," Shelly corrected him.

"Well, 'e thinks 'e is," Deke said, "an' tha's good 'nuff fer me."

"No he don't," Shelly said testily.

"She seh' 'e does," Deke said, pointing at Haddie.

Billy and Ralph both looked at Haddie then Ralph turned to Billy. "When did you start callin' yourself Billy the Kid?" he said at the same time Haddie said, "No I didn't," but nobody paid any attention to her.

Billy glared at Ralph a second and then started walking toward Deke, menace in every step. "I'm gonna take care of this right now, you damn long-haired freak."

"If yer Billy the Kid, then draw!" Deke shouted at him.

"Draw???" Billy said, "I'm not wearin' - "

As soon as Billy said, "draw," Deke went for his gun, but his thumb slipped off the hammer.

BANG!

The bullet whizzed between Billy's legs, barely missing his crotch. Billy jumped higher than when he'd mounted his horse.

"DEKE!" Shelly screamed and everyone else – except Hazel – ducked and covered their heads.

Deke cocked the pistol but before he could get off a second shot, he felt something hard poking him in the back of the head. Deke turned to look and Hazel put the barrel of her .45 right between his eyes and cocked the hammer.

"Drop it," she said.

"Shitfire! Don' shoot me!" Deke cried and dropped his pistol — right on its hammer.

BANG!

The bullet caught Billy's right spur, tore off the rowel and ricocheted into the wood stove. With a loud *PING* it ricocheted again and punctured the picture of Buffalo Bill, shattering the glass and leaving him gutshot and face down on the barroom floor.

Billy jumped even higher than before and yelled, "JESUS H. CHRIST!"

"Don' shoo' me," Deke wailed, "please don' shoo' me! I didn' mean fer it ta go off."

Hazel eased the hammer down on the big Colt, but Deke had little time to enjoy his reprieve. With the dexterity of Wyatt Earp, Hazel executed a 'border roll' and rapped Deke square on top of his cowboy hat with the pistol butt.

Deke went down like a sackfull of wet horseshit.

"OWWWWWWW!" he screamed and crumpled over, his hat falling to the floor.

"How come ya done that?" Shelly hollered at Hazel.

" 'Cause I'm the one holdin' the gun to do it with," she said.

"OHHHHHHH, God it hurts!" Deke wailed, cradling his head in both hands. "Why'd ya hih' me so hard?"

Already a welt was rising up from under his hair.

"OWWWWWWWWW!" he howled again, doubled up in pain.

"Oh, quit your bawlin'," Hazel said, leaning over the bar and looking down at Deke. "You sound like a damn new born calf that can't find its mama. You're not the first man I've buffaloed in this bar and you damn sure won't be the last. Just be glad I didn't shoot ya."

"And that little bump on the head's nothin' compared to what you're about to get from me," Billy growled, stepping toward Deke.

"OHHHHHHH NO! I ken't take no more!" Deke pleaded.

"No you don't, Billy Stanton," Hazel said. "I'm not having you beat on a man who's already down."

"I'll stand him up first," Billy said, taking another step.

"You stay where you are," Hazel said to him, rolling the Peacemaker back to shooting position. "This is my bar and I'm the only one dispensin' justice in it."

"Then I'll wait till they go outside," Billy said, "but he's gettin' a cowboy ass-whippin before he leaves Johnstown."

Shelly thought about stepping over and cold-cocking Billy, but wasn't sure where Hazel would weigh in on that. Plus, Billy was plenty tough and punching him might just make him madder.

Hazel guessed her thoughts. "You'd better load your man up and leave."

Shelly grabbed Deke under the shoulders to stand him up, but Deke's legs were like noodles. She finally got him upright and held him against the bar while she bent down and picked up his dented cowboy hat. She set the hat crookedly on Deke's head then grabbed his change off the bar, leaving two dollars for a tip.

"Thanks," Hazel told her.

Holding Deke upright, Shelly started walking him toward the door, one painful step at the time, Deke exhaling "Ohhh" at each one. When they were halfway across the floor Billy started following them like a tracking hound.

"You get back here right now," Hazel said to him.

"No I won't," Billy told her. "You had your fun with him but he's got some coming from me."

Hazel pointed the gun barrel towards Billy's feet. "You take one more step Billy Stanton and I'll shoot your other spur off." She cocked the revolver.

Fire flared in Billy's eyes. "You'd do that to me?" he said, indignant that the woman who used to babysit him would even consider such a thing. "You might miss and shoot me in the ankle."

"That could happen," Hazel said, "but I'm the law in here, and the *only* law. You weren't totally innocent in this matter yourself and justice has been served." She motioned with the gun barrel for Billy to move away from Deke and after a few seconds he backed off, muttering murder under his breath.

Shelly had a time of it, trying to keep Deke on his feet and get him out the front door, all the while watching out for Billy. She held Deke against the frame with one hand and turned the door handle with the other.

Ralph waved goodbye. Haddie said, "You folks have a nice trip to Montana. If you get back this way, stop in again."

"Thanks, we will," Shelly called back.

Shelly got Deke into the passenger seat and dug the keys out of his front pocket. After stroking the dun mare's neck, she walked around behind the truck and got in the driver's seat. She started the engine, pulled the shifter into reverse and hit the gas. The Ford jumped back, lurched to a sudden halt, and jumped back again, making a loud rending noise followed by clanging. The bumper, now bent to a V, lay in front of the pickup, still hitched to the rail.

"Mah bumber!" Deke yelled.

Shelly started to retrieve it, but Billy was now at the open door, glaring at them. She hit the gas, spun backward onto Main Street and hightailed it to the highway, dusting onto the asphalt without stopping for the sign. As Shelly racked through the gears, Deke looked back at Johnstown disappearing behind them. "Mah bumber!" he wailed.

––––––––––

Hazel stowed her pistol under the bar when she heard the Ford start up. The clatter of Deke's bumper got everyone's attention and Billy ran to the front door. He walked back in a minute later, shaking his head. "That dumbass tied his bumper to the hitching post and now it's layin' in the street."

"I wonder why he did that?" Ralph said, but nobody answered.

Hazel walked around the bar and picked up Deke's pistol. She unloaded it then tied a $50 price tag to the trigger guard and hung it on the nail where Buffalo Bill's picture had been.

Billy was still brimming with unreleased rage. "If I ever see that son of a bitch again, his ass won't be worth rooster shit when I'm done with him."

"You go ahead and crow, Billy," Hazel told him, "but if that first shot had been a few inches higher, your own days of bein' a rooster would've been over."

The door opened and Clem walked in. "I heard the horses coming down the street and figured you were back," he said to Billy, then turned to Hazel. "Did you know there's a bentup bumper out there tied to the rail?"

"We know," Hazel said. "There's a story to it if you want to hear it."

"Don't have time," Clem said. "I've got to get movin'. I have to make three more calls today." He looked at Billy. "Can we get back to your ranch so I can get my truck?"

Billy took a couple of breaths. "Yeah, I guess the horses are rested enough," he said. "Let's go."

After they left, Haddie said to Ralph, "So, you say you've got some good steaks at the house?"

"Two of the finest T-bones you ever sank your teeth into," Ralph told her, as Hazel turned away in disgust.

Chapter 27

Still moaning, Deke leaned his head against the side window. Tears ran down his cheeks. The bump on his head had grown to the size of an egg and each time he dabbed at it with his handkerchief he winced and went, "OHH!"

Shelly was mad at him but also worried. "Are you alright, Deke?"

"Noh, I ain' a'right, wha'ya think?" Deke said between sobs. "She hih' me real har' with tha' big gun. Har' enou' ta kill any normal man."

"'It didn't look like she hit ya all that hard, Deke, but I will agree that yor not a normal man."

"She dih' hih' me rea' har'," Deke protested. "Wha' dah you know abou' how har' she hih' me?" He glared at Shelly then went back to moaning.

"How come you done that back there, Deke? You almost shot Billy."

"Fuh' Billy. Hih' git over it."

"Of all the ig'nernt things I've seen you do, that's gotta be the dumbest, an' all for no reason."

"Ih' weren' fer noh' reason," Deke drunkenly slurred. "You roh' off wih' tha' cowboy an I din' know whe' you was comin' back."

"Why that's jes silly, Deke. We went for a short ride, that's all. There weren't no more to it than that."

"Seem' li' more to it ta me. Jes' the way 'e done it, an' you goin' righ' along wih' 'im." Deke dabbed at his lump and cringed. "At leas' I may' 'im dance. Joo' see the way I may' 'at sum'bitch dance? I fix'd 'at goddam Billy's wagon for 'im."

"Your own wagon ain't doin' too good, Deke," Shelly said.

"Oh be quieh'. I don' wanna hear abou' my wagon."

For a moment Shelly was silent, then said, "I understand people gittin a little jealous now an' then, and Billy was cocky, even rude, but what you did was real scary. Were you really tryin' ta shoot him, Deke?"

Deke raised his head from the window. "When 'e seh', 'Draw' I figger'd 'e was goin' fer 'is gun, so I drew mine too."

"Billy didn't have any gun on. You could see that."

"How'd I know? Yah coul'n' see mine, neither."

Deke wiped the tears from his face and leaned against the window again. "I never eve' got mah' gun back," he said. "I beh' tha' goddam Billy took it." He looked at Shelly. "How come you din' pick it up on a' way out?"

"Cause I was too busy gittin' your ass outa there 'fore Billy whupped on it. An' even if I coulda grabbed it, I wouldn'ta."

"Fuh' ih' all," Deke said. He picked up the calico bundle that held the gunbelt and holster, rolled down the side window and threw it out.

Shelly looked at Deke with disgust: as miserable of a wretch as she'd ever seen and deserving of every bit of it. She stared too long. The giant combine coming around the curve took up half of her lane and the panicked driver was already over as far as he could get. Shelly swerved off the pavement doing seventy. The old Ford jounced like it was hopping logs. Shelly clung tight to the wheel but poor Deke bounced like a bunny rabbit, his head thumping against the side window: whumpwhumpwhumpwhump.

"AHHHHHHHH!" he screamed with each bump.

Lucky for both of them, Shelly didn't panic. She let off the gas and guided the pickup back onto the pavement. After she'd regained control, Deke yelled, "STOP THE TRUCK RIGH' NOW! I feeh sick, awfuh' sick, an' I goh' a' pee real bad, too."

Shelly pulled over right away but the wind was blowing so hard that Deke had trouble forcing his door open and his desperation grew. Once out, the only way he could stay vertical was by holding onto the truck bed. Deke frantically made his way to the back, trying to decide which act to perform first. Hoping he could forstall throwing up for one more moment, Deke decided to pee. With his cheeks puffed out and holding his breath to keep from heaving, Deke fumbled for his fly. He finally got his zipper down then fumbled some more getting 'it' out. As Deke fought to control his stomach, his bladder, desperate for relief and not waiting for orders from mission control, which was temporarily out of service anyway, began spurting its load, which the wind promptly blew back all over his new shirt and Wranglers.

Deke looked down and let out an angry scream. As soon as his mouth opened, the bacon, beans, cornbread, whiskey and beer, along with the slimy baloney and stale crackers, that had been mixing it up in his belly saw their chance to escape and made for daylight. The resulting eruption splattered against Deke's face, shirt and pants in a revolting Technicolor blast. Deke spun around to face away from the wind and went down hard on his hands and knees as vomit and urine streamed out of him. The gusting wind blew most of the spew over his face and hair and saturated his shirt and beard with urine. All of Deke's frustration, rage and pain merged into a cacophony of screams and curses along with his retches and moans.

Shelly watched in the mirror and when Deke's head disappeared from view she pushed the door open and walked back. She rounded the tailgate and saw Deke down on all fours like a dog, dingus dangling and vomit covering him like a beer-battered cod. A pool of puke mixed with urine lay beneath him, the tips of Deke's long hair wicking it up. He quit retching and swearing long enough to look up at Shelly, his sad eyes begging like Old Shep, 'Please, just shoot me.'

A black car approached and came to a stop. "Are you okay?" a Mennonite woman asked Shelly. "Do you need any …" Then she saw Deke and said to the man beside her, "Keep driving Hiram, just keep driving."

Deke vomited again and then had the dry heaves as Shelly stood by shivering. After five minutes she said, "Reckon yor done yet? It's cold out here."

Deke loosed a few more sobs. "I nee' help gittin' up."

Getting Deke back into the truck without getting covered with his mess looked impossible. Shelly took a deep breath and held it. Stepping gingerly behind Deke, she grasped him under his armpits and lifted. Deke got to his knees, steadied himself against the rear tire and pulled himself up with Shelly's help.

"You gonna puke any more?" Shelly asked, as Deke hung onto the bed.

"I don' think so," he answered and eased his way towards the cab.

The wind had blown the door shut so Shelly fought it back open and held it for him. Deke went to climb in and Shelly nodded toward his belt line. "Ya need ta put your horse back in the barn."

Deke nodded assent and fumbled at the task unsuccessfully. In frustration he looked at Shelly but she shook her head from side to side. "I ain't a'gonna do it for ya, Deke," she told him.

Deke moaned and went back to fumbling. After more botched attempts he got his horse back in the barn, but not into the stall, as opening the flap and returning Dobbin to his rightful place in his new boxer shorts was well beyond Deke's current motor skills. Reckoning his Wranglers provided shelter enough, Deke gave up the struggle and raised his zipper. Apparently Dobbin had poked his muzzle out and when it caught in Deke's zipper he let out a truly awful howl. Dobbin would have whinnied too, if he could have.

Shelly winced. "This really ain't your day, is it, Deke?"

"Nohhhhhhh," he answered.

Shelly found a rag in the bed, wiped her hands and got into the cab. The stench was unbearable so she buttoned up her jacket and rolled down the window. Deke slouched against the door, drifting in and out of sleep, his moans alternating with fits of snoring. Half an hour later Shelly pulled into Valentine. There were two motels, but it was only 4:00 o'clock. The map showed that Chadron was two and half hours away and in spite of Deke's stink, she decided to make for it. The further west she drove, the more barren and sparsely populated the country became. The land was drier, more broken, the undulating prairie dotted with old windmills and range cattle. A few miles beyond Gordon, Deke stirred. "I goh' a' pee again."

Shelly pulled over and Deke got out. This time he turned away from the wind, which still blew his stream all over the side of his pickup. Deke muttered, then got back into the cab and fell asleep.

Out past Hay Springs the sky turned ominously dark, the roiling clouds threatening to collapse and crush the prairie. Shelly was freezing from driving with the window open and when Chadron appeared on the flat horizon, she stopped at the first motel and got a room with twin beds. She carried the luggage in and then shook Deke awake. Still unsteady, he could now walk a little on his own but Shelly refused to let him in the room. She propped Deke against the motel wall and said, "Take off all your clothes, right down ta your underwear."

"Noh'," Deke said. "Peo'le ken see."

"Alright, then you can sleep in the truck ta'night or git your own room, but you ain't stinkin' this one up an' gittin puke an' piss all over it."

"Noh, I ain' doin' it."

"See ya in the mornin' then, Deke." Shelly said and ducked into the room and locked the door behind her.

"OOOOOHHHHHH," Deke wailed and pounded on the door. "Leh'me in. Leh' me in."

Shelly opened the door a crack, keeping the chain bolt locked. "I'll let ya in soon as yor undressed," she said, then closed the door again.

Pleading, Deke pounded on the door, but Shelly turned on the television and settled back on one of the beds. Ten minutes later Shelly heard sobbing on the other side of the door so she got up and peered out the window. Deke was crying, but he was also removing his clothes, and just like he'd said, people were watching. Deke knocked on the door again and Shelly opened it. He stood shivering in only his boxer shorts, holding his cowboy boots, hat, wallet and his old belt with the John Wayne buckle.

"C'mon in," Shelly said, "but don'tchoo dare sit down or touch nothin."

She went into the bathroom, turned on the shower then came out and handed Deke a bar of motel soap. "Git in the shower," she said. "An' if there's one speck left on you, yor gonna go right back in again."

Deke stumbled into the bathroom, held onto a towel rack while he took off his shorts, climbed into the tub and plopped on his bottom. "AHHH!"

"You okay, Deke?" Shelly called.

"I fell on mah buh', an' the wah'er hurts mah head," Deke yelled.

"Be shor an' scrub your lump good with that soap," Shelly told him.

Deke sat in the tub, gingerly washing himself and pulled the curtain closed when Shelly came in with a clean pair of boxers. She picked up his old ones with a pencil and added them to the pile outside the door. Thirty minutes later Deke wobbled out of the bathroom wearing his new shorts and Shelly examined him. "Looks like yor clean," she said and squirted a dab of first aid cream on top of his head. "Rub that inta your bump."

"Ih' still reah'y hurts," Deke said, wincing, as he rubbed in the cream.

"Hang on," Shelly said. She got two aspirin out of her suitcase and handed them to Deke, along with a glass of tap water. "You wanta sleep some more?"

"Yeah."

Shelly pulled the covers down on one of the twin beds. "Then git in."

Deke had seen right away that he wouldn't be sleeping with Shelly that night, but when he got into the bed he was hoping for at least a kiss. He didn't get it and gave out one more self-pitying moan before falling to sleep. Shelly went into the bathroom, wiped out the tub with a towel, took a shower and put on clean clothes. When she came out she shook Deke awake. "It's after seven," she said. "I'm gonna walk downtown an get somethin' ta eat. Ya want me ta bring ya anything back?"

"Nohhhhh."

"Alright then," Shelly said, "see ya later."

After walking twelve blocks Shelly found a place called The Stockman's. Taking an open booth she ordered the biggest steak on the menu, a Coors and a shot of whiskey, figuring she deserved it after the afternoon she'd had. Whoever was feeding the jukebox had a refined taste for country music. As Shelly devoured her steak Patsy Cline, Kitty Wells, Pee Wee King and the Louvin Brothers helped put the crazy day behind her. When the music stopped a tall, rangy cowboy wearing a tan Stetson walked over to the machine, stuck some money in and the music cranked up again. As Shelly was tipping back the last of her beer and about to leave, the waitress returned to her table with another bottle of Coors and set it down. She pointed to the young cowboy at the bar who'd just played the jukebox and told Shelly, "Compliments of Jack."

Shelly thought about refusing the Coors. She knew that Jack would follow the beer to her table and she wasn't in the mood to be hustled.

As she was about to tell the waitress no thanks, the song "Wings of a Dove" began playing. Any cowboy who liked Ferlin Husky was worth drinking a beer with.

When Shelly nodded her thanks the cowboy nodded back then lifted his long frame off the stool and sauntered over as Shelly sized him up. He was at least six-four, with dark hair and a craggy, yet pleasant face. He looked a little like the actor Jack Palance, Shelly thought, but without the hardness. Nothing in his dress or manner was affected, like Billy Stanton, but Jack was all cowboy.

"Ma'am, would you mind sharin' some conversation?" he said, touching his hat. "I'll be a gentleman, I promise."

Whether that was Jack's standard pick-up line or not, it wasn't a bad one, so Shelly assented. Jack sat down opposite her in the booth and laid his hat on the table.

"My name's Jack Dillard," he said, sticking out his hand. "I'm the manager of a ranch just west of town."

"I'm Shelly Stamper, an' I'm jes stopping here for the night on my way ta Montana," Shelly told him as they shook hands, letting Jack know right away that a relationship was not in the offing.

Jack saw Shelly looking for a ring on his hand and said, "I'm single. I don't think it's right for married people to cheat on each other." That earned him a point.

Before Jack cornered her with any personal questions, Shelly asked about him. He was born and raised on a ranch in Wyoming, spent several years on the rodeo circuit, mostly on broncs, and had been at his current job for four years. The ranch's absentee owner paid Jack well and he liked the job, but like most cowboys, wanted his own ranch and was saving up to buy one. Jack was a good conversationalist and true to what he had said, a gentleman.

After a while Jack saw an opening and started asking questions. Shelly told Jack where she was from and that she planned to become a truck driver in Montana.

"That takes some courage," Jack said, "going to Montana by yourself to be a truck driver."

Shelly almost let it go. "I ain't by myself, Jack," she finally said. "The guy who's brother owns the truck I'm gonna drive is with me."

Jack didn't say anything but his eyes changed.

"I ain't committed ta nobody, though," Shelly said, and Jack grinned.

"Where is he now?"

"Back at the motel sleepin' off a drunk. He pulled a gun an' near shot somebody at the bar in Johnstown and the bartender rapped 'im on the head with her pistol."

"Your buddy's lucky Hazel didn't shoot him," Jack said and took a drink from his beer. "What'd he pull a gun for."

"Cause me an' one a' the local cowboys went for a horse ride."

"That's not reason enough to shoot somebody."

"I know. An' this ain't the first time he's done somethin' that stupid."

"And it won't be the last," Jack said.

"Likely not," Shelly agreed, and looked down at her beer.

"Sounds like you enjoy riding," Jack said to change the subject.

"When I was growin' up I had a horse an' rode all the time."

"What was your horse's name?"

Shelly's throat seized up. In the five years since Tramp had died, Shelly hadn't said his name once. Her mouth opened, but nothing came out.

"I can tell that something happened to your horse, Shelly, and that it still bothers you," Jack said. "We don't have to keep talking about that."

"His name was Tramp," Shelly said, biting down on her bottom lip.

"Whatever happened," Jack said, "I'm sorry for you. Losing a horse you love is a mighty hard thing."

"I've never told anybody what really happened." Shelly said. "The only ones who know are my own family an' the people who lived near us then."

"I understand," Jack said.

"An' afterwards, nobody ever mentioned Tramp again … cause they knew I couldn't handle hearin' it. Yor the first person I've even said his name to."

Jack put his hand over Shelly's and squeezed lightly. "I've lost horses that I swear I loved more than any human being," he said, "and the hardest part is if they died because of something I did."

Shelly turned her hand over beneath Jack's palm and gripped his hand.

"I didn't fasten the gate good enough, Jack. I was mad about somethin' an' in a hurry an' didn't pay attention. Tramp was real good at gittin' out, that's why the people we got 'im from named 'im Tramp … but I was in a hurry … an' went back in the house, still mad. I went up in my room ta pout an' after a spell I heard truck brakes lock up an' this long skid out on the highway. Somethin' bad happened, I jes knew it, an' when I ran outside an' didn't see Tramp in his corral I knew … I jes knew, Jack. I ran down to the highway at Wimmer Gap an' Tramp was layin' in the middle a' the road. One a' them big coal trucks had come aroun' the corner an' couldn't stop. Tramp was tryin' to git up, but he couldn't. He was ripped open an' two of his legs was broke an' one hoof was tore clean off … but he was still tryin' to git up. He raised his head an' looked at me, Jack … when I went up to 'im … he looked right in my eyes … like he was tellin' me how sorry he was for runnin' away … 'cause he knew this was gonna hurt me real bad … an' I jes stood there screamin' Jack, that's all I could do … stand there screamin'.'"

Shelly stopped to catch her breath.

"Mama heard me screamin', an' must a' noticed Tramp was gone too an' figgered it out, cause when she ran up she was carryin' Daddy's rifle. She told me ta git. She said, 'You go back to the house, right now, you don't need ta see this,' an' soon as I was up the hill an' outa sight I heard that rifle shot. I can still hear that rifle shot ta this day. I hear it right now."

Shelly took another breath and focused her eyes.

"I never saw Tramp again. The state highway people came an' took him away, I guess. Nobody ever told me what they done with 'im. But ev'ry day till the next spring, whenever I went ta school or inta town I'd see that big patch a' Tramp's blood on the road. It wouldn't go away."

The jukebox clinked and Shelly's favorite Ferlin Husky song, "Gone", began playing. An older couple walked out onto the dance floor and with loving, long practiced gestures, moved to the music in each other's arms.

Shelly watched them and lightened her grip on Jack's hand. "You wanta dance, Jack?"

"Sure, Shelly," Jack answered, and they walked to where the other couple was swaying together.

Shelly pressed up against Jack and put her arms around him, trying to think about nothing except the song that was playing. When the music ended and the other couple sat down, Shelly and Jack started walking back to their booth. Halfway there, Buddy Holly's "Peggy Sue" started up.

"Do you jitterbug?" Jack asked.

"I shor do," Shelly answered.

By the second verse every eye in the bar was on them. They danced sharp and quick, like a pair of cheetahs. When the song ended they sat down and Shelly squeezed Jack's hand. "Thanks, Jack," she said.

They sipped at their beers and Jack let Shelly restart the conversation on her terms.

"Where'd ya learn ta dance like that, Jack? Not many men can jitterbug the way you jes did."

"My older sister made me learn. Out there on the ranch she didn't have anybody else to practice with. How about you?" he asked. "You cut a rug better than anybody I've seen in a while."

"My daddy liked ta dance. He had me flatfootin' an cloggin' with 'im when I was still little."

"I've never heard of flat-footin'," Jack said.

"It's kind of a hillbilly thing," Shelly told him, and they both laughed.

"How about another beer?" Jack asked, holding up his empty bottle.

"Alright," Shelly agreed, "but this round's on me."

For the next three hours they talked, laughed and danced when the music was right. They jitterbugged some more, did a few western swings, a couple of two steps and waltzed across a small part of Nebraska when Ernest Tubb sang. As the clock above the bar nudged toward midnight, Shelly said, "I oughta be gittin back to the motel."

Jack looked into Shelly's eyes. "Why?" he said simply, and Shelly couldn't come up with an answer. Every ounce of her recognized that the sensible decision would be to remain right here in Chadron and forget about Troy, Montana and Deke McConahay.

Jack knew that Shelly understood his question, but he laid it out anyway. "You'd be welcome to stay at the ranch, and I don't mean just for tonight. If you're set on being a truck driver, we've got a couple of semis you can drive. I've got my own house out there and it has three bedrooms. You could have your own for as long as you want if that would make you feel more comfortable."

Shelly listened quietly, letting his offer sink in.

"If you'd like some time to think it over I'll stand you at the hotel here in town so we can get to know each other better. And," Jack said, throwing in the clincher, "we've got all the horses you could ever want to ride."

Shelly's brain screamed in confusion. On her first day in the West, she'd gone into a bar and grill for dinner and met the ideal man who'd just offered her the best life she could imagine. And if she walked out the door, she'd be going back to the biggest fool she ever met and heading off to someplace where who knows what, if anything, might happen. She pictured what life would be like with Jack: living and working on the prairie, riding horses together and someday having their own ranch. The thought of it stirred Shelly to the middle of her core, down low. Frankly, she wanted Jack right now. On the pool table if everybody else would get the hell outa the bar.

Then that voice rose up in her, the one that she never could figure out where it came from, just like it had that night back in Norwood when she'd asked Deke if she could go to Montana with him and agreed to be his girlfriend.

"I can't, Jack, an' don't ask me why 'cause I don't even know myself. I jes know I can't."

Jack didn't say anything. In the dim light of neon beer signs he and Shelly looked at each other from across the table. Only a few customers remained in the Stockman's and the jukebox had gone quiet.

"How about one more dance?" Jack said.

"Alright," Shelly agreed, and they stood up.

Jack dropped a quarter into the jukebox, punched a button and he and Shelly walked out onto the dance floor. The record changer clanked as the 45rpm slipped into place and the voice of Kris Kristofferson softly filled the room. Neither Jack nor Shelly said anything as they danced. Shelly buried her face in Jack's shoulder and they gave themselves over to the song, thankful for the moment and ... *'for the good times.'*

Shelly only walked three blocks when the rumpled black clouds that had been hovering overhead all day let loose. The cold rain poured over her and mixed with the tears running down her face but she didn't care. She had just walked away from the best offer in her life and couldn't figure out why. Feeling as drenched and alone as an unwanted cat flung into the river, Shelly walked on through the darkness. Two blocks from the motel she saw the neon glare of its blinking sign and a light came on in her brain. She was seventeen. This was her first day in the West. Her life wasn't meant to be settled … or perfect, at least not yet. Maybe some day she'd come back here and Jack's offer would still be open, but she couldn't accept it tonight, she had too much living in front of her.

On her way to the room, Shelly walked past Deke's pickup, its tired metal glistening in the rain, and she thought of the rainy night she felt sorry for Clete's dripping '49 Powerwagon, not knowing that she'd never see her daddy again. Old Paint, Shelly thought, looking at the discolored Ford; that's a good name for it.

As Shelly was unlocking the door, she saw that Deke's clothing was gone. Somebody was still in the motel office so she went over and asked about it.

"Oh, that," the old desk clerk said, stubbing out his hand-rolled cigarette. "I got so many complaints on the smell that I got a pitchfork and tossed 'em in the dumpster. They're covered up with all kinds a' shit by now."

Deke was sitting up, propped against the headboard, wearing his old clothes and watching a black and white western on TV. With one hand he steadied a rolled up washcloth containing crushed ice on top of his head.

"Whatcha watchin'?" Shelly asked.

"*Have Gun, Will Travel.*"

Shelly thought, In your case it's *Had Gun, Will Travel*, but she said, "Didn't ya get e'nuff a' that kinda stuff today?"

Deke just looked at her.

"How's your head?"

"I'll live. I took two more aspirin."

"I hope you don't wanta watch TV all night," Shelly said, "I'm tired."

"You can turn it off."

Shelly flipped the knob and the screen went black.

"That sure was a long dinner you had," Deke said.

"I was hungry."

"Is that all ya did?"

"No."

Shelly took a toothbrush from her overnight bag, walked into the bathroom and closed the door behind her.

Ten minutes later when she came out, Deke had taken off his clothes and was under the covers. His eyes followed Shelly as she undressed to her bra and panties, flipped off the light switch and crawled into bed. She'd just gotten settled when Deke called over to her. "Shelly?"

"Yeah, Deke?"

"Good night."

"Good night, Deke."

"Shelly?"

"Yeah?"

"I love you, Shelly."

"I know ya do, Deke."

"Shelly?"

"Yeah?"

"I'll do better tomorrow, I promise."

"Alright, Deke."

"Goodnight, Shelly."

"Goodnight, Deke."

Chapter 28

Friday, September 28

Having slept for most of the previous day, Deke woke at dawn, pulled on his old Levis and t-shirt, and popped two aspirin from the bottle Shelly'd left him on the table. He turned on the television but kept the sound off, then lay back down on his bed and watched Captain Kangaroo. An hour later Shelly woke up.

"Good morning, Shelly," Deke said and started to get up.

Fearing he was going to get in bed with her, Shelly jumped from the covers. "Mornin', Deke," she said, grabbing some dry clothes and hustling into the bathroom. When she came out she asked Deke, "How soon you gonna be ready ta leave?"

"Reckon I can leave now," Deke said and reached for his socks and boots.

They went out to the truck and as Shelly was stowing her knapsack and suitcase she asked Deke, "Can you drive okay?"

"Maybe you better drive awhile," he said, "but I am hungry."

"Me too," Shelly said. "We'll stop at the first rest'ernt we see."

They drove into downtown Chadron without seeing any place to eat but as they waited at a stoplight, Shelly glanced over and saw the Stockman's. Deke saw it, too. "Look, the sign in the winda says 'Open for Breakfast'. Let's stop."

"I don't want to," Shelly said.

"How come? It looks okay."

"I ate there las' night," Shelly said as the light turned green, "an' it cost me too much."

An old family-style diner fronted the highway on the western edge of town and they pulled in. After ordering, Deke gulped coffee and tried to make conversation, but Shelly was still mad at him. She also couldn't get Jack out of her mind or the temptation to grab her things from Deke's truck and stay in Chadron. When the bill came, Shelly told Deke to pay it, then went out and got behind the wheel of his Ford.

They continued west under a sky that was overcast and gray, but behind them the sun shone mightily and reflected off a range of high buttes and peaks to the south. Shelly wished they were heading toward them, but they needed to go north. A few miles out of town they turned onto Route 385, and when Chadron disappeared from the rearview mirror, Shelly felt a sense of relief.

"Where's this road go?" Deke asked, after they crossed the White River.

"Up inta the Black Hills. We're gonna see a lot a' perty country ta'day."

"How close are we ta Montana?"

"It ain't that far. We oughta be there ta'day, unless somethin' stupid happens like it did yesterday."

"I ain't gonna do stuff like that no more, Shelly. I'm done with drinkin'." Deke felt his bump. "But I do wish I had me a little weed. That might take some a' the hurt away."

"Yeah, then we could git caught with dope an' go ta jail." Shelly exhaled a long breath. "Deke, you promised me you wouldn't git screwed up no more. You even swore it on my daddy's Bible."

"I'm sorry, Shelly. I didn't mean fer it ta happen."

Shelly turned away, drove and watched the scenery.

The landscape was hilly and broken, but no longer barren prairie, and cattle grazed on the grass of well-tended farms. Still, there was a bigness to it, and Shelly reckoned that all of West Virginia would fit into what she could see around her. The sun had punched holes in the clouds ahead and as they crossed into South Dakota the solid gray layer was breaking up. Further on they topped a rise and saw a range of steep hills in the distance, black against the sky. Shelly stayed on

385 into Hot Springs and after they'd filled the gas tank, drove into the middle of town and parked. "Let's git out an' stretch," she said.

They walked around a bit, but as the town was obviously meant for the tourist trade, Shelly found little to interest her. Deke popped into a small store and came out with a sack of baloney and crackers, a carton of cigarettes and two pints of milk, one of which he handed to Shelly. At an information center Shelly grabbed a dozen brochures on the Black Hills before they went back to the truck.

"I feel good enough ta drive now," Deke said.

Shelly dug in her pocket. "Here's the keys ta Old Paint."

"How come you keep callin' my truck Old Paint?"

"Cause that's what it's got on it, Deke, old paint."

As Shelly navigated them north, the increasing sunlight warmed the countryside and they rolled their windows part way down. After they entered Wind Cave National Park the highway rose in elevation and the land opened to wide vistas of prairie grass. A few miles into the park Shelly saw some strange looking cattle off in the distance and she had Deke pull over. When she saw that they were bison she said, "I think this'll be a good day after all." At the park's visitor center they pulled over and went inside. "You wanta go down inta the caves?" Shelly asked.

"I don't like caves. I'd prob'ly git sick agin," Deke said.

Shelly was disappointed but didn't say anything. After leaving the visitor center they came to an intersection and Shelly told Deke to take Highway 87. They crossed the magnificent arch bridge over Beaver Creek and began climbing to Rankin Ridge. At the top was a trail that went to a fire lookout. "Let's hike it, Deke," Shelly said, "it's only about a mile."

"Naw. I don't feel like it."

"Alright, then, you wait here. I'll be back in a while." Half an hour later Shelly returned at a trot. "Ya should been there, Deke. You can see all aroun' from up there, likely even inta Montana."

They continued into Custer State Park and the land became more forested. At the turnoff for Route 16A Shelly said, "Turn right here, Deke, the brochure says this is a real fine highway." A few miles later they forked left onto the Iron Mountain Road and found that the brochure was not exaggerating. Tucked into its short seventeen miles were 314 curves, 14 switchbacks, 3 tunnels and 3 pigtail wooden beam bridges that turned a full 360 degrees.

As the sun approached its zenith, the clouds scattered, turning the hills and forests into dappled wonderlands. The tourists were long gone for the season and Deke and Shelly had Iron Mountain Road to themselves. Shelly was ecstatic and even Deke was awed. He drove slowly and gawked. At the first tunnel, a square, one-lane cave that punched through rock, they pulled over and got out. Shelly walked to the middle of the road and looked through it. "Hey Deke," she yelled, "come lookit this."

After off-loading some morning coffee Deke joined her and Shelly pointed to a mountain in the distance. "This tunnel's been built so it frames Mt. Rushmore."

Deke looked. "That mountain looks like it's got faces on it," he said.

"Yor right, Deke, it does. Ain't it amazin' what erosion can do."

"Wow," Deke said.

Shelly was holding her stomach to keep from laughing. "Deke, them faces were carved up there."

"Oh … I reckon I knew that."

"Didn't ya ever hear a' Mount Rushmore?"

"Now that ya mention it, I guess so. I musta fergot about it."

Further down the road a dozen elk sauntered across in front of them. With no traffic behind, Deke turned off the Ford and let the elk take their time. "Well, Deke," Shelly said, "there ain't no doubt about it, we're really in the West."

When they arrived at the paying portion of Mount Rushmore, Deke and Shelly got out and debated the matter. Deke's position was clear. "I don't need ta pay money jest ta git closer to it. I can see them faces plenty good from here."

For once, Shelly agreed. "I think yor right, Deke. We done seen it."

They reconnected with Route 385 and drove steady until they dropped into Deadwood. "You'll like this town, Deke," Shelly said. "It was an old gold minin' camp an' a lot a' famous people were here, includin' Wild Bill Hickock an' Calamity Jane."

"Oh, I heard a' this town plenty," Deke said. "It's been in lots a' movies."

"You wanta grab some lunch here an' walk around?" Shelly asked.

"You bet."

They cruised down a quiet Main Steet and parked. Deke grabbed his cowboy hat from off the seat and set it on his head, careful not to disturb the goose egg that protruded from his hair.

"How's your head doin'?" Shelly asked.

"It still hurts but not as bad. I don' wan' nobody ta see it, neither."

Shelly and Deke strolled along the street, peeking into the windows of the tourist shops until they came to Calamity's Café. "Ya wanta eat here?" Shelly asked.

"Fine by me."

They took a table in the middle of a dozen other tourists.

"What?" Deke asked, when he saw Shelly staring at him.

"Deke, I know yor partial ta them old clothes, but that NASCAR shirt looks terrible. It's all faded an' full a' holes."

"I like this shirt," Deke said. "I wasted a bunch a' money on those fancy duds you made me buy …an' I only had 'em fer one day."

After eating they continued down Main Street and passed several establishments that claimed to have histories connected to Deadwood's past. Then they came to the Old Style Saloon No.10. A large sign in the window read: *Have a drink in the saloon where Wild Bill Hickock died. See the chair he was shot in. Look at the famous Aces and Eights he was holding.*

"I wanna go in," Deke said.

"Only ta have a Coke," Shelly told him.

The joint was almost as dead as Wild Bill. Two elderly men in old-style clothes rested their rear ends on stools at the bar and the bartender, gussied up in a white shirt, bow tie and arm garters, tried his best not to look bored. Shelly walked up to the bar and before the bartender even asked, said, "We'd like two Cokes." The two men were drinking whiskey and both looked at Deke with raised eyebrows.

Deke and Shelly sipped at their Cokes and walked around, taking in the bar's attractions. High on the wall, in a glass case, sat the chair that Wild Bill Hickock was sitting in back in 1876 when he was shot in the back of the head by that little coward Jack McCall. Displayed with it were the famous aces and eights that Wild Bill was holding when he placed his last bet.

"Jes imagine, Deke," Shelly said, "what this bar woulda been like a hund'ert years ago. I wonder how much it's changed since then."

"I bet it ain't changed hardly a'tall," Deke said. "Some a' this stuff in here looks real old." He looked up at Wild Bill's death chair then took in the surrounding bar. "I can see myself in here back then. I'd a' been a gunfighter, jest like Hickock."

"Well, you 'bout got shot in the back a' the head like he did," Shelly said.

They went back to the bar. Shelly sat on a stool but Deke stayed standing, as no self-respecting gunslinger would sit down at a bar. "Ya still have a lot a' shootouts in here?" he asked the bartender, as Shelly cringed.

The bartender hesitated. "Not too many," he finally said.

The old guys two stools away looked at each other and one of them said to Deke, "Only about one or two a month anymore."

The other fella looked at his buddy. "Yeah, but it'll pick up again next summer when the cattle drives start comin' up from Texas."

"You're right, Will, we'll have two or three gunfights a week then."

"Remember that Saturday in July, Dan, when three people got shot? What was it, a claim jumper, a sheep herder and a tinhorn gambler?"

"No! It was two gamblers and a sodbuster. We strung up the sheep herder an' run the claim jumper outa town." Dan turned to Deke. "Old Will here's gettin' a little tetched in his old age. He can't remember much anymore."

"Well pardner, if you'd been kicked by as many mules as I have an' run over by an ore wagon, you'd have a hard time rememberin' things too."

The bartender looked at the two retired mailmen who stopped in each afternoon for a drink, shook his head, then turned around and went to dusting off the back bar.

"You guys from around here?" Deke asked.

"All our lives," the one named Will said. "My granddad was one of the original miners in Deadwood."

"Wow," Deke said.

"In fact," he said, and reached over and tapped the bar in front of Deke for emphasis, "he was in this bar when Hickock was killed. He told me all about it when I was a kid."

Deke's eyes got big and the bartender looked over his shoulder at Will.

"Why shitfire, I'd a like'd ta met him," Deke said.

"Oh that's nothin'," Will said. "Dan's grandmother was in here too. She was a whore, the best in Deadwood, they said," he looked over at Shelly and put his finger to his forehead, "pardon my sayin' it ma'am, and she'd just got off Wild Bill's lap, not two minutes before McCall shot him." Will turned around and pointed to the chair in the glass case: "In that chair, right there, that very one."

"Wow," Deke said again as Dan gave Will a nasty look.

"What'd you guys do around here?" Deke asked.

"We're prospectors," Dan said. "Most of the time we're pannin' for gold up in the hills but about once a month I need a woman and Will here needs a bath, so we come to town."

The bartender coughed.

Shelly couldn't take any more. "I'm goin' to the ladies room," she said, "an' freshen up." She looked over at Dan and Will. "I might scrape my shoes off, too, while I'm in there."

As soon as Shelly was out of hearing range, Deke said, "I ain't no stranger ta gunplay, myself. Yesterday I shot up a bar in Nebraska. Some cowpoke was flirtin' with Shelly an' braggin' that he was Billy the Kid so I made 'im dance."

The bartender spun around. "You're not carryin' a gun are you? Sometimes we get idiots in here who think this is still the Wild West." He looked over at Dan and Will and wagged his finger at them to knock it off.

"Naw, I promised my girlfriend I wouldn't do that no more." Deke said, and took a drink off his Coke. "She git's a little nervous about gunslingin'." Then he lowered his head and whispered, "Gimme a whiskey, quick."

The bartender filled a shot glass with whiskey. Deke picked it up and nodded at the two 'prospectors'. "Ta Wild Bill," he said, and tossed it down. If Deke thought he had recovered from the day before, his stomach told him otherwise. The booze barely made it to his throat before Deke gagged, splurting whiskey out of his nose and mouth all over the bar.

"First time?" Dan asked, as the bartender wiped off the bar and put the shot glass in the sink.

Deke was still spluttering when Shelly returned. "You okay?" she asked.

"I'm fine," he said, "jest fine," and took a long gulp of Coke.

After Deke quit coughing, Shelly pointed to a row of t-shirts for sale above the back bar. "Hey, Deke, they got shirts with Wild Bill Hickock's picture on 'em. If I bought ya one, would ya wear it?" When Deke didn't answer, Shelly said, "He looks a little like ya."

Deke eyed the shirt. Wild Bill stood tall and imposing in fringed buckskin, a brace of pistols facing backwards and a large skinning knife in his belt, his long hair falling onto his broad shoulders. "We do look alike, don't we," he said to Shelly. Deke leaned over and looked at Dan and Will. "An' he had the guts ta wear his hair long, just like I do." Deke turned to the bartender. "I take a large."

"If you're interested," the bartender said, as Deke was pulling on his new shirt, "Wild Bill Hickock and Calamity Jane are buried in the cemetery here. It's only a mile or so up the hill."

"Thanks for tellin' us," Shelly said. "I'd like to see that."

As they walked back to the truck Deke told Shelly, "I can't wait ta tell my brother I was in the saloon where Wild Bill Hickock was shot and even saw the chair he was sittin' in and the cards he was holdin'."

"I gotta admit," Shelly said, as she and Deke got into his Ford, "that was impressive, the way they've kept that bar like it was a hund'ert years ago an' hung on to all them things."

Some of the tang might have gone out of their experience if Deke and Shelly had known that the aces and eights displayed in the Old No. 10 were not the actual cards Wild Bill had been holding when he was shot, nor was the 'death chair' the real chair Bill had been sitting in, but only one similar to it. They'd have been even less thrilled to learn that the original Old No. 10 Saloon had burned to the ground many years before and that the bar they were in was not even at the same location. But Wild Bill likely would have taken the ruse all in stride.

An old huckster himself, who once told reporter Henry Stanley with a straight face that he had killed over a hundred men, he would have been amused that an entire town was now making its living on his exagerated reputation.

Deke and Shelly drove up the steep grade to Mount Moriah Cemetery and stood in the warm afternoon sunshine, respectfully admiring the graves of Wild Bill and Calamity Jane.

"I've always kinda liked ol' Calamity," Shelly said. "She was a tough woman when it was tough ta be a woman an' she did whatever she wanted."

Deke looked at Hickock's tombstone and nodded his head. "I've always thought me an' Wild Bill Hickock was a lot alike. Maybe someday they'll bury you an' me side by side too, jest like Wild Bill an' Calamity Jane."

Shelly started to say, Over my dead body, but caught herself in time.

Chapter 29

I don't wanta stay on this damn interstate," Shelly told Deke as they drove onto I-90 north of Deadwood. "Take 85 up here at Spearfish an' we'll jump on 212 at Belle Fourche an' be in Montana quicker'n ya know it."

At the Wyoming border they cheered, but twenty miles later whooped and howled as they crossed into Montana. Three miles in, where, according to Shelly's atlas, a town called Alzada should've been, they saw a bar.

"Shitfire," Deke said, stomping on the brakes, "we gotta stop an' have us a beer ta celebrate gittin' ta Montana."

"Reckon so, but jes one," Shelly said, "an' no whiskey."

"I'm done with whiskey," Deke told her. "It don't even sound good."

Deke pulled in and parked amidst an impressive display of junk, old machinery and battered vehicles. Near the entrance were two hitching rails and as Deke walked by them he looked down to where his bumper had been and frowned at Shelly. Nothing indicated the establishment's name, but above the front door, a crude wooden sign read: *Alzada — conveniently located in the middle of nowhere.* Dirty sawdust covered the uneven floor and dollar bills overwritten with names and good luck wishes served as wallpaper. A mid-day gathering of local ranchers clustered at the bar and Deke and Shelly were not five steps inside when a middle-aged man covered in dust said, "Come on over and join the crowd. We're tired of listening to each other."

Deke and Shelly obliged and when they ordered beers the locals caught their Appalachian accents and wanted to know all about them.

"Goin' to Troy to drive log trucks, huh?" one toothless old cowboy they called Gummy said between drags on his hand-rolled cigarette. "They're all crazy as hell over there in western Montana, ya know."

"Troy, the lowest town in Montana," a rancher named Wiley said.

"Like how?" Shelly asked. "The dirtiest or the toughest?"

"Oh, it's all of those," Wiley told her, "but it's the lowest in altitude."

Walt, the dust-covered man who'd invited them over, said, "I've been to Troy a time or two and it's also the lowest in aptitude." Everybody laughed.

"I'll tell you what," Wiley said, "that logging is a rough business. Falling trees is touchy work and hooking or skidding the logs is even worse. Log truck drivers don't have it much better. They haul all winter long on dangerous roads. I did it when I stayed with my granddad just outside of Libby."

"Purty tough, huh?" Deke said.

"You betcha," Wiley answered. "I came back here where a ranching man can have a drink in the afternoon."

Walt said, "Hell, my cattle got more sense than most of the loggers I've met."

Shelly and Deke finished their beers, said goodbye and were turning to leave when Wiley nodded to the bartender and tilted his head toward Shelly and Deke. The bartender, a slight woman with kindly eyes who'd introduced herself as Diane, set two more beers in front of them.

"Here's a couple on Wiley for the road," she said.

"Thanks, but we don't drink when we're drivin'," Shelly told her. "That's invitin' trouble with the law."

"Not in Montana," Gummy said. "It's legal."

"Ta drink whilst yer drivin'?" Deke said, astounded.

"Yep," the crowd answered, and Diane nodded in ascent.

"Long as you're not drunk," Wiley told them.

"And there's some leeway on that too," Walt said. "You have to be over point one five on the machine and even then most cops'll let you go if you're not being too crazy or an asshole. Sometimes they'll even take you home."

Gummy grinned. "The sheriff drives me home about as often as I drive myself."

"No daytime speed limit, either," Walt added.

"And no law against having a loaded gun with you," Wiley told them. "In fact, you can be driving down the highway at 90 miles an hour, pulling on a bottle of whiskey with a loaded .45 under the seat, and you're perfectly legal."

Deke and Shelly looked at each other.

"No speed limit?" Deke said, almost in disbelief.

"Did you see any speed limit signs when you crossed over from Wyoming?" Wiley asked.

"Come ta think of it, no, " Shelly said. "Just the 'Welcome To Montana' sign."

"Well," Walt said, "Welcome to Montana."

Spirits soaring, windows down, swigging their beers and laughing, Deke and Shelly roared west at 85 miles an hour. Deke flipped his empty bottle back into the bed. "Let's see how fast this baby'll go," he said.

Shelly looked sideways at him

"I can handle it. I use ta be a race car driver, ya know."

"I know all about it. Debbie told me how ya wrecked 'er brother's car."

"But the road's straight an' there ain't a lick a' traffic."

"Go ahead, but jes for a ways." Shelly finally agreed.

Deke depressed the accelerator and the Ford's engine responded, revving smoothly from Cliff's tune-up. Shelly loved speed as much as Deke did and if she'd been at the wheel would've done the same thing. The wind from the high plains blew over their faces, fresh and bold, as they watched the speedometer climb. When it reached 104 Deke ran for a mile then backed off, satisfied. "I think if I tinkered with the mill a'whiles, I could git 'er a little higher," he told Shelly.

After that, 85 didn't seem fast anymore. Montana unfolded around them: open, fenceless and free. Tree-covered hills stretched away in every direction and beyond them, mountain after mountain to infinity. Even the pine-scented wind blowing through the cab screamed freedom. Already, Montana was living up to its hope and promise, and then some. Before they knew it they had breezed through Broadus and were climbing the grade that wound between the conifers of Custer National Forest. After dropping down the other side they passed through Ashland, and though no sign declared it, entered onto the Northern Cheyenne Reservation. Idling slowly into Lame Deer, Shelly said, "These folks look like Indians."

"I think yer right," Deke said, gawking. "What should we do?"

"Well Deke, since there ain't enough of us ta circle the wagons, I reckon we oughta jes keep drivin'." Two blocks later Shelly changed her mind. "Let's drive around town, Deke. I never been on an Indian reservation before."

"I don't think that's safe, Shelly."

"Jumpin' Jesus, Deke. Don'tcha remember back in Ohio when we talked about seein' Indians an' how exited ya were about it?"

"I remember," Deke said, "but I figgered they'd look diff'runt."

"Ya mean like ridin' aroun' on horses wearin' feathers an' warpaint?"

"I don't know," Deke said, " jest diff'runt."

"Well, I reckon they do look a little diff'ernt, Deke, otherwise we wouldn't know they was Indians. Turn down this side street here," Shelly ordered. "They ain't gonna take us captive an' burn us at the stake."

Deke didn't like it, but he obeyed. Other than the Ohio tags, Deke's battered pickup would have gone unnoticed on the rez, but two gawking palefaces cruising at 10 miles an hour drew attention. The elders just stared back, but some of the younger Cheyenne shot them angry looks. Shelly smiled and waved at two high school girls but got glares in return. "Jeeze, Deke, I was hopin' ta git out an' talk to some Indians but that might not be so smart."

They pulled up to a stop sign where two Cheyenne men with long braids stood on the corner, talking. Deke stared, trying to hear what they were saying. The one facing Deke, a tall, powerful man, took several steps over to the truck. He peered down at Deke through his open window. "What's the matter, you've never seen an Indian before?" Then he saw Deke's t-shirt. "Arrhhh!" he yelled, and reached for the door handle. Deke hit the gas, almost clipping the back end of a car passing through the intersection.

"Careful!" Shelly hollered. "We don't wanta have a wreck in this town."

"I wish I still had that pistol," Deke said.

"To do what? Drive aroun' an' shoot Indians?"

"No. I'd jest feel safer with it, that's all."

"I wouldn't feel safer. You dang near shot me with it, an' then tried ta shoot somebody else for no reason an' almost got yor'self shot. How safe is that?'

"I don't care, I still wish I had it," Deke said.

"Lets git back on the highway," Shelly told him. "I think we're makin' the folks here mad."

Fifteen minutes later they passed through Busby and entered the Crow Reservation. Late afternoon was settling in and clouds had gathered in the western sky by the time they reached the Little Bighorn Battlefield, but there was no question about stopping. In the visitor center a ranger gave them pamphlets to help them understand the complexity of the battle. Deke and Shelly looked around the center, viewing relics from the battle, paintings, and written descriptions. From Reno's first charge on the west side of the river to the Reno-Benteen site and Last Stand Hill, the battle took place over a vaster area than Deke and Shelly had imagined. They drove first to the Reno-Benteen Battlefield for a quick look, stopping at Calhoun Hill along the way, then drove back to Last Stand Hill. It was getting late and nearly all the visitors were gone. As Deke and Shelly parked, the last car pulled away, leaving them alone on the battlefield. They got out of the pickup and walked to the 7th Cavalry Memorial obelisk above Last Stand Hill. After looking at the obelisk Shelly and Deke moved over to a smaller memorial stone off to the side and read:

"The remains of about 220 soldiers, scouts, and civilians are buried around the base of this memorial. The white marble headstones scattered over the battlefield denote where the slain troopers were found and originally buried. In 1881 they were reinterred in a single grave on this site. The officers' remains were removed in 1877 to various cemeteries throughout the country. General Custer was buried at West Point."

"Looks like they first buried the soldiers where they fell an' later reburied 'em here," Shelly said, looking out across Last Stand Hill.

Deke turned up his nose. "I'm glad I wadn't around when they dug up them bodies an' re-entered 'em here."

"They was likely jes bones by then, Deke."

"I still wouldn't want ta see it."

"I guess they decided ta bring the bodies here so's they could be ta'gether," Shelly said, "'cept for the officers. Looks like the Army didn't want 'em buried with their own soldiers. They hauled Custer as far away as they could get 'im so's he wouldn't have ta lay with the men he got killed."

Deke and Shelly walked over to Last Stand Hill and its 52 markers: 51 of them white, and one, Custer's, ominously faced in black. They opened a gate in the iron fence that enclosed the hill and entered. Shelly strode into the long grass but Deke looked at the sign warning of rattlesnakes and hesitated. Finally he followed, watchful at every step. They walked silently among the markers and paused at Custer's.

"I've never been to a place like this," Shelly said. "Have you?"

"No," Deke answered, "I sure ain't."

Shelly turned and gazed over the battlefield, trying to take in what had happened nearly 100 years before. The sun squinted through a fluffy layer of clouds on the western horizon and the afternoon breeze came on brisk and steady. She could see the wind coming, swelling in force where the Indian pony herd had grazed in 1876. It hopped Interstate 90 and whipped through the old Indian encampment, rustling the cottonwoods along the Little Big Horn River, then rolled over Greasy Grass Ridge, gathered pace and hurried up the slope, careening through the draws and coulees where the 7th Cavalry troopers had fought with Lakota and Cheyenne warriors, bending the long grass and mustering spirits, whistling around the white markers of the fallen. When the breeze struck Shelly on Last Stand Hill it carried cries and screams, prayers and futile orders, war-whoops of victory and the odors of fear, sweat and blood. Shelly closed her eyes, inhaled, and let the spirits fill her lungs.

"I'm gonna walk down that path we saw over yonder," she said.

"It's gittin' late, Shelly, maybe we oughta go."

"Deke, we ain't very far from towns with motels and we might never get back here. Don't ya find this place fascinating ... and haunting?"

Without waiting for an answer, Shelly began walking to the path that led down Deep Ravine Trail and Deke had no choice but to follow.

They came to the first of the 28 markers for the men of Company E, and Shelly left the path to walk among the white marble stones that stated only a simple fact: *U.S. Soldier; 7th Cavalry; Fell Here; June 25, 1876.*

"This place goes right through me," Shelly said, kneeling down and putting her hand on a marker. "I can see the battle, hear it, and even smell it, like it was happinin' right now. The difference is how hot it was then, real hot, an' ev'rybody was miserable an' thirsty, even the Indians. It's all right in front a' me, the yellin' and shootin', men screamin' in pain, the cavalrymen scared outa their wits and the Indians all excited ta be winnin' for once." She gazed across the battlefield. "It woulda' really been somethin' bein' here on that day, even if ya did get killed."

"Are you alright, Shelly?" Deke asked.

Shelly didn't answer. She stood up and walked on to where another set of markers clustered together. "I swear I can see 'em, the cavalrymen fightin' for their lives an' tryin' ta hide in the brush. I see the Indians too. Shootin' arrows up in the air ta fall on the soldiers, an' the Indians with guns firin' anytime they see somebody wearin' blue."

A quick gust of wind blew Shelly's hair off her shoulders.

"I even see, or more like, feel, the Indians sneakin' up, hidin' and crawlin' in that long grass, tryin' not ta be seen or get shot, an' the soldiers knowin' all the time they're gittin' closer." Shelly brushed the hair away from her eyes. "Jes bein' here, I can tell it wasn't like in any of the movies."

Shelly turned on her heels and looked around, taking in the ravine where the Gray Horse Troop had been slaughtered. "An' then after the battle, I see the soldiers layin' here all cut ta pieces an' bloody, swole'd up an' black till the Army come along an' buried 'em. Can't ya see 'em, Deke?"

"No. An' I don't want to."

"I ain't particularly superstitious," Shelly said, "but I don't know as I'd wanta be out here at night."

"Not fer all the money in the world," Deke said. "Especially by m'self."

A ranger came part way down the trail and called to them that the battlefield was closing.

"Wonder why there ain't any memorials to the Indians here," Shelly said as they were walking back up the path. "Shor'ly a bunch a' them got killed too, an' after all, they did win the fight. Most ev'rywhere's else it's the winners who put up memorials."

Deke shrugged. "I don't know as Indians build memorials, do they?"

Passing Last Stand Hill again on their way to the parking lot, Shelly stopped and turned toward the slope, then gasped.

"What is it?" Deke asked.

Shelly had to catch her breath before she could answer. "I jes saw them cavalrymen havin' to shoot their own horses ta hide behind, an' how hard that was for 'em." She continued staring until Deke touched her arm and said, "We need ta go, the ranger said they're closin'."

They walked silently to Deke's truck. Shelly got in and remained quiet as they drove down the grade leading back to the highway. When they turned onto Route 212, the strange feeling that Shelly first felt at Last Stand Hill left her, as suddenly as it had entered, like it had to remain at the battlefield.

Chapter 30

Deke wanted to put the Ford on I-90 and highball it to the nearest motel off the reservation, but Shelly saw a frontage road just before the interchange and told Deke to take it.

"It might be a dead-end," Deke said.

'Then we'll turn aroun'. I still wanta meet some Indians," Shelly said, "an' besides, I'm hungry."

Three minutes later they came to another I-90 interchange at Crow Agency. "I'm hungry, too," Deke said. "Let's go to the next town and eat."

"We're in a town right now. Let's look for a rest'ernt."

Shelly directed Deke up and down Crow Agency's dirt streets. On every block were run-down houses, piles of junk and derelict vehicles. "I thought we had it bad at home," Shelly said, "but this is even worse."

Despite the poverty, the streets were full of rambunctious children playing and adults talking and laughing. No one gave Deke and Shelly angry looks like in Lame Deer. Just as Deke was saying, "I don't think they got 'em a rest'runt here," they passed one. Deke continued driving, pretending he hadn't seen it.

"Turn around," Shelly said. "I wanta eat there."

Deke looked peeved but did a U-ey and they pulled into the gravel parking lot of a small café called the Crow's Nest. The old wooden building needed paint, but was not unappealing. A sign advertised 'Native Food'.

"I don't think it's open," Deke said, and put the Ford in reverse.

"Yeah it is. See, there's a little sign on the door that says, 'Open'. An' there's a car in the parkin' lot."

Reluctantly Deke shut off the engine and he and Shelly got out. "Make sure yer door's locked," Deke said as he opened the hood to disconnect the battery cables. He dropped the hood. "I'm gonna tie that spare down, too."

"Oh, for the love a' ..." Shelly said, grabbing Deke's elbow and pulling him toward the front door. "Deke, we been through that. We can see the truck from out the window an' nobody'd steal that old tire anyway. Let's go eat."

They couldn't help but notice the other vehicle in the parking lot. "It's a '55 Eldorado," Deke said.

"How can ya tell?"

"Them shark tailfins. Most Eldorados were convertibles, but this one's a hardtop."

It must have been, because the crumpled roof showed that the car had been rolled yet was stalwart enough to remain intact. The two-door Cadillac's original color was yellow but both doors and three fenders were of different colors and other spots on the car had been brush-coated with paint to cover scrapes and rust. Technically, the vehicle still had both headlights but one of them pointed straight down, hanging loose from its socket, secured only by wires. The front grill, with its chrome titties, was miraculously intact but all along the rest of the vehicle a bevy of scratches and dents testified to its turbulent history. The better part of a dozen tires, all on rims, nestled catty-wampus inside the raised trunk, which was secured with bailing twine, and where the back bumper should have been, a personalized license plate was fastened on with wire. It took Shelly a second to figure it out: REZRUNR.

"This car would be a good mate for your truck, Deke," Shelly said, "but I ain't shor what the offspring would look like."

She opened the restaurant door and nearly collided with a short, stocky older man. "Oh, I was coming to turn the 'Open' sign around," he told her.

Deke jumped in. "That's alright, we can go on to the next town."

"No," the man said. "I was in back and didn't see you drive up. You come in. The grill and fryer are still hot." He put one thick, brown arm around Shelly's shoulders and the other around Deke's and with a limp, led them to a booth.

The only other customers in the Crow's Nest were four young tribal men with long, raven hair. Two of them, in their mid-twenties, sat in a booth across the café from Deke and Shelly, while the two younger ones, in their late teens, ran around the restaurant laughing and tussling with each other. Once they knocked over a couple of chairs but the manager wasn't bothered by their horseplay. In fact, he poked and prodded them several times and put one youth in a friendly headlock. After going into the back, he brought Deke and Shelly tall glasses of icewater and pointed to a large sign on the opposite wall.

"There's our menu," he said. "It isn't fancy, hey, but everything is good and if you don't like the food, you can send it back."

"Does that mean if we don't like it we don't have ta pay?" Deke asked.

"No," he said, "you still have to pay, but you can send it back. My chickens will eat it." Then he laughed.

Deke and Shelly looked up at the menu.

"Are your buffalo burgers made from real buffaloes?" Shelly asked.

"Yes," the man said, "and our hot dogs are made from real dogs."

Shelly was pretty sure he was joking, but ordered two buffalo burgers. Deke wasn't taking any chances either and went for the Indian tacos. As Deke and Shelly ate, the two men at the booth looked over at Deke several times and fixed him with hard stares. When the man who ran the restaurant walked by them, the heavy shoulder'd one said something to him and looked directly at Deke. The manager looked over at Deke, shrugged and went into the kitchen. The two younger Crows running around the café also frowned at Deke.

"I don't like the way they keep lookin' at me," Deke whispered to Shelly.

"They do seem ta be givin' ya the evil eye," Shelly agreed.

Deke ate as fast as he could, but Shelly was unconcerned and asked for a second Coke. As she was finishing up, the four men paid for their food and left. Deke felt relieved, but when they didn't get into the Eldorado and started running around the parking lot, scuffling and laughing, he had the disconcerting feeling they might be waiting for him to come outside.

The manager turned the lights off in the kitchen, then came out and sat down by Deke and Shelly, pulling a chair around to face them.

"I'm Lawrence Iron Bull, the owner," he said, and stuck out his hand to Shelly and then to Deke. Shelly was surprised at how gentle his handshake was.

"I noticed your accents," Lawrence said, after Shelly and Deke had introduced themselves. "Are you from the South?"

"Not the real South," Shelly told him. "We're from Appalachia. I'm from Wes' Virginia an' Deke's from Tennessee."

Lawrence Iron Bull nodded his head. "Ah," he said.

"We're hillbillies," Shelly added, by way of further clarification.

Lawrence and Shelly both laughed but Deke remained straight-faced.

"Somebody told me a long time ago – many moons ago -," Lawrence chuckled when he said it, "that Indians and hillbillies are a lot alike."

"Really!" Shelly said.

Lawrence laughed again. "Well, what I think he said was that Indians were the hillbillies of the West."

"I'm not shor I know what that means," Shelly told him.

"Me neither," Lawrence said, still laughing. "I was hoping you could explain it to me."

Deke looked nervously out the window at the four Indians horsing around outside. They were running around his truck as well as the Cadillac.

Lawrence nodded in their direction. "Good kids," he said. "Two of them are my cousins and the oldest one, Melvin Not Afraid, is my nephew on my wife's side." He paused and watched them for a minute. "It's tough for them. Over half the men on the rez don't have jobs; there are no jobs. For many the only way to make a living is to leave, hey, but here is where their families are."

"It ain't quite as bad now where I'm from," Shelly said, "but there's been times when it got like that. My daddy had a job but other miners lost theirs."

Lawence nodded. "When our people leave the reservation, they not only leave their friends and families, they leave their culture. They have to learn new ways that they don't understand and many non-native people don't like Indians."

"I didn't know that," Shelly said. "Where I'm from people think Indians are somethin' special and wanta meet 'em. I've always wanted to."

"Not so much in the West," Lawrence said, "especially near the rez."

The roar of a mufflerless V-8 engine started up outside and the Cadillac backed out of the parking lot. Lawrence followed the car with his eyes. "Melvin told me they lost the muffler coming into town today. The only original parts left on that car are the frame and one fender."

Deke also watched the car leave, and openly breathed a sigh of relief.

"You are happy to see them go," Lawrence said to Deke.

"I don't think they liked me," Deke told him.

"What do you expect, hey?" Lawrence said, and for the first time there was no trace of humor in his voice.

"I didn't do nothin' ta git them riled up."

Lawrence nodded at Deke's t-shirt. "You came in here ... onto the reservation, wearing a shirt with Custer's picture on it."

"HUH?" Deke said. "This ain't Custer! It's Wild Bill Hickock."

Lawrence leaned over and looked at Deke's shirt. "Oh," he said, "you're right, it is Hickcock. From across the room he looks like Custer."

"That's pro'bly why that guy in Lame Deer got mad at ya," Shelly said.

"You wore that shirt in Lame Deer?" Lawrence said. "I'm surprised you still have your hair."

Now that the crew in the Eldorado was gone, Deke was anxious to leave. "It's late, Shelly, can we git goin'?"

"It ain't that late, Deke. I wanta talk ta Lawrence some more." She turned to Lawrence. "Would it be okay if I asked ya some questions? I don't really know much about Indians but I've always wanted to." What Shelly really wanted to tell Lawrence was that she'd found out she was part Indian, but she didn't want to say anything in front of Deke.

"Sure," Lawrence Iron Bull said. "Most of us want non-tribal people to understand what our ways are like." He turned to Deke. "Just like you, Deke McConahay, Crow men like to wear their hair long."

"How come yer hair's short?" Deke said.

"I wore my hair longer than yours when I was young," Lawrence said, "it almost covered my ass, hey. But when I started working here the tribal health inspector, who's so old she inspected Custer's latrine, gave me so much trouble over my long hair that I cut it."

The mention of Custer reminded Shelly of something. "Up at the battlefield, they told us the Crow scouted for Custer an' was on his side. How come your tribe liked Custer?"

"It's true," Lawrence said, "that some of our people scouted for the cavalry and died with Custer, but we didn't like him. We just liked the Cheyenne and the Lakota less. We also fought with General Crook and the Shoshone at the Battle of Rosebud Creek against the Lakota and Cheyenne. That fight was just a few days before the Greasy Grass. At the Rosebud our great chief, Plenty Coups, who we call by a different name, went up against the Lakota Chief Crazy Horse."

"How come ya sided with the Whites?" Shelly asked. "Didn't ya know they was after your land?"

"We knew it," Lawrence said. "Plenty Coups had a dream when he was young that the Crow would be better off not to fight against the Whites. When our old enemies, the Northern Cheyenne and the Lakota came here in 1876, they were invading our land. To us the Army was helping the Crow drive them out."

"Sounds like it's more complicated than the movies make it out ta be," Shelly said.

"Plenty Coups, Alaxchiiaahush in our language, was our greatest chief. He lived to be very old and set our tribe on the best path he could when our world was changing. That's why our reservation is so much bigger than the Northern Cheyenne's. Plenty Coups also said that education is the most important thing to our success, but it is still hard for many of us to learn that." Lawrence shook his head. "I know it was hard for me. I never liked school. Being indoors and sitting still all day does not fit with being Indian."

Deke and Shelly both nodded a big 'yes' to that. "It don't sit well with us mountain folk, neither," Shelly said.

"Maybe Indians and hillbillies are alike," Lawrence said, and laughed.

Lawrence's easy manner made Shelly feel comfortable talking to him and she asked, "Are you called Crows 'cause of your black hair?"

"Oh, no, we're not Crows to ourselves, we are Apsaalooke, the Children of the Large Beaked Bird. The Whites, who like to give other people funny names, turned us into Crows. They did it to other tribes too, like the Gros Ventre. That means Big Belly. Just look at the name

Indian. I've been around Indians all my life and I've never met one who's even been to India."

"Reckon I never thought about that," Shelly said.

"Were you up to the Greasy Grass Battlefield?" Lawrence asked.

"We jes came from there," Shelly answered, "but till they told us that name, I'd always heard it called Custer's Last Stand."

Deke lit a cigarette. "Me too. How come y'all call it the Greasy Grass?"

Lawrence's face lost its smile. "That's how the Lakota and the Cheyenne beat us," he said. "The night before the battle, knowing Custer would attack there, they went up to that spot and rubbed buffalo fat all over the grass so the cavalry's horses would fall down. When that happened the Lakota and Cheyenne warriors moved in and slaughtered all the blue coats and our Crow scouts. It was a dirty trick and even today is hard for us Crow to talk about."

Deke's eyes got big. "Shitfire, they didn't tell us nothin' about that up at the battlefield. I never seen it in the movies, neither."

Shelly laughed so hard her sides hurt. "Deke, Lawrence is joshin' ya."

"Oh."

Lawrence's laugh filled the café. He slapped his knee and reached over and slapped Deke on the knee as well. "We call it the Battle of the Greasy Grass because that is our name for the Little Bighorn River," he said, and then asked, "What did you think of the battlefield?"

"I don't rightly know how ta describe it," Shelly said, "but somethin' strange happened to me up there. It was like I was in the middle of the battle."

"You are not alone in feeling that," Lawrence said, locking eyes with Shelly. "It is common among us tribal people, but sometimes happens to Whites."

"Does anybody ever go up there at night?" Shelly asked.

Lawrence hesitated. "Yes," he finally said. "It is against their rules, but there are those who go to that place at night. I have been there myself."

"You wouldn't ketch me up there fer nothin' in the dark," Deke said. Lawrence kept his eyes on Shelly. "Sometimes we Indians go there on vision quests. That is why I went."

Shelly had never heard the term. "What's a vision quest?"

"We seek our own vision, maybe a spirit guide or our own spirit animal. For me, it was to find my true path." He looked out the side window in the direction of the battlefield. "That is sacred ground. It is different for Whites than for Indians, and different for the Crow than for the Lakota or the Northern Cheyenne, but still a place of much power, big medicine, as we say. You have to be careful up there at night alone. This land is filled with spirits."

"Did ya find your true path?" Shelly asked.

"Better to say it found me. Until I was thirty-five I was a drunk, in and out of every jail from Miles City to Sheridan. I wrecked a dozen cars, not all of them mine. After one bad wreck, I almost ended up a cripple, hey. That's why I limp. Most of my friends were drunks too, and my relatives were worried. They'd seen too many young Crow go down this same path. My aunt, Lucille Iron Bull, made me come and work in her restaurant, this one." Lawrence waved his arm, indicating the Crow's Nest. "But I kept going out and getting drunk, not showing up for work. It was very hard on my aunt, but she wouldn't give up on me.

"My father, Joe Iron Bull, who I did not get along with, came to me one day and said, 'My sister is trying to help you but you are killing her. It is time for you to stop being a fool and become a man.' We had fought many times, even with our fists, but his words hit me very hard. I had heard people talk of the battlefield as a place for visions since I was a child, so that night I went up there. For three nights, I ate nothing and only drank water from the Greasy Grass. In the daytime I hid in the bushes near the river. I will not tell you about those nights or my vision, but when I came back I was different."

Shelly sat rapt, and except for the ceiling fan turning in lazy circles and the buzz of two fat, late summer flies, all else was still.

"When I returned, I learned that Lucille Iron Bull had cancer and was dying. My father knew, but he should not have blamed me. After that I tried to become a good worker and not be wild or get drunk, but sometimes I would fail. My old friends would come around and take me with them and I would stay drunk for days and not come to work. I could see my aunt's life going out of her until she could no longer work. One day I went to see her and she said to me from her bed, 'Lawrence, I am dying soon, but if you don't stop drinking and change your life, you will die soon also. That's why I am giving you the Crow's Nest. Now you have no excuse.' One week later she died and when the wake and the funeral were over I went to that place again, this time for four days and nights. On the fourth night I made a vow that I would never drink again and that I would be a real Crow man and help my people."

"And you have, Lawrence," Shelly said, softly.

"Yes," he said. "Sometimes I think I could do better, but at least I have never taken a drink or hurt anyone since then. I married a good woman, too. She works at the library here in Crow Agency."

Shadows were now creeping in from outside and filling the café. Shelly hesitated to break the spell, but she asked, "Lawrence, can folks other'n Indians go on vision quests and find their true path?"

He thought about the question. "I don't know for sure, but I would think so. But they should not try to do it like an Indian because they are not Indian."

"How would they do it?"

"That is not for me to say, Shelly, but I think they would have to know their own heart and follow that."

Shelly nodded, trying to understand.

"Sometimes White people, especially hippies, come around here looking for medicine men and shamans. They call themselves by Indian sounding names and try to act like Indians. Others tell us they are Indians because they have some tribal blood in them, but they are not Indians because they were not raised Indian. We are usually nice to them but we really want to say, 'Go find your own way, you are not us.' I don't think you are like that, Shelly. You have come to the West for something else."

"Maybe us hillbillies ain't as much like Indians as we were sayin', Lawrence," Shelly said. "We don't have nothin' like vision quests or spirit guides. We got Jesus an' God an' the Bible an' I b'lieve in it an' pray sometimes, but religion's never really come over me the way it has some people. I've seen folks hoppin' up an' down an' rollin' on the floor, an' shoutin' out words ya can't understand. That's never happened ta me an' I don't think it ever will."

"Not all tribal people are strong in the spirit world either," Lawence said, "but we are more connected to spirits and to our ancestors than most people are because we have not become separated from our culture. Your tribal culture is so far in the past that it has been forgotten and even if you knew of it, you could not become part of that world again because that way is gone."

"Sounds like us White folks don't have much of a chance ta connect with our spiritual past," Shelly said, "or with the earth an' animals like Indians do."

"I don't think that's true, Shelly, and I didn't mean to make my words sound like that. The spirit of the earth is in every human being. You can learn things from other cultures but you have to find your own way into the spirit world and each one of us has the ability to do that." Lawrence's face wrinkled into a grin. "Indians and hillbillies."

Shelly smiled back. "Sounds like there's hope for me too, Lawrence."

"There's as much hope for you as any Indian I know, Shelly. Don't put too much faith in my words, though," Lawrenced said, still smiling. "I am not a shaman, hey, or a wise chief like Plenty Coups. I am just someone who used to be a drunk and now owns a restaurant my aunt left me."

"There's nothin' says a rest'ernt owner can't be wise," Shelly said, "an' you were wise enough to quit drinkin'.'"

Deke saw an opening. "Uh, Shelly, shouldn't we be leavin'?"

"I 'spose so, Deke, but it ain't that late. I was still hopin' to see some country aroun' here instead a' gittin on that ugly four-lane."

"There are motels in Hardin," Lawrence said, "only a few miles away."

"That sounds real good, don't it Shelly?" Deke said, grinning.

Shelly didn't answer but Lawrence said, "If you want to see some nice country there's a back road to Hardin. It's not very long and part of it takes you along the Bighorn River."

The smile left Deke's face. "Oh, we ain't got time fer that," he said but Shelly countered, "That sounds great, Lawrence. Where is it?"

"It's only a couple of blocks from here," Lawrence said, and pointed. "Go back to where the frontage road connects with the interstate and take the road that goes beneath the overpass and across the railroad tracks. There's a sign that says, 'Two Leggins'. After about ten miles of gravel road and empty country you come to road 313. Turn right and that takes you into Hardin, eight or nine miles away."

"I don't wanna go on any back roads," Deke said.

"How come? Lawence said we'll git ta see some nice country."

"You r'member that town a ways back where nobody was friendly an' that big In'jun come up to the truck an' yelled at me an' grabbed the door handle?"

"Was that the one you told me about in Lame Deer?" Lawrence asked.

"Yep," Shelly answered. "Near ev'rybody there looked at us real hard."

"That would be the Cheyenne," Lawrence said. "Even though they used to be our enemies, I feel bad for them. The Northern Cheyenne were treated very harshly by the Whites. That's why some of them still have trouble liking White people and who can blame them."

"It gave me the creeps," Deke said.

"I understand why it would," Lawrence told Deke. "And, yes, you would want to be careful on that reservation. We Crow are a little friendlier to Whites. You shouldn't have any trouble here unless you go looking for it. And if your medicine is strong, you might find something special along that road tonight."

With those words Lawrence stood up. After Deke and Shelly had paid, he said, "Good luck in timber country. You will have many adventures and stories."

Deke and Shelly left the restaurant and drove two blocks back to the I-90 interchange and the road Lawrence had told them about. At the corner sat a gas station and auto repair shop. Off to the side was a gigantic conical mound of tires. The beat-up Eldorado was parked at a gas pump and the four young Crows were standing near it, talking with a tall, serious looking man with long gray braids and the face of a hawk. Deke couldn't help but notice he wore a knife on his belt that came halfway down to his knee. Deke turned west, but instead of going under the I-90 overpass he turned onto the northbound ramp of the interstate.

"Oh no you don't, Deke McConahay!" Shelly said. "The road Lawrence told us about goes *underneath* I-90 and I'm takin' it even if I hafta walk it."

This wasn't the first time Shelly had made that threat and Deke decided to find out how serious she was about it so he continued on.

"Stop the truck, I'm gittin' out," Shelly said, and opened her door.

Deke hit the brake. "Shelly, how come we can't go straight ta town, git a motel an' have us a quiet night like the normal people yer always talkin' about?"

"We can do all that Deke. As soon as we drive that road Lawrence said we oughta take."

Deke stared straight ahead, pouting and silent.

"Lookie here," Shelly said, holding the atlas out to him. "This road is on the map. It ain't very far outa the way an' it looks like it goes through some perty country along the Big Horn River. Lawrence said we wouldn't have one lick a' trouble on it an' might even run inta somethin' special." Deke looked at the map as Shelly pointed with her finger. "See Deke, it ain't far ta Hardin a'tall. We got some light left in the sky an' the makin's of a beautiful evening."

Deke looked dubious.

"It'll be fine, Deke," Shelly said and smiled. "An' I'll make it up to ya when we git to the motel."

That did it. Deke made a u-turn and drove back down the ramp in the wrong direction. He stopped at the road to look for oncoming traffic and glanced over at the service station on the corner. All five Crow men had stopped talking and were watching him with flinty-eyed stares as he turned onto the back road.

Chapter 31

Purple evening was settling over the Crow Reservation as Deke and Shelly drove toward the remains of a sunset. The sky overhead was swiftly darkening but a band of yellow light hung on the horizon, dimly illuminating the surrounding countryside, which changed dramatically just outside of Crow Agency. Gone was the rolling grassland, replaced by a desolate plain of barren soil and jagged rock outcroppings. Patches of brush and sage mingled with sparse clumps of prairie grass in the lusterless landscape and sheer, perilous ravines gouged the earth. Gusts of wind blew in like visiting ghosts, rattling the sage and making the prairie grass dance and wave. No posting was needed that this was rattlesnake country.

Deke and Shelly saw no structures or sign of human habitation. Early autumn had dried the entire land to dull sienna, which now took on the grayness of twilight, creating a scene of somber, unforgiving harshness. Shelly thought the rugged landscape was beautiful. "I think these are called badlands. I've always wanted ta see some."

"They give me the willies," Deke said.

He was still unsettled by the Indians at the gas station and every few seconds glanced in the side mirror to see if the Cadillac was following. Even if it had been, Deke would not have seen it, for he clipped over the gravel so fast that nothing showed in his mirror but a cloud of dust.

"Is somethin' botherin' you, Deke?" Shelly asked. "Yor drivin' like a bat outa hell and watchin' that mirror like the Devil's on your tail."

"I jest wanna git to a motel, that's all."

"Well, I'd like ta see this country if ya don't mind."

"Go ahead an' look at it, I ain't stoppin' ya."

"I can't see much the way we're bouncin' around. How come you wanta get through here so fast, anyway? Ain'tcha happy ta finally be in the West?"

"What's that got ta do with it? You know I like drivin' fast."

"This is real cowboy an' Indian country, Deke, an' I figger'd you'd wanta take your time seein' it. You told me how you think a' yor'self as a cowboy like John Wayne an' how you wanted to be in the Wild West where you could prove yor'self an' measure up. Well, this shor looks like the Wild West ta me."

"I am a cowboy, Shelly, an' I do wanna prove myself to ya," Deke said. "You ain't got ta see what kinda man I am when the chips are down. If trouble comes along, I'll take care of things jest like John Wayne would, but right now I wanna git to a motel."

"I don't remember ever seein' John Wayne ridin' like a maniac ta git to a motel," Shelly said.

Deke was about to say something when Shelly pointed ahead. "Deke, you need ta watch the road ... an' slow down."

Coming down a long grade they'd picked up even more speed then shot between the guardrails of a narrow bridge that spanned a sheer-walled gully. Ahead, the road cut through a ledge of jagged rock thirty feet high on the right and was crowded on the left by a boulder the size of a double-decker bus that concealed a sharp right turn.

"OH, SHIT!" Deke yelled.

He was driver enough not to hit the brakes, knowing the Ford would plaster itself against the boulder. Swinging left to flatten the curve, Deke hoped to lateral drift the turn as he slid sideways into the blind corner. In a flurry of dust he goosed the accelerator at the apex and had it made ... until he saw a muffler with four feet of tail pipe still attached lying in the road.

With a loud THWACK! the right rear tire struck the jagged metal. Shelly looked in her side mirror and caught a quick glimpse of the muffler and the tailpipe, now separated, bouncing behind them. Half a mile down the road, she and Deke heard FLOP-FLOP-FLOP-FLOP and the Ford began listing.

Swearing, Deke let off the gas and coasted until he found a level turnoff. "Shitfire! What dumbass left his muffler in the road!"

"Take it easy, Deke," Shelly said. "It ain't the end a' the world. It won't take us long ta change the tire."

"It was them In'juns," Deke said.

"What Indians?"

"Them ones in the Eldorado. Don't ya remember? That guy in the rest'runt told us they lost their muffler comin' inta town."

"It coulda been anybody's, Deke. C'mon, let's git this tire changed."

Seeing the carnage only increased Deke's anger. The tire was shredded and halfway off the rim. "Damn it all ta hell, the whole tar'r's ruint," he raged. "An' we jest bought these in Wes' Virginia."

"That's cause you drove on it after it went flat," Shelly said, "but since I'm the one who wanted ta take this road, I'll buy ya another one."

"A new one?"

"Yeah, Deke, a new one. Soon as we find a tire shop. Where's your jack?"

"It's behind the seat, but let me loosen the lug nuts first."

Deke placed a wooden block in front of each front tire then grabbed the tire tool and cranked the lug nuts a turn as Shelly got the jack. She found the butt end of a 2x12 in the bed and set it under the handyman jack's base plate. "Good thing the flat ain't in the front," she told Deke. "There wouldn't be any bumper ta put the jack on."

Deke did not smile. "You gonna buy me a new bumper, too?"

"We'll talk about fixin' your bumper when we git ta Troy."

Shelly worked the jack slowly, keeping her face away from the handle and watching for sway that could kick it out.

"Ya want me ta do that?" Deke said. "Them jacks can be dangerous."

"I got it, Deke. Daddy taught me all about this kinda stuff."

As the tire cleared the gravel the pickup tilted forward at a steep angle. Shelly saw two 6x8 blocks in the bed and stacked them under the differential as a fail-safe in case the jack fell.

"Good idea," Deke told her, as he knelt in the dust twirling the spanner to remove the lug nuts. He wriggled the tire off and looked at it. "The rim's all bent up, too. Good thing we stopped when we did or it mighta tore up the hub an' brake drum. Damn In'juns."

"Let's git that spare on, it's almost dark," Shelly said. "You stay there an' I'll grab the tire." A minute later she asked, "What part a' the bed's it in?"

"Right on top, where it's always been," Deke called up to her.

"Not any more, Deke. It musta got covered up."

"I never covered it up," Deke said. "Did you?"

"Why would I do that?"

"Maybe you jest can't see it 'cause it's gittin' dark."

"It ain't too dark for me ta see a tire."

"I'll show ya where it's at then," Deke said, getting up.

"You do that," Shelly answered.

Deke climbed into the bed and dug through the clutter, tossing aside junk he hadn't seen for years. After five frantic minutes Deke sat down on the wooden trunk, his shoulders sagging in defeat.

"It musta bounced out," Shelly said, "'cause a' the way you were drivin'."

Deke jumped down from the truck bed. "It didn't bounce out. Them goddam In'juns stole't my tar'r."

"You don't know that," Shelly said.

"I know that spare was in the bed when we stopped ta eat 'cause I was gonna tie it down an' you wouldn't let me." Deke looked at Shelly accusingly. "Then when we was inside, them In'juns was runnin' around my truck an' whoopin' it up – you saw 'em."

"I saw 'em havin' fun," Shelly said, "but I never saw 'em take your tire."

"In'juns are real sneaky about things like that," Deke said. "They git taught how ta do it from the time they're little."

"Taught what, stealin' old spare tires?"

"Stealin' anything," Deke said. "All I know is that when we come out I didn't see my spare tar'r ... did you?"

"No, but I wasn't lookin' for it, neither," Shelly said. "I got more important things on my mind than spare tires."

"Well, that spare tar'r's purty damn important now, ain't it?" Deke said. "Didya see all the tar'rs them In'juns had in their trunk? I bet that's what they do, drive around an' steal spare tar'rs for beer money. First the jungle bunnies steal my batt'ry an' then In'juns steal my spare. Shelly, I don't deserve bein' treated like this an' if I catch 'em there's gonna be hell ta pay."

"Deke, I bet if you walked back on this road a little ways, you'd find your tire layin' right where it bounced out."

"Damn it, my tar'r didn't bounce out! I'd a' seen it in the mirror if it had," Deke said, raising his voice. "Plus, in a few minutes it'll be too dark ta see anything."

"You was kickin' up too much dust ta see it in the mirror," Shelly said, "an' the fact that's it's gonna be dark in a few minutes is *why* you need ta walk back right now an' start lookin'."

"Goddamit, I could walk the whole way back ta Crow Agency an' I wouldn't find my tar'r, *'cause it didn't bounce out!*"

Shelly was quiet for a moment. "Well," she finally said, "if ya did walk back ta Crow Agency, that fillin' station we passed had a big mound a' tires. You know they'd have one for your truck."

"That place'd be closed by now," Deke said.

"There was a little house right behind the station, Deke," Shelly said. "I betcha anything the owner lives there. Jes go knock on the door an' tell 'im ya need a tire. He's pro'bly a real friendly guy."

Deke remembered how the hawk-faced Indian with the huge knife had glared at him.

"Shelly, I can't go all the way ta Crow Agency an' lug a tar'r back here ... even if somebody was there, which ain't likely."

"You got a better idea Deke? Like jes settin' here all night ... an' maybe ta'morrow? We ain't seen another car on this road yet."

Deke didn't answer.

"It ain't all that far, Deke," Shelly said, "only a couple a' miles. You'd be back here in an' hour."

"A coupla miles? It's way more'n that!"

"Not much. An' heck, Deke, you might find your tire layin' some-where's along the way. It might only be a few hund'ert yards from here." Shelly looked at Deke and smiled. "Then we could slap 'er on an' git to a motel."

"How come I gotta be the one ta go?" Deke said.

"Cause it's your truck an' your tire."

"Maybe we could both go."

"An' leave all our stuff out here with nobody ta watch it? You really wanta do that, Deke?"

"No," Deke said, "I reckon not." He thought for a second. "Maybe we could flip a coin ta see who goes."

"Now that's right gentlemanly of ya, Deke," Shelly told him. "I'm shor that's jes what John Wayne would do. Flip a coin ta see whether he goes off in the desert at night ta git help or sends his lady ta do it."

"I didn't mean it like …"

"Deke, you been tellin' me for how long now that you wanta prove up an' show me what kinda man you are when the chips are down? Well, I'd have ta say, lookin' at our situation, the chips are down, wouldn't you?"

"Yeah, I reckon you could say that … but …"

"If yor scared, Deke, jes say so an' I'll do it. All you need ta do is tell me yor too scared ta go." Shelly waited as Deke's tongue flicked in and out of his mouth, moistening his lips. Finally she said, "Alright, Deke, I'll go. Let me grab my jacket an' canteen." She hopped into the bed. "Gimme the key to the trunk."

Deke handed her up the key and watched as she pulled out her jacket and canteen. "I ain't scare't … jest cautious, that's all," he said.

"Whatcha sayin', Deke, that yor *too cautious* ta go?"

Deke hesitated. "That's not what I'm tellin' ya," he said.

"Then what *are* ya tellin' me?"

Deke's hands were trembling as Shelly waited for an answer. "I'm tellin' ya I'll go," he finally said.

"Are ya shor?"

"I'm … sure," Deke said slowly.

Shelly looked down at Deke. "Alright. You'll wanta take some water."

She jumped from the truck bed as Deke got back in and took an Army web belt with a canteen and a hunting knife from his duffel bag. He filled the canteen from their water jug then pulled the knife from its sheath and looked at it. "It's a little rusty and could use a sharpenin', but she'll do."

"Ya oughta take a jacket," Shelly said.

"Naw, I'll jest put a flannel shirt on," Deke told her, digging one from his bag. "It ain't gonna git that cold." After putting on the shirt Deke reached into the bag again and held up his Winchester.

"I wouldn't take that, Deke," Shelly said. "It might git ya inta trouble."

"It might git me outa trouble, too."

"I still don't think ya oughta take it."

"You keep tellin' me ta act like John Wayne," Deke said, "an' John Wayne wouldn't go off without his rifle in In'jun country."

He poked a hand into his bag again and produced a box of ammunition. "I only got twelve cartridges," Deke said as he loaded the tube of his .30-30 and stuffed the rest in his front pants pocket. "I hope I don't git surrounded like Custer did."

Shelly shook her head. "Deke, when are you gonna understand that this ain't a hund'ert years ago?"

"I know that, but there's still no tellin' what might happen out there," Deke said, waving the rifle barrel over the desert. "Leastwise I know enough about In'juns ta save the last bullet for myself."

"Oh, for the love a' ..." Shelly muttered. "I hope you ain't that crazy, Deke. If you do run inta any Indians ta'night, they ain't gonna fill ya full a' arrows an' scalp ya, they'll pro'bly give ya a ride an' help ya find a tire."

"I ain't gittin in no car with a bunch a' In'juns," Deke said, "an' you better not either." He reached down into his duffel bag and came up with the double barrel 10 gauge. "I'm leavin' this with you."

"I don't need it," Shelly said.

"I hope ya don't, but I'm givin' it to ya anyway." Deke pulled a pouch from the bag and hefted it. "I only got a few 10 gauge shells, but they're mighty potent." He broke the gun open, took two shotgun shells from the pouch and inserted them into the twin barrels. "These are three-an' a half inch magnum, double ought buck," Deke said. "The most powerful you can buy." He handed the shotgun down to Shelly. "You know how ta use a hammer gun?"

"We had a 20 gauge double that I hunted with," Shelly said as she took the massive weapon in her hands. "Holy cow, this thing's big as an elephant gun."

"It's too bad you can't see the Damascus barrels. They're real purty."

"An' ya say your gran' daddy killed somebody with this?" Shelly asked.

"My great grand daddy shot a Jenkins with it," Deke said. "Gave 'im both barrels. Folks that saw Jenkins afterwards said he was near blow'd in half."

"Did your great gran' daddy go ta jail over it?"

"They never even arrested 'im," Deke said. "Jenkins had a pistol on an' they was feudin', so ever'body said it was a fair fight."

Deke strapped on his web belt, picked up the Winchester and jumped to the ground. Now that he'd committed himself and was armed with the rifle, a measure of courage came to Deke. "Reckon I better git movin'," he said, looking over the dark landscape. "The light's nearly gone."

Only the dark outline of the surrounding hills and the peaks to the west were still visible. A star spackled sky winked overhead, but no moon had risen. Deke looked at Shelly to say goodbye.

"Yor actin' like a real cowboy, Deke," she said, her face close to his. "I'm proud a' ya an' when we git to the motel, I'll show ya how grateful I am."

Deke tingled with sexual excitement. Any fears he had of going alone into the desert night were gone. Here was his chance to measure up and finally prove to Shelly what kind of man he really was. "I won't come back without a tar'r, Shelly," Deke said, "an' that's a promise." He tipped the brim of his hat. "An' a good tar'r, too, a damn good tar'r. Ya got my word on it as a cowboy."

"Hang on," Shelly said. "I almost fer'got." She opened the truck door, leaned the shotgun against the seat and in the dome light undid her purse and pulled out a bill. "Here's ten dollars," she said, stuffing the bill into Deke's shirt pocket. "They better not try'n charge ya more'n that for a used tire." She leaned over and kissed him.

Deke pulled her to him, pressing their bodies together. When he began groping her butt and getting aroused, Shelly broke off the kiss. "Better head out, Deke," she told him, "the sooner yor back the sooner we can git to a motel."

Calm now and confident, Deke strode into the darkness. After seventy or eighty paces he stopped and turned around. Shelly's form and the outline of his pickup had been absorbed by the night, but Deke called out, "Take care, Shelly, I'll see ya later."

From the blackness Shelly's clear voice came back to him. "You take care too, Deke ... an' don't step on no rattlesnakes."

Deke's bowels turned to water.

Chapter 32

Until Shelly's warning, Deke had intended to walk as fast as he could, but now he stood trembling, too fearful to move. The way ahead was so dark he could barely see the edges of the road beside him. He wanted a cigarette. Taking the pack of Camels from his t-shirt sleeve, he discovered it contained only three cigarettes. He lit one and thought about walking back to the truck for more, but knew he might not have the nerve to leave again. After smoking the cigarette down to the nub, he searched his pockets for more, but found only another pack of matches in his flannel shirt.

As his eyes adjusted to the darkness, however, Deke could faintly see the road for several feet in front of him. Cautiously, he took a step, stopped, carefully scanned the roadbed and took another. In this manner Deke pressed on, but his progress was slow, for in his mind every stick or oblong object was a snake, and he wondered how he'd ever get to Crow Agency at this pace. Wiping his brow with his sleeve, Deke continued at his hesitant pace, hoping that Shelly was right and the spare had bounced out and stayed on the roadbed. After a few minutes he noticed a pale light at the crest of a facing hill and the moon slowly rose, like the head of a bald giant peeking over the mountains. Low clouds blanketed the moon, greatly dimming its light, but Deke welcomed its company. He still examined the road carefully, but now recognized sticks for what they were and walked at a steady pace. Shortly he glanced up from the roadbed and saw the dark outlines of the massive boulder and its opposing rock cliff only fifty yards away.

This strange formation where the road disappeared into blackness gave Deke the creeps. No moonlight fell into its narrow depths. He walked twenty paces and stopped, halted by what he sensed was a haunted presence at this spot. "I think some a' them spirits that In'jun was talkin' about live in there," Deke said, remembering Lawrence's stories. He had been cursed here before and was terrified of entering again. Deke looked at the shaded moon, wishing he could take it with him into the gloom of the canyon.

On that dark prairie, Deke McConahay was not the only creature gladdened at the moonrise. As he worked up his nerve to enter the dark portal, one hundred yards away, a coyote expressed her joy. Her night-rending howl echoed from the rocks and distant hills. Deke nearly jumped out of his skin.

On the other side of Deke, an even louder YIP-YIP-YIP-AAAA-WWWW-OOOOOOO of a big male rose in reply. "Omma God!" Deke gasped, "I'm surrounded by wolves."

Enticed by the male, the she-coyote trotted toward him, calling out, WOOO-YIP-YIP-WOO-YIP-YIP-WOOOOOOOO. The male loped through the sage toward her call, howling back. AAWWOOO-YIP-AAWWOOO-YIP-YIP-AAWW-OOOOOOOOOOO. Caught between them, Deke was panicked. "Shitfire! Them wolves are a'gittin' closer."

Halfway to their tryst, both coyotes scented the frightened interloper and instinctively began working as a team. Low to the ground and silent, they moved stealthily, using the sage for cover. At the road they halted and watched the intruder, who had his back to them. Seing a human alone at night was rare and they were curious. They crept closer.

Paralyzed with fear, Deke stood in the road, mumbling to himself. "Whadamy gonna do? I ain't half a mile from the truck an' already surrounded by wolves ... an' I don't wanna go in that haunted cave. I'm goin' back," he said, and turned around.

When Deke turned, he looked straight into the twin sets of moonlit eyes not twenty-five yards away. Taking his look as a challenge, the male coyote let out his most blood-curdling howl and the female joined in. Deke screamed and his feet took off on their own in the opposite direction. Legs pumping in terror, Deke ran straight into the dark maw of the chasm, his mind reeling with thoughts of pursuing teeth ripping his flesh.

At the curve, where the boulder rose up solid and black ahead of him, Deke saw a horrible form lying directly in his path. Round and thick, dark against the gray roadbed and over three feet long, the snake was coiled into the shape of an 'S', ready to strike. Deke was already on top of the serpent when he saw it and couldn't alter his gait. He screamed "AAAHHHHOOWWW!" as his right heel came down hard on its tail and the snake's head shot up and struck Deke midway on the back of his calf. The rifle dropped from his hands as Deke's momentum carried him several more steps before he stumbled and fell, rolling over and over in the dust. He lay writhing in the center of the road, screaming in terror, closed in by the narrow walls that echoed his screams back to him.

Deke screamed until he lay limp and exhausted, his wails becoming whimpers. Fear contracted his stomach until it ached and he felt like he was going to vomit. He expected the big rattler to slither over and bite him two or three more times just because it had nothing else better to do. Then he remembered the wolves, sure that they'd enter the chasm and tear him to pieces. The chasm itself terrified him, with its sheer, jagged rock jutting up from the edge of the road on one side and the massive boulder, so out of place on the prairie, looming dark and huge on the other. The way the road bent ninety degrees in the middle of the gorge also felt unnatural.

A belt of stars glittered above the narrow walls and Deke looked up at them, wishing the moon would pass over so he could see better. He desperately wanted to know how bad the bite was, but dreaded touching his calf, fearing it might already be horribly swollen.

Deke's fear of snakes was not unfounded. He'd grown up where rattlesnakes and copperheads were common and had had close calls. When he was fourteen, he and a neighbor boy were fishing, barefoot as usual, and the other boy stepped on a copperhead at a spot Deke had just walked through. Deke never forgot the kid's screams or his agony for the next few weeks as his foot turned black and swelled to the size of a canteloupe.

Gritting his teeth, Deke reached down to his calf and gingerly ran his fingers over the bite area. The leg didn't feel swollen, but Deke reckoned that would happen later. Carefully, he rolled his pantleg up and felt again. Some liquid rubbed onto his finger but he couldn't tell whether it was blood or venom.

"I wish I could see it," he said, and then remembered the matchbook in his shirt pocket. He tore one off, struck it, and held the flame close to his calf. The area was slightly bruised but Deke could see only one fang mark oozing a small amount of blood. When the match burned low he dropped it and lit another. This time he was sure there was only one puncture wound. "Maybe it jest got me with one fang," he said, "but I still gotta git that poison out b'fore it starts workin'."

Deke knew how to do that: he'd seen it done in lots of westerns. Sooner or later, every cowboy got snakebit and had to take out the poison or die. The Lone Ranger did it, the Rifleman did it and John Wayne likely did it too, though Deke couldn't recall any specific movie. You sterilized your knife with fire, cut a deep x mark into each fang bite, then sucked out the venom. When finished, you applied a tourniquet and went on your way. With a trembling hand, Deke pulled his knife from its sheath. "I don' wanna do this," he said, on the verge of tears, "but I don' wanna die out here, neither."

He lit a match and held the blade tip in the flame, then a second and a third one. The steel glinted in the darkness, showing patches of rust along its length. "I know this knife ain't very sharp," Deke said, tears running down his cheeks, "but I still gotta do it." Holding his calf tightly in his left hand, Deke touched the blade to the fang mark. "OWWWWWWW!" he hollered. "Sum'bitch, 'at's hot!"

Deke blew on the blade to cool it and after testing the knife-edge with his finger, raised the blade to his calf again, held it there trembling, and then lowered it. "I need a drink first," he said and took a swig from his canteen, wishing it were whiskey. "How come I ain't got no whiskey? Ever' cowboy's got whiskey with 'im fer things like this. If I had me some whiskey, I'd jest pour it on the bite, an' that might take care a' the poison without me havin' ta cut inta my leg."

Deke grasped his ankle and laid the blade along the bite mark. Fighting hard to control his shakes, he willed himself to cut into it. "I gotta do it, I gotta do it, I gotta do it," he said, then pressed down and felt pain. "I can't do it," he cried.

Openly sobbing now, Deke rolled onto his back and looked at the strip of stars overhead. "I'm 'fraid I'm gonna die," he whimpered, "real slow an' painful."

More frightened and exhausted than he'd ever been, Deke was on the verge of giving up. He watched the stars until his pulse settled down. "Maybe I can jest suck 'at poison out," he said. He put the knife in its sheath, took hold of his leg with both hands, pulled it to his mouth and began sucking as hard as he could at the bite mark, looking like he was eating a giant ear of corn on the cob. After he had sucked his leg sore, Deke spat. "I sure hope 'at helps," he said, panting.

Taking out his crusty red handkerchief, Deke blew a snotball into it and then mopped the sweat from his forehead. After rolling his pantleg back down, he tied the hanky snugly below his knee as a tourniquet. "I oughta git up an' go back ta Shelly b'fore this leg gits too bad ta walk," Deke said, but no sooner were the words out of his mouth than the two coyotes took up their serenade just outside the gorge. YIP-YIP-YIP-AAA-WWWWOOOOOOOO.

"Oh shitfire, them wolves are out there waitin' fer me. An' that rattlesnake's likely still back there too. If I git bit agin it'll kill me fer sure."

Deke rested his head on the road and stared at the dark walls that closed in from both sides. "Crow Agency might have a doctor, but it's a long ways off an' my leg's gonna start gittin' bad, I jest know it. I'm already tired an' startin' ta feel sick. Ain't no way I could make it."

A cold gust of wind whipped through the canyon and a shiver vibrated through Deke from end to end. "I'm gittin' chilled, too," he said, trembling. "I think 'at snake poison's gittin to me."

Within a couple of minutes Deke's entire body was quaking and the two coyotes howled again, joined now by several others. "I couldn't be in no worse fix 'an this," he said, his voice but a soft whine. "I don' know what ta do. I couldn't git up now if I wanted to."

Straining to raise his head off the gravel, Deke looked up at the stars again. Crow Agency and Shelly seemed as far away as they were. He watched his chest rising and falling. Every breath was difficult and he could see the pointed toes of his cowboy boots trembling in the dark. "Maybe if I lay here long e'nough somebody'll come along an' help me ... if they don't run over me first."

Deke reached his hand down and felt the embossed image on his belt buckle. In the eerie lonliness of the canyon, rubbing his fingers over John Wayne's face brought him a measure of comfort and after a few minutes Deke let his head fall back onto the road. Then he began shivering uncontrollably. "I don't even care no more," he said, and his mind slipped into a black nothingness.

———————

Get up.

"Huh?"

I said, get up.

"Who is it?" Deke said.

You know who it is. Now get up, before I come over there and kick ya in the butt.

The voice sounded familiar, awfully familiar, but who'd be out here at night on this road, Deke wondered. He turned his head to where the voice was coming from and saw a man's shape outlined against the chasm wall.

You don't lay in the road like a dog when your woman's countin' on ya. Now get up.

The longer Deke stared, the sharper the man's image became. He stood splaylegged and was big, real big; and he was wearing a cowboy hat. But it was his voice that got to Deke. He'd heard it a hundred times, but couldn't place it.

The shadow took two steps toward Deke.

Get up, I'm tellin' ya. NOW!

"AH!" Deke gasped. "John Wayne! Is 'at really you, Duke?"

Who else would it be? Now get on your feet.

Deke looked up at the dark form and wiped the tearstains off his cheeks with the back of his sleeve, not wanting John Wayne to know he had been crying. "I don't think I can get up," he said. "I got snakebit an' I'm a'bout done in."

We've all been snakebit, but we didn't give up. Now put your legs under your backside and get movin'.

"I'll try, Duke, I'll try."

Deke rolled onto his stomach, put his palms against the road and pushed as hard as he could. "Oh-oh-ohhaaa ..." he grunted until his arms gave out and he collapsed back onto the gravel. "I can't ... git up." He looked up at the shadow. "That snake poison's got to me, Duke. I'm sorry ... I jest can't do it."

You CAN do it. You pick up your hat, you put it on, and you get on your feet. It's that simple. It just takes some guts.

Deke felt around in the darkness, found his cowboy hat and put it on. *That's a start.*

He rose a few inches on his hands but the gravel bit into Deke's palms and his arms felt weak as rubber bands. "Ooohhhhaa ... I'm tryin' ... I'm tryin'."

The shadow took a step toward Deke. *Get up or I'll kick ya inta town!*

"Don' kick me, Duke," Deke cried, "Please don' kick me. I couldn't take that ... spesh'ly from you ... you always been my hero."

Then GET UP!

Quick as nothing, Deke's legs bent beneath him, his knees flexed and he was standing upright. Surprised and panting like a winded dog, he took several cautious steps. His leg hurt and he was dead tired, but he could walk. "Thanks, Duke, I needed that," he said, but didn't get an answer. The figure was now so faint that Deke wasn't sure if it was even there any more. After catching his breath, he started walking slowly in the direction of Crow Agency.

Where you goin'?

Deke turned around. The tall, shadowy form was twenty feet behind him.

"Into town, Duke. Shelly's waitin' fer me ta come back with a tar'r."

A man don't walk off and leave his rifle.

Embarrassed, Deke lowered his head. "I'm sorry, Duke. I oughta know better."

It's right over there. The figure raised a shadowy arm and pointed back to where Deke had stepped on the rattler. *Go get it.*

Deke gulped. "Sure, Duke, sure. I was meanin' to. I was jest takin' a few steps ta see if my leg worked okay."

Slowly, Deke worked his way back through the narrow canyon, carefully checking the ground at each step. At the curve where he'd been bitten, Deke began shaking violently and stopped. "I don't see my rifle anywhere's," he said.

Keep lookin' … you'll find it.

John Wayne was now standing in front of him on the other side of the road, but Deke hadn't seen him move. "Alright, Duke," he said, swallowing hard, and took another cautious step. Four excruciating steps later, Deke spotted a straight object in the middle of the road. He edged a few feet closer and peered at it intently. "There's my rifle, Duke, jest like you'd told me it'd be," he said, bending over to pick it up.

"AAAHHH!!!" Deke screamed and jumped back. A foot away from his rifle, the rattlesnake was poised, still in the shape of an 'S', ready to strike Deke's hand as soon as he reached for the gun.

"Ohhhhhh," Deke wailed, "that snake wants ta bite me agin'."

Pick up your rifle, the voice said.

"I can't do that, Duke," Deke pleaded. "That thing'll bite my hand if I reach fer my gun."

You can't walk away and leave it here.

"I know that, Duke … I know that," Deke said, trying not to cry again, "but I gotta think on how ta do it."

Then think about how to do it … I'm not stoppin' ya.

Keeping his eyes on the snake, Deke pondered his options. At twelve, when he started smoking, he and other kids would try to flip lit matches on each other. "I bet if I put some fire near that snake, it'd move," Deke said, pulling the matchbook from his shirt pocket. He tore off a match, placed the head on the striker, and flicked it toward the snake. The match took fire and landed two feet beyond the rattler. He sent another, which flickered out in mid-air. "Damn," Deke said, "I'm a little outa practice."

The third match landed close enough to the snake that Deke could see the rust colored tint on the rattler's round sides in the flame's light. His next match was even closer. "I'm gittin' my aim back," Deke said as he flipped another match through the air. It landed right on the snake's back and stayed lit. "Yessss!" Deke said, "that sum'bitch oughta move now."

But it didn't. Deke moved a step closer and flicked two more match-es. Both landed close to the snake and flickered along its length. The rattler was as thick at its head and tail as it was in the middle. "Shit-fire," Deke said, "that ain't no rattlesnake. That's part a' the tailpipe I ran over. I musta stepped on it when I was runnin' an' it flipped up an' whacked me on the leg."

Deke picked up his Winchester. "I got my rifle, Duke," he said, but the shadow was gone. Still cautious, Deke walked back through the canyon, cradling his Winchester like the old friend it was. Where the huge boulder entered the earth, the sky widened. Glad to be under the moon's faint guidance again, Deke started to pick up his pace when he heard a voice behind him.

Hey.

Deke turned around. The big shadow stood at the chasm's portal. "What, Duke?"

Your woman's countin' on ya, pardner, don't let her down, the shadow said, and touched its hat brim.

"I won't, Duke," Deke said, touching his hat in return. "Ya got my word on it as a cowboy."

Deke turned and walked into the night, heading to Crow Agency to bring back a tire, because that's what he promised he'd do.

"Ya hear that?" he said, looking up at the stars, "He called me 'pardner'. John Wayne called me 'pardner'."

Chapter 33

Not far from the canyon Deke stopped and peered over the guard-rail of a narrow bridge that spanned a sheer-walled coulee. The black abyss below made him shudder. "I sure wouldn't ever wanna be down in a place like that," he said.

Shortly after the bridge, the road began a long, straight climb and Deke was panting and thirsty when he reached the summit. Resting the Winchester against his leg, he got his canteen from the pouch and took a long drink. He wanted a cigarette, but with only two left, reckoned his need would be greater on the trip back. A breeze blew in from the West as Deke surveyed the dark landscape, utterly barren in every direction. The coyotes had quieted and except for the rustle of wind, all was still. He picked up his rifle and holding it in the crook of his arm, set off again, cautious, but resolute.

The road rose, dipped and curved in places, but was mostly featureless. As Deke tramped on through the night, he began to think about what he would do once he reached Crow Agency and how he would confront the tall, grim looking Indian who had stared at him so fiercely. He also wondered why he hadn't yet seen the lights of the town, which should have shown from far away across the dark plain. He took another drink from his canteen and continued on. After some time he trudged up a steep grade and when he reached the top, saw that he was standing on a ridge that had blocked the town from view. Half a mile away were the twin concrete ribbons of Interstate 90 and just beyond, a scattered twinkling of yellow lights.

Crow Agency was even more forbidding at night. The town had no streetlamps or yard lights, as its residents, who had grown up in open country, did not fear darkness. Cottonwoods, plentiful and leafy, absorbed most of the light that escaped from the houses, making Crow Agency look more like an encampment than a town. Deke saw little movement, but the cacophony of sounds that drifted across the prairie gave him cause for apprehension. Dogs barked constantly, horses whinnied, and the voices of people rose up: laughing, shouting and whooping. He even heard a man's piercing scream. Deke feared that he was about to enter a place where anything could, and probably did, happen, and if something went wrong, he was on his own. He faced down his urge for a smoke and took one more drink from his canteen. "Gotta remember to fill this," he said and began walking down the winding grade that led into town.

At the bottom of the grade he crossed a set of railroad tracks and halted in the shadows of the I-90 underpass. On the other side of the frontage road sat the service station, closed and shuttered. As Deke anxiously considered his next move, a northbound semi rumbled over the bridge above, rattling the girders. He listened to the diesel roll away into the night and wished he was behind the wheel, comfy and safe in the cab, instead of standing alone on the dark edge of this reservation town, committed to something he desperately did not want to do. Cautiously, Deke took a couple of steps into the open and began walking toward the gas station, watching for movement. The unsettling sounds of Crow Agency were now magnified. All sorts of uproariousness was taking place on this Friday night, but lucky for him, Deke thought, none of it was happening in his immediate vicinity.

As he approached the gas station, Deke's eyes were drawn to the huge, cone shaped mound of tires off to the side. He'd never seen anything like it and thought it a strange way to store tires. The station itself was well maintained, with only a few scattered vehicles awaiting repair. Above the office door was a large, hand painted sign that read: *Agency Gas and Repair. Tires, new and used. Tobacco, Pop and Candy.*

"I reckon he can't complain about me wantin' a tar'r," Deke whispered. "Says right here he sells 'em. I might git me a pack a' cigarettes and a Coke, too. Maybe even a candy bar an' a Slim Jim fer the trip back."

Keeping to the shadows, Deke walked to the back of the station, looking for the house that Shelly had seen. He spotted the small residence among some trees about a hundred feet back from the main building. The house had no exterior lighting but an outline of yellow shone around the curtained windows, indicating the owner was still awake. Deke swallowed, looked at the house and swallowed again. His pulse quickened and his stomach balled into a knot as he forced himself toward it. He hadn't gone a dozen paces when movement near the front door made him stop. For a moment he was still, then took two more steps and was almost jolted off his feet by the loudest and fiercest barking he'd ever heard. Now he could see the dog. It was huge, and very excited. Deke swiftly backpedaled to his starting point and then some.

He prayed the dog was tied up and hoped the owner would come to the door to see what the dog was barking about, then Deke could call out to him. But the dog soon quieted down and no one came out. Deke thought about hollering out anyway, but feared that would bring the wrong kind of attention and with all the other yelling going on in Crow Agency, the man wouldn't likely notice one more voice.

As Deke stood weighing his options a pair of headlights careened around the corner and turned onto the frontage road, speeding toward him. He ran to a gas pump and hid behind it as an old pickup roared by, tires squealing. From its open windows Deke heard men laughing. Leery of being in the open, Deke got up and ran in a low crouch to the back of the gas station, away from the road. This got the dog barking again. Deke started shivering. "I think 'em chills are comin' back," he muttered. "Goddam dog, anyway."

He eased back around the corner of the station where the dog couldn't see him and it quieted. "Ain't no way I can git close ta that guy's door," Deke said, and looked over at the giant mound of tires 40 feet away. "I bet there's an F150 tar'r right near the bottom. Maybe I oughta go see if I can find one. After I put it on the truck, me an' Shelly could drive back here an' pay fer it then take the interstate up ta Hardin like we shoulda done in the first place."

Deke peeked around the corner to make sure the coast was clear and trotted over to the tires. The dog started up again, but Deke went around to the side of the mound where the dog couldn't see him and the creature shut up.

Working his way around the bottom of the pile, Deke avoided the side facing the owner's house. He quickly eliminated most of the tires as being too big or too small. Whenever he found a 15-inch truck tire he ran a hand over the rim to feel if it had five holes spaced the right distance apart. He quickly found several, but they were either flat or defective. Not wanting to climb the treacherous looking pile, Deke worked his way back, sticking his arm into the stack and feeling around. He found a tire that felt right, but realized how hard getting it out of the stack would be. The tires were not piled haphazardly, but were woven together like a bird's nest. This conical mound of rubber had been constructed with intent. "What a dumb-ass way ta store tar'rs," Deke muttered, as he leaned his rifle up and began digging out a tire his fingers told him would fit.

The tire Deke sought was at chest height and he carefully began pulling out the ones around it. All of the tires were on rims and Deke was soon puffing and sweating from the exertion. He did his best not to make any noise in lowering them to the ground, but one 16-inch Goodyear slipped from his hands, plopped loudly on the hard dirt and began rolling away. Deke took off and quickly retrieved it but not before the dog saw him and started barking again.

Being extra cautious, Deke dug out three other tires to get at the one he wanted, but when he tugged it out, four more came with it, thumping on the ground and knocking over his rifle. The dog began barking again, but this time Deke heard the front door open and the gruff sound of a man's voice. "Be quiet!"

The dog fell silent and Deke held his breath until the door slammed closed. He wiped the sweat from his face and searched through the jumble of fallen rubber. Again Deke was disappointed, for when he found the tire, one spot was so frayed and damaged it wouldn't have lasted five miles.

Deke was in a quandary. Getting a tire anywhere but from the outside layer was too difficult and he couldn't search on the side of the mound where the dog, or worse yet, the owner, could see him. His only option was to go up, and Deke did not like heights.

The summit was perhaps 35 feet in the air, but to Deke it looked like the Matterhorn. He knew the footing would be treacherous and pulling out a tire while balancing on a pile of shaky rubber no easy feat. He'd also have to leave his rifle at the bottom, and Deke didn't like that one bit. He stared at the steep black cone, finished off the water in his canteen, and made his decision. To keep his word and come back with a tire, he'd have to climb the stack. Deke took off his Army web belt with his knife and canteen, set it beside his Winchester, and started climbing.

The first few steps up weren't too bad. At each 15-inch truck tire, Deke held on with one hand and felt the rim holes with the other. He found half a dozen that would fit his pickup, but on closer inspection, each was flat or had a defect. Deke carefully moved along the stack sideways until he'd checked each tire within reach, halted for a minute to steady his nerves and catch his breath then climbed several feet to the next level. When he was 15 feet from the ground, Deke was tired and scared, but forced himself to keep going.

The higher Deke went, the shakier the pile became, but his promise to Shelly drove him on. By the time he was 25 feet up, Deke was quivering so badly he could barely force himself to let go with one hand and feel the rim holes. Finding nothing, Deke sucked in his breath and took one more very cautious step higher. As he was checking the rim of a likely looking tire, headlights approached. "Oh God, please don't let 'em see me."

Arms outstretched, Deke pressed himself against the tires as the car got closer. The highbeams of a station wagon full of laughing women swept the rubber mound only a couple of feet below his boots. After he'd caught his breath, Deke reached again for the truck tire he'd seen, but his searching fingers counted six holes in the rim. "Sum'bitch, I ain't never gonna find me a tar'r."

Deke looked up. The summit was still six or seven feet above his head but the top three feet were all compact car tires. Just below them, though, a nice looking 15-incher caught his eye. Deke looked at the tire for some time, trying to decide if it was worth the risk. "Why don't this damn In'jun put his tar'rs in rows like ever'body else?"

A sudden gust blew in, rustling the leaves of neighboring cottonwoods and whipping back the folds of Deke's unbuttoned flannel shirt.

The top of the pile swayed in the wind. Feeling like he was clinging to the topmast of a clipper ship in heavy seas, Deke shivered and wanted to vomit.

"I can't do this any more," he said and started to take a step down … then hesitated. How would he explain to Shelly that he'd made it to Crow Agency but never asked the old Indian for a tire? But how could he? The goddam dog would eat him before he got to the door. No matter what story he told Shelly, Deke knew she'd see through it and know he'd chickened out.

He looked up at the light truck tire again. It was only two feet above his reach. The tread on it was good and Deke didn't see any defects. "I give Shelly my word … an John Wayne too," he whispered. "I can't go back on it."

Holding his breath, Deke reached up, grabbed hold of a tire for leverage and took two more steps. The narrow spire of rubber quivered as Deke clung precariously to the tires until they quit wobbling. With his boot soles fighting for purchase and his chest mashed against the smelly rubber, Deke knew he could be seen from anywhere below. Grimacing, he clutched the whitewall beside him in a deathgrip while stretching out his other arm and reaching into the rim of the truck tire he'd seen from below. Five holes. He thumped the tire with his knuckes. It was filled with air. He ran his fingers over the tread and sidewall. No defects. All he had to do now was pull the tire out and get back down the steep cone without falling or dropping it. Cold sweat ran down Deke's back and he was exhausted, but he'd finally found a tire. "I'm gittin' this tar'r … if it's the las' thing I ever do," he mumbled as he carefully tried to wriggle it free.

When the tire wouldn't come out, Deke jiggled it a little harder and the entire summit of the pile nearly went over. "Ohh, shit," he said, clinging to the stack with both hands. "This is gonna be real touchy."

Deke put his boot on the tire to his right and eased over onto it to get more leverage on the heavy ten-ply he was after. With only one free hand to work with, Deke struggled to release his tire from the others holding it in place. He gingerly pulled at the smaller tire to its left, then pushed on the tire to its right. He lifted the tire that was resting on top of his selection and forced it back a tad. The spire started to wobble again and Deke shuddered. When it quit shaking, he pulled at his tire and it came out a couple of inches. Twice more he repeated this process and each time it came out of the pile a little further. "I almos' got 'er," he said.

He steadied his footing, wiped a sweaty palm on his jeans and, summoning his courage, reached into the tire and grasped the inside edge of the rim. Holding onto a solid 16-inch Michelin with his left hand for support, Deke tugged at the pickup tire, wiggling it gently as he pulled. Slowly, the tire began to come out of the pile. "See, I told ya I'd come back with a tar'r," Deke said, imagining his triumphal return to Shelly.

From out of nowhere, two cars, tires squealing, engines gunning, turned onto the frontage road, barreling in Deke's direction. "Not now!" he pleaded, as the vehicles sped toward him. They were the same ones he'd seen earlier, but now the station wagon full of women was chasing the pickup with the two men. Deke knew that if anybody in the vehicles looked up they would spot him. As they approached, the driver of the station wagon laid on the horn and rammed the back bumper of the pickup, giving it a jolt. Raucus laughter erupted from the open windows of both vehicles.

As they raced by the gas station the dog on the porch stood up to watch and his eyes caught sight of something he had never seen before; a lone nocturnal alpinist silhouetted against the sky, trying to pull a tire from his master's rubber teepee. The dog let loose with everything he had, baying so loud that every dog in Crow Agency joined in.

Deke clutched at the tire, shaking so badly he could barely hang on and praying the dog would stop barking. But the dog didn't stop. The front door opened and a bright swath of yellow light covered the porch as a harsh voice yelled, "Would you shut up, I'm trying to watch TV!" This time, though, the dog wouldn't shut up and the man did not go back inside.

"I gotta git down from here, right now!" Deke said and yanked out the tire.

When the dog did not obey his command the man on the porch cast his eyes to where his snarling dog was staring. The tire snatcher was already gone, but as the perplexed station owner watched, the top dozen feet of his carefully constructed tower disappeared and he heard the thumps and thuds of a rubber landslide. Over and above the rumble of falling tires came the drawn out sound of a man's wail: "ohhhhhhhhhhhaaaaaaaaaahhhhhhhhh!"

"I think I need to go put on some shoes and get my knife and a flashlight," he said to the dog.

––––––––––––––

For the second time that night, Deke McConahay lay on his back, panic stricken and looking up at the stars. A 14-inch Goodyear rested on his right leg and his left arm was pinned under a Firestone radial. Every inch of him hurt and his breaths came in quick, spasmodic gasps. The dog was still barking and Deke knew the vicious animal and his frightening owner would be coming. The last of his adrenaline kicked in.

Pushing aside tires, Deke got on his hands and knees and hurriedly began searching for his rifle. He saw his scrunched cowboy hat and put it on, then, more by feel than sight, found the Winchester. Using tires for leverage, Deke raised his aching body to a standing position and peeked around the corner of the mound in the direction of the house. At first he only saw the huge barking dog outlined against the light of the open door, then the tall, braided Indian man emerged. He took the snarling dog by its collar and after a dozen steps stopped and looked down at it. "Be quiet, Little Wolf!" he ordered, and rapped the dog on the head with his knuckles. The dog shut up.

Deke stood panting, his mind flooded with terror, not knowing what to do. Sweat ran down his face and back. His heart pounded and his guts were so tight they ached. He almost started running, but his body was too sore and exhausted. Whatever direction he went, he'd have to cross open ground and knew the Indian would sic the monstrous dog on him. Staying in the shadows, Deke knelt down behind a stack of fallen tires and quietly levered a .30-30 cartridge into the chamber of his Winchester. The dog heard the sound and barked twice.

"Quiet," the man said.

Deke laid his rifle across a tire and peered through the iron sights. "I don' wanna do this," he whispered, trembling, "but I don' wanna be tore ta pieces neither." Both man and dog were backlit from the open door. There wasn't enough light for accurate shooting at distance, but if he could control his shaking and wait until they were within 10 or 15 paces, he couldn't miss. Maybe I oughta take out the dog out first, Deke thought, cause it'll come at me as soon as I shoot the man ... unless he's got a gun ... then I oughta shoot him first. As they drew closer, Deke held his breath. Oh Lord ... I really ... really don' wanna do this ... but I ... I ... Deke's thoughts trailed off into an incoherent tangle of fear.

Man and dog were now within 15 yards of Deke. The man's eyes had not yet adjusted to the darkness, but the dog could see both Deke and the rifle. He barked and tugged at his collar. The Crow man knew his dog was trying to warn him and he pointed his flashlight toward where Deke crouched.

Shaking, Deke tried to hold the rifle sights in the middle of the man's chest and pressed the Winchester down on the tire to keep it steady. If he turns 'at light on me I gotta shoot 'em. If I don't, that dog'll kill me fer sure.

The Indian stopped walking and shook his flashlight. Deke heard him say, "Dammit, the batteries are dead." He turned to his dog. "Let's go find out what knocked my tires down." The man began walking toward Deke again, but the dog barked and resisted at each step. "All right, then," he said to the dog, then laid the flashlight down and pulled the huge knife from its sheath.

Deke could see the steel blade glinting in the starlight and he put his finger against the trigger. That In'jun's got his knife out. I really ain' got no choice now.

Stealthy and alert, just the way Deke imagined an Indian would move when stalking an enemy in the dark, the man continued toward him. The dog now crouched low, its muscles bunched, ready to attack.

Despite his trembling, Deke tried to keep his rifle steady. He's gonna see me in a second, an' when he does ... I gotta shoot.

The Indian started to take another step but stopped and looked in Deke's direction. "Who's there?" he called into the darkness and the dog backed him up with a low, menacing growl.

Deke's finger tightened on the trigger and he almost choked with fear and sickness at what he was about to do. Then, nearly sobbing, he took his finger off the trigger. I can't do it ... I can't shoot a man over a tar'r, no matter what happens to me. It wouldn't be right.

Not pulling the trigger might have been the closest Deke McConahay ever came to being a real cowboy, because he did it for the best reason of all: it wouldn't be right.

"It's me," Deke called back, as if that answered the man's question. "Who else could it be? Now get out here where I can see you."

Deke did not want the Indian to see his rifle, fearing he would set the dog on him. Thinking fast, Deke undid his leather belt, opened his jeans and stuffed the Winchester down his right pantleg, zipped up and buckled his belt again.

"Come out here, now," the man ordered, "or I'll send the dog in to hurry you up." The dog eagerly barked.

"Don' do that!" Deke yelled, painfully raising himself. "I took a bad fall an' its hard fer me ta stand up."

"Little Wolf will help you stand up," the man called, laughing harshly as the dog snarled.

"I'm comin' … I'm comin' … righ' now," Deke yelled frantically and stepped away from the mound of tires, dragging his stiff leg.

As soon as the station owner saw Deke he pointed to a spot about ten feet away with his knife. "Stand over there," he said, "so I can see you."

Visibly shaking, Deke hobbled to where the man pointed. "You don' need that knife," he said, "I come in peace, Kemosabe."

"What's this 'Kemosabe' bullshit?" the man with the gray braids said. "I'm not the Lone Ranger. I'm the Indian here." Deke took two more steps. "What happened to your leg?" the man asked.

Deke stopped and looked down, as if he'd forgotten. "Oh yeah, my leg. I got that in Viet Nam. I was one a' them Green Beer-rays an' I got shot by some Viet Congs … that is … jest b'fore I shot them … an' a bunch more, too."

"All right, Chester, if you say so," the old Indian said, and laughed. Then he quit laughing and ordered, "Stop there."

Little Wolf tugged at his collar and snarled at Deke. Up close, the dog was even more frightening. The beast was certainly part wolf, but of a size that suggested its mother had mated with a grizzly bear. "Don' let that d-dog go," Deke pleaded, "I don' want no t-trouble."

"You stand still," Gray-braids said to Deke, "and don't move." He turned to his dog. "And you stand still, too." He let go of the dog's collar.

"Nohhh!" Deke said, nearly wetting his pants as the dog growled and took a step toward him.

"SIT!" the Indian commanded and pointed toward the ground with his finger. The dog sat, but he was not happy about it.

"If he moves … take him," Gray-braids said.

Grrrrrrrr …

Holding his huge knife in front of him, the old Indian approached Deke.

"Ohhhhh n-n-nohhhhh!" Deke pleaded, shaking so hard his knees were knocking. "Don' skin me alive or scalp me … I din' mean no harm … I swear it."

"Hmmm," the Crow man said, "your long hair would look good hanging on my mantel," and chuckled.

Deke let out a plaintive wail as Gray-braids held the knife an inch from his nose and grabbed a fistful of hair. "You better not move, not even one inch," he said and nodded toward the dog.

Tall as Deke was, the hawk-faced Crow stood several inches over him. His hands were the size of coal shovels and he seemed possessed of an ungodly strength. Tightly gripping Deke's hair, he peered into his eyes. "Now I remember you," he said. "You and the girl drove by here in the Ford pickup."

"That was me," Deke said.

The Indian frowned. "You're the one Melvin Not Afraid said was wearing the Custer t-shirt."

"That wadn't me," Deke said, "that w-wadn't me."

"Melvin Not Afraid does not lie," the Crow man said angrily, and moved Deke's flannel shirt aside with his knife blade. "That looks like Custer to me."

"It ain't! I swear it ain't," Deke spluttered. "It's Wild Bill Hickock."

Gray-braids looked closer. "No matter," he said, "I don't like Hickock either." Raising the knife to Deke's face again, he asked, "What are you doing here on my property at night … and on my tire stack?"

Deke gulped, trying to swallow, but his throat wouldn't co-operate.

"Answer me!" Gray-braids said, tightening his grip on Deke's hair.

"Me an' Shelly had a f-f-flat … an' somebody stole't my spare."

"Heh heh heh …" the man laughed menacingly. "And so you were going to steal a tire from me?"

"Oh no … nothin' like that a'tall. I was gonna come up ta the house an' pay ya soon as I found one."

"Why didn't you come to the house first?"

"Oh, I wanted to. I even tried to … but that dog was gonna tear inta me."

"Hmmm … and how would it have been different *after* you took a tire?"

"I don' know," Deke said. "I hadn't thought it out that far."

"Heh heh heh …" the old man laughed again and nodded toward the pile. "You wouldn't have found a tire in all of that stack. None of them are any good."

Deke looked at what remained of the pile. "What is that thing, anyway?"

"You don't know?" the Indian asked, as if it was obvious "It's a giant lodge – a teepee – made out of tires so it will last forever."

"What for?"

"It is a monument to my people," Gray-braids said, looking toward the pile of black rubber. "Long after I am gone … maybe even thousands of years from now, someone will discover it, like the pyramids, and know who the Apsaalooke were and how we once lived." He turned back to Deke and his look was angry. "Now, because of you, I'll have to rebuild it and that's a lot of work."

"I didn't mean ta knock it down," Deke said hastily, "an' I'm sorry as all git out. I was jest des'prit for a tar'r an' figger'd there'd be one in that big pile."

"I keep all of my good tires in the station," Gray-braids said, "so people like you can't steal them." He turned the knife slowly in front of Deke's face.

"Listen," Deke pleaded, "if ya don't kill me or scalp me or nothin' … I'll buy a tar'r from ya. I'll even pay ya twice … or three times what it's worth." Deke looked at the glinting blade, an inch from his nose. "In fact, it'd be my p-p-pleasure ta pay ya two or three times what ya normally git for a used tar'r … for yer trouble an' all."

"Heh heh heh …" Gray-braids laughed. He let go of Deke's hair and put the knife back in its sheath. In truth, he just wanted to be done with this fool of a White man and get back to the house and finish watching *Kojac*. He took hold of his dog's collar and told Deke, "Walk over to the gas station ...slowly."

Trying to make his stiff leg look natural, Deke started walking toward the station, but he could see that the old Indian was watching him closely. When they got to the front of the building Gray-braids said, "Hold up, Chester. Why is that bandana on your leg?"

"It's a tourniquet," Deke said. "I got snakebit earlier."

"I know a lot about snakebite. Let me take a look."

"Oh no!" Deke said quickly. "It's okay now. I sucked out all the poison!"

Before Deke could react, the Indian knelt down and clasped his huge hand around Deke's ankle. Quick as lightning the big knife was in his other hand and he looked up into Deke's panicked eyes. "Now I know why you limp, Chester."

Gray-braids stood up. "If he moves an inch," he told the dog, "kill him."

Grrrrrrrrr.

In one swift motion the Indian sheathed his knife, grasped Deke's frayed belt in his iron hands and ripped it in two, popping the snaps off of Deke's jeans and tearing them open. Deke's John Wayne belt buckle fell into the dirt.

Deke stood rigid as a tree while Gray-braids reached into his pantleg and pulled out the .30-30. "Were you going to shoot me and my dog over a tire?"

"I'd never do n-nothin' like that," Deke blubbered, "not in a m-million years."

"Then why did you bring it?"

"It's fer the wolves ... an' the snakes an' things out in the desert. I git k-kinda scared by myself at night in pl-places like that."

"And maybe a little scared of Indians, too?" Gray-braids said and chuckled. He held the rifle up and looked at it in the starlight. "Hm-mmm ...nice," he said. "A Winchester 94, pre 1964 model. Good steel in these." He looked closer. "This gun is cocked. Is it loaded?"

Deke nodded.

"You had a loaded and cocked rifle down your pants?"

"Yeah. I r-reckon so," Deke said.

"You're even dumber than you look," the Indian said, easing down the hammer and shaking his head in disbelief.

"I been t-told that b-b'fore," Deke answered.

"You stand right here," Gray-braids said and walked to the front of his station. He unlocked the door, opened it, flipped on a light and looked at his watch. *Kojac* was just about over but *McCloud* would be starting soon.

"Come," he said to the dog. Little Wolf got up and snarled at Deke as he trotted by him. "Now you come over here," Gray-braids ordered Deke.

Deke bent over to pick up his belt buckle but the dog gave a ferocious bark and lunged at him. Jumping back, Deke let out a yelp.

"Stay!" Gray-braids called, then took two steps and grabbed the dog's collar. "What are you doing?" he said harshly to Deke.

"Pickin' up my belt buckle."

"Leave it."

Deke straightened up a little and looked back at the tall, braided man who stared at him with hawk-like eyes.

"I ain't leavin' it," Deke said. "This buckle means a lot ta me."

They glared at each other until Gray-braids said, "Alright, pick it up. Then get over here and no more silliness."

Deke picked up the buckle and stuffed it into his back pocket. He started to walk to where Gray-braids stood by the door, holding Little Wolf, but he had to clasp the front of his pants together with one hand to keep them up.

"Heh heh heh ..." Gray-braids chuckled. "In there," he said and nodded for Deke to go into the gas station.

Deke took a couple of hesitant steps into the station. Gray-braids followed him in and placed Little Wolf in the center of the doorway. "You stay here," he told the dog then pointed to the double car-bay. "Go in there," he ordered Deke.

A shudder of panic shot through Deke as he thought, Is this where's he's gonna tie me up an' skin me alive an' take my hair!

"W-w-what for?" Deke said.

"I thought you wanted to buy a tire."

"Oh ... I sure do," Deke said, "More'n anything in the world, 'at's what I wanna do ... I wanna buy a tar'r."

"Well," Gray-braids said, pointing into the garage, "that's where they are."

Two walls of the repair shop were lined with tires and a Chevy stepside with its hood up sat in the far bay. Between it and the near hoist lay a dozen of so tires in a jumbled heap. "These just came in today," Gray-braids said. "I didn't have time to put them away before *The Price is Right* started, but there's one in there that will fit your Ford." He gestured toward the pile with Deke's rifle. "Go get it if you want it."

Deke walked over to the tires, thinking he'd seen them somewhere before. He lifted a couple from the top of the pile and saw a 15-inch B.F. Goodrich on a five-hole rim. Deke bent down and looked closer. "That's my spare," he said, then looked up at Gray-braids and said it again, louder. "That's my spare tar'r!"

"No," Gray-braids answered, "that's *my* tire. I got it from Melvin Not Afraid earlier today."

"But he stole't it from me!" Deke said indignantly. "An' he likely stole these others, too."

The Crow man stiffened and his dark eyes flashed at Deke. "Melvin Not Afraid does not steal. He finds these tires around the reservation or people give them to him. He brings them in and I trade him for gas or parts."

"Well, he stole't this one from me," Deke said, now angry. "Took it right outa my truck whiles we was in that rest'runt."

"Yeah ... he might have done that," Gray-braids said and shrugged, "after he saw your Custer shirt."

"Godammit," Deke said, "it ain't Custer, it's Wild Bill Hickock!"

"Heh heh ... no matter," Gray-braids said. "Anyway, Chester, if you want the tire, you can have it for thirty-dollars."

"What!" Deke yelled and stood up, then had to quickly grab the front of his pants to keep them from falling down. "That's my tar'r. I shouldn't have ta pay nothin'."

He looked down at the worn spare on the rusty rim. "An' it ain't worth more'n ten dollars at most."

"You told me just a few minutes ago that you would pay three times the worth of a tire. The words you said were, 'it'd be my pleasure'."

"Well it ain't my pleasure no more," Deke said, "an' you can jack my rabbit, cuz I ain't payin' no thirty dollars ta git my own tar'r back."

Gray-braid's face darkened and he took a step toward Deke, then his sharp features relaxed into a smile. "Oh, okay," he said, and shrugged once more. "Let me get my phone."

"Phone?" Deke said, "fer what?"

"To call the Tribal Police and have them take you to jail. I caught you trespassing, armed with a rifle and trying to steal from me." The old man's mouth curled into a grin. "It's Friday night," he said, "you'll be sharing the drunk tank with fifteen or twenty Indians for the weekend. I think I'll hear some funny stories about that next week." He turned and started back to the office.

Deke's stomach came up into his throat. "Hang on there," he called, holding up his pants and hobbling after Gray-braids. "I mighta got a little hot there an' spoke too soon. Maybe we can work somethin' out."

"What we can work out is this: you pay me thirty dollars for the tire, then get off my place." He stared at Deke with his raptor eyes. "I am older now and have mellowed. If I had caught you doing this when I was young … heh heh … things would have gone much different for you."

Deke shivered. "Reckon I'll take 'at tar'r after all," he said.

"Good decision," Gray-braids told him.

Deke went back and got his old B.F. Goodrich, fumbling to pick it up and carry it to the office with one hand while he held his britches with the other. After he'd dug out his wallet and paid for the tire he said to Gray-braids, "Could I buy me some cigarettes an' a Coke. Maybe a Slim Jim an' a candy bar, too?"

"No!" Gray-braids said and looked at his watch again. Nothing would be on now but re-runs. With some luck they might be showing *The Addams Family*. "Get over here," he said to his dog, which still guarded the doorway, "so Chester can go back where he came from."

The dog got up, growled at Deke, and walked over and stood beside his master. Deke looked at the open doorway, but didn't move.

"Go," the tall, braided man said. "What are you waiting for?"

"I'm waitin' fer you ta give me my rifle back," Deke said.

"You're not getting it back," the Indian told him, surprised that Deke would even ask for it.

"My daddy give me that gun," Deke said, "jest b'fore he died."

"Then he should have taught you not to take it onto other people's property when you are trying to steal from them," Gray-braids answered.

"This ain't right," Deke said.

"A lot of things aren't right, Chester. Indians learned that a long time ago."

Deke grabbed his jeans with one hand, hefted the spare with the other, and silently vowing to get his Winchester back, shambled into the night that soon swallowed him.

Chapter 34

Muttering aloud, Deke tramped beneath the I-90 underpass, clutching the heavy ten-ply against his side with one hand while squeezing the front of his jeans together with the other. After he crossed the railroad tracks, he sat the tire down and looked back at Crow Agency, gathering his breath and concocting wild schemes of how he would get his Winchester back. When his breathing settled, Deke peered into the black wasteland that lay ahead of him. He was thirsty and exhausted. The lump on his head from the day before still hurt and the rest of him ached from his tumble down the mountain of tires. "Dammit" he said, "I left my knife an' canteen back 'ere, too … sum'bitch."

Alone and facing a bleak journey, Deke inhaled the darkness and looked around. Except for the cloudbank shielding the nearly full moon, stars twinkled overhead. Nearby hills bordered the horizons and Deke realized with a start that the ones to the southeast were the Little Bighorn Battlefield. A breeze came up, rattling the brim of his cowboy hat, and Deke remembered the wind blowing over the battlefield earlier that day and Lawrence Iron Bull's words about this land being filled with spirits. A sudden chill darted through him and he ran his tongue over his dry lips.

He desperately wanted his rifle. It couldn't protect him from demon spirits but he still had the unfriendly natives and wolves to worry about. Yet here he was, facing a difficult journey through a hostile land with nothing but his bare hands to fend off the dangers of the night, and when Deke thought about it, he really only had one hand to fend off danger with, because he needed the other one to hold up his pants. Deke dug a booger out of his nose and wiped it on his jeans. "I think I'll have me a smoke," he said.

He unrolled the crinkled pack of Camels from his t-shirt sleeve and using both hands (letting his pants fall to his knees), carefully tore the paper open and peeled the foil back. His last two cigarettes had been shredded into loose tobacco and torn paper from his tumble down the mound of tires. Deke sniffed the fragrant tobacco, trying to figure out how he could light it and inhale at least a few sweet puffs, but the next gust of wind blew the mixture away.

"Fuck!" Deke hollered, for there was simply no other word to express how he felt. He pulled up his pants, sat down on the gravel road-bed and started sobbing. "I ain't got no cigarettes … I ain' got my rifle … or my knife … or any water." Deke picked up a handful of gravel and threw it as hard as he could into the darkness. "I ain' even got any snaps on muh' pants or a goddam belt ta hold 'em up with." Tears fell from his cheeks and plopped in the dust. "Ever' bit a' me hurts. I'm tired an' thirsty as hell … an' gittin' hungry too. Some baloney an' crackers sure would taste good right now … an' a Coke."

He wiped his shirtsleeve across his face. "But that goddam In'jun wouldn't sell me a Coke … or any cigarettes … or even a Slim Jim an' a candy bar. Whadoo I have? I don' have shit. That sum'bitch back 'ere took it all … an' thirty dollars too." Deke craned his neck and looked at the lights of Crow Agency. "An' fer what? Jest so's I could git muh own fuckin' spare tar'r back."

He turned back around and rested his hand on the tire. "I knew I shoulda tied you down, pardner, but Shelly wouldn't let me." Running his palm over what remained of the tread, Deke said, "We been t'gether a long time, you an' me, through thick an' thin. You were on the first truck I ever owned an' now yer all I got left."

Deke undid the handerchief from around his calf and wiped the tears and sweat off his face. He wadded the red hanky into a ball, stuffed it into his back pocket and realized that he did have something else left. "At least 'at damn In'jun didn't git this," Deke said, "but he tried."

Holding the brass buckle in his hand, Deke rubbed his fingers over John Wayne's face and looked around him, hoping to see the tall shadow again. When nothing appeared, he stared at the buckle for a few seconds and then shoved it down his front jeans pocket as far as it would go. Clutching the front of his pants together with his left hand, Deke stood up, walked over to the ditch and made water. He went back to where his spare tire faithfully waited for him and picked it up. "C'mon, Goodrich," he said to the tire and began the long walk back to his truck and Shelly.

Sustained only by his resolve, Deke trundled along. Every hundred yards or so he would take a short rest, then carry the tire with the other arm for a while. Having to hold his pants up added to the awkwardness of his gait and after only half a mile his arms ached and his hipbones hurt from the tire resting on them. "Sum'bitch, but yer heavy," he said to the tire. "Maybe I'll roll ya for awhile."

This proved no easy task either. Keeping the tire moving straight required profound concentration and most of Deke's concentration already went to watching for snakes. On level ground the tire was relatively cooperative, but going up a grade he had to push it along a few inches at a time and made little progress. On the downhill slope, the B.F. Goodrich wanted to run off without him. Being tall, Deke had to bend over to roll the tire, and this put a crick in his back. After a while, though, Deke found that alternately carrying, then rolling the heavy tire worked best, but he still had to rest often.

Since leaving Crow Agency, Deke hadn't heard any "wolf" howls, but the further he intruded into the wasteland the greater his sense of dread became, and he sensed that *things*, not animal in the usual sense, were watching him from the blackness. With each step, his fear worsened, until he could no longer sit down while resting, feeling vulnerable when his legs were not beneath him, ready to run.

Besides westerns, Deke had watched many science fiction and horror films when he was a child, joining his older brother on the couch when everybody else was asleep. When the movie was over Deke had to go into his room alone at the end of the dark hallway, where he would lie awake, shivering in fright with the covers pulled over his head. Certain scary movies were still strong in his memory, and now, alone in the dark and desolate wasteland, those movies were coming back to him. "I wonder how come so many scary movies, like *The Blob*, happen at night in the desert?" he said, looking up for falling meteors.

The most terrifying movie that Deke remembered was called *Them!* It was about giant ants, grown monstrous from radioactivity out in a desert – just like this one. They always made this strange clacking sound when they attacked. One guy had tried to stop them with a Winchester, but they chewed up the rifle and pinched him to death. The only thing that would kill them was a flamethrower, and if somebody had offered one to Deke right then, he would have gladly taken it, despite the extra weight.

When Deke looked into the murky wasteland, he became almost nauseous with fright. On the roadway, he could see for a little ways, but on either side of it the darkness felt alive, itself some vast, horrible creature, waiting to consume him. Deke feared that if he ever had to go out into those hideous shadows and precipitous coulees, his heart would give out. "I don' like this, Goodrich," he said to the tire. "I don' like this at all. Let's git outa here."

The night wore on and Deke trudged along until he drooped from fatigue and was nearly mad with thirst. He didn't wear a watch but guessed he'd been walking for hours. The trip into Crow Agency now seemed like a jaunt in the park compared to this excruciating nightmare. "We been out on this damn road fer'ever," Deke mumbled to his tire. "We gotta be gittin' close. I don' know as I can go much further."

Too worn out to carry the tire anymore, Deke pushed it along, shuffling beside it, stopping to rest every few minutes. Just when he thought he'd reached his limit, the road began to climb. "Shitfire, I can't take no more a' this," he groaned after twenty paces.

But he had no choice. Deke ascended the grade one agonizing step at a time, his exhaustion and thirst so complete that he nearly forgot his fear. The tire had to be shoved and goaded up the hill, resisting him every inch of the way, and whenever Deke stopped to catch his breath he had to take care that the tire didn't roll backwards. "Don't you even think a' backslidin' on me, Goodrich," he warned it.

The urge to give up was overwhelming and just as Deke was about to say, the hell with it, and stretch out on the gravel, the tire quit fighting him and rolled easily along. Deke stopped and looked up. The horizon ahead was open; he had finally made the summit. Gasping for breath and soaked with sweat, Deke gazed to where stars met the western mountain peaks. So exhausted he wanted to throw up, Deke pulled out his hankerchief, mopped his face and ran his parched tongue over his lips. After a few minutes, the cool air blowing along the top of the ridge revived Deke a little and as he peered into the distance, a jumbled mass of stone began to take shape. "Why hell, them rocks where I met John Wayne are jest at the bottom a' this hill ...right after that bridge over the gully." Deke straightened up, inhaling the night air. "I think we got this, Goodrich," he said to the tire. "It ain't that far to the truck."

He gazed over the dark prairie below, resting his aching muscles and catching his wind for the last leg of the journey. "When we git back," he told his round companion, "the first thing I'm gonna do is have me a long drink a' water from the jug an' light up a Camel. Then I'll stick you on an' hightail it to a motel. I might even let Shelly drive so's I can rest up for when we git there."

Deke patted the tire solidly a couple of times. "I'm glad I got ya back, Goodrich," he said to it, "but you ain't worth no thirty dollars an' a rifle."

He turned around and looked back in the direction of Crow Agency. "I ain't done with that sum'bitch back there, not by a long ways. An' b'fore this is over, I'm either gonna git my Winchester back or fix his wagon but good."

Deke wiped his face again and turned back around. "Alright, hoss," he said, "it's downhill from here, let's go," and reached down to set the tire rolling.

For several seconds Deke's hand waved about in empty air. Thinking the tire had perhaps fallen over when he patted it, Deke looked at the ground. Then he looked down the road and saw a round outline against the backdrop of stars, freewheeling silently away from him.

"Holy shit!" Deke yelled and took off after his spare.

The tire was not far down the hill or its speed so great that he could not catch it, but in his excitement Deke forgot about his missing snap and let go of his pants. They immediately dropped to his knees and Deke went tumbling in the dirt. Cursing, he fought to get to his feet but his fallen Levi's had entangled his legs and he thrashed about in the dust, trying to pull them up. When he at last became vertical, Deke saw his tire, now well down the slope, rolling easy over the gravel and gathering speed.

"GODDAMIT, GOODRICH, GIT BACK HERE!" Deke hollered, as if he expected the tire to stop rolling downhill, turn around and obey him.

Skedaddling with the resolve of a petulant child whose feelings have been hurt, the tire easily outpaced Deke, who was trying to run and hold his pants up at the same time. "Ohhhhhohhhhh ..." he wailed, "it's gittin' away!"

With Deke huffing in pursuit, the tire ran true and straight until it neared the bottom of the grade, where it struck a small rock, veered to the right, hit the ditch at maximum velocity and continued on into the dark prairie until Deke saw it no more. Panting, he ran to where he had last seen his spare, now worth a good deal more to him than he had valued it only two minutes before. Deke stood looking forlornly into the black and forbidding wasteland, then his legs buckled under him and he went down on his knees, then on his belly, where he lay with his face in the dirt, sobbing and pounding his fist into the sand.

For ten minutes Deke cried into the gray dust. Finally he sat up, his tear-stained face covered with grit. "Oh God, I wanna drink a' water," he moaned, wiping his nose on the sleeve of his flannel shirt.

Deke picked up his fallen hat and put it on. "What am I gonna do now?" he said. "I don' wanna go out there." Taking a pebble from the edge of the road, he chucked it into the darkness. "I could go back to the truck, git me some water an' cigarettes an' my shotgun, then come back here an' start lookin'. Shelly might even help me." He flung another pebble into the night. "Naw, she can't leave the truck with all our gear in it." Deke wiped the tears away with the back of his fist. "Dammit anyways, I give Shelly muh' word I'd come back with a tar'r, an' I can't let 'er down."

He peered into the darkness. Much of the prairie was barren but other spots were covered with scrub brush and jutting rocks. "If my tar'r hit somethin' rightaways it might not a' gone all that far. Reckon I could look a little bit."

Deke got to his feet and walked slowly along the roadside, but saw nothing. "I reckon it wouldn't hurt ta walk in there a few feet, long as

I stay close to the road," he said, and took a stride over the shallow ditch. Careful to step only where the moonlight shone upon the sand and pea gravel, Deke treaded cautiously around any brush or rocks where snakes could be lurking. When he was about fifty feet from the road, he began walking parallel to it, but saw no tire.

"That tar'r could a' gone a long ways in here if it didn't hit nothin'," Deke said, and reluctantly forced himself deeper into the prairie. He constantly fought back his terror of the dark and avoided outright panic, but whenever a rise or rock outcrop blocked Deke's vision of the road, his heart raced until it came back into view. After ten minutes of searching, Deke's nerves were shot. "Jest a little more an' that's it. This place is really givin' me the spooks."

As he was about to give up and head back to the road, Deke came to a steep gully. He remembered the bridge just past the bottom of the hill, not far from the rock chasm and when he looked in the direction of the road, could dimly make out the steel railings. Unlike at the bridge, here Deke could see to the bottom of the ravine, which was bare sand, and guessed that the dry watercourse became shallower the further it got from the road. "Fast as that tar'r was movin', it coulda made it this far, an' if it did, it'd be down there," he said, and shivered at the thought.

Stepping carefully, Deke walked along the rim of the steep arroyo and after about 100 feet he spotted a dark, circular object lying on the sandy bottom. He got down on his belly and peered over the side to get a better look. It was a tire, but was it *his* tire? Deke knew he could get down into the ravine, but wondered if he could get back out, especially lugging a heavy tire. "Dammit anyway, how come 'at tar'r couldn't a' stopped rollin' up here?"

Still on his belly, Deke turned around and let his feet hang over the lip, then pushed against the ground with his one free hand. He dropped so suddenly that he let go of his pants and clutched at the dirt, digging the tips of his cowboy boots into the gravel to slow his descent. The sandy soil crumbled so easily that he slid clear to the bottom, howling the whole way down as his bare thighs scraped against the rough earth.

"I sure hope 'ere ain't no snakes down here," Deke said, jumping to his feet and quickly pulling his pants up over his skinned thighs. He walked over and examined the tire. It was his lost B.F Goodrich, but Deke's joy was dampened by his terror of the ravine and the knowledge that the soil was too loose for him to climb back out. "You ain't gittin' away from me agin', Goodrich, no matter what," he said, then stood the tire upright and started pushing it in the direction he hoped the ravine would level out.

The tire was difficult to roll in the soft, uneven sand and soon Deke was puffing with exhaustion and had to rest. Five minutes later he stopped again to catch his breath. "Dammit all ta hell, this gully ain't flattenin' out a'tall. I might be trapped down here fer'ever," he said, now truly terrified. But sixty yards later he came to a spot where the dry watercourse widened and was not as steep. Deke carefully laid the tire on its side and walked over to check it out. He climbed half way up without too much difficulty, then went back down to retrieve the tire.

Holding the tire in one hand and his pants with the other, Deke had to fight for every vertical foot. He made it halfway to the top, but then the slope became steeper. Breathing hard, Deke rested against the side of the gully, consumed by thirst and thinking about what would happen if he couldn't get out. He stuck the toes of his boots into the dirt, trying to force his way upward, but the soil was too loose and with no free hand to help him climb he went nowhere and was soon winded. "If I didn't have ta hold my pants up I think I could git it. Maybe I'll jest let 'em fall and the hell with it."

Deke let go of his britches and used his left hand to help pull himself up while his right clung to the tire. He kicked his toes into the soft soil and pushed, but his Levis dropped to his knees, binding his legs and making them useless. He slid two yards back down the hill. "Sum'bitch," he cried, "how come nothin' ever goes right fer me?"

Out of breath and frustrated, Deke tried to think of a solution. "I know what I need ta do," he muttered after a few minutes, "but I sure don' like the idea."

Dropping down to where the slope wasn't as steep, Deke carefully scooted the tire to a stable spot, then took his wallet and John Wayne belt buckle out of his jeans and put them in the front pockets of his flannel shirt and buttoned them tight. He took off his boots, tugged his pants off and put his boots back on. Now unimpeded, Deke scrambled up the slope to where the top was only a few feet above his head and flung his Levis in an arc over the rim. He eased back down, grabbed the tire and began working his way up the side of the arroyo. Deke struggled to the spot he had tossed his jeans from, but the remaining several feet of the ravine was nearly vertical.

The only way he could see of getting the tire to the top was to lift it above his head and push it over the rim. Deke dug his boots into the yellow dirt until he found toeholds that felt solid, then groaning, pulled the heavy ten-ply up a few inches at a time until he got it head-high. Crooking his neck sideways, Deke balanced the tire on his shoulder against the side of the gully, put both hands beneath it and pushed up as hard as he could. Just as his arms were about to give out, Deke gave a final shove and the B. F. Goodrich tipped above the edge. He pushed it a few more inches to be sure, then leaned against the steep wall, his sides heaving. When he felt strong enough to pull himself up, Deke raised his legs, kicked new toeholds into the dirt and climbed to the top, completely exhausted. He pulled the tire back from the lip of the ravine then laid his face and shoulders across it, gasping for air. "You sure put me to a lot a trouble, Goodrich," he told the tire, "but I gotcha now."

For some time Deke rested on the tire, panting and desperate for water. When he finally sat up and looked into the dark prairie, he had the unnerving feeling that he was *not alone* and that he was being watched. Try as he might, Deke could not stop the memories of the old horror movies from entering his brain or keep his hands and bare knees from shaking. "I need ta find my pants an' git back to the road, right now," he said, and started to stand up.

From behind him came a strange clacking sound. Something large or *some things*, were trodding on the gravelly prairie surface. He spun around quickly and saw half a dozen amorphous dark shapes, each with a set of large, glowing eyes, coming at him.

"OH GOD, IT'S *THEM!* IT'S THEM BIG ANTS!" Deke screamed, grabbed the tire and took off.

Heedless of direction, Deke ran as fast as he was able, too panicked to even watch for snakes. Lugging the tire, his gait was no more than a ponderous lope, and even fueled by adrenaline, his exhausted body could not carry him far. After a couple of hundred yards his legs and lungs gave out. Deke dropped the tire and fell to the ground, chest heaving, his leg muscles on fire. He looked behind him, horrified to see that the creatures were still coming on. "I can't let 'em pinch me in half," Deke moaned, and tried to get to his feet but was too spent.

He struggled again to get up but collapsed back onto the hard ground, painfully retching. The monsters continued their advance, moonlight glinting off their bulbous eyes. "Ohhhhhh," Deke wailed feebly, "I don' wanna die like this. Go away … jest go away … I never hurt no ants in my life … I swear it."

The creatures stopped and stared at Deke then the lead one turned sideways and casually began walking off. The others followed and Deke saw their profiles against the night sky. "Why shit," he said, "they ain't nothin' but cows." Deke watched the curious little herd of range cattle trail off into the prairie then let his head fall back onto the sandy ground. "I can't keep goin' like this, I'm plum wore out," he mumbled.

The night air helped rejunvenate Deke but when a breeze whipped up, his sweat-covered body chilled and he knew he had to start moving again. With sore, stiff muscles, Deke slowly got to his feet. "Now I even lost muh' pants," he said, looking down at his trembling legs.

Deke wiped his nose, and then his brow, on the sleeve of his flannel shirt. He leaned over, set his spare tire upright and sat down on it. "I'm glad I found ya, Goodrich" he told it, "but now I got no idea where the road is … or even where that gully's at." The wind came up again and Deke shivered. "I can't set here fer'ever. I'll freeze ta death or die a' thirst … maybe even both. But I'm 'fraid if I start walkin' I'll jest git even more … *lost*."

The word terrified Deke. He'd seen enough movies to know what happens to people who get lost in the desert at night. The chill wind gusting over the landscape whipped through the juniper and underbrush, making strange noises. Deke's imagination soon turned them into eerie wails. "This place ain't far from that battlefield over yonder," Deke said, watching the rustling bushes. "Who knows what all goes on up 'ere when it gits dark? Even that In'jun in the rest'runt said that place was full a' dangerous spirits."

Deke cradled his head in his hands. "What'm I gonna do?" he moaned. "I wonder if …." He unbuttoned his shirt pocket, took out the brass belt buckle and rubbed his fingers over John Wayne's face. "Duke?" he called, "I sure could use some help right now."

Deke peered into the darkness, looking for the strong, familiar figure. Near a stand of junipers Deke thought he saw a wavering shadow. He rubbed the buckle harder. "Is 'at you, Duke? Could ya come help me agin'?" No answer. Then the shadow faded to an indistinct mass and disappeared.

"I reckon you ain't gonna help me no more, Duke," Deke said dejectedly, and put the buckle back in his shirt. He had no tears left to cry, but his guts wrenched dry spasms.

"Oh, Lord, help me find a way outa here," Deke pleaded … and he saw the light.

At first he thought it was a brilliant, newly risen star on the horizon, but it moved so rapidly that Deke knew it was no star. The light quickly grew in size and was definitely coming toward him. Deke prayed it was not coming *for* him. "Ohhh, shitfire, I sure hope it ain't one a' them yoo-oh-eff things from outer space. That's the last thing I need right now," Deke said, trembling.

The single beam ran linear for a stretch, wavered and straightened out again. Frozen with horror, Deke watched the oncoming light. The craft briefly rose to a higher plane and then began to descend, its shining eye pointing earthward. Deke knew running would be futile and he was far too tired to even try. As the object came closer, Deke saw that it didn't have one light, but two. The second one pointed straight down instead of forward and Deke's first thought was that it was for spotlighting earthlings.

As his heart was about to give out Deke realized that the object was not in the sky at all, but on the road, and was coming down the hill where his tire had taken off. In a flash it roared by and Deke saw the dark silhouette of a battered Cadillac Eldorado, barely more than 100 feet away, throwing up a roostertail of gray dust in its wake.

"C'mon, Goodrich," Deke yelled, grabbing his spare tire. "We ain't very far from the road … an' they're a'headed right fer Shelly."

Deke ran no more than a dozen steps before he had to put the heavy tire down and roll it over the uneven prairie. Every yard was a struggle. His lungs wheezed like a bellows and his legs ached fire, but Deke soldiered on. When he reached the road, Deke took half a dozen gulps of air, picked up the B.F. Goodrich and tried again to run with it. Twenty steps later he almost collapsed. He set the tire down and rested his forhead against the tread, gasping for breath. "We gotta git to the truck righ' now," Deke panted. "There ain' no tellin' what them In'juns migh' do ta Shelly."

Staggering with exhaustion, Deke goaded the tire along, resting every twenty or thirty paces. He came to the bridge over the ravine, inhaled a few quick breaths and pushed on. At the bus-shaped boulder and eerie rockpile that formed the canyon, Deke entered without hesitation. He rolled the tire between the dark walls, not letting his fear of snakes slow him down. The tailpipe was no longer lying in the road but Deke gave the matter little heed. Shortly after leaving the chasm he saw the red glow of taillights ahead and continued until he was close enough that he could hear voices. Easing the tire into the ditch, Deke laid it flat and whispered, "You wait here, Goodrich."

Moving in a slow crouch Deke went another 25 yards and then got down on his hands and knees. The Cadillac was parked directly behind his pickup, its forward pointing headlight throwing a yellow beam over the Ford. The dangling headlamp cast a downward glow that allowed Deke to see what was taking place around the Eldorado. "I gotta move quiet, like an In'jun," he said to himself, and edged closer.

The voices were louder now but Deke still couldn't make out any words. He attempted to crawl, 'Indian style', like he'd seen in the movies, but the stones scraping against his naked legs hurt so much he nearly cried out in pain. After only a few feet, Deke stopped crawling and watched.

Shelly was leaning in the front passenger window of the Eldorado, talking. Suddenly she turned and ran for the pickup. Both doors of the Cadillac flew open and four Indians jumped out and followed in pursuit. Hurry Shelly, hurry! Git in the cab. Don' let 'em gitch ya!

Shelly made it to the truck cab as the Indians became engaged in taking Deke and Shelly's personal possessions from the wooden trunk in the pickup's bed and loading them into the back of the Eldorado. Damn thievin' redskins! They're a'takin' ever'thing we got.

After they'd cleaned out the trunk the Indians went to where Shelly was holding out in the cab. Three of them blocked the passenger side where Shelly was sitting and the solidly built leader stood by the driver's door so she couldn't escape. Ohhhhhh, nohhhh! Now they got 'er surrounded.

Shelly grabbed the shotgun. That's it, Shelly! Use the 10 gauge ta hold 'em off.

Quick as a wink, the leader opened the driver's door and took the gun from Shelly's hand before she could react. "Ohhhhhhhh," Deke moaned in a low voice, trying to stifle his anger.

Shelly got out of the truck carrying her canteen, then walked back to the Cadillac, closely guarded by three of the Indians. They must be a' takin' 'er a long ways if she's packin' water fer the trip. Likely ta trade 'er off ta some other tribe ... after they've all had their way with 'er.

One of the Indians opened the car door and motioned for Shelly to get in. When she turned to resist, he put his hand on top of her head and forced her into the back seat. Deke's gut churned with fury and he almost charged in to save her, but being unarmed and outnumbered four to one, knew he wouldn't stand a chance. Helplessly, Deke lay in the dirt as two Indians climbed into the back seat, one on either side of Shelly, and the other two got in the front and the Cadillac sped away, throwing gravel.

When their taillights vanished into the night, Deke got to his feet and let out an agonized scream. He was faced with a harsh and undeniable fact: the girl he loved had been taken captive by Indians.

"I'm gonna gitch ya back, Shelly, jest like John Wayne did with Debbie in *The Searchers* ... no matter how long it takes or if I die tryin. Ya got my word on it."

Chapter 35

Shelly watched Deke's form dissolve into the darkness, wishing she were the one going off into the prairie, but Deke had to go. The truck was his responsibility and he needed to learn to deal with his fears. She let the darkness drape over her and sat for a while in the pickup with the door open, but the prairie was too alive for her to stay in the truck. Knowing she couldn't go far, Shelly strolled several hundred yards further down the road. She walked into the dark prairie and on her way back to the truck examined plants and smelled sprigs of sage. The moon appeared over the distant hills and Shelly saw the outline of Deke's Ford, but continued on through the wasteland. When the coyotes started in with their yelps and howls, she listened, entranced by their music, wishing they would come closer so she could see them. "I sure hope Deke is enjoyin' this," she said.

Continuing on, she saw the silhouette of the rounded boulder and jagged rock where Deke had hit the muffler. The howling seemed to be coming from near there, so Shelly made her way toward the mysterious looking jumble of stone. As she got closer, she saw movement among the sage and got down on her hands and knees, approaching quietly and trying to stay hidden. The two coyotes were engaged in other matters and didn't notice Shelly until the wind blew her scent to them. They turned to look and their gleaming eyes met hers. "Hey there," Shelly called to them, "you two make a cute couple." The coyotes looked at her curiously and trotted away for privacy.

She stood up and walked to the dark entrance of the little canyon, marveling at how the road entered the vertical walls. The chasm certainly looked spooky and Shelly thought about going in, but she was already too far from the pickup. "I bet there's been some strange goin's on in there," she said and reluctantly turned around. If she had entered, Shelly would have seen a strange thing going on at that very moment: a grown man lying on his back, maniacally sucking on his bare leg.

Shelly returned to the pickup, sat in the cab for a while, then became impatient and climbed out again. Deke's likely in Crow Agency by now, she thought. He shoulda made good time with nothin' ta slow 'im down.

She walked out into the scrubland again, then wandered back to the truck, climbed into the bed and sat on the wooden trunk. Every fifteen minutes she pressed the light on her watch and checked the time. When Deke had been gone for close to three hours she began to seriously worry if he was okay. She walked to the mysterious canyon again but this time she entered.

"This place is really cool," she said, looking up at the band of stars between the sheer rocks. At the spot where the road curved, Shelly saw the "S" shaped tailpipe and kicked it off the road. "Somebody not too smart could mistake that thing fer a snake."

She walked as far as the bridge and looked over the guardrail into the black gully. "I hope Deke didn't end up down there," she said and went back to the truck.

The wind picked up and Shelly leaned against the bed and listened to it blow through the prairie. On the far horizon a small cluster of stars rose above one of the dark hills. "Wow, it's the Pleiades," she said. "In a while Orion oughta be tailin' along." She found the Big Dipper and followed the pointer stars to Polaris and then in the other direction to Leo. Cassiopeia twinkled above her, impressive as always. Shelly remembered that the Great Square of Pegasus was nearby. It took a minute, but she found the winged-horse and thought of Tramp, the horse that had given her wings. Off to one side was the fuzzy little dot of the Andromeda Galaxy.

All of this, Shelly had learned from her father. He knew every constellation and the stories behind their names. Even into her teens, Shelly would join Clete in the pasture behind their house and they'd stand in the dark, talking and looking at the sky. The Andromeda Galaxy was Clete's favorite.

"There's billions an' billions a' stars in that little fuzz ball," he'd say, "an' likely a whole lot a' worlds in there too. Jus' imagine, Shelly, what all might be happenin' right now in that little splotch a' light up there."

Eyes sparkling, Cletus would tell his daughter, "People live under the sky their whole lives an' hardly a one knows anything about it. Ah'm gonna teach ya the stars an' constellations, Shelly, so whenever ya look up at night, you'll have frien's in the sky."

Seeing the stars over Montana reminded Shelly of how far she was from home and how much she'd lost and left behind. She shook her head to clear it and looked at her watch. Twenty past eleven and Deke had been gone for over three and a half hours. In all that time no cars had come by and now she was more concerned about Deke than their belongings. She decided to go look for him.

Shelly filled her canteen and drank what little water remained in the jug. Taking a piece of blank paper from the glove box, she started to write a note to Deke when she heard a motor in the distance. A single headlight shot out of the slot canyon and the engine's roar filled Shelly's ears. "Good," Shelly said, "maybe Deke's gittin' a ride back."

She stepped away from the pickup and waved to the car as it approached. The Cadillac screeched to a stop behind the truck and Shelly went back to see if Deke was inside. She leaned into the open front passenger window but saw only the four Indian men who had been in the Crow's Nest.

"Howdy," she said. "Y'all seen Deke anywhere along the road?"

"What's a Deke?" the man closest to her said.

"Deke," Shelly answered. "The feller who was with me when we saw ya in Lawrence's rest'ernt."

"No," the driver answered, "were we supposed to be looking?"

"What happened to your truck?" the skinny kid in the back seat asked.

"We ran over a muffler back in them rocks an' got a flat," Shelly said, pointing down the road. "Then our spare tire came up missin'. Deke hiked in to Crow Agency ta git another tire at that gas station where we saw ya parked."

The four men in the Cadillac exchanged looks and the other kid in the back seat said something that Shelly didn't understand.

"Can ya speak up?" Shelly said to him. "It's kinda hard ta hear 'cause your car ain't got no muffler."

The men looked at each other again.

"How long has he been gone?" the driver asked.

"It's been close ta four hours," Shelly told him.

"Hmmmmm," the driver said. "He should have been back by now."

"Maybe he interrupted one of Sam's favorite TV shows," the older of the two kids in the back seat said and laughed. "Then Sam would've just slit his throat and gone back in the house to finish watching the program."

"That could've happened," the skinny kid in the back agreed.

"What!" Shelly yelped. "We need ta go back there right now an' find out."

"Two-dogs was only joking," the man beside the driver said. "Sam Black Eagle is gruff and would be dangerous if pushed too far, but he is not as mean as he looks. Anyway, we just went by his place a few minutes ago and everything was quiet."

"Except the top of his Teepee-to-the-Sky fell down," the guy in the back seat said. "He won't be happy about that." He looked at the man in the front seat. "And stop calling me Two-dogs. My name is Charlie."

"But you have two dogs," the man said to him and laughed.

"I know I have two dogs, dumb ass, but that's not why you call me Two-dogs, so stop it."

Trying to get back in the conversation Shelly said, "Could ya drive me in ta Crow Agency so's I could check on Deke?"

"No," the driver said. "We're on our way to a powwow and we want to get there before it's over. We've already missed most of the dancing." He leaned across the seat and looked at Shelly: "Why don't you come along?"

"Thanks for the invite," Shelly said, "but I don't wanta in'trude. 'Sides, I oughta go look for Deke."

"You should come. This is just a small powwow among friends, not a big event like Crow Fair," the front passenger said, "and you would be welcome."

"You'd have a good time and would meet a lot of people," the kid in the back seat told Shelly. "If that Deke guy was at Sam's we would have seen lights. He wasn't on the road, either, so there's no use of you walking the whole way in."

"Jeremy's right," the driver said. "You could join in the dancing."

Shelly's heart jumped. Going to a *real* powwow and dancing with *real* Indians was beyond her greatest dream. "I'd love ta come," she said, "but Deke would freak out if he got back an' I was gone."

"You can leave your friend a note, telling him where you're at and how to get there," the front passenger told her. "The powwow is only a few miles from here. You turn right on the road to Hardin and in a little way there's a bridge and a camping area on the Bighorn River called Two Leggins. It's right beside the road and full of teepees, you can't miss it."

"The dancing ends at midnight," the stocky man behind the wheel said, "and then we have the Buffalo Ceremony, but that does not last long. If your friend does not show up by then, we will all go look for him. I'm sure others at the powwow would help look for him too." The other three men in the car nodded their heads.

Shelly thought the offer over. "It sure sounds fun, but I don't know about leavin' me an' Deke's stuff here in the pickup."

"I don't think anyone else will be along tonight," the driver said, "but we can put your things in the car trunk. No one will bother them at the powwow."

That did it. "Alright," Shelly said, "c'mon an' help me git our stuff."

Excited now, Shelly trotted back to the pickup as the four men piled out of the Cadillac and followed. "You wanta grab ev'rything outa that wooden trunk in the bed while I write a note ta Deke," she told them.

Shelly jumped into the cab and began writing. The two younger men hopped into the truck bed and passed everything in the wooden box down to the others, who carried it back to the Cadillac. When they were done three of the men went up to where Shelly sat with the dome light on, finishing her note, while the thick-set Crow man walked to the driver's side of the pickup. "Is there anything else?" he asked Shelly.

She picked up Deke's shotgun. "Here, ya better take this, but be careful, it's loaded."

The driver opened the pickup door and took the gun from Shelly's hand. "I'll put it in a place that's safe."

Shelly left the note to Deke on the seat then got out of the truck. "Is there anything I could contribute to the powwow?" she asked.

"It's traditional for a guest to make an offering of tobacco," the driver said. "Do you have any cigarettes?"

"I don't smoke," Shelly said, "but Deke's got most of a carton here that you can have. He's always got plenty with 'im so he won't need 'em." She opened the glove box and handed over Deke's carton of Camels.

"Thank you," the driver said. "I will pass these out at the powwow and tell everyone that it is a gift from you."

After grabbing her canteen, Shelly walked back to the Cadillac with the three Crow men while the driver carried Deke's shotgun to his car and stowed it under the front seat. The older of the men opened the door for her then held the front seat so she could get into the back. Shelly turned to say "thanks" and almost hit her head on the roof as she got in.

"Watch your head, tall-girl," he said, and put his hand on the back of Shelly's head so she wouldn't bump her noggin.

The two younger men climbed in the back seat with her, and as the Cadillac sped away with all four windows down, Shelly hollered over the engine's roar, "My name is Shelly Stamper an' I'm from Wes' Virginia."

Next to her, the youngest and skinniest of the four stuck his hand out and said, "I'm Jeremy Old Crow." The other young Indian in the back seat extended his hand. "Charlie Whitebear," he said.

"My name is Robert Backbone," the man riding shotgun, who looked in his mid-twenties said, and turned and shook Shelly's hand. The driver, who looked about the same age as the man beside him, also turned around and offered his hand. "I'm Melvin Not Afraid," he told Shelly.

Just like with Lawrence Iron Bull, Shelly was surprised at the gentleness of the men's handshakes. "Lawrence told me some a' y'all are related to 'im," she said, trying to be conversational.

To Shelly's discomfort, the driver remained looking at her. "Lawrence Iron Bull is my uncle," he said. "My mother is his sister."

"I see," Shelly said, but she was thinking, This guy drives like Tommy Kegley.

Charlie Whitebear said, "Lawrence is my cousin, and Jeremy's too."

"Are you and Jeremy cousins?" Shelly asked him.

"Probably," he said.

"A lot of people on the rez are related," Melvin said, still turned toward Shelly.

Shelly nodded, but her eyes were focused on the bullet riddled yellow sign in the Cadillac's headlight indicating a sharp curve.

Melvin glanced at the road, slid sideways through the curve without slowing down and turned back to Shelly. "That's what makes our people so strong … that and our shared culture and history."

"How come yor so late gittin' to the powwow?" Shelly asked.

"We were there earlier today," Melvin said, "helping to set everything up. Then we decided to go back to Crow Agency and get something to eat at the Crow's Nest."

"Is that when ya lost your muffler an' tailpipe?" Shelly cut in.

"How did you know about that?" Robert asked her.

"Lawrence told us," Shelly said.

"Oh."

"After we took the tires we had collected to Sam Black Eagle to trade for gas," Melvin said, "we were going to come back here, but just after you saw us at his station, someone came by and told me my aunt had lost her medicine and needed more. She's old and diabetic."

Melvin drifted another curve then looked at Shelly again. "She's forgetful too and sometimes loses her insulin. By then the pharmacy in Hardin was closed so we had to drive into Billings. After that we had to drive my aunt's medicine to her in Lodge Grass. We're just getting back from there now."

"That was mighty good a' ya ta do that," Shelly told him, but her eyes were glued to the stop sign ahead where the road ended in a 'T'.

Without looking for traffic or slowing down Melvin wheeled through the intersection and sped north as cold air blasted through the car. Chilled to her bones, Shelly was about to ask if the car had any windows when the Cadillac shot over a bridge and whipped into an open area covered with teepees and giant cottonwood trees. The car bucked and bounced over a rough dirt track until Melvin stopped in the midst of a cluster of randomly parked vehicles. Robert Backbone and Melvin hopped out and Melvin held the front seat forward for Shelly and the others to exit.

Shelly's first impression of the camp was that she had dreamed herself back 100 years in time. Scattered among tall, straight cottonwoods, the dark outlines of 25 teepees rose from a haze of wispy smoke and the flickering light of half a dozen small, untended campfires. At the far end of the encampment was the glow of a much larger fire and near it the movement of people and the sound of drumming. Just beyond that, the Bighorn River flowed by, swift and deep, stars and moonlight glinting off its black water.

As Shelly walked with the four Indian men toward the sound of the drumming, the odor of wood smoke filled her nostrils. Dogs ran helter-skelter through the camp, barking and growling. Once or twice she heard the voices of children in the lodges they passed. She thought of how the Indian camp on the Little Bighorn, not many miles away, must have been much like this one the night before Custer attacked, but a hundred times bigger. No one spoke as they walked and the drumming became louder until Shelly heard singing and saw the dancers.

Near the river a group of cottonwood trees rose so high into the night that it looked like their top leaves brushed against the sky. On one side of them was the fire and in the center of an open circle sat the drummers, two men and two women, around a large powwow drum. Each drummer beat upon the drumhead with only one stick and sang as they played. Circling the drum clockwise were perhaps 30 dancers, both men and women, and another 20 people watching from the side. As Shelly and the men made their way to the dancing, nearly everyone who was watching turned and acknowledged them with a nod of the head or a soft, spoken greeting.

The dress of the dancers varied considerably but nearly everyone had some type of dancing gear. Some were only partially arrayed but others were dancing in full regalia. Many were also wearing paint and had rattle sticks.

"Is there a name for this kind a' dancin'?" Shelly asked Melvin.

"There is a name for each style," Melvin said, "and for each dance. If we had been here earlier you would have seen the difference between Fancy Dancing and Traditional Dancing. My favorite is the Hot Dance because it is a dance of the Crow tribe. Bigger powwows have many kinds of songs, like welcome songs and going home songs or even sneak-up songs and the dancers compete, often for prizes or money. But our dancing here is not a competition so we don't have any dancing rules. The only rule we have for this powwow is no alcohol or drugs."

"What kind a' dance are they doin' now?" Shelly asked.

"We do the different styles and dances early," Melvin said, "and after a while the drummers play what they want and people can dance in their own fashion. This dance is similar, I suppose, to what we call an Intertribal, but even more informal. As you can see, some of the dancers are still in their regular clothes. We just want everyone to join in and feel comfortable here."

"I really like some of those costumes," Shelly told him.

"We never call them costumes," Melvin said. "Costumes are for Halloween. Sometimes we say outfit or rig, but the proper term is regalia." Melvin held up Deke's carton of Camels. "I'll be back in a minute," he said, and walked off.

The other three men had also gone so Shelly turned to watch the dancers, fascinated by the regalia: beads, face paint, metal bells, tin cones, feathers, bustles, rowels, elk teeth and roaches. The colors of the dresses, breeches and breechclouts were also striking. Shelly soon became mesmerized by the drumming and singing and the intensity of the dancers. They seemed in another realm, a spirit world that she herself had felt or dreamt, but never fully entered. She was snapped from her reverie when a middle-aged couple walked over and stood quietly, waiting to speak to her.

"Hello," Shelly said to them.

"Hello," the woman replied. "Welcome to our powwow."

"Thank you for the tobacco," the man said to her.

"Oh, sure," Shelly said, not quite understanding.

Then she saw Melvin Not Afraid passing out packs of Deke's cigarettes and pointing to her. Several other people also walked over and thanked her. After he had given out all of the cigarettes Melvin came back and stood beside Shelly. "You would have been welcome here anyway," he told her, "but giving out the tobacco showed everyone that you are considerate and respectful."

A young woman about Melvin's age with long, braided hair, strong features, and deep-set black eyes danced over to him. She wore tall moccasins and a red velvet dress covered with small tin cones that jingled when she moved.

"Where have you been?" the woman said. "The dancing is almost over."

Melvin told her about getting his aunt's medicine.

"Sometimes you're too nice, Melvin. People get you to do things that they could do for themselves because they know you will not say no to them." She looked at Shelly. "Who is this?"

"Her name is Shelly Stamper and she's from West Virginia," Melvin said. "She was stranded along the road. And this is Sharon Goes Ahead," Melvin told Shelly, "but everyone calls her Shar."

"With a last name like Stamper, you should be a good dancer," the woman said without smiling, then turned back to Melvin. "The drummers might go a little longer since you and the others just got here, but you need to get dressed and join us. Where is your rig?"

"It's in my lodge," Melvin said, "but I won't have time to put everything on. I'll grab what I can and be right back."

Melvin hurried away and Shar turned to Shelly. "Come with me."

Her manner left little room for argument and as Shelly followed along Shar said, "I have a dress in my lodge that you can wear. It will make you feel more comfortable dancing with us."

Shar entered a teepee and Shelly ducked low and went in behind her. The inside of the lodge was so dark that Shelly stopped at the doorway, afraid of tripping or stepping on something valuable. It was her first time in a real teepee and Shelly was awed. This wasn't like a movie teepee at all, but had a very lived-in look. Dresses and clothes were draped over the liner or hung from a rope stretched between poles. Blankets and buffalo hides covered the floor, and assorted crates and chests were scattered about.

Sharon Goes Ahead came back to where Shelly stood, holding a white, beaded dress in her hand. "Take off your jacket and put this on over your clothes," she told Shelly.

Shelly took the dress, patterned throughout with beaded designs, in her hands. "That's the softest leather I've ever felt."

"It's brain-tanned buckskin," Shar told her. "That's how I make my living."

"You made this?" Shelly said, amazed at the dress's beauty.

"Yes, now put it on, I want to get back to the dancing."

Shelly took off her denim jacket and slipped the dress over her head. Shar was thicker but shorter than Shelly so the long dress came only to Shelly's knees, but looked striking on her. "I don't know as I should be wearin' this, Shar," Shelly said. "It's mighty nice, I wouldn't wanta git it dirty."

"Don't worry, it'll be fine," Shar said. "Now let's go."

They walked back to the dance circle and Shar said, "This dance is a Celebration Dance so any type of dancing is acceptable. Just pick someone who's style you like and try to emulate what they are doing." Then Shar danced away.

Shelly let the singing enter her head and began moving her feet to the drummer's rhythm while watching the other dancers, glad that they paid little attention to her. She saw Robert Backbone and Charlie Whitebear, both with face paint and feathers, but they did not look at her. Only Jeremy Old Crow, wearing ankle bells and a bustle, glanced over and smiled.

Melvin Not Afraid sooned joined the dance circle, wearing moccasins, a porcupine broach that came to the middle of his back and a tail bustle of feathers sticking out in every direction. Shelly immediately sensed a change in him. No longer just a man trying to make his way in a hard world, Melvin's steps were forceful and sure, his spirit as powerful as his stocky body. Each time his moccasin hit the dirt, Melvin connected with the earth and with his ancestors who had danced on this same ground for many generations.

Shelly danced to the drumming, watching for someone she could follow. A small, wiry man in full regalia and shaking a rattle stick danced nearby. His rig was not colorful or fancy, but looked like he had created it long ago from items he had collected from the land. Yet with his weathered vest and leather leggings, bone breastplate and feathers, he cut an imposing figure. He danced with such intensity and power, that only when Shelly got close enough to see his face in the firelight did she realize he was old. Fascinated, Shelly tried to watch the man without being too obvious or rude, but whenever she started to get his steps down something would change in his dancing. Sometimes he would even put his feet down on the offbeat. Shelly was about to move off and try to follow someone else when the old man looked into her eyes and smiled. Gazing into those penetrating eyes, Shelly felt that the man was not old so much as *ancient* and that she was looking into a time before the reservations or the coming of the Europeans, almost before time was thought of as time, and that his eyes held those memories. He circled away and Shelly forgot herself and just danced.

Hearing nothing but the singing and the drumming, Shelly danced and danced. The drumming became the heartbeat of the earth and through her feet she felt the roundness and the immensity of the planet beneath her and knew that it had a spirit and a life within it, just like her. The stars moved and under her feet the earth turned and Shelly felt the circle of all things and understood that the circle she danced in was but a part of many other, greater circles, a cycle of life that came back on itself again and again and time was no longer something to be measured or feared. When the drumming and singing abruptly stopped, Shelly had no inkling of how long she had danced. People slowly began walking to the outside of the circle. Shelly saw Melvin Not Afraid and Robert Backbone standing with some other people and walked over to them.

Sweat beaded on Melvin's brow and he was breathing hard. "Did you enjoy the dancing?" he asked Shelly.

"I felt like I was in a trance," Shelly said, and pointed to the old dancer who had smiled at her. "I think that man put a spell on me."

Melvin laughed. "That's George White Clay, but I don't think he would have done that."

"Somethin' happened when he looked at me," Shelly said, "'cause I don't know if I danced for ten hours or ten minutes."

"That happens to a lot of dancers," Robert Backbone told her. "George White Clay is one of our most respected elders, but he's very quiet. Some people say he is a shaman, but he has never said that himself."

"Can I meet 'im?" Shelly asked.

"I can introduce you to him," Melvin said, "but he may not say much."

"That's okay," Shelly said. "He just spoke ta me with his eyes, anyway."

As they walked over to where he stood, Melvin told Shelly, "When George was young, he knew many of the Crow warriors who fought with General Crook and scouted for Custer. He was a friend of Chief Plenty Coups."

"Lawrence Iron Bull told me about Plenty Coups," Shelly said, "and what a great chief he was."

"Sometimes," Melvin said, "if you can catch him in the right mood, George will tell you stories of those days and the people he met."

"I'd shor love ta hear that," Shelly said.

Melvin and Shelly went to where George was standing quietly with a small group of people. He turned to face them, the top of his head barely reaching Shelly's shoulders. "George," Melvin said, "this is Shelly Stamper from West Virginia. I invited her to the powwow."

George smiled at Shelly and stuck out his hand. "You enjoyed the dancing," he said to her.

Shelly eased off from her usual robust handshake and smiled back, captivated by the old man's eyes. Hidden in their depths were memories and mysteries she wanted to know, but all she could think of to say was, "Thank you for helping me."

George's face crinkled into a grin and he was about to say something else when a group of people came up and said, "The Buffalo Ceremony is starting."

Melvin, George, and the others began walking toward the big teepee in the center of the camp. "Is the Buffalo Ceremony part of every powwow?" Shelly asked.

"Oh, no," Melvin explained. "As far as I know, this is something we only do here. This powwow began about the time I was born and my family was part of getting it started. I don't know whose idea the Buffalo Ceremony was, but it has been a tradition since the beginning." He turned to George White Clay. "Maybe George knows. You were at the first one, weren't you, George?"

"Yes," George said. "That was in 1946. Some of the families who had sons in the service started this powwow to celebrate those who came home from the war and to remember and honor those who didn't.

The Buffalo Ceremony was their way of doing that, but after that first year it became what it is today."

"Were you in the service?" Shelly asked.

"Yes," George said quietly, "I was in France during World War I."

At that moment Sharon Goes Ahead caught up to them. "I like your bustle," she said to Melvin. "Is this the first time you've worn it?"

"I finished it last week so it would be ready for tonight's dancing."

"It looks good on you," she told him, and hooked Melvin's arm in hers as they walked to the main lodge. Outside the doorway, Melvin took off his bustle so he could sit down, then laid it on a nearby picnic table and ducked into the doorway. Shelly followed, and after stooping to get through the entrance, straightened up and stood awed at the scene before her.

The interior of the lodge was hazy with smoke but not as dark as Shar's, for in the center a fire of leaping yellow flames sent light and dancing shadows off the white sides, highlighting the running bison painted on the teepee's outer surface. Unlike Sharon Goes Ahead's smaller teepee, this one did not have a liner and people sat almost to the edge of the perimeter. Over fifty Crow of all ages, many of them painted and in regalia from the dance, sat cross-legged in a circle and once again Shelly had the sensation that she had been transported in time.

Shelly sat down with Melvin and Shar a few rows back from the center of the lodge. Nearly everyone in the lodge was talking and Shelly heard speech she didn't recognize and realized some of the Indians were speaking Crow. Several people seated nearby nodded to her or said hello and a couple of the men shook her hand. She felt a sharp poke in her ribs and turning, saw that the middle-aged woman seated to her right, also wearing a buckskin dress, but not as fancy as the one she had on, had elbowed her. "Shar must like you a lot to loan you that dress," the woman said.

"It was mighty nice a' her ta do that," Shelly told her.

The woman elbowed her again. "Buffalo meat," she said and nodded toward the fire. "Smells good, hey? This is my favorite part of the powwow."

A very large and ancient cast iron kettle hung from a tripod above the fire, wisps of steam slipping from beneath its heavy lid. "Oh, yeah," Shelly said to her, and suddenly felt hungry.

People quieted down and when an elder wearing a vest decorated with shells and medals stood up, everyone became silent. "That's Alvin Yellowtail," Melvin whispered to Shelly. "He was one of the people who started this powwow. His son was killed in the war."

Alvin Yellowtail cleared his throat and began speaking in a hoarse, but strong voice. "Thank you for coming to the powwow," he said. "This is the twenty-eighth year of the Two-Leggins gathering and my hope is that the younger members of our tribe will keep it going for many more." Throughout the lodge, people nodded or said, "Yes," to assure Alvin Yellowtail that would happen.

"I am told," he said, "that we have a guest tonight. A young woman from the eastern mountains far from here." Alvin turned to Shelly. "Welcome," he said, "and thank you for your gift of tobacco."

The woman to the right of Shelly poked her in the ribs again, lifted a pack of Camels from beneath her dress and showed them to her.

Alvin continued. "The dancing went well tonight and we thank the drummers." Nods and mumbles of approval went around the lodge.

"We also want to thank those who helped slaughter the buffalo and cook the meat that we are about to eat." He lifted the heavy lid from the iron kettle and sat it on the ground then took out a chunk of meat the size of a man's fist. The aroma from the pot filled the teepee as Alvin held up the steaming piece of bison.

"We give our thanks to the buffalo that has been the strength and lifeblood of the Apsaalooke since Old Man Coyote created the world and in eating it, this animal will now become a part of each one of us." Alvin took a bite. "Tonight we share this meat in the company of our brothers and sisters who are still here and we honor the spirits of those who have gone. As we eat, let us remember them and be grateful for the contributions and sacrifices they made to keep our people strong and free." Alvin took another bite and sat down.

George White Clay stood up next and took a piece of bison from the kettle. But George did not speak. Instead, he turned in a slow circle and looked at the seated members of his tribe. He made eye contact with each person in the lodge and for the brief second his eyes met hers, Shelly felt his spirit pulse through her. Then George sat down and started to eat.

The elder beside George, a thin, dignified looking woman wearing a blue dress and long hair that came nearly to her waist, then stood up. But before she could speak, two dogs came through the lodge entrance, which had been left open. The larger one was brazen and headed directly toward the cooking pot but the smaller one slunk into the shadows, hoping no one would spot him.

Robert Backbone, who was seated two people away from Shar, turned around and called to the back of the teepee. "Hey Two-dogs, get your mutts out of the lodge. We're trying to have the Buffalo Ceremony."

Charlie Whitebear scowled at Robert but got up and chased the dog nearest the fire out the door, but the other one avoided him until Charlie finally cornered the cur and grabbed him by the hair on the back of his neck. Snapping and growling, the dog tried to bite whoever he could as Charlie dragged him to the teepee door and sent him scurrying with a moccasin to the ribs.

"Robert hates that dog," Melvin whispered to Shelly. "Slinker bit him last year at Crow Fair so he calls Charlie 'Two-dogs', just to make him mad."

"How come that makes him mad?" Shelly asked.

The woman beside Shelly poked her again. "Because it's short for Two-dogs Fucking," she said, loud enough for the people around her to turn and look.

"Oh," Shelly said, a little embarrassed.

Shar leaned in front of Melvin's chest. "It's a stupid joke that White people tell about how Indians get their names," she whispered.

"Oh, I see," Shelly said, even though she really didn't.

Alvin Yellowtail cleared his throat again for silence as Charlie Whitebear returned to his spot. After the woman in the blue dress took a chunk of bison meat and gave a blessing in Crow, several other elders, both men and women, stood up in turn and went to the kettle. Each took a piece of buffalo and made a short speech. When the last elder had sat down, Alvin Yellowtail rose again. "Let's have our guest from the east come up now," he said, and looked at Shelly.

The woman beside Shelly elbowed her. "He means you," she said.

As Shelly started to stand up, Melvin leaned close to her ear. "You are expected to introduce yourself," he said, "and say a little bit about why you came to Montana, because people will want to know. We Crow are very curious."

"What Melvin means is we're nosy and like to gossip," Shar whispered.

Shelly carefully stepped between the people seated on the ground to the center of the lodge and stood beside Alvin Yellowtail. Outside, one of Charlie Whitebear's dogs started barking. Everyone in the lodge ignored it and Alvin motioned for Shelly to take a piece of meat from the kettle. She picked up a chunk of bison and almost dropped it because the meat was so hot, but as the other people had held it in their hands, Shelly forced herself to do the same.

"My name's Shelly Stamper an' I'm from Wes' Virginia," she said. "I'm headed to Troy ta be a log truck driver." She switched the buffalo meat to her other hand. "I wanta thank y'all for makin' me feel welcome here, especially Shar for loanin' me this dress. This is jes about the best git-ta'gether I've ever been to an' the folks back in Peapatch won't b'lieve me when I tell 'em about it."

"You are brave," Alvin said, "to come all the way out to Montana by yourself."

"I ain't really by myself. A feller named Deke is drivin' out with me."

"Where is he tonight?" Alvin asked. "He would have been welcome also."

Shelly switched hands with the meat again. "We had a flat tire an' Deke walked in ta Crow Agency ta buy a spare. He ain't back yet an' I'm kinda worried about 'im."

"Oh, yes ... I would think so," Alvin said to her. "If he does not show up by the time the Buffalo Ceremony is finished, some of us will go look for him."

"I'd appreciate that," Shelly said. "I know Deke shor would like ta meet all of ya. I wish he was here right now ta be a part a' this."

"I hope we will get to meet your friend later," Alvin Yellowtail said and smiled. "Now go ahead and eat. I can see that you want to taste the buffalo."

Shelly bit into the bison and the warm juice ran down her chin. "That's the best meat I ever tasted," she said, just as a piercing scream, followed by a thunderous explosion, shattered the night outside the teepee.

Chapter 36

Deke hurried back to the spare tire and rolled it to his abandoned pickup. His parched mouth screamed for water and Deke feverishly dug the jug out of the truck bed, but barely enough drops came from the spout to moisten his cracked lips. He cursed and threw the jug back into the bed. "Alright," he said, "there ain't no water but I can have me a cigarette."

He opened the side door and pawed through the glove compartment, then cursed again in disbelief and frustration. "What'd I do ta deserve this? Them thievin' In'juns stole all my cigarettes. They likely drank up the water too, jest so's I couldn't follow 'em … but I'll show 'em. They got no idea who their a'dealin' with. I'll track them sum'bitches to Hell ta git Shelly back."

Muttering, Deke slammed the door and went to the rear of the pickup. He knelt down, hurriedly unscrewed the lug nuts then plopped the spare on the rim and twisted the nuts back on. The tire tool was still lying in the dirt where Deke had left it. "At least the In'juns didn't take the tar'r tool an' the jack," Deke mumbled as he tightened the nuts. He let the jack down, heaved it into the bed, then ran to the cab and opened the driver's door. The dome light came on and Deke saw Shelly's note lying on the seat.

Deke
Those Indians in the Cadillac are taking me to their camp just up the road. Turn right at the T and you'll see a bunch of teepees by the river. Come as quick as you can before the dancing is over.
Shelly

"Oh, Shelly ... brave Shelly. Even surrounded by wild In'juns she got a note off to me." He read the note again. "I need ta hurry. I know all about what In'juns do ta their captives after they're done dancin'."

Surprised to find the keys still in the ignition Deke started the Ford and shoved it into gear. He let out the clutch but the truck didn't move. He gave it more gas. Nothing. Reverse. Still nothing. "Shitfire! What's goin' on?" Deke opened the truck door and looked back. His tire was spinning but the truck stayed in place. Then he remembered the blocks Shelly had put under the differential in case the jack slipped.

"Dammit all ta hell, I ain't got time fer this kinda shit."

Deke shut off the truck, ran back to the bed and swiftly dug out the jack. When the back tires were above the gravel Deke got down and pulled the blocks from under the rear-end. He tossed them in the truck bed, lowered the jack, got back in the cab and restarted the Ford. HMP-HMP-HMP-HMP! The old truck rattled and bucked its rear end in the air like a bronc, but didn't go forward.

"Goddammit, what now? I ain't a' gittin' nowhere!" Deke wailed. He put the Ford in neutral, set the brake and hopped out. Finding nothing at the back end he ran to the front and saw the two large wooden blocks, one in front of each tire. Swearing wildly, Deke grabbed the chocks and hurled them into the truck bed. "I bet them In'juns are havin' their way with Shelly right now," he muttered and tore off down the gravel road.

Just like Melvin, Deke blew through the intersection but when he crossed the bridge and saw the dance fire he killed his headlights and let off the gas. Blacked-out, Deke coasted in neutral past the encampment then turned quietly into the rutted dirt path where he pulled his pickup off to the side and shut it off.

Before getting out, Deke took off his white hat. With senses on high alert, he scurried from tree to tree in the darkness, checking to see that the Eldorado was among the parked vehicles. As he reached the first teepee, Deke heard the sound of drumming and dropped to all fours. Silently, he crawled past the lodge, hoping no one was inside but soon he was surrounded by other lodges. The hard dirt was painful to his bare knees, but he was too afraid of being seen to walk upright. In some of the teepees Deke heard voices and tried to stay as far away from them as he could. He also heard dogs running around the camp and that scared him even more than the voices. I sure don' need no more trouble with dogs t'night, he thought.

As Deke scrambled past a traditional lodge made of hides, something near the entrance caught his attention. He crept a few yards closer, glanced around, then crawled to only a couple of feet from the buffalo hide flap that served as a door. Trying not to make any noise, he picked up the bowl in both hands and greedily drank. Deke heard a rustling noise inside the teepee but couldn't force himself to stop drinking. "Why are you drinking my dog's water?" a voice said.

Deke almost jumped out his boots. He looked over and saw the face of a small boy, about seven or eight years old, peeking at him from the opening of the teepee. After recovering from his shock, Deke gave the only answer he could think of: "Cuz I'm thirsty."

"Oh, okay," the boy said. "What are you doing, playing dog?"

"Yeah," Deke answered quickly, "that's it. I'm playin' dog."

"Where are your pants?" the boy asked.

"Dogs don't wear pants," Deke said.

"Would you like some dog food?"

"Uh, no thanks," Deke said, trying to keep his voice low. "I already had some jest a while ago."

"Oh."

"Listen," Deke whispered, "you go back ta sleep. I'm gonna go over here a ways an' play dog some more."

"Okay," the boy said. "Don't bite anybody."

More cautious than ever, Deke scrambled to where the cottonwoods grew thicker and cast their shadows. He crept closer to the drumming and the fire but now his knees were beginning to ache badly. When he got to where he could see the dancers, Deke crawled further into the shadow of the trees, moving slow and furtive, only a few feet at a time. He made his way to a large cottonwood and rested behind it. The next tree was 30 feet away and after working up his courage, Deke flattened out and slithered to it on his belly. Panting hard, he lay prone until he caught his breath, then peered carefully around the thick trunk. He now had a good view of the dance and what he saw sent shivers up his spine. Over two dozen Indians wearing feathers, bones and face paint danced in a circle, stamping their moccasins and shaking sticks, while other Indians beat on a large drum and chanted something that sounded to Deke like, "Hoka-hey-hey-hey."

He quickly ducked back behind the tree. Oh, God, he thought, they're doin' a war dance. I thought this kinda stuff only happened in the movies. He peeked around the tree again. I'd bet anythin' they're goin' on a raid when the dancin's over an' that's why Shelly said ta come quick.

Deke looked for Shelly among the group who were standing outside of the circle, watching the dance, but he couldn't find her anywhere. "They likely got Shelly tied up to a post somewhere's," he whispered. "If I can find 'er, maybe I could untie 'er an' we could git away an warn the settlers aroun' here."

Both horrified and fascinated, Deke continued to watch the dancers. One dancer, whose back had been to him, turned and now danced facing Deke, the firelight shining on her face and beaded buckskin dress. "Ohhhhhhh nohhhhh," Deke moaned, choking back a scream. "It's Shelly … an they've already turned 'er into an In'jun." Deke watched Shelly's face as she danced. "She don' even look like she knows where she's at. I bet they done some a' their In'jun voodoo on 'er."

Shelly turned and danced away.

"I'm gonna gitcha back, Shelly, I swear it," Deke muttered, striking the dirt with his fist. "Ohhhhhhhh, I hope they ain't forced 'er ta coperlate with nobody yet."

As Deke watched, Shelly danced around the circle half a dozen more times. Each time her face came into the light, his agony increased. Deke concocted scheme after scheme to rescue Shelly but he knew none of them stood a chance. There's jest too many of 'em … an' I ain't got nothin' ta fight with.

Suddenly the drumming and the dancing stopped. The dancers and onlookers talked for a few minutes, likely makin' plans for the raid, Deke reckoned, and started walking toward the large teepee near the center of the encampment. As the Indians began filing into the lodge, a plan formulated in Deke's mind. He belly-crawled back to the big tree 30 feet away and stood up.

I gotta git Shelly outa that teepee right now. They might not be in there very long b'fore they head out to attack. He thought for a second.

If I can git back ta where them cars are parked without gittin' caught … I might jest have a chance.

Deke peeked around the cottonwood until he was certain no one was looking his direction. His knees now hurt way too much to crawl back to the parking area, and besides, it would take too long. "I seen Tonto do this once," Deke whispered, "walk back'ards so nobody can track 'im. I'll use these In'juns own damn tricks against 'em."

Gingerly back stepping along the dark edge of the trees, Deke went about 20 paces and then cut through the encampment toward where the cars were parked, hoping no one was about. After he had passed several teepees, a voice behind him said, "Why are you walking backwards?"

"OHH!" Deke yelped, and jumped a foot in the air. He turned around and saw the same little boy who had been peeking out of the teepee.

"Are you a Contrary now?" the boy asked.

"Yep, that's jest what I am," Deke said in a low voice; "one a' them."

"I've never seen a White man who was a Contrary before," the boy said.

"Well, I'm the first one," Deke told him. "Somebody had ta be first, an' I reckon that's me." He looked at the boy and said, "How come you ain't back in yer teepee sleepin', like ya should be?"

"Because the drumming stopped," the boy said. "That means the Buffalo Ceremony is starting and everyone goes to the Buffalo Ceremony."

"Ever'body in the whole village?" Deke asked.

The boy shook his head. "Yes."

"Well, that's good," Deke told him. "I'm real glad ta hear that."

"You should come, too," the boy said. "Buffalo is good meat."

"I'll be along d'rectly, but I gotta git somethin' first."

"Okay," the boy said, "maybe I'll see you later."

"You kin count on it," Deke told him, and continued walking backwards.

When he came to the parked vehicles, Deke went straight to the Eldorado and untied the baling twine holding the trunk down. His duffle bag and Shelly's knapsack and suitcase were stuffed inside, along with other items, but Deke didn't find what he was after. Remembering that the thickset driver was holding the 10 gauge when he got back into the front seat, Deke opened the driver's door and looked around but didn't see the gun in either the front or the back. I wouldn't mind findin' my cigarettes, neither, Deke thought, but I don' reckon I got time fer a smoke right now, anyways.

Figuring there was only one more place the shotgun could be Deke slid his hand under the front seat and his palm bumped against the the barrel. "I hope it's still loaded," he muttered as he pulled out the weapon and smiled when he broke the gun open and saw brass in both chambers. "I only got two shots, but I'm a'bettin' them In'juns'll give Shelly up without a fight when they look down these barrels an' know I'm serious."

He started walking backwards again, but after a few steps realized that walking backwards to and from the same place left the same tracks as walking forwards so he turned around and followed his former path back through the camp. "Maybe they'll think there's two of us now," he said.

The camp was dead still as Deke stealthily crept through it. When the big teepee came into sight, Deke stiffened with anxiety and looked at the gun in his hand. "I can't make no mistakes," he muttered as he hunkered behind a smaller teepee and watched the shadowy movement of the people inside the lodge. He heard them talking, which, in the still night, sounded like the buzz of a swarm. To Deke, the lodge looked like a giant hornet's nest, and he was about to stir it up. "I gotta do this right now or I'm gonna change my mind," he whispered and carefully moved into the open.

As he crept closer, Deke's breaths came in nervous gasps. Fifty feet from the teepee, he got down on his belly and crawled, pushing the shotgun ahead of him. He'd only gone about 15 feet when two dogs trotted around the side of the lodge and went through the open flap. From his position, Deke could see that it caused a commotion in the proceedings. One dog was swiftly chased out and ran off but when the other one was booted, he continued to prowl near the entrance.

Deke eyed the dog, not happy about its presence, but he was too committed to change his plan now. Slowly, he crawled closer to the lodge opening, but with 25 feet to go, the dog raised its ears and looked at him, then started barking. "Shhhhhhhh," Deke hissed and put a finger to his lips.

The dog stopped barking but gave up all interest of sneaking back into the lodge and concentrated on Deke. Weasel-faced and lean, mottled with blue and black spots, the creature known as Slinker didn't come straight at him, but with a low, menacing growl, circled around behind. Sum'bitch, Deke thought, now I gotta watch out fer this goddam dog b'sides ever'thing else.

Deke could see through the open flap into the teepee, but reckoned no one on the inside could see him lying in the shadows. Still, he knew it would be too risky to get any closer before he made his move. If I can make it inside that door an' git the drop on them In'juns an' tell 'em I'm takin' Shelly back, I think it'll work. Ain't nobody in 'is right mind would go up aginst this 10 gauge.

Shelly was now standing in the center of the teepee, holding something in her hand and speaking. A tall Crow man who looked like a chief was standing beside her, also talking. Deke couldn't make out their words, but it looked to him like Shelly was taking some kind of oath. I bet this is where they're makin' her part a' the tribe. I can jest about guess what they'll make 'er do next.

Behind him, Deke heard a snarl. He turned his head and saw the dog sneaking up. All too aware that his bare legs were a tempting target, Deke snarled back, "Go away mutt or I'll blow yer head off."

The dog bared its teeth but didn't come closer. Deke turned back around. Inside the teepee Shelly was still standing with the Indian chief. "I need ta git her outa there now," Deke whispered. "If I only do one thing right in my life, it's gotta be this."

Deke put his feet underneath him and rose to a low, crouching position. "I'm goin' in on the count a' three."

"One." Deke cocked the right hammer of the 10 gauge and took a breath.

"Two." He cocked the left hammer. Behind him Deke heard a "grrrrrrrrr," but he had no time to deal with any damn dog right now.

"Three!" Deke said, and stood up. He took a step but Slinker took five and sank his long canines into Deke's bare thigh, right below his skivvies.

"OOOOOWWWWWWWWW!" Deke screamed as his hand clamped down on the shotgun.

KAAABLAMMMM-MMMM!!!! Both barrels went off at once, sending a mighty flash of flame and smoke into the night sky. The gun recoiled upwards with such force that it smacked Deke squarely in the forehead, knocking him senseless and felling him over backwards like an old-growth Ponderosa pine, squashing the dog beneath him.

The ancient Damascas steel barrels, never meant to handle the pressure of modern magnum loads, burst asunder like two exploding cigars, but not before sending 36 pellets of double-ought buckshot skyward, where they scored a direct, if unintentional, hit at the top of the teepee where the poles came together. Splintered fragments of wood flew in all directions.

The roar of the shotgun echoed through the lodge and then all went quiet ... for about three seconds, until the fractured poles fell inward and the entire structure collapsed, plunging the closely packed crowd into a maelstom of darkness and confusion. The plummeting lodgepoles and canvas knocked over the kettle of buffalo meat and snuffed the flames, sending a blast of ash and smoke throughout the lodge. Everyone's eyes and lungs quickly filled with acrid fumes as parents, children and friends frantically called and groped for each other. Adding to the pandemonium, the poles and thick canvas pushed down on those trapped inside with a crushing weight, making movement almost impossible, especially for the elders and children.

Those seated around the perimeter desperately tried to get out, but the bottom of the teepee was securely pegged to the ground on the outside and others trying to escape piled on top of them. When they could not exit from the sides, people began crawling toward the front opening, but they collided in the dark and were soon tangled in a mass of choking, suffocating bedlam. The trapped Crow helped each other as much as they could, but as the smoke increased a natural panic ensued and a cacophony of yells, coughs and screams arose from the writhing pile of canvas.

The area around the entrance had been left empty so that people could come in and when the teepee collapsed an eruption of smoke and soot belched out the opening, but then it collapsed as well. Now, as the canvas rose and fell like a bellows from the human turbulence inside, the doorway flap partially opened at regular intervals and released puffs of gray billows. To anyone outside, the teepee would have resembled a giant, spasmodic amoeba blowing smoke out of its ass.

The first person to emerge was little George White Clay. He crawled through the flap during one of the teepee's smoke farts, blinked and coughed a couple of times, took a breath and stood up. Then George turned around and lifted up the canvas as high as he could and said calmly to those still inside, "The door is over here."

Two women scrambled through and lay on the ground hacking and then Melvin Not Afraid came out, pulling Shar by the hand. Shelly was right behind them and several others followed in single file. After he'd gulped several quick breaths, Melvin Not Afraid got to his feet and said loudly to all those who were outside, "Stand up! We have to go and pull up the pegs so those trapped at the edges can get out."

Melvin, Shar and Shelly, along with several others ran around the perimeter of the lodge, yanking up the wooden pegs that held the canvas loops to the ground. Then they lifted up the sides of the teepee and men, women, and children piled out in droves, all of them gagging and gasping for breath. Melvin told Shar, Shelly and two men, "Hold this side up as high as you can," and he got down on his hands and knees and went back into the teepee to see if anyone remained inside. Satisfied that the lodge was empty, he crawled back out and said to everyone who was able to stand, "We need to pull the lodge away from the fire before it starts to burn." Thirty people took hold of the canvas and dragged it away from the firepit then went back to help those who were still recovering.

In the middle of this frenzy Deke came to, more or less. The dog lay unmoving beneath him and in the darkness and flurry of excitement, no one had noticed him lying on the ground. A great throbbing pain pulsed in the middle of his forehead. Deke didn't fully know what had happened, but he could see the commotion going on nearby and was cognizant enough to know that he was likely the cause of it. *I need ta git outa here,* was Deke's only thought, as he rolled off of the dog and painfully crawled away.

After the teepee had been moved away from the fire and everyone accounted for, people began discussing why the lodge fell. There was agreement that the scream and the explosion were linked to the collapse, but no one could coherently put those events together. People spread out, looking for evidence, and when Jeremy Old Crow called, "There's something very strange over here," the others came to see.

They looked down at the unconscious, but still breathing dog, and the exploded shotgun in front of him, trying to reason an explanation. Robert Backbone turned to Charlie Whitebear. "It looks to me, Twodogs, like Slinker got mad because he was kicked out of the teepee and he went and got a gun and shot the lodge. The recoil must have knocked him out." Everyone looked at Robert, who just shrugged and said, "Does anyone have a better guess?"

"No, Robert, I do not think that is what happened, even if it does look like it," George White Clay said.

Then Melvin Not Afraid came up, along with Shar and Shelly, and looked down at the dog and the gun. Melvin bent and picked up the shotgun with its frayed barrels and held it up. Shelly looked at the gun, and then Shelly and Melvin looked at each other. "Deke."

Alvin Yellowtail, who was standing a few feet away, looked at the assembled group of Crow men and women. "Go find him," he ordered.

The hunt for Deke McConahay was over in two minutes. In his dazed condition Deke had only crawled 30 yards. Robert Backbone and Jeremy Old Crow found him in a lodge, trying to hide under a baby blanket. They dragged him back by his armpits, whimpering and blubbering the entire way. The Crow had once again gathered and when Deke saw them, many still painted and in regalia, or what was left of it after the disaster in the teepee, he tried to scream, but didn't have the energy. "Ohhhaahhh," was all that came out.

Slinker was now gone. When everyone left to search for Deke, he had seen his chance to escape and taken it. Alvin Yellowtail picked up the broken shotgun and his face was grim with anger. He looked into Deke's eyes. "Why did you shoot our lodge?" Alvin said, his voice hard.

Still held up by Robert and Jeremy, all Deke could offer in answer was a string of incoherent mumbling. The bump in the middle of his forehead had already discolored to a purplish blue and in the darkness, looked curiously like a third eye. Along with the lump that Hazel had given him the day before, Deke's face had a distorted, alien appearance and the people stared at him in wonderment, as if he had come from another planet to attack them.

"Take him over to the fire," Alvin Yellowtail said to Robert and Jeremy, and pointed to where the flames still burned by the dance circle. "And put more wood on it."

"Ohhhhhh nohhhhh!" Deke pleaded as they hauled him in tow across the camp. "Don' burn me at the stake ... ohhhhh please, don' do that, I jest hate fire!"

"Maybe fire will help get some answers out of you," Robert Backbone told him.

"I just want to be able to see him better," Alvin said, and Deke breathed a small sigh, until Alvin added, "so we can decide what to do with him."

With Alvin Yellowtail leading the way, Robert and Jeremy lugged the whimpering Deke back to the dance circle and held him upright as more wood was tossed onto the fire. "Why don't you stand up on your own, like a man?" Robert Backbone said to him, but Deke only looked at him and babbled.

Alvin Yellowtail took Deke's chin in his hand. "Now tell us," he said, "why did you shoot the lodge while we were having the Buffalo Ceremony?"

"Buhwuhwuhwuhwuhhhh," Deke said, trembling from head to heel.

"Why isn't he wearing any pants?" someone asked. "Is he a pervert?"

Everyone turned and looked at Shelly for an answer.

"Uh, not that I know of," she said. "We ain't been ta'gether long enough for me ta really find out."

Shelly was in a pickle. Indirectly, she had brought this calamity upon the pow-wow and felt awful about it. Still, she understood that some comeuppance was due to Deke and was mad enough at him that she wouldn't mind joining in.

Alvin turned Deke's face to his. "Why aren't you wearing pants?"

"Mahwuhmahmahwuhhhh," Deke told him.

"He told me he took his pants off because he was a dog," a voice said, and a small boy stepped forward from the group.

"You know him, Willie?" Alvin Yellowtail asked the boy.

"I met him twice tonight," the boy said. "The first time he was drinking from my dog's water bowl and told me he was playing dog. The next time he was walking backwards and told me he was a Contrary."

The boy picked up a stick and walked up to Deke, who winced, thinking the boy was going to strike him. But Willie only touched him lightly on his bare leg. "You are a bad man," he said, "for shooting our lodge and I count coup on you." He dropped the stick and went back with the others.

A couple of people in the crowd made circles around their temples with their index fingers and said, "Ummm, maybe he's just crazy."

Once again everyone looked at Shelly. "Is he crazy?" Alvin asked her.

"Uhhhhh … uhhhhh … " Shelly didn't know how to answer.

"We're not going to kill him," Alvin told her.

Robert Backbone looked at Alvin. "We're not?"

"No, Robert, we're not," Alvin told him.

"Oh," Robert said, sounding disappointed.

"Before we decide anything," Alvin said, "we need to know what happened and why."

George White Clay stepped forward. "Let me look into his eyes," he said to Alvin, "and see what kind of man he is."

Deke shuddered as the small man wearing the ancient bones and weathered buckskin looked deeply into his eyes. Trembling, he tried to turn his face away from the old man's piercing gaze, but Alvin Yellowtail's gnarled hand tightly gripped his chin. "Keep your eyes open," Alvin said sternly and squeezed, forcing Deke to look at George White Clay.

After a long minute George's knees began shaking and he made a choking sound. "What is happening to George?" people whispered quietly to each other.

No longer able to contain himself, George White Clay turned away from Deke and broke down in outright laughter. He said nothing, but continued laughing as he took his place back in the crowd.

Shar, who was standing beside Shelly, turned to her. "You need to get him to talk," she said. "He has to tell us why he did this."

"Yes," other people said to Shelly, "maybe he will talk to you."

Still wearing Shar's beaded dress, Shelly approached Deke.

By now, Jeremy Old Crow and Robert Backbone were tired of holding Deke upright. "Can we drop him in the dirt?" Robert asked Alvin Yellowtail.

"No," Alvin said. "Someone find a chair."

Melvin Not Afraid went and got a metal folding chair. After Robert and Jeremy lowered Deke onto the seat he relaxed a little. When Shelly walked up and stood before him, Deke looked up at her and swallowed. "Can I have a cigarette?" he asked in a feeble voice.

"You know I don't smoke," Shelly told him and felt someone poke her in the ribs. She turned and saw the woman who had been sitting beside her at the Buffalo Ceremony holding out a pack of Camels. "Here, he can have one of mine," the woman said.

Deke reached for the pack but his hands were shaking so badly Shelly tapped out a cigarette and stuck it in his mouth. Alvin Yellowtail lit it for him.

The Camel noticeably calmed Deke's nerves and after a few puffs Shelly said, "Alright, Deke, we need ta know why ya shot the teepee."

The way Shelly said "we" further convinced Deke that Shelly was now part of the tribe. "I did it ta save you, Shelly," Deke finally said, "but it looks like I'm too late."

"Save me from what, Deke?" Shelly asked, astounded.

"From bein' taken captive. I seen 'em force ya inta that Cadillac."

"They didn't force me inta nothin'," Shelly said. "Melvin an' them invited me to the pow-wow. I left a note so's you'd know where I was."

"Well, that note made it sound like you'd been taken prisoner, Shelly. An' look at ya now, all dressed up like some squaw."

Murmurs rippled through the crowd and Alvin Yellowtail stiffened.

"Don'tchoo say that word no more, Deke," Shelly told him. "That ain't a nice word an' you shouldn't be talkin' like that."

"I didn't know that, Shelly," Deke muttered, as tears rolled down his dirty cheeks. "There's times I don't think I know anything, anymore. I was jest tryin' ta do what I thought was right." Deke started sobbing and some of the Crow turned away so as not to see the disgusting sight of a grown man crying.

"All I wanted … all I wanted was ta git to a motel t'night and git me a little rest an' be with you … but we hit that muffler an' got a flat

… an' I had ta walk in ta git another'n cuz them In'juns in the Cadillac stole't the spare … an' then a pack a' hungry wolves chased me inta that little canyon where I got bit by a rattlesnake … but thank God John Wayne come along an' saved me … an' when I finally got ta that scary town there was this gret big mean dog at the fillin' station … an' I fell off that big rubber teepee an' knocked it over … an' the big In'jun with the knife got mad an' ripped muh' belt off an' took the rifle that my daddy give me jest 'fore 'e died … an' made me give 'im thirty dollars jest ta git muh own tar'r back … then wouldn't even sell me a Slim Jim or a Coke … an' I had ta walk all the way back holdin' muh' pants up an' carry'n that heavy tar'r with no water … an' Goodrich got mad cuz I told 'im he weren't worth no thirty dollars an' run off on me … an' I had ta go down in 'at awful gully ta find 'im an' take muh' pants off ta git back out … an' then I got chased by these giant ants till I couldn't run no more … an' I was lost in the desert an' dyin' till this spaceship come outa the sky an' showed me where the road was … an' when I got to the truck, them In'juns was takin' you captive … an' all the water was gone an' I was about dead a' thirst … an' they took all our stuff … an' I didn't have no cigarettes." Deke stopped to catch his breath. "All I wanted ta do, Shelly, was take ya back an' save ya from bein' a captive."

Some of the Crow listening to Deke's story muttered, "Crazy," but a few, including Melvin Not Afraid, looked at the bruised, barely coherent wretch and felt sorry for him.

Shelly let out a long breath. "All that still don't explain why ya shot the teepee, Deke."

"I didn't mean ta shoot it," Deke said, "I truly didn't. I was jest gonna run in holdin' the shotgun an' take ya back, but that damn dog bit me in the leg an' the gun went off." Deke lifted his leg off the chair to show the puncture marks.

"I knew that dog had something to do with this," Robert Backbone said. "We need to go find that mutt and take care of him once and for all."

"No!" Charlie Whitebear said, and stepped out of the crowd. "Slinker shouldn't be blamed. He saw what this man was about to do and bit him to stop it. My dog is a hero and should be honored. He might have saved lives. Think what could have happened if dickhead here had come into the lodge with a loaded and cocked shotgun."

Shelly turned to Charlie. "How'd you know his name was Dickhead?"

"Is that his real name?" Shar asked, and Melvin Not Afraid said, "Is that what 'Deke' is short for, Dickhead?"

Robert Backbone looked at Deke and shook his head. "And White people think Indians have funny names."

Alvin Yellowtail interceded. "We can't blame the dog," he said. "This man, Dickhead, is the one who came into our camp with a loaded gun and shot the lodge, whether he meant to or not." The other Crow nodded their heads in agreement. Alvin looked around. "What should we do with him?"

"Let's make him run the gauntlet," Robert Backbone said.

"Ohhh, I can't do that," Deke whimpered. "I'm too weak ta run, all I can do is crawl."

"All the better," Robert told him, "we can hit you more."

"Ohh ... muhwahbahwahwah," Deke blubbered.

"Robert," Alvin Yellowtail said, "we don't do that anymore." He looked at Deke. "Maybe we should call the tribal police and have him taken to jail."

"OH NO!" Deke sobbed. "I'd rather crawl through 'at gauntlet'n do that."

In the end, it was Melvin Not Afraid who saved Deke McConahay. He stepped forward and addressed Alvin Yellowtail and the rest of the Crow.

"I can't let this man take the blame by himself," Melvin said. "If we had not taken Dickhead's spare tire, none of this would have happened. It was also my muffler that he hit. We should have stopped and picked it up after it fell off instead of leaving it in the middle of the road. I apologize to all of you ... even Dickhead."

"Why did you take his spare tire, Melvin?" Alvin Yellowtail asked. "That's not like you, to steal."

"We did it mostly as a joke," Melvin answered. "When we saw him in the Crow's Nest, we thought he was wearing a t-shirt with Custer's picture on it. We were on our way to Sam Black Eagle's to trade him some used tires for gas so we just threw his spare tire into the trunk along with the others to have some fun ... or maybe teach him a lesson

... I don't know. I guess we just weren't thinking, but it was wrong anyway."

Alvin Yellowtail bent down and opened Deke's flannel shirt. "That's not Custer, that's Wild Bill Hickock," he said to Melvin.

"We know that now," Melvin said, "but from across the room it looked like Custer."

"Even so, you should not have done it," Alvin said. "Some of our ancestors fought alongside Custer and died with him."

Melvin lowered his head but after a few seconds raised his eyes and looked at the other members of his tribe. "I will do whatever I need to in order to make this right. I will pay for any damage to the lodge and make some new poles. I will also help Sam Black Eagle rebuild his Teepee-to-the-Sky."

"What about him?" Alvin Yellowtail asked, pointing at the pathetic, pantless figure in the chair, shivering and mumbling incoherently to himself.

"I'll put him in my lodge tonight and watch him so he doesn't cause anymore trouble," Melvin said.

Alvin Yellowtail glanced at his watch. "It's late and we are all tired," he said, looking at the other people. "We still have one more day of the pow-wow left. If we rebuild the lodge we can finish the Buffalo Ceremony tomorrow night."

"I will work all day to help," Melvin said.

Jeremy Old Crow and Charlie Whitebear spoke up. "This was partly our fault also," each of them admitted, "and we will work tomorrow." They looked at Robert Backbone.

"I will help too," Robert finally said.

Deke had another cigarette and with Shelly's assistance was able to stand up and walk. As people went back to their lodges, Shar leaned close to Melvin and said in a low voice, "Why are you so nice, Melvin? I would have trussed Dickhead up like a pig and thrown him into the Bighorn."

Melvin shrugged his shoulders.

They went to Shar's teepee and Shelly gave the buckskin dress back to her. Shar handed Shelly two heavy blankets. "Take these," she said, "Melvin never has enough blankets in his lodge." Then she said to Melvin, "They'll be okay by themselves tonight."

Melvin thought it over. "I gave my word I'd watch Dickhead."

"Maybe I'd better help watch him, too," Shar said, and picked up a heavy rolled-up bison hide. "This is what I sleep in," she told Shelly as they ducked out of the low opening to go to Melvin's teepee.

Melvin's lodge was not as orderly or well appointed as Shar's. "See you in the morning," he said to Shelly and Deke, and without further ceremony lay down on a red woolen blanket.

"You can sleep any place you'd like," Shar told Shelly. "There's another buffalo hide over there. Melvin doesn't use it unless it's twenty below." She lay down beside Melvin Not Afraid, her body snug against his, and pulled her buffalo skin over her.

"Thanks," Shelly said, and walked around the dark teepee until she found a large rug that looked comfortable. "You lay down here," she told Deke and when he was settled, covered his shivering form with the blankets that Shar had given her.

"You gonna sleep here with me?" Deke asked.

"Nope," Shelly said and went to the other side of the teepee. She unrolled Melvin's bison hide and spread it on the ground, sat down, took off her jacket and boots then lay back and wrapped the hide around her. The odor in the hide was strong, and as her body heat warmed the fur, Shelly felt like she was sleeping in an animal that was still alive. She thought of all the Indians who had ever slept in lodges, wrapped in buffalo skins, just like she was doing tonight, and wondered how many generations it had been since there was a full-blooded Indian in her Melungeon ancestry. The words of Lawrence Iron Bull came back to her: "If your medicine is strong, you might find something special along that road tonight."

This night had certainly been special and Shelly was not sorry Deke had hit the muffler or that Melvin Not Afraid and his friends had taken the spare tire. Her first day in Montana had been crammed full of adventure, surprise, and magic. Wrapped snug and warm in this animal that was, as Alvin Yellowtail had put it, "the strength and lifeblood of the Apsaalooke," she wanted nothing more.

Chapter 37

Saturday, September 29

Crystal shafts of light streamed into the lodge, rousing Shelly from her sleep. Across the teepee Deke snored beneath his blankets. A bison hide still covered Shar, but Melvin was gone. Shelly put on her jacket and boots and slipped outside into the chill morning air. In the trees back from the dance circle was a rickety outhouse and after using it, Shelly strolled along the river as the sun rose over the hills and spread light across the camp. She walked out onto a gravel bar, knelt and rinsed her hands then splashed cold water over her face. The biting water rolled down her cheeks and chin, washing away the last traces of slumber. Here, the Bighorn flowed swift and was deep enough that Shelly could only see the bottom near the banks. Sunlight from the new day played over the sparkling surface and filled the depths with incandescent green light.

As Shelly gazed into the river, she had the same vision as when she had looked into George White Clay's eyes the night before while dancing; that this river held the memory of ancient days, even of the first people who had come to its banks, and Shelly wanted to know their stories. After a few minutes, she stood up and started toward camp.

Smoke drifted from scattered fires and again, Shelly had the feeling that this is how the encampment would have been on that morning nearly a hundred years ago before the 7th Cavalry attacked. Halfway back to Melvin's lodge, Shelly met Shar.

"Let's go get breakfast," Shar said and they walked to where a dozen people had gathered around a fire. Two large kettles hung suspended over the low flames and Shar filled two plates and handed one to Shelly. They sat down on a log and after a few bites Shelly said, "This is good, what is it?"

"Potatoes, eggs and antelope, seasoned with sage."

"I saw a lot a' sage on the prairie las' night," Shelly said. "It smells like the West to me."

Shar nodded.

A few bites later, Shelly asked, "Where's Melvin? Is he around the camp somewhere's?"

Shar shook her head. "Melvin got up before it was light and left. He didn't say where he was going but told me to tell you not to leave until he got back."

"We can't leave," Shelly said. "Melvin's got our stuff in 'is trunk."

As more Crow arrived from their lodges, Shelly and Shar helped with the breakfast chores until most of the camp had eaten. They were talking with Jeremy Old Crow and Robert Backbone when they heard the Eldorado on the highway. A few minutes later Melvin Not Afraid joined them and Shar got him a plate of food. "Did you get what you wanted in Crow Agency?" she asked him.

"How did you know I went to Crow Agency?" Melvin said.

"Because I know you, Melvin," Shar told him, "and I think I know why you went there, even though I would have told you not to."

"Umm," Melvin said, and turned to Shelly. "Is Dickhead up yet?"

"Not yet," Shelly said. "He's perty whupped after las' night. The day before didn't go too good for 'im, neither."

"Is that when he got that other lump on his head?" Shar asked.

"Yep," Shelly said. "He got real drunk an' sick, too."

"If Dickhead stays around today, he might get another lump on his head and make it three in a row," Robert Backbone said.

"We're leavin' soon as I can git 'im movin'," Shelly said. "An' his name ain't really Dickhead. That's jes what people called 'im back in Norwood."

"Oh," Melvin said, "we were wondering. It didn't seem quite right."

"It seems right to me," Robert said. "I'm still going to call him Dickhead."

"Anyways, I better go wake 'im up," Shelly said and turned to go.

"I'll go with you," Melvin told her, "and take him some breakfast."

Shar watched with disgust as Melvin, carrying a plate of food and a cup of coffee, headed toward his lodge with Shelly. Twenty minutes later, they returned, Shelly and Melvin walking in front and Deke, head down, trailing behind. Shelly said goodbye to everyone who was present and thanked them again, especially Alvin Yellowtail and George White Clay, as Deke stood shivering by himself, wrapped in Shar's blankets. Shelly, Melvin and Deke started walking toward the parking area and Shar said to Jeremy and Robert, "I'd better go along and get my blankets back and make sure Melvin doesn't give Dickhead his car."

Melvin had parked the Cadillac beside Deke's pickup. He reached through the open back window and took out Deke's web belt with his knife and canteen. "Here," he said, "Sam Black Eagle found this when he went out this morning to look at the damage to his Teepee-to-the-Sky. It's broke and he doesn't want it."

Deke took the canvas belt. One of the metal buckles was snapped off and the belt was useless. "I didn't mean fer that big rubber teepee ta fall down," Deke said to Melvin, "I really didn't."

"I promised Sam I'd help him rebuild it," Melvin said, "and that made him feel a little better."

"If we were stickin' around, I'd help too," Deke said, looking at the belt. "He didn't give ya anything else a' mine, did he?"

Melvin studied Deke's face, as if making a decision. He opened the front door of his car, reached under the seat and handed Deke his Winchester.

Deke took the rifle in his hands and ran his palm over the barrel. "This ain't jest a gun ta me," he told Melvin. "It's the las' thing my daddy give me b'fore him an' Mom got killed in a car wreck. I really do appreciate ya gittin' this back for me."

"I heard you say that when you told your story last night," Melvin said, closing the door. "This is as much as I can do for leaving my muffler in the road and taking your tire. Sam wouldn't give me your thirty dollars back. He said it will cost him a lot of time to rebuild his tire teepee, even with my help."

Deke nodded. "I'm jest glad I got my rifle back."

"Oh wait," Melvin said, glancing at Deke's bare legs, "I almost forgot. I have one more thing for you, Dick."

"It's Deke," Shelly said.

"Oh, yes, Deke. I don't know how you lost your pants, but I guess that was partly my fault, too."

"What are you going to do now, Melvin," Shar said, "take off your pants and give them to him?"

"Not the ones I'm wearing," Melvin said. "I went by my place and got an old pair that he can have."

Melvin reached into the back seat again and pulled out a rolled-up pair of faded jeans. "Take those blankets off and put these on. They're old pants, but even old pants are better than no pants."

Deke removed the blankets and handed them to Shar, who looked at them and curled up her nose. He took Melvin's Levis and pulled them on. The legs were wide enough that Deke didn't need to take off his boots but when he let go of the waist they fell to his ankles.

"I have an idea," Melvin said. He went to his trunk, got some baling twine, then took out his folding knife and cut off two lengths. He tied a strand to one of the front belt loops on the Levis, ran it over Deke's shoulder then tied it to a belt loop in the back. He did the same on the other side, creating a pair of baling twine suspenders. "That works," he said.

Melvin had cut the twine too short and the oversized Levis hiked halfway up Deke's chest. He was also a good five inches shorter than Deke, and whereas Deke's height was in his legs, Melvin's was in his trunk. Six inches of white, hairy leg showed between the frayed bottoms of the jeans and the tops of Deke's cowboy boots. The Levis were clean, but years of use had left them faded and full of holes, which Melvin had crudely sewn over with different colored patches.

Deke looked at his new britches. "Uh, thanks … I think."

Shar looked at Deke and shook her head in disbelief. Shelly had to cup her hand over her mouth to keep from laughing. "We oughta load our stuff back in the truck an' git goin'," she said, when she was able to talk. "Why don't you git in the bed, Deke, an' I'll hand ev'rything up to ya."

As Shelly was getting their belongings from Melvin's trunk, he said to Deke, "When you were watching us giving Shelly a ride last night, I'll bet you thought we were a bunch of thieving redskins stealing your things."

"Oh, no," Deke said, "I didn't think nothin' a' the kind. I knew you was just takin' our stuff ta keep it safe ... an I thought it was mighty nice a' ya."

Melvin laughed and winked at Shar.

After everything was secured in the big wooden chest Deke took out the key he had hidden under the seat and started the pickup. Shelly walked over to Shar and Melvin. "I'm sorry 'bout all the trouble that happened at the Buffalo Ceremony. But even so, las' night was one a' the best nights I've ever had in my life." She paused. "I don't know if it's right for me ta say this or not, but a few days ago I found out from my Grammy that I'm part Indian. I know I ain't a real Indian, raised to it like y'all were, but las' night was still mighty important to me an' I won't ever fer'git it."

Shar and Melvin nodded that they understood, but didn't say anything.

"I don't know if y'all hug or not," Shelly told them, "but I can't help my'self." She threw her arms around Melvin's thick shoulders. "Thanks for takin' our tire, Melvin," she whispered to him. "This wouldn't a' happened ta me if ya hadn't."

Then she hugged Shar, who hugged her back. "Thanks so much Shar, for loanin' me that beautiful dress. It made me feel like part a' the pow-wow. I don't wanta say goodbye 'cause I hope ta see ya agin' sometime."

"You will be welcome here whenever you want to visit," Melvin said.

"Yes, come see us," Shar said. "I'll loan you my dress again."

Deke stayed silent as they drove away from Two-Leggins toward Hardin. So much needed to be said and finally Shelly looked over and asked, "How ya doin', Deke?"

"How the hell you think I'm doin'? I'm so tired I can't think straight. Ever' inch me hurts like a sum'bitch an' muh head wants ta explode."

"You want me ta drive?"

"No. It gives me somethin' ta do b'sides think about las' night."

"You wanta talk about las' night?" Shelly asked.

"No," Deke answered. "An' I don't wanna hear about it, neither."

"Okay," Shelly said and looked out the side window.

In Hardin Deke pulled into a gas station and convenience store. He put on his cowboy hat and opened the truck door. "You wanna fill 'er up," he told Shelly. "I gotta use the bathroom an' git me some cigarettes."

After topping off the tank Shelly washed the windshield and looked at the old spare, chuckling that Deke paid thirty dollars to get it back. As she walked into the store, Deke was coming out of the bathroom. The place was busy, mostly with local ranchers and travelers from the nearby interstate. Deke got a can of Coke, a bottle of aspirin and two Slim Jims then got in line behind three people at the counter. Shelly grabbed a can of Coke and joined Deke in line. At the counter Deke asked for two packs of Camels as Shelly dug in her pocket and gave him money for half the gas and her Coke. As she turned away, Shelly saw that people in the store were staring at them, especially at Deke.

One burly rancher in particular, wearing a Stetson and a Carhartt jacket, kept looking over at him. A boy about ten years old stood beside him in a small group of other ranchers. Every time he looked at Deke he'd say something to the other men. When Shelly and Deke started walking toward the door, the man broke from the group and planted himself in front of Deke. Oh shit, here's trouble, Shelly thought, but the big rancher grinned, said "Howdy," and stuck his hand out for Deke to shake.

Deke forced out a "Howdy," then stuffed his cigarettes, Slim Jims and aspirin in one of the pockets of Melvin's pants and shook the man's hand.

"My boy, Dusty, over there," the man said, nodding toward the kid, "just thinks the world of you guys. Could you come over an' say 'Hi' to him?"

Before Deke could answer, the man's beefy hand was between his shoulder blades, guiding him over to where the half dozen ranchers and the boy stood watching. Shelly stayed put, sipping her Coke and listening closely.

"Shake his hand, Dusty," the man said to the boy. "You always said you wanted ta meet one of these fella's."

The kid politely removed his cowboy hat then shyly offered his hand. Deke took the kid's hand but all he could think of to say was, "Hi, Dusty."

As they were shaking hands the boy looked at the purplish lump sprouting beneath the brim of Deke's hat and asked, "Did you get kicked by a bull?"

Deke was flustered. "Uh … well … uh … somethin' like that."

"Wow," the kid said, "that musta really hurt."

"Oh yeah," Deke told him, "it really hurt, alright."

"Hey," the rancher said, and elbowed Deke. "Do something funny."

"Huh?" Deke said.

"Do something funny for Dusty," the man said again. "Make him laugh."

Ten feet away, Shelly wondered where this was going.

Deke hesitated. "I don't know offhand what I could do that would be funny."

"I thought you'd have all kinds of funny things you could do to make kids laugh," the guy said, sounding a little put out.

"Well … I don't," Deke told him. "What makes you think I could do somethin' funny?"

"Ain't you a rodeo clown?" the man asked.

Deke heard a snort and turned to see Shelly choking and blowing Coke out of her nose. He turned back around and saw that all the ranchers were looking at him, waiting for an answer.

"Uhhh … not really … at least not that I know of," Deke finally said.

"Wait a minute," the rancher said, "you mean that's your normal get-up … what you wear every day?"

"Well, not ever' day … jest t'day," Deke said.

"What's special about today?" one of the other ranchers asked him.

"Well … uhhh …."

The time had come for an intervention. Shelly forced herself to stop laughing, wiped her nose and quick-stepped over to the group. She took Deke by the elbow and pulled him away.

"C'mon, Dudley," she said, "let's go. I promised the staff I'd have you back by noon." Before the ranchers could ask any more questions she had Deke out the door and in the truck.

Deke downed four aspirin with a swig of Coke, lit a Camel and started the engine. "Them assholes thought I was a clown."

"At least it was a rodeo clown," Shelly said. "They're perty cool."

"What's the next big town?" Deke asked, and bit off part of a Slim Jim.

"Billings."

"Well, we're stoppin' so's I can git some new pants."

"How come ya didn't want any new pants before?" Shelly asked.

" 'Cause I wadn't wearin' clown pants then," Deke said. "And stop laughin', it ain't funny."

After they got on westbound I-90 Shelly said, "Hey, I got an idea, Deke. You don't like new britches so maybe we could go to Goodwill or a Salvation Army store an' find ya some used Levi's like the ones ya lost. They'd be real cheap, too."

"Yeah," Deke said, "I like that idea."

"We also need ta git us another tire, Deke. That spare ain't very good an' I said I'd buy ya a new one."

Deke drove a couple of miles in silence. "How far is it ta Billings?"

Shelly opened up her atlas. "Maybe an hour away."

"Now I got an idea," Deke said. "Since we gotta stop anyway's an' git us a tar'r and shop for pants, why don't we jest take us a motel an' call 'er a day."

"Deke," Shelly said, glancing at her watch, "it won't be much past nine o'clock when we git ta Billings. We can't waste a whole day in a motel."

"I don't know as it'd be wasted," Deke said, and winked at Shelly. "An' you keep sayin' you ain't in no hurry ta git ta Troy."

"No," Shelly said. "We ain't stoppin' at nine o'clock in the mornin'."

Deke went into a pout.

"Listen, I know you had a rough night," Shelly said, "so we'll stop early ta'day an' find us a real nice place ta stay. I'll even pay for it."

"Alright," Deke finally said, and managed a smile. "It's a deal."

In Billings Shelly bought a new tire and rim and Deke spent 15 minutes tying Goodrich down in the bed of the pickup. After that they found a Goodwill store and Deke picked out a pair of used Levis and a belt that he could attach his John Wayne buckle to. "I want a t-shirt, too. Bill Hickock got me in too much trouble," Deke said, and bought a shirt with Daffy Duck on it. "Nobody'll mistake him fer Custer."

Back on I-90, Shelly got out her atlas and studied what lay ahead. Deke was tired and drifted out of his lane several times. They stopped in Columbus for Cokes and a bathroom break and Deke got two more Slim Jims. When they got back in the truck, Shelly said, "We oughta go to Yellowstone National Park."

"Today?"

"Yeah, Deke. This is the day we're goin' right by it."

Deke glanced over at the map. "We ain't goin' right by it," he said. "It's clear to the south." He looked closer. "It ain't even in Montana."

"A little bit of it is," Shelly said.

"No ... we ain't doin' it."

"Deke, it won't be that late when we git ta Yellowstone. We'll see a few things an' maybe even find a motel right in the park."

"No, an' that's final," Deke said and started the truck.

Now Shelly was pouting and stared at the passing landscape in silence.

Deke was fighting exhaustion from his rough night and after he'd crossed the center line and drifted off the pavement several times, Shelly said, "Yor scarin' me. If we weren't on a four lane you'd a kill'd us by now."

"That's why I wanted ta stop at a motel back there in Billings," Deke said.

"That ain't why you wanted ta stop at a motel, an you know it."

A few miles outside of Big Timber the unfinished interstate reverted to a two-lane. Twice Deke almost drove into the ditch and once he crossed the centerline when a semi was coming. Shelly grabbed his shoulder and shook him hard. Deke looked up, bleary eyed.

"Dammit ta hell, Deke!" she screamed. "I didn't come to Montana ta die. You pull over right now an' let me drive."

"Alright ... alright," Deke said and pulled off the road.

Shelly took the wheel and a mile later Deke was snoring, his head propped against the side window. The day grew increasingly colder, the sun rarely popping out from behind the ceiling of gray clouds. Snow flurries kicked up intermittantly, but the road remained bare and dry. Traffic was light and Shelly was able to watch the scenery as she drove, which was somewhat subdued, as dark billows obscured the distant mountains.

Deke dozed for an hour and a half then awoke on a beautiful stretch of winding two-lane road that ran beside a river. The sun had temporarily come out and glinted off the swift-flowing water. He yawned a couple of times but didn't say anything, content to watch the river and the distant mountains. After a while he asked Shelly, "Has the interstate been two-lane ever' since I went ta sleep?"

"It went back ta four-lane for a ways," Shelly said.

A few miles later they crossed a bridge that said, "Yellowstone River" and a mile further passed a road marker that read, '89'.

Deke looked at it and turned to Shelly. "Where are we now, anyway?"

"On our way ta Yellowstone Park," Shelly said, "an' we're almost there."

"What! I thought you said we were stoppin' early t'day."

"It ain't late," Shelly answered. "We can see some a' the park, then git us a motel an' be all set."

"We ain't doin' it!" Deke yelled.

Shelly stared at the pavement and kept driving.

"Didya hear me, godammit?" Deke hollered. "We ain't goin' ta Yellowstone. We're turnin' around and headin' back to the interstate."

"The interstate's a long ways back," Shelly said, still watching the road, "an' we're dang near to Yellowstone Park."

"I don't care!" Deke screamed. "Turn around right now!"

"I wanta see the park," Shelly said, still looking at the road.

"Well, ya ain't seein' the park, cuz yer stoppin' the truck an' turnin' around b'fore we git there."

Shelly looked at Deke. "I'm seein' the park."

"Not in my truck, ya ain't," Deke said. "This pickup goes where I say."

"That's simple, Deke. Jes say it goes ta Yellowstone Park."

"It ain't goin' ta Yellowstone Park. Not no way an' not no how."

Shelly kept driving.

"Godammit, pull over! I want my truck back, right now! It's my truck."

"We had this conversation once before, Deke, in a dump truck."

"You stop right now or I'm takin' the wheel," Deke screamed.

"You gonna show me how ta drive a truck like ya did with the Brockway?" Shelly said, but she let off the gas and pulled to the side of the road. She turned off the Ford, took the key out of the ignition and opened the door.

"You don' need the keys," Deke said.

"Yeah, I do."

Shelly climbed into the bed as Deke got out and walked around to the driver's side. She unlocked the wooden trunk, took out her knapsack and suitcase and jumped down. "See ya," she said, handing Deke the keys.

She put on her knapsack, walked about four car lengths ahead, then set her suitcase down and stuck out her thumb, even though no vehicles were in sight.

"This is stupid," Deke called to her. "Git back here right now!"

"Where we goin'?" Shelly yelled.

"We're goin' back to the interstate, where d'ya think."

Shelly picked up her suitcase, walked four more car lengths, set it down and stuck out her thumb again. Deke climbed into his pickup and started it, gunned the engine and did a one-eighty, throwing gravel and leaving a pair of tire tracks on the asphalt.

After seven or eight minutes a southbound car with a man and woman in front and three kids in the back approached. They slowed and looked at Shelly but didn't stop. The next two vehicles were northbound but five minutes later a newer Dodge pickup came along and braked as soon as the man at the wheel saw her. The driver stopped a few feet ahead then leaned over and opened the passenger door for Shelly to get in as she cautiously approached. The Dodge had Wyoming plates, but the truck bed was empty, so Shelly guessed the driver was likely not a rancher or even a workingman. She walked to the open door, regretting she hadn't taken the Buck knife out of her knapsack and put it on her belt, and looked at the driver. He was middle-aged, clean-shaven and wore a buttoned down shirt with a bolo tie. "Need a lift?" he said and smiled.

"You goin' inta the park?" Shelly asked.

"Sure am," he said. "I'll take you wherever you want to go."

Shelly studied the man. He was middle-sized with a slight gut on him and didn't look particularly tough or dangerous. If he got aggressive, Shelly reckoned she could handle him, or at least put up such a fight he'd back off.

"Alright," Shelly said, and took off her knapsack. As she was getting into the Dodge someone behind them started honking their horn.

"Yeah, yeah," the driver said, looking in the rear view mirror. "Stop honkin' and go around."

Shelly stood up and looked back. It was Deke's Ford. He leaned out the open window and called, "I'm goin' ta Yellowstone Park. Ya wanna ride along?"

"Thanks for stoppin'," Shelly told the driver of the Dodge, "but I know this guy," and she trotted back to Deke's pickup.

Shelly locked her gear back in the wooden trunk and got in the cab. Deke pulled onto the roadway like nothing had happened. "I hope we see Yogi Bear," he said.

"He lives in Jellystone Park, Deke, not this one," Shelly said. "But I would like to see a bear, especially a grizzly."

"I reckon that'd be okay," Deke said, "as long as it was far enough away."

When they reached Yellowstone, Shelly paid the entrance fee and the female ranger told them, "It's late in the season, so nearly all the services inside the park are closed for the winter. We're also expecting a storm tonight, so you might want to be outside of the park by dark."

After taking in the Mammoth Hot Springs area Shelly and Deke drove east on Grand Loop Road to Tower Junction and to the Grand Canyon of the Yellowstone. Shelly got out to look everytime they came to something spectacular, which in Yellowstone National Park, was often. Deke didn't argue or complain and each time they stopped he got out of the truck and joined Shelly. More than once, Shelly said, "I really want ta come back here an' do some hikin' an' explorin' when the weather's nicer." By the time they drove to Canyon Junction and visited Inspiration Point, twilight was coming on and snow was falling.

"I'm gittin' mighty hungry," Deke said. "We didn't stop for lunch."

"You was dozin' then," Shelly said, "an' I figured you needed the sleep."

At Norris Junction they looked for someplace to eat, but everything was bolted up for the winter. Snow was now sticking to the road and Deke had to turn on the headlights. When they reached Madison Junction only a vague remnant of light remained in the sky and they faced a choice. Shelly wanted to see Old Faithful, but she and Deke were seriously hungry and the snow was falling harder. Shelly studied her map under the dome light. "We better not go ta Old Faithful," she told

Deke, "it's too far away. Reckon we oughta take that ranger's advice an' git outa the park 'fore it gits dark an' that storm gits too bad."

But as they followed the Madison River toward West Yellowstone, the sky turned black and the snow came down heavier until the road was covered. When the lights of town came into view, Shelly said, "I kinda pulled a fast one on ya back there, turnin' off the interstate, but I appreciate ya drivin' back to git me, then not complainin' about stoppin' ta look at things in the park. An' to show my gratitude, Deke, I'll pay for a nice motel an' the best steak dinner in town."

"Ummmm," Deke said, "they *both* sound real good right now."

"Let's stop an' fill the gas tank," Shelly said, "an' we can ask at the station about a good place ta stay and where the best steak is."

They pulled in at the first service station they saw in West Yellowstone and an old cowboy about sixty came out and pumped their gas. Shelly was feeling generous and paid for the gas then asked about a steak and a place to stay.

"Only one place to go if you're after a good steak," he said, leaning his face in the side window, "and that's the Elkhorn Lodge. They got a 24 ounce ribeye that'll knock your socks off an' it comes with a salad bar and a baked potato the size of a football."

"That's what I'm havin'," Deke said.

"Where's a nice place ta stay?" Shelly asked.

"Same joint," the attendant said. "It's a lodge. They've even got a few rooms with private hot tubs."

Deke turned to Shelly with pleading eyes. "Can we?"

"Yeah, I reckon so, Deke; you've had a rough coupla days. A good hot soak would do us both some good."

"They got beer?" Deke asked.

"Yup," the man said. "The place has a nice bar. They probably even have the fireplace going tonight."

"Any problem gittin' a room?" Shelly said.

"Naw. They're not too busy this time of year. You'll be fine."

"Where is it?" Shelly asked.

"Well, now, it's a little bit outa town," the man said, "about twenty miles. It'll take you a half an hour in this weather, but it's worth it. And besides, there isn't any other place around to get a good steak."

"Let's do it, Shelly," Deke said. "I can already taste that ribeye."

"Okay," the man said, "you take this road you're on, U.S.20, west out of town, and after you get over the pass, take a right at the next road. You go over another pass nine miles after you turn and it's just down the hill on the left. You won't miss the place, it's all lit up."

Wet snow fell from the inky, starless sky as Deke and Shelly left the lights of West Yellowstone behind. Two miles from town Shelly said, "Are you okay gittin' ta that lodge, Deke? I didn't git much sleep las' night either an' I wouldn't mind kickin' back b'fore we git there."

"You bet, Shelly," Deke said and winked. "You git rested up fer later on."

———————————

Shelly leaned her head against the side window and soon was fast asleep. A few miles later the highway began climbing up what Deke guessed was the first pass. The higher he got, the harder the snow fell and the worse the visibility became. Since leaving West Yellowstone he hadn't seen any other vehicles and there were no tire tracks in the new fallen snow. By the time Deke topped the grade his wipers and defroster were having trouble keeping up. He hunched over the steering wheel, wiping wet fog off the glass with his bare hand and trying to see the white-covered roadway ahead.

Coming down the other side Deke shifted into second so as not to pick up speed or have to use his brakes on the icy roadway. He hoped the snow would let up at the bottom of the pass but it didn't. Visibility was now down to two car lengths and Deke guessed that snow was covering the headlights. He thought about getting out and brushing them off, but the weather was so miserable he slowed down to 30 and decided to ride it out. After several miles Deke started wondering where the road was that the filling station attendant had told them to take. The guy didn't say how far it was from the pass, just that it was the first road to the right. Three miles later Deke was ready to turn around but then a road to the right appeared. He gently tapped the brake and turned onto it, still making virgin tracks in the snow.

This road was narrower, with deeper ditches on the sides, but Deke kept to the middle and plugged along. Once again, Deke thought about wiping off his headlights, but decided not to since the lodge wasn't far ahead. When he had gone seven or eight miles, Deke began to wonder if he was on the right road, but then it started to climb and he figured this must be the second pass that the old cowboy had told them about. This grade was steeper and narrower than the first pass, and with the building snow, the pickup's rear tires began slipping.

"Don't fail me now truck," Deke said quietly. "That lodge is jest on the other side a' this hill."

Spinning and sliding, the Ford topped the crest and Deke breathed a long sigh of relief. Descending was just as treacherous and when the road leveled out, Deke started looking for the lights of the lodge. Still wiping condensation from the windshield, he crawled through the deepening snow. Five miles went by yet Deke saw no lights. "Shitfire, I shoulda seen it by now," he muttered.

"What'd ya say, Deke?" Shelly said, opening her eyes and sitting up.

"I said we shoulda been there by now," Deke told her.

"Did ya go over the pass an' take that right turn?" Shelly asked.

"Yeah, but it was farther than I thought it'd be."

"Did ya go over the second pass the man told us about?"

"Sure did, about five miles back."

"Oooh ... that ain't good, Deke. That feller said the lodge was jes down the hill an' on the left from the second pass. When's the last time ya saw lights?"

"About two miles outa town."

"An' none after that?"

"Not a single one. Whadaya reckon we oughta do, Shelly?"

"Let's give it another mile or two, Deke."

Ten minutes later Shelly and Deke looked at each across the dark cab. "Let me wipe off them headlights so's we can see the road better," Shelly said.

Deke stopped and when Shelly got out of the truck she almost went down. "It's slip'ry as hell out here," she hollered after catching herself on the open door.

"I know," Deke said, "that's why I'm drivin' so slow."

Shelly edged to the front of the pickup and wiped off both headlamps. With her boot, she scraped away some snow, which was over six inches deep, down to the bare roadway. "Hey, Deke," she called, "this road ain't even paved, it's gravel." She got back in the cab and closed the door. "I don't think some nice big lodge would be on a gravel road."

Deke ran his tongue over his lips: he could almost taste the ribeye. "Naw, I don't reckon so," he reluctantly agreed. "What're we gonna do?"

They sat for a moment and watched the falling snow. "We ain't got a choice, Deke," Shelly said. "We gotta turn around. You mighta missed a turn back there or taken the wrong road. Roll your winda down an' I'll git out an' guide ya."

Shelly cautiously walked to the front of the pickup. "Since yor already in the middle a' the road, Deke, you only got seven or eight feet to the ditch."

"Alright," Deke hollered back, and put the truck in gear. He cranked the wheel to the left and eased out on the clutch, giving the Ford only a little gas. The back tire spun a couple of times then caught traction and the pickup moved.

"Stop!" Shelly yelled, but when Deke touched the brake the truck slid until it was two feet from the ditch. "Whew! That was close, Deke. Back up."

Again Deke worked the clutch and accelerator gently but the road-bed was graded higher in the middle so he had to back slightly uphill. The rear tire spun in futility as the truck slipped toward the berm.

"Stop!" Shelly yelled. The front tire was only inches from the ditch.

Shelly looked at Deke through his open side window. "This ain't gonna work. Ya got any tire chains?"

"No."

"Then we need ta git creative. Ya got a shovel in the back?"

"No."

Shelly rummaged in the bed of the pickup until her hand fell upon a piece of angle iron about two feet long. "This might work," she said, and called to Deke, "Ya got a bucket back here?"

"No."

"How come you got ev'rything in this heap 'cept what we need?" Shelly hollered, and then remembered the water jug. She took the lid off the two-gallon plastic container, inched to the side of the road and slid down the ditch on her butt. After clearing away a patch of snow, Shelly dug out some gravel and dirt with the angle iron and filled the bucket with her bare hands. "Brrrrrr … this is cold on the fingers," she called to Deke.

Setting the jug on the roadway, she climbed out of the ditch on all fours and pulled herself upright using the front fender. With one hand clinging to the truck, Shelly went to the rear and carefully spread the dirt and gravel beneath the drive-wheel and in a line about two feet behind it. She dropped the angle iron in the bed but kept the jug with some gravel still in it. "Now try it," she said.

Deke edged the shifter into reverse, took his foot from the brake, and before the truck could slide forward any further, gently goosed the gas pedal. The back tire spun and spun but the pickup started to inch downhill toward the ditch. In desperation Deke gunned the engine and as the tire whirled in reverse Shelly tossed the rest of the dirt and gravel underneath it.

The tire instantly found traction and before Deke could let up on the accelerator the Ford shot backwards across the road. He hit the brake but the pickup continued sliding on the icy surface. Fast as he could, Deke clutched, rammed the gearshift into second and tried the get the tire spinning forward, but he was already too late. With a loud "WHUMPPP" the Ford dropped into the far ditch, its back bumper slamming against the embankment, and there it came to rest, stern down and bow tilted upward like a sinking ship.

Chapter 38

Shelly watched the pickup slam into the ditch and expected a loud string of profanity from Deke, but he calmly put the Ford into neutral then laid his head on the steering wheel and began sobbing. Stepping gingerly across the slick roadway, Shelly assessed the calamity. "You need ta git out an' look at this, Deke."

"I don' need ta look at nothin'," Deke said, wiping the tears off his face with the back of his hand. "What I need is to git ta that lodge an' have me a big ribeye an' a tater the size of a football."

"That ain't gonna happen, Deke, so you might as well git out an' look."

Deke opened the door and got out. Holding onto the truck he carefully walked over to where Shelly stood. The situation was obviously hopeless. The ditch was three feet deep and the truck had bottomed out.

Shelly looked across the road. "If there was a stout tree over yonder, we could use the handyman jack as a come-along if ya had a cable or a strong rope."

"I don't have a cable," Deke said, "or near 'nough rope ... but it don' matter cuz there ain't no tree."

A gust of wind blew the falling snow sideways. "Let's git back in the truck," Shelly said. "It's gittin' colder out here."

They got into the idling pickup and Shelly turned on the domelight and got out her atlas. "I see where we *might* be Deke ... an' if I'm right, we're a long ways from anywhere."

"I got a feelin' that even if yer wrong, we're still a long ways from anywhere," Deke said. "Whadaya think we oughta do?"

"Ain't much we can do, Deke. We can't start walkin', we'd freeze ta death, an' we don't even know where we are. Somebody'll come by ta'morrow."

They sat for a while with the heater on, watching the snow swirl and build up around them. "Listen," Shelly said, "it's gonna git a lot colder 'fore this night is over an' we can't keep the motor runnin' or we'll run outa gas. We oughta grab whatever heavy clothes we got out a' the trunk in the back right now, 'fore the snow gits any deeper."

Deke shut off the engine and he and Shelly climbed into the bed and dug through their things, pulling out all the warm clothing they could find. When they got back in the cab, Deke had his Winchester.

"How come ya got that?" Shelly asked him.

"I jest wanted it up here with me ta be safe."

"Anytime you got a gun in your hand, Deke, the last thing I feel is safe."

Deke slid the Winchester under the seat and started up the truck again. He and Shelly put on whatever sweaters and jackets they had and when they were bundled up Shelly said, "I think we oughta turn off the engine for a while."

"Alright," Deke said, and lit up a cigarette.

Shelly cranked the window down a little to let out the smoke. "We should try'n git some sleep. Time'll go by faster an' maybe when we wake up in the mornin' somebody'll come along an' pull us out."

"I know a better way ta make the time go by fast," Deke said slyly. "We could start up the truck an' git it warm in here agin, then do what we woulda done if we'd a got ta that lodge."

"You mean have a steak dinner?" Shelly asked.

"No ... I mean like we'd a done later on ... up in the room."

"Deke, even with the heater goin' it ain't exactly warm in here. You can take off all the clothes you want, but I'm stayin' dressed."

"There's things you can do with yer clothes on," Deke said.

"Nothin' along them lines that I'm gonna do right now, Deke."

"But Shelly, you said we'd do all kinds a stuff once we got to a motel."

"Deke, I hate ta pop your balloon, but we ain't in a motel."

"Well, it's kinda like a motel, ain't it ... a little."

"Maybe where you come from, but the motels I've seen generally have bathrooms an' beds. Deke, let's jes try an' git some sleep." With that, Shelly rolled up the window, leaned against the door and closed her eyes.

Deke watched her for a little while then slid down in the seat and closed his eyes as well. The Ford's windows quickly fogged over as the temperature dropped. Each time the wind kicked up, puffs of cold air blew into the cab. Shelly had a blue stocking cap on and a sweatshirt under her jacket with the hood pulled up over her head, but Deke only had his ratty straw cowboy hat. After a while, a shivering Deke sat up, took off his hat and got the Wild Bill Hickock t-shirt that he had stuffed under the seat and wrapped it around his head. He leaned back and tried to sleep again, but his teeth wouldn't stop chattering and his feet were freezing. "Sh-shelly?" Deke said. "Are you asleep?"

"Not now."

"It's c-c-cold in here, ain't it?"

"I reckoned it would be. That's why we got our clothes outa the trunk."

"I can't feel my t-toes."

"That's 'cause those cowboy boots are pinchin' your feet."

"I'm turnin' the truck an' the heater b-back on," Deke said, starting the engine.

Shelly sat up, looked at Deke and giggled. "You look like a swami with that shirt wrapped aroun' your head."

"What's a swami?"

"I don't rightly know for shor, but you look like one," Shelly said.

"I can't help it," Deke said, "I'm fr-freezin' my ass off."

"If that's the case, you got that shirt on the wrong part a' ya," Shelly said, grinning.

"It ain't f-funny. I wish we had us a blanket."

"Me too, Deke. I almost brought one, but I wanted ta travel light."

"It'd be warmer fer b-both of us if we huddled t'gether," Deke said.

"It'll warm up in a minute," Shelly told him. "That heater's jes gittin started. Take them boots off an' rub your feet. That'll help the blood flow to 'em."

Deke tugged off his cowboy boots and a great stench filled the cab.

"Light a cigarette, quick," Shelly said, choking.

"Can you rub muh f-f-feet for me?" Deke said, after he lit a Camel.

"No! They stink," Shelly said.

Deke stuck his feet under the heater and massaged them until Shelly said, "We better turn off the truck an' try an' sleep some more."

"I ain't warm yet," Deke said.

"Deke, if we use up all the gas, we really will freeze."

"Alright," Deke said, and reluctantly shut off the engine.

As the night deepened the temperature fell and Deke shivered pitifully whenever the heater was off. He kept starting the truck and wanted to run the engine continually but as the gas gauge dropped Shelly made him shut it off. She said nothing, but feared for them if no one drove by the next day. The snow was now over a foot deep and though it had let up some, was still falling.

A few minutes before 5:00, Deke began muttering. "I can't t-t-take it no more. We need ta turn the truck b-back on agin."

"Maybe fer a while, Deke, but the gas is gittin' low."

Deke unwrapped the shirt from his face and started the engine. "I don' think anybody's g-g-gonna come."

"Sure they will, Deke."

"I ain't so sure. What if this is one a' them b-back roads that nobody uses in the winter? There might not be anybody come through here till spring."

Shelly also had considered that possibility "Well, I'm a little worried too, Deke, but if nobody comes along, we'll figure somethin' else out."

"Like what?"

"I don't know, but we ain't a'gonna die 'cause I won't let that happen."

"B'sides freezin'," Deke said, "I'm starvin'."

"Try not ta think about it, Deke."

"How can I not think about it? We didn't have no lunch or dinner. I'm thinkin' about baloney an' crackers so much I can smell the baloney."

"I don't think that's baloney yor smellin', Deke."

"It is too. I know the diff'runce b'tween my feet an' baloney."

"Well, I hope so, 'cause if there ain't no diff'ernce I'm never eatin' baloney again. I think yor havin' a mirage, Deke, 'cept yor smellin' the mirage instead a' seein' it."

"I'm tellin' ya, I can smell baloney." Deke took a deep whiff. "It's on yer side a' the truck." He leaned over and stuck his face in front of Shelly's knees and sniffed. "It's right around here," he said.

"There ain't no baloney here, Deke," Shelly told him, "an' I don't much care for the inference."

Deke reached under the seat beneath Shelly and pulled out a rolled up paper bag. He looked inside and smiled real big, then stuck his hand in the sack and pulled out an open pack of sliced baloney.

"Oh, jeeze, Deke, you bought that back in Nebraska from that shyster who sold ya the pistol."

"Morgan wadn't no shyster," Deke said. "That was a good pistol."

"Well, it didn't do *you* no good. An' if yor dumb e'nuff ta eat that baloney, it won't do ya no good either. That stuff was spoil't three days ago."

Deke flipped on the dome light and held the baloney up for inspection. "It don't smell all that bad," he said. "I'm gonna eat it." He looked at Shelly, "You don' want any, do ya?"

"Let me see it a second," Shelly said, and held out her hand.

Deke glared at Shelly like she'd just asked him for his magic ring, but after a long hesitation, handed over his precious baloney.

Shelly held it up to the light. "Deke, this stuff's green an' got slime on it."

"I don't care," Deke said, "I'm gonna eat it anyway … give it back."

Quick as a flash, Shelly opened the truck door and tossed the pack of baloney as far as she could.

"Ahhhhhhhhhhh!" Deke screamed. "What'd ya do that for?"

"Ta keep you from gittin' sick," Shelly said. "Now shut off the truck an' go ta sleep, it'll be light perty soon."

Pouting, Deke wrapped the Wild Bill shirt around his head but didn't shut the engine off. Shelly leaned over and turned the key. As the motor spluttered to a stop, Deke reached down to start the truck again. "Don'tchoo do it," Shelly warned him, "we're low on gas."

"Dammit, I'm cold," Deke said.

"I feel for ya, Deke, but there's nothin' I can do about it."

"Yeah there is. We could cuddle up t'gether. Yer s'pose ta be my girlfriend, but most a' time, like now, you don't act like it."

"I slept with ya two nights in a row didn't I?"

"Yeah, but ya ain't done it since."

"An' who's fault is that? One night you was sick drunk an' last night ya knocked yor'self out. I was gonna sleep with ya at that lodge tonight if we'd a got there, an' I'll sleep with ya at a motel ta'morrow night before we git ta Troy. I'm keepin' my side a' the promise, Deke, it's you that ain't holdin' up your end."

"I'm takin' ya to Montana with me like I promised, ain't I?"

"Yeah, but part a' your promise was that ya wouldn't git drunked up or do crazy shit no more an' you shor ain't lived up ta that side a' the bargain."

Deke looked down and rubbed his freezing feet. "Is that the only reason ya sleep with me …'cause you promised ya would if I took ya ta Montana?"

Shelly stared out the side window at the falling snow.

"Other'n sleepin' with me them two nights," Deke said, "you never have acted like a real girlfriend. Sometimes I think you don't even like me all that much."

"I tried, I really did," Shelly said and looked at Deke, "but then you went an' almost shot a guy jes for takin' me ridin'. Last night some real nice people invited me ta join 'em for a pow-wow, an' you ruin'd it. How can I be your girlfriend when ya do stuff like that?"

"Is that the only reason?" Deke asked.

"No. You said you'd clean up, start brushin' your teeth, trim your hair an' beard, shower more often, start wearin' nicer clothes. The only time you done any a' that was when I made ya."

"Anything else?"

"Yeah. The way yor prejudiced against people who are diff'ernt than you. I won't put up with that. What you did las' night woulda never happened if you weren't prejudiced against Indians."

"I thought I was savin' ya, Shelly," Deke said. "Ever'thing I know about In'juns came from the westerns I watched."

"We all grew up watchin' westerns, but most of us figger'd out they weren't real. An' that don't account for how you feel about Black people or folks who are gay."

Deke dropped his head. "Does that mean you won't ever be my girlfriend?"

"How can I, Deke, unless you change?"

"What're you gonna do when we git ta Troy. Don't ya still wanna learn ta drive my brother's log truck?"

"You know I do. But I can't go back on what I b'lieve is right."

"I want ya ta learn how ta drive Zeke's truck too, so we can be log truck drivers t'gether, Shelly," Deke said. "I'm sorry for all a' them things I did an' said. I don't mean no harm ta the people you say I'm prejudiced aginst. That way a' thinkin' came from my aunt an' uncle."

"We been through this before, Deke. Yor a man now and responsible for how you think an' what you do. You *can* change if ya really want to."

"If I stopped bein' prejudiced right now, Shelly, promised ta never say another bad word, or even think a bad word, about In'juns an' colored's, an' even queers, would ya at least give me a chance."

"I don't know, Deke, there's all them other things too."

"When we git ta Troy it'll all be diff'runt, Shelly, I swear it. I'll git new clothes and clean up, all on my own. An' you won't have ta worry about me drinkin' or smokin' dope 'cause Zeke made me promise I wouldn't do none a' that or he won't let me drive his truck. All I'm askin', Shelly, is ta give me a chance."

"You promised all them things before Deke, and didn't live up to 'em. What yor askin' for isn't a chance, but another chance." Shelly turned away and looked out the side window. It was no longer snowing and the first shards of light had crept into the cold sky. "Alright, Deke," she said, "If you live up ta them promises, I won't walk out on ya, even when we git ta Troy, but if you wanta be my boyfriend, then yor gonna have ta make *all* a' them changes we jes talked about, includin' no more lyin'. Startin' now."

"I'll really do it this time, Shelly, you'll see. I'll even swear to it on my John Wayne belt buckle if ya want."

"That's alright, Deke, you don't need ta do that."

"Uh …Shelly?"

"Yeah, Deke?"

"We're still sleepin' t'gether at the motel t'morrow night, ain't we, jest like you said a minute ago?"

Shelly hesitated. "Since I said we were, I reckon so, Deke."

"Uh …Shelly?"

"Yeah, Deke?"

"Can we turn the truck on? I'm cold."

"Jes for five minutes, then we should try an' sleep till it gits light out."

Half an hour later, in the gray dawn, Deke reached over and shook Shelly awake. "I'm freezin' agin an' I need ta use the bathroom."

"We don't have one in here," Shelly told him.

"I know that," Deke said, "but it's cold out there."

"Well, ya ain't doin' your business here in the cab, so jes git out an' do it."

"We got any t.p.?"

"No. There might be some oily rags in the trunk."

Deke looked through the back window. The wooden trunk was covered with a foot of snow. "Dammit, anyway."

"You still got that ol' snot rag in your pocket?"

"No. It was in muh pants when I lost 'em."

"Here ya go, then," Shelly said and yanked Deke's t-shirt off his head.

"I can't do that ta Wild Bill Hickock, he's a hero a' mine."

"Well, Wild Bill didn't do ya any good back there on the rez," Shelly said, "he might as well help ya out now."

"Can I start the truck so it's warm when I git back in?"

"No, we're too low on gas."

Deke sat upright and looked at Shelly with a pinched face. "I can't wait no longer." He flung his door open, grabbed Wild Bill and pulled his Winchester from under the seat.

"How come yor takin' that?" Shelly asked through the open door but Deke was already scrambling up the ditch.

"Don't you watch," he called as he hurried through the snow.

"That's the last thing in the world I wanta do," Shelly hollered back as she leaned over and pulled the door closed. A few minutes later she heard a muffled cry and rolled her window down. This time the scream was loud and clear and Shelly jumped out to see what was happening. Deke was standing in the open with his pants down, yelling at the top of his lungs, his rifle raised to his shoulder. Sixty yards away, a humongous grizzly bear ambled towards him.

"Don't shoot the bear!" Shelly hollered and took off towards Deke. She expected to hear a shot but instead heard Deke swearing violently as he worked the lever action.

When the bear was halfway to him, Deke reached down, tugged up his pants and made for the truck. The bear shuffled after him, gaining ground as Deke struggled through the snow clutching his pants with one hand and holding his rifle in the other.

"AAAHHHHHH!" Deke screamed, and in his desperation to out-run the bear, tripped and pitched face first in the snow.

"Go away, bear!" Shelly yelled, and started chucking snowballs at the oncoming grizzly. Ingoring Shelly's barrage, the grizzly came on as Deke scrambled to his feet, grabbed his pants with both hands and ran right past Shelly. Shelly was about to run, but the bear stopped, sniffed at something in the snow, ate it, then turned and shambled back to the woods. She walked over to where Deke had fallen and picked up his rifle. "Here ya go," she said, handing Deke the gun when she got back to the pickup.

"Thanks," Deke said sheepishly, and stowed the Winchester under the seat. "That damn In'jun at the gas station took the bullets outa my gun."

"I'm glad he did. That ol' bear wadn't after you a'tall, it just smelled that rotten baloney a' yours that I threw out. It's pro'bly off in the woods gittin' sick right now."

"That was real brave a' you comin' ta help me like that," Deke said.

"I never gave it a thought. You was in a fix, with your pants down an' all."

"Yeah, I reckon so," Deke said, and looked away, embarrassed.

Shelly smiled. "We both said we wanted ta see a bear. I guess we saw one."

Since he was wet from falling down, Shelly let Deke turn the engine on. Ten minutes later she leaned over and shut it off.

"I'm still wet an' cold," Deke said.

"I know, but if we use up all the gas, you won't ever git warm again."

"What're we gonna do, Shelly?"

Dawn was upon them, though the sun only peeped through the clouds periodically. The air had warmed from it's pre-dawn chill but was still well below freezing and what direction the weather would take was anybody's guess.

"Listen, Deke," Shelly said, "I've been doin' some thinkin'. It's at least twenty miles to the highway, an' you might be right about this bein' a back road that nobody uses in the winter. We can't stay here another night with no gas, it could git a lot colder."

"I can't walk that far in the snow with these cowboy boots, Shelly."

"I know ya can't, Deke … but I pro'bly can."

"What if the weather turns real bad?"

"That's a chance I'll hafta take. But if nobody comes by, we'll be in real trouble."

Deke ran his tongue over his lips. "How soon ya leavin'?"

"It'll be slow goin' in this snow an' I might need the whole day ta git to the highway." Shelly looked at her Timex. "It's a few minutes after seven now, so I better git on with it."

Shelly got out and climbed into the pickup bed, scraped the snow off the trunk and unlocked it, then got her Buck knife out and attached it to her belt. She jumped down and opened Deke's door. "I'll bring some help back, Deke, ya got my word on it," she said and smiled.

"What am I s'pose ta do if somebody comes by?" Deke asked.

"That's easy. If they're comin' from the East I'll be with 'em an' if they come from the West, you git in with them an' pick me up on the road."

"Yeah, I guess that'd be right," Deke said, then asked, "Do I git a kiss?"

Shelly leaned over and put one on his lips, then started down the road.

Deke stepped out of the truck to watch Shelly go. Just before she disappeared over the top of a rise, she called, "Take care, Deke, an' don't use up all the gas."

"You take care too, Shelly," Deke hollered back, "an' watch out fer grizzly bears."

Deke climbed back in the pickup and locked both doors. He looked at the ignition key but didn't turn it on. Ten minutes later his toes were numb and he was shivering. Half-crazed with hunger, by 8:00 Deke was having doubts if he would live through the day and couldn't take his eyes off the key. At 8:25 he said, "I'll jest turn the truck on fer five minutes," and cranked over the motor. Five minutes later, as the truck cab was starting to warm up, Deke said, "I'll let it go fer another five minutes."

The engine's steady purr was comforting and the warm air pouring from the heater felt good on his toes and damp legs. Fifteen minutes passed. Deke looked down at the ignition key but made no move to turn it off. A few minutes later he thought his engine was getting louder then realized that another rumble was coming from outside. Cautiously, he rolled his window down and looked out. Over the top of the rise came a massive piece of equipment, plowing snow from the road like nobody's business. Deke turned off the truck, opened the door and stepped out. The machine hove to beside the pickup and Shelly hopped down from the high cab.

"Lookee what I found, Deke," she said, laughing. "Ain't she a beaut?"

And indeed she was: a big, yellow Galion road grader with all six tires chained up and a 14-foot snow blade attached to the front. The operator, a stocky guy wearing blue coveralls, unlaced Sorrel packs and a Stormy Kromer hat climbed down and stood beside Shelly. "I'm Glenn," he said, staring at the black and blue lump protruding from Deke's forehead. "Shelly tells me you two spent a cold night out here."

"We sure did," Deke said. "An' a starvin' one, too."

Glenn leaned forward and drizzled a long brown line of snoose saliva into the snow. "You're lucky you didn't do this three months from now or you two woulda been Popsicles. This is the coldest spot in Montana and a lot a' times the coldest place in the country. Thirty below's nothin' around here."

"Glenn's gonna pull us out, Deke," Shelly said. "He's plowin' the whole way over to Monida on the interstate an' says we can follow 'im."

"Speakin' of," Glenn said, "let's tug that old beater outa the ditch. We need ta get movin', I got a late start today. The wife and me went out for steaks last night at the Elkhorn Lodge then had a few beers afterwards by their fireplace. Man, they got a 24 ounce ribeye you wouldn't believe."

"So we've heard," Shelly said.

"Where in blazes were you folks headed on this road last night, anyway?" Glenn asked as he was getting back into the grader's cab.

"Troy," Shelly told him.

"You shoulda asked somebody local. There's better ways to go."

Glenn pulled the Galion ahead of Deke's pickup then climbed out again. "I pull half the people in this county out of the ditch every year," he said as he uncoiled the heavy chain wound around the grader's rear deck and handed one end to Deke. "You hook up your own truck, that way I'm not responsible." He spit another load of juice in the snow. "Looks like somebody already latched onta your front bumper."

"That was my doin'," Shelly said.

Deke took the chain, got down in the snow and attached it to his pickup.

"Put it in neutral and let's go," Glenn told him.

The grader pulled Deke's Ford from the ditch like it was a Tonka toy and as Deke was unhitching the chain, Shelly asked Glenn, "How far is it ta Monida?"

"Close to forty miles."

"Is there a gas station there?"

"Sure is," Glenn answered.

"Good, 'cause we only got a quarter of a tank left," Shelly said, "unless Deke used some more up."

"Oh no," Deke said, "I didn't use any."

"That's the good news," Glenn said. "The bad news is that it's not open today. This is Sunday and Solly will either be out fishin' or trappin'. The nearest gas if you're headed north is in Dillon and that's a hundred miles from here."

"We can't make it that far," Deke said. "A quarter tank is seventy-five miles at most."

"Well, I don't know what to tell you," Glenn said as another brown blob dribbled from his mouth, "unless you go back to West Yellowstone."

"I hate backtrackin'," Shelly said. "How far is it from Monida ta Dillion?"

"Around sixty miles."

"I got an idea," Shelly said. "How 'bout we jes stay hooked on ta your grader an' you tow us?"

"I can do that," Glenn said. "It'll be around two hours until we get there."

Shelly turned to Deke. "Why don't ya let me drive? It's gonna be cold with no heater goin' and you'll wanta rub your feet." She took off her jacket and handed Deke her hooded sweatshirt. "Put this on under your jacket, it'll help keep ya warm."

"What about you, Shelly?" Deke asked.

"I got warmed up walkin', I'll live."

Freewheeling along behind the Galion, all Shelly had to do was steer and tap the brakes whenever they went down a hill. A little ways up the road was a sign that said, 'Lakeview' and they passed a cluster of scattered houses. Beyond that were several ranches.

"Looks like there's a few folks on this road after all, Deke," Shelly said. "Glenn told me the county plows it so the school bus can come out here."

Before they were even halfway to Monida, Deke was a shuddering wreck. He had the hood of Shelly's sweatshirt drawn up so tight that only his nose was showing and was sitting on his bootless feet to keep them warm. "I'm starvin' an' freezin' both, Shelly. Please, can't we start the engine fer jest a few minutes?"

"I ain't runnin' the motor, Deke, or we'll run outa gas on the interstate. Rub your feet an' stop complainin', we'll be in Dillon 'fore ya know it."

When they reached Monida, Glenn towed them through the decaying little burg then stopped the grader near the I-15 on-ramp. Shelly hopped out to thank him and unhook the tow chain and heard the Ford start up as soon as she closed the door.

Chapter 39

Sunday, September 30, 1973

Northbound from Monida Pass, the wind whipped over the bleak hills and bullied the Ford with such rudeness that Shelly fought to keep the old pickup in its own lane. The sun, afraid to show its face, cowered behind the clouds. Deke stuck his frozen feet next to the heater vent and moaned in pain as they thawed while Shelly drove in silence.

Matching the gray weather, the snow-blown landscape rolled by, barren and cold, with little of interest to look at except the railroad tracks beside the highway and the white-capped peaks far in the distance. Twenty-five miles from Monida Deke lowered the sweatshirt hood and put his cowboy hat on. "I finally got warm," he said, "but I'm still starvin'."

"You ate the same time I did yesterday," Shelly told him.

At the north end of Clark Canyon Resevoir the Beaverhead River emerged and the highway became more scenic, twisting beside the river through miles of craggy buttes. After a while the wind died down and the sun felt safe enough to come out. Fifteen miles from Dillon the gas gauge settled on empty and Shelly, temporarily tired of adventures, prayed the fuel would last. At the first exit to Dillon she pulled into a service station.

"Can you fill the truck up?" Deke said and ran inside.

Shelly topped off the tank and cleaned the windshield then went in. Deke was walking away from the counter with a carton of Camels and a box of saltines under his arm, ripping a pack of baloney open with his teeth. As she was paying for the gas, Shelly asked about the best place in town for breakfast.

Back at the truck, Deke was furiously stuffing his face with baloney and crackers. "You might wanta hold off, Deke," Shelly told him, "there's a good breakfast spot jes two blocks from here."

"Unh-huh," Deke said, and crammed more baloney into his mouth.

Three minutes later Shelly parked in front of the Conestoga Café. "You still hungry?" she asked Deke.

"You bet," Deke answered, wiping his sleeve across his greasy mouth.

After they'd finished the Cattleman's breakfast and three cups of coffee Shelly said, "This place is perty nice, Deke, and the bathrooms are clean. Let's git our toiletries outa the truck an' do a good wash up and brush our teeth."

"Can't it wait till we git to a motel? I thought we were stoppin' early."

"It's barely past noon. We might as well be clean for the rest a' the day."

Deke lit a cigarette and motioned for the waitress to bring him another cup of coffee. "You go ahead," he said. "I'll clean up at the motel."

Without saying anything Shelly got up and went to the truck. Twenty minutes later she came out of the ladies room. "Well, let's go," she told Deke.

"Gimme the keys, I'll drive now," Deke said. He walked around behind the pickup to get to the driver's side and stopped. "Shitfire, lookit this."

"What?" Shelly asked, and walked back to look.

"One taillight's broke and the backend's all dented up from where we went in the ditch." Deke tugged on the tailgate. "The goddam tailgate won't open now." Deke got into the cab and slammed the door so hard the windows rattled. "This truck's gonna be a wreck by the time we git ta Troy."

Deke pushed the truck at a steady 85 over the blustery expanse of steppe north of Dillon. After a few miles the Pioneer Mountains encroached from the west and a short while later Deke and Shelly crossed the Big Hole River. As the day got on the weather warmed and Shelly cranked her side window halfway down, partly to take in the pure Montana air and partly to alleviate Deke's b.o. Well before they reached Interstate 90, all trace of snow was gone and a brilliant sun radiated over the land. Shelly spread her atlas across her knees. She and Deke had not talked much since leaving Dillon and to be conversational Shelly said, "Butte, Montana's about 10 miles east a' here. It's kinda famous."

"What for?" Deke asked.

"Somebody back in Ohio told me they got the biggest open pit mine in the world an' a whole lot a' bars."

"That'd be a good place ta stop fer the night," Deke said.

"Deke, it's still way too soon ta stop an' Butte's in the wrong direction. I don't like backtrackin'."

"What about that trip we made clear outa the way ta Yellowstone Park?"

"That wasn't backtrackin, that was sidetrackin' an' that's diff'ernt."

In spite of the sunshine, the landscape had a dreary, withered look, like it had once been beautiful, but had been scoured. The chilly, incessant wind buffeted the pickup until Shelly had to roll her window back up. At the exit for Anaconda they saw a sign pointing out the World's Largest Smokestack. Shelly considered asking Deke if he wanted to go look at it up close, but changed her mind. Her heart was no longer in extending the trip, she just wanted to get to Troy and start her new life.

The sun came on brighter with each mile west they drove and the unrelenting wind subsided as the countryside became more forested and hilly. By the time they got to Drummond, Deke and Shelly had their jackets off and the windows rolled down.

"This has turned inta one mighty fine afternoon, Deke," Shelly said. "It's hard ta b'lieve we were worried 'bout freezin' ta death las' night."

"That's a cold, damn place down there by Yellowstone," Deke said. "I don't need ta go there no more."

Throughout the day the unfinished interstate had alternated between two and four lanes, but Shelly's atlas showed it being a divided highway the rest of the way to Missoula. Her mind began figuring the distances and times. "Deke," she said, as they passed Clinton, "let's stop in Missoula and fill up the gas tank an' you can call your brother an' let 'im know we'll be there ta'day."

"Huh?" Deke said, and looked at Shelly like she'd just whacked him with a stick. "What're you talkin' about? Troy's still a long ways from here."

"It ain't that far a'tall, Deke. We can be there by a little after six."

"We'll need ta stop an' eat," Deke told her.

"Okay, we'll be in Troy by seven. Or, we could git us some burgers an' eat on the way. You like ta do that an' then we'd be there aroun' six-thirty."

"This is Sunday," Deke said. "Zeke goes ta bed early cuz he's gotta git up an' haul logs on Monday."

"He don't go ta bed at seven," Shelly said, "'cause you called him later'n that from my place in Norwood an' he was still up."

"I jest don't know as goin' there t'night's a good idea," Deke said.

"It's a great idea," Shelly persisted. "We can ride with 'im in his truck ta'morrow."

"I thought we was gonna stop early an' git us a motel."

"There ain't no sense in that. We'll be at your brother's by six-thirty."

"Yeah … well … I guess so … but somehow it jest don' seem …"

"Deke, this whole trip you been wantin' ta make straight for Troy an' now it sounds like yor tryin' ta stall."

"Oh, no … nothin' like that, Shelly. It's jest that …"

"Zeke's expectin' us, ain't he?"

"Uh … yeah …"

"Good, it's settled then. You call your brother in Missoula," Shelly said, smiling. "I'm excited about learnin' how ta drive that big Peterbilt log truck, ain't you, Deke?"

"Well … yeah …"

East of Missoula they passed a billboard: *MURRAY'S TRUCK STOP. Full Service. Gas and Diesel, Phones, Restaurant. I-90 and US 93.*

"That's where we wanta stop," Shelly said, pointing at the billboard. "Highway 93's where we git off the interstate to go ta Troy."

At the first Missoula exit Deke said, "Can't we jest stay in Missoula t'night, I'm tired?"

"I ain't a bit tired," Shelly said. "I'll drive us the rest a' the way. I can't wait ta meet your brother an' see his truck."

At the Highway 93 off ramp Shelly pointed at Murray's Truck Stop. "It's your turn ta buy, Deke, I paid for the gas in Dillon."

Deke didn't say anything as he pulled up to the pump and shut off the engine.

"I'll go inside an' git us some burgers an' Cokes ta go while yor pumpin' the gas an' callin' your brother," Shelly said and hopped out of the pickup.

From the restaurant Shelly could see the gas pumps. After Deke filled the tank he paid in the office and then got back into the pickup. "Could ya give me two dollars in dimes an' quarters?" Shelly said when she paid the waitress.

Toting a grease-stained paper bag, Shelly walked to the pickup and set it on the seat beside Deke. "Didja call your brother?"

"Uh … I tried, but didn't git no answer … an' now I'm all outa change."

"I got change, Deke. Gimme Zeke's number an' I'll call 'im."

"Oh, don't do that," Deke said quickly. "I'll try agin."

Shelly handed Deke her change, and as he slowly walked to the phone she wondered why he was so reluctant to call. She had the urge to go over to the booth and listen in, but reckoned that would be rude. Still, she watched closely as Deke dialed, then fed change into the slot and started talking.

Zeke knew it was his brother when the phone rang. "Hello, Deke. Where are ya?"

"I'm in Missoula at the truck stop."

"Did ya have any trouble on the way out?"

"Uh … not really … one flat tar'r was all," Deke said, and then he remembered the lumps on his head and reckoned his brother would ask about them. "Oh, an' I fell down on the ice."

"Where'd that happen?"

"Down by Yellowstone Park."

"What were ya doin' down there? That's clear outa the way."

"I always wanted ta see it, Zeke, so I swung by … an' then it snowed an' got icy."

"Did ya get hurt when ya fell?"

"I got a bump on my head … well, actually I got two."

"From one fall … that don't sound right."

"Well ... I guess I fell twice."

"You ain't changed much, have ya, Deke?"

"In some ways I've changed a lot, Zeke."

"Like how?"

"I don't drink ... least hardly a'tall ... or use dope or tell lies no more ... or git myself inta bad fixes like I used to."

"I'm glad ta hear that, Deke, 'cause that's how it's gonna hafta be if you're stayin' here."

"I know it is, Zeke ... an' I'm glad yer puttin' them rules on me."

"You're only about three hours away, Deke. You should be here by six-thirty. We'll wait dinner on ya. We can talk for a while an still get ta bed early an' you can go with me in the truck tomorrow."

"Well ... uh ... that's what I wanted ta talk to ya about, Zeke. I think I'm gonna stay in a motel t'night."

"In Missoula?"

"Uh ... no ... up there in Troy."

"Deke, there's no reason for that. We moved both boys inta one bedroom and got a room waitin' for ya."

"Well ... I'm kinda dirty ... an' tired an' all ... an' I jest figger'd it'd be better if I rested up after this long trip."

"We got a shower you can use, Deke, but I understand ya not wantin' to get up real early after you jest got here. Tomorrow I'll be back at the house for lunch around noon an' you can go out with me for the afternoon haul."

Deke was silent.

"Did ya hear me, Deke?"

"Uh ... yeah ... uh ... how about I come ta yer place b'fore noon after I check outa the motel?"

"You sure are set on stayin' at a motel. What's the deal, anyway? How come you wanta throw money away like that?"

"Uh ... well, ya see ... I never got ta stay in motels b'fore this trip ... an' I kinda like 'em. I jest wanna spend one more night in a motel."

"That's the dumbest thing I ever heard of, Deke, but it sounds like ya got your mind made up."

"Yeah, jest this one more time, Zeke. You got a motel up there, don't ya?"

"We got a couple. The best one is the Starlight. It's jest after the Lake Creek bridge comin' inta town. I'll call an' have 'em save a room for ya."

"Thanks a lot fer doin' that, Zeke."

"Are you comin' by the house when ya get in?"

"Likely not, Zeke. Like I said, I'm real tired an' I wanna stop an' have dinner and see a few things on the way. This is real purty country."

"Alright then, Deke, I guess we'll see ya around noon tomorrow. I live at 115 Second Street an' you got my phone number."

"I'll be there, Zeke … an' I really appreciate this."

Deke got back in the pickup and Shelly handed him a burger from the sack and a can of Coke. "How'd it go?"

"We're all set," Deke said, "but we won't be stayin' at Zeke's tonight. He said it's gittin' kinda late an' he needs ta set ever'thing up at the house first."

"Well, where we stayin', then?"

"Zeke's gonna reserve us a room at the Starlight Motel comin' inta Troy. He said it's real nice."

Deke bit into the hamburger and started the truck. When he let out the clutch, the pickup hesitated, so he gave it more gas. It slowly moved forward and Deke tromped on the accelerator. The motor revved and the pickup gained some speed but both Deke and Shelly felt the slippage.

"What's wrong with the truck?" Shelly asked.

"I don't know," Deke said. "It feels like somethin' ain't catchin' in the tranny or the drive train."

Deke coaxed his old rig up to 60 on the highway north of Missoula but when they started up Evaro Hill the truck slowed down, even though the engine was running strong. Halfway to the top their speed was down to 25.

"C'mon, baby," Deke pleaded as the Ford dropped to 20, 15 and then 10 miles an hour. When the road leveled out Deke got the truck back up to 50 and then goosed it to 70 on a downgrade.

Shortly they passed a sign that read, 'Entering the Flathead Indian Reservation'. "Shitfire," Deke said, "I hope the truck don't break down on an In'jun reservation agin."

"I hope it don't break down a'tall," Shelly told him.

Highway 93 stayed mostly level, but the pickup steadily lost momentum. A few miles later the truck was topping out at 20 and by the time they hit Ravali, 30 miles north of Missoula, the truck was barely moving.

"Dammit all ta hell," Deke mumbled. "Why's this kinda shit always hafta happen ta me?"

"I been kinda won'drin that my'self, Deke," Shelly said, "but you need ta pull over so's we can take a look."

Deke coasted into a wide turnout at the south end of Ravali and stopped in front of an establishment that had a large sign with a white buffalo painted on it that read, 'Big Medicine Tavern'.

"Leave it runnin' and open your door so's we can talk," Shelly said as she got out. She went around to Deke's side and lay down in the gravel beside the pickup. "Put it in third an' let the clutch out real slow."

Deke followed her instructions, but the truck didn't move.

"The drive shaft is turnin' jes fine," Shelly hollered up, "but it don't seem ta be connectin' inside the differential."

"Now what're we gonna do?" Deke said.

"We could pull out the drive line," Shelly said, "an' try ta see what the problem is. Ya got any tools?"

"A few," Deke answered, "but not enough to …uh …Shelly?"

"What, Deke?"

"There's …uh … two great big In'juns comin' this way."

"Good," Shelly said. "Maybe they got some tools an' can help us."

Two men approached from the direction of the tavern, looked at Deke in the cab, then walked around to the back of the truck and looked at the license plate. After checking out the contents of the bed, they came and stood above Shelly.

Deke was right; they were big Indians. Both were at least six-foot three and built like athletes. They also looked very much alike except one of them was wearing an Oakland Raiders hat and holding a can of Rainier beer and the other had on a Pittsburgh Steelers cap and was drinking Olympia.

"Howdy," Shelly said, looking up at them. "I'm Shelly Stamper an' that's Deke in the cab."

"Howdy, back," the one on the right said. "We're Beavers'."

Shelly didn't know what to say. She thought perhaps the men were drunk or that they identified with beavers as their spirit animals. Then the man on the left said, "I'm Allen Beavers and this is Arlen. We're brothers."

"Most of the time, anyway," Arlen said. "What's going on, did your truck quit running?"

"It shor did," Shelly told them. "It started actin' up as we were leavin' Missoula an' then quit movin' all ta'gether."

A third man appeared on the far side of the truck and said, "At least it broke down in front of a bar."

"That's Joe," Allen told Shelly.

"Is he a Beaver, too?" Shelly asked.

"No," Arlen said, "he's a horse's ass."

Shelly stood up and saw that a dozen people were coming towards the truck from the bar. About half of them looked tribal and nearly everyone was holding a beer or a drink. "Don't make any sudden moves, Deke," Shelly said, looking at the crowd and grinning, "they got us surrounded."

"Damn straight," a skinny woman with foliage woven throughout her blonde hair said. With one hand she clutched the tailgate and saluted Shelly with her tequila sunrise in the other.

A dark-haired woman wearing thick glasses walked up. "What's going on out here?"

"These folks drove all the way out from Ohio just ta go tits up in front of your bar, Bonnie," the blonde told her.

"Well, when you're done doin' whatever, drag 'em in for a drink," Bonnie said and went back inside.

"Does anybody here have a decent set of tools?" Shelly asked the crowd.

"Arlen should have," Allen said, pointing to his brother. "He's borrowed enough of mine over the years and never returned them."

"What about my air compressor?" Arlen said.

"You don't need it," Allen told him, "you make enough air on your own."

"I'll go get my tools," the short, dark-skinned man named Joe said, and walked over to a 1960's Dodge four-wheel drive pickup. He came back lugging a large metal toolbox and set it down beside Deke's Ford, along with his can of Pabst Blue Ribbon. "What's your truck doing, or not doing?" he asked Shelly.

"The motor runs good an' the drive line turns," Shelly told him "but the back end don't wanta go."

"I have an' idea what the problem might be," Joe said, then leaned into the passenger window and told Deke, "Shut the engine off and put the truck in gear with the parking brake on."

He crawled under the truck and Shelly got down in the gravel beside him. Joe took several wrenches and a ballpeen hammer from his toolbox and started taking off the driveline as the crowd around the truck exchanged observations, advice and insults. Most returned to the tavern when their drinks ran dry.

As Shelly helped, Joe's dexterity with tools reminded her of her father. "You must be a mechanic, Joe," she said to him.

"I do some now and then, but I'm a contractor."

Together, Joe and Shelly tugged the grease-covered drive shaft out of the differential housing. Joe looked at the rear part of the shaft. "Just what I thought," he said, removing a tattered piece of metal, "the housing sleeve is torn up."

"Is there any way ta fix it?" Shelly asked.

"I'll make a new one," Joe said. "Hand me my beer."

Shelly grabbed the can of Pabst and gave it to Joe, who drank the beer then took out his folding knife and cut both ends off the can. He sliced it lengthwise, wrapped it around the end of the driveshaft, peened it tightly into the grooves and cut off what was left over. With Shelly's help he slid the shaft back into the differential housing and hooked the driveline back up. "Start it up and see if it goes," he said to Deke, after they'd stood up and wiped their hands with a shop rag from his tool box.

Deke cranked over the engine, put the Ford into second, and the truck went forward with no slippage. The scrawny blonde was still hanging onto the tailgate and tumbled into the gravel.

"Are you okay, Moonflower?" Joe asked her.

"Thank God my drink was empty," she said, getting to her feet with the help of Arlen and Allen.

Deke put the truck into reverse and backed up, careful not to run over anyone.

"Are we done here?" the blonde asked.

"I am," Joe told her, and carried the toolbox back to his pickup.

"All right, then, let's go have a drink," Moonflower said, and holding her empty glass in front of her, followed it to the bar as if it were a beacon.

Allen Beavers put his arm around Shelly's shoulders. "Bonnie said to drag you two in for a drink and nobody at this bar argues with Bonnie." Arlen reached into the Ford and grabbed Deke, who throughout the affair, had stayed in the cab, staring silently ahead, and pulled him right out. With Joe bringing up the rear, they trooped to the Big Medicine's front door.

Shelly was not overjoyed to be waylaid on the last leg of the trip, but she understood barroom civility. Deke kept his mouth shut and hoped for the best. "Git your wallet out," Shelly told him, "we're buyin' a round for the house."

Deke frowned and Shelly said into his ear, "It's way cheaper'n callin' a wrecker an' goin' to a repair shop."

After the drinks were served and the money collected, Shelly raised her Coors to the 15 or so people in the bar. "Thanks for the help, especially to Joe."

From her stool on the other side of Deke, Moonflower held up her tequila sunrise. "Here's to synergy and symbiosis," she said. Then, smiling at Deke, asked, "Where are you guys from in Ohio?"

"We're not really from Ohio," Shelly told the bar in general, "we were jes workin' there. I'm from Wes' Virginia an' Deke's from Tennessee." Knowing somebody would ask, she explained that they were on their way to Troy to be logging truck drivers.

"Crazy place," Bonnie said. "Those loggers know how to drink and fight."

"They shoot each other on a regular basis, too," Allen interjected.

"Usually only once, Allen," Arlen corrected him.

"Are you from Ohio?" Deke asked Moonflower.

"No friggin' way," she said, "I'm from California. But when I was sixteen I was hitchhiking through Ohio on my way to Woodstock and got really stoned and drunk in a place called Celeryville with a bunch of Mexicans."

"Was the taco-bender here one of them?" Arlen asked her, pointing at Joe, who was standing to his right.

"He might have been," Moonflower said to Arlen, looking past Deke and Shelly, "there was a multitude." She turned her attention to Deke. "How'd you get that bump on your head, cowboy? Defending your lady's honor?"

"Uh … well … yeah … " Deke said, "somethin' like that."

"I like your belt buckle," she said, and began giving John Wayne a facial massage.

"The Duke is purty special ta me," Deke said, with a big smile on his face.

"I'll bet he is," Moonflower agreed.

Deke leaned over and smelled the greenery woven throughout Moonflower's long yellow hair. "Ummm, that smells good. What is it?"

"Cilantro," she told him. "I wear a different plant or flower every day depending on my mood."

"One day she came in here with a head full of knapweed," Bonnie said.

"That wasn't a good day for me," Moonflower admitted. "But today is!" She held her empty glass in front of Deke. "And I'd like another sunrise."

Deke hurriedly dug for his wallet. "A drink fer the lady here," he told Bonnie, "an' I'll have another Budweiser."

Shelly watched this spectacle unfold, not sure if it was funny or revolting, then walked around the Beavers to talk to Joe. She reckoned she owed him more than one drink for fixing the truck. "Can I git ya another beer, Joe?"

"Naw, I'm set," he said. "Tomorrow's a work day."

"Are you really from Mexico?" Shelly asked him.

"Hell no!" Joe said. "I was born in Pablo, just up the road. The stumpchewers here are always givin' me shit because my last name is Alvarez and my ol' man is half Mexican. I'm three-quarters Salish."

Allen and Arlen Beavers were now laughing. Shelly and the three men continued talking and joking and when Shelly looked over, saw that Deke and Moonflower had disappeared. Ten minutes later they came in the back door together and Moonflower was leaning on Deke's shoulder.

"Have fun?" Shelly asked Deke.

"Uhhhhhhhhh … yeahhhhhh," he answered. Deke's eyes looked like frosted glass and the reek of marijuana smoke was so strong on him that it cancelled out his b.o.

"Another one for me, Bonnie, " Moonflower said and slid her empty glass across the bar.

"Me too," Deke said, setting down his empty bottle.

"No ya don't," Shelly told Deke. "It's time ta hit the road."

"Well, I want one, anyway," Moonflower said.

"Oh, sure … sure," Deke said and pulled out his wallet. "Another one fer Moonflower an' a twelve pack of Bud cans ta go."

Shelly scowled at him.

"Fer when we git to the motel," Deke said.

"It's time for us to go, too," Joe said, and turned to Allen and Arlen. "Are you two fur-hats ready? We've got a sewer line to put in tomorrow."

"You guys work together?" Shelly asked, surprised.

"The three of us have a contracting business," Arlen answered.

"It's even worse than that," Allen said. "He's our brother-in-law."

"Wowwwww," Deke said, leaning over the bar in front of Shelly and looking at the two brothers; "Both a' you are married to his sister?"

Everything went quiet and for a second Shelly had that 'Oh shit' feeling in her stomach. "That might be how you do it in Tennessee," Arlen said to Deke, "but out here he's married to our sister."

"Ohhhh … yeah," Deke said. "I guess that would be right."

"Time ta go," Shelly said, pushing Deke toward the door. "Thanks agin," she called to everybody. As they were walking to the truck Shelly told Deke, "I don't think you should be drivin'."

"Why, I only had two beers."

"An a whole lot a' somethin' else."

"I only took a coupla tokes … jest ta be polite."

"That's you all over, Deke … Mr. Consideration."

"Well, I'm drivin'," Deke said, and dropped the twelve-pack into the truck bed. He jiggled his roped down spare. "At least the goddam In'juns didn't steal my spare tar'r this time."

"No," Shelly told him, "the 'goddam In'juns' fixed your truck for free an' you never even said 'thanks'.

Shelly climbed into the cab and closed the door. When Deke got in he had two Budweisers in his hand. "You want one?" he asked, holding out a can.

"No." Shelly said icily.

Deke popped the pull-tab and started the pickup. "What?" he said, as Shelly glared at him. "It's legal ta drink while'st yer drivin' in Montana."

"It might be legal, but right now it ain't smart," Shelly said and rolled the window down.

The sun rested against the mountain peaks as Deke and Shelly started west on Highway 200. A few miles beyond Dixon the Flathead River came alongside the road and the view spread before them like a picture postcard. Just past Perma Deke drained his beer, flipped the empty into the bed and opened the other one. Shelly, who hadn't said a word since they left Ravali, looked at him and growled.

"You mad at me?" Deke asked.

"Urrrrrrrr."

"Yer jealous, ain't ya?"

"Jealous! I'm mad 'cause yor gittin' fucked up an' we got a ways ta go."

"Yer jealous cuz I slipped out back with Moonflower," Deke said, "an' yer won'drin what we did. Jest like I wonder'd what happened when you rode off with that sum'bitch that called himself Billy the Kid."

"Nobody called him Billy the Kid but you, Deke, an' I don't give a damn what you an' Moonflower did. I jes want ya to stop drinkin' 'fore ya kill us both."

"Don't you wanna know if we did anything 'sides smoke some weed?"

"No. If ya didn't do nothin' there's nothin' ta know. An' if ya did do somethin' it's likely disgusting an' I don't need ta hear about it."

"I still think yer jealous," Deke said.

"An' I think yor an idiot, so let's jes drop it," Shelly said and turned away to look out her side window.

East of Paradise the Clark Fork River flowed up from the south and merged with the Flathead to become the largest river in Montana. They crossed it on a long, narrow, silver-girdered bridge, set only a few feet beside a massive, black railroad truss. The speed limit sign coming into Paradise said 35 but Deke blew through the little railroad town at 60. Rolling into Plains six miles down the road he finished his Bud and backhanded the can into the bed. "I gotta take a leak," Deke said and pulled into a Conoco station.

Shelly was waiting to give him an ultimatum if he grabbed more beer from the half-rack in the bed, but when he got in the truck all he had was a Slim Jim in his hand.

"You want a bite?" Deke asked.

"I'm fine," Shelly said, and went back to looking at the scenery.

Plains itself rested in a wide, grassy valley of rounded hills but to the West trees covered every vista, and rocky, sharp edged mountains loomed. The sun had dropped from sight behind those mountains and their ridges glowed with yellow and crimson light. In every direction the sky was clear, deepening to amethyst as evening bore down. Several miles from town the Clark Fork River met up with the highway and ran beside it, then disappeared and re-appeared at regular intervals.

The farther west they went, the more Shelly was enchanted with Montana. The air had not yet cooled and she had her window down. The sweet, fresh wind whistled through the cab, and Shelly felt like sticking her head out the window like a dog and letting the air blow against her face.

"Are you excited ta be gittin' close ta Troy?" Deke asked as he lit a cigarette from the dashboard lighter.

Now that he'd stopped drinking Shelly lightened up a little. "Yeah. I been wantin' ta drive a semi truck for a long time an' this'll be my chance. I'm also excited to start a new life out here in the West. What about you, Deke?"

"Yeah … well … I wanna do all that, but what I meant was, are you excited cuz we're gittin' close to a motel?"

"Oh, that," Shelly said. "What's excitin' about stayin' in a motel?"

"Well … I jest thought you might be excited cuz you an' I git ta …"

"Look at that!" Shelly yelled and pointed to her right. "Pull over, Deke. I've never seen any a these critters before."

Deke coasted into a wide turnout. Eighty feet away, in a flat, open field stood a herd of bighorn sheep. The solid, adult rams had full curls and stared at Deke and Shelly with curious, pale eyes.

"Now this is somethin' to git excited about," Shelly said.

"It's alright, I reckon," Deke answered, barely looking up.

Twenty minutes later, driving through downtown Thompson Falls, they saw a neon 'Open' sign in the window of Mona's Café.

"Let's stop," Shelly said. "I'm hungry."

"You buyin'?"

"I reckon I owe ya for makin' ya miss dinner last night," Shelly said.

Thinking of what he'd missed the night before, Deke ordered the ribeye steak with a baked potato and a beer. As the waitress was taking their empty plates away Shelly asked her, "Where can we see the falls? I've never seen a waterfall on a big river before an' I'd like ta see it."

"No big falls around here that I know of," the woman told her.

"Then how come they call this place Thompson Falls?"

"Oh, that," she said, and laughed. "There used to be a falls on the river here but they built a dam over it a long time ago."

"How far ta Troy?" Deke asked Shelly when they were back in the truck.

"Less'n eighty miles."

"Ummmm," Deke said, raising his eyebrows. "We'll be there in an hour. I can hardly wait."

"You might wanta drive a little slower, Deke, we're losin' the light."

"We'll be fine. I got a feelin' in my gut that all our troubles are b'hind us."

"That feelin' in your gut is from all the beer ya drank," Shelly said.

Just west of Thompson Falls they drove across the high bridge over the Clark Fork River and into the shadow of a steep ridge that descended to the highway. The river flowed alongside the road and to the north the southern edge of the Cabinet Mountains poked into the darkening sky. Deke glanced down to turn on his headlights as they rounded a curve and when he looked up saw that rocks the size of softballs were strewn across the highway. He managed to swerve around the bigger ones but there was no way to miss them all and the Ford bounced several times. "Shitfire, we don't need no more flats," Deke yelled, but two miles down the road the tail end of the Ford was sagging and Deke had to pull over.

"You whore-hoppin' sum'bitch!" Deke hollered, when he saw the deflated right rear tire, the very one that Shelly had bought in Billings yesterday. "Why's this happen ta me? All I wanna do's git to a motel." Deke kicked the tire. "God damn you anyway!"

"Let's git it changed 'fore it's too dark ta see," Shelly said and hopped into the truck bed and untied the ropes that secured the spare.

"You gonna buy me another new one?" Deke asked when she handed Goodrich down to him.

"Nope. This one ain't my fault. I told ya not ta drive so fast."

"I ain't gonna have me a penny left when this trip is over," Deke muttered, as he pulled out the handyman jack from behind the seat.

When the old spare was lugged tight on the axel, Shelly ran her fingers over the thin tread. "This ain't a very good tire, Deke. I hope it makes it ta Troy."

"It better. I paid that damn In'jun thirty dollars ta git that tar'r back."

"I hope your spare knows it's worth that much," Shelly said.

Dusk was now upon them. Out past the cluster of houses known as White Pine the open countryside ended and thick forest edged right up to the highway. Deke had slowed a little since having the flat but was still cruising at close to 80 when a deer bounded from the woods and ran in front of the truck. He slammed on the brakes and swerved to the right, missing the buck's behind by inches. Shelly bounced against the dash as the pickup nearly went into the ditch.

"Dammit, Deke!" she yelled. "You need ta slow down!"

Deke dropped his speed to 75 but every deer in the forest was on the move. Four more came out of the shadows before they reached Trout Creek. "Yor still goin' too fast," Shelly said and braced herself against the dash.

The deer were nearly as suicidal near Noxon. Twice, Deke had to hit the brakes to avoid collisions. Beyond Noxon the forest retreated as more buildings sprang up alongside the road and Shelly and Deke knew they were in logging country. The yards and lots were littered with skidders, yarders, jammers, and log trucks. Most of the equipment was old and much of it derelict. The majority of the ramshackle houses looked handbuilt, often tacked onto singlewide house trailers. Crammed in among the structures and equipment were long abandoned cars and pickup trucks.

"This place looks like home," Deke said.

"It is home, Deke," Shelly reminded him.

Between Noxon and their turnoff at Highway 56 Deke and Shelly didn't see any deer and relaxed a bit. The final shreds of light deserted the sky as they drove north along the lower reaches of the Bull River. On the east side of the river, the dark bulk of the Cabinet Mountains rose sheer and rugged as more stars popped into the sky with every mile they drove.

Deke sped up again and Shelly kept her side window halfway down, preferring the rush of cool air to Deke's b.o. At the bottom end of Bull Lake the road ran beside the water and starlight glinted off the black surface against a silhouette of mountains. Near the north end of the lake they came to a bar called the Midway where a dozen vehicles were lined up out front.

"Looks like a purty cool joint," Deke said as he slowed down.

"We don't need ta be stoppin' here," Shelly told him.

"Yer right," Deke said, and sped up. "We got beer in the back an' we'll have us a whole lot more fun at the motel than we will here."

"How long's it been since you've seen your brother?" Shelly asked when the highway turned away from the lake.

"Jest after he got outa the Army. He stopped ta see us in Rogersville b'fore he came out here ta haul logs with that guy he knew in Viet Nam," Deke said. "That'd be goin' on five years now."

"Rogersville?" Shelly said. "I remember you sayin' you were from Kingston Springs, near Nashville."

"I am," Deke said, "but after our folks died, us kids went ta live with our aunt an' uncle in Rogersville in east Tennessee."

"Is Rogersville anywhere close ta Sneedville?" Shelly asked.

"Jest south of it. Our schools played each other in sports."

"Didja ever hear of Melungeons?"

"Why sure," Deke said and laughed. "Ever'body around them parts knows about Melungeons."

"What do ya know about 'em?"

"I know 'nough ta stay away from 'em," Deke said, still laughing.

"How come?" Shelly asked.

"Cuz they ain't no good."

"Didja ever know any Melungeons?"

"Hell no, an' I don't want to neither. They ain't nothin' but piss-ig'nernt liars an' thieves. Melungeons ain't no better than ... well, you know what I mean."

Shelly's face flushed hot with anger. "I wish I didn't know what ya mean, Deke, but I do," she said, "an' I've had it with ..."

The deer came out of nowhere, in front of the truck before Deke or Shelly even saw it. Shelly felt the sickening thump of steel against flesh as the poor animal was knocked 30 feet down the road. When she jumped from the truck and ran back to it, the doe's legs were thrashing, its bloody mouth opening and closing in silent agony. Helpless to end its suffering, Shelly could only watch as the deer's legs convulsed slower and slower until only the hooves were twitching. A few minutes later they stopped moving and the animal's eyes clouded over. Memories of the day Tramp was killed flooded over her and Shelly started to cry.

Down the highway, Deke stood in front of his pickup, raving like a lunatic. Shelly didn't want him to come back and rage at the deer. She put her hand on the animal's flank and shook it to make sure it was dead, then grabbed the back hooves and dragged the doe to the side of the road. She rolled the doe off into the ditch so no one else would hit it and walked back to the pickup.

"The deer is dead," she told Deke, wiping her eyes.

He didn't seem to hear her or to care. His swearing was more profane and violent than Shelly had ever heard from him, filled with an anger that nothing could soothe. She looked at the truck. The engine was still running and the radiator looked intact, but the left fender and headlight, as well as part of the hood, were demolished.

"Does your truck still run?" Shelly asked blankly.

"Yeah ... but it's a fuckin' wonder it does."

"Then let's git on down the road," Shelly said and got into the cab.

Deke reached into the bed. "I need me a beer ta calm down after all that," he said, but he had two in his hand. He tore the tab off one and took a long drink then tossed the other can on the seat. "I ain't gonna have a fuckin' truck left by the time we git ta Troy."

For several miles Deke continued ranting but Shelly said nothing. Running with only one headlight, visibility was decreased but Deke drove 80, like he didn't care anymore. To take Deke's mind off his anger, Shelly said, "Are we gonna ride in your brother's truck with 'im ta'morrow?"

"Huh?" Deke said, turning to look at her.

"Are we ridin' with your brother ta'morrow?"

"I'm goin' over to his house at noon an' ridin' with 'im on his afternoon haul," Deke said.

"What about me?" Shelly asked.

"The truck's jest got one passenger seat, so only one of us can ride at a time."

"Are we gonna take turns then?"

"Uhhhh … I ain't thought that part out yet," Deke said.

Curious now, Shelly asked, "Are we gonna be stayin' at Zeke's place?"

"I been meanin' ta tell ya about that," Deke said. "I'll be stayin' with Zeke cuz I gotta git up real early ta go out with 'im, but you can stay at the motel so's you can sleep in. But that'll jest be fer a little while, till we git our own place."

Deke drained off the Budweiser, rolled down his window and flipped the empty out, then opened the second can. "But I'll come see ya at the motel ever' night after I git back from ridin' with Zeke an' we can … you know … drink a few beers an' have us some fun."

"So when do I start ridin' with Zeke?" Shelly asked.

Deke was starting to calm down from hitting the deer, but Shelly's questions were irritating him. "I don't know fer sure, but it'll be soon, real soon. Maybe I could learn how ta drive Zeke's truck first, then teach you, jest like I did with the dump truck."

"What's Zeke gonna do while yor teachin' me, sit home an' watch TV?"

"Uhhhh … I ain't thought that part out yet, either," Deke said.

"Well, I'll go over at noon with ya ta'morrow an' ask 'im," Shelly said. "I wanta thank Zeke for his generous offer of teachin' me ta drive 'is truck."

"Oh, there ain't no need fer that," Deke spluttered. "In fact, maybe you oughta hold off on meetin' 'im fer a little while. Zeke tol' me on the phone that I should drive first … jest ta check things out, ya understand."

"I think I understand," Shelly said slowly. "Let me see if I got this right. You'll be stayin' at your brother's an' I'll stay at the motel."

Deke nodded.

"You'll go out with Zeke ev'ry day and learn how ta drive his truck while I hang out in the motel room by myself."

Deke nodded, but not as much.

"At night you'll come over to the motel an' drink beer an' screw me."

Deke didn't nod.

"I 'spose you'll want me ta buy the beer, too," Shelly said.

"Well … it ain't quite like that, Shelly," Deke said, "an' it'd only be fer a short spell …jest until …"

Deke continued talking but Shelly didn't hear him. She was looking out the side window at the dark outline of the Cabinet Mountains looming up to her right and shaking her head. They began descending a long grade and Deke downshifted into third. How could she have been so dumb, so naïve? Deke's brother had no idea she was with him and wouldn't approve if he found out. Somewhere in the middle of Deke's rambling she heard him say, "Things'll be jest fine, Shelly, I got it all worked out."

Shelly turned and looked at Deke but didn't say anything. Funny, she thought, now that the truth was out, she wasn't even mad and she wasn't a bit surprised. Deke McConahay is what he is and always will be. The other truth that she had to admit to was that she'd done her part in finagling Deke into it.

Deke depressed the clutch, took his foot off the gas and applied the brakes. They came to a stop at the 'T' where Montana Highway 56 met US Route 2. In front of the shadowy forest facing them, the Ford's single headlight shown on a large, green highway sign that read, 'Troy – 2', and an arrow pointing to the left and 'Libby – 16', with an arrow pointing to the right. Beneath that sign was a smaller, blue sign that read, 'Kootenai Falls – 4', and had an arrow to the right.

"We made it, Shelly," Deke said, and in spite of all his woes, he smiled.

"Yeah, Deke, we made it," Shelly answered. She opened her door. "I need ta git somethin' outa the back," she said. "Hand me the keys to the trunk."

"Can't it wait till we git ta the motel?"

"Nope. I need it now." Shelly stepped onto the road and held her hand out.

Seeing that Shelly wasn't going to get back into the truck until she got what she wanted, Deke turned off his one headlight, shut off the motor and gave her the keys. He heard Shelly rummaging around in the back of the pickup and when she jumped down, Shelly was wearing her knapsack and had her suitcase in her hand. Her Buck knife was on her belt.

Shelly reached into the truck and handed Deke back his keys. "Thanks for the ride," she said, and closed the door.

Deke fumbled to get the key back into the ignition in the unlighted cab but by the time he got the truck started and the headlight turned on, Shelly had disappeared into the dark forest on the other side of the highway.

Chapter 40

Stumbling and bumping into trees, Shelly struggled through the brush and dog-hair lodgepole until she was sure Deke couldn't see her and then turned east toward Libby. Tripping at nearly every step, she lugged the suitcase in one hand, feeling her way through the dense forest with the other. Through the screen of trees, she dimly saw the Ford's single headlight cruising slowly by on Highway 2 and heard Deke yelling her name.

As her eyes adjusted to the darkness walking became easier and after a while the heavy understory thinned out as the lodgepole became mixed with Douglas fir and larch. Stars glittered overhead and enough of their light trickled through the canopy for Shelly to see the forest floor and avoid most obstacles. Deke's headlight raked the edge of the forest again, this time coming from the east, then Shelly saw his pickup no more.

The last thing she wanted was to get lost in this strange forest at night so when Deke's truck disappeared Shelly veered to the right until she saw the highway. She went on for some time, keeping the road in sight, but the Sunday night traffic was so sparse that Shelly finally came out of the woods and walked along the edge of the asphalt. The few times that vehicles approached she quickly ducked back into the trees to avoid any unpleasant encounters.

The highway was fairly level and Shelly walked steadily along, switching her suitcase from hand to hand every few minutes to give her arms a rest. To her left was a wall of trees and on her right, the dark bulk of the Cabinet Mountains rose like huge, black temples. From somewhere behind her, a light became brighter and brighter until it illuminated the forest ahead. A low, heavy rumble grew to a roar of motive din, and Shelly knew a railroad was not far off in the trees.

Twenty minutes after the train passed, the mountains receded and the moon, full and brilliant, rose through a gap in the peaks. A half-mile later Shelly passed in front of a ridge and the moon vanished, but soon appeared again over a tree-lined hill. Up to this point, Shelly'd seen no structures or lights, but now to her right was a building, set on a thin strip of ground between the mountains and the road. The Buckhorn Bar and Restaurant was completely dark, inside and out, and Shelly was a little disappointed, for if it had been open she would have gone in and tried to get a ride to Libby where she could get a motel. The evening was unseasonably mild and she still had her hooded sweatshirt, stocking cap and cotton gloves in her pack, but whether that would be enough for a night outside was a question that now crossed her mind.

She'd been walking for over an hour when a set of headlights jumped out at her from up ahead. Shelly hadn't seen them approach and scurried into the woods, barely making cover before they washed over the trees beside her. Guessing there must be a sharp curve or hill ahead that kept her from seeing the lights sooner, she stayed close to the edge of the forest after the car passed. A few minutes later she saw a faint yellow glow and quickly darted into the woods. Again, headlights appeared from nowhere.

Shelly continued hugging the treeline and in a while heard the sound of rushing water to her left. Trees blocked her view, but Shelly knew this was no creek, for it thundered in the darkness far below. The road here was being squeezed like it was entering a giant funnel. A double set of railroad tracks had come up beside the highway and the mountain to Shelly's right was pushing closer and closer. Where there'd been an open corridor ahead of her, now all Shelly saw was a wall of blackness.

Two hundred yards later the roar coming up from the river filled the night and Shelly soon saw why. On the other side of the railroad tracks the land dropped away and the Kootenai River rushed foaming through a twisting gray-walled chasm. The moon lit the stone and reflected off the whitecaps that danced in the rapids. Shelly sat her suitcase down and watched the show. At this spot, there was no forest beside the highway and when the headlights jumped out at her from whatever obstruction lay ahead, Shelly had no place to go.

The blue pickup lurched to a stop one hundred feet down the road. Shelly grabbed her suitcase and started walking away from it, just to let whoever was in the truck know she wasn't interested in a ride. It started backing up and Shelly got off the road as far as she could, but when the dented and dirty truck stopped beside her, all she had at her back was the railroad tracks and the gorge.

The old Dodge flatbed was piled high with cedar fence rails. On top of them were two chain saws, mauls, axes and a peavey. A heavy-faced man in his twenties rolled down the side window. "Need a ride?" he asked and grinned, displaying several missing teeth.

"Nope, but thanks for stoppin' an' askin'," Shelly said, then started walking again to show that the conversation was over.

The truck continued backing along beside her.

"You shouldn't be out here all alone at night," the man said.

"I'm my fav'rit person ta be alone with," Shelly said and kept walking.

"There's a lot of scary things out here in these woods."

"Nothin' that I'm scared of."

"We're headed to Troy to have a beer. Why don't ya come along?"

"You mighta noticed, I'm goin' away from Troy, not t'wards it."

"Where are you goin', anyway?" the driver said, leaning over as he continued to back up.

"I got some friends up here I'm stayin' with," Shelly said.

"Who are they?" the man closest to her asked.

"None a' your fuckin' business," Shelly said, "now take off."

"No need to get nasty," the driver said. "We're just tryin' to help."

The door opened and the passenger stepped out. He was huge, not just big: tall and over 300 pounds. He reminded Shelly of a fairytale ogre. In the truck's domelight, Shelly could see that the driver was also massive and resembled the other man in the face. In the back window was a rifle rack with two guns.

Shelly's reaction was automatic. She set her suitcase down broadside in front of her to act as a barrier, then slung her knapsack around and held it against her torso as a shield. The Buck knife was in her hand. "I might not git both a' ya," she said, "but I *will* git one a' ya … ya got my promise on it."

Balanced and ready, Shelly didn't hold the knife in front of her like an amateur where it could be easily taken, but kept it protected along the back of her thigh, blade down, ready to slash or stab at whatever target presented itself.

The giant took two steps toward her but Shelly held her ground, waiting for him to reach down and move the suitcase and leave himself open. When he tried to walk around it, she circled, keeping the suitcase between them.

"I'm tellin' ya … if ya git close I'm gonna kill ya," Shelly warned him.

"I ain't gonna hurt you. I just want you to go have a beer with us," the man told her, but he didn't back off.

Then the driver got out and walked around the front of the truck.

Now Shelly really was worried. Fighting off one monster was bad enough, but she didn't stand much chance against two of them, especially if one got behind her. She thought about dropping her knapsack and running for the railroad tracks. Both men were extremely bulky and she guessed she could outrun them, but the second it would take to turn around would give the man in front of her a chance to grab her from behind. She made her decision. She'd try and kill the one closest to her and hope for the best with the other one. Maybe he'd just get a gun from the cab and shoot her, but that would still be better than what she reckoned they had planned. For the briefest flash, Shelly's mind reflected on the irony of coming all the way to Montana just to have her new life cut short on the first night. Then she went into action.

Shelly feigned like she was going to toss her knapsack at the man's face and his hands went up. She planned to toss it at his groin and when his hands dropped to block it, step in and slash with all of her strength at his throat. Her knife was sharp enough to shave the fine hairs on her forearm, and if the man didn't react fast enough he was about to be dead. Shelly stepped around her suitcase to throw her knapsack.

"Lyle!" the other man called to him.

The man in front of Shelly turned around. "What, Lon?"

"Get in the truck, Lyle. The girl doesn't want to have a beer with you."

"But I want her to," the man said and turned back around to look at Shelly.

They stared at each other and Shelly saw the dullness in his eyes. He probably wasn't cruel, but still dangerous.

"Lyle, get back in the damn truck before she sticks you like a pig."

"All right, Lon," the man finally said and walked back to the Dodge.

As they drove off Shelly's wind went out of her. She wanted to sit down, but this spot was too exposed. Grabbing her suitcase, she started walking as fast as she could, the knife still in her hand.

Just ahead the highway bent away from the railroad and the river and Shelly saw what had obstructed her view. A giant slab of rock jutted from the mountain, forcing the road to make a sharp S curve around it. After it straightened, the forest once again came alongside the road and Shelly walked into the cover of the trees, glad to still be alive. Strange, she thought, how people were afraid of the woods at night, when it was humans you had to fear the most. She put her knife back in its sheath and started walking, lugging her suitcase through the trees and brush.

The highway continued straight and when Shelly knew she could see headlights far enough away to duck into the forest, she went back to walking along the edge of the road. She'd only gone a short distance when she came to a trail, wide enough for vehicles, winding into the woods. Wondering where the little road went, Shelly set her suitcase down and looked around. On the other side of the highway was a small signpost and she walked over to it. The faded white lettering read, 'Kootenai Falls Viewpoint'.

She followed the track into the trees and after about 100 feet it looped back on itself. In the center of the loop some of the trees had been cleared away and there were two picnic tables. Shelly set her suitcase on one of the tables and walked over to read a sign nailed to a Douglas fir. 'No Overnight Camping'. The sound of rampaging water filled the darkness, but she saw no waterfall, or even the river.

On the north side of the clearing the forest fell away, exposing a view of the mountain across the valley. Moonlight fell on its steep flank, turning the talus to a deep, pinkish gray. A rustic fence, made from the same type of rails that were in the back of the blue Dodge, had been constructed along the edge to keep people from falling into the ravine. Shelly walked over to the railing and looked into the canyon where frothing white water churned through the gorge at a furious pace. The nearby brush and small trees were cut away to present a view, but either they'd been carelessly thinned or else had grown back, because only a short stretch of the river was visible.

Through openings in the branches, Shelly could see water spilling over a ledge, but the vision was indistinct. A crude trail, cluttered with brush and deadfall, led down the slope. Shelly retrieved her suitcase and hid it behind a larch where the trees were thickest. Tightening the straps on her knapsack, she walked back to the cedar railing, climbed over, and started down.

Using bushes and small trees as handholds, she descended into the canyon, inching her way over exposed roots and tangled vines in the dark. After a hundred and fifty yards or so the forest opened, but not to the river. In a wide clearing, moonlight glinted off the white gravel ballast and steel rails of double railroad tracks. Shelly crossed them, fought her way to the top of a brush-tangled embankment and there was the Kootenai. Her wonderment at suddenly confronting the brilliant white river in the darkness left her breathless, like she'd surprised a dragon. She was instantly seized with the feeling that the river was waiting for her and shivered with an eerie rush of foreboding.

Powerful and swift, the river blasted against the gray stone walls, twisting and leaping through the labyrinthine gorge, dangerously alive and strangely terrifying. Shelly stared at the pounding water, fighting back her fear, and nearly turned around and climbed back up the wooded slope to the highway. But this river had drawn her here, and Shelly knew she had to find out why. Slowly, she started walking toward the water.

Shortly the ground cover gave way to flat, dark stone tilting toward the shear-walled gorge. Shelly stepped carefully to the brink and looked into the rushing water below. To her right, a narrow outcrop of stone led precariously down to the river. Grasping chunks of rock to keep from falling, Shelly edged her way down, one treacherous step at a time, until she stood beside the rapids. The leaping, plunging water, crashing through the canyon in the otherwise still night charged her with excitement, and Shelly inhaled the river's energy.

She worked her way upstream over the slick rock to where a large boulder blocked her path. The boulder contained enough indents and handholds for her to attempt a climb and after several tries, Shelly pulled herself to the top and saw the falls, two hundred yards away. Staying close to the river, she continued along the bank until she stood on a slab of stone at the edge of an eddy, twenty-five feet from where the river tumbled over the ledge. The water fell sheer and straight, pure white as it dropped from the rim into a churning maelstrom thirty feet below, then charged downstream like a thousand white horses. To the right of the roaring wall of water a vertical scarp of jagged rock ran to the top of the falls.

Delicately stepping along the wet stone, Shelly approached the falls and stared at the rock wall. The face was too obscured in shadow to tell if it was climbable but she resolved to try. After testing several stones that jutted from the cliff she reached overhead and pulled herself up. The toes of her boots scraped against flat stone until they found purchase on a horizontal runner barely an inch wide. One tenuous hand and toehold at a time, Shelly went up the rock face, pulling with her fingers and pushing with her toes, until her hand felt the top of the ledge and she pulled herself over. She stood up, only a couple of feet from where the water plunged over the brink, and saw Kootenai Falls in its majestic entirety.

The falls did not extend across the entire river. At intervals, rocks and ledges interrupted the drop and on the far side, much of the water funneled into a steep channel, crashing into an island the size of a battleship. Downstream, more islands divided the Kootenai into channels, each with its own drops and rapids. On the far side of the gorge, the pinkish grey mountain rose straight from the riverbank, making the canyon inaccessible from that side. Upstream, the river was wide and flat, falling over a series of small ledges that gave little indication of the cataclysm that lay ahead.

Shelly took off her knapsack, placed it on a patch of stone away from the water then sat down and scooted to the very edge of the falls. Seated only inches from the rushing water she let her legs and feet dangle in mid-air, nearly touching the cascade. Below her the river churned and frothed, spewing mist high into the air that blew back onto her face. The river's pounding tumult filled every crevice of the night and shook the entire gorge. Rumbling vibrations bounced off the canyon walls, echoing the water's driving power, like the mainspring of a giant clock pulsing life through everything around it. Shelly listened, trying to hear the river's voice, wanting to understand what it was saying.

Here was a river she knew nothing of, except that its name was the Kootenai. She didn't know where the river came from or where it went, but tonight, that didn't matter. No one else was around and the falls was hers. Overhead the stars competed with the full moon that shed enough light to see the gorge but still keep it veiled in mystery. Through the cloud of spray, Shelly watched the roiling water, shimmering white, like the flowing robes of a wraith in the wind.

Then Shelly was no longer looking through the mist, but peering into it. She could distinguish each tiny droplet, glistening with moonlight, as it rose above the falls, danced briefly in the night sky, then returned to the river. In the center of the glittering spray, a shadow wavered, flickered mysteriously, then formed into a perfect moonbow. Shelly had heard of moonbows, but had never seen one, and the sight struck her as an apparition. Ethereal, pale gray, yet with each color distinct, the arch hovered so close that Shelly felt she could leap from her perch and swing from it.

The longer Shelly gazed at the moonbow, the more distinct the river's voice became. What she'd heard as a steady roar was really a series of individual sounds: rumbles and reverberations, echoes and re-echoes, the low boom of rock on rock, and the crashing rapids, all singing a mighty aria in the water's depths. No refrain was ever twice the same and once performed was never sung again, yet neither was it lost, for the river built each new song upon the one before. The river's song became her song and her pulse merged with the river's pulse.

The river's tone changed and suddenly Shelly was in the center of the mist, surrounded by millions of tiny phosphorescent swirling lights. All around her a dazzling array of glistening orbs lept in frenzied circles and elipticals. The moonbow now loomed above her and before Shelly knew it she was pulled through and lost all sense of self or separation from the twinkling particles. Immersed in the cloud of spray, Shelly twirled and spun, oblivious to everthing but the moment. Direction and time were meaningless. There was no up or down, no east or west, only the buoyant, whirling dance between river and sky. In every direction, as far as she could see, glowing spheres spun in freewheeling orbits, each tiny droplet its own star, holding within it the essense of life. Reverberating through it all was the roar and pulse of the falls.

For what felt like eons, Shelly floated free among the moonlit specks of mist. Around her, particles fell away and disappeared by the thousands, while others sprang from seemingly nowhere to take their place, but on she danced, cloaked in the spray.

Without warning, she felt weary, no longer weightless, like she was winding down. Her movements became slower and slower until they stopped altogether. Around her, the other phosphorescent orbs continued leaping and spinning in their delirious orbits but she had come to a standstill. She began falling, faster and faster, out of control, until a band of darkness appeared in front of her and she plunged into black silence. There was no sense of sight, sound, or touch, only her own disembodied consciousness, floating in an endless realm of nothing. She waited … and waited … with no concept of how much time had passed, for there was nothing to measure time by or to know if time even existed in this void.

Enveloped by empty silence, Shelly began to fear this dark realm had no end, and she wondered if she had died, toppled into the foaming river from her perch beside the falls and this lightless, soundless nothing was death. Maybe this was Hell: not a fiery inferno, but simply being conscious in the middle of nothing at all, forever and ever.

Trapped in unrelenting isolation Shelly had an even more terrifying revelation: that this monstrous entity into which she had been sucked was the inevitable end for everyone and everything and that the river, the earth, the galaxy, even the entire universe would eventually be consumed by this black horror from which there was no escape. This void, the Nothing, *was* reality, the natural state of the cosmos. Matter, energy and life were but a brief and deviant blip in eternity.

Fighting to control her rising terror, Shelly knew she was peering into the dark heart of reality, a chill and ghastly truth, the great mystery hidden behind the guise of nature, utterly unfathomable, yet undeniable. The other undeniable truth was her own mortal consciousness, yet nowhere in this empty realm was there anything to explain by what charm the void had given rise to her conscious mind, the ability to think and feel, the gift of imagination or the blessings of love and mercy.

When Shelly looked into the billions of years past and the billions of years to come and on into forever, she was not there and her own existence seemed impossible. Yet here she was, a living awareness in the midst of endless nothing and the unanswered paradox whirled in her mind.

More alone and desperate than she'd ever been, and fearing her short life was over, Shelly's memories turned to home: her brothers and sisters, Ethel and her daddy, whom she'd never stop loving. She thought of her free-roaming childhood in the mountains and of Tramp, the gentlest, most beautiful spirit she'd ever known. Summoning all of her faith, not knowing if she could even speak or be heard in this lightless vacuum, Shelly called out, "Please, Lord, show me the way," and was startled to hear her own voice in the darkness. She knew not to whom or what she prayed, whether it was the God she'd prayed to in the little Shiloh Church or the spirit of the river, or some ultimate, unknowable force, lying beyond time and creation; maybe they were all the same. All she knew was that as soon as she uttered the prayer, her mind quieted and the terror overtaking her subsided.

For a long while Shelly waited. Just as her fear was returning she detected a slight palpitation in the surrounding darkness, but it quickly faded. A span of time passed before there was another. The next one came sooner. Shelly couldn't hear the pulsations, only *sense* them as ripples and she thought the sensation might be her imagination, but shortly they built to a steady, faint thrumming. As the vibrations intensified they rumbled through the darkness with a low throb. The throbbing wasn't frightening and as it grew in strength the more comforting it became, like the universe was purring.

The swelling current rippled through Shelly like a great tendril of living energy. Darkness itself had come alive and just like with the river, Shelly's soul pulsated along with it. Whatever was happening could never be named or understood, only experienced and Shelly learned a new truth: this living thread had always existed, coursing through the fabric of reality before there was a universe, and would continue after the light of the galaxies had gone out, carrying within it the promise of Creation that will come again and again, forever. She finally understood what her father had tried to describe to her of standing alone in the still blackness at the bottom of a mineshaft and letting the darkness flow through him. "Jus' me an' God," he'd told her; "Nobody else aroun'."

There was still no explanation to the paradox she had witnessed earlier, of how, out of all the possible ages throughout infinity, only at this one infintesimal, fleeting speck of time, did she exist, a warm drop of consciousness in a cold sea of eternity. But Shelly no longer needed to know the answer to the mystery, because there was no answer and never would be. It was enough to know that in some way, against impossible odds, she had been given a living body and a brain that generates consciousness and could act upon its own will, *her* will, for this life was hers and the time to live it was *now*. By some unknowable magic, she had been blessed with a gift beyond measure, a soul that could see Creation and hear Glory sung all around her, and for the first time in her life, Shelly understood the true meaning of the word *Miracle*.

She could feel her heart beating and warm blood coursing in her veins. Droplets of mist spattered her face, solid stone was beneath her and Shelly knew she was back at the falls. She looked down at her legs dangling over the rushing water and gazed into the rising spray. The tiny droplets of mist still glowed with shimmering moonlight, but the moonbow was gone. Overhead, the stars had wheeled through the heavens and the moon had crossed the sky. Leaning over, Shelly dipped her hand in the water pouring over the ledge and felt its coolness, then looked downstream to where the rapids thundered through the canyon.

The night air had grown cold and a breeze gusted along the riffling water above the falls. Shelly reached for her knapsack, pulled out her hooded sweatshirt and slipped it on underneath her jacket. She dug into the pack for her hat and her hand lit on a cool metal cylinder. After tugging the ball cap down snug on her head she took out the can of Falstaff she'd found in the back of her fridge when she was packing up in Norwood.

Shelly pulled the tab and the beer fizzed as foam bubbled up through the opening. The tangy aroma of malt and hops met her nostrils and

Shelly watched the sudsy bubbles roll around on the top of the can before she tipped it back. For a while she gazed intently at the water heading downstream and into the future, just like she'd done at the little spectral glade near Peapatch. She finished her beer and stuffed the empty can back into her pack then glanced down at her watch and pressed the button that lit the dial: twenty minutes after four. Shelly stared at the hands for a few seconds. It was now Monday, October 1st, and she'd just turned eighteen while sitting on the edge of a waterfall in Montana.

The improbability of all that had happened to bring her here made her throw back her head and laugh. Shelly jumped to her feet and began dancing on the lip of the falls, whirling and spinning like when she'd been one of the glistening orbs of spray hovering above the water. Raising her arms skyward, she clapped her hands in rhythm with the falls and the river, dancing and laughing in the moonlight.

There really wasn't anything else to do but dance and laugh. Laugh until it rang from the mountains and forests and reverberated off the canyon walls. Laugh until it carried into the night sky and the moon, the planets and the stars heard the sheer joy that could spring from one person's soul. Laugh until it merged with the roar of the falls and became part of the river's song. Laugh, and cry out, *"THANK YOU!"*

The End

About the Author

Ohio State business grad Rube Wrightsman quit his job at age 24 to become a saddle tramp. Riding a shaky BSA Lightning, he headed west with his pardner, a 6'4" biker who went by the name of Bruno Degenerati. After 10,000 miles of adventures and flopping as a Nashville songwriter, Rube settled in northwest Montana.

For most of the next 25 years he lived without electricity or plumbing in a tiny earth-sheltered cabin he'd built in the mountains outside of Paradise, making mead and doing every dirty, dangerous, low-paying job that nobody else wanted. Between jobs he traveled, wrote a newspaper column and magazine articles. At age 50, on a lark, he infiltrated the local police department as a reserve officer and somehow ended up as Undersheriff of Sanders County. Now retired and very happily married, he decided to write a novel about the Appalachian and western characters he loves so well.